Rebels
Of
Sabrehill

Rebels
Of
Sabrehill

Raymond Giles

A FAWCETT GOLD MEDAL BOOK

Fawcett Publications, Inc., Greenwich, Connecticut

REBELS OF SABREHILL

ISBN 0-449-13695-7

Printed in the United States of America

10 9 8 7 6 5 4 3 2 1

. . . and for Maggie
yet again

I am one, my liege,
Whom the vile blows and buffets of the world
Have so incensed that I am reckless what
I do to spite the world.

—Shakespeare, Macbeth, III, i

Rebels
Of
Saberhill

PART ONE

Predators

One

She didn't even hear them coming up behind her.

She had been walking along the dry-rutted road, hardly feeling the chill of the day as she pulled the old piece of blanket shawllike about her shoulders, thinking of nothing but when she would see Lize and Theron again. Remembering the dancing the night before—dancing with Theron, giggling and exchanging a few shy kisses in the dark. Dreaming now, and humming a little tune. And looking forward to the warmth of supper, evening laughter with her father and friends, and settling into bed for more dreaming.

Then they were on her, the horse almost running her down and the white man cursing her. "Goddam, nigger, what the hell do you . . . ?" She jumped aside, heart lurching and slamming, as the buggy whipped by; she stumbled and nearly fell. The horse protested as the white man seized the reins from the Negro driver and viciously yanked at them, bringing the buggy to a rattling halt.

The white man turned and looked back at her. She waited, suddenly frozen, by the side of the road.

"You! You, wench! You come here!"

She wanted to run for the woods. She knew the voice and the face.

"I'm telling you, nigger, come here!"

She did as she was told. Reluctantly, fearfully, dragging her feet, she walked to the side of the buggy and looked up at the long forbidding face, gray as the November sky.

"You hear me coming, nigger?"

"No—"

"I yell at you, you don't hear?"

"No, master."

The white man's face worked with anger; his eyes were black ice. Ettalee stood utterly still, as if that might render her invisible, but she felt that he could see her heart pounding.

13

Then, slowly, the face settled, and something new came into the dark eyes, something like cruel interest. "I know you, don't I," Mr. Skeet said after a moment, and it was not a question.

"No, master, sir."

"I know you."

And he did. Ettalee remembered a day in summer more than a year before when *they* had been looking for a runaway white woman, and *they* had come to her father's blacksmith shop at Sabrehill. *They* had all stared at her, and Mr. Skeet and Mr. Jeppson had searched everywhere while Mr. Bassett had told her what he was going to do to her—he and all the others—if the runaway were not found. The terrible thing had not happened, but she had been so frightened that she still had an occasional nightmare.

"What your name, gal?"

"Ettalee, sir."

"Where you heading for?"

"Sabrehill, sir."

Something like fresh recognition came to the dark eyes, something like a smile to the narrow lips. Yes, he knew her now.

"Show me your pass."

"Ain't got none, master, sir," Ettalee said miserably. "Don't need none."

Mr. Skeet looked pleased. "Now, what you mean, you don't need no pass? You go away from your plantation, you need a pass. How come you ain't got none? 'Course you need a pass."

In Ettalee's experience, that was not precisely true. The law might require a pass, but if the people of a plantation wished to visit their neighbors on a Saturday night or a Sunday, who was to stop them? And where was the harm? The people of Sabrehill often visited their friends on the Kimbrough and Devereau and Buckridge places, and their friends came to see them. Of course they did. Tears gathered in Ettalee's eyes.

"I said, how come you ain't got none?"

"Was just out walking, master, sir." She fought the

tears; she would not cry before this white master, she would not!

"Just out walking from where to where without no pass? Just out walking where?"

Ettalee knew he was toying with her. He had recognized her and knew she was from Sabrehill. But did he *really* know? What if she claimed to be from Kimbrough?

"Just out walking, master," she pleaded. "Ain't going nowhere. Just out walking."

" 'Ain' gwi-i-ine nowhea-ah,' " he mocked. "You telling me you a Kimbrough nigger?"

She took a chance. "Yes, master."

"Then what you doing on Sabre property—without a pass?"

The charge was stunning. It was true that she had no firm idea of where the border between the plantations lay, but she was only a few hundred yards from the Kimbrough field quarters, on the road that ran through the two properties. She had walked the road often, and she knew where she was.

"Ain't on Sabrehill," she managed to say.

"Oh, ain't you? Well, now, that's too bad. 'Cause I coulda swore you was a Sabrehill nigger, and what's a Sabrehill nigger doing on Kimbrough property without a pass?"

"Ain't—ain't Sabre—"

"Ain't Sabre, ain't Kimbrough. Ettamae, or whatever your name is, I don't think you know what you are. And that being the case, I think you better just climb up on this here buggy with me."

"Please, master—"

"*Up!*"

There was no choice. And she refused to be dragged kicking and screaming to the Skeet place, much as Mr. Skeet might have enjoyed that. As she reached up, a large hand enfolded hers, and she was lifted almost gently into the buggy and placed like an object on the seat between Mr. Skeet and the impassive driver.

The driver quickly found a place to turn the buggy and headed back westward, toward Redbird, the Skeet plantation. Mr. Skeet grinned at Ettalee.

"Sabrehill nigger," he said with satisfaction. "Long time since I had me a Sabrehill nigger. Know what I'm gonna do with you, Etta—Ettamae?"

"Yes, sir."

Yes, she knew, or thought she did. All the colored people of the countryside knew about Mr. Skeet and others like him. If they caught you without a pass, they didn't simply take you home and send for your master. No, they put you to work in the daytime and locked you up at night and never told anyone, and weeks might go by before your master learned where you were and came for you. And while they had you, they could be so cruel. . . .

"Yeah," Mr. Skeet said, gently patting her thigh, "yeah, reckon you know what I'm gonna do with you," and Ettalee shuddered at his touch.

The light of the gray day failed quickly, and it was almost dark when they at last arrived at Redbird Plantation, but not even the darkness could hide the shabbiness of the place. Everything had a gray, moldering, unpainted look. Roofs of the outbuildings sagged. A few hands stood about, looking ragged and sullen. The courtyard, if such it could be called, was overgrown with weeds. The most substantial looking building was a plain brick structure with barred, unglazed windows; that, Ettalee thought, must be the Skeet nigger-jail she had heard so much about. She shivered under her scrap of blanket, and her heart ached to be back at bright, clean, warm Sabrehill.

"We here," Mr. Skeet said.

He climbed down from the buggy and, almost courteously, helped Ettalee down, took her by the elbow, and led her toward a small building, which she took to be the plantation office. Inside the office the only light came from a few embers glowing in the fireplace. Mr. Skeet knelt before them and quickly, expertly began building them back into a fire.

"Hungry?" he asked as he worked. "Want something to eat?"

"No, sir."

"Left some johnnycake there on the desk, you want it. Or you can have a sip of whiskey, it'll warm you up."

"No, sir."

The fright, the urge to cry, would not go away. Ettalee pulled her blanket more tightly about her shoulders. The fire bloomed, and looking about, she saw a table, a desk, several chairs, and all the mess and clutter—account books, broken tools, dust—of perhaps half a century. But there was no warmth in the room, no hiding place, no escape.

Mr. Skeet arose from the fire and turned toward her. He didn't bother with any lamps, and with his back to the fire, she could barely see his face. "Well, now," he said, tossing his hat and jacket onto a chair. "Well, now."

She could hear the grin in his voice, and she found herself slowly backing away from him. She knew he wanted something from her now, but she didn't understand what, and she didn't want to understand.

"How old you, Etta—Ellamae?"

"Sixteen." Her voice was a broken whisper.

"Sixteen. Well, that's plenty old enough, ain't it, Ella-mae?" He took a step toward her. "Sure you don't want that drink, Ellamae? Might as well be friendly, you and me. I can be friendly as the next man to the nigger gal that's nice to me, but on the other hand . . ."

She understood then in spite of herself. But she still didn't want to believe it was going to happen.

"Ellamae . . ."

He took another step toward her. Involuntarily she cringed and pulled the scrap of blanket more tightly about her shoulders. Mr. Skeet saw the movement; he quickly stepped forward, tore the blanket away from her, and threw it to the floor.

"Ellamae, ain't no good you trying to get away from me. Now, if you is nice . . ."

There was no way to evade him. As she backed up, the table blocked her, cutting into her legs. She could step to neither side without Mr. Skeet stopping her. He was a tall dark shadow between her and the firelight, a shadow that threatened to envelop her at any instant.

"Please . . . please, master . . . sir . . ." She put her hands up against his chest, holding him off.

He laughed and brushed her hands aside. His own hands suddenly caught the front of her dress and pulled it open, ripping the cloth, and his fingers closed on her bare breasts.

The shock almost stopped her heart. Breasts turned cold, tried to wither and vanish. Nipples wanted to recede, to invert themselves, to hide. Breath stopped for a long aching moment, then returned like a claw in her throat.

"By God," Mr. Skeet muttered thickly as he kneaded her flesh, "by God, you may be black as sin, but you really got 'em, you really got what a man needs."

She tried to thrust him away, tried to escape him, but he only pressed closer, pinning her to the table's edge.

"If only you was nice to me, Ellamae . . ."

"Please, master . . . no . . ."

Abruptly he stepped back from her, his hands leaving her breasts, and for an instant she thought he was heeding her pleas. But then he reached down and lifted the front of her skirt. He laughed as he gazed at her: "By God. A nigger wearing drawers. Now I seen everything."

He reached for her waist. The cloth was old and soft and no stronger than paper: with one sharp tug he ripped it entirely away from her.

It was then that she screamed, then that the tears came at last, and she began to fight him. Because she knew: the terrible thing was going to happen. Dream was becoming reality. Mr. Skeet was going to make the nightmare come true.

He tried to ignore the soft but persistent knocking, tried to dream that it was nothing but a woodpecker and that he was lying in the woods with Zulie on a warm spring day, but the quick tap-tap-tapping brought him gently up from sleep. By the time the sound stopped, he was awake; he had the feeling that he had not slept more than an hour. Ah, well, he thought, rolling toward Zulie in the bed, so much the better. He could enjoy drifting off to sleep with her all over again. Under the blankets, he put an arm around her, pressed against her bare back, and kissed the nape of her neck.

The tapping started again, harder, louder.

Oh, hell.

Reluctantly Jeb pulled himself up from under the blan-

kets and into the cold night air and tried to bring himself
further awake. He looked down at Zulie, who lay quietly,
her back still to him. He smiled. Her dress was thrown
over a chair, and her shoes were placed neatly beside his
bed, but she still wore a yellow silk scarf around her head
and some kind of conjure-charm around her neck. He
leaned down and kissed her cheek.

Tap-tap-tap-tap-tap!

All right!

This sort of thing, being awakened in the night when
you were with your woman, was to be expected if you
were the overseer; and being black, he was far more ap-
proachable than any white overseer would have been. But
just the same, he thought, it had better be important.
Shivering, he swung his bare legs over the side of the bed,
and as the knocking was repeated yet again—all *right*,
you son of a bitch!—he pulled on pants and a shirt. Walking barefoot through the front room, he picked up a jacket
and threw it over his shoulders. When he opened the front
door, he found himself looking at a full, graying beard
and a pair of worried eyes.

"Saul, what the hell?"

"I sorry, Jeb, but I got to see you."

"About what that can't wait until morning?"

" 'Bout my Ettalee, Jeb. I—I don't know where she be!"

The floor cold under his bare feet, his breath a white
cloud, Jeb stepped out onto his small veranda. His house,
at the head of the east service lane, faced the courtyard
of the Sabrehill mansion. The plantation office, at the
near end of the mansion, and the kitchen house, at the
far end, were dark, and some lights in the downstairs of
the mansion itself were just going out. That meant that
Miss Lucy was retiring for the night, and Jeb hoped he
would not have to disturb her.

"All right, Saul," he said, "sit down and tell me about
it."

Saul did not sit. A short, heavy man, all bone and
muscle, made for his hammer and anvil, he moved nervously about like a menacing shadow. Jeb was one of the
tallest and strongest men on the plantation, but it occurred
to him that he would not care to cross Saul. Ordinarily

the blacksmith was the gentlest of men, but if anyone ever hurt one of his children, Jeb hated to think of what his vengeance might be.

"Tell me, Saul," he repeated.

"Ettalee go over to Kimbrough yesterday. Me, I give her little pork ration, say she can stay the night."

"Stay with whom?"

"Friend Lize and Theron. They got nice folk. I say, stay the night but come back today while the sun still high—"

"And she didn't come back."

"No! She don't come back, she *still* ain't come back. Jeb, she ain't *never* done like this!"

Well, there's got to be a first time, Jeb thought. His impression of Ettalee was that she was a considerate, well-behaved girl, deeply attached to her family. But when a girl started cutting her strings, you could never tell what she might do.

But he could hardly say that to Saul. Instead, he said, "Well, I wouldn't worry. Most likely, they asked Ettalee to stay for supper, and she lost all track of time. And they didn't want her to head back home in the dark—"

He broke off. Saul was shaking his head and trying to interrupt. "No, Jeb, it ain't so! I been there to Kimbrough. Can't stand waiting no more, so I go run all the way there and just now come back. And, Jeb, they say she go home long, long ago—she head straight home, but she never get here! So I come right to you."

That put the matter in a different light. The girl might have had an accident or been picked up by the patrol. Almost better, Jeb thought, to step on a copperhead than to encounter a certain type of pattyroller.

He considered. He looked at the big house and saw that all of the lights were now out. He groped for something encouraging to say.

"Just the same, let's not expect the worst. Now, you did the right thing in coming to me, but there's nothing we can do tonight—"

"I got to get her back, Jeb, I got to! Going out of my head!"

"The first thing in the morning—"

"No! Please, Jebediah, I ain't never ask much of you. Go talk to Miss Lucy. Tell her."

Jeb shook his head. Miss Lucy was the sole owner and mistress of Sabrehill, the final authority and last recourse for her people. But at this hour she could do little or no more than Jeb could.

"Saul, we can't search all the fields and woods between here and Kimbrough in the dark. And we can't wake our neighbors and search their peoples' quarters—they wouldn't stand for that, and you know it. But the first thing in the morning—"

"You ain't going do nothing?" Even in the dark, Saul's eyes were fierce, and his voice was incredulous.

Jeb began to feel impatient. "I told you, there's nothing we can do. Now, you get some sleep—"

"You tell me get some sleep, my gal out there somewhere?"

"I know how you feel—"

"You don't know nothing how I feel! And plenty you can do, you want to—you just got a woman in your bed, and you don't give a damn!"

"Saul—"

Jeb tried to put a hand on the blacksmith's huge shoulder, but the man angrily shrugged it away. He stomped down the steps from the veranda. He turned and looked up at Jeb, his eyes still burning.

"Boy, I 'member when they buy you here. 'Member when you is a fighter and a runner. How they break your foot and put that cut on your face. How you got more stripe on your back then any black man I ever see. But stripe on your back, whip-cut on your face, broke foot, they don't mean nothing no more. You just like a lot of people say now."

"And what do they say now?" Jeb asked wearily, and instantly wished he had not.

"They say big Jeb, he something back then, oh, he truly something to see. But he ain't nothing no more. He just another—" Saul's voice shook with fury "—just another—*white man's nigger!*"

Jeb felt the words like the whip that had put the diagonal blaze across his face. His eyes were again filled with the fire of that agonizing moment, and when the fire died, Saul had disappeared into the night.

A white man's nigger.

Jeb found that he was shaking, and not from the cold. So that was what they thought of him—some of them, anyway. If Saul had the guts to say it to his face, others were saying it behind his back. Actually Saul had merely said what Jeb had already sensed.

A white man's nigger. Why, the dirty, ungrateful . . .

Had they so easily forgotten what he had done for them? Had they forgotten what it had been like under the last overseer? The long hours, the cruelty of the drivers, the sexual exploitation? When Jeb had taken charge, he had stopped all that. No man was a slave by choice, but Jeb figured that if a man were forced into that condition, he should still try to make some kind of decent life for himself. And that was what he had struggled to achieve— for himself and for every other slave at Sabrehill.

To hell with them, he thought, if they didn't appreciate what he had done for them. He didn't have to stay here—Miss Lucy would give him a pass north anytime. She wouldn't like doing it, she thought she needed him; but she was also grateful for all he had done for her, and the pass was there for the asking. And one of these days he was going to take it, and the Sabrehill people could damned well get along without him.

Still angry, he reentered his house, and stubbing his toes in the dark did nothing to improve his temper. He slipped back into bed, sitting up, without removing his clothes. Zulie muttered something about his "letting the cold in" and curled up against him. Sleep had never seemed more distant.

Where the *hell* did they get off, calling him a white man's nigger! How many of *them* had been sold from plantation to plantation, been whipped to the point of madness, lived under the constant threat of castration? How many of *them* had had a father left by the master to die in agony and a mother driven to suicide? Did they think he didn't have many a night when the old bitterness welled up so that he dreamed—surely far more than they—of some black avenging angel who would burn the big houses, raze the countryside, make the white masters pay in blood for the long years of pain? Of becoming that avenger himself—someone like the near-legendary Black Buck? Black Buck—outlier, thief, killer? Christ, in the early days that Saul had spoken of, he had prayed that Black Buck would come right here to Sabrehill.

And they dared call *him,* Jeb Hayes, a white man's nigger!

"Jeb, you stop kicking about? You letting all the *co-o-old* in!"

He reached under the blankets to rub Zulie's back. "I'm sorry, honey."

"Only reason I'se here, I do like a warm body on a cold night."

"Yes," Jeb said bleakly, "I know."

Zulie laughed and snuggled closer to him. "Now, don't you be sad; you my sugar. How come you got clothes on?"

"Saul was here. Seems that his Ettalee went to Kimbrough yesterday and hasn't come back yet."

"Well, Ettalee growing up. Reckon she found herself a warm body too."

"No, I don't think so. She started home from Kimbrough, but she never got here. Sounds like someone picked her up."

He felt Zulie stiffen against him. "Somebody like that Mr. Bassett, that Mr. Skeet, they mighty bad."

"Yes, they are."

"Saul, reckon he sick with worry."

"Yes, I think he is."

"Anything happen to Ettalee, it kill him."

Jeb stared into the darkness.

Well, where was Ettalee? If she were with a boy—which Jeb doubted—there was no way to find out before morning. If a patroller or a white master had carried her off, it might take even longer. And if neither were the case, then there was a good chance that the girl was lying in some field between Sabrehill and Kimbrough, or maybe she had tumbled into a creek bed, and she might have broken a leg or been bitten by a snake, she might be cold and frightened and in great pain—

"Zulie, am I a white man's nigger?"

Zulie didn't seem surprised by the question. She sounded half-asleep again. "Now, why you ask a thing like that?"

"Am I?"

"Well . . . you *is* the overseer."

"Yes, and I work directly for Miss Lucy. You figure because of that that I don't care about my people? That I don't do my best for them?"

"Reckon you do. You a good man, Jeb. A mighty good man."

Jeb turned from Zulie and once again swung his legs over the edge of the bed.

"Hey, where you going?"

"I've got to find Ettalee."

Somehow she had slept, and now she did not wish to awaken. She lay perfectly still, her face against the rough boards of the jailhouse floor. For a few seconds she felt nothing; then, abruptly, every ache in her body returned. Her eyes were still closed, and she sensed that one was so swollen that she would not be able to open it. Her entire face was bruised, and when she moved her tongue in her dry mouth, she tasted blood from a split lip.

There had been three of them. First, Mr. Skeet. Then, sometime later, another white man. And then a black man called Shadrach. Not once, but again and again. She did not want to, could not bear to think about it, but it was burned into her mind forever.

She heard soft moans, curses, the clatter of chains. From the far end of the room came a muttering in Gullah. She did not understand it, for little Gullah was spoken this far inland on the longer-settled plantations. Chains rattled again. She heard the woman hum a scrap of mournful tune. Yes, there was actually another woman here, she remembered, a tall hard-eyed woman, bigger than any of the men.

She felt cramped, and in spite of herself she stirred. The barred windows of the jail had no shutters, and the night had been cold. To keep warm, she had only a blanket the overseer had given her and her torn dress; even her shoes were gone. Only exhaustion had allowed her to sleep.

"You 'wake, little one?" the woman asked. "You best wake 'fore he come, he kick you gut out."

Fear. She was still capable of fear, and she forced herself to sit up and look about with her one good eye. It was dark within the jail, but distant lamplight filtered in from outside. Aftter a moment she could make out the two Sea Island blacks, still whispering in Gullah. Near the big woman sat a bald little man, half her size; he seemed to be weeping. Two other black men sat in stony silence, as if listening to the sounds of morning. All but she, Ettalee saw, had chain hobbles, and each huddled under a single blanket.

She shook violently. Her lips moved silently for a moment before she made a croaking sound.

"Say what?" the woman asked.

"Want . . . want . . . go home."

The woman laughed. "Now, why you want go home? Ain't Mr. Skeet so-o-o nice to you? Then maybe you ain't nice to Mr. Skeet."

"Go home."

"Honey, master send you here to Redbird, you don't go home till you a goo-ood nigger, don't you know that? How come you here? What kind bad nigger you?"

"Ain't bad."

" 'Course you bad, we all bad nigger here. Sass the master, steal the hog, piss in the food." A couple of the others chuckled quietly. "Master send us here, Mr. Skeet get free hand for field, and master don't have do no whipping. Master, he say what a ki-i-ind master he be, and nice white lady in the big house, they don't hear no scream from the quarter. Oh, he a ki-i-ind master."

The woman wasn't telling Ettalee anything she didn't know; what black of the countryside didn't know about Mr. Skeet, the "nigger-breaker"?

"Kind master," one of the men said. "Going kill my kind master, I get out here. Going kill my kind master, then come back here, kill Mr. Skeet."

"Mr. Skeet break you," said the small bald man, "you ain't going kill nobody."

"Ain't going break me. Think he break me, but I come back."

"How come you here?" the woman asked.

"Wife dead, boy and girl-child sold, nobody left but me. So I get drunk, go after master with axe."

"Ho! No wonder you here!"

"Next time I ain't drunk. Next time I kill him. Burn big house, barn, stable, everything. Then I come back here. Pay my respects to Mr. Skeet."

"And what you do then?"

"Take off into swamp. Go join up with Black Buck and the maroons. Burn every goddam thing in sight."

The remark brought more laughter and quiet applause, and Ettalee felt the hatred, the bitterness, the latent violence that flooded the room. But what did it have to do with her? What did Black Buck, that vicious marooner, have to do with her? She would have been terrified of such a man. She was no "bad nigger." She had not been sent here by Miss Lucy or Mr. Jeb. They would never have sent her or anyone else here, and surely they would appear at any time now to take her back home.

But it was not Miss Lucy or Mr. Jeb who appeared. A lock rattled, and the door was pulled open. Even in that dim light Ettalee recognized the black man, Shadrach, from the night before, and she cowered away from him. That drew his attention; grinning, he came for her and yanked her to her feet. He snatched away the blanket, pulled her out of the jail, and shoved her into the hands of the white overseer.

She was dragged cringing, trying to keep her torn dress closed, toward the office. She had a wild hope that Miss Lucy would be waiting for her, that help had come at last. But there was no help, she saw as she was thrust through the doorway; there was only Mr. Skeet.

He looked at her with disgust. "Christ, I musta got drunk. Forgot you was such a mess." He turned to the overseer. "Go on, I changed my mind, take her away. I don't want her."

"Spancel her?"

Mr. Skeet shrugged. "Why bother? She ain't running nowhere."

"Where you want to work her?"

"Anywhere that no snooping Sabrehill nigger is going to see her. The gin house maybe. Let that damn Sabrehill bitch sweat a few days for losing one of her niggers."

The overseer grinned appreciatively. He looked at Ettalee's torn dress and yanked her hand away from it. His eyes brightened as it fell open.

"You don't want her, you mind if I . . . ?"

"Hell, no." Mr. Skeet shrugged again. "That's what nigger wenches are for. Just keep her the hell out of sight."

They ain't never going find me, Ettalee thought despairingly, *ain't never!*

Hauled by her elbow, she stumbled half-blindly after the overseer, who led her to a small cook house in the ramshackle field quarters. There she was handed a shingle with some mush on it and commanded to eat. She tried eating with her fingers but immediately began to retch and dropped the shingle into the dust. For this she was given three blows of a whip across her back and told she would have to go hungry for the rest of the day.

She was put to work, helping load the gin, though she was almost too weak to move. Cold through every bone, shaking uncontrollably, she wept with gratitude for the feeble heat of the rising sun. But the chill of the night had taken its toll, and suddenly her back muscles began to tighten and go into spasms. She could barely stand, let alone work, but that did not stop the whip when she hesitated, and the day became an utter agony.

Twice during the day the overseer came for her, took her into some woods not far from the gin house, and did as he pleased. The second time, Ettalee did not even try to resist. She no longer thought of her father or Miss Lucy or Mr. Jeb or anyone else she had ever known. All she knew was this.

And this was hell.

And everyone knew that hell was forever.

. . . burn the big houses, raze the countryside, make the white masters pay in blood . . .

All through that day Black Buck dreamed of the moment. Hidden away in Quashee's cabin, waiting for night-fall, he lay in a light catlike sleep, dreaming: he saw the house burning, he heard the anguished cries of the whites, and he laughed silently to himself. Tonight. The raid. The fire.

But it was not this plantation's big house that he dreamed of burning. No, it was another, far away. It was Redbird.

Every time he burned a house, it was Redbird. Every time he stole, it was from Vachel Skeet. Every time he fired a gun at a white man, it was Vachel Skeet he hoped to see fall.

Someday, Buck told himself, he would go back to Red-bird. Until now he had never dared. But someday . . .

The sun lowered. Blue dusk spread across the planta-tion. The raid. The fire. It would soon be time.

Two

"Saul's Ettalee is missing," Jebediah said. It should not have been an overly worrisome statement, but somehow it was.

It was odd, Lucy thought: so often trouble would ex-plode in one's face without the slightest warning, while at other times she seemed to know instinctively that something had happened or was about to happen. In fact, it seemed to her that there were times when she knew even *before* she knew: there were little signs that spoke to her, as if trouble were whispering into her ear, almost unheard.

So it had been that morning. It was cold, even for mid-November, but when she had awakened at dawn, no one had yet started a fire in her room. And when she had dragged herself shivering from her bed and glanced out the window, she had seen two boys standing on the green parkland that sloped down to Sabre's Landing and the river. They should not have been there; never in her recol-lection had she ever seen two boys down there on a

Monday morning at that hour. It was a little detail that meant nothing in itself but which had set off half-recognized alarms in her mind.

She had splashed water—cold water—on her face and dressed hastily. The morning sounds, as she had hurried down the stairs, had been subtly wrong, and now her overseer and her housekeeper stood on either side of the dining room table, while Lucy sat at its head and poured her own breakfast coffee.

"Sit down, both of you," she said, "and have some coffee. Jebediah, you don't look awake yet. Now, tell me about Ettalee."

It seemed that Jebediah, far from not being awake yet, had been awake most of the night. He told the story of Ettalee's visit to the Kimbrough plantation and her disappearance when she had set out to return. The search he had instituted last night had turned up nothing. Using mainly youngsters whose daytime duties were light, he had gone through all of the Sabrehill quarters and the various outbuildings, and then had covered a great deal of the land between the Sabrehill and the Kimbrough field quarters.

"What do you propose we do now?" she asked.

"Oh, the girl will probably turn up perfectly all right sometime today, but meanwhile we'd better go over the same ground in daylight. And we'd best keep widening the search. We can send a few boys out to each of our neighbors and ask for permission to go through the quarters."

"You ain't saying what you really thinking," Leila, the housekeeper, said. "If Ettalee start home without a pass and don't get here, it's a good chance she was picked up and carried away. Could have been the patrol or a nigger-stealer or, just as bad, goddam Jeppson, somebody like that."

It was true, Lucy thought. They were making all this fuss about a girl who had spent the night away from home, as if this were the first time that such a thing had ever happened. But from all she had heard, and from what she had seen of Ettalee, it simply wasn't in the girl's character to disappear like this. Her sense of something being badly amiss, perhaps even more so than they knew, was gradually deepening.

"You're both right," she said, "But there's nothing to do for the moment but hope for the best and keep looking. Jebediah, you organize the search and send your people to me for passes. We don't want any more of them picked up. Then you'd better put someone else in charge and get some rest. You look tired."

"Yeah, yeah," Leila said, smiling, purring, "here it is, past day clean, and it sure is too bad your bed done got cold."

Something steely flashed between the overseer and the housekeeper. Jebediah rose from the table and left the room, and a moment later Leila followed him.

Lucy poured another cup of coffee.

More problems, she thought. No end to the problems. Perhaps she was a damned fool to think she could go on solving them all, with only her people to help her. Certainly that was what most of her neighbors thought—damn-fool Sabrehill widow-lady, thinks she can run one of the finest plantations in South Carolina without a husband, without even a white overseer. Sits up there, only white person on the whole property. Doesn't know how to discipline her people, lets them run wild, take advantage of her, set a bad example for *our* people! No wonder we got that Jeppson crowd out stringing up niggers, when she can't keep discipline! Besides, everybody *knows* that a mere lady can't possibly run a plantation—makes no more sense than mixing petticoats and politics. It's a damn shame, a fine plantation like that—it won't last a year.

Well, Sabrehill *had* lasted a year—it had lasted a good deal longer. Since her husband had died and she and Jebediah Hayes had taken over its management, they had worked hard and learned much, and in this, the year of Our Lord, 1834, they had a record crop. And they weren't living off their factor's money, as so many planters did. The neighbors had largely been forced to keep their peace.

Not that she could expect them to do so indefinitely,

of course. The next time there was trouble, it would start all over again: That crazy Miss Lucy! That fool scar-faced bitch! A widow living alone like that, nobody around but them buck niggers, why, it's scandalous. You remember how wild she was as a girl? Listen, it ain't for nothing the things they call her behind her back. Why, I remember back ten or twelve years ago . . . when that cousin of hers, that Justin Sabre visited down here. . . . Whispers, scandal, gossip. Entertainment for the long dull weeks between trips to Charleston and Columbia. Stones to be hurled at a scapegoat for their own sins, their own mistakes, their own problems.

Lucy sighed. Don't start pitying yourself, my girl. You're no bondwoman. You're here because you would rather be here than not. Because even on the weariest morning you love the place.

And as for this morning, it may be a bit chilly, but the wind has blown the sky clear, and the sun is rising, and it looks like a radiantly beautiful day. And that pretty little Ettalee will no doubt come rambling home any hour now with a guilty smile on her sweet face, and God bless her, she'll be just fine.

At least, Lucy hoped so.

"Ettalee! We done found Ettalee!"

It was the middle of the afternoon when the two boys came stamping breathlessly into the office. Only fifteen and thirteen years old respectively, they were bursting with excitement.

"Where?" she asked, closing the door. "Where is she?"

"Mr. Skeet place," Tad, the elder, said, and Nemo added, "Mr. Skeet, he done catched her!" and Lucy's worries were confirmed.

"You're sure?" she nevertheless asked. "There's no mistake?"

"Seed her!" Tad said. "Sneak over there, look 'round, don't want Mr. Skeet catch us. Seed her with Mr. Skeet in some trees out back the gin house."

"Wasn't Mr. Skeet," Nemo said indignantly. "That there was Mr. Dinkin, Mr. Skeet overseer." He gave Lucy a broad but embarrassed grin. "Ettalee, she ain't got her no dress on!"

The grin faded as Lucy stared at him. A sickness spread through her like a paralytic poison, and she sank into a chair.

"She—she pull it back on while we watching," Tad said nervously. "Pull it back on, and Mr. Dinkin, he drag Ettalee back to the gin house."

"Was she . . . did she seem to be hurt in any way?"

Tad shrugged. "Guess not. We wasn't so close. But that was Ettalee, I tell you that."

"I see. And nobody there knows that you saw her?"

"No, ma'am. We sneak 'round, we ain't going get caught by no Mr. Skeet, not even with pass. That a me-e-ean man! Soon Ettalee and Mr. Dinkin, they out of sight, we come right to you, don't talk to nobody!"

"You did the right thing. Don't tell anybody, not even Ettalee's papa." Lucy closed her eyes and put a hand over them. What now?

Well, she would simply have to go get Ettalee. But *how* to get her? Go demand her from Vachel Skeet? No, she preferred not even to set eyes on the man if she could help it. She would simply go . . .

"Tad, I'm afraid I don't know where Mr. Skeet's gin house is. Can you take me there?"

"Oh, yes'm."

"Is there any kind of road leading to it?"

"Old wagon path," Nemo said quickly, bound not to be left out. "Go from the road to the gin house."

"Good. Nemo, you run tell Zagreus that I want a carriage ready just as quickly as possible. Maybe that old landaulet. Then tell Ettalee's papa that I want to see him."

"Yes'm."

"And Tad, you go find Mr. Jeb. Tell him I must see him at once."

The boys departed at a run, leaving the door open.

Lucy sat for a time, fighting the sickness, fighting her own weakness. She did not look forward to the possibility of facing either Skeet or his overseer. It had been over three years since Skeet had last picked up a Sabrehill hand, and then there had been men here—white men—to handle the problem. And it was, after all, what they called "man's work."

Should she ask for help? she wondered. She would not have hesitated to ask her neighbor to the east, Mr. Paul Devereau, to accompany her to the Skeet place. Paul was not only an old friend, but also a lawyer and in her debt —he was usually eager to do what he could to assist her. But unfortunately he was in Charleston at present. That léft such neighbors as the Buckridges, farther to the east, and the Kimbroughs, to the west; and while she was on perfectly friendly terms with them, they would take any request for help as a sign of weakness—proof that a lady was incapable of conducting the affairs of a large plantation.

And, Lucy thought wryly, they just might be right.

She would have to take care of this matter herself.

But she had no intention of facing a man who was much larger and stronger than herself, and who was known for his violent ways, without a certain amount of protection. And of course, she could not ask her people to protect her. No, she needed something that would assure her of reasonably good control of the situation.

She found it in one of the two desks that stood against the office walls: an old six-barreled pepperbox. The last time anyone had tried to put it to serious use, it had proven most unreliable, but Jebediah had said that he had repaired it, and checking now, Lucy found that it was loaded. Thanks to her father's coaching, she knew how to use it.

"Ma'am?"

Lucy looked around to find Saul staring at the weapon in her hand. She quickly put it down and began pulling on a coat.

"I have good news for you, Saul. Two of the boys have found out where Ettalee is. I just wanted to relieve your mind."

But of course, Saul was not relieved any more than she was. She saw that in the worried eyes, the desperate pull of the mouth.

"Where she? Miss Lucy, where my Ettalee?"

"Now, don't you worry. I'm going to go get her right now."

"Where my Ettalee?" In an instant, worry had been replaced by something like rage, and Lucy found herself drawing back as Saul seemed to grow taller, larger, more powerful before her very eyes.

But she could not let him see that he frightened her, not even a little. "Your Ettalee," she said firmly, "is perfectly safe, and I'm going to fetch her. She's at the Skeet—"

"Skeet!" The word was poison in Saul's mouth. It was a blasphemy, a curse. He knew quite well the kind of man Vachel Skeet was.

"Now, don't you worry," Lucy said gently, trying to soothe him. "Ettalee is going to be all right. I'll bring her right back to you."

"I go with you. He touch my Ettalee—" Saul seemed to have trouble breathing; even in the cold room there was sweat on his forehead. "He touch her, I kill him—"

"You shut your mouth!" Lucy threw herself in front of Saul, threw her own gaze of blue fire into his dark eyes, and it was his turn to back off, startled. She had to do it. When a black man said such words, she heard the twang of the hanging rope and smelled burning flesh. "Saul, you shut your damn mouth, and don't you ever again let me hear you say you'll raise your hand against a white man, you hear me?"

"He touch her—"

"You'll kill him! All right, you kill him, but *don't you ever say it!*"

The fury in Saul's eyes refused to die down, but after a moment, understanding her, he nodded. Lucy went back to the desk. She picked up the pepperbox again and thrust it into her coat pocket.

"I go with you," Saul said.

There was no stopping him, Lucy saw. "Very well. Very well, you may come along. But you must promise me that you will do exactly as I tell you."

Tad drove the carriage, with Jebediah sitting on the high seat with him, and Lucy and Saul sat behind. The disappointed Nemo had been left at Sabrehill. Saul sat hunched and brooding, emanating anger and fear, his silence quieting the others.

The leaves were autumn sere, the air crisp. They passed fields of corn stubble; field hands bringing in cotton occasionally waved from a distance. Hardly a cloud hung in the sky, not a thing on this brilliant day to block God's eye. They would find Ettalee. Only a few more weeks until Christmas, Lucy thought, and everything's going to be all right, everything's going to be just fine. Ettalee won't have been too badly hurt, and by Christmas she'll have forgotten whatever abuse she's been subjected to. We'll take the poor child home and help her to forget.

Skeet. Vachel Skeet. What in the world had happened to make him the person he was? She could understand the meanness of so many of the sandhillers, the rednecks, the poor buckra, with their frustrations and envy and desperation as they sought to scratch a living from the soil. No wonder they hated those Negroes who lived better than they did. She could even understand those successful farmers, such as Balbo Jeppson, who felt forever excluded from the ranks of the aristocracy—forever condescended to and looked down upon, whatever their successes might be. But Vachel Skeet?

Simply a little crazy, she supposed. Touched. Like his father before him. She remembered her own father telling her what a fine family the Skeets were—or had been until . . . something to do with Old Man Skeet losing his wife. Lucy could not remember. He had gone downhill after that, and so had his plantation. He had taken to "breaking niggers" to get extra help, and his rages when drunk were notorious. People had whispered that he was somewhat deranged.

But for a long time none of that had appeared to affect Vachel. Though she had never paid much attention to him, he had actually seemed to be one of the nicer young men who a dozen years ago had come calling at Sabrehill. She remembered him then as being somewhat shy and inarticulate but very ambitious. Unable to afford a university education, he had pored over books, borrowing dozens of them from her father, and discussing them

with him eagerly. Her father had at that time been quite
fond of Vachel. And Vachel had had such plans for his
plantation, such plans to renew the soil scientifically, to
renovate the big house, to make Redbird, as both mansion
and plantation were called, its former glorious self.

But something had happened to Vachel. Lucy supposed
that there was some truth in the saying that "blood tells,"
for suddenly, almost overnight, Vachel's nature had
changed, and he had become very much his father's son.
Indeed, if the elder Skeet had died first, Lucy would have
sworn that his spirit had entered into the son's body.

And as a result of that extraordinary change . . .

But Lucy had no wish to think back on those painful
days; she had not done so for a very long time. There
came a point, in her view, when old accounts should either
be written off or be marked "paid in full" and the books
closed on them forever.

The jolting of the carriage brought her out of her rev-
erie, and she suddenly realized that they had left the road
and were on a wagon path. Immediately ahead of them
stood the Skeet gin house. Cotton waste tufted the surrounding ground, a couple of mule-drawn wagons stood
nearby, and half a dozen hands, male and female, stared
curiously at the approaching landaulet.

Ettalee, Lucy thought, feeling herself tense; where is
she?

Jebediah leapt from the high front seat of the carriage.

Lucy somehow knew that he must have seen Ettalee.
She did not hesitate; she too jumped from the carriage
before it came to a stop, and Saul followed. She saw Jebediah run through the doorway of the gin house, and seconds later he emerged, an arm tightly around the battered
girl.

The overseer followed them, shouting and shaking his
whip, but Lucy hardly heard him. She stared at the half-
naked girl. Ettalee's dress hung from one shoulder, and
she did not seem to know how exposed she was. One eye
was closed behind swollen purple flesh, the other barely
open; she stared from it as if seeing nothing. A dribble
of blood from her mouth was smeared over her chin, and

a thin wail came from her throat as Jebediah led her toward the carriage.

Lucy did not have to lift the girl's skirt to know what had happened, but she did it anyway. Stepping between Ettalee and her father, she unhesitatingly lifted the tattered cloth, knowing that the girl was beyond humiliation.

And saw the sticky mess. Saw that the girl was still bleeding.

She may have said something then, must have said something, but she did not know. She dropped the skirt, and her eyes closed, or perhaps she went blind for a moment. She felt her hand tightening around the butt of the pepperbox in her coat pocket without knowing that she had reached for it.

"Well, now," a voice said. "Well, now, thought I saw we had company."

Lucy raised her head, and she was seeing again. Saul, his anguished moans muffled, had Ettalee in his arms. Tad, still on the landaulet, looked frightened. A snakelike vein pulsed on Jebediah's temple. A smile cracked Skeet's long gray face, and behind him his overseer grinned nervously.

Lucy stared at Skeet. It seemed odd that a day such as this could be so cloudless and bright. Somewhere a bird sang, sweet indifferent notes.

"Well, now," Skeet repeated. "Funny way to come visiting, Miss Lucy. Riding up to a man's gin house without a by-your-leave. You got business with me, you know you're always welcome at my door."

"Mr. Skeet," Lucy said, as if she had not heard him, "if you ever again touch one of my people, I'll kill you."

Skeet's smile faltered. His face darkened. "Now, that ain't no way to talk to a neighbor." His voice took on a sneer. "No, ma'am, not to an old friend of the family like Vachel Skeet."

"I'll kill you. If you take another one of my people—"

"I found a nigger wandering around without a pass. If she was one of yours, you ought to teach your people better. And if you can't do that, what the hell's a woman doing running a plantation anyway? Why, you ain't even got a proper overseer. . . ."

But Lucy was already speaking to Saul, as if she were indifferent to anything Skeet might say. "Get her into the carriage, Saul. Let's get her back home as fast as we can."

"Now, wait a minute, Miss Lucy." Skeet stepped forward, unwilling to end the encounter so quickly. "You just wait a minute. Ain't you forgetting something? I don't like to remind a lady, but don't you owe me something?"

Lucy paid no attention. She watched as Saul helped Ettalee toward the carriage.

"I said, *you owe* me, Miss Lucy!" As if infuriated by Lucy's apparent indifference, Skeet rushed toward the carriage. In an instant he had torn Ettalee from Saul's arms and thrown her weeping to the ground. He turned on Lucy again. "You just listen, you hear? I pick up your runaway nigger, I keep her here for you, I feed her, you owe me. Maybe I wouldn't even say nothing about that, but you take on your snotty Sabre ways with me—"

He broke off as he saw the six barrels coming up toward his chest.

For a moment they stared at each other. Lucy felt beyond anger now, her mind as blank as the cloudless sky. She only knew that she was going to bring something to an end, if necessary, and Skeet was waiting to see if she really meant it.

Using both hands, she raised the pepperbox higher and thumbed back the cock.

He saw then that she did indeed mean it, that she would do it, that she would seize on any excuse, or perhaps needed no further excuse at all to blow a hole clean through him. No—six barrels, six holes. She was about to shoot him, and with a cry he threw himself back from her, his arms raised as if they might fend off the lead ball.

She never knew if she would actually have shot him, never knew her own deepest intention. Jebediah said, "No, Miss Lucy," and suddenly her hands were knocked high. The gun discharged deafeningly, its echo racketing across distant fields.

"You fucking bitch!" Skeet's eyes were wide with fear, his voice childishly cracked.

Lucy calmly thumbed back the cock again, to use her

second barrel. Still using both hands, she brought the gun back down to bear on Skeet's chest, holding it perfectly steady. This time Jebediah made no move to stop her.

"Never again," she said. "Don't you ever again touch one of my people."

When the gun didn't go off, Skeet at last found his voice. "And you get off my place! You ever come on my place again, God damn you—"

But Lucy did not hear. She lowered the pistol and carefully put down the cock. She went to Ettalee and helped Saul lift the girl from the ground. She was through with Skeet. Skeet no longer existed, would never again exist—until the next time she had to deal with him. Her only concern now was to get Ettalee safely home, where, Lucy hoped, everything that had happened to the girl might be forgotten.

Skeet watched. He stood, chest heaving, as the white woman and the bearded nigger got the wench into the carriage, and the tall black climbed up front with the boy. Sweat ran down his cold gray face, and he felt shriveled with humiliation that he should be treated thus before his overseer and his people. At the last moment, as the carriage turned and headed back along the wagon path, he tried to save dignity by yelling: "You hear me, now. You stay off my place, and you keep your goddam niggers to home. Or it ain't you gonna do no killing. You gonna have riders all over Sabrehill. Won't be the first time Sabrehill niggers was strung up, you hear me?" And one last shot: "You hear me, you *whore of Sabrehill?*"

The carriage rolled on.

Skeet forced himself to grin at his overseer. "Goddam bitch, pointing a gun at me. Guess I told her."

The overseer obediently returned the grin. "Guess you surely did."

"You notice how that nigger didn't dare let her use the gun?"

"She wouldn'ta had the guts anyway."

"Can't never tell with a woman. And them goddam Sabres, so high and mighty. But she ain't nothing but another scar-face bitch to me."

The overseer ran a finger down the right side of his

face, temple to jaw, as if tracing Miss Lucy's scar. "She's marked pretty bad. How she get that?"

"Husband, they say. If you can trust nigger-talk."

"Knew she was a widow—what happened to her husband?"

"Kicked in the head by a horse. They was only married a few months, two, three years back."

"Bitch like that, maybe he was lucky."

"If it was me done it," Skeet said passionately, "she'd be marked a hell of a lot worse than that. With me, ain't *no*body gonna look at her. Leastwise, not without puking up."

The overseer laughed. As they watched the carriage become smaller in the distance, Miss Lucy's image remained clear in Skeet's mind: a tall blond woman with so-blue eyes; high cheekbones over near-hollow cheeks; delicately fluted nose and a firm jaw. And he heard again her voice, low and husky, that had once been the sweetest music he had ever known.

Well, now, Miss Lucy, he thought. Well, now.

His heart was slowing, his palms drying, the sense of humiliation fading away. By God, he had told her. All these years she had acted as if he weren't alive, as if he had never existed for her. When he had arrived at Sabrehill with a posse or a patrol, she had never given him so much as a glance. She had acted as if there had never been anything between them at all, as if he were dirt and had always been dirt, and dirt was beneath her notice.

And him with a game right leg, a bad limp, to this very day because of her. Because he had defended her honor, had fought for her.

Yes, she owed him.

And today he had reminded her. She couldn't put him out of her life like that. After a dozen years, he was back in her life whether she liked it or not, and after today, by God, she knew it. And he didn't think he was going to let her throw him out of her life again.

Funniest goddam thing. He felt as if she still belonged to him.

Well, how do, Miss Lucy.

He looked around. His niggers were staring, but for

once he just laughed. "What's the matter? You all never see a crazy woman before? Get your black asses back to work."

How do, Miss Lucy!

The young ones didn't know, Zulie thought bitterly. They thought they knew, because of the tales they had heard. Oh, yes, they had heard of hangings and burnings and merciless whippings, they might even have seen an occasional cropped ear or a branded forehead. They had heard all about Mr. Skeet and his kind, and they might know something of vicious overseers; Sabrehill had once had one. But most of them had had little personal experience of such things. They thought they knew. But they didn't.

No, to them it was merely an excitement, a game. Mr. Skeet, he done got Ettalee, but now Miss Lucy, she going get Ettalee back. She tell old Mr. Skeet. Hear tell she got old pepperbox gun in she pocket, tell him good! Excitement. Fun. Something to laugh about for the next few days.

But then, well into first dark, when the lights were on in the quarters and the big house, the carriage appeared at the gate. Distant shouts, down by the road, greeted it, and children came running behind it. It came up the long sloping avenue, up between the lines of great live oaks until it reached the circular path of the courtyard. It turned toward the east service lane, where Zulie stood waiting, and the people—cheerful, many of them grinning, expecting a triumphant return—yes, the people came running and gathered round. The carriage came to a halt before the blacksmith shop.

And then they saw Ettalee.

There was an appalled silence as Miss Lucy handed the girl down to Zulie and light from the surrounding shops hit the girl's face; then a universal gasp, a groan, the sounds of disbelief, shock, horror. Zulie yelled, "Shut your fool heads, get your asses out of here! Goddam it, Jeb, can't you get these people *out?*"

She was in charge now, unless Miss Lucy said otherwise. She grabbed the battered girl before the girl's feet had hit the ground, "Get these peoples 'way from here!" and led her, or carried her, to the quarters at one end of the blacksmith shop.

Ettalee's pallet was in a loft over the room, but Zulie, without bothering to ask, now put her into her father's bed. She shooed Saul from the room, and he reluctantly left. Then she went to work, silently, quickly, tearing the girl's tattered dress from her body, scrubbing her, cleansing, healing. One of the women, Binnie, had already brought Zulie's ointments, salves, herbs. Momma Lucinda, the cook, and as much a healer as Zulie, worked with her. Miss Lucy watched silently from the doorway. Ettalee, half-conscious, barely whimpering, seemed to have little idea of what was going on.

They finished. Zulie gave Ettalee a potion to help her sleep, and Momma Lucinda tucked the girl deeply under covers. Binnie burned the ruined dress, except for one bloody strip that Zulie kept for her own conjure-woman reasons. The light was put out. Momma Lucinda, Binnie, Miss Lucy, like the crowd outside, vanished quietly into more distant shadows. Zulie, wrapping a spare blanket around herself, left the room and found Saul sitting on a bench outside of the shop. Coatless, he seemed unaware of the cold.

"She going be all right, Saul."

Saul gave no indication of hearing. He sat hunched, as he had been in the carriage, and stared into the darkness. Zulie sat down beside him, patted his hand, and repeated: "She going be all right."

He stirred. She felt the tensions that flowed through his rock-hard body: tensions of hatred, fear, sorrow. *What had that white man done to his daughter?* And what would be the result? A different Ettalee, perhaps, scarred within and ridden by demons implanted in her by Skeet? A girl forever wounded, forever maimed? A child unwanted, since there was no sure way to prevent one? He had seen these things before; he knew that the pain, the wounds, the suffering could go on for generations.

But Saul, she wanted to tell him, it don't *got* to be

that way. Many a black woman, she live through worse, yes, and white woman too. And come out singing!

But you couldn't say that to Saul, not yet. First he had to have his time of grief and anger. And the most you could do for now was to pat his hand and say one more time: "She going be all right." And then wait. Wait until he was ready to speak.

"Should killed him," Saul said at last.

"No, Saul."

"Should killed him right there with my own hands."

"Then they string you up, what good that do Ettalee?"

Perhaps she should not have said even that; she felt his frustration and shared it. And that brought on the dream.

Adaba, she thought. *Adaba!*

Everyone, it seemed to her, had to have some kind of dream at times like this, in order to survive, to keep on going. And Adaba was hers. She had had many dreams —she had dreamed of being rich and free in Charleston, she had dreamed of being sent north, all the way to Canada. But at the worst times, when there seemed no other way to escape the pain of being black and a slave, she dreamed of Adaba.

Adaba, the outlier. Adaba, the maroon leader, the slave-thief, the rescuer. Adaba, who came in the night and silently led slaves away, never to be seen again, who led them through swamps and forests, who led them north to freedom. . . .

Of course, there were many who said he didn't even exist. After all, who around these parts had ever seen him? He was a rumor, a myth, a tale told after dark. But she had heard white masters curse him—*That damned Adaba! Freed more niggers than all the Quaker abolitionists you'll ever meet!*—and that made him seem real.

Trying to share the dream, Zulie smiled and put an arm around Saul's shoulders. "Well, one of these days," she said, "maybe old Adaba come, carry us all away."

Saul made a sound of contempt. "Ain't no Adaba. That just dumb field-nigger talk."

"Can't never tell. Maybe one these days I just conjure him up." But hadn't she already tried and failed?

"Ain't no Adaba," Saul repeated after a moment. "You go conjuring, you bring us Black Buck."

So that was his dream, the dream that helped him to keep going. She had hers, and he had his—and perhaps his was the better dream. While she longed for a savior who would carry her off, he prayed for an avenger. Not an outlier who merely stole away slaves, but one who stirred up rebellion, one who raided and plundered and killed.

"But there ain't no Adaba, Saul, what make you think there a real and true Black Buck out there?"

Saul turned toward her on the bench. He frowned at her. "I *know* Black Buck," he said. "Why, I know Buck since he ain't hardly a pickaninny. Ain't no blacksmith at Skeet plantation, Buck he bring the work here for me. Buck drive Mr. Skeet here, he come calling. Why, back then you see Buckley Skeet yourself."

Maybe she had, she didn't remember. She had been only fifteen or sixteen when Buck had run away from Redbird. There had been a tale at the time that Mr. Skeet, so angry with Buckley, had offered a huge reward for him. But how did all of that prove that Buckley Skeet and Black Buck were one and the same? It was just a tale that people told, like the tales of Adaba.

Anyway, what did it matter?

"Guess he ain't never going come back here," she said. "Not so Mr. Skeet can catch him."

"You bring him back here, Skeet don't catch him. He take care Mr. Skeet."

"Me bring him back?"

"You a true conjure-woman, ain't you? Witch-woman like your momma? And her momma too?"

"Yes, Saul—"

"Then you bring him back! Or you don't want do that, then you put the badmouth on Mr. Skeet, Zulie! Put the voodoo spirits on him, curse him good!"

Saul's dark gaze held Zulie's, and she saw the pleading, the depth of his hope. But he didn't really know what he was asking. A healing potion, a simple love spell, a good luck charm—they were one thing. But a true badmouth, a serious curse—that was quite another. The gods sometimes exacted strange and unexpected payments for their favors, as she had learned from bitter experience, and a curse on one's enemies might turn out to be no better than a curse on one's self.

Still . . . not always, not always.

And Saul was not asking for trouble at Sabrehill but at Redbird. Maybe that would make a difference.

"You sure, Saul? You sure that what you want?"

"Got to do something," Saul said, "got to. And ain't no angel with a fiery sword going after Mr. Skeet. Zulie, you do this for me."

"I do it, I do it for Ettalee. And for all of us."

He took her hand. "Then you going—"

"Ain't said that. Me, I got to think about it."

Yes, she had to think about it. And yet, sitting there in the dark lane with Saul, the night growing colder around them, she had the feeling that some decision had already been made, some corner turned. And there would never be any going back again.

They talked a little longer, saying nothing more about voodoo or Black Buck. Saul wanted Zulie to spend the night with Ettalee in case the girl awakened and needed her. Zulie agreed. Saul climbed up into the loft over the bedroom, and a moment later Zulie undressed and slipped between the covers with Ettalee. She untied from her waist the long, thin, razor-sharp knife she always carried under her dress, and put it under her pillow where she could easily reach it.

She closed her eyes.

Adaba, she thought, as she had so many other nights, *Adaba, Brown Dove, come to me. Come to me and take me, take me far away, take me.* . . . And she had a feeling of being enfolded in softness, a sensation of being lifted, of being carried gently, swiftly, sweetly, far away, never to return.

But her sudden, last vision, just as she fell asleep, was not of Adaba. It was of an angry black face, a triumphant face, a savage face—a face lit up by fire as gunshots rang out and a plantation big house burned.

Yet somehow she was not afraid.
She smiled.
Black Buck, she thought. And she slept.

Three

The raid. The fire. It was time.

Buck knew it was time even before Quashee returned to the cabin. He stirred and came out of the light sleep he had been in for most of the day. He stretched, yawned, sat up, and slowly brought himself fully awake in the darkness of the cabin. He was good for many hours now. It was well, because the others had had little chance to rest today, and he would have to keep them going at least until dawn.

Arising from the bed, he found his pistol and his hatchet and strapped them on. He already wore his knife; he was seldom without it. He pulled on his coat and slung his big leather poke from a broad strap over his shoulder. He put on his old black hat with its broad slouch brim. He now carried most of his possessions in this world, and they were more than he needed to survive in almost any circumstances he was apt to meet.

Though he was alone, he moved soundlessly about the dark cabin—a matter of habit. The same set of habits made him look carefully from the edge of a window and then open the cabin door slowly. The slave-quarters street, with its rows of facing cabins, appeared to be deserted. Most of the cabins were dark, and in the mansion a few hundred yards away the only lights were from a couple of upstairs windows. There was not nearly enough light from the buildings to obscure the brilliant stars, and looking up through the doorway at the heavens, Buck smiled. He read the stars well, and they would make the getaway tonight much easier.

He stepped out of the cabin and stood waiting, breathing deeply of the crisp, invigorating air. A shadow appeared at the far end of the quarters street, and Buck could tell by its stride that it was Quashee. He noted with irritation that there was someone following him. Quashee's wife, Nita? No. It was the youngest of their party, Henry, a three-quarter hand. Buck didn't like that. If he was to lead this bunch of niggers to freedom, he expected them to obey his every order to the letter. As a matter of fact, he didn't like the way Henry had been behaving at all, but this was no time to raise hell about it.

"Ready?" he asked, as the pair arrived at the cabin.

"Got four mule loaded." Quashee was so excited he could hardly keep his voice down. "Got smoke meat, corn, sugar, salt, don't know what all."

"Ogden clean out his carpenter shop?"

"Got axe, draw knife, chisel, adze—man, we got everything we can put on four big mule!"

"Not overloaded," Buck cautioned.

"No! Man, I know them mule. Strong, fast, and big heart."

It sounded good. Buck turned to the boy. "What you doing here, Henry? You supposed to be with the others, over by the creek, watching the mules."

"He still don't like the fire," Quashee said.

"Well, now, that is plain too damn bad!"

"Don't need no fire!" Henry said plaintively. "Can go now, go in the dark, and they never know. Ain't no need for no fire!"

Buck restrained his temper. "I told you. Fire keep them busy. While they fighting the fire, we get away."

"But they don't know we running tonight, ain't no need—"

It was an old story. The boy might dream of rebelling against his masters, he might dream of burning the entire countryside. But not *his* big house, not *his* plantation, not even if he were running for his freedom. His life here, his work, had made the place in some measure *his,* and to destroy it was too painful.

But Henry was wrong. The masters would never let him have what was his, and there *was* a need for fire.

"Quashee," Buck said, "you still want to burn the place?"

"Burn it," Quashee said passionately. "Burn it to the ground. Then burn overseer house too. Burn it all."

"And I reckon Nita say the same thing, and Ogden and Joe too. So that what we going do, Henry. No need for you to help, but you just stay clear." Buck's hand dropped to the butt of his pistol. "You make me, I shoot you fast as any white man."

"Aw, ain't no need for that," Quashee said. "You get to the creek, Henry, help with them four mule. We meet you all there real soon, and then we be on our way. You shoo now, real fast."

Reluctantly the boy turned away. He headed between the cabins, off toward the creek. Buck and Quashee watched until he had disappeared into the darkness.

"He gonna be all right?" Buck asked.

"Aw, sure," Quashee said. "Sure, he be all right."

How many plantations had he raided? How many slaves had he led off to maroon camps and sent on their way north? He honestly had no idea, for it had never occurred to him to keep track.

He might never have survived after running away from Redbird if he had not happened onto Adaba. He had known how to hunt and fish, but he had had no weapon of any kind and virtually none of the skills of the fugitive. By sheer luck he had stumbled exhausted onto Adaba's camp, and the latter had taken him in and taught him all that he needed to know. They had traveled together for several years before Buck started wandering up and down through the coastal states on his own.

Like Adaba, he learned to move freely and easily, avoiding patrols and leaving no trail behind him. He lived off the land when he had to and stole when he could. He spent many a night in slave quarters, eating well and sleeping easily, unbeknownst to the masters. And always, while traveling, he kept his eyes open. And listened. And asked questions.

Thus it was that he had the Courtney plantation in mind long before he ever set foot on it. He had heard that old Courtney was overly strict and that his overseer, a man named DeGraff, was feared, which suggested that there was a lot of discontent on the place. He knew that it had been raided before, but not for several years, which meant that it was probably not on its guard. And most important, it was several days from the nearest maroon community. Buck was always careful not to cause trouble for his places of retreat; ironically, those plantations closest to outlier camps were often the safest from them.

Yes, Buck decided one day, it was time for a raid, and the Courtney plantation was a good bet.

Ordinarily, he might simply walk into a slave quarters late at night, keeping on the alert, but with little worry; he had an instinct both for trouble and for safety. In this case, however, he watched the fields and outbuildings from behind thickets and hedges for most of two days, and it did seem that what he had been told about the Courtney plantation was true. He watched while one of the drivers, for no apparent reason, made life hell for a young cotton-picking field hand called Henry. He saw how the other hands, particularly the young women, reacted when DeGraff, the overseer, appeared. It soon became evident to Buck that this plantation, far more than most, was anything but a happy place.

On the evening of the second day, as the hands were leaving the fields, Buck made his presence known, casually joining Henry. Henry was not surprised—Buck was just another black man passing by, the latest of many.

"Seen you with that driver," Buck said, grinning. "Want me kill the sonabitch for you?"

After that it was easy. He had supper with Henry and some of his friends. He impressed them with his "educated" talk—he had spent much of his boyhood in a big house—and amused them with his stories of life in the wilds. They believed his stories too—he had the look. He was a solidly built yet lean man, weathered beyond any field hand, and narrow-eyed. His beard was a short, narrow spike below his chin; his mustache, twin spikes hanging at the corners of his mouth. He knew how to laugh heartily, but he had the kind of eyes that could threaten death without his ever saying a word.

He called himself Buck. Just Buck, nothing more. But he was Black Buck, and everybody knew it.

Through Henry, he met Quashee and Nita that same first night. He saw at once that Quashee was the right-hand man, the driver, that he needed for this raid. The man had been trying to protect his wife from DeGraff for three years and with only limited success. Complaints to the master had gotten the overseer away from Nita for a time, but they had also brought the whips down on Quashee's back unmercifully. The man was ready to march through hell to claim his vengeance and to take his wife away from this place. All he needed was a leader, someone to show him the way, and now, as if in answer to years of desperate prayer, Black Buck had come at last.

Quashee, in turn, soon led Buck to Ogden, the carpenter, and to Joe, who worked with the mules. Ogden had no woman, and Joe's wife was dead. Both men were loners and had little in the way of ties on the plantation. Henry, an orphan, said he wanted to join them, and that gave Buck five followers—an easily manageable group.

He set Monday night as their time of departure, a few days hence. Meanwhile the group set out quietly to make its thefts—a tool here, a bit of food there. Some things, such as tools from the shops, could be stolen only at the last moment; any earlier, and their absence would be noticed. But at last, tonight, they were ready to go. The mules were packed. Nita, Ogden, and Joe had them ready by the creek, where they were all to meet, and Henry was on his way there.

"You know what to do?" Buck asked Quashee, as they stood by the cabin.

"I know."

"The torches ready?"

"They waiting, and I got this to fire 'em." Quashee showed Buck the stolen flintlock. It looked like a small barrelless pistol.

"Then let's go."

They walked slowly along the quarters street. If anyone saw them, he paid them no attention, or pretended not to.

Quashee knew the way best, of course, and led. The night was now brilliant with stars, revealing mansion, outbuildings, and landscape with perfect clarity. They passed

barns, stables, shops, and circled the big house, keeping a
good distance from it. Twice, dogs barked at them, but
Quashee, who knew the animals, quickly silenced them.

Like so many plantation big houses, this one was built
facing a river, and they circled to the river side, where,
at this hour, they were least apt to be observed. From under some brush, at some distance from the house, Quashee
produced two torches and handed one to Buck. Two more
torches were hidden near the overseer's house.

Until this moment, Buck had felt perfectly calm. But
now he felt a trembling deep within himself as tension
mounted. He felt the familiar weight of stick, cotton, and
straw in his hand, smelled the familiar perfume of turpen-
tine and tar. And thought of Redbird.

"We do it," Quashee said quietly, as if he needed one
last affirmation.

"Yeah. We do it."

Torches in hand but still unlit, they walked purposefully but unhurriedly toward the piazza of the big house.
Now the house showed no lights at all. Buck felt his nerves
drawing still more taut.

They crossed the piazza. Quashee cautiously tried the
door. As expected, it was unlocked—they usually were.

Quashee took the flintlock from his pocket. He stared
at it for a few seconds, as if realizing that once he used
it there would be no turning back.

He drew back the cock and snapped it, releasing a
small brilliant spray of sparks. Tinder flamed, straw
flamed. The torch flared up, and suddenly the brilliant
night around them turned dark.

Buck's knees shook. His mouth was dry. He lit his own
torch from Quashee's, and again he thought of Redbird.

"Now," he said.

He threw open the door and led the way into the house.

The only light came from their torches, flickering and
flaring, but Quashee had told Buck what to expect. The
house was like a great many others, large and small, in the
South. It was organized around a large central hallway, or
passage, which ran through the house from one side to
the other, to permit a cooling draft during the hot sum-
mers. Rooms on each side of the hallway were intercon-

nected. A staircase in the hallway led to the upper storeys. Buck needed no diagram to tell him where to go.

Once in motion, he had no nerves, no fear, only a kind of ferocious joy. He took the left wing; Quashee took the right. They moved silently. The place would be afire and they would be gone before anyone knew. Buck had not even drawn his pistol.

He found himself in a music room: a large piano stood on one side, a gilded harp on the other. He moved at once to the windows. He opened them silently, then fired the long heavy drapes that hung beside them. Almost at once there was a low, dull roar as the flames began to leap and climb.

Buck smeared his torch against a sofa and a couple of chairs and moved on to the next room. Again he opened windows and put the torch to the heavy drapes. Through an open doorway nearby, he saw the glitter of glass and crystal, and he had an impulse to smash it. But no: the house was burning, and there was still no alarm. The longer before the fire was discovered, the better.

It was all going so beautifully: the recruitment, the thefts, the fire.

He stepped back out into the central passage and waited by the staircase, near the door. Quashee had not yet reappeared from the right wing of the house. An instant later, he appeared in the glow of his own torch. He wore a wild grin, a triumphant grin.

The grin disappeared. Quashee's eyes were suddenly wide.

Buck knew in that instant that something had gone wrong. He knew it even before the pistol shot from the staircase. He saw the ball thud into Quashee's forehead driving him backward and down as the torch flew from his hand. Then the white man was down the stairs in one bound and twisting toward Buck. Courtney, the master— a blond bear of a man, shaggy mustached, eyes of green fire. The gun in his right hand was smoking, and the one in his left was coming down level, was swinging toward Buck, was aiming—

Buck had no time to draw. He was a dead man and knew it. Unless—

There was no time even for terror. Buck threw his torch in the man's face. At the same time he twisted away toward the door and dropped to one knee. He saw the door flung open in the very instant that he felt the ball blaze over his head. The overseer stood there, gun in hand, his face blank with surprise as Courtney's slug drilled into his chest. Buck was through the door, knocking the overseer to one side, before the body could fall.

Then he was in the darkness, running—running, still blinded by the brilliance of the flames. Behind him a gun slammed—probably the overseer's pistol in the master's hand. The shot didn't come close.

No time to fire the overseer's house now. No need to. The bastard was probably dead. Buck sucked air, sobbed, ran. Cursed himself. Wished now that he had taken a chance, taken ten seconds more, killed Courtney. Two dead white men were not too many for one dead nigger. But he had panicked, and now it was too late.

Into darkness. Run.

The yard was lit by torches. A few flames and a good deal of smoke still showed at the windows, but most of the light in the house now came from lamps. The people kept running into the house with their buckets of water, and it seemed to Courtney that they were enjoying the mess they were making. They acted as if this were some kind of picnic. No matter what you did for the black bastards, no matter how puppy-dog loyal they seemed, you could never tell when the damned savages would turn against you. You could treat them well, teach them discipline, keep them in their natural place, and they'd still help some damned outlier to burn your house down.

At his side, Courtney's wife sobbed for her poor house. He put an arm around her shoulders and patted her, but his throat was tight with rage. He looked around. Furniture and clothing had been carried out of the house to save it from smoke damage. DeGraff and Quashee had been dragged away from the house and laid out on the grass, where they were hardly distinguishable from the piles of clothing. Young Henry, lugging buckets of water, was the one live nigger who looked miserable.

Well, Henry, at least, had proved loyal, if only at the last moment. There had been no time to prepare a real defense. All Courtney had been able to do was send the boy for DeGraff and then wait on the second floor, hidden from view, pistols in hand. And the two men had entered so suddenly that there had been no chance to take them before they started the fire.

And now he had a half-ruined house and one dead overseer and one dead nigger on his hands. And—Henry had not been too coherent—evidently he had lost several other niggers as well. In other words, he had lost several thousands of dollars in valuable property.

Someone was going to pay.

It had been a long time since he had last been raided, but altogether this was the third time, and he was determined, by God, that it would be the last. The damned runaways and outliers, they would learn that if any one of them set foot on Courtney land somebody was going to die for it. The maroon camps could be found, if anyone really took the time and trouble to look for them, and the only way to deal with them was to wipe them out completely. He was going to get this Black Buck, or whoever it had been, and if he could not get Black Buck, he would kill a dozen others.

He heard a long anguished wail, a woman's cry of grief.

It was Quashee's woman, kneeling over his body. What was her name? Anita? According to Henry, she had been in on it with Quashee, and there was probably plenty she could tell. Courtney strode over to her.

"He got your husband killed, Anita," he said harshly. "Yes, your nigger outlier friend did that, didn't he? He went and got your Quashee killed."

The woman did not appear to hear. Courtney supposed he should feel some sympathy, even if she were involved in the plot, but somehow her keening just made him angrier. God, he thought, these people even grieved like savages.

"Anita."

He reached down, grabbed a handful of her hair, and

yanked up and back. The torch light caught her face, wet with tears.

"Now, you listen to me. I said, that nigger that came here got your husband killed. Isn't that right?"

The woman did not answer. He tightened his grip on her hair and shook her. "Yes, that's right. He got Quashee killed. But now I'm going to get him killed, and you're going to help me. You and Henry. You're going to tell me everything you know about that murderer, everything you know about his plans, every single thing you heard him say. You're going to tell me right now. Tonight. And then I'm going after him."

And get him.

He had no illusion that it would be easy. It might take days or even weeks. But he would have the entire countryside alerted by dawn. He would have plenty of men willing to ride with him—hell, he would pay them if he had to, to keep them riding until the job was done. They would soon pick up a lead, they would stop at every plantation, they would talk to the blacks in the quarters and in the fields. The blacks would try to lie, but he, by God, would whip the truth out of them.

And sooner or later Black Buck would die.

Four

Run.

That was what they had to do now, in the darkness, as fast as possible. Put distance between themselves and the Courtney plantation. If they were lucky, whites from miles around would soon be fighting the fire, and it might be hours before pursuit could be organized.

Buck and Ogden each led a mule; Joe, the most experienced man with the animals, led two of them. They were headed northwest, upcountry, through the lower pine belt. The land was slowly rising, and over their heads the great long-leaf pines frequently obscured the stars.

This was farming country, plantation country, but there was nevertheless a great deal of forest. As much as possible, Buck planned to stay in the woods, toward the upper pine belt and then the hills. In the woods skirting the desolate white-domed sand hills, they would find their maroon camp and, with any luck, Adaba.

Buck had no difficulty in keeping Ogden and Joe going; they understood well the importance of traveling almost at a run through the night, pausing only to rest, feed, and water the mules. And Quashee had been right about one thing—the mules were strong and bighearted, and they never balked.

They traveled well into the next morning. While staying back among the trees whenever possible, they saw hands coming out into the fields. The day warmed. Ogden's and Joe's faces were creased with fatigue, and at last the mules showed signs of refusing to go further. They still had to feed themselves and improvise a temporary camp, and with one silent accord they came to a halt.

Buck took the first watch and slept the last, and as happened so often, his sleep was haunted. He was back in the Courtney big house, reliving that terrifying moment when Quashee had appeared and gazed up the staircase at the end of his life. But then Buck realized that he was not in the Courtney big house at all, he was back at Redbird, and it was not Courtney coming down the stairs, it was Vachel Skeet. It was Vachel Skeet, grinning, who fired the pistol into Quashee's head, drilling a hole through his brain. It was Vachel Skeet, who then turned the same pistol, somehow reloaded, on Buck and deliberately aimed it low at Buck's guts.

He awakened sobbing as Joe tugged at his arm.

It took a moment. His head whirled, he was lost and scared. Then he realized.

They were being watched. They had been seen. Seen not by one person but by half a dozen or a dozen or even more—God only knew how many. Sitting up, gathering his wits, Buck saw that it was sunset—and that they were surrounded. Blacks were moving by at a distance, staring at them for a moment, then looking away.

He realized what had happened. It was the end of the workday, and these people were headed back toward their quarters. In moving from one field to another, they passed through this patch of woods. In his fatigue that morning, Buck had failed to see the signs.

If they had been seen by only two or three blacks, he would not have been very much concerned. But to be seen by so many was a different matter. Word would quickly get around, there would be talk in the wrong places, and their pursuers could hardly fail to pick up some information. The blacks might play dumb and lie like hell, but Courtney would at least have confirmed that Buck and the others had passed by and were heading for the upcountry.

The last of the blacks disappeared from the woods.

"All right," Buck said, "let's go. Fast."

They continued traveling mostly at night for three days, always pressing themselves, making almost as good distance in the dark as they could have in the daytime. Looking back from the tallest pines they could climb, they saw no signs of pursuit, and Buck sensed a rise in his companions' spirits. They were seen again, more than once, but the farther they got from the Courtney plantation, the less that worried Buck.

The land kept rising. There was more oak and hickory among the pines. But by Friday morning the pines had thinned; the land had become white and infertile, the trees scrubby and stunted. Buck turned northeast, staying close to the pine belt. He allowed only a morning rest and then, in the early afternoon, urged the mules back into motion. He hoped to reach Adaba's camp—or one of them—by evening.

He no longer took any particular pains to keep them hidden; boldness was safer. He led his party past shacks and shanties and tried for a swagger as the whites came out to stare at them. The women shooed the ragged children back indoors ("Nigger steal you off to a maroon camp!"); the few men nodded, perhaps muttered a greeting, and gripped their ancient muskets with white knuckles. These, Buck knew well, were among the poorest whites in the Carolinas, the true po' whites, the po' buckra, the sandhillers. They lived in a kind of armed truce with the nearby marooners, hating them and often envying them, and yet in a kind of secret, unspoken alliance with them. They had a common enemy in "the quality," "the chivalry," the well-to-do, and a common interest in the burden carried by the mules.

What was that burden? Treasure. Perhaps a few bolts of cloth, perhaps seed, perhaps tools. Center bits for a beam drill, a chisel axe head, a hay knife or two. Anything that might help a runaway black—or a white man in the hills—to survive. And all of it probably stolen from whites who lived miles from here. Why else would three blacks have four heavily loaded mules in these parts? The marooners at the camp would keep what they needed for themselves and trade the greater part of it to the whites for more-needed supplies—an axehead or a saw for corn or fruit. Treasure. The whites watched, sullen-eyed, but alert with greed.

Buck took only one precaution. He did not draw his pistol: that would have been too aggressive. But walking on the near side of his mule, he kept a slight, twisted smile on his face, and he carried his unsheathed axe in his left hand. The axe was somewhat different from most. Basically a shingling hatchet in design, it had a heavy poll, unlike, say, a hatchet meant for hewing or lathing. This gave it a balanced head and made it possible to throw the axe, edge forward, with great accuracy. With a little luck, Buck could split a man's skull at more than a dozen paces. He knew. He had done it.

Nobody approached them or interfered with them, and in the late afternoon they reached Adaba's camp.

Dark clouds boiled and tumbled in the sky, and a cold breeze cut through Buck's clothes. A storm was building, a thunderous storm, more like spring than winter.

Adaba's face was grim, his eyes implacable.

"You dumb son of a bitch," he said. He spoke slowly and distinctly but so softly that perhaps only Buck could hear him. "You goddam stupid bastard."

He sat in a chair out before his little cabin. He was a lean, hard man, big boned, big handed, ruggedly handsome; smooth cheeked, but with a muzzle of thick black beard. Buck sat on the ground a few yards in front of him. He sat there because Adaba had told him to sit there, and the eyes of the armed blacks around them had defied him to do otherwise. It had the effect of making Buck feel very young, much younger than Adaba, though both men were in their fourth decade. But then Adaba often made him feel young.

Adaba: the Brown Dove. Some people said his real name was John Dove and he was from somewhere to the north, Virginia or perhaps Maryland. Others said his name was Johnny Edisto and that he was from the Sea Islands, though he didn't speak like an Island black. In all the years he had known Adaba, Buck had never learned his story.

Now Adaba sat in his chair like a magistrate listening to evidence and passing judgment. The armed men, who had surrounded Buck and the others and brought them into camp, stood at a distance with Joe and Ogden and pretended to pay no attention to what was going on. The moment was critical. Buck had counted on Adaba's help— Adaba, who more than any other black knew the escape routes that led to the north. Adaba, who had the friends and the trust. But Adaba's face was stone.

"Buck, I ain't seen you in 'most a year. You forget everything I teach you in that time?"

"Ain't forgot nothing, Johnny. It just work out that way."

"It didn't 'just work out that way,'" Adaba said scornfully, "not from what you tell me yourself."

"If wasn't for that Henry—"

"Now, don't you go blaming some poor nigger boy that can't stand to see the place he lived all his life burned down."

"He didn't live in no big house."

Adaba angrily waved the contradiction away. "Don't give me none of that shit, you know damn good and well what I mean. You was a fool, Buck, a fool!"

"Should kept my eye on him—"

"Damn right you should have. One mistake after another. But your big mistake was in firing the big house."

"But we had to do that," Buck insisted vehemently, knowing that this was his weakest argument. "We had to! Some nigger run tell them we was gone that night, they come after us. The fire was to keep them busy—"

"Ah, shit! Always more shit! You and your friends, all you got to do is take a quiet little walk in the night. Take a quiet little walk, and nobody know a damn thing till the next day. Nobody get hurt, nobody get killed, and you have five niggers with you 'stead of two. Fact is, you the kind of runaway nigger that just got to burn, burn, burn, no matter what. And this time you got black and white both killed, and don't tell me those white bastards ain't coming looking for you."

"But they ain't found me."

"Yet."

"Ain't going to find me. Wasn't nobody after us. I swear it, Johnny, we got away safe and free."

Adaba shook his head. "I ought to string you up myself. Ought to drive you out of this camp."

Another gust of wind blew through Buck's clothes, and the clouds thickened. There was nothing more to be said. In the long silence, Buck lowered his eyes to the ground and waited for judgment, knowing that his argument had gone badly.

"But," Adaba said at last, "wouldn't do no good, would it? Whatever you done, good or bad, it's done."

Buck looked up slowly, still not sure of the verdict. But Adaba's hard eyes softened. He shrugged and grinned. "Aw, hell," he said, "whyn't you get up and call your friends over here?"

Buck felt a surge of relief, and suddenly he wondered why he had ever doubted that Adaba would help them—give them sanctuary in his camp and help Ogden and Joe to go north. Of course he would—because he was Adaba.

Adaba stood up from his chair. He ruffled Buck's hair and slapped his shoulder, as he had so often done, once again making him feel very young. "Been worrying about you, son. Glad to see you still kicking."

Lightning broke distantly, and with a mutter of thunder, the storm rolled closer.

Sandhillers, Courtney thought contemptuously. Sandhillers, the dregs of the earth. There were half a dozen of them, men and boys, standing before the cabin—ragged, scared, craven—more animals, he thought, than men. Such creatures were put on earth, like niggers, only to do as they were told. He himself had brought three men with him and two boys near grown, and today he had met up with four patrollers. That meant a party of sixteen, including the sandhillers, and surely he could find still more men in these hills if he needed them.

"Now, the runaways came this way," he said. "We know that. And we've talked to people that saw them. And we've known for years that there was an outlier camp up this way somewhere, and now we aim to find it."

"Mister," one of the sandhillers said nervously, "we don't know nothing 'bout no outlier camp. Why, we don't even see hardly no niggers hereabouts."

"Not many, but I figure you've seen three of them in the last day or so. And you know which way they were heading. You've got an idea of where that camp is."

"Never seen no camp. Mister, we wouldn't never dare go looking for no camp back in them woods—"

"So it's back in the woods, and you've got an idea of *where* it is back in the woods, because you don't dare go there. Well, you're going to show us where."

Another man shook his head. "Could be there's a hundred niggers back there. Some say two hundred or even more. Why, you go back there, they kill you off so fast— you go in them woods, ain't nobody never going see you again. Why, there's hundreds niggers back there."

This was nonsense, and Courtney knew it. There wasn't a single camp of "hundreds niggers" anywhere from Maryland to Georgia. A camp of such size would be almost impossible to hide, and it would never have been tolerated. But a camp of a dozen or even two or three dozen, yes, that was possible. Most likely this camp had at best ten or fifteen men and boys who could put up a fight and maybe a few women and their pickaninnies.

But he did not say that. He said, "You mean to tell me that any white man isn't as good as any ten niggers? Why, I've seen little white children ordering a dozen black boogers out of their way, and you mean to tell me that all of us here can't go in and clean out a few dozen or so half-starved, lice-eaten, dirty black savages? You mean to tell me—"

"Black Buck," one of the men said, "he ain't your ordinary nigger."

Courtney smiled. It was the first time the name had been mentioned.

"So you've seen him."

He was dreaming when they came.

It was an old dream, often repeated. He was bound to a chair in the office at Redbird, and this time there was the sound of thunder and the drumming of rain on the roof. His ankles were secured to the legs of the chair, and his arms were tied around the back, and no matter how he tried, he could not get loose. With each distant scream—someone was screaming, and his own throat was raw—he pulled, strained, tore at his bonds, his muscles in knots, but he could not get away. And he had to get away, had to, because very soon, any time now, Vachel would be back, Vachel and Mr. Jeppson and maybe the others, and then they would—

He had failed. He would never escape. And now, somehow, he had been moved to the table. He lay naked, stretched out over it, faceup, still tied, still straining at the ropes. His legs, spread wide, were tied to the legs of the table, as they had been to the chair. His arms, stretched above his head and bent down over the edge of the table, were tied to the other two table legs. But he could still lift his head, and as he did so, he saw Vachel Skeet approaching, knife in hand. Buck cried, *No, no, no, no!* but Vachel only laughed and kept coming closer. The ropes cut into Buck's arms and legs as he pulled at them, *No, no, no, no!* and nothing he could do would free him or stop Vachel from carrying out his threat. He strained first to one side and then to the other. He lifted his entire body from knees to shoulders from the table; he made the table rock and shake, *No, no, no, no!* but Vachel only laughed the harder and, *No, no, no, no!* seized Buck's entire cock in a brutal grip and, *No, no, no, no!* pressed the steel into the flesh and began cutting, cutting, cutting—

Buck was sitting up on the pallet in the very instant that the first shot went off. "Out!" he heard Adaba calling to him. *"Out!"*

The terror of the dream was still with him as he reached for his boots. Fortunately he had fallen asleep with most of his clothing on, and his pistol, axe, and knife were, as always, right at hand.

As he leapt to his feet, the terror of the dream and the terror of the raid became the same thing: he was going to die here. He was going to die here in the dark, perhaps shot in the guts, perhaps captured, tortured, mutilated, unless he ran. He was out through the door of Adaba's cabin before he had his weapons strapped on.

The rain had stopped, but the sky was still cloud blanketed. Lightning struck nearby, illuminating a pair of running figures, then leaving the night darker than ever. An instant later, thunder cracked, but not so loud as to cover a woman's screams. Two pistol shots flashed.

Buck felt Adaba grab his left wrist, heard him say, "Come on!"

He was still disoriented. He did not know what, where, how. Adaba pulled at him and said, "Run, God damn you, *run!*"

There was nothing else to do. More shots rang out, and Buck had an impression of dark figures dashing by them, but he had no idea if they were friends or enemies. Adaba had posted guards, but obviously something had happened to them—they had been captured or killed. And now the entire camp was disorganized, and the gunfire suggested that to surrender was to die.

Buck followed the hand that kept pulling at his left wrist. If anyone could get them safely away from the camp, it was Adaba. With his free hand Buck drew his pistol and looked for a white face, any white face, but all he saw was the wet darkness.

Then he was alone.

He didn't know the exact moment that he lost Adaba. The fingers had slipped from his wrist and hadn't returned to it. He kept plunging forward, hitting trees, thrusting himself through brush, while pistol shots cracked behind him and lightning lit up the forest. And Adaba was not there.

Buck had to go back. There was no choice. He had brought this destruction, this death, to the camp, and he damned well knew it, and now he had lost his best friend, really his only friend in the world. If Adaba had been wounded, Buck had to help him. If he had been killed, Buck had to know. He had to do something about it. Terror at last vanished as Buck hurled himself back the way he had come.

He found Adaba within fifty feet. As lightning flashed, Buck saw the big man lying on his side, while a white man bent over him, arm cocked back, ready to plunge a knife into Adaba's throat. Buck's pistol was drenched from his run through the wet forest, but by some miracle it went off, and in the last flare of lightning, he saw the white man straighten and fall like a rag doll kicked in the face.

"You run, boy," Adaba said, as Buck reached him, "you run."

Buck ignored the order. He yanked Adaba to his feet. "Where you hurt?"

"Left leg. Left side."

Buck pulled Adaba's left arm over his shoulder, put his own right arm around the man's back. "Ain't going nowhere without you," he said. "Now, come on, damn it, we run together."

The rain began again at dawn, thin but steady. In the dim light, they could see what they had done.

They had managed to cut the throat of the one guard they had found. A second guard had seen them, but by then it was too late. They had fanned out and simply shot at or stabbed anything seen moving from the cabins. They had lost only one man, a sandhiller, and a couple of others had been wounded.

Obviously some of the blacks had gotten away. There were about fifteen cabins, well spaced from each other, which meant that the camp had probably had a population of at least that many blacks and possibly three or four times that many. But when they gathered up the bodies and dragged them to the middle of the camp, they found they had only twelve.

Courtney looked at them: twelve black bodies lying in the steadily falling rain. Twelve, including Ogden and Joe. Well, he'd promised himself a dozen, hadn't he? And yet he felt sick.

"Any of 'em look like your Black Buck?" one of the men asked.

"I didn't get too good a look at him," Courtney said. "He threw his damn torch in my face before I could. But . . ." He pointed to one of the bodies. "That could be him there."

"Just 'could be.'" The man sounded disappointed. "Hell, then he could be Adaba, for all we know."

"Nah," another man said, "Adaba got a black beard. Suppose to hide a birthmark on his left cheek. Ain't no Adaba here."

Twelve black bodies lying in the rain. Something disturbing was happening to Courtney. He was beginning to wonder why the hell he was here. Because a white man and a nigger had been killed on his plantation? Because his house had been damaged by fire? Because a couple of his niggers had run off? Those had seemed adequate reasons a few days ago, or even a few hours ago. But now, looking at the twelve black bodies lying in the rain, they no longer seemed so important. He didn't even care much if none of these was Black Buck.

Twelve black bodies.

What the hell was it with a nigger when he didn't know he was well off? What the hell was it that some of them preferred to live like savages in the woods and the swamps rather than be kept warm and clothed and well fed by a kindly master? Courtney did not regard himself as an unkind man, even if he did keep his blacks securely in their place. Most masters were decent, godfearing men. Then what the hell was it?

He looked more closely at the twelve bodies, as if seeking a clue. And for the first time he saw the thirteenth body.

There were eight men and two boys. There were two women. One of the women had a small dead child tucked under her arm. The woman had been shot, but the baby's throat had been cut, the head almost severed.

Courtney felt himself trembling. "Who did that?" he asked. His voice shook. "What rotten son of a bitch would do that to a child?"

"Why—why, she done it herself, Mr. Courtney," one of the sandhillers said, almost apologetically. "She was screaming something 'bout her baby not gonna be no slave, not never gonna be no slave, and she cut its throat before I could shoot her."

The rain kept falling, steadily, indifferently.

"Thought we ought to keep the two together," the sandhiller added awkwardly after a minute.

Courtney nodded. He said, "Let's bury them."

But he had to get away from the others for a while. It was time to go back home, he decided. He had got his revenge, and how the hell did he like it? If Black Buck was not among the dead, then let the bastard go. Courtney was tired of chasing him. Let the bastard go.

The rain, softer now, came steadily down on the roof of the old shed. They had found it none too soon, because even with the rain, the hands were beginning to appear in the fields and going about their chores. Fortunately the shed had a long-deserted look, and Buck was reasonably sure they would not be disturbed.

Adaba lay stretched out on the rough plank floor. His eyes were closed and his breathing deep, but Buck could not tell if he was conscious or not. He did not move as Buck carefully unfastened his clothes to inspect his wounds. As he had said, there were two of them, a bullet hole through the left thigh and another through the left side; fortunately both balls had gone clear through, and the holes looked cleaner than Adaba had any right to expect. No bones were broken. They were only flesh wounds, however painful and crippling. But he had bled a great deal, and of course there was always the chance of festering and fever, of gangrene or the dreaded lockjaw. With luck, a man might survive a couple of wounds such as these, but if his luck ran bad, even a scratch might kill him.

And it's my fault, Buck thought, *all my fault.*

There was time now for bitterness and anger and guilt. He had led Quashee to his death. He had failed to shake Courtney off of his trail. He had led the whites to Adaba's camp, and God only knew how many had been killed. And now Adaba.

There was no way to get justice, it seemed to Buck. No matter how you tried, no matter how many houses you burned, no matter how many white men you killed, they kept coming after you, you could never defeat them, the score was never settled. But the need to settle it remained. Somehow he had to defeat them, he had to win, he had to have justice for everything that had happened, all the way back to—

To Vachel Skeet.

Twelve years, and Vachel was still never far from his thoughts.

"It's all right, Buck," Adaba said, as if he knew what was in Buck's mind. He spoke softly, his lips hardly moving, and he never opened his eyes. "It's all right. Gonna be all right."

"That's right, Buck," another voice said, a white man's voice.

Buck looked up. He looked toward the door of the shed. The white man stood there, a ragged old man with a gleeful look in his eyes and an old blunderbuss in his hands.

"That's right, just don't you move, Buck," he said. "Just don't you move, and everything gonna be all right."

Five

Now at last the young ones were beginning to learn, Zulie thought with grim satisfaction. And the older ones had been reminded. No matter how well clothed and fed they might be, no matter how light the work demands, no matter what rewards and satisfactions they might be given, they were still slaves.

Everybody in the field and big house quarters knew what had happened to Ettalee, and not only in the quarters at Sabrehill, but at all the surrounding plantations as well. The day after her return, dozens of the people stopped by Saul's shop to find out how she was, and in the evening perhaps a hundred or more came by. They came from the Kimbrough and Devereau and Buckridge plantations, and a few came from as far as the Pettigrew and McClintock quarters. Grim-faced and bitter, they expressed their sympathy to Saul and muttered their deepest grievances to each other.

Zulie listened to the complaints and encouraged them. Let the people hate, she thought. Let the people hate, and then one day they will rise up.

Some of them at last turned to her. "Whyn't you do something to old Skeet, Zulie? You a conjure-woman, ain't you? Whyn't you sicken him for what he done, sicken him to the grave, he ain't no good. Whyn't you?"

Yes, why didn't she?

Late Tuesday evening, when every light was out, she crossed the lane to the coach house, where her older brother, Zagreus, lived in an upstairs room with his wife, Binnie. When she had entered and called up the stairs a few times, she heard the trapdoor entrance above opening, and Zagreus came down where she could see him in the starlight. He was a handsome man, in spite of a lash mark over his eyes, and the person she loved most in all the world—loved even more than Jebediah Hayes. She saw the worry and disapproval on his face. He already knew.

"Zagreus," she said, ignoring his look, "I sorry I bother you. I want a horse—"

"Thought you wasn't going to do no more badmouth, Zulie. You know what happen the last time."

Yes, she knew: death and near death; every hope, every dream, in ruins.

"Going be different this time," she said.

Zagreus shook his head. "Ain't going be no different."

"Then . . . maybe last time was all for best."

He saw then, as she knew he would, that her mind would not be changed. He was a strong man, but of the two of them, she was the stronger.

He nodded slowly. "You want a horse tonight?"

"In a little while. And don't you worry none, I put him back in his stall myself."

"Any special horse?"

"Thunder." She had already decided. She had chosen Thunder because he was associated with death. He had once shied at a snake and thrown his rider, killing him instantly.

Zagreus nodded again. "I get him for you."

But there were spells to be prepared first, magic to be made. Taking leave of Zagreus, Zulie hurried out to her cabin at a far corner of the field quarters. It was distinguished from the other of the older and shabbier cabins, of the quarters in only two ways. It was cleaner and better maintained, and the roof extended in front for some feet, making a kind of small pavilion with a floor of beaten earth. Actually this was a peristyle, which made the cabin a voodoo temple—though, fortunately, few white people who had seen it thought of it as such. At one time it had had a center-post around which voodoo ceremonies had been performed, but voodoo had been discouraged in South Carolina by the whip and the gallows, and Zulie performed the ceremonies only rarely. The services of a witch were in far greater demand at Sabrehill than those of a priestess.

She didn't bother with a light; she had known every inch of the cabin from childhood. It took her only a few seconds to locate a small cloth sack of cornmeal, several candles, and flint, steel, and tinder. With these in hand, she left the cabin and hurried across the fields to an old graveyard for slaves. There she quickly located a certain great elm tree near which her mother and her grandmother had been buried.

Carefully she sprinkled the cornmeal about the roots of the elm. Then she lit the candles and placed them upon the roots, securing them with their own drippings. With the candles in place, Zulie knelt and prayed to Momma Brigitte, wife of Baron Samedi, lord of the cemetery. When she had finished, she carefully gathered up handfuls of dirt from around the elm tree and put them into the sack in which she had brought the cornmeal. She hurried back to the east service lane, where Zagreus awaited her in front of the stables with Thunder.

She knew the countryside, and she rode well. Much sooner than Miss Lucy on the previous day, she was within a thousand yards of the Skeet big house. There she tied up the horse in a clump of woods and, the sack of dirt in hand, continued toward the house on foot. She traveled at a steady, tireless lope, an even run, that carried her across fields like the shadow of a deer.

She stopped a hundred yards from the house. She sniffed the air, as if for danger. Then she proceeded with greater caution, ever alert, aware of every sound in the night. Oddly enough, the dogs did not bark as she approached the house. They whimpered and slinked away.

The old shambles of a house loomed up against the night sky. Zulie stopped for a minute at the edge of the final clearing. She crossed the clearing and stepped onto the piazza. A board creaked under her weight, and she froze.

It seemed to her that if she listened hard enough, she might hear Mr. Skeet's night breathing behind the closed door, might even hear the beat of his heart.

She opened the sack and scattered the graveyard dirt before the door.

It was done.

She left as quietly as she had come.

Dirt on the piazza: Skeet was suddenly aware of it that morning, as the scattered bits grated and ground and compacted under his boots. Puzzled, he stared down at it. It was no surprise that the piazza was dusty, for it was never swept; but how had fresh *dirt* come to be scattered about it? What the hell had the niggers been up to?

Nothing. It was not worth thinking about, and he put it completely out of mind. Since the evening before last, Skeet had been able to think of only one thing.

Miss Lucy was in his thoughts as she had not been in years—both the Miss Lucy of his young manhood and the Miss Lucy who was now mistress of Sabrehill. After she had left Redbird on Monday evening, his anger had quickly dissipated, leaving only a kind of pure, sharp awareness of her presence in his world.

And she was aware of him too—he was certain of that. She might continue to feign indifference to him, she might pretend not to see him in the streets of Riverboro, but she would know he was there. After the incident on Monday, she *had* to know. And he had no intention of letting her forget him, not ever again.

Suddenly he had dreams again, he had plans. There was certainly no reason at this late date why he and Miss Lucy should remain enemies. What was past was past. Why, she had been married and widowed since that business with Justin Sabre so long ago, and she probably hardly even remembered it. He himself seldom gave it thought anymore, except on the rare occasions when he saw Miss Lucy—that is, he seldom had until she had come to his gin house, gun in hand, to get the girl. But that, it seemed to him now, was a minor incident, masking a much more important reality: their awareness of each other. He could easily forgive her for their trivial quarrel as long as it was clear that he still—or once again—occupied an important place in her life.

Yes, he thought, there was no reason in the world why he should not have a place in her life. There she was at Sabrehill, no man to take care of her, the only white person on the whole damn place; it was a situation that had caused more than a little scandalized talk. Why, she needed all the friends she could get. And had he not been a friend—yes, *more* than a friend—until Justin Sabre had spoiled it all? Had not he and old Aaron, Miss Lucy's father, been the very best of friends? He remembered the hours in the Sabre library with Aaron, the shy encounters with Miss Lucy, the wonderful expectations he had had in those days. Looking back on them now, it seemed to him that those days had a glow and a warmth almost too sweet to describe.

And why shouldn't he and Miss Lucy share such friendship again? Now that the past was so distant, why shouldn't Vachel Skeet once again go calling at Sabrehill on a Sunday afternoon? Why, he would probably be

welcome. It had been a long time since there had been
any talk about her and an acceptable bachelor, a long
time since her marriage, and from what he had heard,
she had very few gentleman callers. She was probably
very lonely. After all, most of the young bucks of her
generation had been married off years ago, and that scar
on her face wasn't exactly an advertisement for marriage.

Not that she was such a bad-looking woman if you
could ignore the damned thing. In fact . . .

Vachel Skeet was a lonely man, a solitary man. It
wasn't difficult for him to imagine a reconciliation with
Miss Lucy. *Vachel, I'm so glad you stopped by . . .
this quarrel has been so silly . . . you don't know how
lonely I've been . . . need a man at Sabrehill so badly
. . . need a man . . . you don't know how difficult it
is for a widow-lady, Vachel, all alone . . . need a man
. . . need a man. . . .*

Within twenty-four hours of their meeting at the gin
house, Skeet was wondering what it would be like to bed
Miss Lucy. Not simply to take her and use her like some
damned nigger, but to be wanted by her, to be loved by
her. And he calculated that of all the men in the world,
he was the one most likely to succeed with her. By the
next morning, when he stepped out onto the dirt-strewn
piazza, the thought, the hope, had become in his own
mind almost a certainty. He and Miss Lucy . . .

He saw her again that afternoon in Riverboro.

He had gone into town ostensibly to purchase supplies,
but actually with the thought that he might encounter
Miss Lucy. Of course, he knew that that was most unlikely, and yet—there she was, one of her wenches at
her side, in the same carriage in which she had been
driven to Redbird. The gods, it seemed, were smiling on
Skeet.

She did not appear to notice him. He watched as the
driver reined up a hundred feet ahead. Miss Lucy stepped
out of the carriage without waiting for assistance, and the
wench followed her. They crossed the board sidewalk
and entered a dry goods store.

For a moment Skeet stood paralyzed, palms sweating,

afraid to risk his dreams. But he knew that if he did not speak to Miss Lucy now, he might never do it.

He forced himself to walk. He walked slowly toward the store. All he had to do was appear to meet Miss Lucy by chance. He would greet her warmly and respectfully. If the matter of Etta-whatever-her-name-was came up, he would apologize. Yes, by God, he would, he would apologize for getting so damned angry and talking that way to a lady. He would ask her if he could be of any assistance to her at Sabrehill. He knew how difficult it must be for a lady to run a big plantation like that on her own, yes he did, and he had a lot of respect for her for doing it. Yes, sir, it would take more than a fine lady, it would take a *real* woman, like old Aaron's daughter, to do that, and he really admired her.

He approached the door of the store. He felt sick with anticipation. But he would smile and tell her—

She came back out of the door. He barely had time to step in front of her.

"Miss Lucy . . ." He remembered to snatch off his hat. He tried to smile. "Miss Lucy . . ."

He had forgotten that those eyes, so large and so very blue, could be so cold. He had forgotten that they could be so indifferent, so uncaring. He froze before them. His very brain seemed to congeal, and he became an unthinking object—a mere obstacle to this woman and in no way whatsoever a human being.

As insignificant as a nigger.

Her lips moved—one side of her upper lip lifted slightly. Her voice did not bother to conceal her contempt and hardly bothered to express it. In little more than a whisper, yet quite distinctly, she said, "Get out of my way."

He felt his smile becoming a painful rictus, a sick parody of itself. He tried to say her name again but could not. Somehow he found himself removed from her path as she swept by him. She entered the carriage, assisted by her wench, and the wench followed. Skeet watched, powerless to move.

The carriage rolled away.

Every dream he had had, every hope, mocked him.
She would never be friend or lover or even, truly, acquain-
tance to him. She had made a fool of him in his own
eyes by revealing his self-deception. Now she was disappearing down the main street of Riverboro, and he
could believe that she was giving him not the slightest
further thought. No, it was not she who was disappearing,
it was *he*—as she banished him from her mind.

But he would not be banished.

He refused. She had done that to him once before, but
never again. He refused to submit to such humiliation—
as if she could wipe him out of her life like a smear of
chalk from a slate. By God, she would learn that one
way or another *she had to pay attention to him.*

And there were ways to teach her. He knew that now.
There were ways.

On Wednesday evening, Theron and Lize, Ettalee's
friends from the Kimbrough plantation, sprinkled flour
around the elm tree in the cemetery, and Saul placed
candles on its roots—all in accordance with instructions
from Zulie. Other offerings, other sacrifices, were also to
be made. Momma Brigitte acted, when she acted at all,
only in return for payment, and Zulie had promised not
only her own but also those of others who were interested
in avenging Ettalee.

The next few days were difficult. Ettalee rarely left
her bed, rarely spoke. Zulie spent almost every hour with
her, feeding her, comforting her, trying to tease a smile
out of her. But Ettalee slept most of the hours away, and
when she was awake, she seemed to be in a zombielike
trance. Before long, Zulie felt the walls closing in on her,
and by Saturday evening she felt an urgent need to get
away. She tried to get Ettalee to go out to the field quarters with her, but the girl merely shook her head and
turned to the wall. Zulie went alone.

As it turned out, very little of interest was happening
in the field quarters. There was none of the usual dancing
that night and little music. Zulie heard a number of
complaints about Skeet and his kind, and there was talk

of rebellion—talk which, Zulie reflected sourly, would probably never come to anything.

At length, bored, she left the field quarters and went to Jebediah's house. She found a book, threw herself down on his bed, and spent an hour practicing her reading. As if he knew precisely when she had grown tired of that, Jebediah then plucked the book from her fingers, opened her dress, and began to pleasure her.

An hour later, while she still lay in his arms, he asked her to be his wife.

She looked up at him with astonishment. Fond as she was of Jebediah, it had never occurred to her that he might ask her to marry him. Marriage rarely figured in her thoughts, and besides, he was already getting what he wanted, wasn't he? They were both getting what they wanted.

"Why?" she asked. "Why you want to marry me?"

He smiled down at her. The arm around her shoulders pulled her closer, and his hand stroked her neat, close skullcap of curly black hair. "Because I love you, Zulie," he said, his lips touching hers. "I love you, you must know that."

She found that she was immensely pleased, but she said, "Don't mean you got to marry me."

"If I don't, sooner or later you're going to marry someone else. And I'm not going to like that one damned bit."

"Thought you was going up north one of these days."

"I am. And I want you to go with me."

"Now, how can I do that? Maybe Miss Lucy let you go free, but I *belong* here. They don't let no nigger buy hisself free no more, and even if they do, I ain't got no money."

"But I have. I can pay Miss Lucy for you, and she'll give you a pass to go with me. She'll let you go if I ask her."

So the rumor Zulie had heard was true: Miss Lucy paid Jebediah wages, which were put into a bank somewhere. She had heard of masters paying wages to their people, but it was very unusual, and she had never known it to happen at Sabrehill.

"Marry me, Zulie," Jebediah said. "Marry me, and when I leave here, go north with me."

She reached up and stroked his cheek. He had a good face, she thought, even with its broken nose and the whip-blaze that slashed across it. It had once been a handsome face, and in a way it still was. Certainly it made him no less attractive to the women of Sabrehill, and he could have had almost any girl he wanted for a wife. But he was asking her.

And she had love for him, a great deal of love.

Then why did she hesitate to accept him? Why did she feel underneath her pleasure an odd sense of dismay?

Somehow she had to delay, had to put him off. "Jebe-diah," she said teasingly, "you been at your Saturday night jug?"

"You know I haven't. Zulie, please—"

"Must been. Here you so smart, so educated, talk so good—why you marry a little old ignorant darky gal like me?"

"Don't talk like that, Zulie. You have a good mind, a fast mind, and when you've read more—"

She laughed and moved against him, trying to arouse and distract him. "It my *mind* you like, honey-child?"

He smiled. "Well, I like the rest of you too. So marry me, Zulie. Marry me."

"I think about it. Now, come on, honey, come on. . . ."

He sighed as she moved against him, bringing him to life again, and there was no more talk of marriage that night.

The next afternoon, a week almost to the hour after Ettalee had been stolen by Mr. Skeet, Zulie walked far out into the fields to visit her "dreaming tree." It was a gnarled old oak, so bent that one could easily climb the path of its broad trunk and sit comfortably in the spread of its branches—and dream. It seemed to hold her like a great gentle hand. As she watched the setting sun, she thought about Jebediah's proposal.

She supposed she would be a fool not to seize upon the opportunity. To be the wife of someone like Jebediah Hayes was almost as good as being free—insofar as any married woman, black or white, could be free. She would be the wife of the overseer of a great plantation, and how many women ever attained such heights? And he had money; Zulie had little doubt that if he did go north one day, he would be able to arrange for her to go with him. She had long dreamed of traveling far and seeing the great cities, and with a husband like Jebediah, the only limitation to achievement and happiness would be the simple fact that they were black. Somehow she didn't think that Jebediah would let that hold them back much. Oh, she would be a fool, no doubt, not to marry him.

And yet, and yet . . .

Somehow she had the feeling that if she married Jebediah, she would be trapped. She wondered how many other women, faced with marriage, had the same worry. She had a genuine love for Jebediah, but she also had the impression that he was hoping to receive from her far more than she had to give. If that were the case, she would eventually make him very unhappy, and she could look forward to a long waste of days as they slowly drifted apart.

The fact of the matter was that Zulie simply was not a particularly passionate woman. She was passionate neither emotionally nor physically except, perhaps, in her hatreds. She enjoyed her admirers' attentions, yes; they flattered and warmed her. She enjoyed the pleasure she gave and took in Jebediah's bed; she was always the happier for it. But beyond that, she had no great need, no great desire. Her instinct was to disdain emotional ties, to remain defiantly independent. Only once in her adult life had she experienced real passion for someone outside of her immediate family, and she had no wish to experience it again.

Or perhaps she felt that if she married Jebediah, she might never have the opportunity to experience it again.

She shook her head wearily. She didn't know, she just didn't know, and the setting sun had begun to hurt her eyes. She had best be getting back home. Yes, time to get back to Ettalee.

Zulie stood up from her place in the old bent oak. One small step at a time, carefully, she worked her way down the sloping trunk. She jumped the last few feet to the ground.

That was when Skeet seized her, clamping a hand over her mouth before she could scream, and—

—And Skeet screamed as the bitch bit into his hand, screamed and pulled away from her, tried to thrust her away, threw her a dozen feet into the dirt—

—And he couldn't believe it. The bitch had a knife in her hand, eight inches of thin, gray carbon steel. Pulled a knife on him she had, but she was getting to her feet, and when she saw he was a white man, she would drop it and run, and he would catch her, and—

—But no, she was not running away, she was not dropping the knife. She was lifting it, she was coming toward him, left arm up to guard, right in position to slash. She was coming at him teeth bared and eyes mad, she was throwing herself at him, she was going to—

—Jesus Christ!

Skeet turned and fled.

He couldn't believe that a mere nigger, and a wench at that, would actually pull a knife on him and come at him. But it was happening, this tall bitch, almost as big as he was and a hell of a lot faster, she was coming at him, and he would have sworn at that moment that she had fangs. She was coming at him like a rabid bitch dog, and he had no weapon, and he had to get to his horse, had to—

With his bad right leg, he felt as if he were trying to run through swamp muck. As he reached his horse, he saw that the wench was right behind him, and he wheeled the horse just in time to put it between them. He threw himself into the saddle, kicking out at the woman as he brought his leg over. She ducked, drew back, but only for an instant. That instant was all he needed, and he was on his way, riding, riding like hell for Redbird.

But when he looked back over his shoulder, the wench was still pursuing him across the field, still pursuing him along the road, falling back but still pursuing him, like a nightmare he would have for the rest of his life.

On Sunday afternoon, Lucy learned from Irish, the houseboy (or butler, as he preferred to be called), that Paul Devereau had returned from Charleston and, in fact, had been back for several days. She immediately dispatched Paris, Zulie's youngest brother, with an invitation to supper, and late that afternoon he appeared at the courtyard door. She kissed his cheek and led him into the library.

Paul Devereau was her neighbor, her lawyer, her friend. He might under the right circumstances have been her enemy, as she knew well, but at present that was irrelevant; whatever their differences in the past, they had made their peace, and she was genuinely glad to see him. In his middle thirties, he was a solidly built man, not much taller than she, with a full head of shaggy white hair and piercing eyes under heavy brows. His manner was somewhat theatrical, and he frequently made good use of the fact.

"Your note," he said, "sounded somewhat urgent."

After pouring two glasses of sherry, she told the story of Ettalee's abduction by Skeet and of how she herself had retrieved the girl. She told the story in full, stressing the girl's youth and her good character and omitting nothing. She tried to be as cool and precise as possible in her narrative, but she felt her indignation returning in full force.

"Now, I can't let that man get away with such a thing, Paul," she concluded, "I simply can't. Something must be done about him, or he'll do the same thing again. But what can I do, what can I—"

"Nothing," Paul said flatly, and added slowly as if teaching a child, "you—can—do—nothing."

"But Ettalee was dragged off—she had obviously been abused—"

"Oh, now, was she?" Paul lifted an eyebrow; his eyes had a satiric glint. "Now, I don't want to shock you, Lucy, honey, but we all know the nigger he just animal, honey, he get drunk on the Lawd's day, go chasing after white man, nigger gal she—"

Lucy's temper flared. "Paul, that is—that is obscene!"

"Of course it is. My point is, that is what Skeet will say. He picked up a wench away from home without a pass, as he was entitled, nay, was obliged as a good citizen to do. Perhaps she got drunk. In any case, she was in rut, and she no doubt took on any buck she could find—any and all. You, behaving like a harridan, came to get the wench, and he gladly released her to you, and good riddance."

"But it wasn't that way at all! Oh, I certainly behaved like a harridan, and I don't regret it one bit. But I happen to know that Ettalee does not drink—she did not drink while in the Kimbrough quarters, she was not drunk when I went to get her. She was bloody, she had been hurt, she was out of her mind with shock. Anybody could see what had happened—"

"But nobody did." Paul Devereau made a point of looking and sounding bored. Lucy stared at him, and he repeated, "Nobody—did."

"My people—Jebediah, Saul—"

"Jebediah and Saul are niggers, Lucy. A Negro cannot testify against a white man, and therefore for all practical purposes they saw nothing. And of course, neither Skeet nor his overseer saw anyone abusing Ettalee. But Skeet *does* have a witness to the fact that you threatened him with a gun—that you took a shot at him, as a matter of fact. I dare say the only reason he hasn't put the law on you is that he doesn't want to press his luck."

Lucy knew all of this. These were the kinds of facts that she had been brought up with. She had heard them all her life. And yet somehow she had hoped . . .

"All right," she said, "there are the technicalities of the law. But there is also common sense."

"Oh, good God, Lucy, what common sense? Sometimes you talk like a woman. Not often, but occasionally."

"I thank you for that."

"Now, don't get on your high horse. You keep too damned much to yourself, Lucy—don't you know what the hell is going on in the world around you? I've just come back from Charleston—the nullification talk there is stronger than it's ever been before, far stronger than it is around here. And the insurrection fears are as bad, if not worse—worse than they've been since back in the Vesey days. And every paleface fool just seems to be looking for an excuse to flog a nigger. And sometimes the blacks *do* lose their heads and fight back. They waylay mail riders, they burn barns. . . ."

Paul seemed unable to contain himself. He stood and

paced about the library. "Lucy, I have a pretty good idea of what you think of me. You think I'm an opportunist and something of a knave, and to hell with most of the chivalric pretensions. Well, maybe you're right. Maybe I've had to be that way to hold onto my place in this world. But if it's true, it's forced me to be clear-sighted and honest with myself, and the hypocrisy, the sheer stupidity I see around me is absolutely appalling. How often have I heard a slave-owner preaching the loyalty of our Negro people, how they love us, how faithful they are, how they'll fight with us to the death against the goddam Yankees. And the next instant the same fool will be telling you that, thanks to the abolitionists, the dirty goddam niggers are going to rise up any night now and murder us all in our beds." He shook his head. "We're getting almost as hypocritical as the goddam Yankees—who want to free all the niggers as long as they don't have to live with them."

Somehow Paul's outburst had calmed Lucy. She smiled. "You keep thinking along those lines, Mr. Devereau, and eventually you are going to become an Idealist and espouse a Great Cause."

Paul made a sour face. "God forbid—"

A door banged loudly as it was flung open in the passage, and from somewhere in the house there was a sound like a cry of baffled rage. Feet thumped in the passage, and someone cried out, "Miss Lucy, where you?" Lucy was about to call for Leila, when Zulie burst into the library, and rarely had Lucy seen one of her people more furious.

"Miss Lucy, ain't you going do nothing 'bout that man, ain't you going do nothing?"

"Zulie, what in the world—"

"That Skeet is what, that goddam Skeet. and you ain't going do nothing!"

"Mr. Skeet—what has he done now—"

"First Ettalee, then me, and all the others before, and nobody don't do nothing! What a nigger got to do? I work for you. I work hard. I tend Ettalee, I tend all the sick, I tend 'em till I sick myself! I work the laundry, I help the kitchen garden, I work like hell, and what the fuck I get

for it? What I get is Mr. Skeet trying grab me, Skeet grabbing Ettalee, dragging her off—"

Lucy tried to interrupt, but Zulie was not to be stopped.
"And you don't do nothing! Oh, you go get Ettalee, but
not 'fore she all messed up, and nobody do nothing about
Skeet, nobody stop him grabbing *me!* What the hell the
matter with you, you don't take care your people! *I* don't
ask to be no fucking slave! You want me work for you,
goddam you—"

"Zulie, where did this happen?" Paul cut in strongly.
"Were you away from Sabrehill?"

"No! He come right on Sabrehill and grab me! He come
to my dreaming tree where I watch the sun go down, he
grab me from behind, but I bite him. I show my knife, I
run him off!"

"Oh, Christ," Paul said. "You pulled a knife on him?"

"Well, what else could she do?" Lucy asked. "What
else?"

But Zulie did not appear to hear either of them. She said
a few more words, barely distinguishable, and bursting
into tears, ran from the room.

"Maybe she's right," Lucy said after a long silent moment. "Maybe everyone is right—what's a woman doing
running Sabrehill? If Zulie had been one of your people,
Vachel Skeet wouldn't have dared to try such a thing."

"I'd like to believe that, but I know it's not necessarily
true."

"On your own land, Paul?"

Paul shrugged. He looked as if there were something he
hesitated to say, but he said it anyway. "Lucy, I don't
suppose you know what started Skeet off again, do you?
Was it just a chance encounter with Ettalee, or did you
cross him in some way—"

"Started him off?" Lucy was startled. "I don't understand."

"Well, it's no secret that he's had bad feelings toward
the Sabres for years, but he hasn't picked up any of your
people before Ettalee for quite a while, has he? Of course,
he's always given you more trouble than he has anyone
else—"

"Trouble! I don't know that he's given us any more trouble than he has any of our neighbors."

"Well, he has. My God, you must know that. It started with that business with Justin."

"Oh, that was long ago!"

"Yes, it was." Paul looked at her oddly. "I'm sorry, Lucy. I've always known you didn't care to talk about it, and perhaps I shouldn't have mentioned it. But just the same, that *was* where it all started."

She stood up and hurried to the door. "Paul, let me see if supper is ready."

He was right, of course, and she was ducking the subject. There was so much in the past that she did not care to look back upon. But the past was inescapable, she should know that by now; and you could not always, as she had hoped, simply write it off. It was as if the past always lay in the future, waiting to recapture the present. More than once before, it had suddenly sprung out at her, to bring her new suffering, and it could do so again. Perhaps the only hope of escaping the past lay not in evading it but in facing it. Perhaps she would have to go back.

But not now. Later. She had a guest.

"Supper, Paul."

"He's not going to hurt you, Zulie, he's not going to hurt you. You're here with Jeb, and he's not going to hurt you."

Jeb rocked the sobbing Zulie in his arms, and his heart swelled. She had needed someone, and she had come to him. He had had little love in his life, and the last was long gone, and he needed Zulie. He needed her, he sometimes thought, far more than she needed him.

"Your Jeb will take care of you. You stay with your Jeb, and you'll never have to fear again."

But was that true?

How could it be? How, when the Skeets and the Jeppsons and the Bassetts were at large in this world?

He held Zulie tighter. Maybe Saul was right. Maybe he had turned out to be a white man's nigger. But no more. Not when one of them touched his woman. Give him the chance, and he'd kill the son of a bitch himself. There was no need for a Black Buck at Sabrehill.

He rocked Zulie in his arms, and he had never been happier, or angrier, in all his life.

"Mr. Skeet . . ."

Dinkin was a shadow in the open doorway of the office. Skeet sat in the darkness, nursing his hand and his humiliation. To have been run off by a mere nigger wench: the thought was sickening. His bandaged hand throbbed, and he gripped his left wrist and rocked in his chair. Nigger bite. He had soaked and medicated it, but everyone knew that a nigger bite was poisonous. It was almost as bad as a copperhead.

"Mr. Skeet, sir."

"Yes, Mr. Dinkin."

He had spent hours of each day away from Redbird, crossing and recrossing Sabrehill, looking for his chance. And when he had seen the wench, he had been so certain that this was it at last. A good-looking wench, by God, almost as tall as a man and as broad shouldered. He had followed her across the field, hardly believing his luck. He had watched her climb that tree, wondering what the hell she thought she was doing. He had come up behind her and waited patiently, and when she had come down . . .

". . . still going on," Dinkin said, stepping through the doorway. "More talk than ever, the drivers say."

"What talk, Mr. Dinkin? What the hell are you talking about? What's going on?"

"About them conjure-people over at Sabrehill. I told you about it the other day. They say they're making these spells on us, 'count of the wench."

"Oh, for Christ's sake. You believe in that shit, Dinkin?" Skeet did not, or at least he told himself that he did not, but for some inexplicable reason he thought of the dirt strewn over his piazza.

"No, sir, I don't believe in it, but—"

"But what?"

"I still don't like it. It ain't Christian."

Skeet laughed and shook his head. "Forget it, Mr.

Dinkin. Every little farm around here got some old man or woman who makes spells. You can flog hell out of them, they still gonna make spells in secret. Don't mean a thing."

"Just the same, I don't like it. We got spells up in Tennessee too, but there ain't no voodoo there. Voodoo, obeah, all that—that's different. Like I say, it just plain ain't Christian."

"What's this voodoo supposed to be doing to us, Mr. Dinkin?"

"Don't rightly know. But there's talk now about some Black Buck coming back soon. Mr. Skeet, just who the hell *is* Black Buck?"

Skeet slowly looked up from his aching hand. "Black Buck?"

"Yes, sir. Ever heard of him?"

Something like joy entered Skeet's heart. "Why, I surely have, Mr. Dinkin. Black Buck and me is old friends."

"Friends, Mr. Skeet?"

"Every few years there's talk about old Black Buck coming back here, but it ain't ever happened. Reckon it could happen, though, sooner or later, and I surely do look forward to the day."

"Reckon you must be pretty good friends." Dinkin sounded dubious.

"Oh, you can bet we are. Leastwise we are if Black Buck is the Buckley Skeet I used to know. Oh, Buck and me is such good friends I've had a reward out for him for years. *Big* reward. Why, I'd give my heart and soul to see old Buck again."

"Well, then, Mr. Skeet, I surely do wish you luck."

"Thank you, Mr. Dinkin. Thank you very much."

Dinkin left. Skeet rocked in his chair, gripping his left wrist, nursing his hand.

Buck, he thought, smiling in the dark. *Good old Buck.* Yes, it seemed to him that if only he could see good old Buck again, all of the humiliations and defeats of the years past could be wiped out and forgotten. Get that bastard Buck, and all scores would be even again. He would once again be young and strong, and the past could truly be forgotten. After all, it was Buck who had given him the greatest humiliation of all, one far greater than any that Miss Lucy or any miserable black bitch had given him. Buck. His old friend.

Yes, Buck, yes, he thought, taking comfort in the dream, *time you came on back. Been waiting for you all these years, Buck. And I'm still waiting. . . .*

Six

The whip came singing through the air and cut like a dull knife across Buck's shoulders.

There was absolutely no reason for it. His wrists were tied behind him with rawhide, his ankles were shackled, and a length of rope with a noose at each end led from his neck to Adaba's. Both of them were helpless. But the whip sang again and cut through flesh, and a sudden darkness swept over Buck like a roaring sea wave.

Another wave came pouring over him, and he found himself lying full length, like something beached by the sea. He might have strangled on the water that had been pitched in his face, but Adaba was shaking him, pounding his back, helping him clear his head. Young Lute Rogan, gap-toothed, grinned down at them.

Somehow that brought back to Buck where they were. They were on a wooden pier, a river landing. Lute Rogan, whip in hand, stood nearby. Some distance off, Lute's father, Silas Rogan, stood in conversation with another white man. There were a number of slaves on the landing, and Buck saw that they had gone to work, loading a long flat-bottomed boat, or "cotton box," with cotton bales that were brought up in mule-drawn wagons.

How had they come to be here? It was a jumble in Buck's mind. That first morning when they had been caught was clear enough. The Rogans had acted quickly and efficiently, with the viciousness of the fearful. Two runaway niggers, that was not much to worry about: put them on their knees and keep them there; rarely was any nigger foolish enough to raise his hand against a white man. But Silas Rogan had heard Adaba address Buck by name, and that had aroused both suspicion and hope.

"Buck, huh?" Silas had grinned, and he had even fewer teeth than his son. He was a gnarled, red-bearded man who could have been anywhere from forty to sixty years of age. "Buck, huh? Runaway nigger. Say they's a big feller, Black Buck, up in the hills sometimes, not so far from here. Hear tell there been a reward on him for a long time now. Where you come from, Buck?"

Playing at stupidity, playing the ignorant savage, had been no help. The Rogans themselves were too stupid, too savage to be deceived. They wanted Buck to be Black Buck, and this led them to think of Adaba for the role of Adaba, for the two maroons were frequently mentioned together. When the Rogans had tied them up, Silas had spread the beard on Adaba's left cheek.

"See, Lute? See that there mark, like a bird with his wings stretched out? That there how he get the name Adaba, the Brown Dove, when he a pickaninny. What we got us here is the Brown Dove!"

"Don't know no Brown Dove, master, sir," Adaba had whined. "Don't know no Adaba, sir!"

"Shut your mouth, boy!" The whip had come blazing down, as it had so many times since. "Shut your mouth!" The dream was not to be threatened. The Brown Dove and Black Buck—to have them in captivity surely meant the Rogans' fortune. The chances, of course, had been that this was neither Adaba nor Black Buck, but the Rogans had not wanted to think that. And ironically, they had been right.

Buck and Adaba had been fed. Mrs. Rogan, a worn-out shadow of a woman, had tended Adaba's wounds, though she hardly knew how to cope with them. They had then been allowed to rest, locked in a woodshed until early the next morning, when the male Rogans had started them on this journey.

The time since then was a muddle of fatigue and pain. The Rogans had ridden in a mule-drawn wagon, but Buck and Adaba had been forced to walk behind, tied to the wagon by their double noose. When Adaba had stumbled and fallen, he had been dragged behind by the neck, Buck powerless to help him and almost too parch-throated to cry out. After that, Lute had ridden in the back of the wagon, and each time one of them had stumbled, the whip had flicked out, a tongue of fire.

Mile after mile . . . a day, two days . . . cold nights, each with a single thin blanket, huddled together for warmth, still shackled and tied, and always guarded . . . the Rogans surlier and more vicious than ever the next day, because of their lack of sleep. At last they had arrived here, on the river landing.

Silas Rogan and the other white man nodded briskly at each other, evidently having struck a bargain. The other man, Buck guessed, was the owner of the crop and the big "box" that would float it downriver to market. Silas turned away from him and, a satisfied look on his face, came over to Lute.

"Got it all fixed, honey-boy," he said, "and it ain't costing us nothing. Our two here," he indicated Buck and Adaba, "they gonna pole and paddle. Save the man two hand he can leave home and don't have to bring back. Don't need 'em to paddle back, 'cause he break up the box and sell it downriver."

"Don't cost us nothing," Lute said, delighted, "and we come back rich."

"We sure do. Now, get them niggers on their feet, 'cause they gonna help load this here cotton."

Somehow Buck managed to get to his feet. It seemed hardly believable that in their condition they were ex-pected to work, but Lute's whip made it plain that they were. They were driven to the edge of the landing, and there, with scarcely the strength of a half-hand between them, they were set to tumbling the bales onto the boat and shoving them into place.

As if it were his turn to escape into oblivion, Adaba gave out first; there was a grayness about his eyes, and Buck caught him as he folded. As he lowered Adaba gently onto a bale, the whip came down again, for what seemed the thousandth time, and Buck heard it slice air as it was raised for another blow. But the blow never came.

"All right, boy, no more of that."

Buck looked around and saw that the owner of the cotton box was holding Lute's arm. Lute looked surprised.

"Just driving 'em, mister. Making 'em earn their way."

"They ain't no good to me nor you neither, they dead. You too damn quick with a whip, boy. Now, you going down the river with me, you be a little more careful with that whip."

"These bad niggers, Mr. Tradwell," Silas Rogan said. "Got to keep 'em in line."

Tradwell released Lute's arm. "They your niggers, Mr. Rogan, but on my box you better be a mite more careful of 'em. You just let 'em be, and let 'em rest till we leave."

Buck might have been grateful to Tradwell, white man or not, but he hardly had strength even for that. He was as close to despair as he had been in years. Since Redbird.

He tended to Adaba. He wasn't certain that the wounds were healing properly—he was afraid they were not, but at least there was no lockjaw yet and no stink of rotting, a smell that could portend death. He tried to rest, tried to sleep, but his very fatigue seemed to keep him awake. When the sun was well down, the Rogans brought them a supper of dry bread, and they were allowed to quench their thirst with river water. They were then separated; Buck was put on the left side of the raft, facing downstream, and Adaba on the right. Large iron staples secured their chain hobbles to the deck. And under his thin blanket, Buck at last found sleep.

Pain began again the next morning before dawn. A boot-toe kicked into Buck's shoulder—kicked and kicked again. "Come on, nigger," Lute Rogan said, "move your ass. It 'most first light, and you got work to do."

They were on their way before sunup. After another meal of dry bread washed down with river water, Buck and Adaba were given poles, and the order was given to cast off. The Negro patroon at the tiller yelled, "Hard

with them pole 'gin the bank! Hard with them pole!"
and they began the trip down the river.

To Redbird, for Buck; to Charleston, for Adaba. To
death, more likely than not, for both of them.

The work, at this point, should not have been hard.
The shallow-draft barge never touched bottom, even this
far upstream. Including Buck and Adaba, there were
six hands, and they were required only to keep the barge
clear of the banks and in those channels known to the
patroon. But the Rogans were after Buck and Adaba
from the time they were awake, and they never let up.
The whip snapped, and Buck felt his back bleeding.
Adaba slipped and fell to his knees, and Silas immediately
kicked him in the belly. Before long, the pain was again
unending, each blow merely a surge in its flow.

The sun rose, the day grew older. The boat stopped at
a landing, picked up some men, let them off at another
landing. Slowly the river widened. Buck remembered
years ago at Redbird reading about the river Styx—how
men were ferried by Charon into the everlasting darkness
of the underworld. This, it occurred to him, could very
well be the last trip that he and Adaba would ever make.

But he was not ready to die. He could not allow himself to think that there was no escape.

Was there the slightest chance at all that someone on
the raft might be of help? There were four slaves, two
on the forward corners and two toward the rear. They
were not chained, and they were no doubt trusted. The
chances were that they would do nothing to assist an
escape attempt, but neither would they interfere.

There was the patroon, probably a slave to Tradwell.
But slave or free Negro, he was not going to risk his
position. He seemed to enjoy his work too much.

That left Tradwell. Tradwell was sympathetic, he did
not like to see them abused, but helping them to get
away was a different matter, a criminal matter. And he
was white. Could a black possibly expect help from a
white slave-owner?

Buck turned to look at Tradwell.

Then, for the first time, he noticed another white pas-
senger. He had no idea of how long the man had been

traveling with them—perhaps from the very beginning of the trip. The man was seated on a cotton bale beside Tradwell. Tall, lean, about Buck's age, he wore a wide-brimmed hat and leather clothes. A holstered pistol showed under his jacket on his left side, and on his right a rifle leaned against the bale. His face was blank and un-smiling, his deep-set eyes disinterested, but he was looking steadily at Buck.

I know him! Buck thought.

I know him, and if he knows me, we're dead!

Justin Sabre kept his face carefully blank when his eyes met those of the Negro. There was no point in offering compassion when there was not a damn thing he could do to back it up with active help. He merely turned to Trad-well and said, "Those two hands will be lucky if they live to reach market."

"You damn right," Tradwell said angrily, "and it serve the goddam Rogans right if the niggers die."

Yes, Justin thought, it would serve the Rogans right. And a hell of a great consolation that would be to the niggers.

"They really expect to sell those two?"

Tradwell shrugged, knowing what Justin meant. "They lucky they get five cents on the dollar value, I tell you that. Say they're selling 'em 'cause they mean. But who want to buy a mean nigger, who want to buy a nigger all cut up and whip-marked? I ask 'em, they say don't give a damn, just want to get rid of 'em."

"Yet they're taking them all the way down river. Going to all that trouble."

"Only part way. Man gonna buy one of 'em. Least that's what they say."

"How do they know that? How do they know they have a sale?"

Tradwell said nothing.

"Looks to me more like they're returning runaways. Like they don't care what condition the men are in, be-cause they're going to be paid anyway. But if that's the case, why don't they just say so? Have they got some fool idea that someone might steal the niggers?"

"Could be. None of my business."

"That one on the starboard there. On the right, the heavy-bearded one. He looks to be in really bad shape."

"He . . . I think . . ." Tradwell was hesitant. "I think he's been shot."

"Shot?"

"Something old Rogan said. Shot twice, in the side and the leg."

Justin was incredulous. "And they think they can sell a slave with a couple of bullet holes in him? Before he's healed?"

"Maybe I heard wrong."

Maybe, but Justin was remembering something he himself had heard. Only a few days ago, a maroon camp had been located and destroyed. A dozen or so blacks had been killed, but almost certainly, a number of others had escaped, some of them perhaps wounded.

Justin Sabre had owned a number of slaves in his time, but he had never considered slaveholding to be a God-given right. He was also the kind of man who at bullfights cheered for the bull.

"Well," he said, "I reckon it's none of my business either," but he was uncomfortably conscious of dissembling. He had no interest in being anyone else's conscience, but how could he say it was none of his business when he saw two men, black or not, slave or free, being abused for no good reason? If it got any worse, he might just make it his business.

But to hell with that. He turned his attention away from the Rogans and their slaves to watch the banks of the river drift by. An occasional redbird flashed crimson in the sunlight, and gray titmice screamed at each other: *Peter! Peter! Peter!* The patroon yelled, "Hard on the right!" and the raft started smoothly around a curve in the meandering river.

Sabre country, Justin thought.

He and his immediate family were Virginians, but there were more Sabres down this way, in South Carolina and Georgia, and he had always thought of this as Sabre country. Of course, many of the Sabres were only distantly related, but related they were; they were family. And

family was very important in the tidewater. Justin tried
to remember all the Sabres he had been told about, many
of whom he had never met.

Aunt Sally Sabre . . .

Ben Sabre . . .

Old Garland Sabre . . .

Mary Buchanan Sabre—called "Buck" Sabre, of
course . . .

Lewis Sabre—Lew, with his nigger wife, seldom mentioned by the rest of the family . . .

Aaron and Joel Sabre—among the best of the Carolina
planters . . .

And Aaron's daughters, Dulcy, Amity, Lucy . . .

Yes, Lucy Sabre. He had hardly thought about her in
years, had made a point of not thinking about her, and
yet she was the first to come to mind, she had been in his
mind all the time that he had been trying to recall the
others. Perhaps the others were just an excuse to think of
Lucy.

This was her country, this was her river. He had
thought never to return here, but in the days ahead he
would float downriver, would float past Sabrehill and Sabre's Landing . . . would float past, and Lucy, wherever
she might be after all these years, would never know.

And most certainly would not care.

The Rogans were after their slaves again, cursing and
beating them with no apparent provocation. Old Silas had
uncorked a jug, and he and young Luther were passing it
steadily back and forth. The more they drank, the more
abusive they became.

Justin decided that if this kept up he would have to do
something about it.

It kept up.

In the late afternoon Tradwell tried to make the Rogans
temper their behavior toward their two blacks. Justin
watched from the rear of the raft while Tradwell went
forward. The planter gesticulated and pounded his fist
against his palm, obviously trying to keep both his voice
and his temper down while laying down the law, but old
Rogan, now quite drunk, merely shouted back at him.

When Tradwell returned red-faced to Justin, Lute made
obscene gestures behind his back while Silas guffawed his
approval.

"Old bastard said we made a bargain," Tradwell said
angrily. "All but threatened to shoot at us from the bank
if we put 'em ashore. Son of a bitch if I don't think they
would too."

"Well, I wouldn't worry about it. The way they've been
drinking, they'll probably pass out before long."

The Rogans continued to drink, but they did not pass
out. Evening came, and they neglected to feed their two
blacks; Tradwell fed them himself. Finally, well after dark,
the patroon piloted the boat to a big square landing on the
left bank of the river. A torch burned on the landing to
show that they were expected.

"This here is my main plantation," Tradwell said. "We
load early and try to get off before full light, so you want
to be here."

"Anywhere I can get a hot meal and some whiskey?
And maybe a place to sleep for the night?"

Tradwell pointed the way. "They's a tavern just up the
road a short piece. I'm a partner in it. Pleased to have
you."

"I appreciate that. And if you'll tell your watchman to
turn a deaf ear on the Rogans and their blacks and me
tonight, I'm sure that tomorrow will be a happier day."

Tradwell looked sharply at Justin, then, understanding,
nodded.

A couple of boys arrived with some covered pots—a
late, extra meal for the patroon and the crew. Tradwell
gave his instructions: except for the patroon, who was to
be allowed to sleep through, the crew was to take turns on
watch during the night; the watchman was to stay near the
foot of the landing. Mr. Sabre and the Rogans and the Rogans' men were to be allowed to come and go as they
pleased.

"Our niggers," Silas Rogan growled, "they ain't going
nowhere."

Tradwell left. The patroon and crewmen gathered at
one corner of the landing and ate their meal. Justin went

to another corner and looked down on the raft where the Rogans lay stretched out, their jug between them.

"Gentlemen," he said jovially, "I understand there's a tavern near here. I suggest that you join me, gentlemen, for a bit of the cup that cheers."

"Got to stay here," Silas said. "Got to keep an eye on these here niggers."

"They're well chained."

"Don't matter. Damn tricky niggers. That Adaba, he . . ." Silas hesitated, as if he had made an inadvertent slip. "I mean . . . damn tricky."

"Suit yourself. Anything left in that jug?"

Silas picked up the jug and sloshed it. "Some. Not much."

"Give it to me. I'll get it filled up."

Silas started to hand up the jug, but then chuckled wisely and pulled it back. "You ain't going run off with our whiskey, mister."

Justin laughed. "There's surely no fooling Silas Rogan! For that, Mr. Rogan, I'm going to buy us all another jug and bring it back here!"

There was no difficulty, no problem. When Justin reached the tavern, he had scarcely stepped through the doorway when the publican saw him and placed a jug on the counter. He refused payment: Mr. Sabre was Mr. Tradwell's guest for the night, and a room awaited him whenever he wanted it. Justin took the liquor and returned to the raft.

"Drink up, gentlemen! For how's a man to travel through this godforsaken country without his booze!"

The first jug was finished off and the second one hoisted in the flickering light of the landing torch. "Smooth!" said young Lute Rogan. "Smoo-ooth!"

Deceptively smooth. The Rogans were good for one jug, but not for two. The torch on the landing soon burned low, but the Rogans burned out first.

Justin sat quietly for almost an hour, watching the stars wheel in the firmament. If the snores of the Rogans left something to be desired, the music of the spheres more than made up for it.

At the end of the hour, Justin stood up. He kicked each of the Rogans in the ribs a couple of times. This altered their harmony somewhat, but left their basic melody undisturbed.

The blacks too were asleep. It had not escaped Justin that not one of them was snoring. This struck him as most unusual and most considerate. "Now that we are all nicely asleep," he said chattily, in a normal daytime voice, "I suggest that we had all damn well better stay that way."

Nobody moved. The Rogans' snores should have awakened the dead.

Now Justin needed some kind of tool. He was in luck. In a box at the helm he found a number of tools, including axes, some wedges and dogs, and a shipwright's adze. The adze had a spur, or punch, rather than a poll, and should do nicely. He thought a couple of wedges might also be helpful.

He carried the adze and wedges to the right side of the raft, where the wounded black lay chained. He knelt and shook the man's shoulder. Eyes opened at once and held Justin's, steady and unblinking. Half a dozen questions raced through Justin's mind, but he knew they were largely irrelevant: either he was going to do this or he was not.

Nevertheless, he asked, "What are they going to do to you in Charleston?"

"Hang me, I reckon," the black answered softly.

"What for?"

The black's lip curled. "For being a man, Mr. Sabre, if that's your name. For being a man."

Justin smiled. "Then I reckon you belong to that maroon camp that got shot up last week?"

The black didn't answer.

"All right, Adaba—if that's *your* name. I guess you don't figure on going to Charleston, do you? Figure on getting away and killing a lot of whites up and down this river for revenge, is that it?"

The depth of contempt on the black's face was startling. "Mr. Sabre, sir, has a nigger ever before told you that you are a goddam fool?"

Justin laughed with genuine amusement. "Not often,

I'm afraid. What are you going to do when you get away from the Rogans?"

"I'm going to hightail it for the upcountry, is what I'm going to do. My friend and me, we're going to disappear so fast!—the Rogans, they're going to think that we're something they must have dreamed, and nobody is ever going to see us again."

"You talk pretty well for a po' ig'orant nigger boy."

"I talk the way I have to, according to the circumstances."

"And say what you have to."

The black was silent for a moment. "What do you want from me, Mr. Sabre?"

"Just what you said. I want you to disappear. Are you sure you can do it?"

"I'll find a way."

Justin held up the adze and the wedges. "I think you ought to be able to get your shackles off with these."

"Like I said. I'll find a way."

"And no killing."

"Not if I can help it. You have my word. I'm not a murderer, Mr. Sabre, no matter what you may have heard."

Justin stood up. Adaba inserted the spur of the ship-wright's adze under the staple. Two sharp pulls on the handle, and the staple was drawn out of the deck.

The Rogans snored loudly. The black grinned.

They crossed the raft to where the other captive lay. He looked up at them as if he could not quite believe what he was seeing. Adaba laughed. "We on our way, Buck! On our way!" With no wasted time or motion, Justin drew the staple.

"Now I'm going to leave," he said. "I'm going to talk to the guard for a minute or two, try to distract him. I don't think he'll try to stop you even if he sees you, but it'll be better if he doesn't. We don't want to make any more trouble for anyone than we have to."

"Ain't gonna be no trouble for no one but them Rogans," Buck said, reaching for the adze. "But they ain't gonna see another sunrise—"

"Now, look you!" Justin knocked the adze from Buck's

hand and whirled him around. "You're not killing anyone! I'm not setting you loose to kill, not even the Rogans. You touch anyone, black or white, and so help me God, I'll chase you down——"

"Old Buck, he ain't gonna kill nobody, Mr. Sabre," Adaba said, "I promise you that. Ain't gonna be no killing, Mr. Sabre."

Justin looked hard at Buck, exacting a promise. After a moment Buck nodded. He indicated Adaba. "I do like he say."

Something nagged at Justin. He never really knew why he did what he did next.

He nodded at Buck, acknowledging the promise. He turned to Adaba.

"Listen," he said, "if you head back upriver toward the hills, that's exactly where everybody will be looking for you. But if you head downriver . . ."

"Might be best," Adaba said, considering it.

"There's a place downriver on this side called Sabrehill. It belongs to cousins of mine. I wasn't planning to stop there, but if I met you there, maybe I could help you. Take you to Charleston as my servants and put you on a packet north."

Adaba frowned. "Why you doing this? You abolitionist?"

"What's the difference? I'm not going to beg you. Make up your mind."

"All right. Yes, we meet you there."

"Good. I reckon it'll take you a few days to get there. Hide in the field quarters——I guess you know how to do that——and wait for me. If you're sick or hurt, there's a woman there called Aunt Zule who can cure anything. It'll be better if the Sabres don't find out about you, but if they do, tell them you're waiting for me. Tell them I'll explain everything."

Adaba laughed. "Yes, sir, Mr. Abolitionist."

"And remember," Justin turned to Buck, "no killing."

He stepped up onto the landing and went to find the guard. They chatted for a few minutes, and Justin heard a sound that might have been a rattling of chains.

Why the hell had he done it, he wondered. To set free a couple of blacks who were in danger of being beaten to death by redneck savages, that was one thing. But to send them to Sabrehill and promise them further help, that was quite another.

And if there were any one place in the entire wide world to which he did not want to go, it was Sabrehill. It was the one place in the world where he had the least right to go, the place where he was least wanted.

But now he had committed himself.

Well, hell, he thought. And suddenly he was angrily, perversely glad to be going back. After all, not all of the wrong had been his fault and on his side. And the most the Carolina Sabres could do was shoot him.

On the boat the Rogans snored.

Buck couldn't believe it. He had waited to be recognized:

Yeah, I know him now, that's Buckley all right. I don't give a damn how often he denies it, I know Buckley Skeet. Runaway, is he? Outlier? Bandit? Might have known it —like master, like nigger, bastards both of them. Never mind how the Rogans are treating 'em, Tradwell, you just see that they don't get away. You know, the Rogans are right, there's a price on Adaba's head too. Now, if we could get rid of the Rogans . . . Yeah, take Buckley to Redbird and claim the money, then take Adaba to Charleston. . . .

He had waited for that, for something like that, because it had to happen—and yet, miraculously, it had not. As if he had been Adaba himself, Justin Sabre had set them free, and it had to be some kind of trick, a trap, a cruel joke. There would be a shout, guns would explode, men and dogs would come rushing toward them—

Nothing. There was silence. The moon and stars made the night day-bright. Buck and Adaba quietly appropriated the Rogans' blanket rolls and supply pouches. Buck touched Lute's rifle, but Lute stirred and almost awakened, and Buck drew back. Like more sensible men, the Rogans slept on their weapons, and nothing was more apt to awaken them, even from drunken sleep, than trying to steal them. If only Adaba had not promised that they would not kill . . .

Well, they could do very well with what they had. They stepped up onto the landing. Justin and the guard stood not a dozen yards away, chatting casually, neither of them bothering to look toward Buck and Adaba. Softly the river lapped at the piles of the landing.

Just walk away. That was all they had to do. A dozen careful steps, and they were out of sight of the landing. Another dozen steps, through the concealing brush, and they were that much closer to Sabrehill. Another dozen steps and another . . .

And they were that much closer to Redbird too.

Adaba stumbled. Buck tried to put an arm around him, but he insisted that a hand on Buck's shoulder was all the help he needed. They hurried on.

Going back, Buck thought, going back. He had long looked forward to this return, looked forward to it and dreaded it. It was a journey into the hell of the past, and Buck began to remember. . . .

Vachel . . . Old Man Skeet . . . Miss Lucy . . . Going back . . .

PART TWO

Lovers

One

Going back . . .

There was one particular spring day, Buck remembered, when everything changed. Until that day, life was sweet, if occasionally uncertain, and every day was full of promises. On that day he got his first glimmering of the fact that every promise was going to be broken.

His memory of that day began with Vachel and himself sitting in the plantation office. What they were doing there he could not have said—probably just dreaming and planning and having a small whiskey together; only a small one, because there was to be a party that evening at Sabrehill. It was in honor of a distant cousin, one Justin Sabre, now the new overseer of Sabrehill. And of course, Vachel was invited. The Old Man was invited too, as a matter of form, but he seldom went anywhere.

They were in the office, then, when they heard the screams—more of anger than of pain—and heard the Old Man a-roaring. Even from there they could hear his whip; between blows, he cracked it, making a sound like a pistol shot. Vachel said, "Oh, Christ," lowered his boots from the table, and ran out the door, with Buck close behind.

They found the Old Man not far away, behind the nigger jail. He was red faced and reeking, staggering in circles, and chasing the hands about. As they ran, he yelled, "Come back here, you sons a bitches," cracked his whip, and sent it out toward any back he could reach. He drew it back to whip Vachel, but Vachel grabbed him in time to stop the blow.

"Leggo me, nigger!"

"Pa, it's me!"

"You don't leggo me, nigger, I kill you!"

"Pa, pa, it's me—Vachel!"

"Vachel?" The Old Man blinked and stopped struggling to use the whip.

"Yeah, pa, Vachel! It's me!"

"Watchoo doing buncha nigger?"

"I ain't doing nothing, pa! It's you that's doing! Why you whipping them, pa?"

"They ain't doing no work!" the Old Man said indignantly. "They all coming out of the field!"

"Well, 'course they are, pa! It's Saturday afternoon!"

The Old Man blinked again, harder. "Saturday afternoon?"

"Saturday afternoon, pa. It's time to quit work. Time for all the niggers to come out of the fields."

The Old Man squinted. "Saturday after*noo-oon?* You sure, Vachel?"

Vachel nearly bent double with laughter. "I'm sure, pa."

"Saturday afternoon. Well, I swan."

Both Buck and Vachel knew the Old Man was going, though neither of them spoke of it. It was not just the liquor, though that was a large part of the problem. Something had broken in him when Vachel's mother died. That was when he had started letting Redbird go to ruin, even before he had started drinking. Redbird had been one of the larger plantations in those parts, with its own gin house and over a hundred people; but the Old Man had sold off most of the people, reduced the acreage under cultivation, and eventually taken to "nigger-breaking" to make ends meet. He had even sold some of the land to a neighbor, Balbo Jeppson, and Vachel had had to fight to keep him from selling more.

"Think you need a little nap, pa."

"Yeah, guess I do. I been working mighty hard . . . mighty hard. . . ."

The whip dropped into the dust, and Buck picked it up. Vachel took his father's right arm, and Buck walked on his left, in case the Old Man should stagger that way, and together they all walked toward the big house.

Balbo Jeppson was waiting at the door.

Vachel did not like Jeppson, and Buck liked him less. He was a craggy, red-faced man, heavily built and barrel-like, who moved his body like a physical threat. He was a successful planter by almost any standard, but no aristocrat, and he made a point of the fact that he was "just a simple farmer." In fact, if there was anything he disliked more than a "bad nigger," it was a wealthy aristocrat, and he took ill-concealed pleasure in the fact that, while he had risen in the world, the well-born Skeets had come down.

He saw at once that the Old Man was drunk. "Well," he said jovially, "how is my good friend Mr. Skeet?"

"Working mighty hard, Balbo," the Old Man said, his head lolling on his shoulders, "working mighty hard." Buck's face warmed with embarrassment—embarrassment for the Old Man, for Vachel, for himself.

"Hey," Jeppson said to Vachel, with a pretense of lowering his gravelly voice, "want me help tuck him in for a nap?"

"Just don't get in my way, Jeppson," Vachel said, hard faced. "We don't need no help from you."

" 'Course not," Jeppson said. "I'll wait for you right here."

Vachel pulled the Old Man into the house, and the latter's legs nearly gave out under him. Buck helped to lug him up the stairs and into his bedroom. Vachel dumped him, muttering, onto his bed and turned him over. By the time Buck had pulled his boots off, the Old Man was asleep.

Vachel, hands on hips, stood by the bed for a moment. He sadly shook his head. Buck knew that, in a way, Vachel had said good-bye to his father a long time ago.

When they went downstairs, Jeppson was no longer, as he had promised, at the door. That would have been cause for relief, except that his horse was still tied to a post. They hurried to the office, and there, as they expected, they found Jeppson. Snooping around. Fingers riffling through odd papers on the desk.

"You want something in here, Jeppson?" Vachel asked with no pretense of friendliness.

"Yes, sir, young fellow, I do." Jeppson took a last glance at a scrap of paper and flicked it aside.

"What is it? We're pretty busy."

Jeppson thumped his broad ass into a chair. He glanced at Buck. "Don't know as I care to talk in front of a nigger."

Buck felt a tightening in his chest. Somehow he felt a

tightening in Vachel too, and saw it in his face. Vachel took a deep breath before answering.

"Jeppson," he said, " 'nigger' is just a word. I use it sometimes myself. But coming out of some mouths, it's a dirty word."

Jeppson grinned. "It sure as hell is, and it's meant to be. But me, I got nothing against niggers long as——"

"——long as they stay in their place, I know, I've heard you say that before. You'll be happy to hear that Buckley is in his place. Redbird is his place, and he's my friend——"

"Well, now, course he is! Nothing wrong with having a nigger for a friend, why, *good* niggers make *good* friends, and some of the best boys I know——"

"——are niggers. Fuck you, Jeppson. Get out of here."

In a split second, Jeppson's eyes turned hard as stone and winter cold, and Buck thought he was going to explode out of the chair. He saw Jeppson begin to rise. But the big man fell back, laughed explosively, and slapped his knee.

"Why, good for you! I always say a man should stand up for his niggers, especially in front of 'em!" He looked at Buck. "You got a good master here, boy. Better remember that."

"Jeppson . . ." Vachel wiped his face with a hand, trying to restrain himself. "I don't think you and I have any business. I told you, we are not going to sell them forty acres."

"I been thinking and figuring, and I'm ready to make you a new offer——"

"I don't even want to hear it. Why should I? I don't need your money. We had a good crop last year, Jeppson, and we're gonna have another this year. And sooner or later the price of cotton is going up. Santee and mains, short-staple, sea-island, they're all going up, and Redbird is gonna do all right. And we ain't fattening up the bird just to sell her off."

"Ain't asking you to sell her off. Just asking you to sell me that land that's rightfully mine on account of how it sticks into my property. Now, you know I got right on my side, Vachel. I had your pa talked into selling me that land, and you talked him out of it——"

"That's right. You bought your last piece of Redbird. Now, I told you we're busy. . . ."

Balbo Jeppson was a stubborn man, used to getting his way; but Vachel could be just as stubborn, and Jeppson was the last man in the world he wanted anything to do with. For a few minutes, Buck thought the two men might come to blows, but Vachel finally succeeded in getting Jeppson out of the office, and he and Buck watched as the man mounted his horse and rode away.

"And there," said Vachel, "goes a disappointed man."

"But he'll be back. It ain't just a little forty-acre patch he wants, Vaych, it's everything. All of Redbird."

"Yeah, but he ain't gonna get it. The last two, three years, we really been coming back up in the world, Buck, and now that pa is leaving all the planning to me and you . . ."

Vachel suddenly whooped with happiness. He grabbed Buck by the waist and whirled him around a couple of times in a kind of dance, then let go of him and grabbed the jug.

"What the hell! It's Saturday afternoon—let's have us another one!"

Vachel poured, and they both sat down at the table, facing one another. Vachel's face seemed to glow, and he grinned at Buck. Buck's face flushed warm, and he grinned back. Sometimes he felt like a mirror to Vachel. When Vachel was happy, he was happy. When Vachel was unhappy or worried or afraid, Buck broke out in sweats.

They sipped their drinks. "Yes, sir," Vachel said. "We really been doing things with Redbird, and we gonna do a lot more. You and me, Buck. Before long we'll have as much land in cotton as we ever had, and we'll take care of it right, rotating and fertilizing. But we got to get more people to do that, good people who act right and get treated right. This nigger-breaking pa does, that ain't no way to run a plantation. . . ."

Vachel talked on, and Buck smiled and nodded from time to time, but he hardly listened. He had heard all of this before. Instead, he simply basked in the warmth of the other man's happiness and felt good for him. He admired Vachel tremendously. He and Vachel *had* worked hard together, they *had* done a great deal toward restoring Redbird's former glory, but the inspiration and ambition had all been Vachel's. Buck had merely reflected and helped to implement Vachel's dreams.

And so he smiled. And hardly listened. And he almost missed the all-important words: ". . . thinking of getting married."

He sat there, suddenly numb faced, feeling oddly as if he had been slapped.

Vachel laughed. "Well, now, what's so surprising about that? If you could see the look on you!"

Buck groped for words: "I . . . don't know . . . just . . . we never talked about it before."

"Guess a man's got to sometime." Vachel's face reddened, as if the subject were somewhat embarrassing. "You ought to give it some thought yourself. Find yourself a nice gal. . . ."

"Who you thinking of marrying?"

"Oh, now, you know."

"No, I don't."

"Why, Miss Lucy. Who else would it be?"

Yes, who else would it be?

And yet Buck could hardly believe that he had understood correctly. The idea that Vachel might marry anyone as grand, as superior, as *high* as Miss Lucy of Sabrehill—could Vachel really believe such a thing?

It was not that Vachel was not worthy of Miss Lucy, of course. But who besides himself knew just how worthy Vachel was? Almost every Sunday afternoon Buck delivered his friend to Sabrehill, and—he could not deceive himself—Vachel simply did not *shine* among the many callers on Miss Lucy. He was earnest, he was sincere, he was . . . dull. He was unfashionable. He was inarticulate. He could speak well enough when talking to a Jeppson, he could speak as properly as Mr. Aaron Sabre, when he tried. But with Miss Lucy . . . he lacked wit, grace, fluency. Buck knew, because Mr. Aaron let him prowl about the library, and Buck saw. Hell, *Buck* could talk to the ladies better than Vachel could! And he was always relieved for Vachel when Vachel had paid his respects to Miss Lucy and stammered a couple of compliments and escaped to Mr. Aaron in the library to discuss Voltaire and Plato and what's-the-price-of-cotton.

Was he actually under the impression that he had been *courting* Miss Lucy?

"Well," Vachel laughed, "who else would it be?"

"Why . . . I don't know."

"Been calling on her all this time."

"But," said Buck carefully, "all them others been calling too."

Vachel made a gesture of dismissal. "Them others don't mean nothing to her. She says to me, she says, 'Vachel, the way you and my papa talk, I sometimes think you are the only young man around here with a brain in your head. South Carolina is full of fools and popinjays.' She said that exactly, last Sunday."

It didn't exactly strike Buck as a declaration of love. "Have you spoken to Mr. Aaron yet?" he asked.

"No, but I'm going to, real soon. Won't be no problem there. You know how good Mr. Aaron and me get along. Why, aside from you, he's about the best friend I got."

That was true enough: aside from Buck, Mr. Aaron was about the only friend that Vachel had.

"You asked Miss Lucy if you can speak to her papa?"

"Not yet, but I'm thinking of doing it. Real soon now."

The whole conversation had a feeling of unreality to Buck. Vachel could not be serious. In all of the many visits they had made to Sabrehill, Miss Lucy had hardly noticed Vachel. And now he expected . . .

But supposing that Vachel were right? Supposing that it were Buck's perception of reality that was flawed? Supposing that Vachel asked Miss Lucy for her hand, and Miss Lucy agreed, and Mr. Aaron gave his blessing? What then?

A single question suddenly pounded through Buck's brain.

What will happen to me?

He was not as other niggers: that he knew. For fourteen, almost fifteen years, his black hide had been like Vachel's shadow. Even before that, they had been raised together, raised virtually from the cradle, since Buck had arrived only a few months before Vachel. His earliest, happiest memories were of their laughing mothers together, in the days when Redbird gleamed with white paint and it never thundered without one mother or the other close by for comfort.

That innocence had ended when he was seven years old.

"You just 'nother nigger," the older boy, Jared, had sneered on that hot Sunday afternoon. "Think you so special, you house nigger, you fancy clothes, fancy talk, but you ain't nothing but a dirty nigger!"

He had not understood the ferocity of the boy's attack; he had not understood the attack at all—the hatred, the resentment, the viciousness in Jared's voice. True, Buckley was a house servant's child. He ate different food, had better clothes than the children of the field quarters. He talked somewhat differently, even felt himself to be somewhat different. But what had he done to deserve this?

"You got black skin, you just a nigger, you a dirty nigger *slave!*"

The boy had then dragged him through a manure pile. Dragged him in his best Sunday clothes. Dragged him, beaten him, sent him bawling back to his mother in the big house.

Vachel's mother had been furious, even more so than his own mother. She had insisted that Jared must be punished, that he must be publicly whipped. And it was done. Usually the discipline of a child was left to its parents, but in this case the Old Man—even over the protests of Buckley's mother—had tied the boy over a barrel on that sunny Sunday afternoon and wielded the whip himself.

Buckley had watched, appalled, strangely guilty, almost wishing he could take the whipping for Jared.

Afterward he had asked his mother, "Is it true? Am I just a nigger? Am I only a slave?"

And she had bitterly replied, "Yes. You are a nigger and a slave. And don't you never forget it."

Soon after that, he had come to an important realization: his safety, his future, his hope depended upon Vachel. Vachel was his one true friend, and nothing must ever separate them. They must be loyal to each other forever.

And so they had continued to live together—to eat together, to sleep together, to study Vachel's lessons together. And when, one fall just before first frost, the same fever took both of their mothers, they were thrown together still more—like brothers, almost, white and black.

But still, dimly, the words of Buckley's mother had echoed in his memory: *Yes, you are a nigger and a slave. And don't you never forget it.*

Never.

Not quite.

Resentment ate at him. It was a quite irrational resentment, he knew, but he could not subdue it. He felt that Vachel was seeking to replace him. His love, his friendship, his fidelity had been forgotten, or at least casually set aside.

"Don't know why they giving a party for a new overseer, though," Vachel said for the thousandth time, as Buck drove through the Sabrehill gate. "Never heard of giving a party just for a new overseer."

Buck restrained an impulse to cry out that Vachel was a goddam fool. He merely said, as he had said before, "Well, him being a cousin and all . . ."

"Yeah, but such a distant cousin, from what I hear tell. Why, they ain't even hardly related."

"One excuse for giving a party is good as any other, I reckon."

"I reckon."

But that was not true. The Sabres did not look for excuses to give parties, and these Saturday evening occasions were rare. Why, then, give one for a new overseer who was merely a "distant cousin"?

Buck drove up the long avenue of oaks to Sabrehill's courtyard. It was growing dark, and most of the guests had already arrived. Lights glowed, and music came from the big house. Vachel jumped down from the carriage, and Buck drove off without a word toward the east lane.

It's Saturday night, he thought, *and I'm going to have me a good time.*

Alone!

Yes; for once, alone.

He turned the horse and carriage over to Old Walter, who had charge of the stable and who whined and complained at all he had to do, until Buck shut him up with a few sharp words. Buck's resentment toward Vachel made him feel aggressive—he would not have minded a fight—and oddly enough, rather horny. He wandered back toward the courtyard to see what he could find of interest.

Saturday night.

The kitchen house, on the far side of the courtyard, was flooded with light; there would be plenty of refreshments for the guests. There was usually plenty going on around the kitchen on an evening like this, and Buck crossed the yard.

He knew, more or less, most of the people he found there, and they came and went in a swirl of activity. Maids and houseboys hurried back and forth along the portico that led to the house. Fayanne, the cook, stood jealous watch over her stoves, and Eben, the butler, put in a brief dignified appearance. Lida, an attractive young woman who worked in the laundry, came by to give Buck an interested look and to chat with Cheney and Lucinda. She gave Buck another look as she left, but he had other ideas.

Cheney was a driver, a bull of a man only a little older than Buck but already going bald; he seemed to have designs on Lucinda, but she put him off, and he soon departed. Lucinda was Fayanne's daughter; a handsome widow in her late twenties, she was "momma" to Miss Lucy's younger sisters, Amity and Dulcy. Ten-year-old Amity, blond and beautiful, was screaming orders at the younger Dulcy, until Dulcy heaved a bored sigh and left for the field quarters with Irish. (Buck *thought* Irish was Lucinda's little boy, but the relationships were sometimes difficult to keep straight.) Amity departed in another direction with her playmate, Leila. Fayanne had already gone down into the larder, and Buck suddenly found himself—

Happily, unbelievably, miraculously—

Alone with Lucinda.

He leaned back in his chair and waited for Lucinda to look around at him.

When she did, she at first appeared shocked, then burst out laughing.

"Why, Buckley Skeet, shame on you!"

He stood up, trying to look very wise and experienced, and shifted his hips suggestively from side to side. "Shame on me for what?"

"Why, for looking at me like that!"

"Ain't no other way for a real man to look at you, Lucinda."

"For a real man, huh?" Smothering her laughter, Lucinda looked him up and down. "Well, I do thank you for the compliment, Buckley, but you don't watch out, you gonna bust your pants."

"I do, it be your fault."

"What I *mean,* Buckley, you getting too big for your britches!"

"Then maybe we better go some place and take 'em off, honey—you can measure me for a new set!"

"Now, Buckley—"

Buck reached for her, and there was a great deal of Lucinda to reach for, very little of it fat. She was tall, she was big boned, she was strong. Laughing, she slapped his arms aside, slipped away, made him chase her. She allowed herself to be caught, slipped away again. Buck pursued, whispering endearments, praising Lucinda's charms. But she showed no sign of yielding, and it soon became evident that he was eliciting more laughter than passion.

"Buckley," she said gleefully, "you are a fool!"

Buck was becoming desperate. "Lucinda, why you do me this way! You see I dying for love of you!"

"Oh, I see, 'deed I do! But you just come back in

five, ten years. Whenever you grow up and don't need Mr. Vachel to hold your hand while you doing it—"

"*Wha-a-at?*" Buck was brought up short. His ears burned. "*Wha-a-at?*"

"That's right. When you don't need your Mr. Vachel."

"Lucinda," Buck said, "what the hell you talking about?" Though he knew perfectly well what she was talking about.

"I'm talking about them baby games you play with Mr. Vachel, you and him always together. You think I don't know about that?"

Goddam niggers, Buck thought furiously. *Goddam niggers, can't keep their mouths shut!*

"Well, Vachel ain't here right now!"

"Good thing too. You think I want to take you both on? Not even one of you, till you grow up, Buckley—"

Fayanne appeared at the head of the larder stairs. "Lucinda, you be careful how you talk, you hear me? Ain't proper, how you talk!"

"Yes, momma. Nighty-night, Buckley."

His face hot, Lucinda's grin like a brand between his shoulder blades, Buck stepped out of the kitchen house and into the courtyard. He turned toward the head of the west service lane, as if wishing to hide in its darkness.

So they knew. Word had gotten around.

Goddam jabbering niggers!

Well, what did he care? It wasn't as if he had really done anything so wrong. It was just that . . .

He and Vachel had done almost everything together, for most of their lives. Everything! They had eaten together, been bathed together, gone swimming and riding together. They had slept in the same bed—until Buck had built his own bed in the same room. They had worn the same clothes and shaved with the same razor.

They had attained their manhood together.

They had made the same frightening discoveries and performed the same experiments—together. That was hardly unusual; other boys did the same. They had grown bolder together. They had gone venturing in the quarters together on Saturday nights, had approached the same girls and experienced the same rebuffs.

And at last they had found willing partners. Partners willing to join their play, partners willing to be exchanged.

That was hardly unusual either. But it had gone on that way, had gone on year after year.

And what was so terrible about that? That fact was that it was simply more *fun* when they were together. It was not as if either of them ever gave any great importance to a particular woman. They enjoyed them all, enjoyed them thoroughly, felt from time to time that they had to have them. But that was all. Their own friendship, their plans for Redbird, their great future together—that had been much more important to them.

Until now.

Suddenly—he wasn't sure why—Buck felt excluded, left out, unwanted. He even felt his exclusion from the Sabrehill mansion: for once he couldn't go in and prowl about the library while he waited for Vachel. For once he was conscious of being a nigger and not a guest.

No one wanted him, not even Lucinda.

He walked through the darkness toward the west service lane, seeking greater darkness.

"Buckley, honey," a soft voice whispered beside him, "what you doing out here all by yourself?"

And so he took her. Took Lida. Took her not out of any love or tenderness or even need, though he was aroused, or even out of a sense of fun. Took her simply because she was there in the dark with him, and he needed an object to assault.

Clinging together, they moved along the deserted lane, past gardener's cottage, spinning house, wash house. Halfway to the mansion quarters, he began to undress her; she did not resist, but did the same to him. They hardly cared who saw them. The long brick building was dark. The moment they entered her room, he threw her onto the bed.

He took her—but tortured her. Took her, but made her squeal, made her beg, as they separated to pull their clothes off in the dark. Took her again, but deprived her, silenced his own curses as she clawed for him, resisted the temptation to slap her bloody. Used his cock as a weapon to degrade her by reducing her to his will. Took her, spent himself in her—and then began all over again.

It was rape, though she would never know that. Rape, because he had no wish to please her, only to make her submit, to deprive her of all choice. Rape, because, whether she knew it or not, she was his victim.

So much, the thought came unbidden, hours later, *so much for Vachel Skeet!*

"So much for Vaych," he muttered, and the woman beside him stirred and spoke, "Say what, honey?"

"Nothing."

He was half-propped up on the bed, the woman against his side, and he stretched and yawned, feeling powerful in his nakedness, powerful even through his depletion. He laughed silently. So he needed Vachel to hold his hand, did he?

Odd, but he no longer felt disturbed or angry, as he had earlier, and he could not even quite remember what had been the matter. Vachel had said he planned to marry Miss Lucy. Well, if he insisted on marrying, Miss Lucy was probably his best possible choice, a decent, reasonable lady, not at all like some of the shrill nigger-slapping buckra bitches he had known. Anyway, what the hell, nobody was going to take Buck's place at Redbird.

"What you laughing for?" Lida asked.

"Ain't laughing."

"Oh, yes, you laughing—what for?"

"Thinking, what if Vachel was to marry Miss Lucy."

"Ha!" The woman quivered against him.

"Now what you laughing for?"

"Mr. Vachel marry Miss Lucy! Ha!"

"What you ha-ing about? What funny 'bout that?"

"Like mating a weasel with a mare. Where you get such a 'diculous idea?"

Buck was offended. "Ain't ridiculous. What you mean, calling Vaych a weasel? You mean he ain't good enough for your dead-ass Miss Lucy?"

"That ain't dead ass, boy, don't let them icy blue eyes fool you. That gal can't hardly keep her drawers on."

"Shee-it!" Buck had seen too much of Miss Lucy to be

taken in by such nonsense. If Miss Lucy were anything, she was grand-lady proper.

"Anyway, your Mr. Vachel ain't going get no chance to tug 'em off. Mr. Justin going do that, if he ain't already."

"What you mean," he asked carefully, " 'if he ain't already'?"

"I was in the house in Charleston last winter. Don't know when we had such a time. Balls and dinners and the music and the racing. And Miss Lucy and Mr. Justin, they was *always* together, sneaking off like it was Saturday night in the quarters. Why, you never seen two had such eyes for each other! My, that gal, she ain't got no icy eyes then—"

"Mr. Justin? He in Charleston?"

"Mr. Macy Sabre, him and his family come down from Virginia to visit. Mr. Aaron and Mr. Macy, good friends long ago, and now Mr. Macy got a family. And when Miss Lucy see Mr. Justin!—ain't see her catch fire like that since she growed up."

"Lida, you know what the hell you talking about?"

"I hear Mr. Aaron say, 'Macy, we going lose our overseer real soon, got to find a new one. But you know how hard to find a good overseer, most them just trash.' And Mr. Macy, he get that funny smile, and he say, 'Come spring, whyn't you let me send one my boys down? Justin, he help you out till you get you a overseer.' And Mr. Aaron, he say, 'Like that fine, if'n he ain't got better to do. I think Lucy like that too. She ain't got nobody 'telligent to talk to at Sabrehill. Young men 'round there, they ain't worth fish to fry, not a goddam one of them.' "

"He say that about Vachel?" Buck felt the poison of betrayal sickening him.

"Well, he *don't* say, 'Not a goddam one 'cepting Mr. Vachel,' I tell you that."

"He can't mean Vachel."

Lida shrugged. "I only know what I tell you. And I tell you what happen. Since Mr. Justin come here, him and Miss Lucy been chasing each other 'round and 'bout like two happy squirrel in springtime."

It was all going wrong for Vachel. Buck knew it, he

could feel it, and goddam all arrogant, patronizing Sabres. Christ, didn't Vachel realize that Miss Lucy didn't even know he existed?

Suddenly Buck had to get to Vachel. He had to get to him before it was too late. He had to save him from whatever humiliation the Sabres had in store for him.

"Where you going, honey?"

Buck was off of the bed, reaching for his clothes in the dark, hurriedly pulling them on. "Late . . . Vachel waiting for me. . . ."

He gave the woman a quick indifferent kiss and left the mansion quarters. Ahead of him, beyond the end of the service lane, he saw lights burning, but the courtyard seemed to be a mile away. He hurried toward it, ran toward it, knowing that he could not get there fast enough.

Something was happening in the courtyard.

He saw it all, took it all in, in one instant.

Vachel was drunk. He was very drunk. Eben, the butler, and Mr. Aaron were helping him toward his carriage. A boy sat in the carriage, holding the reins, ready to take Vachel home. Most of the guests had already left, but a few stood nearby, laughing and joking as they waited for Old Walter to bring their carriages.

And near the door of the big house stood Miss Lucy and Mr. Justin. The man could have been none other than Mr. Justin—no other could have been so handsome, no other could have taken such complete possession of Miss Lucy. She stood beside him, a hand tucked under his arm, quite unconscious of the impropriety. And coldly indifferent to the spectacle of the drunken Vachel Skeet being helped into his carriage.

Buck hated her.

He hurried across the courtyard. He reached for the startled boy in the carriage and lifted him down. He circled the carriage, shoved Eben out of the way, and pushed Vachel the rest of the way into the seat. He became aware that the other guests had fallen silent and were staring at him. Mr. Aaron's sympathetic eye caught his, and that just made him the angrier.

"Don't need no help," he said to Eben, "just get your ass out of my way and let me take him home."

He climbed up beside Vachel. He drove away from Sabrehill, hoping with all his heart never to see it again.

He knew what had happened. He knew as well as if he had been there himself, following Vachel into the Sabrehill big house and looking over his shoulder. Vachel had taken one look at Mr. Justin and Miss Lucy, he had taken one look at those blue eyes that were so icy and blind except when they were turned on Mr. Justin, and he had known—known that he was a self-deluded fool. Known that his love for Miss Lucy was unrecognized, unvalued, unwanted. Known that his suit, to fine people such as these, could be nothing more than a joke.

And so he had proceeded to get drunk. Not amusingly drunk, as a gentleman might well be expected to do at a party, but disgustingly, wretchedly, offensively drunk.

He vomited over the side of the carriage as they rode back to Redbird.

Just as well, Buck thought. Just as well he knew the truth about his fine Miss Lucy, and now they could go back to being just the way they had been before. Just the two of them, him and Vachel, putting Redbird back into shape again. Making it as great a plantation as it once had been, a plantation every bit as successful as Sabrehill. So to hell with Miss Lucy and all the other Sabres.

And yet Buck could not escape the feeling that in some way everything had been changed forever.

A couple of dogs barked as they reached Redbird, and that brought a sleepy-eyed boy to the stable to care for the horses. Buck helped Vachel down from the carriage; he could not tell if Vachel were awake or not. He took his friend's arm and steadied him as they walked toward the house.

Home again, he thought. Home again, and it felt good. The long drive back in the dark and the cool of the night had soothed him; he would not have to lie awake, pained by the thought of Vachel's disappointment and humiliation.

He steered Vachel to the door of the house. He opened the door. Inside the passage a lamp burned, just for them. Buck tried to help Vachel through the door.

"What you doing?"

Vachel was awake, his eyes red rimmed. His voice had sounded startlingly like the Old Man's.

"Just helping you into the house, Vaych. Just helping you to bed."

"Don't need no help."

"Fine. Let's go up——"

"Don't need no help."

Vachel was holding back in the doorway. Buck tightened his grip on his arm. "Now, Vaych——"

"Don't need no help!"

"Vachel, I'm only trying to——"

"What the hell's the matter with you? You don't hear me?"

Buck looked at Vachel with astonishment, not quite able to believe that he understood what was happening. Never before had he heard such anger in his friend's voice, never seen such hatred in his eyes.

"Why, sure, I hear——"

"Then let *go* me!"

Vachel pulled his elbow free. In the same instant he shoved out with both hands. He caught Buck squarely in the ribs, a solid blow, sending him tripping, flailing, sprawling back out into the dark.

"Let *go* me, *NIGGER-R-R-R!*"

Buck fell to the ground.

The word seemed to roar endlessly through the night: *NIGGER-R-R-R!*

And with a sound like thunder, the door of the big house slammed closed.

Two

Perhaps the only hope of escaping the past lay not in evading it but in facing it. Perhaps she would have to go back. . . .

But what did Lucy remember of Vachel Skeet that she had not already recalled? What had she known even then,

those dozen years ago? For a time, he appeared regularly
at Sabrehill, along with the other young men who came
calling, but he did little more than stammer a salutation
before disappearing into the library to talk to her father.
And on reappearing, he usually bobbed his head, muttered his farewell, and rode away as quickly as possible.
No, Lucy really had nothing to do with Vachel Skeet, nor
he with her.

Or was she deceiving herself? Was there an undercur-
rent when she was in Vachel's presence, a hint of a problem that she wished to evade? Was she, perhaps, in some
obscure way just a little frightened of him? She would
always remember that one particular Sunday that he called
at Sabrehill and that puzzling moment when he had seemed
to be trying to tell her something. . . .

But of course, the day had a far greater meaning for
her than Vachel Skeet could ever give it.

Justin. Justin gave it meaning. He was in her bones,
in her blood, as no other man ever had been. He was in
her thoughts almost every minute, he was something warm
deep down inside her, and even in church that morning,
when she was supposed to be thinking about God, all she
could think of was Justin. She sat and sweated and almost
fainted with the June heat, and thought: *Justin.*

As usual in hot weather, Fayanne served a light dinner.
Lucy could hardly eat, and the moments seemed to drag
on endlessly, moments that kept them apart, even though
they sat at the same table. *Please, Lord,* she thought,
turning her thoughts to God at last, *let this meal end,
and let me be with him!*

The Lord cooperated. The meal did at last end. Papa
and Uncle Joel stood up from the table, Amity and Dulcy
ran from the room, and Lucy started to follow Justin.
They could be alone now. They could be alone together.
They could be sweetly, beautifully, miserably alone—

"Justin, don't go yet. I want to talk to you." It was her
father, speaking in that flat tone that meant he had something serious in mind. "No, Lucy, not you—this is
between Justin and me."

Delay. Wretched, insufferable delay.

And as if that were not enough, Vachel Skeet had to

appear at that moment, which meant still *more* delay. "Come into the library, Vachel. Justin, you might as well come too. We'll talk as soon as Vachel and I have finished." She was left outside of the closed library door. Waiting.

Well, she would go to her room and change her clothes, she decided. She had been planning to do that anyway, planning to do it hastily, but now she would dally over the task, use it to take up time.

She even started up the stairs slowly. Up two, down one. Up two, down one. But she would feel like a fool if anyone saw her—she ran the rest of the way.

Ran into her room and closed the door. And got out of her Sunday best. Piece by piece. Slowly. Until she was stark, jaybird, birthday-suit naked.

God, it was hot. She poured water from a pitcher into a pan, dipped a cloth into it, and bathed her wrists and elbows and her throat and neck. Even the water was hot, but it helped. She leaned, head down, against the table, and watched a drop of sweat roll down the curve of her belly into the blond thatch.

And thought about Justin. And how he had held her and kissed her. And how she had felt—drunk and hot and honey-heavy in every part of her body.

Am I wanton? she asked herself. *Am I really so wicked?*

Yes, she answered, not displeased, *I guess I really am.*

She went to an open window. She peeked out carefully first to be sure that there was no one on the parkland down below. Then she opened the curtains and raised the blind and stood there, naked to the great outer world. She closed her eyes and let the breeze sweep over her and whispered, "Justin . . ."

Justin was waiting, even as she.

She closed the blind. She put on an old dress and an old pair of shoes, nothing more. She took out an old rice-straw hat, wide brimmed, that would protect her from the sun. She went slowly down the stairs, still thinking, *Justin.*

"Miss Lucy."

Vachel Skeet's voice so startled her that she jumped. She had been so absorbed in her own thoughts that she had failed to see him standing in the passage, and for a moment she could only stare. His own gaze swept up and down her body, as he stood there clutching his hat, and she was suddenly conscious of her nakedness beneath her dress. She thought of herself standing naked at her bedroom window and of Vachel Skeet somewhere in the distance, down by the landing, watching her. That was quite impossible, of course. He had been in the library with her father and Justin, presumably until within the last few minutes. He could not have seen her. And yet . . .

She had the odd feeling that he had looked at her that way—seen her naked—many times. And a sense of outrage came to her, a sense that built instantly to a fine anger. She tried to contain the anger, but she felt her body growing cold and her eyes hard.

"Yes, Mr. Skeet?"

Vachel Skeet's hands were ruining his hat. He tried to smile at her. He tried to say something.

Lucy no longer had any Sunday afternoon callers. Some had drifted away soon after Justin had appeared at Sabrehill, as if they had realized that their suits were useless. Others had disappeared with the hot weather and the "sickly season." Now there was only Vachel, and she did not like to think of him as *her* caller at all; but since the party a few weeks ago, when he had got so drunk, he had paid much more attention to her, as if trying to make amends. And now he stood before her, still trying to smile, muttering something inane about how hot it was.

"Yes, Mr. Skeet, it certainly is hot, and now if you'll excuse me . . ."

But he did not want to excuse her. He stood there, trying to hold her in conversation. His eyes no longer saw her naked, but seemed to be pleading, trying to tell her something that he could not put into words. Asking her to be patient, asking her to understand.

But she *did not want* to understand. She was not interested in Vachel Skeet or in any other young man, aside from Justin Sabre. And, yes, she was just a little frightened by Vachel Skeet's strange intensity.

". . . nice to see you. Papa always enjoys your visits. And now . . ."

Vachel Skeet was embarrassed. He gathered up three borrowed books, said his good-bye, and hurried out into the courtyard. Lucy, watching him ride away, felt a moment of shame: *He's a nice man, he's papa's friend. Why couldn't I have been kind?*

But she had no intention of allowing her afternoon to be spoiled by Vachel Skeet. She hurried out to the kitchen house, looking for distraction.

She found it. Fayanne was off taking a nap, but Lucinda was there, just finishing the after-dinner ridd-up. She glanced at Lucy, then looked again harder, frowning slightly.

"What you up to?" she asked.

Lucy smiled. "What do you mean, what am I up to?" The hazy, lazy, honeyed feeling that Vachel Skeet had driven away was returning.

"I mean," Lucinda said distinctly, "what do you think you are going to do?"

Lucy stretched and yawned. "Oh, I don't know. Just laze around, I guess. Maybe take a little walk with Mr. Justin."

"Take a little walk with Mr. Justin, huh?" Lucinda looked at her critically. "What you got on under that dress?"

The question surprised Lucy. But Lucinda so often seemed to know more than she had any right to know. "Nothing much. It's such a hot day."

"You got nothing much *what* on under that dress?"

"Nothing much. Lucinda, it's so hot—"

"Pull up that skirt, let me see."

Lucy raised her skirt a few tentative inches.

"*Up,* I said! *Up!*"

"Oh!" She angrily jerked the skirt up over her knees.

"The day ain't the only thing around here that's hot," Lucinda said. "Now, you get back in the house and put on some drawers."

Lucy sighed dramatically and lowered her skirt. "Please don't talk to me like that. I am not a child."

"That's just the point, honey. You ain't a child and ain't been for some time now. And you ain't gonna walk around with no gentleman without no drawers on."

"Do I have to remind you that you are not my mother?"

"No, but I took a lot of care of you all these years, and I ain't stopping now. You just go do like I say."

Her rebellion was like a gun going off, surprising even Lucy. "Ain't gonna do it!"

"Is!"

"Ain't!"

Mighty arms folded under an Amazonian bosom. *"Is!"*

Tears suddenly flooded Lucy's eyes. "My papa is the only one who can tell me what to do!"

"Your papa is the one that gives you girls too many privileges," Lucinda snapped. *"I* am the one that takes them away!"

Lucy shook her head fiercely and tried not to sob. She seldom wept, and for the life of her, she could not understand why she felt so emotional today. Here she was, all grown up and most of her friends married, and it was utterly unfair that Lucinda should make her feel like such a child.

But suddenly Lucinda softened. She took Lucy's shoulders and shook her gently. "Oh, now, look, honey," she said, "you like a little sister to me, and I *got* to take care of you. And I know you ain't planning nothing bad, but something in you is looking for something good, and maybe you ain't ready for that yet."

Lucy tried to pull away. "I don't know what you're talking about."

"Oh, yes, you do, honey, 'cause you and me, we talked about it lots of times. And you know I ain't real strict like some, that ain't got no juice nor joy left in 'em. But on the other hand, I do know something about men—"

"I love him." She hadn't meant to say it, but the words burst out.

"I know you do. And maybe he told you he love you too."

"He told me—"

"I ain't asked. All I know is, I ain't heard him shouting from any housetop he love you. He ain't told your papa, he ain't told me, he ain't told your Uncle Joel—"

"That doesn't matter."

"Honey-child, *that matters.* You ain't no man's woman

till he tells the world. Till then, you just his plaything, and he'll up and ride away anytime he feels like it. Now, I ain't saying nothing again' your Mr. Justin, not yet. But till he is ready . . ."

Lucinda's voice drifted off as footsteps sounded in the portico that led to the big house, and Justin stepped into the kitchen. He wore no jacket, and his shirt was open at the throat, showing smooth sweat-shiny skin. *Salty,* she thought, remembering. But when she looked up at his eyes and smiled, he did not smile back.

He dropped into a chair. Dropped like a defeated man.

"I've just been talking to your father," he said to Lucy. He glanced at her, then pulled his eyes away.

"Yes . . ."

"We talked about several things, but mainly about . . . about you."

Lucy felt a kind of dread building. "You . . . you don't have to tell me."

"Oh, yes, he does," Lucinda said quietly.

"What he said really made a good deal of sense, Lucy. I knew about the callers you had this spring, of course, and he told me how he discouraged any he didn't approve of. And how any young man would have to watch his step with you until . . . well, you know."

"I know."

"And he pointed out that I was in a rather special position here. I'm living right in the house, I see you every day, I could make tongues wag without half trying."

"I guess you could." Lucy hated the way Justin was avoiding her eyes.

"And I guess I haven't been exactly discreet . . . going into town with you with hardly a proper chaperone sometimes . . . things like that. . . ."

Lucy didn't think she could stand the welter of her emotions much longer. Anger was returning. "So you promised papa that you would be a good little boy and exercise greater discretion hereafter."

"No, as a matter of fact, I didn't. But he said that in view of the situation here and my own patently offensive behavior, it was time I declared my intentions." For the first time, Lucy realized that Justin was having difficulty in keeping a straight face. "So I said, 'Hell, Cousin Aaron, I aim to marry that gal—I hope with your permission, sir, but come hell or high water—' "

With a cry, Lucy threw herself into Justin's arms.

"He said it was all right with him," Justin added a minute later, "but that you might be hard to convince."

Lucinda laughed softly, a low velvet sound. "Whyn't you two get out of here. Go take a walk somewhere. Me, I want to finish my work and have my Sunday rest."

And so it happened. Happened not because Lucy planned it, even then, but because—so it seemed to her —it had to be.

Hands clasped, happy beyond speech, they walked out the west service lane, out beyond the little guest houses and the mansion quarters. The incident with Vachel Skeet and the altercation with Lucinda were almost as forgotten as if they had never occurred. The only thing that mattered to Lucy now was that Justin was hers, hers forever. Even the hot sun that bathed them in sweat seemed to burn in celebration, and every rank scent of weed and dust and wildflower was a lover's perfume.

By unspoken agreement, they walked toward "their place," a line of trees where a stream swelled to a small pool. There, sheltered, unseen by the outside world, Justin at once took her into his arms; her lips swelled as she brushed them against his, her legs trembled. But there was time for play first, both time and need, and after that first kiss, she pushed him away. With a look that was a challenge, she kicked off her shoes, gathered up her skirts, and leapt into the water.

Justin took the challenge. He pulled off his boots and went after her. She ran from him, turned and splashed him, and ran again. But he caught her, as he was meant to do, caught her and they struggled. She broke away. Her skirt fell into the water, and when she stopped to lift it again, lift it still higher over glistening wet legs, his arms again encircled her. She moved her body against his, strained to break free, knowing he would only hold her the tighter. He lifted her in his arms and carried her up onto the bank of the stream.

He laid her gently, carefully, in the grass and took her again into his arms.

This moment would never come again, she thought, as they kissed. She hardly knew what she meant. This moment would never come again, and it should not have to. Once in a lifetime was enough. It had to be right this time, because another time could never be like this.

And she must give herself to it—all of herself.

There was no holding back then, and her only further thought was to give and to take love. Never before, even with Justin, had she been more free, as she shook herself into greater disarray and invited his caresses. Never before had she surrendered herself to her emotions, her needs, her desires so completely. There could be no stopping what was happening, no end to this except one. She tried to draw him closer and still closer, but suddenly—

He swung away from her. They were apart, and she saw only his broad back as he sat there, his head hanging low. She felt betrayed.

"What is it?" she asked weakly.

His voice was muffled. "Lucy, you've got to understand . . . I love you . . . and each time we're together like this . . . you don't know what it does. . . . If only I didn't want you so much . . ."

Then she understood. She smiled.

"Justin," she said, "you come back here to me, you hear?"

And he did, instantly, as she had known he would.

She did not have to say anything more. Closing her eyes, she reached for him. Once again, desire mounted like a thunderhead, like a storm.

And it happened.

She owed him.

Yes, she owed him, and she always would: he thought it then, as he would years later. You could not long for a woman, court her, fight for her, without her forever owing you something. Even if she refused to acknowledge the debt.

As she had refused that afternoon at Sabrehill. He had waited for her in the passage after leaving the library, waited nervously, hoping to exchange a few pleasant words and maybe a smile or two. But when she came down the stairs, her eyes hardened. She had never looked more desirable to him—there was something summery and free and half-naked about her, something that brought a catch to his throat and made him want to reach for her—but as he looked at her, her eyes widened and turned cold. They excluded him from her life utterly, made him feel no less a stranger than when he had first seen her.

He was embarrassed. A few mumbled words, and he bolted from the house. Could it possibly be true, what the niggers said about Miss Lucy and Justin Sabre? Never. And yet he had to find out.

He drove down the long avenue between the oaks to the main road and turned west. He continued on for several minutes. Then, at the edge of a long open expanse that stretched hundreds of yards to the south, almost to the river, he stopped. And waited.

The niggers always seemed to know more than any white man what was going on. And it was said that for about three or four Sundays now Miss Lucy and Mr. Justin had been wandering out unchaperoned to a certain patch of woods together, and that . . .

Vachel would not believe it. Of course, they had appeared in town with only a child or two for chaperone several times, but that was a different thing from venturing out alone into the woods, and—

He saw them.

There was no way he could know for certain that it was they. The distance was too great; they were like something being blown slowly along the horizon by a breeze. Yet he knew.

He waited until they had disappeared into the trees, then urged his horse forward. A couple of hundred yards to the west he came to a bridge over a stream.

Now all he had to do was get down from the phaeton, tie up the horse, and follow the stream on foot. He would enter the woods that bordered the stream. He would go silently, always keeping hidden, until . . .

Most likely, they would simply be strolling through the woods, talking. And he would follow them, for the rest of the afternoon if need be, their unseen chaperone. And nothing wrong would happen, nothing at all, because Miss Lucy was much too smart for that, much too *good*. She was strong minded, independent, and sometimes unconventional, as everybody knew, but those were the marks of a truly grand lady. Nobody would ever suspect the cool-eyed Miss Lucy of—

Suddenly he remembered Lucy's eyes as she had looked at Justin on the night of the party.

He remembered how she had looked as she had come down the staircase less than an hour ago—her face flushed, her lips full, her eyes eager.

He remembered the tension he had felt between her and Justin every time they had been in the same room together.

The pain hit Vachel so suddenly and so hard that he cried out aloud and bent double. He knew what he would find if he followed the stream through the woods, knew beyond any doubt, and he couldn't stand it. Couldn't stand to see it or to hear it—the fierce abandonment on Lucy's face as she cried out for more from Justin, her cries as she strained for fulfillment, Justin's moans as he pleasured her.

Because that was what was happening right now, perhaps at this very moment. The two of them were together, and he could see them doing it, half-clothed or naked, rolling in the grass, doing it joyfully, obscenely, like animals, and he couldn't stand it, he would kill them, he would have to kill them—*kill them, kill them, kill them!*

He tried to stifle his sobs. He forced himself to straighten up. He wiped his face with one arm, pulled the other arm tight across his belly as if to contain the pain.

No, it was not happening. Miss Lucy would never do such a thing. She would never let such a thing happen.

But he knew he could never go into those woods to find out.

He drove on.

Three

He was a nigger: Vachel had said so. Worse, Vachel had made him feel like a nigger, which was a far greater betrayal. But Buck could take that, because he knew that Vachel was in pain, and any creature in pain was likely to strike out, even at a friend. His concern, for the moment, was far more for Vachel than for himself.

Still, things were changing, and Buck felt a little bit as if he were living on the edge of a precipice. What would Vachel decide, determine, give, or take next? The day after the Sabrehill party, he said, "Whyn't you move into another room? We got plenty room in this old place, no need to crowd up." So Buck moved into another room, which was all right with him—grown men should have their own rooms anyway, and at least Vachel was not throwing him out of the house. But it was a change.

One thing did not change. Sunday a week later, Vachel cheerfully announced that they were "going to go call on Miss Lucy." And when Buck looked surprised, Vachel added with a strained smile, "Well, get a move on, boy— she be expecting us!" For the first time, Buck realized the depths of his friend's self-deceit, and it frightened him. Vachel had *seen* what was happening between Miss Lucy and Mr. Justin (Buck himself had, in an instant). He *knew* that his was the least successful of suits, but he had put all that firmly out of mind. He simply denied it. Everything was just as it had been before Justin's appearance: Miss Lucy eagerly awaited Vachel's call, and one day soon he would ask for her hand. The Sunday visits continued.

But they continued after that Sunday without Buck. It was as if Vachel read the truth in Buck's face and therefore did not want him along.

Buck watched as Vachel's drinking increased. His drinking was always heaviest on Sunday evenings, after calling on Miss Lucy, as if he had to ease the strain of maintaining his illusions. Then he would abuse Buck as he never had before in his life, cursing him, calling him a "nigger," and ordering him out of the house.

And finally one evening it happened: he took a whip to Buck.

He had returned from Sabrehill that afternoon, carrying three of Mr. Aaron's books, which he simply dropped in the middle of the passage. Without a word, he turned around, left the house, and headed for the office. Buck picked up the books, automatically noting the authors: Locke, Irving, Milton. He put them on a shelf—he had long done most of the housekeeping, though he was beginning to despair of keeping the place neat—and then followed Vachel. He found him, as he knew he would, taking the evening's first drink, straight from the jug.

He tried to stop Vachel from drinking, or at least slow him down, but it was not use. Vachel sat right where he was, rarely answering Buck, and repeatedly lifting the jug.

The supper hour came. Buck brought a plate of food, which Vachel, now thoroughly drunk, refused to eat. When Buck insisted, Vachel threw the plate at him. He was getting more and more like the Old Man, Buck thought —the Old Man, who had been up in his bedroom, drunk all day. In fact, with every passing week the resemblance grew more frightening.

Late in the evening Vachel at last appeared to be on the verge of passing out. He stood up from the table and took a few steps, yawing from side to side, and Buck, who had been keeping a careful eye on him, sighed with relief. Standing himself, he said, "Come on, old Vaych, let's get our asses up to bed."

It was the wrong thing to say.

Vachel roared, a sound somewhere between pain and fury. His face was twisted, his eyes mad. By now, Buck was used to Vachel's whiskey angers, but he had seen nothing like this before. While he watched with astonishment, Vachel snatched a whip from a peg on the wall and sent it lashing out.

The room was small but not small enough to stop the blow; the whip cut across Buck's shoulders. His howl was like Vachel's: of both pain and fury. He saw the whip rising again, and knowing he could not stop the blow, he ran for the door—but too late. The whip hit him with such force that he fell to the ground outside. Then Vachel was standing over him, and the whip came down again, and again, and again.

How he got to his feet under the rain of those blows, he would never know. Somehow he found himself struggling to his knees, found himself clinging to Vachel, and then he was supporting Vachel and tearing the whip from his hands. Vachel at once began to sob, began to blubber out a drunken plea for forgiveness, but Buck had no forgiveness in him; he felt the blood running down his back, and he had only hatred.

In that moment he might have killed Vachel. He might have taken the man's head in his hands and broken his neck. He might have thrown him to the ground and whipped him to death. In that moment.

But the moment passed.

Poor goddam stupid cunt-crazy Vaych, he thought. *Poor fuck-sick bastard. But if you ever lay a finger on me again . . .*

"All right, goddam it, let's get your ass to bed."

Somehow he maneuvered the staggering man to the big house. Somehow he got him up the stairs and into his room, the room that Buck had shared with him for so many years. In another room the Old Man snored loudly. Buck toppled Vachel onto the bed, then lifted his feet onto it and pulled off his boots, and Vachel joined the snoring.

Buck stood by the bed and watched him for a moment. Though the will-to-murder was gone and pity had returned, some of the hatred he had felt out by the office remained. Buck wondered if in some part of himself he had not always hated Vachel Skeet.

Thirteen days later, on Saturday afternoon, Buck and Vachel rode into Riverboro together. The trip was a welcome relief for Buck. He had hardly been off of Redbird in weeks, and he had spent too many hours with a sullen, depressed Vachel, feeling powerless to help him. But Riverboro was bright and cheerful, and Buck felt his spirits rising. He noted with satisfaction that even Vachel was smiling and looking about alertly; he looked better than he had in several days.

They made their few purchases and afterward, as usual, stopped by the Carstairs tavern. Trade was brisk. P. V. Tucker was there, and young Taggart Bassett, and a number of other men known to Vachel and Buck wandered in and out. Truman Carstairs, the proprietor, entertained the customers with gossip, while his daughter, Claramae, filled and refilled glasses and tankards, and even her lazy brothers, Caley and Rowan, did some work. Buck sat quietly by the door until Vachel handed him a glass, then went outside to sit on a bench and enjoy the brew.

When she had a free minute, Claramae came out to speak to him.

"Mr. Skeet looking better today, ain't he?"

It was impossible that Riverboro and the countryside knew nothing of Vachel's long suit and his failure, and with anyone else, Buck might have been offended by this reference. But not with Claramae, a seventeen-year-old blond girl with an attractive freckled face and a sunny disposition. He had known her all his life—his mother had helped deliver her—and he knew she wished Vachel only well. He smiled and said, "Yes, he is looking better today, Miss Claramae."

"You take good care of him, Buck, you hear me?"

"I certainly shall, Miss Claramae, unfailingly."

She grinned, spreading the freckles. Buck loved it when she grinned. "You do talk grand when you want to, Buck," she said, and she went back into the tavern, leaving Buck feeling better than ever.

Feeling better than ever, that is, until he saw Miss Lucy and Mr. Justin coming down the other side of the street. Little ten-year-old Amity and her Negro companion, Leila, were with them, their only chaperones.

Suddenly depressed, Buck drained his glass and went back into the tavern. Vachel was sitting alone at a table at that moment. He was slightly glassy eyed from his whiskey, and he smiled from some distant corner of his mind as Buck set down the empty glass.

"Well, would you look at that," Taggart Bassett said in

a voice that was meant to be heard. He was standing in the open doorway, looking out into the street, and somehow Buck knew what he was looking at.

"What's that, Tag?" Truman Carstairs asked from the back of the room.

"It's Justin and Miss Lucy again, and nobody with 'em 'cept little Amity and that nigger kid."

P. V. Tucker went to the door to have a look. "He's a high-and-mighty God-would-kiss-his-ass Sabre," P. V. said. "Where you get off calling him Justin?"

"He's a overseer, ain't he? Let the niggers call him mister. One overseer's same as any other to me, don't give a damn if he is a Sabre." Tag nudged P. V. "Hey, you reckon old Justin's getting into that stuff?"

"Mmmm." P. V. pretended to consider. "Reckon he would be, if he could thaw that pussy."

"How 'bout you? Think you could do it?"

"Me, I never even called on her. Never figured she had a hole to get into—"

The tavern was filled with a sudden roar of laughter. Buck looked at Vachel. He was still smiling, but his eyes were glassier than they had been.

"But now that Justin's opened her up," P. V. went on, "reckon I could get my share."

"Yeah, the cold ones, once they find out what they been missing, they worse than niggers."

"Actually, Tag . . ." P. V. pretended to consider the matter further. "Actually, maybe Miss Lucy ain't cold as you think. You probably don't remember, you was only twelve or thirteen, but a few years back some McCloud people was visiting the Sabres down here. And this young buck they had with 'em, they say Miss Lucy was something scandalous with him. Lots of people will swear that he was fucking her regular all the time he was here, and her only about fifteen years old at the time. Yes, sir, he fucked her—"

"Oh, well, now," Tag cut in, "if he fucked her, and fucked her that early, reckon she's been getting it pretty regular since."

"Yeah, I reckon I was a damn fool not to think about that. Heard from my nigger foreman she was running off into the woods with Justin Sabre, but I hardly believed it. Now, if I'd thought about it, reckon I'da dragged her off into the woods myself."

Vachel sat perfectly still. Claramae had come into the room unobserved, but now her eyes met Buck's and held them: *We got to do something, Buck, we got to—*

"Well, maybe you'll get your chance yet, P. V. I mean, a woman like that, one man just ain't gonna be enough for her, ain't that right?"

"Reckon so. But in that case, I wonder who's been giving it to her all this time since that McCloud fella."

"Well, she got niggers on her place, ain't she? That's what these quality ladies do to get their satisfaction, they fuck their niggers. Now, you ask Buckley over there—"

He exploded. The table was flung away from him, the table, the chairs, he exploded and filled the room, a rushing, smashing, savage force. He felt Buckley and Claramae reach for him, felt them claw at his arms, saw them being hurled aside.

There was a roaring in the room, a roaring in his own ears. Dimly he heard Carstairs shout. Claramae screamed. Tag Bassett seemed to be laughing, there was a wide grin on his face, but laughter and grin faded as Vachel exploded through the room. Tucker tried to stop him but vanished as Vachel brushed him aside. Bassett threw up his hands, but too late—Vachel's left fist shot past them, and Bassett's head was like a melon hit by a bullet. He seemed to splatter against the wall.

Hit. Kill. It was all he knew. He looked around for someone to hit, to kill, Tucker, Carstairs, even Buckley, it didn't matter, but somehow in the haze of his anger and hatred he saw no one.

He stepped out through the tavern door, out of the shaded room and into the glare of the day.

And saw Justin Sabre.

Miss Lucy and the two children were nowhere in sight. Justin strolled on the other side of the street like a man at leisure, a man just waiting.

Vachel knew what he had to do.

"Sabre!" he shouted. *"Sabre!"*

Justin Sabre stopped in his tracks and looked at Vachel. So did everyone else who had heard that cry.

Vachel walked across the street, boots pounding, head throbbing. There was a terrible pain in his left hand, as if he had broken something, but it hardly seemed to matter. All that mattered was his anger, now cold and deadly and completely under control.

Justin Sabre waited, face carefully blank, feet apart, arms hanging loose, as if he knew.

Vachel stopped immediately in front of him. He stared at Justin Sabre for a few seconds. Then, using his right hand, he gave Justin a backhand blow across the face with all his strength. Justin staggered back against a storefront.

Vachel said, "I am calling you out."

Justin recovered his footing. He looked shocked. "Mr. Skeet, I think you may know, sir, that I do not duel. It is a matter of principle. I respect those who see the matter differently and do fight. However, I—"

Vachel brought up his right hand again, this time in a forehand slap that sounded like the crack of a whip.

"Mr. Sabre, I am calling you out!"

Justin blinked the tears from his eyes. His mouth was already swelling from the two blows, and his cheeks were streaked with red. "May I ask why you are issuing this challenge, sir?"

"Because you—you dirty up a woman—you—you damn—"

Vachel could not hold himself back, and did not want to. He brought up the backhand again, a blow that ripped across Justin Sabre's face and left blood streaming from his nose. His eyes were closed, as if he were in exquisite pain. And yet the eyes opened again after a few seconds, and he asked in a completely different, almost conversational tone of voice, "What the hell are you talking about, boy?"

"You know goddam good and well what I'm talking about!" Vachel said furiously, preparing another blow. "You know goddam good and well! The Sabres are my friends—Mr. Aaron, Miss Lucy!—then you come along.

You make Miss Lucy the laugh of this town with your carrying on, you go about with her so free, like she was the village whore, you have everybody in the world talking dirty about her, and you—"

Vachel brought the hand up again, another backhand, but something had happened, something quite unexpected. Justin Sabre caught his forearm with his right hand and held it immobile. His face was totally changed, a mask of fury matching Vachel's own.

"I said I don't duel! But you touch me again, you stupid son of a bitch, and I'll kill you here and now!"

Vachel had never before heard such a voice, a voice so taut with anger that it barely rose above a whisper. It reminded him of the sound a cornered wildcat might make, and the shocking thought hit him, *My God, he means it! He just might kill me!*

But he didn't give a damn. He was ready to die if need be. Looking Justin directly in the eyes, he said, "Maybe you didn't hear me. I said, you make Miss Lucy a whore in people's eyes. And I say you're a goddam disgrace to the name of Sabre. I say—"

The blow was blinding. It caught Vachel across the face before he realized what was going to happen. Justin had released the forearm and had grabbed Vachel's shirtfront in his left fist. Then, after the first blow, he brought up a backhand and another forehand slap, three blows for Vachel's three. But he wasn't done. His right fist shot into Vachel's belly, and Vachel felt as if he had been destroyed. His breath went out of him, and he seemed to be strangling on his own guts. Straining, retching, thinking he might truly be dying, he fell to his knees on the sunlit street. He bent double, and his face ground into the dust.

Gradually he regained control of his breathing. He managed to look up. Justin Sabre seemed to tower over him. All the world, Vachel knew, the whole goddam world was watching just the two of them—Justin standing there, and him, Vachel, in the dust as if he were groveling.

"Skeet," Justin said quietly, "you will never again say Miss Lucy's name. You will never again insult that name by saying it aloud in another person's presence."

"To hell with you," Vachel sobbed. "Say what I please
. . . all your fault . . . make her a fucking whore. . . ."

Justin kicked him in the mouth, but it was a light kick,
hardly more than a gesture of contempt. "I've warned
you, Skeet."

"Whore," Vachel cried defiantly, "whore! Miss Lucy
. . . whore, whore!"

"Very well," Justin Sabre said, "you shall have your
duel. And," he added, "I shall kill you."

It was hours before she even knew what was wrong.
There stood Justin on the sun-baked street, his face red
welted and blood streaked, but he would tell her nothing,
nothing. Every wide, curious eye regarding them as they
stood there knew more than she did.

"Justin, if only you would tell me—"

"Lucy, I can't . . . not . . . not yet."

As soon as they arrived home, Justin disappeared into
the library with her father and her Uncle Joel. Half an
hour later messengers were sent out to various neighbors
—Kimbrough, Devereau, Buckridge. Supper was eaten,
or nibbled at, in silence—only Uncle Joel showed any
taste for his food—and Lucy had no opportunity to talk
further with Justin. He seemed to be avoiding her.

Neighbors appeared. There was another meeting, of
almost an hour, in the library. The neighbors left. And
Lucy at once entered the library to force an interview with
her father.

"Papa, you have got to tell me what is going on!"

Aaron Sabre was a tall, lean man, his thick hair already
going to white, though he was still in his early forties.
He tried to smile at his daughter, but his eyes had no
smile in them. "I'm sorry, Lucy. I don't think any of us
have trusted ourselves to speak, but you're right—"

"Then tell me!"

"Vachel Skeet has challenged Justin to a duel. And
Justin has accepted."

Lucy felt as if somehow she should have known; duels
were common enough, and one almost took them for
granted. But that did not make the shock the less.

"Why?" she asked. "What in the world do they have to fight about?"

"That's between them."

"But I don't understand! Justin doesn't fight duels, any more than you do. It's a matter of principle with him!"

"And with me. But I might fight—in special circumstances."

"In what circumstances?"

But her father would say nothing more, except to add, "I know it's useless to tell you not to worry, but I'm sure you realize that most challenges come to nothing. We'll meet with Vachel's seconds tomorrow, and the whole matter will probably be resolved quite peaceably."

Somehow Lucy did not believe him. She had a feeling about Vachel.

Her Uncle Joel was more sanguine about the whole affair. A husky, chunky sportsman who had five times left the field of honor a victor, he was quite looking forward to the duel.

"Now, I wouldn't worry, honey. Vachel ain't a bad shot, in fact he's fast and he's accurate. But the little I've seen of Justin, he ain't bad neither. And neither of 'em fought before, so you might say it's in the hands of the Lord."

Lucy hurried away.

She at last found Justin, alone and brooding in the formal gardens at the east end of the house. She followed him into the darkness of the gazebo.

"Justin," she said, "you mustn't fight this duel with Vachel Skeet. I don't know what it's all about, but I do know you must not fight!"

"I have no choice, Lucy."

She strained to see his face in the darkness. "Of course you have a choice. Justin, you are gambling not only with your own life but with my happiness. And I am very selfish about my happiness. What right have you to risk it?"

"None. But again, I have no choice."

"Justin, I beg you."

He did not answer but merely gathered her into his arms and held her close. Tears came to her eyes.

"At least tell me why you must fight."

"I can't do that."

And she knew he never would. Would never explain and would never turn his back on the duel, even though he might hate the duel in principle. She sensed that he was caught up, trapped, in some conception of honor and duty that was more important to him than his disapproval of the *code duello,* and if need be, he would die for it.

She left his arms. There was no lovemaking that night, no secret visit to her room or his, and there never would be again until the duel was either fought or stopped. It was as if her life and her happiness had come to a complete standstill.

Her hope lay in the meeting of the seconds. Justin, her father, and her uncle rode into Riverboro the next afternoon, and she prayed that when they returned the matter would have been resolved.

It had not been: she saw that on her father's face as he stepped down from the carriage. "I'm sorry, Lucy. Vachel was quite adamant, and so was Justin—no concessions, no compromise. I confess I no longer understand Vachel."

"When?"

"Tomorrow. At dawn."

And still she did not know what it was about. No one would tell her, not even her Uncle Joel, and he remained the one person who seemed to be enjoying the affair.

"They're both determined, just determined," he said when she cornered him by the east lane barn. "Don't think anything could stop either of them now—why, they'd as soon shoot each other down in the streets. No, this ain't no little matter of 'first blood and honor satisfied.' They gonna keep right on shooting till somebody is dead!" He saw her stricken look. "Aw, now, Lucy— now, don't you worry."

She stood it as long as she could. Somehow she got through the grim evening meal, but when she found Uncle Joel humming cheerfully to himself as he sat in the north parlor inspecting his matched dueling pistols, she could stand the inaction, the waiting, the strain no longer. She had to know what the duel was about. And she had to try to stop it.

"Come, Lucinda, we are going to Redbird."

She knew that neither her father nor Justin would approve. She knew that what she was about to do was unconventional, unladylike, perhaps unforgivable. She was intruding into a man's world, where it would be said that she had no right to be. But to hell with that, she thought furiously—men made too many of the rules. It was *her* life as well as Justin's and Vachel's that they intended to shape by gunfire.

It was sundown when she told Old Walter to hitch a fast horse to the cabriolet, and well into dark when they reached Redbird. Lights burned in the big house. An obviously surprised Buckley met them at the door and led them into a parlor, where a moment later Vachel appeared, looking no less surprised.

For all the tumult in her mind, Lucy found she had no idea of what she was going to say, no wildest plan. She found herself saying, "Mr. Skeet—Vachel—you intend to kill my cousin Justin."

"Yes, Miss Lucy," Vachel said, "I do."

"But why? Why? The Skeets and the Sabres have always been friends. You and I have been friends."

Something hardened in Vachel's eyes. "Have we, Miss Lucy?"

"Why, I always thought so. You wouldn't be welcome at Sabrehill otherwise, and we've always made you welcome, haven't we? And is this how you repay us? By challenging my cousin to a duel?"

Vachel stared at Lucy as if trying to puzzle her out. "Who sent you here? Mr. Justin? Mr. Aaron?"

"Nobody sent me here."

"Wouldn't have come on your own."

"But I have. Vachel—"

"*He* sent you, I guess—Justin. Trying to hide behind your skirts."

"Now, why would he do that? I assure you—"

Vachel laughed harshly. "Because he's a goddam coward, Miss Lucy, if you'll excuse the language. A goddam coward who would disgrace a woman's name, then pretend he got principles against dueling so that he don't have to answer for it. But he's gonna fight me all right."

"What in the world are you—"

"And him saying *I* ain't supposed to say your name aloud no more! Like *I* was the one disgracing you! You damn right I intend to kill the son of a bitch. You talk about the Skeets and the Sabres being friends—it's *because* we been friends that I got to kill Justin, and I don't know why Mr. Aaron don't understand that."

Lucy hardly heard what Vachel said next; his words seemed almost beyond comprehension. She finally interrupted.

"Mr. Skeet—Vachel—did I understand you correctly? Are you saying that *I* have something to do with this duel?"

Vachel's eyes grew wary. "I guess they told you all about it."

"No. No, they did not."

"Then I guess it ain't right that we should talk about it."

She stared at him. Suddenly she understood. *Goddam coward who would disgrace a woman's name . . . like* I *was the one disgracing you. . . .* She was the woman Vachel had referred to. And the men of her family had refused to tell her the reason for the duel, because even to speak of such a thing was an embarrassment; they would not trouble her with the thought that someone had cast a shadow over her name.

But if someone had clouded her reputation, what had that to do with—of all people—Vachel Skeet?

"Vachel," she said carefully, "are you under the impression that you are defending my honor?"

Vachel abruptly turned away from her. He pursed his lips and lowered his eyes. He looked like a small boy, afraid of being rebuked. At any other time the effect might have been comic, but now . . .

"Because, if you are," Lucy went on in the face of his silence, "I really do not think it needs defending."

"Miss Lucy, you don't know the talk he's caused."

"I am not interested—"

"It's him—Justin—his free and easy ways with you

that's caused it all. You just walk down the street in Riverboro, and somebody like Tag Bassett or P. V. Tucker sees you, and you don't know the things they say about you. Terrible things, Miss Lucy, terrible, filthy—"

"Mr. Skeet." Lucy found that she was beginning to tremble in spite of all determination to remain calm. "I have no interest in what a Mr. Bassett or a Mr. Tucker may say. If you have any quarrel with what they say, I suggest that you take it up with them—"

"No!" Vachel whirled on her. "Because they ain't quality! They just dirt, but Justin Sabre is quality, and so am I, by God. Skeet is good as Sabre, and I'll have my satisfaction from *him!"*

"But I don't understand!" Lucy said desperately. "What has all this to do with *you?"*

Vachel shook his hands before her, all but wrung them. His eyes pled for her understanding. "Miss Lucy, it ain't only people like Bassett and Tucker. You think the Pettigrews and Kimbroughs and all them ain't going to hear too? 'Cause he even got the niggers talking, and you know how niggers spread tales. The niggers spread it all around how just last Sunday afternoon he coaxed you off into the woods, and the Sunday before that too."

"He—he did what?"

"He coaxed you off into the woods."

"He did nothing of the kind, Mr. Skeet!"

"Aw, now, he did, Miss Lucy, 'cause I saw him myself, both times. Now, I ain't saying *you* done nothing wrong, but I *saw* him taking you off into those woods way out west of your big house. . . ."

Vachel's voice died away. He stared at Lucy, as if he knew he had gone too far, had said much more than he had intended to say.

"You what?" Lucy asked in a whisper. The trembling was worse now, far worse. "You what, Mr. Skeet?"

Vachel said nothing. He might have been stone.

Lucy closed her eyes for a few seconds. She knew she must remain perfectly calm, but it was hard. She put her hand to her face and took a few steps about the room. She realized that Lucinda and Buckley were still there, carefully blank-faced, silent witnesses. Bracing herself, she turned again to Vachel Skeet.

"Mr. Skeet, I think we should understand a thing or two. I appreciate your concern for me. But it is not your place to defend my honor."

"Your pa can't do it, or your uncle. I can understand that, it would be Sabre against Sabre, but I—"

"Please listen to me, Mr. Skeet. I like you. My father and my uncle like you. You are a very nice young man, a neighbor who comes calling at Sabrehill and borrows books. But nobody appointed you the guardian of our customs, manners, and morals, and this duel is quite unnecessary."

Vachel shook his head. "If we don't stop Justin Sabre, before long it'll be somebody else."

"Somebody else doing *what,* Vachel?"

Vachel Skeet was silent.

Lucy laughed; she couldn't help it, though she was on the verge of tears. "Vachel, what must I tell you to stop this nonsense?"

"It'll all be over in the morning, Miss Lucy," Vachel Skeet said quietly.

She understood then: nothing was going to stop Vachel from fighting this duel. There was some kind of madness in him that called for it, and nothing she might say or do would make the slightest difference. And yet, as a madness of her own seized her, she had to try.

"Vachel, would it make any difference if I told you that Justin did not, as you put it, coax me off into the woods, but that I coaxed him?"

"Now, don't you talk like that."

"But it's true. Would it help if I told you that I love him, that we plan to marry, that I hope to bear his children?"

"You're only trying to save him."

"Yes, I am! Because who the hell are you, almost a stranger, to try to destroy my happiness?"

"He ain't your happiness, Miss Lucy. You'll come to know that."

"Oh, he *ain't* my happiness! I guess you didn't get very

close to us in them there woods, did you, boy! You did, you'da found out what happiness is!"

"I told you, don't talk like that!"

She rejoiced in the pain she saw on his face. "You'da found out all right, 'cause *I* sure did, and I sure as hell learned him!"

"Don't—"

"Why not? 'Fraid you'll find out I ain't worth risking death for, Mr. Skeet? 'Fraid you'll find out I ain't nothing like what you thought? Think I should be 'shamed for shucking down and spreading for my man, Mr. Skeet?"

Vachel Skeet's face was like raw meat. "Miss Lucy! You talking like a whore!"

"Whore! Why, what a thing to say, Mr. Skeet. Lucinda, honey, am I talking like a whore? Then I guess I am one, but bless my ass, ain't nobody gonna die for a goddam—"

The blow took her solidly across the face and sent her slamming back against the wall. Lucinda cried out. Buckley grabbed Vachel.

"Whore!" he cried in pain. "Whore! But if you a whore, it's 'cause he made you one! The whore of Sabrehill! And for that, I'll kill him! I'll kill him!"

She had failed. There was nothing more to be done. Her knees buckled, and she began to slide down the wall to the floor, but Lucinda caught her. She closed her eyes to shut out Vachel Skeet's twisted, unforgiving face, and she let Lucinda guide her out into the passage and out of the house. The cabriolet was right where they had left it, a boy holding the horse. Lucinda helped her in, then took the reins herself. Redbird was left behind.

The whore of Sabrehill, he had called her. She had never before been called such a thing, but it was as if he had branded her. She might bury the memory, she might cover the scar, but her enemies would fling the insult at her, again and again, down through the years.

Lucinda whipped the horse back to Sabrehill. Lucy's father and uncle and Justin were in the torchlit courtyard with a dozen or more of the people. Lucy leapt from the cabriolet and hurried to her father.

"Lucy, where in God's name have you been? Did you go— We all have been out of our minds!"

She flung herself into his arms. "I'm sorry," she wept, "I'm sorry!"

He did not sleep that night. He spent it checking and rechecking his pistols, sipping an occasional drink, and thinking about Miss Lucy.

"I guess you didn't get very close to us in them there woods, did you, boy! You did, you'da found out what happiness is! 'Cause I sure did, and I sure as hell learned him!"

She had lied. He knew she had lied, though at the very same moment he knew that she had *not* lied. He broke out in a sweat and told himself that she had lied to save Justin, even as he imagined the two of them naked together and coupled. Naked, sweat-slippery, writhing . . .

He would kill Justin Sabre. He would kill the son of a bitch, and then, yes, Lucy would know who the better man was. She would learn to appreciate Vachel, and he would take Justin's place. He would take Justin's place over that naked, lusting female body.

He had at last dozed off on a couch in the parlor, when Buckley shook him. "Come on, Vachel. It's time to go."

Why did so many duels take place at dawn, Buck wondered. Duels, hangings, and natural deaths. Maybe that was the answer—it seemed natural, just as it seemed natural and right that birth should take place at dawn or shortly before. You got life or death, not after a last day, but after one last night.

The duel was to take place at the fair grounds, out behind the race track—a stretch of land that had soaked up a lot of blood. Dawn was breaking, and within minutes it would be light enough to shoot. Buck looked around. There were a number of people who had no business being there, people like young Paul Devereau and Balbo Jeppson and P. V. Tucker. Dr. Ewell and Dr. Paulson were there, one for each principal. The judges, Captain Kimbrough, old Mr. Devereau, and Mr. Breakline, stood together under an old live oak, conferring. Justin stood off to one side with his seconds, Aaron and Joel Sabre. Buck looked over at Vachel's official party.

Dr. Ewell, Mr. Pettigrew, Mr. Haining. There was not a one of them, Buck thought bitterly, who would not rather have been there for Justin Sabre. Oh, they would do their jobs, all right, because they were honorable men. Any one of them would kill Justin on the spot for breaking the rules. But just the same, in their hearts they hoped for Justin and not for Vachel.

Aristocrats. Gentry. Chivalry. All the bitterness and anger and pain that Buck had felt in recent weeks found a new focus, a new thrust. Vachel did not have a single friend in this whole crowd except for Buck and the Old Man. Buck hoped he would blow Justin Sabre's goddam head off.

". . . get to it. We're not going to prolong this. We're not going to waste any time."

The time had come, too soon. It was Captain Kimbrough speaking. He was a tall man with a very military bearing; even his straight black bar of mustache was military. Buck and the Old Man moved closer so they could hear what the captain was saying.

"I'm going over the rules we've agreed on. If there's any disagreement, any argument, state it now. . . . Back to back, pistols cocked and at ready. Ten full paces as I count should put you approximately at the markers. After the tenth step, you may fire, while I continue the count, one to five. If either man fires after the five, the other man's second shall shoot him dead. But if I see that the first man to fire has scored a hit—not a scratch but a palpable hit—I shall begin the one-to-five count over again."

"What if it turns out you're wrong?" Vachel asked. "What if that first hit turns out to be nothing at all? Like he fakes that he's hit bad—"

"Mr. Sabre is a gentleman, sir," the captain said coldly. "If there is a mistake, that is an act of God. And if *you* cannot behave as a gentleman in this affair, you will no doubt be killed. By one or another of us. Are there any further questions thus far?"

No one spoke.

"Very well. If neither man falls and cannot rise after the first round, both men will remain in position by the markers. Each will be given another pistol, loaded and cocked, by his second. Mr. Aaron Sabre and Mr. Pettigrew will handle the pistols. They will exchange the empty pistols and reload them while I give the signals for the second round—'Ready, aim, fire'—followed by the count to five. The same rules remain in force for the second round, as they do for a third and any other rounds. Questions?"

Silence. There was enough light now for the fight to begin, Buck judged. The morning was warm, and yet his teeth chattered and his knees shook.

"Very well. We shall toss a coin to see whose pistols are used on the first round and who gets first choice of pistols."

The captain tossed a coin, and Vachel called it right. He chose his own pistols. The captain tossed again, and Justin Sabre called it wrong. Vachel picked his favorite pistol. Buck smiled; he took that to be a good omen. Justin was left to pick his own favorite of the Sabre pistols for the second round. If there should be one.

"Gentlemen, take your positions . . . back to back."

Dawn. The two men in shirt sleeves. The east red now, though the west was still sunk in darkest blue. A faint breeze made waves through the long grass of the meadow. Somewhere, distantly, a cock crowed.

"On your marks, gentlemen."

The judges and doctors stood together under the great oak. To one side stood Mr. Justin's seconds—Mr. Joel aiming a cocked pistol at Vachel, and Mr. Aaron holding a second pistol for the second round. On the other side stood Mr. Haining and Mr. Pettigrew, doing the same thing for Mr. Vachel.

"On your marks . . . *ONE* . . . two . . . three . . . four . . ."

Even over the pounding of the hoofs and the rattle of the cabriolet she could hear that loud, piercing voice: ". . . three . . . four . . . five . . ."

Once again she had been unable to wait. It was impossible. She didn't care what anyone might say about her, what anyone thought—this dawn brought death, and the full light of day might bring a hearse bearing Justin's body, and she couldn't wait for that. If he died, she had to live every last second with him, and so she had whipped the horse, yelled at it, urged it on at a murderous, carriage-wrecking gallop.

". . . six . . . seven . . . eight . . ."

She was out of the cabriolet and running, running toward Justin—

". . . nine . . . *TEN!*"

She might have cried out, might have screamed in spite of herself, if Lucinda had not grabbed her and put a hand firmly over her mouth. She saw it all so clearly: on *ten,* Justin came down on his left foot, turned clockwise smoothly, and leveled his pistol. But Vachel, coming down on his right foot, merely twisted to the left, brought his pistol down to his shoulder, and instantly squeezed off his shot. The ball seemed to lift Justin off of his feet, to lift him into the air, and Lucy felt her heart crash—

"One . . . two . . . three . . ."

Justin fired.

Vachel swayed, rocked, as a red mark appeared on the side of his white shirt, appeared and spread.

Oh, Jesus, Lucy screamed silently, *it's over, please, God, make it be over!* But she knew it was not, because the voice of God or her uncle or somebody boomed in her head: *gonna keep right on shooting till somebody is dead!*

Her father ran to Justin. He took the empty pistol and handed Justin a loaded one. Then, striding back to the sideline, he saw Lucy. Ash-faced, he stared at her a few seconds, but there was no time for more. He hurried to Mr. Pettigrew, exchanged empty pistols with him, and they began reloading.

"Ready . . ."

Lucy moaned under Lucinda's tightly clamped hand.

". . . aim . . . fire."

Both pistols seemed to go off at once. Justin swung to his right and bent double. Vachel screamed and fell to the ground.

It was over now. Vachel was down, and it had to be over, it had to be. She tried to run to Justin.

But Lucinda held her back. Vachel was struggling to

his feet and yelling, "Gimme a gun, gimme a gun, goddam you all, gimme a gun, and I'll kill the bastard!"

And he got his gun. There was no haste, but there was no delay either, and a pistol was pressed into his hand, and another into Justin's.

"Ready . . ."

The guns were up and cocked. Both men swayed.

". . . aim . . ."

The guns came down level.

". . . fire. . . . One . . . two . . ."

Vachel's ball cut across Justin's chest and left shoulder. Justin swayed and glanced down at his chest, but nothing more. He steadied his pistol again, and the captain started a new count.

"One . . . two . . ."

Vachel stared as if he couldn't believe that this was happening, as if he knew that this was the end.

". . . three . . . four . . ."

"Oh, to hell with it," Justin said, and raising his pistol, he fired into the air.

"Justin!"

Lucy pulled Lucinda's hand from her mouth and screamed the name. Justin turned toward her, saw her. His eyes widened, and his lips moved silently. He might have been saying, *I'm sorry . . . good-bye. . . .*

"Justin!"

She had to be with him, had to be, for whatever time was left. She would give the rest of her life for those last precious seconds. She tore herself free from Lucinda at last and ran toward him.

But she was too late. His eyes closed. His knees gave way, and he crumpled to the ground.

Four

And then Aunt Zule was there. Aunt Zule, or Momma Erzulie, as her voodoo followers called her, widowed mother of young Zulie and three sons. Tall and lean, with fire in her eyes. Conjure-woman, it was said, and healer of the sick, who struck bargains with gods and devils.

God only knew where she had come from or how she had got here, but she had a way of appearing when she was needed—or where she had something to gain. Most likely she had been somewhere nearby since long before dawn, waiting for this moment. And now Lucy found herself being lifted from Justin's body by Aunt Zule, and thrust into Lucinda's arms.

"Take her. Keep her with you, you hear me?"

"I take care her."

Lucy was borne back away from the others.

"Is he dead, doctor?" someone asked.

She heard Dr. Paulson: "Not dead, but more dead than alive. That third shot didn't do much, but the first ball went through the ribs into the back of the chest. Lucky if it didn't get the lung. The wound in his side is bad too, and he's losing blood fast. Not much I can do."

"But you've got to try." It was her father's voice.

"If I can stop the bleeding fast enough and get the balls out—"

"I can stop that bleeding," Aunt Zule said. "You all get out of my way. Let me do what I can."

"Auntie," Dr. Paulson said, "I seen you do it before. I ain't about to stop you now."

So there was hope. Not much, perhaps, but hope. Lucy wiped her eyes and watched as Aunt Zule knelt down and bent over Justin.

"I *stop* it," the woman muttered, as if she could staunch the flow by an act of will. "I *stop* it, I *stop* it, I *stop* it."

Time values became strangely jumbled: moments seemed like hours, hours rushed by too quickly. None but those who were called for dared to go anywhere near the kitchen house where Dr. Paulson was operating, yet it was the focus of attention of most of Sabrehill. Even the hands in the fields knew: a duel had been fought; a man dying, perhaps dead by now, lay stretched out on a table, while the doctor probed with his long knives. His only assistants were Fayanne, preparing hot water and bandages, and Aunt Zule whose strong hands held Justin's body and who stood by to stop any further bleeding.

Lucy waited on the kitchen house steps. Twice, when Justin cried out, apparently regaining consciousness, she thought that she herself might die. But Lucinda could not drag her away. Her father and her uncle waited in the office, across the courtyard. The children instinctively kept their distance, only occasionally raising their voices.

Dr. Paulson at last appeared in the doorway of the kitchen house. His shirtfront was stained with blood, and his arms were red to the elbows. "Well, at least his heart is still beating," he said. "Lucky for him, he's a mighty game cock."

Justin was carried to the downstairs bed chamber in the big house; Dr. Paulson wanted him carried no further than necessary. A second bed was set up in the chamber, and it was arranged that either Aunt Zule or young Zulie would be with him day and night. A quiet settled over the house—over all of Sabrehill. There was nothing to do but wait.

She could not sleep. The man she loved lay in a bed in the room immediately below hers, and at this very moment he might be dying. She had to know, she had to see him, she had to be with him.

Lucy silently crept from her bed. She pulled on a robe and went out onto the U-shaped landing that led to the second-floor bedrooms. Looking down into the well of the passage, she saw only a dim light. The house was as quiet as it had been all day.

Going down the two flights of stairs to the first floor, she saw that the bed chamber door was partially open and that the light came from it. She crossed the passage and tapped on the door. It at once opened further, but Aunt Zule blocked the view. Lucy caught a glimpse of young Zulie as Aunt Zule stepped out into the passage.

"Now, what you doing down here?"

"Please, Aunt Zule, I saw the light—is anything wrong? Is he—"

"No, that just so we can watch him. Child, you go to bed."

"But can't I see him? Just for a minute?"

Aunt Zule considered, and shrugged. "But you can't go in," she said, and pushed open the door.

Justin lay perfectly still, as white as if he had lost every last drop of blood. It was hard to believe that he was not already dead. Young Zulie, standing by the bed, looked out at Lucy with a face that told nothing, and after a moment Aunt Zule slowly closed the door again until Justin could no longer be seen.

A terrifying certainty shook Lucy. "He's going to die, isn't he, Aunt Zule!"

Aunt Zule shrugged. "Reckon he could."

Lucy felt shock at that coolness, that apparent lack of concern. But it was typical of Aunt Zule. She had always been a good servant, and she was the best healer at Sabrehill, but Lucy had never felt that she had any great love for her masters. Lucy had, in fact, always been a little bit frightened of her.

"But can't you save him?"

"Me? Not that Dr. Paulson?" Aunt Zule's smile was good-humored but held a measure of contempt.

"Papa says you know things most doctors don't know. You save lives here every summer."

"Yeah, black nigger lives. But I don't go outa my way for no buckra."

It was the kind of remark that might have gotten Aunt Zule disciplined on many a plantation—more than the remark itself, the tone in which it was delivered.

"But you did this morning, Aunt Zule, when you stopped the bleeding."

Aunt Zule laughed silently; her high, pointed breasts shook. Her laughter seemed to confirm to Lucy that there was something she could do to save Justin, if only she would.

"Please help him, Aunt Zule, please! For me!"

The older woman looked away as indifferently as if she had not heard Lucy. She opened the door a little farther and looked into the bed chamber. She was a tall woman and regal in her bearing, broad shouldered and long legged, with a narrow waist. In her early forties, she looked a good ten years younger than she was. She awed Lucy, never more than now.

"'Please, Aunt Zule,'" she said softly, mockingly. "Nigger child, white child, all alike. 'For me, for me, for me.'" She turned her mocking smile on Lucy. "Tell me, child, what you ever done for *me?*"

"I'll do anything!"

"Anything?"

"Well . . . almost anything."

Aunt Zule threw back her head and laughed again, quietly. "Almost anything! Why, how sweet for me, Lucy-child!"

"Please, Aunt Zule!"

Aunt Zule smothered her laughter. Still smiling, she said, not unkindly, "All right, missy, I make a bargain with you."

"Yes!"

"I do my best to make your Mr. Justin all well."

"Oh, my dear—"

The smile faded from Aunt Zule's lips. "Now, you listen," she said seriously. "I *try* to make him well. He make you happy, give you a good time, put a baby in you—"

"Aunt Erzulie!"

Aunt Zule reached out and took Lucy's shoulders. "Now, ain't nothing wrong with that, child. That what you want, ain't it?"

"Yes!"

The older woman gave Lucy a little shake. "All I saying is, I try my best for you. But what you got to do for me is take care my children."

"Why, we always take care—"

"No! Now, you listen! I see trouble for my children, bad trouble, and I ain't always going to be here to help 'em. Maybe not long now. I see my own death coming."

"Aunt Zule, you aren't going to die!"

Aunt Zule shrugged. "Everybody die. Me, sooner than some we know. And when the trouble come for Zulie or Zagreus or Paris or Orion, you don't turn again' 'em. You help 'em like they was your own brothers or sisters. Or like you was their mother."

"I will! And I'll never forget!"

"You don't have to 'member, child." There was a hint of threat in Aunt Zule's voice, a glitter in her eye. "You just do it."

"I will. I promise."

Aunt Zule did not smile or loosen her grip on Lucy's shoulders, and the glitter lingered in her eye, and Lucy realized, as she had not before, how utterly serious the woman was. She really did foresee her death, or thought she did, and she was providing for her children. Nothing could be more serious than that, nothing more to be respected.

"I promise," Lucy repeated, placing her right hand over the other woman's. "Aunt Zule—I do promise."

A faint smile appeared on Aunt Zule's lips, a smile without mockery, and perhaps even with some liking. "Thank you, Lucy-child," she said. "You growing up."

"I am trying."

The smile grew warmer. "Lucinda learning you the things you s'pose to know?"

"Yes."

"You come to me. Soon. I know things even Lucinda don't know."

"All right."

"Saving 'em for all my daughters, and I only got one." Aunt Zule laughed. "Now, whyn't you get yourself up them stairs to bed."

"Can't I help?"

"No, you and him had a long day. You go have yourself some sweet dreams, child. Good night, now."

Aunt Zule went back into the bed chamber without waiting for Lucy's good night. *She likes me,* Lucy thought as she went up the stairs. *She never did before, but now she's starting to like me.* The thought gave her a warm feeling.

And then, as she slipped into bed, it struck her that she was no longer afraid. She was tired and sleepy and very happy, and somehow she had no doubt that Justin would be all right. They would both live long. He would give her a child. . . .

With the thought of that child, she fell asleep.

He knew, if he thought about it at all, that Claramae was doing her best in changing the bandages. Where it was obvious that they were going to stick, she moistened them first. She allowed them to soak for a few minutes. She then pulled at them quite carefully. And yet, as she tried to remove the bandage around his waist, the cloth stuck, he started and gasped, and the slight pain seemed to rocket to his broken right leg, where it exploded like a bomb. His gasp was followed by a scream, and the pain grew even worse. He found himself howling at Claramae, cursing her, mouthing every obscenity he could think of, striking out at her with one arm—and all the time the pain grew. Tears came to Claramae's eyes. She held her cheek, where Vachel had hit her. She tried to apologize, tried to soothe Vachel, but at last his curses sent her weeping from the bedroom.

He tried to relax, tried to ease the pain by an act of will. Gradually the blast of agony reduced to a pounding throb, and then settled, little by little.

Vachel lay perfectly still on his sweat-soaked bed. The windows were open, but not the faintest breeze gave relief from the July heat. He wondered if Justin Sabre were suffering as much as he was.

But no. That wouldn't be. Justin didn't have a broken leg, just a couple of ribs, from what Vachel had heard. He would be lying in a nice cool room at Sabrehill—it would always be cool at Sabrehill in the summer, even if it were hell everywhere else in South Carolina, just because the Sabres were the goddam Sabres.

Justin had won. No matter what Buck might say to gloss that over—and Buck was staunchly loyal—it was nonetheless clear to Vachel. Justin had won, first, in the main street of Riverboro, where he had beaten Vachel into the dust in front of God only knew how many witnesses. And he had won again on the field of honor.

He had won by the very simple expedient of throwing away his last shot. He was against dueling, and everybody knew it, and everybody also knew that he had been more or less forced into the duel against his principles. At least, that was the way people saw it. And then, hit three times, when Vachel had been hit only twice, he had refused his chance to get even. Refused his chance to kill Vachel, which, despite his principles, he had promised to do. Terrified though Vachel had been at that moment, it now seemed to him that that had been the ultimate in Sabre arrogance.

He took it all away from me, Vachel thought. Miss Lucy might have been Vachel's even yet. Three years of courting her, three years of hard work rehabilitating Redbird and the name of Skeet, and he was worse off than when he had started. No better than dirt.

Buckley came into the bedroom. Sent by the whining Claramae, no doubt. He had a little smile on his face, a nigger smile. Vachel wondered why it was that he'd never noticed before that Buckley was so goddam *nigger*.

He pulled up a chair and sat down. "How you feeling?"

It was a stupid question, unworthy of an answer. Vachel glared.

"Gotta change them bandages, Vaych," Buck said gently. "They get to stinking too bad, and you know what that means."

"She hurt me." Vachel hated himself for sounding childish.

"She didn't mean to. Sometimes them bandages gonna stick, no matter what. But we *got* to get 'em off. She's doing the best she can."

"She's a clumsy bitch."

"Vaych." Buckley patted his shoulder. "She don't have to be here. She come out here with her maid-gal out of the goodness of her heart, just 'cause she likes you—"

"She come out here 'cause old Truman Carstairs says, 'Get your ass out there, gal, and make yourself useful. That dumb son of a bitch, Vachel Skeet, is helpless now, but if you can help him get better enough to bed you, you'll be a planter's wife and have old Redbird for yourself.' *That's* why her and her gal come out here, Buckley!"

Buck laughed. "Well, maybe so. But you don't have to bed her, Vaych, and meanwhile, she's a mighty handy gal to have around, and she *does* have a good heart, and she *does* like you, and you can't deny she's a pretty little thing."

"With all them freckles?"

"Yeah, with all them freckles."

Vachel sighed. Buck was right, of course. The bandages did have to be changed, and they were lucky that Claramae had offered to come out to Redbird with her gal and be of help.

"Tell her I'm sorry," he said, "Ask her to come back in here."

Buckley left. A few minutes later, Claramae reentered the room, and Vachel saw that her face was still tear streaked. "I'm sorry, Claramae," he said. "Ain't none of that true that I said. It's just that the discomfort and the pain and the lying here drives me plumb out of my head."

She smiled. She had a sunny face, even with the tears on it. "That's all right, Mr. Skeet," she said. "I understand."

She likes me, he thought wonderingly. *She really likes me.*

Well, then, she can't be worth much.

He was going to live. Not only had Aunt Zule all but promised, but Lucy *willed* his survival—willed it with such strength, such ferocity, that if Justin died, she was certain that she would die with him. Aunt Zule, who seemed to understand, regarded her with a warmth she had never shown before. "You breathing life back into him, missy," she said. "You may not know, but you sure breathing it back. And maybe he never know how much he owe you. Maybe more to you than to me."

The jumbling of time continued: days seemed like months, a week passed in a matter of minutes. Lucy hardly noticed Independence Day. The important thing was that Justin was suddenly showing a new alertness, even if he was still sleeping most of the time. There was no fever or inflammation; the wounds were healing well; and Dr. Paulson stopped calling on Justin daily.

Justin began to talk more. He referred for the first time to the duel, asking how Vachel Skeet was. He was relieved to know that Vachel was going to live and that his leg was on the mend. The whole unhappy affair was becoming a thing of the past. Justin was cheered.

But, though he was improving rapidly, he was by no

means past all danger. This was the worst time of the year for sickness, and there was always a chance of complications and a relapse. Therefore, whenever thoughts of love crept into Lucy's mind, as they did increasingly with Justin's improvement, she hastily suppressed them. There was no time for thoughts of love now, no time for thoughts of past or future. There was time for only one thought: *You are going to live!*

Letters were dispatched to Virginia almost daily, informing Justin's family of his progress, and his older brother, Zachary Sabre, soon appeared at Sabrehill. Zachary fretted and fumed: "Ma worried sick. And what was your goddam duel about? Musta been something goddam stupid. All goddam duels are stupid. . . . You sure you're getting better? You sure you're feeling better? . . . Got to get back home. I'm a working farmer, not a goddam absentee landlord. Besides I'm running for Congress next election, did I tell you? Goddam idiots in Washington." Zachary secured Justin's promise that as soon as he could travel, he would return to Virginia and demonstrate to the rest of the family that he was well and sound. He then departed in a swirl of dust and scattered "goddams."

At last came the evening that Lucy would always think of as the turning point in Justin's return to health. Dr. Paulson announced that it was safe to move the patient now and that he would be much better off in an upstairs room where the night air was safer. "We don't want him inhaling some miasma and picking up a fever."

And so they made the trek up the stairs to Justin's former room, Lucy leading the way, Lucinda and Aunt Zule supporting Justin ("I don't know what the fuss is! I'm quite capable of walking by myself!"), and the children following. Dulcy and Irish jumped on the bed, and Amity and Leila snooped in the wardrobes, until they were all shooed out, and Justin was tucked in again. He would still need some weeks of rest, Dr. Paulson warned, before he could travel, but in another week or so he could leave his bed for an hour or two at a time. Rest at this stage meant everything. Justin groaned. How dull.

That night Lucy could not sleep, and in fact, she did not really want to. She preferred to sit up in bed, her arms around her knees, and wiggle her toes. Thunder rumbled softly in the distance, and rain began to fall gently—not such a storm as to disturb the children, but a pattering more like a lullaby. Now, once again, she could think about her love, about herself and Justin . . .

. . . and about that Sunday afternoon when he had first taken her . . . and the afternoons since in hidden groves and distant fields . . . and the nights, oh, yes, the nights when he had come to her . . . and the laughing, breath-taking, nigh-unbearable ecstasy of those most intimate moments. . . .

Ah, if only they had known—all those dull young men who had called on her, all their simpering sisters and their very proper mommas and papas, who saw her as the overly intellectual and chilly-hearted Miss Lucy Sabre. If only they had known how in her wildest heart she scorned their rules and laws and proprieties. If only they had known what a pagan, woodland creature she really was! Would they ever have guessed her secret? that she was insatiable, inexhaustible, and gloriously happy? and served nightly by that naked godlike creature with the powers of a ram?

She laughed quietly.

She lifted her head from her knees and listened. The rain continued to fall gently. There was no other sound. All lights had long been out. But was Justin all right? Aunt Zule and her daughter were no longer sleeping in his room, and if he needed something . . .

But she needed no excuses or rationalizations for visiting Justin. She got off of her bed and went out onto the dark landing, where she paused to listen again. No sound, other than the rain. Her father's three rooms were at the west end of the house, her uncle's at the east. The children were asleep in the two bedrooms overlooking the courtyard. Justin occupied the room directly across the landing from Lucy's. Silently she crossed the landing, entered his room, and went to his bedside. When she slipped under the sheet with him, he stirred. She kissed him lightly, carefully, trying not to disturb him.

Not tonight, my love.

Sleep, my love. . . .

Five

Each night she went to him.

There was never any difficulty. She merely waited until she was quite sure the children were sleeping and then crossed the landing. After that first night, the night of Justin's return to the upstairs room, he was always awake and waiting for her. She slid into bed with him and, in a little while, slipped off her gown. And he made love to her. Made love, calling her by a secret love-name. *Luz*. Never would she let another call her by that name. *"Ah, Luz,"* he sighed in the night, *"ah, Luz . . . Luz . . . Luz . . ."*

They would be married—of course. In their world there was no other way they could go on being together like this, no other way they could be together forever. He would make the obligatory trip up to Virginia to show his family that he was well recovered from his wounds and to inform them of his and Lucy's intentions. He would then return at once, and they would hold the wedding as soon as possible, either in Charleston or at Sabrehill.

But the wedding was weeks away, even months, and months might as well have been centuries. They could not wait, and saw no reason to. Their nights, while the rest of the world slept, were filled with love and play and secret laughter.

Sometimes she worried. Was this good for Justin? Or was she, Delilahlike, draining him of much-needed strength? Aunt Zule was now training her in the healing arts, and Lucy put the question to her as discreetly as possible, pretending to refer to another patient: was it good for the recuperating man to sleep with his wife? Aunt Zule laughed. "Lucy-child, you can pleasure that man of yours all you wants at night, long as you lets him get his rest in the daytime."

Lucy flushed crimson. "Oh, I didn't mean——"

"Oh, yes, you did. Never mind, I ain't going tell."

She worried too, though not often or very deeply, about the possibility of having a baby before she was ready for one. She followed Lucinda's instructions in this regard, but rather carelessly, since Lucinda herself had said, "Most of all, you just got to *hope!*" But it would be no great disaster if her firstborn were to arrive a little early. Though it was never openly admitted, such arrivals were so common in some good families that they practically became a family tradition—which showed that one could live with these little irregularities quite nicely.

The day came when Justin could be out of bed for an hour, then for two hours. The day came when his bandages were no more than a few scraps of cloth, then the day when they were taken off altogether. He still had to rest most of the time; exercise was kept at a minimum. But at Aunt Zule's urging, he began to walk out of the house, taking Lucy with him, and each day the walk grew longer. Lucy realized that she could count the hours until Justin would be leaving for Virginia.

They made the best of those hours, and Lucy began to wonder how in the world anyone could miss seeing what was going on. Aunt Zule had guessed, of course, and Lucinda had her suspicions, to say the very least; but no one else—her father, her uncle, the house servants—seemed to have the slightest idea.

Or perhaps they were merely discreet.

In the early morning hours before Justin's departure, she lay in his arms.

"I'll die without you."

"No, you won't."

"I won't live until you return."

"I'll be back soon—as soon as I can."

"If only you could tell me exactly . . ."

Teasing: "There's nothing certain in this world."

"Oh, don't say that!"

"But it's true."

"Not of my love. My love is certain. Our love."

"Yes . . ."

And so Justin Sabre departed from Sabrehill, while from the cupola that crowned the house, Lucy watched his carriage grow smaller in the distance. *But he'll soon be back,* she told herself, *he'll soon be back.* She clung to the thought as to life itself.

In the deepest heat of August, the Old Man died. He died suddenly and instantly, like an old tool, not much used anymore, that simply breaks. Like an old axe handle might break, clean, just below the head.

He fell down, and was dead.

He died in the evening and was buried the next morning. Buck arranged almost everything, as was only fitting. "Now, Vachel, you shouldn't *have* to do anything. Just tell me what you want, and I'll take care of it." He arranged to have the coffin made, he arranged for the hearse and the preacher, and he saw to it that the word was spread: the Old Man had died, and the burial would take place in the graveyard of Riverboro's Episcopal church in the morning.

The whole business was mercifully brief, yet without apparent haste. Buck was surprised at how many people attended, both quality and common. Sabres, Pettigrews, McClintocks, Kimbroughs, Hainings, Buckridges, Paulsons—all of the leading planters. Tag Bassett was there, bearing no grudge, and P. V. Tucker, and of course, Balbo Jeppson. And Truman Carstairs and his two sons and Claramae. All kinds of people. Buck looked around for Justin Sabre, but didn't see him, then remembered that Justin was said to have departed for Virginia some time ago. Buck was just as glad. A duel was supposed to square all accounts, and most duelists wound up getting drunk together, but Vachel and Mr. Justin sure as hell hadn't. Buck would be perfectly happy never to see Mr. Justin again as long as he lived.

They had no sooner got the Old Man deep-sixed than Claramae came scurrying over to Vachel and took his hand right in front of God and everybody, and it occurred to Buck that while she might be cute as a hound dog's pup, she was getting to be a bit of a pain in the ass. It happened to be the custom in that part of the country, as in many others, for neighbors to go to the house of the deceased after the burial and offer condolences to the many bereaved relatives, tell quiet jokes, and get drunk. Since one could hardly ask the bereaved to take the trouble of throwing the party, neighbors usually came with a dish of this, a platter of that, a jug of something else. Now, in this particular case, the fact was that nobody had given much of a damn for the deceased in years, and the only bereaved, if any, was Vachel and maybe (just a little) Buck. But the freckle-faced pain in the ass had taken it upon herself to *make sure* that half of the county showed up at Redbird, dishes, platters, and jugs in hand. And when Buck tried to say that it wasn't really necessary, Vachel silenced him with a shake of his head and told her how grateful he was.

And so, suddenly, *Miss* Claramae was in charge of the house that day, welcoming the guests for Vachel, setting out the food, giving orders to her brothers, to her father, *even to Buck,* for Christ's sake—"Buck, *do* get more wineglasses from the pantry. And *do* open this here bottle of Madeira for me. And *do* take back these here tumblers and wash them—whatever will our guests think!"

Quality and common passed through the house in affable proximity, only occasionally with a touch of unease. The Bassetts and the Tuckers tended to stay outside under the shade trees and to leave quickly. People like Aaron Sabre and Owen Buckridge, however, were reluctant to show unseemly haste in departure. Mr. Carstairs, as father of the unofficial hostess, made himself quite at home. The food was eaten, the drinks were downed. And Vachel retired to a corner of the parlor to get quietly and thoroughly drunk, as befitted the occasion.

And so the afternoon passed.

And it was nice. Finally Buck had to admit it, it was nice. And it had been nice of Claramae to arrange it.

The guests began to depart. They left slowly, one or two at a time at first, saying good-bye to Vachel; later, as if on signal, the remainder departed almost all at once. By that time Vachel was nowhere to be seen, and Buck found himself alone in the house with Claramae and her father.

"Miss Claramae, it sure was nice of you—"

That was when they heard the distant scream, and Buck had the horrible feeling that, oh, Jesus, he had lived through all this before, and he had thought it had ended, but it was going on and on and on. He did not know what the feeling meant, he simply had it, like poison in the gut.

The scream, the wail, the cry was repeated. Without another word, Buck ran out through the passage and into the courtyard. There were more cries, and they seemed to come from the field quarters. Buck ran toward them.

Yes, he had lived through all this before, almost exactly. There was the Old Man—bent, staggering, whip in hand. There were the people, a dozen of them, in a circle around the Old Man, but now taking care not to get within range of the whip. There were the threats, the angry defiance, the smothered laughter behind the Old Man's back. *"Come back here, you black bastards!"*

But of course, it wasn't the Old Man. It was Vachel— Vachel as piss-eyed drunk as the Old Man had ever been, Vachel doing exactly what the Old Man would have done in his place.

Buck ran to him. "Vaych! Vachel, what's wrong?"

"Putting 'em to work!"

"But, Vachel, it's the end of the day almost. Besides, we just buried your pa today. It ain't right they should work."

"You tell 'em that?"

"Yeah, I did—"

"And who the hell told you you could let my niggers off? Who the hell told you—"

"Vaych, please!"

"Please, my ass! Who the hell told you, black boy? Who the hell give you the right—"

Truman Carstairs laughed—approvingly, it seemed to Buck. Buck tried to put an arm around Vachel's shoulders. "Come on back to the house, Vachel."

Vachel shrugged the arm away. "Get your goddam hands off me. You don't know better'n touch a white man, boy?"

"Vachel—for God's sake!—this is me!—Buckley!"

"I know you, goddam you, you . . ."

Vachel staggered a few steps from Buck. Carstairs stood nearby, grinning, and Claramae was wringing her hands with worry. Vachel looked at the black faces around him, faces filled with anger, amusement, disgust.

"I got something to tell you all," he said. "I got something to tell you all, and I want you all to listen."

"Yes, master," one of the hands said softly, a jeering note in his voice, "you tell us."

"Guess you all know the old master died. Guess you all know he done died and been buried."

"We know, master," another hand said, "we know."

"And I guess you think that now that the old bastard is dead, things is gonna change."

"Don't look like it, master."

"That's *right!* That's *right!* Ain't nothing gonna change, and don't you forget it. You think you gonna lay on your lazy black asses from now on, you dead wrong! You gonna sweat lard like always to earn your keep, or I flay your goddam hide off. *Ain't nothing gonna change!*"

No, Buck thought, as the sickness in him grew, ain't nothing gonna change.

Everything already had.

He'll be back.

But when? He had been able to tell her only that he would return as soon as possible, and she eagerly awaited his first letter: *"I am coming. Now. I have told my family. They send their love. In a matter of weeks, of days, we shall be married."* But first he had to make the trip up to Virginia, and then he had to find the proper moment to tell his family (a papa who might have his own plans for Justin, a momma who could be difficult). And the mails could take such a long time.

But meanwhile, she, at least, could write to him, and she did—almost every day. Five pages out of six were torn up and thrown away, and damn the expense. She had a flood of passion and plans for him, a treasure of dreams and memories, which she found herself committing to paper, but which she would never have dared to mail. A brother, a sister, a mother might happen upon those pages, and she would be disgraced forever. Against every inclination to pour her heart out, she struggled to be discreet.

He'll be back . . . and his letter will come soon.

She fought the temptation to count the days and the weeks. The simplest and most effective way to do this was through hard work, work that occupied the mind as well as the hands. She began spending more time with Lucinda, helping take care of the children. Momma Lucinda, as she was often called, watched after not only Dulcy and Amity and her own Irish, but also the orphaned Leila and a number of other children whose parents were at work. Lucy learned a great deal through assisting Lucinda, knowledge she would use as Justin's wife; she had decided that they would have at least half a dozen children.

But that brought her back to thoughts of Justin.

Better to work with Aunt Zule, she decided. The healing arts were important to any conscientious plantation wife, not only for the sake of her immediate family but for all of her "colored family" as well. And now was the time to learn, when the annual illness was at its worse and would continue bad until well into the fall. And Aunt Zule kept her busy every moment, telling her what to look for, what to do about it, how to do it—and then seeing to it that she did it right. There was little time for romantic thoughts when one was comforting a sick child or trying to keep an old man from spewing out his life. It was hard, dirty work, and work that had to be done.

But at night it was impossible not to think about Justin. . . .

But she would not have romantic loving thoughts, she determined—they were too self-torturing. She would have nothing but eminently practical thoughts.

Where would they live, how would they arrange their lives? They would not live on the Virginia plantation; that would eventually go to Zachary, and Justin had made it quite clear that he would be satisfied with no less than a plantation of his own. Well, that was quite possible. He would have a certain amount of money, and she would bring money of her own to the match. He had spoken of going west to the rich lands of Alabama or Mississippi, and if that was what he wanted, she would go with him.

Still, she harbored a secret hope that one day they might return to Sabrehill, that Sabrehill might be theirs. And why not? In time, her father and her uncle would wish to retire from the active management of the plantation, and it seemed unlikely that either would ever produce a son. And there should always be a Sabre at Sabrehill. And since Amity would probably marry the richest, handsomest, most sought after male in the region (Lucy already suspected), and since papa had plans for sending Dulcy north, why shouldn't Sabrehill go to her and Justin? She was the oldest sister. Yes, it seemed very likely that one day Justin and she would be master and mistress of Sabrehill.

And then, she thought (tossing about, restless in her lonely bed), they could go once again to their favorite places . . . return to that bower by the creek where she had tempted him . . . where he had first kissed her breasts and thrown off his clothes . . . where they had, for the first time . . .

She could *not* keep her mind off of that! She could *not!*

And so, from time to time, she gave up trying. In the nights, before sleeping, she submitted to the torture and remembered every kiss, every caress, every delightful moment of their love, and she looked forward to those yet to come. On afternoons when she could escape for a time from her work with Aunt Zule and Lucinda, she returned to those woodland places where they had made love, there to sit about with bare legs and breasts while she played with memories and dreams. *I am a wild thing,* she would think. *And he is a demon. And nobody, nobody, has ever loved as we do. Nobody ever dreamed of such a love.*

But *why* didn't he *write?*

He did. The letter lay in a silver salver on a small table in the passage, placed there by Eben, the butler. It lay there like an object of such magical potency that she hardly dared touch it. But she did, after a moment, pick it up. She carried it without haste up the stairs and into her room. She closed the door and threw herself onto her bed.

She was smiling slightly as she opened the envelope. She never entirely stopped smiling all the while she was reading the letter. She read it all the way through four times.

When she had finished, she put it back into its envelope and looked about for a place to hide it away. She ended by folding it and tucking it into the bosom of her dress.

She left her room. She went back downstairs and looked about for Lucinda. She finally found her, with some of the children, in the east gardens. She waited until the children were at some distance, then sat down with Lucinda on the steps of the gazebo.

"A letter came from Justin today," she said.

"I know." After a moment Lucinda asked, "What's wrong, Lucy-child?"

"He's not coming back. He's marrying somebody else. Wouldn't be surprised if he'd done it by this time."

Lucinda said nothing. Lucy began to rock back and forth on the step, rock with the pain that was only beginning to grip her. Her eyes blurred.

"And what's more," she added, her voice breaking, "I'm going to have a baby."

He was not at all sure why he was doing it. There were other women available, safer women, black women. He was drunk, of course, but that was not the reason: this night had been inevitable; he had known for a long time what he was going to do to Claramae. Not that he had consciously planned it, he had not; but it had been there, in the back of his mind. It was as if he had been waiting for it to happen. It was too bad, perhaps, that it hadn't happened at Redbird, where it would have been easier and safer, but he hadn't been ripe for it then. And perhaps Claramae hadn't either. Now they were. Both of them.

And so he was going to have her, right here in the Carstairs tavern, right in her own home. With her idiot family snoring their heads off only a few yards away.

But why her?

Because, he thought dimly, she was a goddam fool.

Because she was, in common phrase, a dumb fuck, and she loved him. And that made her a natural victim.

"Mr. Skeet," she sobbed, more in agony than in pleasure, "Mr. Vachel, honey . . . no more . . . oh, please . . . no more. . . ."

It was so easy. He had never before been so deft with a woman, never before so sure of himself. Contempt gave birth to mastery: a touch of the thigh under the table, a breath in the ear, a word of love, a kiss on the throat. She was his.

"Oh, Vachel, Vachel . . . no more . . . I'll call pa, I'll call. . . ."

But she would not call, and he knew it; she did not want to summon Truman Carstairs from his bed any more than he did. They had been left alone in the common room of the tavern for over an hour now, an hour in which he had stoked every fire in Claramae's hot little body. He touched fires every time he caressed her, hot coals in her breasts, flames in her nest. His own need had become painful, and yet all the time he remained calculating, amused, and utterly cold—cold even in his iron-bar erection.

"No!"

She tore herself away from him, shoving her skirt back down between her legs. Her chair fell with a crash as she leapt to her feet, but there was no answering sound from any other part of the tavern. They might have been the only creatures in the world—two animals in heat in this dimly lit cave of a room.

"No, please, Mr. Skeet, no more!"

He watched her, swollen lipped and dazed, her eyes unfocused, as she stumbled away from him, stumbled in full retreat, and he nearly laughed aloud.

And he knew the time had come.

He got up from the table slowly, careful not to frighten her off further. "Guess you're right," he said. "But you do like me, don't you, Claramae?"

"Oh, Mr. Skeet, you know I do! But I . . . I just can't. . . ."

"But you're my gal, ain't you, Claramae? Ain't you?"

"Oh, Vachel . . ."

He kissed her, moving the full length of his body against hers, and her body answered, legs shaking and mound lifting against him. And from that moment on she seemed to have no will of her own.

As he guided her toward the stairs, she picked up the lamp. An arm around her, he all but carried her, swaying, up the stairs. They swayed along the hallway to the room he customarily used at the tavern. He pulled her into the room and closed the door. He threw off his shirt. She put the lamp on a table and, with a moan, moved into his arms again. Her dress was already loose, and as his mouth closed on hers, his hand bared a shoulder, a breast, and seconds later she was naked.

It was so easy, he thought as he moved her toward the bed, so goddam easy. He laid her down, kicked off his boots and pants, and moved up onto the bed over her. So goddam easy, he could have any woman in the world he wanted, and to hell with Miss Lucy of Sabrehill.

But why had he suddenly thought of her? He did not want to think of her anymore, ever. To hell with her and her father and her uncle and all the other Sabres in the world. To hell with the goddam whore of Sabrehill. He had—

He had Claramae. She cried out as he broke through, taking her, for, yes, by God, she was a virgin. Which was more than the whore of Sabrehill could say.

"Oh, Vachel," she whispered. "I love you so much!" Her face was lovely in the lamplight, lovely, freckles and all; freckles like a sprinkling of gold on a face lovely with love. But he didn't want to think of that. All he wanted to think was that he had *got* the stupid little bitch. While she whispered, "And, Vachel, I loved you for so long!"

Yes, she loved him, most likely she really did. And now she had him, and the pain of the first taking was not too bad, as she made clear when she began panting again and working on him. It was all he could do to keep from giggling out loud. *Stupid little bitch!* Thinking she was getting love when all she was doing was dancing, squirming, humping beneath him like a goddam fool. Thinking she was *making* love, while he laughed at her lonely carnal spasms!

"Vachel—oh, my sweet Vachel . . ."

He did nothing to help her. Nothing. He lay over her, his weight on his elbows and his knees, poised above her like a spider. He felt no urge to help her come or to achieve his own satisfaction. He wanted only to laugh at this ridiculous bitch. Until—

"Oh, *please,* Vachel, *do* it to me. Do it, *please!*"

Claramae, but not Claramae. Lucy. Miss Lucy Sabre, dancing beneath him, no longer jeering at him—*You'da found out what happiness is, 'cause I sure did*—but instead begging him to *Help me, love me* as he rolled her naked in the grass of the Sabrehill woods. Miss Lucy Sabre, face strained with passion, breasts flying, thighs locked around his waist, subjected to his will and his weapon as he began thrusting into her again and again. Miss Lucy Sabre, reduced, demeaned, degraded, as she exploded in climax, because she was nothing to him now, nothing but a victim. Miss Lucy taken, Miss Lucy had, Miss Lucy fucked. And to hell with Miss Lucy, and if only he could . . .

But he couldn't. He kept trying, but he couldn't. Maybe it was the liquor, maybe something else. But try as he did, he couldn't, until—

Raising up, he slapped her hard across the face. Lucy's eyes—Claramae's—widened with shock. And somehow that did it. Victory at last. He had it all then, every last bit of it, she was his, and he poured out into her, poured out every last drop of his bitterness and hatred. Poured, thrusting, poured, poured, poured . . .

And it was over. He had what he had wanted. He had invaded her home, invaded her body, made himself her master. She didn't matter anymore.

He let himself settle down on her body, crushing her with his weight, and when she protested, he rolled aside. The lamplight, once soft, now seemed to glare, and he shut his eyes tightly against it. He would rest for a few minutes and then leave.

The glare against his eyelids disappeared: blessedly,

Claramae had blown out the lamp. She curled up against
him, her head on his shoulder. She loved him, she said,
oh. yes, she did. And was he happy now? As happy as
she was? Oh, yes, yes, he was happy. And now all he had
to do was rest. He sank peacefully, peacefully, into darkness. . . .

He sensed the light even before he heard Claramae's
little cry, but it was the cry that brought him up onto his
elbow, blinking away sleep, to realize that the blaze of
full day streamed through the window. There was the
light, the startled cry, and then the shuffling of feet—and
finally the realization that he had slept through the night
and been caught.

Yes, caught. There they were in the doorway, crowded
together—an indignant Truman Carstairs, his boy Rowan
wearing an uneasy grin, and a planter named Buckridge,
his face carefully blank. And behind them, Buck. Buck,
come to look for him. Buck, frightened and angry.

And Vachel understood.

The victor victimized, the seducer caught. Truman
Carstairs had planned well. What better husband for a
respectable tavernkeeper's daughter than an ambitious
young planter?

Vachel Skeet, to his own surprise, burst out laughing.

She was no special thing, she knew now; nothing
special at all. No wild thing with a demon lover, no woodland nymph pursued by a godling, no Juliet, no Isolde, no
Helen of Troy. She was not the grand exception, above
and beyond rule and custom and law, her acts sanctioned
by love. She was ordinary. She was that common case, the
willful adolescent girl who got herself pregnant by a
passing dandy and had to be sent away. The ignobility of
it, the very commonness shattered every flattering illusion
she had about herself.

But how could she have been so mistaken about
Justin? How could she have mistaken his attentions for
love? Why would he have fought a duel for her? But of
course, he had not fought it for her, not really—he had
been forced into it, a matter of circumstance and anger
and pride. Could it be that Vachel Skeet—poor, deluded

Vachel—really had been the one true defender of her honor? She read and reread Justin's letter—that stilted, awkward, painful letter—looking for a clue. But there was none, none at all.

It was decided: yes, she would be sent away. "See England," her father said with a wan smile, "first England and then France—even Italy if weather and politics permit. As for trying to lose the child or having it, you needn't decide at once. I'm sure Lucinda or Aunt Zule can help you."

Her father, her understanding father. At least he had the grace not to blame himself. ("Oh, I let you girls run too wild," he had so often said.) He had been close to killing Justin ("I've always been against dueling, but I'm quite capable of murder"), but she had had to say *no* to him only once. There would be no more duels, no murder, no killing. Justin and his family would simply be eliminated from the world of Sabrehill. They would cease to exist. No letters would be written or answered, no names spoken. They would never be heard of again.

As it turned out, she did not have to go to Europe. On a beautiful evening in early autumn, in Charleston, she lost the baby. How convenient. On the other hand, she also missed an opportunity to see a lot of lovely ruins.

The pains were not bad, a mere gripe, a nausea, the result of eating bad food perhaps. Or perhaps it was simply nature—so many babies were lost before they were ever really formed. Or perhaps Lucinda had followed Aaron Sabre's suggestion or taken it upon herself. Lucy would never know.

Afterward she wept for the first time since learning of Justin's desertion. The child they might have had was dead—and with it a thousand dreams.

Six

Caught. Trapped. Truman Carstairs had worked it well. Vachel had known the old boy was after his ass to put into Claramae's hope chest, and he had damn well got it. There they were in the doorway, the father, the brother, and a witness from outside the family. And Buckley as well, come to fetch Vachel home. Yes, Carstairs had got him. But he didn't know what kind of prey he had captured.

Grim-faced, the tavernkeeper stepped into the room. "Reckon you know what this means, Vachel."

Vachel laughed, a single rough bark. "Truman, you old bastard, I know better than you what it means."

"It means you're gonna have to do right."

"And you're gonna have to pay for it, you know that, Truman? *You're* gonna have to pay, not me. Now, why don't you all get your asses out of here and let my *wife* and me get dressed."

For an instant Carstairs looked uncertain. "You ain't in no position to threaten, Vachel."

"Get out."

Carstairs turned away. "Ten minutes. I give you ten minutes to get downstairs, both of you."

Vachel laughed again. "Go suck an egg, you fucking weasel."

The moment the door was closed, his grin vanished. He rolled from one elbow to the other to face Claramae. Behind her freckles she was milk white, pale with fright, and her eyes, meeting his, widened.

"Well?" he asked.

She moved quickly away from him and sat up, her back to the wall. She held the sheet up in front of her naked body. She shook her head. "Mr. Skeet, I didn't mean him to catch us! I really didn't, honest to God, Mr. Skeet!"

Her eyes pled for him to believe her, and what she said was probably true. Everything he knew of her suggested that it was unlikely that she would collaborate in such a trap. But there was no point in telling her that. His answer was to reach over and grasp the sheet, and snatch it away, as if to expose her lie.

"You fucking little bitch. You goddam little liar."

"No!" Claramae wailed. "No, Mr. Skeet, I love you! Oh, Vachel—"

"Don't worry, Claramae, I'll marry you. Hell, I been thinking about getting me a wife. Need some more help out at Redbird, and I reckon you'll do good as any. Now, pull on your dress, and let's get downstairs. Your old man is a windy bastard, and I ain't got all day."

Carstairs and his two sons were waiting in the shade of an oak out behind the tavern, a place where they could talk uninterrupted. Vachel looked around for Buckridge, the planter, but evidently he had departed; it was just as well. With a flick of his hand, Vachel indicated to Buck and Claramae that they were to stand over to one side; he himself hunkered down under the tree with the other three white men.

"Vachel," Truman Carstairs said, shaking his head, "I never thought I'd see the day you'd abuse the hospitality of my house. Makes me almost glad the little gal's maw ain't alive to—"

"Truman," Vachel cut in angrily, "don't waste my time with a lot of shit. You been wanting me to take your gal off your hands, and I intend to. Only question now is how you're gonna make it worth my while."

Rowan Carstairs' eyes widened. "Make it worth *your* while! Vaych, you done dirt to our sister, and now you better make it right!"

"Truman, you gonna stop that jackass braying? Or do I just turn my back and walk away?"

"You ain't going nowhere!" Rowan rose to his feet. "You ain't going nowhere, Vaych."

" 'Cause it's either that, or he gonna be picking his teeth out of his brains."

"Rowan, keep your goddam mouth shut. You ain't the head of this here family, I am." Truman turned again to Vachel. "Now, what the hell you talking about—'make it worth your while'?"

"Just what I said. I don't figure I'll ever marry no bitch don't bring a damn good dowry with her. I mean, hell, man—"

"Why, you sonabitch!" It was young Caley Carstairs' turn to be angry. "You see-duce our sister, and you expect—"

"Truman, do shut that boy up."

Truman's backhand caught Caley in the mouth and set him back on his ass.

"Thank you, Truman."

Truman Carstairs glared. "After what you done, you expect me to pay you?"

"Well, what the hell did *you* expect? I was gonna take her off your hands for free? You got some damn fool idea, old man, you got me by the balls just 'cause you let me sample the goods? How many others sampled the goods afore me, Truman, and turned 'em down?"

Claramae cried out as if she had been slapped. Truman Carstairs' face went blank. For a moment no one spoke.

"Vachel," Truman Carstairs finally said, "we been friends a long time. Your pa and me was friends long before that. We even talked about getting you and Claramae together, when you was both nothing but tykes. Now, maybe you and me got a little something to settle between us, a little friendly dickering to do, but that's all right. No need to make it so that me and the boys got to kill you."

Vachel grinned. "Then start dickering."

Buck watched Claramae cringe, as they stood there together in the hot morning sunlight, and he shared her humiliation. She was a pain in the ass, yes, he thought; but even so, she shouldn't have to go through this— hearing Vachel and her father bargaining over her as if she were a piece of livestock. What was her worth? For how little could her father and her brothers get her off their hands?

No, Buck thought, *it ain't right.* And he said quietly, "Miss Claramae, why don't you and me go get out of this sun?" But her face screwed up, and she shook her head as if defying anyone to hurt her. *Sticks and stones can break my bones, but names* . . . He tried again, in a different way. "Gonna be nice out at Redbird with you there, Miss Claramae," he said softly. "Gonna be real nice. Place needs a woman's touch, you know that. I'm gonna fix it up real nice for you, and I'll change things around any way you want 'em. You're gonna like it at Redbird, Claramae."

Suddenly she was in the curve of his arm, weeping against his shoulder, trying to stifle her sobs. *God damn them all,* Buck thought dully. *God damn them all.*

It was settled. He was going to marry Claramae, and do it with all possible dispatch, and to hell with what the gentry or the plain folk or anyone else might think. He no longer gave a damn about that. He had the kind of wife that suited him now, no two-faced, snotty, hypocritical "lady," but a plain, ordinary tavernkeeper's daughter, and furthermore, she was bringing fresh capital to Redbird. And that was all that mattered. He felt very well satisfied with himself.

In fact, that morning when he was discovered with Claramae, he felt better than he had in weeks. He felt as if every last illusion and false hope had been burned away. It was as if, after years of struggle to turn himself into something he could never be, he could at last relax and simply be himself.

The next afternoon, Vachel had an inspiration. It hit him as he was watching Buck move from the big house to the old disused overseer's house. "Buckley," he said, almost before he knew what the words would be, "we gonna give a party!"

"A party, Vaych?"

"You damn right, a party. A party for the bride, right after the wedding. And it's gonna be bigger than any party ever at Sabrehill or Kimbrough Hall."

"If it's gonna be that big, you gonna have to wait till November, after the frost comes. Most people are still away for the summer."

Vachel shook his head. "The Sabres are here, and the Buckridges and plenty of others. And Truman Carstairs, not many of his friends go away for the summer. And Balbo Jeppson is here, and P. V. Tucker, and the patty-roller crowd, and . . ."

Buck looked as if he could not believe what he was hearing. "You gonna invite *them?*"

Them: Not merely the gentry, not merely the honest tradesmen, small farmers, and mechanics. No, "the pattyroller crowd" as well. The yahoos, the bullyboys, the nigger-haters. All those who were Buck's natural enemies and who had once been Vachel's.

Vachel grinned. "Yeah, Buck, *them*."

And to hell with Buck and anyone else who did not approve. He knew now that he would never be worth anything in the eyes of Miss Lucy Sabre or anyone like her. He was by birth and property and heritage a planter and a gentleman, but he would never be anything but the least of such creatures—self-educated, inarticulate, quietly scorned.

But not scorned by the pattyroller crowd. Not by the Tuckers or the Bassetts. Not by the nigger-haters and lynchers. He could speak their plain, blunt language far better than he could speak the language of the aristocracy, and if they could not understand that, he could always beat them to their knees, as he had beaten Tag Bassett. To *them* he was a prince, and with the possible exception of Balbo Jeppson, there was none he could not dominate. Of that he was confident.

"Yeah, Buck, *them*." Vachel tapped Buck's chest with a knuckle. "You know something, Buck? The wise man is the one that knows who his real friends are."

For the first time in years, Vachel Skeet was a truly happy man.

The wedding party was, Buck supposed, a huge success. Certainly it was from Vachel's point of view. The ceremony was held in the large parlor at Redbird, and Vachel amused himself by asking Tag Bassett to stand up with him. The party followed immediately afterward, a barbecue of steer and hog, with the liquor flowing freely. There were whispered rumors, of course, that Vachel had been caught bedding Claramae—that kind of rumor was hard to avoid—but if anyone questioned the propriety of a wedding so soon after the Old Man's death, he was wise enough to keep his mouth shut.

The guest list was, as Vachel had promised, completely indiscriminate. Mr. and Mrs. Pettigrew viewed the scene sourly, soon made their excuses, and left. Captain Kimbrough, who had come without Miss Adamina, looked about with purse-mouthed disapproval. Joel Sabre, who apparently saw nothing at all unusual about this feast, dug into the hot, spicy meat and the liquor with gusto, and soon had his voice raised in song with Truman Carstairs. Aaron Sabre, who seemed to know exactly what was happening, greeted Buck kindly and watched Vachel with a sad sympathetic smile.

"Look after him, Buckley. Look after both of them."

"I've always tried to look after him, Mr. Aaron."

"So have I, when I could."

As was expected, the gentry left early; even the Sabres, though Mr. Aaron had to drag Mr. Joel off, and he made a special point of wishing Claramae well and saying a courteous good night. At that point, Buck saw a definite shift in the character of the party: the stuffed shirts had all left, and the plain folk, by God, could enjoy themselves.

And Vachel could let it be known, lest anyone doubted it, that he too was just plain folk. "Now, goddam it, ain't nobody else gonna leave 'less I say so! Ain't nobody else gonna leave here 'til he goddam drunk! Y'all hear me? I'm gonna shoot the first sonabitch tries to leave here, he ain't drunk! Rolly, lemme fill your glass." Oh, let no one forget that he was Mr. Vachel Skeet, a planter of good family. But just the same. "Why, he's just like us!" Buck heard it said. "Just like us, just common!"

Hell of a good fellow. Just common.

"Claramae, goddam it, fill up this man's cup! What kinda bitchin' wife you gonna make, you can't keep our guests drinking, honey? Come on, move your lazy fuckin' ass, sweetie."

Buck watched Claramae go pale, watched her try to smile. She had married above herself, had married an aristocratic planter. Now she knew how an aristocratic planter addressed his bride in front of the rabble . . . if he were a hell of a good fellow and, at heart, just common.

In the early morning hours, she pled weakness, pled a woman's frailty, begged to be allowed to go to bed. Vachel, with an angry curse, gave consent, but of course he had to stay up with his roistering, singing, drinking guests, begging them to stay longer and still longer yet.

They finally left at dawn, only to return minutes later to fire pistols into the air and give the bride and groom a noisy serenade. Buck watched from the veranda of the overseer's house. They might have dragged the bride and groom from their bed, probably would have, if Balbo Jeppson had not maintained some control of the crowd. Actually the charivari was an honor—a testament to the success of the party and the esteem in which Vachel was now held.

Buck retired to his bed.

It looked as if Vachel were getting what he wanted, he thought as he stared at his ceiling. He knew who his friends were. But Claramae . . .

His last thoughts were of Claramae as he fell asleep.

How, Buck wondered, could a man change so completely? How could a kindly, generous, always thoughtful young man change so quickly into a coldly brutal, sneering, demanding bully? Surely this new Vachel was the product of some madness.

Or was he? Was the change really so great? Had there been some hints of this Vachel all along in the streaks of meanness that sometimes appeared after a few drinks? Or in the arrogance with which he had sometimes treated the black women they had shared? Had the kindly, generous Vachel been merely a mask for the real Vachel, the brutal Vachel—a curtain which had now, once and for all, been torn aside?

And, if so, why hadn't Buck long ago guessed as much?

Because he had not wanted to. Because he had wanted so badly to believe in Vachel, the friend, the partner, the protector.

But there was no longer any room for such a belief. Vachel seemed to have changed permanently, and as he had changed, so had Redbird. In the fields, if the Old Man had been a hard taskmaster, Vachel more than matched him. For a chief driver, he relied increasingly on a muscular young bull named Shadrach, who was much too fond of using the whip. The women especially suffered—the women and those hands who had been sent to Redbird to be broken. Buck saw them coming in from the fields each evening, the backs of their shirts streaked with blood.

Those who worked in and around the big house and its immediate environs were fortunate: they saw the least of Vachel. But they prayed for his departure each morning and dreaded his return each night, for he always managed to find fault, always found a way to mete out punishment. Claramae seemed to be his most sought after victim, and Buck his least, but not even Buck entirely escaped his wrath.

"Buck! Buckley, goddam you, get your black ass in here!"

A sick feeling in his stomach and a sour taste in his mouth, Buck hurried into the big house passage to find Claramae cowering before Vachel as if she expected to be beaten.

"Buckley, you bastard, does this house look clean to you?"

Buck glanced about. "Why, I don't know, Vaych—"

"It's a pig pen. It's a sty. Now, ain't it?"

The house looked all right to Buck, but he was not about to contradict Vachel when the latter was in this mood. "Well . . . I suppose there's always room for improvement."

Vachel turned on Claramae. "You see? Even a nigger knows dirt when he sees it. Not even a clean nigger would live in this dirt, and if you ain't dirtier than some dirty niggers I seen . . ." Vachel swiped a hand across a table and looked at his finger tips.

Tears flooded Claramae's eyes. "Mr. Skeet, I'm sorry, I do my best."

"Maybe you let your pa and your brothers live in a sty, but you ain't gonna do that to me. You got a couple of wenches to help you, ain't you?"

"Yes, but—"

" 'Cause if you don't know how to whip their asses in line and get 'em to do the work right, I'm gonna have to whip yours. I mean that, Claramae, you gonna pay with raw butt-skin unless you start doing right. You understand me?"

"Yes. Yes, sir."

Buck was too embarrassed even to look toward Claramae. "Mr. Vachel, sir, if you ain't got no more use for me, sir—"

"Buckley, sir, you bet your left ball, sir, I got some use for you. You ran this here house for a long time. Didn't I tell you to teach Claramae how I like it?"

"Why, sure, Vaych—"

"Well, it appears to me that you done a goddam poor job. Now, starting tomorrow morning I want you to *show* Claramae how it's got to be done, *tell* her how it's got to be done, and make her do it *right*. And do that every goddam day until I'm sure she knows what the hell she's doing."

"Aw, Vaych, I got work to do! The gin needs fixing—"

"To hell with all that. You teach Claramae what she got to know. That comes first, and I goddam well mean it."

Vachel strode out of the house, and the sickness in Buck's stomach was worse than ever. He had to force himself to turn toward Claramae. "Now, don't you worry, Miss Claramae, we'll get everything fixed up."

Claramae didn't hear him. With a small cry of pain, she hurried up the stairs, no doubt to find a pillow to weep on.

Thus it was that each morning after breakfast Buck reported to the big house. And thus it was that he had to spend hours of each day with Claramae and could not always avoid witnessing Vachel's attacks on her.

"Woman," Vachel said abruptly one evening about a month after the wedding, "how many our people we got in the sick house?"

"Ten, Mr. Skeet," Claramae said meekly, sensing from his tone that an attack was coming. They were sitting at the dining room table. Buck was present, having come to report on some repairs in the field quarters.

"Ten, you say. And how many we have yesterday?"

"Nine."

"And how many at the beginning of the week?"

"Eight."

Vachel exploded. "And now we got *ten* sick niggers in the sick house! Now, how come we got so damn many sick niggers around here, Claramae, how come? What the hell you trying to do, ruin me?"

"Mr. Skeet—"

"Your pa said you know how to cure. Ain't that right, Buckley? Didn't he say that, that morning we sat out under the oak behind the tavern and dickered? Didn't he?"

"Yes, Mr. Vachel," Buck sighed.

"He said it, Claramae, and you supposed to be getting them niggers well. Instead, they getting sick faster than you cure them. Now, what the goddam hell is going on here?"

Claramae was left speechless before the unfairness of the attack. How did one present a logical answer to an utterly illogical argument? And of course, if she tried, *she* would be accused of childish illogic: that was how women and niggers were kept in their place.

Vachel threw his napkin onto the table. "Mrs. Skeet, honey, let me tell you something. If half them niggers die, what you brought to Redbird ain't no way gonna pay back their cost. And ain't a damn one of 'em don't earn his keep around here better than you do, and that's a fact." He stood up. "You need me for anything, I'll be over at Jeppson's."

And he left.

That was the way it so often happened: Vachel would attack and insult her in front of Buck and any other servants who happened to be nearby, then leave her alone with the witnesses to her humiliation.

But not every humiliation had a witness. In the mornings Buck approached the big house with a kind of dread. More often than not, he heard raised voices behind the closed door, the male voice dominant. When the door opened to his knock, there would stand Claramae, with red eyes and tear-stained face, and Vachel, angry, yet somehow cheered and exhilarated by his first victory of the day. If there was ever any loving, any shared pleasure between them, Buck saw no sign of it. If anything, the signs were to the contrary.

About two weeks after the incident concerning the sick slaves, Buck and Vachel went to the kitchen house to inspect some repairs that had been made on the ovens. Buck saw, however, that Vachel had little interest in the ovens. A sly grin had come over his face, and Buck followed his gaze out the open doorway. A young girl, sweet looking, child pretty, with a budding figure, stood about twenty feet away. Aware of Vachel's attention and the quality of his grin, she was slowly moving away, with an air of wanting to hide herself.

"Who's that?" Vachel asked softly. "That Minnie's gal? Serena? By God, she growed up in the last year or so, ain't she?"

Buck didn't like his tone. He looked around nervously for Minnie, the cook, but fortunately they were alone in the kitchen at that moment. "Ah," he said, "she ain't nothing but a child."

"Wouldn't say that. I'd say she's just about ripe for busting, wouldn't you?"

"Vaych! Serena ain't more than thirteen, fourteen year old!"

"That's old enough."

Buck was shocked. If Vachel wanted a change from Claramae, there were plenty of wenches who would be glad to spread for him, especially if he favored them with some little gift, some little privilege. Of course, such wenches were, for the most part, a dull bunch, but some, like Lida of Sabrehill, weren't bad at all. Vachel didn't have to go after thirteen-year-old innocents.

"How about it, Buckley? Want to help me bust her? If she ain't busted already?"

"Aw, no . . ."

"Been a long time since you and me had a wench together."

"Vaych, you don't want that. She's just too young. Hell, Vachel, you married now, you got your own woman."

"To hell with that. White woman get married, she gets to thinking she's a goddam lady, she's too goddam good for spreading. What a man needs is something like that out there, something with real bitch nature to keep him happy." Vachel started out of the kitchen. "Come on, we'll get us Serena and maybe another, and we'll take turns on 'em like we used to."

"Vachel, I ain't gonna do it."

Vachel turned back to face Buck. His eyes were as hard, as implacable as Buck had ever seen them.

"You what?"

"I just ain't gonna—"

"Buckley, I tell you do something, you do it. Ain't that right?"

"Well . . . yeah . . ."

"I tell you to spread that little gal in front of God and the whole congregation, you damn well spread her. Now, come on."

Buck wiped his face with his hand. His eyes felt tired. Every part of him felt tired.

"Buck?"

"No."

Vachel's hard eyes never wavered; he never blinked. After a moment, he shrugged. "Aw, hell. What the hell's the use of wasting stuff like that on you, anyway? I tell you something, Buckley, you ain't got what you used to. Now, that Shadrach, *he* is some stud. When him and me take a little time off, midday, go get us a little something, *he* is three times what you ever was and damn near good as me. You hear me, Buckley?"

"I hear you, Vachel." So it was Vachel and Shadrach now. Once, not so long ago, Buck would have felt bitterly jealous. At this moment he felt nothing but a deep sadness.

"Yes, sir," Vachel said, "when Shadrach and me get us something . . . Ah, to hell with it."

He shrugged again and walked off.

It was a farewell, of sorts.

Buck had just finished his breakfast and was standing in the darkness outside of the kitchen house when they heard Claramae scream. They had heard cries, wails, from the big house before, but never like this. Minnie, the cook, moved to the door and looked toward the lighted second-story window of the big house.

The scream was repeated, distant, yet harsh enough to be heard and to set the heart to pounding.

"He whipping her," Minnie said. "My God, if his maw know what he come to . . . *Buckley!*"

But Buck was beyond heeding any warning. Nothing in the world could have kept him away from the big house now. He felt as if he were floating, his toes barely touching the ground as he rushed toward the door, and the angle of wooden floor and wall muffled the sound of a third scream.

The door was unlocked. Buck threw it open, threw himself into the dark passage.

"Oh, please! Mr. Skeet, please, please, please!"

Claramae in a nightgown was like a ghost on the staircase, a ghost fleeing some evil darker spirit. "Mr. Skeet, *please!*"

The whip came down, hardly visible in the darkness, cutting across Claramae's back. She cried out and, halfway down the stairs, fell the rest of the way, tumbling to the floor of the passage. Vachel came after her, raising the whip again.

"Vachel," Buck yelled, "Vachel, no!"

Vachel showed no surprise and never broke stride. "Nigger, what you doing in my house!" he said as he stepped toward Buck, and the whip cracked around Buck's shoulders and across his back. "Nigger! Goddam nigger!" And the whip cut across his back again, almost putting Buck on his knees.

And Vachel was gone, the door of the passage still standing open.

Claramae lay on the floor, weeping. The pain in Buck's back eased. He went to Claramae.

"Why he do that?" he asked. He found he was panting. "Miss Claramae, why he do that?"

Claramae shook her head.

"He hurt you bad?" Buck touched the back of her gown. He saw no blood, felt no dampness. "Don't reckon he cut you."

"Ain't so bad now," Claramae sobbed. "Ain't my body he hurts most."

"I know. Here, let me help you."

He began lifting her to her feet, slowly, carefully. "He hates me," she said, "oh, how he do hate me! I can't do nothing right for him, Buck, nothing at all. And I love him. Buck, I loved him for years and years, I dreamed about him, I love him so!"

"I know. I love him too."

"I know you do, we the two people love him most in the world, maybe the only people! *Oh, Buck!*"

Her tears did not diminish. Her sobs grew louder, and she went into the fold of his arm, as she had that morning behind the tavern. She cried his name again and again, and he drew her closer to whisper comfort into her ear. He stroked her shoulder, stroked her back and her side through the thin gown, kissed the tears from her face.

"Oh, Buck . . ."

"Yes, Claramae. Yes, honey, yes . . ."

And it happened: the forbidden, the unthinkable. He felt the hot rush of blood, the lurch of his flesh, at the same instant that the quality of her sobbing changed. She pressed harder against him, her breast flattening, her nipple like a pebble between them. His hand moved from her shoulder to her other breast. She shifted slightly, moving a thigh up between his legs.

When she raised her face from his shoulder, there in the dimness of the passage, he could hardly see what was in her eyes. Something between horror and astonishment? Or between astonishment and joy?

They should tear themselves from each other, he knew. They should run for opposite ends of the earth. They should deny this moment, should never think of it again, should forget that it ever existed. Because in this world they had not a chance in a hundred of surviving together, not a chance in a thousand, and they both knew it.

Perhaps a chance in ten thousand.

She moaned and moved her thigh against his hardened

flesh. He pressed his mouth to her face, moved his hand down her body.

They were doomed.

Seven

And so they made love. Made it fiercely, desperately, with no thought of the danger, because at that moment it had to be done. The starving must eat. The thirsting must drink.

They did not pause even to close the passage door. He drew her into the greater darkness by the stairs. It was she who lifted the hem of her gown, she who tore open his clothes to return his caresses. She dropped her gown from her shoulders, moved her breasts hard against his chest, and then, because she could not wait, pulled him toward the stairs. Her gown about her waist, she lay back on the stairs, bracing her feet on different levels, and arched high. He descended upon her.

That quickly it happened—quicker than with Lida and even more brutally. But there was no rape of the woman this time, no torture, no degradation—only the mutual striving, the hard, driving effort to give the gift and to receive it. There was no thought of revenge, no bitterness behind the act. Vachel Skeet, for all that he had helped to cause it, had become irrelevant to this moment. All the world, it seemed, had become irrelevant. Only the shared want, the need, the hunger remained, and when, so soon, she cried out her joy, he let himself go, *made* himself go, threw himself into that long drumming moment of fire, holding back nothing.

The moment passed. The fires died, leaving embers still aglow. Buck felt on his bare skin a breath of cool air from the passage doorway. He heard Claramae's heavy breathing and felt her final clasps on his softening flesh. "Oh, Buck," she sighed, "oh, my sweet Buck . . ."

And it was over.

And how did he feel now?

Happy. He had never before in his life felt so happy. He felt relieved and tender. He felt deeply grateful. He felt protective. He felt that he was holding, beneath his body on the stairs, a treasure that he never wanted to lose. He had never experienced such a feeling with a woman before in his life.

"Oh, my sweet Buck," Claramae sighed again. "Oh, Buck, honey-love, we really *done* it!"

Buck smothered laughter against her shoulder, tasted the salt of her flesh. "Yes, Claramae, we really done it."

"I never knew . . . I never thought . . . it could be . . ."

"Neither did I."

"Honest, Buck? Really and truly?"

"Really and truly, Miss Claramae."

She giggled, and he felt her clasp again. "That's funny! You calling me *Miss* Claramae, after."

"Lots of people, even married, say Mister and Missus all their lives."

"Yes, but not my sweet Buck, not to me." She pulled his head down and kissed him gently on the mouth. In the gray dawning light, he saw a faint worry come into her eyes. "Buck, it ain't . . . it ain't just for this one time, is it?"

"Not if you want me, Claramae."

"Do you . . . do you want me?"

Sanity was returning. He was remembering that for all of his privileged position at Redbird, he was a black nonetheless. And he had committed what to many whites was the most intolerable of crimes: he lay here now with a white woman in his arms, a white man's wife, his flesh still deep within hers. If he were caught, God alone knew what would happen to him. He might be tortured, mutilated, hung—the dangers were almost too grim to be contemplated. And yet he could answer truthfully: "Claramae, I swear to God there ain't another woman in the world I want after you. I want you and only you forever."

"Oh, Buck!"

"But not on these goddam stairs—*they are killing me, Claramae!*"

Her explosive laughter threw them apart. He slipped away from her and rolled, tumbled, to the floor of the passage.

Doomed.

Or perhaps not doomed. There was always that one chance in ten thousand. There were those lovers who were never discovered, and those others who slipped away into what remained of the wilderness, never to be seen again . . . perhaps to emerge as different people in different places, free to live out their lives.

Those few.

But Buck and Claramae (Buck thought later) began their affair with incredible recklessness, an insane recklessness, as if they had no choice. For each a dam had been burst, and the rush of that passionate tide carried them as if they had no will of their own.

There was that first morning: the madness of it. Half-naked, the passage door open, a servant likely to walk in at any moment, they had made love lying on the stairs, with no thought of possible consequences. Moments later, Buck left, closing the passage door behind him. He went to the kitchen house and told Minnie and all others within hearing that Miss Claramae was ill (presumably because of the whipping) and that neither the maids nor anyone else was to enter the house until she called for them; she wanted to rest. He then attended to a few chores, managed to disappear, and circled the house to enter from the river side. Claramae, now completely naked, awaited him in her bed.

He had a strangely anguished moment as he entered that room, an unexpectedly painful moment. He remembered the boy Vachel with whom he had lived all those years and whom he had come in some manner to love, and he felt like a betrayer, a Judas. He felt it deeply and poignantly, like a dream of old grief. Then, almost immediately, he remembered: *that* Vachel was dead. Vachel the boy was dead, and the dead do not care. And only an hour ago he had ceased to give one last damn about Vachel the man, whose wife now lay naked in bed awaiting her black lover.

He closed the door behind himself, but there was no safety. A maid might ignore, or never learn of the order not to enter the house. She might listen at the door (for didn't they all?) or enter without knocking. She might inadvertently, or because of a grudge, get word to Vachel. Or Vachel himself, varying his habits, might return to the house and find them together. They were playing the deadliest kind of game.

It did not matter. The only thing that mattered was what they were about to do. His flesh already rising for her, his clothes falling away, he went to her. In seconds, he too was naked on the bed. In minutes they were coupled. And they made love again, long this time, as long as either of them had ever been linked with another, and without thought of the living or the dead or of the rest of the outside world or of anything but each other. They made love and then made love again, in the full strength of their youth, joyously, holding back absolutely nothing, as if defying the angry gods to tear them apart.

That afternoon they gave the gods another chance. Again the order went out that Claramae was not to be disturbed, and Buck, unseen, entered the house. Again they twice made love, taking their time, and hardly giving a thought to the risk.

And again that night.

They would have to hurry, Claramae said, when she arrived at his house. She had thought Mr. Skeet to be in a drunken sleep, but he had roused up and asked her where the hell she was going, and she had said to the necessary house, and he had asked why the hell she din usa cham'er pot, and she had said she didn't like to use a chamber pot, and she *thought* he had fallen back asleep, but still they had best hurry, hurry, hurry.

They did not hurry. Buck made love to her twice yet again, seven glorious times in a single day, seven lusty, jubilant celebrations of life.

She had fallen asleep in the necessary house, she later explained to Mr. Skeet, hiding laughter.

Their lives had the quality of a game after that, a most dangerous game of high adventure and unequaled delights. Where and how could they meet? Where could

they make love and how often? The big house was much
too risky for regular meetings. A drop of laudanum in
Mr. Skeet's last drink at night put him soundly to sleep, but
still . . . Any regular pattern of behavior might give them
away. They had to seek new places, new opportunities.
And thus . . .

Seeing him enter the stable, she waited a few minutes,
then followed and found him alone. Here? Now? Quickly,
quickly! Love in a stall, leaning against the rough boards.
Love in a stolen moment, on the run. Oh, Buck! Oh,
my sweet Buck, I do love you. . . .

Done once again, then. Love stolen, filched, thieved.
And . . .

Mr. Skeet wanted his midday meal delivered to him in
the fields, she told Buck. She would take it to him herself.
And on her way back they met in some woods, far from
the work gangs, safe from all but the most casual wan-
derers. Got plenty of time this time, Buck. An hour, two
hours . . . make love slow and easy . . . but do it soon
so we can do it again . . . and again . . . oh,
Buck. . . .

Love in the seed house . . .

"How come you like most to be on top, Buck?"

"So if old Vaych catches us at it, he can kiss my ass."

Laughter, wild laughter, quickly choked back, and then
lost in the glory of the moment.

Love in the wash house . . . love in the barn loft . . .
all hot flesh and smothered laughter and praise and won-
derment . . . love seized where it could be seized, at the
risk of horror and death.

And Buck in all his life had never been happier. He
felt like a child again and, at the same time, that he was
at last truly a man. This was the love he had been born for,
not the shared adventures with Vachel, not the random
rapacious acts with girls like Lida. He was a man who
had found his woman.

But how could they keep their secret? Most likely, Buck
thought, they could not. The days went by, a week passed
and more, and the house wenches had to notice. Sooner
or later there were bound to be whispers. Fortunately for
them, however, even a Shadrach would be reluctant to be

the bearer of ill tidings to Mr. Skeet. What Mr. Skeet did not know could hurt nobody.

So they had time, at least a little. And in that time plans had to be made.

He told her one night as they lay in his bed, their hunger for the moment satisfied. The orange light of the lamp flickered over her naked body, and sitting up, he reached out to her. His fingertips drifted over her smooth cheeks, her full lips, her throat. They drifted over her lightly freckled chest and settled for a moment into the softness of a breast, nipple to palm. They moved on, over quivering belly and high blond mound, to touch the lips and mouth that gave so much pleasure. So much pleasure, and yet . . .

"And yet, I want more than this, Claramae. I love this, I love what we got, but I want the between times too. I want to go where we can maybe work our own patch of land together, spend our whole days and nights together, even raise a family. Pleasure each other when we please and not have to grab what we can and run. You're my woman, Claramae, and a man wants to make a home for his woman. Hell, even an ignorant field hand wants that. But they're gonna take away what little we got."

She touched his cheek. She smiled, but there was worry in her eyes. "You want to run away, then. You have any idea when?"

"I don't know. Just lately I been thinking and thinking on it. Wait till spring weather, when it's warmer? Or go right soon, when the goddam patrol don't feel like working?"

"You run off with a white woman, they'll follow you anytime."

"I suppose. And then there's how to do it. I can write a fake pass, of course. But we'll need money—if we steal something, can we sell it?"

"Pa says anything worth four dollars is grand larceny, and they can hang you for that, Buck!"

"Hell, honey, they likely to hang me anyway and maybe you too. . . . Claramae, there's holidays coming soon. That means I can get away for a while before any of our niggers even notice. Could you maybe give Vachel enough of that laudanum so he gets a nice long sleep? So he don't even know you're gone for a couple of days?"

"I don't know. If I tried, I might kill him."

Buck laughed mirthlessly. "That'd really get us hung."

Claramae stroked his cheek for a moment, and the worry in her eyes deepened. "Buck, I know just one thing. One of these days I'm gonna catch me a baby. I try and try not to, but I'm gonna, and it's gonna be yours. And we better get us away from here, honey, while I can still travel and before it comes."

The thought had never been far from Buck's mind, but with it was another and even more bitter thought: "No chance it might be his?"

Claramae shrugged. "Less chance all the time. He don't like me except to hurt me, and I heard the gals whispering about how he likes to spread the nigger wenches. Say he's been spreading that poor little Serena. Him and that Shadrach, taking turns on her."

Buck winced and shook his head. The thought of Vachel treating young Serena as he had other, older and more willing girls made Buck sick. Serena, he knew, would be unwilling but too frightened to offer much resistance. And the idea of turning her over to the more brutal Shadrach . . . *God*, Buck wondered, *what pleasure could I have had in those old times with Vachel? Why, they don't even compare with what I got now. Vachel, whatever happened that we went such separate ways?*

"Aw, now, Buck," Claramae whispered, "don't you brood on it. Pleasure me right, now, and I ain't gonna let you think about Mr. Skeet no more."

And she didn't let him think about Mr. Skeet. They kissed and caressed and touched and tumbled, bringing back the hard, aching, driving desire, until they could wait no longer. He tossed her onto her back and climbed over her, her knees at his shoulders. She brought the spike to its place, and he drove it all the way, gripping her shoulders, kissing her lamplit face, pressing his mouth to her ear. He waited for his panting to ease so that he could whisper to her.

"Claramae, I'm just a half-educated nigger boy, never had nothing of my own. But I'll take care of you. I swear to God I will. I'll take you away from here, and ain't nobody ever gonna hurt you again, ain't nobody gonna harm you. You are my woman now, Claramae, and I'm gonna keep you safe forever. Do you believe me?"

The way she was breathing, simmering under him, clasping at him, he wasn't sure she had even heard him, let alone understood. But she managed a smile, a whisper. " 'Course I believe you. But you ain't no boy, Buck. You are a *man!* You are *my* man, Buck, and . . . oh, my sweet Buck. . . ."

And once again they defied the world and stole the prize.

While Vachel Skeet watched.

Stood outside the window and heard not a word that was said, but through a narrow slit saw absolutely everything.

He wanted to kill them both, here and now. He wanted to go find an axe, to return to this house, to burst in on the lovers, to swing the axe down on their terrified faces.

He had known that something was going on. Claramae had not been acting right. There had been something about her, a glow, a barely hidden happiness that had no apparent cause. And a wife should not act that way, not the kind of wife he aimed to have. You never saw that kind of happiness on the faces of the wives of his new-found friends. She acted almost like . . . like Miss Lucy in those last months. And Vachel did not like it at all.

And so he had begun to observe—observe without consciously meaning to. And he found that somehow Claramae was not always where he would have expected her to be. When habit and pattern told him she would be in the kitchen, it would turn out that she had been in the wash house. When he should have found her in the wash house, it seemed that she had been in the office instead. Something in their little world was slightly askew.

And why had she stopped looking on his drinking with resentment, when she knew it usually made him dog mean? Why did she even sometimes fill his glass?

And when she did fill his glass, was his sleep deeper, longer, more drugged?

Tonight he had drunk less than usual. Hardly knowing why he was doing it, unwilling to hazard a guess, he had staggered about the house, glass in hand, and had secretly disposed of most of the whiskey. And when *she* had handed him a glass, he had drunk nothing from it at all.

Later, he had lain perfectly still in their bed, breathing deeply and faking sleep until she had left the room. Then he had hastily pulled on clothes and followed her through the dark night, here to the overseer's house. And now, watching the pair on the bed, he knew. He had been betrayed.

Betrayed by Buckley Skeet!

And by Claramae too, of course. This was how she repaid him for having the decency and the kindness to marry her. This was how she repaid him for making her a respectable planter's wife. By getting hot for black cock and spreading for the best nigger-friend a man ever had. It so enraged Vachel that he wanted to cry out, as he sometimes had in their wenching days: *"Go ahead, Buckley, make her scream for it! Ram it to her, goddam bitch. Fuck her! fuck her! fuck her!"*

Vachel sobbed. This was the second time in his life that he had been betrayed by a woman, and both women, with the help of their lovers, had destroyed his vision of himself, his vision of the life he was trying to build. But this time he would not let the vision be destroyed. This time he would destroy the destroyers. He would get the axe and return to this house and burst in and send the heavy blade smashing down.

But no.

There was a better way, a safer way, a much more satisfactory way. He would have a revenge that only the dead would ever forget. If he could just restrain himself. If he could just wait.

He watched the rise and fall of the lovers in the lamplight.

"Go ahead, Buckley, make her scream! Fuck her! fuck her! fuck her!"

He felt ash-cold, burned-out, every illusion gone. He felt as if his youth were long behind him, though in fact most of it still lay ahead. His mouth was like a sagging weight on his face, a face that actually felt gray. And when he looked at the niggers and asked where Jeppson was, his gaze seemed to freeze them.

He found Jeppson overseeing a half-dozen hands who were felling dead trees and sawing and splitting cord wood. Jeppson looked at him with interest as he dismounted. The two watched the gang for a few minutes, and when Vachel turned away, Jeppson followed him. The two of them sat down on the trunk of a fallen tree.

Jeppson continued to regard him curiously. "You ain't looking so good, young Mr. Skeet. Look about like P. V. Tucker on Sunday morning. You feeling poorly?"

"I'm feeling fine, Jeppson, just fine." Vachel's voice was strange, even to himself; it had a quiet, rumbling threat in it that had never been there before.

"Got something on your mind, though."

"Yes, I do. Want to have a little confidential talk with you, Jeppson, and you ain't gonna say nothing about it to nobody till I give you leave."

Jeppson grinned. "Oh, my. That do sound serious."

"It is." There didn't seem to be much point in farting around, so Vachel got right to it. "Jeppson, what you do about a nigger fucks a white woman?"

The broad red face stiffened, as Vachel had known it would. "You mean he rapes her?"

"Hell, no, he just plain spreads her. And, hell, she loves it. What you do about him?"

Jeppson's jaw moved from side to side for a moment, as if he hardly trusted himself to speak, and when he did speak, his voice shook. "Goddam, boy, I think you know what I say about that. And I don't give a goddam if they do call theyselves man and wife or what the law of South Carolina allows—"

"They ain't man and wife. Fact is, she's married to a white man."

"Then there just ain't no question. That boy got to die. Can't have a nigger messing around with a white man's wife. You got to make an example by cutting it off of him first, take it off one way or another, then you got to hang him up. Or burn him or flay him or whatever you want to do. But he got to die, no question."

"And the woman?"

Jeppson looked around at the work gang, thought about it, scratched his chin. "Well, now . . . that depends. You got to consider what her husband wants done to her. For a lot of 'em, a good thirty-nine stripes will do."

"I don't ever want to see her again."

Jeppson's gaze turned slowly back to Vachel. He stared. The chunk of the axes and the burr of the saw made a slow rhythm.

Jeppson said, "Well, I'll be goddamned."

The words had slipped out before Vachel had meant to say them, but that didn't matter. He said, "Want her punished good like she should be, and then I don't ever want to see her again, Jeppson. I want to know that *no*body ain't never gonna see her again."

"Truman Carstairs' little gal," Jeppson said wonderingly. "Little Claramae. . . . And who's the nigger?"

"Buckley."

Jeppson nodded. "And you always treated him 'most like a white man. Always said that was a mistake."

"You was right."

"You sure you want her done like you said?"

"I'm sure."

You went to different people for different things. You went to Captain Kimbrough to find out about the militia and to the Devereaus to find out about the law and to Aaron Sabre to borrow books. When you wanted certain things done, you went to Balbo Jeppson.

Jeppson liked to ride with the local patrol. He was that kind of man. The patrolmen tended to be drunken scum, nigger-haters whose excesses were too often overlooked, and he could easily have afforded to pay for a substitute to fulfill his obligation for him. But patrol duty, when his turn came, gave him the opportunity and the excuse to visit every plantation on the beat about once a month and thus engage in his favorite occupation of "nigger-watching." He liked to brag that no one knew more slaves by name than he did, and that no one was better at keeping slaves disciplined and "in their place."

But there were some things that not even the hated pattyrollers could do. Balbo Jeppson and his friends— masked, for a pretense of anonymity—could and did.

"Well," Jeppson sighed, "reckon something just could happen to the sinning pair. Could happen right soon. Best, though, if they got caught in flagrant. What that means is—"

"I know what it means."

"Good. They get caught that way, there just ain't no doubt in nobody's mind why they being punished." Jeppson grinned nastily. "Besides I reckon a nigger boy ought to be allowed to pop his load one last time before he gets it torn off, ain't that right?"

Vachel did not smile. He stared at the earth between his feet.

Jeppson gave him a friendly slap on the knee. "Vachel, I want to tell you something. There was a time when some of us didn't know what to make of you. I mean, you cozying up to the Sabres and the Buckridges and all them, goddam snot-noses, never soiled a chamber pot. I know, you come from a family good as any of them— so do *I*, truth was known—but it just didn't seem right. Not for old Mr. Skeet's boy Vachel.

"But then you finally found your own. After you got around to shooting that goddam Justin Sabre. Yes, sir, you found your own, and it was just like you come home. And the way you are handling this here business proves you are just as good a man as—as P. V. Tucker or Rolly Joe Macon or Tag Bassett—and now *you are one of us!* You understand me, boy?"

Vachel nodded.

Jeppson gave him another slap on the knee. "Now. When the time comes, do you want to be part of it or not?"

"I want to be part of it."

Jeppson smiled. "Yes, sir. You are one of us."

And so it happened. There were no miracles in store

for them, and what was one chance in ten thousand? Inevitably it happened, as it had uncounted times in the past, would again uncounted times in the future. Nigger with a white woman. Nigger with a white man's wife. The ritual of pain and terror and death had to be played out.

At least they were spared the indignity of being torn naked from each other's arms. They had made love, and then, in the chill of the night, Claramae had pulled her gown back on. Buck had pulled on a shirt and pants and had even slipped his feet into his boots. The lamp turned low, they sat at the head of the bed, Claramae curled up under his arm, and they talked. Talked softly and made plans and dreams.

And then it ended. All of it. There was the heart-jarring sound of a door being thrown open, and Buck leapt from the bed and stepped toward a window. The glass shattered, and a rifle barrel was thrust in toward his chest. Boots pounded, and a hooded man ran in through the bedroom door, and Claramae screamed—the mindless, despairing scream of one who knew there was nothing more left, nothing but the agony that would come before death.

No, Buck thought, *no, not like this,* but he knew it was going to be like this: nothing left but the final horror.

Despite the dimness of the lamp, he saw everything in the room with amazing clarity. A hooded man was coming at him. Without ever thinking of what he was going to do, Buck caught the man's raised arm with one hand and slammed the other hand into the man's belly, throwing him toward the window where the rifle barrel intruded. More glass broke. The rifle went off as Buck grabbed the barrel and pulled it through the window. Two other men had grabbed the screaming Claramae and were dragging her away, and Buck brought the rifle stock down on the head of one of them: he fell to the floor and rolled, clutching his skull.

But then the room was filled with men, hooded and masked, rushing at them with a kind of goblin fury, making no sound but the thump of boots and the hiss and rasp of excited breathing. Buck raised the rifle again, but someone grabbed it. He brought a boot up solidly between an attacker's legs and got a harsh scream. Some-one cursed, spoke at last, in a white man's voice, and Buck let go of the rifle barrel so that he could throw a fist solidly into the masked face. His arms were grabbed, held, twisted. He tried to kick again. Somewhere Clara-mae was still screaming. Buck felt a cry burning up from his own throat, but it turned to a whimper as something hard, the rifle barrel perhaps, hit the back of his head. The room went gray, and Claramae's screams faded.

He came to in the office. Water was thrown in his face and a drink of whiskey forced between his lips, choking him, and he found himself leaning back against the table. Hands were pulling his clothes away: shirt, pants, boots. He tried to tear away from the dozen or more hands that held him, and found he could hardly move.

The men in front of Buck drew back, and there was an odd pause, an instant of anticipation. Vachel stepped directly in front of Buck; he was masked, but—that stance, those hands—he could only be Vachel. The hands held something up for Buck to see, held it out as if it were a gift.

It was a piece of thin steel wire, about forty inches long, such as might have come from a piano. At one end there was a small loop, a noose.

Vachel leaned forward and, with a delicate surgical touch, fitted the noose over Buck's genitals and drew it tight. Buck fought back a scream.

"Oh, now, don't you worry, boy," Vachel said in a soft, almost tender voice that Buck hardly recognized. "You ain't gonna lose this yet. Maybe not for quite a while. But just don't you forget that you could, anytime you don't do like you're told."

"I still say we should take care of him first." It was Balbo Jeppson's voice. "Take care of him, and make the gal watch."

"No, no, she's just a woman. It's our *loyal* friend Buck-ley who's gonna do the watching."

They dragged him to the side of the room and slammed him down on a straight-back chair. His wrists were quickly tied behind the chair back and his ankles to the legs. Claramae, on the other side of the room, was sobbing, her eyes blank with terror. Vachel pulled over another chair and sat down beside Buck. Gently, carefully, he pulled on the wire. Buck clenched his teeth and held his breath as he felt the loop tighten.

"Good wire," Vachel said. "Won't break, won't slip off. Just cuts in. Reckon I could hang you up by this wire, and you'd just dangle there till the wire cut through. Ain't that right?"

Buck could barely see Claramae through his blurred eyes. His throat was as tight with pain as if the wire had been there.

Vachel gave the wire a sharp tug. "I said, ain't that right?"

"Yes."

"Yes, what, Buckley?"

"Yes, sir . . . master, sir."

"Speak up, can't hear you!"

"Yes, sir, master, sir!"

"That's better. Now, Buckley, you pay real good attention. All of us here, we gonna do some real nice things to that there nigger-hot wench of yours. Since I reckon they're pretty much the same things you been doing to her, she ought to have herself a real fine time, best time of her life. But we don't want you to feel left out, Buckley, we want you to have a good time too. So we're gonna let you enjoy yourself by watching. And anytime you feel a little bit sleepy or bored, we're gonna rouse you up by—"

Vachel began pulling on the wire. The horror was far greater than the pain. Buck slid forward on the seat of the chair, but Vachel continued to pull. Buck lifted his hips. His body was bathed in sweat, but Vachel was right: the wire did not slip off but only dug in further. Buck arched up out of the chair.

"Got the idea, Buck?"

Somehow he had thought he would never beg, no matter what. Now he said, "Oh, yes, God, please!"

Vachel eased the wire. Buck sat again, and his head fell to his chest.

"Not like that, boy."

Vachel tugged at the wire, and Buck's head snapped up. "That's right. Now, you watch."

Buck watched. All of it.

He watched as they tore Claramae's gown off of her, threw her onto the table, and raped her. Each in his turn, each at least once, some more often. He watched, trying not to hear her cries, her sobs, the little animal sounds that signaled the coming of madness. Even Vachel took his turn: a man raping his own wife, or the woman who had supposedly been his wife. But Vachel, no less than the others, kept his mask on the whole time. The masks were meant to terrify, but perhaps even more to hide each man's secret self from the others. They all knew who they were, and they all knew what they were doing and what they were going to do. But without the masks, some of them might not be able to face the others the next day. A few might not be able to face themselves.

Buck watched it. He watched as Claramae's body grew battered and bruised. He watched as her cries grew weaker. He watched as they threw water over her to bring her back to consciousness and spilled whiskey down her throat to give her strength. He watched until she lay limp and half-broken, unresponsive to slaps and blows.

"All right," Vachel said, "get her out of here."

"What for? We ain't done with her yet!"

" 'Course you ain't. Take her to the kitchen or back to the overseer's house. Take her wherever you want, but get her out of here. I'll come with you later. Jeppson . . ."

"Don't worry. I'll take care of everything."

And they left.

It was true: he had thought that he was not as other niggers, that he was something special. Jared, that other black boy years back, had told him otherwise: *"You got black skin, you just a nigger, you a dirty nigger slave!"* And his mother had warned him: *"You are a nigger and a slave. And don't you never forget it."* But he had forgotten. Oh, he had always known that he was black, yes. But not a nigger. Not even a true slave. For hadn't Vachel

Skeet practically made him an honorary white man? Hadn't he been accepted as a member of the enemy camp?

Yes, he had forgotten. For all of Vachel's recent abuse, he had never *really* thought that this could happen to him. And now he sat tied to a chair, head tumbled to his chest, staring at his wire-bound genitals. The wire blocked the flow of blood, giving him an erection, a vicious parody of desire.

Vachel chuckled. "We wouldn't want it to drop off too soon, would we?" He held Buck with one hand and with the other loosened the wire. The hands lingered almost lovingly for a moment, then slipped away.

"Want a drink, Buck?"

Buck didn't answer. He felt the throb of life-giving blood in his softening flesh and wept with relief. He heard the scuff of Vachel's boots and the clink of jug on cup. Vachel sighed his pleasure after a deep swallow and poured again. Boots scuffed again. A hand lifted Buck's head by the hair, and the cup was pressed to his teeth. Vachel's mask was gone, and he was smiling.

"Drink it, Buckley, it'll do you good."

Buck swallowed, felt the whiskey burn its way down. Vachel finished the cup and poured some more. "Hope you don't mind," he said. "Never let it be said that you and me is too good to drink from the same cup with a friend. Ain't that right, Buck?"

Buck wanted to be left alone. He wanted to close his eyes and to sleep and to be forgotten.

"I said, ain't that right, you goddam black Judas?"

"That's right, Vachel."

"Others wanted to do the job right there in the overseer's house. No, I said, me and my old friend Buckley spent many an hour in the office house, planning what we do next, how we gonna make Redbird grow. Got to have one last talk with my old friend Buckley in the plantation office."

Vachel settled himself comfortably into the chair beside Buck and put one boot up onto the table. He poured more whiskey and set the jug on the floor at his side.

"Want another drink?"

Buck shook his head. Vachel sipped.

"How come you done it, Judas?"

Buck's voice hurt him, like something caught in his throat. "You changed, Vachel."

"*I* changed! *I* changed!" Vachel sounded genuinely astonished.

"We both loved you, Vachel, but—"

"You got a great way of showing it."

"But you treated her so bad."

"I treated her how she damn well deserved to be treated. The way she damn well ought to be treated, the way a woman *needs* to be treated."

"No, Vachel."

"You don't know a goddam thing about it, boy. You talk about love, and you don't know a goddam thing about love or—or friendship or loyalty—and like any nigger, you dirty up the words when you use them. You know about 'em in a nigger way and a nigger way only, and my mistake was in not realizing that. Thought we was something special, Buckley. Thought you and me together was something special."

"We was, Vaych!"

"Goddam fucking nigger Judas."

A sob broke from Vachel's throat, and Buck saw with amazement that he was weeping. What did you say to a man who felt so betrayed that he would torture and kill you? you and the woman you loved? you and the wife he hated? Did you say, *I'm sorry*?

Buck said, "I wish I could change things back for you. Back the way they was a couple of years ago. Back the way they was when we was kids."

"Well, you can't."

"I know that. Can't never change nothing back, can't undo nothing you did, got to keep right on going—"

"Until you die." Vachel wiped his eyes with the back of his hand. He grinned. "Until you die, Buckley. That wipes out everything."

"You got to kill her too, Vachel?"

" 'Course I do!" The grin widened, and Vachel sounded

downright cheerful. "She gonna die and die hard, and ain't nobody even gonna *see* the bitch again. Gonna be like she never was. Have a drink, Buckley."

Buck shook his head.

Vachel talked. He drank. Buck hardly listened. Maybe Vachel is right, he thought. It's me that's changed, more than him. Or maybe it's that what we was all the time underneath has finally come out, and now neither of us *wants* to change anymore.

"Let me go, Vachel."

"No."

He hadn't even planned to speak, but the words sprang from his lips. "Let me and Claramae go, and—"

It was as if, somewhere far away, she had heard her name and was responding to it—responding with a long, rising animallike scream of pain.

Vachel thumped his boots on the floor. He picked up the jug and stood up. "Sounds like Claramae done rejoined the party. Time I got back to it too."

The cry was repeated. Buck tugged at his bonds with all his strength, heart pounding as if it might burst.

"Jesus," Vachel said, "I wonder what they doing to her now."

He went to the door. The scream tore through the night a third time.

"Vachel, stop them!" Buck cried. "Stop them!"

Vachel turned back from the door. He was smiling. He put the jug down on the table. He returned to Buck. Buck didn't know what he was going to do until the last moment.

Again he leaned down, reached between Buck's legs, and held him with one hand. But this time the other hand drew the wire tight, tighter, tighter than it had been before.

"There," he said, straightening up, "you like that, don't you? Now, you just sit there and watch your brown nigger dong turn purple, and when I get back, we'll finish you off."

Picking up his jug again, Vachel left the office.

Buck's screams so blended with Claramae's that he could hardly tell them apart.

Fingers dug into his shoulder. The hand shoved at him, shook him.

"Vachel? You hear me, Vachel?"

Jeppson's voice in his ear, setting his head to thudding. Where the hell was he, and why was Jeppson waking him? Mouth and throat were parched. Had he got drunk at Carstairs' tavern?

"Vachel, boy? You wakening now?"

It came back. What had happened. Part of it, some of it, most of it. But not all of it.

He opened his eyes slowly. Jeppson looked down at him with a condescending, faintly ironic smile. Vachel looked around and saw that he was lying on a sofa in his own parlor. His aching head pounded harder when he saw the blood on his hands. God, he thought, Claramae's blood. Didn't even wash it off. Could be all over the place.

"Well! You awake now, young Mr. Skeet?"

Slowly, carefully, Vachel sat up. "I'm awake."

But why couldn't he remember more? He had drunk so much it had blotted part of his memory out.

The light at the window seemed oddly wrong. "What time is it?" he asked.

"Just sundown. You passed out last night and slept all the day."

"Wish somebody'd wakened me before."

"Wasn't for not trying."

Vachel looked at the blood on his hands. "Claramae? . . ."

"Claramae? What about Claramae? Come to think of it, I ain't seen Claramae since I come over here to see how you was. How *is* Miss Claramae these days, Vachel?"

Vachel was certain he was going to be sick. And yet he felt pleased, deeply pleased. Everything had gone just as it was supposed to go. Now it was as if Claramae had never existed. She was punished and gone out of his life.

"And Buck?"

"Oh, Buck? I'm glad you asked me that," Jeppson said heartily, "I am truly glad you asked me that. Want you to come with me, Vachel, want to show you something."

"But you . . . we . . ."

"Now, I ain't gonna answer no more questions yet, Vachel. I mean it! Now, I want you to come with me! Ain't gonna take but a minute!"

The man was jovial, and yet there was a snap of anger in his voice. He was giving commands, and in Vachel's own house, but Vachel felt too ill to argue with him. Head pounding, he followed Jeppson out through the passage into the courtyard.

Jeppson led the way to the plantation office. The door stood open, and a light was burning within.

"Take a look," Jeppson said.

Vachel wasn't certain he wanted to. He could not remember what, if anything, they had done to Buck right there in the office; he was not sure what he would find. But when he stepped into the room, he saw nothing alarming. The only sign of Buck was the scraps of rope on the floor.

"Well, Jeppson?"

Jeppson was now openly angry. "Well, Mr. Skeet, you don't see your goddam nigger anywhere, do you?"

Vachel began to understand. "You mean he—"

"I said, 'Take care of the nigger first.' But, oh, no, you had to take care of the woman and make the nigger watch. Then you had to send us all away and wander off yourself, leaving the nigger alone."

Vachel still could not quite believe it. "But he couldn't have . . . couldn't have slipped those bonds."

"Didn't slip the goddam bonds—*busted 'em!*"

"*That rope?*"

"Vachel, you scare a man enough, even a nigger, and he can do things he can't do no other time. Now, that boy was plumb terrified, and with good reason. '*Course* he busted the goddam ropes, what the hell you expect? Maybe the minute you walked out the door. And it was a long time before any of us got back here to take care of Buckley. By that time, that coon was halfway to Pennsylvania."

Now Vachel's head was pounding and his belly was sick, and it was not just the liquor. Claramae dead, but not Buck. Buck escaped. The best part, the most important part of his revenge gone.

"Anybody looking for him?"

"Damn right we're looking for him. And you better notify the patrol that he run off. And we're gonna bring that black son of a bitch back here and fix him right."

"Yes," Vachel said. "Yes, we are."

"Can't let the bastard get away with this."

"No, we can't." Vachel was panting. "Jeppson, I want him back. I want him back so bad. . . ."

"He ain't gonna get away. Some of them men with us last night, they was so mad, they gonna shoot him down on sight."

"No!"

"I know what you're thinking, but they shoot him in the belly maybe and let him linger, teach him that's a hard way to go too."

"No! I don't want him hurt! I don't want a single damn scratch on that boy that I don't put on him myself, you hear me?"

"I hear you. But I don't think you gonna—"

"You tell everybody I'm offering five hundred dollars for the return of Buckley Skeet. Five hundred dollars for that nigger alive and unharmed, and not one goddam penny for him dying or dead. Jeppson, I don't care what I got to do to get him, you bring him back here to me!"

At the mention of $500, a new light had come into Jeppson's eyes. "For that kind of money, you just might get him."

True. That kind of money might very well bring Buckley back to Redbird alive and unharmed within a week. Jeppson himself was ready to go out and beat the bushes. But what he did not know was that if the money did not produce Buckley within a week or a month, Vachel was prepared to increase the reward. If he had to, he was willing to offer five or even ten times the amount.

He was ready to give up his very soul, if he had one, to get Buckley back.

"Then get the word out, Jeppson. Get the word to the whole damn countryside, to all of Carolina, to the whole goddam South. And never let 'em forget. If it takes the rest of my life—*I want Buckley Skeet!*"

PART THREE

Fugitives

One

"Well, you're damn well gonna get Buckley Skeet!"
Get him after all these years, when you least expect it.
Get him when you've probably given up all hope.

It was a promise Buck had made to himself repeatedly over the years, and he reaffirmed it as he and Adaba moved through the darkness away from Tradwell's landing. He had heard of the rewards that Vachel had offered for him—twenty-five hundred dollars, and then thirty-five hundred, and then an almost unheard of five thousand. Five thousand dollars reward for the return of Buckley Skeet—alive. *By God,* he thought now, *maybe I'll just claim that reward myself. Yes, sir, old Vaych is gonna get his wish—and die of it!*

Once they were well away from the landing, the first thing they did was use the adze and wedges to rid themselves of their shackles. *And we're free again,* Buck thought happily, *about free as we ever been.* Even the air smelled sweeter.

But they were still far from safe, and he knew that the odds were distinctly against them. They were both dizzy with the fatigue of the last few days, both battered and whip-sore, and Adaba still had two unhealed wounds. They had a night's run ahead of them, after a day with little rest, and this part of the country was dangerously crowded for runaways. And they had no material with which to forge passes. But they had their stolen supplies, a few hours start on the Rogans, and a lot of experience at maintaining their freedom.

"Well," Adaba said softly, "we can't just stand here. This here is your part of the country. Wasn't Sabrehill where—"

"That was where. I told you about it, long ago."

"The man that helped us—"

"Was Mr. Justin Sabre. He don't remember me, but I

215

sure as hell remember him. He was the one that shot the shit out of old Vaych. Pity he didn't kill him."

Adaba laughed. "He a good man?"

"Hell, Johnny Dove, he's a *white* man." Buck considered. "Still, Sabrehill might not be a bad way to head. Like Mr. Justin said, throw the Rogans off our track. And there used to be some damn good black people there. That Aunt Zule he talked about, that conjure-woman can fix them wounds of yours faster than anybody you ever know."

Adaba laughed again and slapped Buck's shoulder. "Conjure-woman! Just what I need! Like I said, this is your country—how we get there?"

"Think we best head inland, way 'round the river plantations, and stay off the roads. It maybe take us a little longer, but we be safer."

"All right, you lead the way."

Inland they went, guided by the stars and the tall trees, black against the night sky. All too conscious that less than a week before he had led pursuers to Adaba's camp, Buck battled his fatigue to keep every sense alert, so that he could hear any distant hoofbeat or the cracking of a twig, smell a dog or a horse or even a man upwind. Any failure of alertness could lead to their capture. Or it could lead to their roaming the night in great futile circles.

It struck Buck then, in a strange, nightmare way, that he *was* running in a circle; that for a dozen years he had been running in a vast circle that had started at Redbird and that inevitably returned to it. For the first several years after his escape, he had continued to live with the horror of Redbird, until time and distance had diminished it. But the horror had never entirely vanished; it had always been on the horizon, on the far side of the circle. And for the last several years, the horror had been growing again as he reapproached it. That was why it was increasingly necessary to take revenge on the whites —to burn and kill, anything to lay the awful past to rest. And now, in a few days, he would return to the very heart of the horror.

He remembered—he would never forget—how the circle had begun. Claramae's screams still echoed in memory, still haunted his dreams, sounding louder now than they had in years.

"Jesus, I wonder what they doing to her now."

"Vachel, stop them!" he had cried. *"Stop them!"*

But of course Vachel had not stopped them. Instead, he had crossed the office to where Buck sat naked, tied to the chair. He had grinned. And he had reached down and drawn that wire loop tighter than ever. And as Vachel had left the office, Buck's screams had blended with Claramae's.

And then, suddenly, he was free.

But at that moment he had no thought of freedom or escape. He was aware only of that terrible wire that bit into his manhood. He pulled his right arm away from the slackened ropes, and then his left. He found the wire and, with shaking fingers, clawed at it, tore at it, somehow managed to get it off. And threw it across the room.

His scream died away to a whimper.

Now came thoughts of flight. Vachel might return at any minute—Vachel and Jeppson and all the rest. And when they did return . . .

It seemed to take him forever to untie his legs, and his whimper nearly became a scream again. He grabbed shirt, pants, and boots, but he did not stop to dress, did not look for a weapon. He went to the side of the doorway and peered out. He could see nothing. He slipped quickly through the doorway and hurried around the office, putting the building between himself and—he hoped—the lynch party.

Claramae's scream pierced the night again, freezing him there behind the office for a moment, but there was nothing he could do to save her, not a thing in the world.

He ran for darkness, headed into it, tried to bury himself in it. He hardly felt the earth under his bare feet. He was a quarter of a mile east of the office and in some woods when he finally paused to pull on the shirt, pants, and boots. Even there he could hear Claramae's screams, and he knew he would always hear them, would hear them in memory and madness and dreams until the day he died.

A thumping at the door brought Justin Sabre up out of sleep, and at his answer, a man entered the room and lit a lamp. It was not yet dawn. Justin requested some hot water. Quite likely this morning would be his last opportunity for several days to get a decent shave. Odd how being clean and well shaved seemed to affirm his moral superiority over the Rogans.

After a hasty breakfast he checked his weapons one last time, hauled his roll of gear up onto his shoulder, and headed for the landing. It was still dark when he arrived, and the boat was being loaded by torchlight. Tradwell, at the edge of the landing, greeted Justin with a nod. Then, without a word, he pointed toward the Rogans, who were just stirring.

"Looks like they're missing something," Justin said. He put down his gear. He shifted his rifle to his left hand and kept his right hand near the opening of his jacket.

"Looks like I'm missing something too," Tradwell said. "An adze and maybe a couple of wedges."

"I suppose somebody owes you for something like that."

"I get rid of them Rogans, I ain't gonna worry much about it."

Silas Rogan sat up. He held his head as if it might fall off, and considering the liquor he had consumed, Justin figured that to be a very real possibility. Silas kicked at young Luther.

Justin and Tradwell waited.

And at last Silas Rogan saw. He looked where the two chained blacks had been. Bewildered, unable to believe that they were really missing, he turned and looked about the boat. Then he seemed to realize the blankets and supply pouches were missing. In a panic, he felt about the area immediately surrounding him, as if seeking his gear and his blacks by touch. He clutched at his rifle and stared at it, realizing that it was all he had left. Tradwell laughed softly, but somehow Justin did not find the sight amusing.

Silas kicked at Lute again and climbed slowly to his feet. He stumbled over to where Adaba had been chained, stared at the staple holes, leaned down to touch them.

He crossed the boat and looked at the place where Buck had been chained. He raised his head slowly to look into Tradwell's eyes, into Justin's, into Tradwell's again. The pain in his own washed-out eyes was so visible that Justin could almost feel it.

"My niggers gone," he said.

Tradwell said, "So I see."

"Where they go?"

"They your niggers. Reckon you know better'n me where they gone."

Silas's eyes shifted again: to Justin, to Tradwell, to Justin.

"They got away," he said.

"Looks that way, Rogan," Justin said. He noted that Lute was now on his feet, aware of what was going on, and clutching his rifle.

"Got away or been stole," Silas said.

"I suppose that could be."

Silas shook his head and looked about as if bewildered. It was as if only slowly was the enormity of his loss dawning on him. "Took everything we had with 'em," he said. "Everything but our guns."

Lute shook his rifle with both hands. "Anybody touch my gun, I kill 'em! I kill 'em!" He seemed to expect the threat to cause a change.

"Even the money for the mule," Silas said. "Sold a old mule up at your other landing."

"I know that," Tradwell said.

"Money was in my poke. Ain't many people up our way got a mule. Sold that old mule, figured after we got rid of the niggers we get a better mule. Be rich then. Now we ain't got the niggers nor the money from the mule neither."

"That's too bad, Mr. Rogan."

Silas blinked back tears. His voice shook. "Mister, I guess you just don't know. Them niggers and that mule was just about all that me and my missus and our honey-boy got. Ain't got hardly no crop this year, ain't got no money now. Man and his woman and his boy, they work hard year after year trying to scratch up a living. Raise a little cotton, raise a little corn, snare a rabbit, somehow get through the winter. Always think that someday you gonna have something. Only you don't, never. Just get a little older, and you know the sand's a-running out. Then one day you got your niggers, and you gonna—you gonna sell them niggers—and you gonna have what you never had in your life before, and . . ."

Silas's voice faltered and quit. Justin understood. Silas recognized Tradwell and Justin as belonging to a superior world, the world of the competent, the successful, the wealthy. And if Silas could just explain his situation clearly, perhaps they would make things right for him again. If only the gods would take notice! But gazing into Tradwell's and Justin's eyes, Silas saw no hope. And so he lowered his head and wiped his tears.

"Guess you purely don't give a damn if a poor man's niggers is stole," he said.

"Mr. Rogan," Tradwell said, "I don't hanker to see no escaped niggers running around the countryside, thieving and making mischief. But the way you was treating them two boys yesterday, I can't grieve to see 'em get free, neither. Why, damn it, man, you was killing them boys—"

Tradwell broke off as Lute stepped forward, lifting his rifle. His eyes were too wide. Justin eased his hand closer to his pistol.

"Don't you do nothing foolish, young fellow," Tradwell said.

"Our niggers," Lute said. "You let 'em go. You—you didn't do nothing to stop 'em."

"And don't say nothing foolish neither. You was guarding your niggers last night. They got away, you got only yourself to blame."

Which, Justin had to admit, was not altogether true. It was most unlikely that the blacks would have escaped without his help.

"Rogan," he said to Silas, "why were you treating those two so badly? Was it simply because you were drunk? A man doesn't ruin his own people unless there's something wrong with him—certainly not if he wants to get a good price for them. Were those men runaways you were taking back? Maybe from that maroon camp that was raided last week?"

"None of your damn business!" Lute said. "Don't you tell him nothing, pa! Those is *our* niggers, and we aim to find 'em and get 'em back!"

"Well, I wish you plenty o' luck," Tradwell said, "and if you'll excuse me, I got to see to loading this here box. Don't reckon you'll be traveling any further downriver with us, Mr. Rogan?"

"Don't reckon," Silas said. "Ain't got no niggers to work our way for us now, anyway." He still appeared stunned by the loss.

"Well, you don't want to look for them downriver anyway," Justin said, feeling almost guilty. "They're going to head toward the high country, where they have the most chance of getting away. That was where you were bringing them from, wasn't it?"

"What you know about it, mister?" Lute said almost hysterically. "What you know about it?"

Silas shushed him, and they had a whispered conference. They found themselves in the way of the hands who were loading the bales of cotton, and they moved up onto the landing. They stood about, looking aimless, as if after their sudden reversal of fortune they had not the slightest idea of what to do next.

Finally Tradwell took pity on them. He spoke to one of his hands and then went over to the Rogans. "Don't like to see no one have bad luck when they traveling with me. You follow that boy up the road a piece to the tavern. He'll have 'em give you a good breakfast and put a little food in a poke to get you started on your way home."

Silas mumbled his thanks, and he and Lute followed the hand off of the landing. Dawn was just beginning to fight the torchlight, and Justin and Tradwell watched until the Rogans disappeared into the shadows.

Justin remembered yesterday's drunken threats. "Think they'll make trouble?" he asked.

Tradwell shrugged. "I doubt it. They ain't gonna have time. Put a meal in their bellies, and they'll go chasing back up the river after their niggers. Just might catch 'em

too, though I hate to think it. Getting caught by the Rogans now is gonna be a lot worse than being picked up
by any goddam patrol."

"And I suppose the patrol will probably pick the blacks
up."

"Most likely, with them beaten up so bad and one of
'em wounded. Could be it's the best damn thing that could
happen to 'em. Niggers got no damn business running
around loose, 'cept when they getting away from the likes
of the Rogans."

Justin found himself hoping like hell that Adaba and
Buck would make it to Sabrehill.

All dreams of love ended like this: in terror. Vachel
would allow them to end in no other way.

Buck heard a scream, a scream of such horror that he
hardly recognized Claramae's voice. It made no difference that he knew he must be dreaming. His heart raced,
his blood pounded in his ears. He heard the scream again,
and he ran toward the overseer's house, not daring to guess
what he would find there.

Claramae met him at the door. Tears ran down her
agonized face, and she could not speak. She pointed into
the house and followed as Buck entered.

It was the loop of wire. That was the first thing he saw
as he entered the room: the wire noose that had pursued
him through the years and filled dream after dream with
anguish; the wire noose that threatened to take not only
his physical manhood and his life, but his moral manhood
and his soul; the wire noose that carried the message:
nigger is beast.

But the loop was not fitted to Buck this time.

Vachel lay naked on his back on a bare bed. His body
was wet with sweat, his face beaded. His eyes were half-
closed, like those of a man in fever. A small, ghastly grin
twitched his mouth. And the loop of wire was tightly
drawn around his swollen genitals, the end of the noose
firmly in his right hand.

That same wire noose. Buck had awakened from it,
shaking with terror, so many times. He had often wished
he had kept it that night when he ran away from Redbird,

so that one day when he returned he could exact this very same payment from Vachel. But now—

Vachel pulled slowly, steadily at the wire, tightening the loop.

"*Jesus God, Vachel, no!*" Buck thought his heart would explode. Somehow he had to save Vachel. Somehow they had to save each other.

"You just keep back," Vachel whispered. "You just keep away from me."

"Don't do it, Vachel!" Buck pleaded.

"Don't you tell me don't do it, nigger boy," Vachel said. "Don't you tell me."

"But why, Vachel, why do such a thing?"

"You know goddam well why, you goddam Judas, don't you ask me why."

Buck took a step into the room. "No, I—"

"*Don't!*"

Buck stopped short as Vachel gave the wire a sharp, hard, brutal tug. The wire dug into the flesh. Vachel's grin stretched tightly, and his eyes rolled up in their sockets with what might have been either pain or ecstasy.

Somehow Buck had to stop Vachel. He had to save him. If he failed to get that wire loop off, if he failed to get it off in time, he would never forgive himself. But Vachel's right hand, tight on the wire, trembled with anticipation, almost with challenge, and there was no way he could be saved. Somewhere behind Buck, Claramae wept.

"Vachel, please! Please, please, please, please!"

Vachel laughed softly. He lay perfectly still on the bed, except for that trembling right hand and the tormented flesh.

He tugged at the wire again.

"No, Vachel!" Tears ran down Buck's face.

A tug at the wire.

"*No!*"

Buck could not help himself. He took another step into the room. Vachel's eyes widened, and he pulled harder. Buck tried to draw back, but he could not make himself do so. He *had* to get that wire off of Vachel before it was too late. He *had* to get it off—and so he threw himself at Vachel, knowing even as he did so that he was causing the wire to cut deeper, knowing that if he failed he was more executioner than savior.

And he failed.

Somehow he could not reach Vachel. Buck stretched out his arms, but Vachel slid away. Buck cried out to him, ran after him, strained every fiber to get to him, but Vachel eluded him. He heard Claramae behind him, trying to help, and felt her hands on his shoulders, but she only held him back. Vachel laughed, his eyes rolling wildly, and pulled at the wire with all his strength.

Buck could stand the horror of it no longer. Blood was flowing from the mangled flesh, Vachel was laughing, and all hope was gone. And Buck dropped like a stone into the black hell of grief and guilt.

"Oh, it ain't fair," Buck wept like a child in the darkness. "It ain't fair, it ain't fair, it ain't fair." Claramae held his shoulders, shaking them gently, trying to comfort him, but after a moment he knew it was not Claramae, it would never be Claramae again.

"No, Buck," Adaba said gently, "it ain't fair."

"It was *me* he done it to, not him! It was Claramae he got killed, not hisself!"

"I know, Buck, I know."

"It ain't fair!"

Adaba let him weep it out. When he awakened from these dreams, it often seemed that all the sins of mankind from the beginning of time rested on his shoulders, and . . . it wasn't fair.

Somehow he managed to calm himself, breathing deeply of the cool evening air. He had picked their resting place well, and no one had disturbed them, and *It was a dream,* he told himself repeatedly, *only a dream.* Ignorant old people in the slave quarters thought that dreams gave clues to the past and the future and to the truth of the present; but he knew that they meant nothing at all. Let all evil dreams be laid to rest.

"Better now?" Adaba asked.

"Yes."

"Still have them."

"Some."

"Worse, I think."

"Oh . . . sometimes."

"Had one the night we was raided, didn't you? I heard you."

Buck did not answer. The feelings of grief and guilt lingered after the dream like a sickness, and he felt exhausted. He had told himself that he needed only a long day of undisturbed sleep to be as good as new again, but now he felt as if he might never again move.

"Well," Adaba said, "about time we sent you up north, I reckon."

Buck was startled. "What? What you mean, up north?"

"Man like you don't want to spend all his life always on the run. Man like you ought to go up to Canada, maybe. Find you a nice little gal—"

"Johnny Dove, what the hell you talking about?"

"About sending you north, son. About your time to go, ain't it? You earned a little peace and quiet."

Buck made a sound of disgust. Indignation brought new life to his body, and he sat up. "I don't want to go up to no Canada. It's *cold* up there, man, all that ice and snow! Besides, I was born and raised in Carolina, man, this is my home! I *own* Carolina like them others ain't *never* gonna own it!"

Adaba laughed. "Guess you do, at that. But just the same—"

"Ain't no 'just the same.' Don't hear *you* talking about going to no Canada."

"I ain't the one with the bad dreams."

The remark took the wind out of Buck; he could not have said why. He did not wish to believe that the dreams had any great importance.

"I am sorry I cried out," he said.

"That's all right."

"No, it ain't. Man on the run cries out in his sleep, he can be heard. You right about that. But I can keep from doing it. I ain't gonna do it again."

"It ain't just that, Buck."

"Then it ain't nothing I want to talk about." Buck climbed to his feet. "Now, unless you want to rest some more, we got a hard night's travel ahead of us."

"Reckon we best travel."

After a fast meal from the Rogans' supplies, they hoisted the straps of their stolen gear to their shoulders and were on their way. One more good night's run, Buck thought, without too much delay hiding from patrols, and they would be well on their way to Sabrehill. And once they reached Sabrehill, Aunt Zule could take care of Adaba. Aunt Zule, he remembered, had no great love for whites: she had taken risks for more than one black man in trouble; she could be trusted.

And with Adaba in safe and caring hands . . .

Then it would be time for his return to Redbird. He would bury Vachel Skeet, he swore, and with Vachel all the evil dreams that had haunted him through the years. He would have his revenge and be freed from the past forever.

At Redbird.

Silas Rogan was stunned. After a lifetime of poverty, he had had a fortune virtually in hand, or so he had thought, and as suddenly as it had appeared, it had vanished. He had no idea of what to think about it or what to do about it. The great good luck he had had in capturing Black Buck and Adaba now no longer seemed entirely real.

On the morning of their loss, Silas and Lute followed the black stevedore from Tradwell's landing to the tavern. The stevedore murmured a message to a Negro woman who stood blocking the doorway and looking at them contemptuously. She said, "Wait here," and they understood that they were barred from the tavern. She reappeared a few minutes later with two plates of food which they ate standing on their feet in the open air. When they were finished, the woman again came to the door, took the plates, and thrust a poke of food into Silas's hands. "Ought to hold you a day or two," she said, hard-voiced. "Now you better be on your way. Mr. Tradwell, he don't like nobody with no business hanging around here."

And what kind of nigger, Silas wondered dully, talked that way to a white man? What kind of nigger kept a white man standing outside the door? What kind of nigger lived better, in all likelihood, than Silas Rogan lived? Silas stared with sullen hatred at the woman. With the two captured blacks lost, hatred was about all he had left, his sole legacy, and he felt it growing in his guts. Hatred for the nigger. His grandchildren might grow rich and his great-grandchildren powerful, they might become industrialists and senators and generals, but he would give them hatred of the nigger forever.

The door closed. The last thing Silas saw was the black woman's look of contempt.

"Black Buck and Adaba," Lute said. "We got to get 'em back, pa! We got to get 'em back!"

Yes, but how? That man called Sabre had said the blacks would probably head for the high country, and the chances were he was right. But how could Silas and Lute possibly search every bit of woods, every slave quarters, every hiding place between Tradwell's landing and the high country? Only the patrol could do that. But if they notified the patrol and it then captured the runaways, it would not return them—not to the likes of the Rogans— without some proof of ownership, which the Rogans, of course, did not have. And if the Rogans told *why* they had no legal papers for the runaways, no proof of ownership, the pattyrollers would then claim the rewards for themselves. There seemed to be no way out of the dilemma. And Black Buck and Adaba were getting further away by the hour.

Silas tried to think it out. Meanwhile, he led the way back home by the fastest, most direct route, and Lute asked every white they met, "You seen two runaway niggers, two niggers without passes?"

And he got such answers as: "Ain't seen no strange niggers at all. You told the patrol?"

"Don't need no patrol. Just two dumb niggers, ain't got no sense, we'll find 'em sooner or later."

Silas warned: "You oughtn't talk about them two, Lute, get everybody looking—"

"But, pa, *we got to find 'em!*"

The food they had been given did not hold out, but Lute shot a couple of rabbits: two shots, two rabbits, because a poor man could not afford to miss. On Sunday afternoon they slouched, hungry and weary, across the last stretch of open ground to their mud-chinked, sag-roofed, one-room house.

Mrs. Rogan had seen them coming. She stood within the open doorway of the house, the old blunderbuss in hand. She lowered it when she recognized them. She knew that something had gone wrong. Why else would they be back so soon and with such an air of defeat.

"What happen?" she asked. "Where's them two niggers? Why you—"

"Woman," Silas said, "don't you say nothing, don't you ask nothing. We been traveling hard. You get us some food."

She did as she was told. The fire was already going, and she built it up. Dried meat and water went into a pot. Later she added some rice, beans, and corn. It was almost an hour before the food was ready, and in all that time she never said another word. And neither did Silas or Lute.

They ate: Silas and Mrs. Rogan at the ends of the plain deal table, Lute at the side. Mrs. Rogan hardly touched her food. When Silas and Lute had finished, she said, "And now, Mr. Rogan, kindly tell me about it."

And Silas told her. Told her most of it.

For a time afterward, Silas thought his wife had been struck dumb. She merely stared at him, dry-eyed and un-blinking, her cheeks resting in her palms. Then, finally, tears came, and she covered her eyes. "Oh, you dang . . . fools," she sobbed, "you God . . . dang . . . fools."

"Now, Mrs. Rogan—"

"All our lives we been poor. And all the time we been together, I prayed the good Lord He would put something good into our hands. And He did. Finally. He did. After all these years, the good Lord made it up to us by putting into our hands those two niggers so we could be rich. Rich the rest of our lives! *And you lost 'em!*"

"But it weren't our fault, ma," Lute said, stricken.

"Weren't your fault?" Mrs. Rogan looked at Lute, looked at Silas again. "Weren't your fault?"

"No, ma—"

"Don't you even know *you was took?*"

Silas licked his lips. His mouth was dry, and for some reason his food sat heavy in his stomach. "Took? No—"

"Took! Cheated and stole from!"

"It could be, pa," Lute said. "I always thought so."

"Mr. Rogan, you had them niggers fastened so they couldn't never get away. But they *did* get away. Now you tell me who *helped* 'em get away?"

"Nobody. They . . . just . . ."

"You sure you didn't tell nobody who they was, Mr. Rogan?"

"No—no, we surely didn't, Lotte Anne." But the heaviness in Silas's stomach was turning cold. He remembered a drunken slip: *"Damn tricky niggers. That Adaba, he . . ."* The name of the black would be known, and so would his value. And Black Buck would be recognized too, just as Silas and Lute had recognized both men.

"Then they must have guessed who they was," Mrs. Rogan said, "knowing you was taking 'em down Redbird way. Or maybe they stole 'em without even knowing."

"They knew," Silas said, feeling certain. "They knew."

"Didn't you even look anywhere for 'em?"

"That other man, that Mr. Sabre, I think he was called, he said they'd probably run for the hills."

Mrs. Rogan laughed mirthlessly. "Mr. Sabre! Him and that Mr. Tradwell was most likely in on it together. Don't you know there's a big Sabre plantation down beyond Redbird? Over two hundred niggers there, some say, maybe three hundred or even more. Mr. Sabre, he steals your niggers and adds 'em to Sabre niggers, who's to know the difference? Rich man like him, who's gonna say he stole some of his niggers? And if he finds out he got Black Buck, he just takes him to Redbird and collects the reward—*your* money, Mr. Rogan—and with that he can buy ten more prime field hands and get richer still, while the likes of us starves."

Silas had no doubt that Mrs. Rogan was right: the two

blacks had been stolen. He saw it all so clearly now. Tradwell or Sabre had recognized the blacks even before he, Silas, had made his slip. Sabre had encouraged him and Lute to get drunk, even bringing them a fresh jug from the tavern. He and Tradwell had then stolen and hidden the blacks, and had stood by, laughing silently, when Silas and Lute had discovered they were gone. Sabre had even sent Silas and Lute off in the wrong direction—upcountry—no doubt laughing at them all the time. The blacks had then been put back on the raft and floated down the river. They would stop at Redbird Plantation, turn over Black Buck, and collect the reward. They would then continue down the river with Adaba and find out what kind of reward they could get for him.

For Black Buck, five thousand dollars. For Adaba, Silas had no idea. A thousand dollars? Another five thousand? Ten? A total of ten or fifteen thousand dollars, or even more? In any case, a fortune. And it had all been his, Silas's, and it had slipped through his fingers.

He closed his eyes. He lowered his head. The rich people, the gentry. And the niggers. They were in a conspiracy to defraud Silas Rogan, to cheat him, to steal from him, to keep him forever poor.

"They ain't gonna do it," he said.

"What, pa?"

"They ain't gonna do it. We ain't gonna let 'em take what's ours. We ain't gonna let 'em cheat and steal from us."

"What we gonna do, pa?"

"We gonna get what's ours. We gonna go get them niggers or our money, one or t'other. We gonna go all the way to Redbird, all the way to that Sabre place, gonna keep on going till we catch up with Mr. Tradwell and that Sabre man. And then . . ."

"Yeah, pa?"

Silas opened his eyes and raised his head. All the frustration and bitter anger of a lifetime seemed to be rising in him at this moment, preparing him for what was to come.

"And then," he said, "we make 'em pay, Lute. We make 'em pay, and pay, and pay."

Two

On Sunday afternoon, Zulie went to the meeting.

Exactly when the meetings had started or how they had gained their present character, Zulie had no idea. She did know that they had begun as religious occasions. On most of the plantations of the region there was religious worship on Sunday mornings, though this was worrisome to many of the whites, and therefore carefully watched. Perhaps for that very reason there had developed clandestine meetings on some of the plantations, and the texts for these meetings increasingly tended to be quite different from those of the Sunday morning worship: "And the children of Israel sighed by reason of the bondage, and they cried, and their cry came up unto God by reason of the bondage." What had begun as worship, then, moved toward subversion—and the whites were quite right to be worried by black religious teachings.

For the most part, people attended the meetings, if they attended them at all, on their own plantations. But there was a certain amount of ranging about from plantation to plantation, as people visited old friends and found new, congenial companions. On a plantation as big as Sabrehill, there might be several meetings going on at the same time. But the one that Zulie attended that afternoon was quite different from the others.

It was different in that the great majority of the people there were not even from Sabrehill. They were people who had stopped by the blacksmith shop to ask about Ettalee and to whom Saul had said, "We got to talk . . . little later . . . we got to talk."

Zulie and Saul both recognized that there was such a thing as a fullness of time, a time when certain events moved people toward action. The abuse of Ettalee appeared to be such an event. It had done what any number of whippings had failed to do: brought a large number of black people together in a common resolve to act on their anger.

But to act how? to do what?

The meeting was held deep in a large patch of woods far to the north of the field quarters and the main Sabrehill buildings. People attended other meetings, then drifted out to the woods, two or three at a time, keeping a wary eye for whites and especially for Mr. Skeet. It had been two weeks since he had picked up Ettalee, but the indignation had not died down, and Zulie saw that the meeting was even larger than it had been the week before. There must have been twenty people there, perhaps more—a dangerously large number. For the most part, they had come in pairs, some of them surprising distances, and at no small risk. Zulie knew most of them: Primus and Scipio from the Pettigrew plantation; Sarah Jane and Athena Rose from the McClintock plantation; Theron and Hector from Kimbrough Hall; Brutus and Faith from over Devereau way; and Cudjoe and Knowledge from further down the river at the Buckridge place; Tabitha Lu from the Haining plantation; and Cato Weston from Redbird. And there were a couple of others from Sabrehill, and some, whom Zulie did not recognize, from other plantations. If the masters were to discover the meeting of such a large group from so many different plantations, if there were an informer in their midst, these people would undoubtedly be accused of being insurrectionists. And would that have been so far from wrong? They wanted change, justice, freedom, and some would do almost anything to get it. And for that, Saul and Zulie and some others would almost certainly be hung, and the rest would be whipped and transported— sold out of state. In coming together in this way, these people were gambling with their futures, with their lives, and they all knew it.

There were no prayers today, no sermon, no discussion of the Gospel. People sat in small groups, two and three together, on the ground and on fallen trees, under the bleak late-autumn sun. Saul asked some of the younger men to keep a lookout, then turned to address the crowd.

"Now, you all know why we here," he said, "you all

know what you want, what I want. What I want is no
more Skeet, nor more nigger-jail, no more Redbird. No
more grab my Ettalee nor other black gal. Why, after
my Ettalee, he even try to carry off Zulie here. And he
still trying—next time he get *you*, Athena Rose. *You*,
Tabby Lu. He keep trying and trying, and what I want,
O Lord, strike that man dead! Use my own hand, if
Thou wilt, O Lord, and strike that man dead, and Mr.
Jeppson, and Mr. Tucker, and all who stand in our way
—and set Thy people free!"

"Set them free for what?" Brutus of the Devereau
plantation asked dryly. He was known as a loner, almost
as mean as he looked, but his intelligence was respected.
"Free for what?"

"Why, free to run away! Free to run to their freedom!"

"And leave their family behind?"

"Ain't nobody in that jail house ain't going run away,"
Cato Weston of Redbird said. He was a ginger-headed
man who looked more white than black. "Ain't nobody
less'n it's Sarah Jane's man."

Zulie was surprised. "Your man there, Sarah Jane?"

"Three days," Sarah Jane said bitterly. "Three days
now, 'cause them McClintock boys was pestering me,
and twice he run 'em off and got whipped for it, and
this time master send him to Mr. Skeet to get busted.
And who going keep them McClintocks away from me
now?"

"I get him out of that nigger-jail, you and him run
away?" Saul asked.

"Him and me run, and Athena Rose here, and maybe
lots more McClintock people!"

"And Pettigrew people!" Scipio said.

"And Buckridge people!"

"And Devereau!"

"And Kimbrough!"

"And Redbird too," Cato Weston said. "It ain't just
people in that jail going run off. There's me and more
like me. Get rid of that Skeet and that Dinkin and that
Shadrach, and ain't nobody going see our tracks. Head
north out of bondage!"

There were cries of approval, but Brutus's voice broke

through them. "Now, you all wait a minute. I want to get away same as all you. Maybe more than most—how many *you* had your wife and child sold away from you? But *how* we get away? How we going do it?"

"Why, we *go*, man!" Tabitha Lu said enthusiastically.

Brutus shook his head with disgust. "Little Tabby Lu, don't you know most any runaway get picked up?"

"They go north all the time!" Faith declared.

"No, no, they don't. The ones know *how*—*they* go north. But *you* know how? You got maps in your head? You know the trails to go and the houses is safe? You *hear* 'bout niggers go to North and freedom, but how many you *know*? The master so sure you going be picked up, he can even sell you *after* you run away. 'Nigger running—For sale!' 'Nigger running—Sold!' "

"So you scared to try?" Tabitha Lu asked.

"Ain't scared. But when I try, don't aim to get caught."

"Thing is," young Cudjoe of Buckridge Plantation said, "we got to do this all together. What everybody forget is, they is one hell of a lot more of us than they is of them."

Before the sounds of approval could start, Brutus cut in: "But they got the guns, man."

"Don't matter. 'Cause they is so many of us. Just from our own plantations, we all go together and they don't dare do nothing. Why, we just go marching straight up north, take what we want, take what we need—"

"Oh, my Lord," Brutus said, "where this boy been? He ain't never heard 'bout up in Virginie? Old Prophet Nat? Went marching and got 'bout hundred'n twenty nigger killed off?"

"That was different," Cudjoe objected. "Old Nat, he went and killed a lot of white folk. I ain't talking about we kill nobody."

"Well, I am," Cato Weston said grimly. "You ain't going get nobody out of the Redbird nigger-jail without you kill somebody. And you get 'em out, *they* going do some killing. They's a big old gal in there and a couple Gullah, they soon kill a white man as look at him. That bunch of nigger start marching for their freedom, don't you think they ain't going be no killing."

"Then we all going die," Brutus said. "That's all. We all going die."

"It be good a way as any," Faith declared, "and better than most."

"No," Saul said flatly. "Ain't no good dying when you can live. Plenty of time left for dying. I ain't trying get my Ettalee well just so I kill her taking her north." He looked at Primus, a Pettigrew driver, who sat off from the others. "What you think, Primus? You always got something to say, but now you don't say nothing."

"Maybe you don't like what I say."

"That don't matter. We got to hear."

"Thing is, most of us, we been thinking about this all wrong. We talk like we going *rise up!* Going *march!* Like all we go to do is link arms, sing *Glory, Hallelujah!,* and go marching into the Promised Land, all us together."

"Well, we is!" Cudjoe said.

"No." Primus stood up and went to the middle of the gathering. "No, 'cause like Brutus say, it ain't no good marching. We done had all the marches we need. We hear 'bout the Stono march in the old days and 'bout Camden and 'bout all them others—and what good all them marches do? They set theyself free? No! They die off, and the masters make new laws to hold us down more. And here we is, brothers and sisters, and don't talk to me 'bout no marches! Maybe the time come, but it ain't here now!"

"Then what we going do?"

"Brothers and sisters, we all know our people do go north! Oh, yeah, plenty get caught, but every year more go, and how they do it? Not marching north like an army. They go quiet! One or two or three together, hardly never more."

"But how we going do that?" Cudjoe asked. "Guess all us here, we know hundred, maybe two hundred folks want to go north tomorrow."

"Good! But not all same time. Send out two, three, they find out where the marooners is, people who can help us—"

"They get caught," Brutus said.

"Maybe so, then we send out more. Find the way, and

come back and tell us. Find the Underground Railroad. More and more us go—"

"Oh, we most be dead 'fore we get north that way, man! We be old with a beard like Saul!"

"But you be alive to enjoy your freedom. Telling you, this like I say the only way colored folks ever get north."

"Telling *you*, we got to find a better way!"

The talk went on . . . and on . . . and on. . . .

And Zulie understood: that was all it would ever be—talk. This was indeed the fullness of time; the moment to act had arrived. But it was passing. And nothing would be born of it, nothing would happen. There would be more meetings, more discussion, more arguments. But there would be no rebellion, no escape north, no end to Skeet and his nigger-jail and the life they represented. In the end, everything would go on exactly as it had before.

Because the only thing these people knew, in a vague sort of way, was that they wanted to rebel, they wanted to escape from their masters. But they had no real idea of how to go about it. Their failed escapes, their scars of retribution were proof of that. Most were leaders on their own plantations, but each knew of the others' failures and was unyielding in his own views; there was no one person among them who could unify them with a single well-defined purpose and plan. It would take a kind of magic to do that, and it was a magic that neither Saul nor Zulie, the conjure-woman, possessed. And so these people were risking a conspiracy charge here today, were risking the most savage punishment—for nothing.

Zulie's heart went out of her. She could listen to the others no longer. It was one of those times when it seemed easiest simply to give up hope, sink down onto the earth, and wait to be buried. She quietly, unobtrusively, moved away from the meeting and started back toward Sabrehill.

She came to a young man who was supposedly standing guard. Listening to the debate, he had grown careless. Zulie looked over his shoulder and beyond the trees about a hundred yards to see a man sitting on a horse.

A tall man with a long gray face. Instinctively she reached for the knife under her dress.

"Go tell the others shut their mouth and scatter 'bout," she told the guard. "Mr. Skeet nosing 'bout here, looking to make trouble."

The guard hurried toward the meeting. Mr. Skeet rode slowly on.

And he ain't even on the road, Zulie thought. *Go anywhere he want, riding on Sabrehill like it was his very own. Like he own Sabrehill and us and all the world.*

And so it would always be: Mr. Skeet over all the world forever, and freedom an idle dream.

On Monday morning at dawn, Adaba felt the wings of the Angel of Death.

At least he thought it was Monday morning, not that it really mattered. He could no longer tell if they had been running four nights or five or even six. Everything was growing muddled in his mind. He could no longer remember.

He lay quietly on the ground, feeling those wings brush over him. He knew what they were. He had felt a change in his body that morning, not a pain, not a slackening, just a change, and he knew instinctively what it meant. In a matter of hours now, perhaps not this morning or even tomorrow morning, but soon . . .

Rain was threatening, and Buck was building a lean-to of branches and leaves and grass to shelter them. He was building it right over Adaba. "Don't need your help, Johnny," he had said. "This here adze is all I need. Now, you just rest easy and get back your strength." In a way, the rain would help. People would tend to stay close to their roofs, and he and Buck were less apt to be discovered while they slept.

What will happen to Buck when I'm gone? he wondered.

The same thing that had been happening all along, no doubt. Driven by his deep angers, he would grow increasingly careless of his own life and the lives of others, and he would die at the end of a rope—or as Adaba was dying, with a couple of bullet holes festering in him. The real question was, how many, black and white, would he take with him?

Well, Buck you took me.

Now, you be careful of that, he told himself; *don't you go blaming Buck. You chose this way of life, and Buck is as good a friend as you've ever had. You got to die sooner or later, and don't you go out with a goddam whine on your lips.*

Anyway, he thought, who was to say that Buck was wrong? Follow Black Buck, and every Negro in the country would end up dead, and wouldn't that solve a lot of problems? Kill off all of one race or the other—it did not matter which—and all the hatred and fear, resentment and envy, of the one for the other would disappear. The surviving race would then be much freer to live in love and charity for the rest of time. And if, as Adaba believed, there was no essential difference between men, whatever their skin colors might be, what the hell difference did it make which survived, black or white? So go ahead, Buck, and get all your nigger brothers and sisters killed, and improve the moral condition of the human race.

Adaba grinned sourly. The only trouble was, he did not care to have his brothers and sisters killed.

Buck had finished work on the lean-to. He crawled in on his hands and knees and sat beside Adaba. "Hey," he said, "you supposed to be sleeping."

Adaba shook his head. He wondered how to tell Buck. He said, "Buck, how much farther you reckon we got to go?"

"Can't be much farther."

"Didn't somebody we met a night or two back say it was five or six days?"

"Oh, hell, he didn't know nothing."

Adaba decided there was only one way to tell him, and that was straight out. "I don't think I'm gonna make it."

Buck stared at him. "What the hell you talking about?"

"I feel that Angel coming for me, Buck. Could be I ain't gonna get to your Aunt Zule in time."

"You talking crazy." Buck sounded scared. "You talking crazy 'cause you got a little fever, is all, and you ain't—"

"Now, now. I ain't dead yet. And I ain't giving up. I just said, that goddam Angel been fluttering mighty close this morning. Don't want to waste no time getting to that Aunt Zule. But, Buck, if I do die off—"

"You ain't gonna!"

"That's right, but if I do, I want you to promise me something, Buck."

Adaba waited for some sign that Buck was willing to make a promise on that basis, but the man's eyes were as hard as if he were an enemy.

"A promise, Buck? A deathbed promise?"

"Tell me what it is."

"Want you to give up this here life we been living. Want you to go north for good—"

"I ain't never going north for good, not while there's a slave nigger in this here country."

Adaba shook his head. "You go north, Buck. Get yourself a good little gal and do all the things I want to do if I live. Like having a good hot meal by a fireside and afterward maybe some loving. That's two things neither of us had much of in our whole lives, Buck, hot food and nice loving, and I figure we earned them. Now, ain't that right?"

Buck's hard eyes turned away. "I reckon."

"So if I die, you got to go north for good and have them things for both of us. I want you to promise."

"That what you gonna do if you live?"

"Yes, I surely am."

"You're a goddam liar."

"Buck, please—"

"You gonna be down here helping niggers north till the day you die."

Adaba laughed weakly. "Well, right now it do look that way."

"But you ain't gonna die yet. Not for a long time yet."

"But if I do. Buck, promise me."

"All right," Buck said harshly, "I promise," and he moved quickly out of the lean-to without looking back.

No, you don't promise, Adaba thought. *It's you that's the goddam liar. And I got to look after you.*

So go away, Angel. Ain't ready to die yet. Somehow got to keep on going.

The rain was falling now, gently, but Buck, sitting outside the lean-to, hardly noticed. Grief put a pain in his throat and an ache in his gut. *Got to save Johnny,* he thought. *Got to. Can't let him die on me.*

Losses. First his father, and then his mother, so long ago. Died in bondage. *A nigger and a slave. And don't you never forget it.* . . . And then the young Vachel, the betrayer, who might just as well be considered dead . . . and then Claramae . . . dead, though she still haunted Buck . . . and now Adaba, Johnny Dove.

Can't let him die!

But how to save him?

Of course, if Adaba did die, Buck had not the slightest intention of keeping his promise. If Adaba did die, Buck would have one more reason for staying in the South. He was not here merely to help blacks escape north, but to exact payment, to get his revenge. That, it sometimes struck him, was the most important thing: *somebody had to pay!*

Yes: it struck him again, that simple, mind-clearing thought: somebody had to pay. Nat Turner had known that, and his men had taken half a hundred lives. Denmark Vesey had known that and had planned the murder of all whites except for a few supporters. Gabriel Prosser too had known and had planned to kill most whites. Whites were right to fear slave revolts. Freedom and revenge went together, and given the chance, many black men would kill.

The thought grew clearer: an uprising, a bloody, murderous insurrection. Wasn't that really the answer, the only answer? How else were blacks ever to be free? He and Adaba had been leading blacks to freedom for years, and what good had it done? A handful of lives taken to the North—while more black babies were born, and there were more slaves in the South than ever.

But the more slaves, the greater the army of vengeance: an army that would grow even larger as it marched, an army that would sweep the countryside, sweep the cities, an army that would strike down the whites and break the chains and make every black forever free.

What was Adaba's life compared with that? What was his own? For that, he would gladly die.

He lifted his face to the gentle rain and smiled. The pain in his throat had eased. Insurrection: it was only a dream, of course, but it was a healing dream, and one day there would come an hour and place when the great march was ready to begin. And if only he, Black Buck, could be there . . .

He moved onto his hands and knees to crawl back under the lean-to. He had to get his rest. Neither he nor Adaba was ready to die yet.

The early morning rain soon ended, leaving a silver gray sky. The river banks moved steadily by, as the long, narrow, shallow-draft vessel made good time under the patroon's skilled commands, and watching the men at the poles, Justin was reminded of ancient galley slaves.

After having spent a number of years out of the South, it was an odd sensation. The western world, as most intelligent people realized, was undergoing some of its greatest changes in a thousand years. Kings might remain, but divine right was dying. Industry was growing by leaps and bounds, and iron and steam would very soon rule. And in a matter of a few generations, slavery had become almost unthinkable to millions of people—they wondered how it could have been tolerated for so long. *We are modern now.* And yet sentiment in the South, and most certainly in South Carolina, was going increasingly against the tide of the times. Here cotton would always be king (or rice, if that was your crop), and slavery was a positive good and a God-given right. And here he stood, Justin Sabre, watching galley slaves at work, as if time had forever stood still.

He was glad he had helped the two blacks to escape. But to help them escape was one thing; to suggest that they meet him at Sabrehill, where he himself was unwelcome, was quite another. Why in God's name, he wondered repeatedly, had he ever done such a thing? Couldn't he have found other ways, possibly even better ways, to help the pair? Well, it was too late for misgivings. Adaba and Buck might be waiting for him at Sabrehill at this very moment.

He did not really expect Cousins Aaron and Joel to shoot him down, or even to drive him off of Sabrehill after all these years; but he could hardly help Adaba and Buck without his cousins becoming aware of what he was doing. And how could he explain? Aaron would understand Justin's feelings in the matter much faster than Joel would, but even he would hardly approve of aiding and abetting runaways. If Justin remembered correctly, helping a slave to escape in South Carolina was considered to be the same as stealing him; and the penalty for that was death. And the penalty for harboring an escaped slave was a fine of up to $1000 and imprisonment at the discretion of the court. Justin had not been overly worried about being caught helping with the escape, but he had no right to ask his cousins knowingly to harbor fugitives. And when they found out . . .

Why the *hell* had he sent the two blacks to Sabrehill! Suddenly he thought of Lucy. Yes, perhaps that was the answer. He had no right to return to Sabrehill, and he had wanted an excuse. An excuse to find out about Lucy. For years he had carefully kept her out of his mind, hardly giving her so much as a random thought, and God knew how difficult that had sometimes been. But now, finding himself so close to Sabrehill . . .

Or was he merely "finding himself" so close? Had not Lucy been in the back of his mind during the whole trip down from Virginia? Even after all these years, didn't conscience still haunt him? Of course, it was highly unlikely that she would still be at Sabrehill, but at least Cousin Aaron could tell him, yes, she married a good man and has fine children and could not possibly be happier.

But he did not care to dwell on that likelihood. Love was long over, stifled by time and infidelity and a desperate act of will; yet he wanted to think of her as he had once known her: young and eager for life, with all of her illusions still intact. Too bright, too untamed, too much woman for the lads around her . . . and yet ready . . . oh, yes, so ready. . . .

He smiled to himself. *Damned near too much woman for me too, truth to tell. As much woman in her way as any I've ever known.*

Damned near too much woman, but not quite. He remembered that hot Sunday afternoon when they had first consummated their love . . . lying in the grass together by a lazy stream . . . her dress slipping from her shoulder, her bare breast dazzling him . . . his lips touching the pink crown . . . his unbelieving hand moving from knee to thigh to hip, finding only smooth bare flesh. He had wanted her as he had wanted no other woman in his life, and he had hesitated for only a moment.

"Justin, you come back here to me, you hear?"

He had understood then. The prize was his. He had won it. And if he failed to take it, he was not the man for Lucy Sabre.

He had returned to her in a rush, tossing away his clothes, and together they had pulled off her dress. All secrets had been revealed at last, all questions answered, and he could have sworn that as he took her she cried out "Hallelujah!"

She had been his, from then on, more fully than he would ever have believed possible. She had crept into his bed that very same night, and he into hers the night after. They had sought opportunities every day, at their leisure when possible, in haste if necessary, the risk, the adventure, spicing their love. She had been his ally, his conspirator, his lover, his very dearest friend. She had been his hands, his body, his life. He had never known that a woman's love could be so unqualified, so unstintingly given, so fierce and uninhibited. And in all his life he had never been happier.

And then that damned fool Vachel Skeet had challenged him to the duel that had nearly ended both of their lives.

He had learned something more about Lucy then.

"She breathe the life back into you," Aunt Zule had told him, when the darkness had cleared. "Her more than me save you. She breathe the life back in you, boy, and put a little piece of her soul deep down in you, or you be dead by now."

He knew that was true. From the moment he had opened his eyes, he had felt her *lifting* him back toward life, *insisting* that he live, *thrusting* the life back into him. When he had been unable to fight off death, she had done it for him. And when the battle was won and she returned to his bed, it had been as wife as much as lover.

He had found a treasure such as he had never in his life had any right to expect.

And he turned his back on it.

For another woman.

The silver gray sky darkened like tarnish as the day waned, and the patroon commanded the craft closer to the left bank. "Just ahead," Tradwell said. "You'll see it just ahead. Like I say, far's I know the Sabres still run it."

Justin did not remember having seen Sabre's Landing from the river, and yet he recognized it: the boat house and the broad wharf and the line of trees behind. The great house, high on the bluff, seemed lonely and ghostlike in the evening light.

"Keep an eye open for those Rogans when you go back up the river," Justin said. "I don't think they'll bother you, but you never can tell."

"I'll do that."

Justin was ready when the cotton box scraped by the landing. He threw his gear ahead of him and, rifle in hand, jumped onto the wharf. He turned and waved to Tradwell, and for just an instant he had an impulse to leap back again. But of course, he could not do that. The boat moved on.

He hoisted his gear to his shoulder and crossed the landing and a rutted wagon path and went through the row of trees. He stopped and looked up the broad green slope of park. It was just as he had remembered it: a great brick house, two and a half storeys, eight tall columns before the piazza. Elaborate formal gardens at each end, each with its gazebo. Lucy had loved working in the gardens. The passage door was open, and a light burned within, but that was the only light he saw from the house. From where he stood, he could just make out the roof of the plantation office, to the right of the big house, but none of the other outbuildings.

He put down his gear and his rifle and stood there for many minutes, feeling tired and dispirited and a little sick at the prospect of what might lie ahead of him.

At length he picked up gear and rifle and started walking slowly up toward the house.

Because of Ettalee.

Why was it, Lucy wondered, that she felt a small, sneaking resentment against the child, though the child was the altogether helpless victim? If anyone were blameless, it was surely Ettalee. And yet there it was: *Why did you have to let yourself get caught? Why can't you behave like a normal child again and let our people forget?* Lucy felt ashamed of herself.

But it was true: Ettalee was not surviving her wounds of the soul. And the people of Sabrehill knew it and were not forgetting. And Lucy felt it and saw it wherever she went. All of Sabrehill was infected with hatred and sickness and despair.

Even Leila, the housekeeper, and Momma Lucinda, the cook. Lucy had thought she had grown close to Leila in the past couple of years, but now the small beautiful black woman avoided her eyes and retreated to a world of her own. "Leila, have I done something to offend you?" "Course not, Miss Lucy, why you say that?" And she would hurry from the room before Lucy could answer. And Lucinda, who had been so close to her, Lucinda, who had been like an older sister, had become silent, pensive, and somehow aloof. *My God,* Lucy thought, *I don't even have a woman here I can depend on anymore.*

After supper, eaten in the office while she worked on the plantation records, she pulled a shawl over her shoulders and went out to the blacksmith shop to see Ettalee. A little light from the various buildings touched the lane, but it seemed empty and bleak. Saul greeted Lucy with a curt nod at his door and silently stood out of her way as she entered his room. Ettalee was dressed, but she was huddled at the head of the bed, a blanket around her.

Lucy was shocked. She had looked in on Ettalee only a few days before, but in that short time the girl had obviously lost a lot more weight. Her eye sockets were hollow, her face blank except for a permanent shadow of fear.

Lucy sat down on the side of the bed. Ettalee showed no sign of knowing that she was there. When Lucy touched her, fingers gentle on her cheek, the girl did not move.

"Ettalee . . . Ettalee, I do hope you're feeling better."

The girl might have been a statue carved in dark wood.

"Ettalee, please do feel better."

There was still no response.

"Ettalee . . ."

"Answer Miss Lucy," Saul said.

And at last the girl's lips moved. "I'se better." But the voice was only a whisper.

"You've got to get better, Ettalee. You've got to get better, for all of us. For the sake of your father, for me, for all—"

"It wasn't her done what was done to her," Zulie's hard voice cut in, and Lucy turned to see her for the first time, standing tall in a corner of the room, her arms folded under her high, pointed breasts. "It wasn't her done it."

"I wasn't blaming her, Zulie," Lucy said, but she felt a pang of guilt.

"It wasn't her done it, it was Mr. Skeet, and ain't nobody going forget that."

"I 'member more'n year back," Saul said quietly. " 'Member patrol come here, big patrol looking for white woman. And Mr. Skeet and Mr. Jeppson and Mr. Bassett, they come to this house. And Mr. Bassett, he say what they going do to that white woman. And he say they don't find that white woman, they going do it to my Ettalee. My Ettalee dream bad after that. She dream and dream and dream and . . ." Saul began to shake. Over his thick beard, his face was pinched with pain.

"And now Mr. Skeet do what they say, and *nobody make him pay!*"

And nobody ever would, Lucy knew, in spite of all the laws against the abuse of slaves that might be passed. Nobody ever would.

"I'm sorry, Saul."

"Sorry!" Saul said contemptuously. "Sorry be fine medicine for my Ettalee!"

Lucy turned to Zulie. "Can't you help her? Isn't there anything you can do?"

"Do what I can," the woman said sullenly.

"Is there anything *I* can do?"

The silence in the room was the answer. It said, *You are not wanted here. You are in a black man's house, and you are white.* It said, *We may be slaves, but our lives are our own, and you are intruding on us.* It said, *Turn your back. Hide your face. Go away.*

She wanted to say, *But I am your friend. I have never been your enemy. I've always done the best I could for you. There has even been love between us—some of us.*

The silence said, *That does not matter now. Love is not enough. Your love, Miss Lucy, warms nobody but yourself.*

There was no answer to that, and nothing more to be said. Lucy turned back to Ettalee and started to kiss the child's cheek, but they, their silence had made her feel that she had no right. She stood up from the bed.

"In any case, let me know if there *is* anything I can do. And let me know every day how Ettalee is. . . . I am speaking to you, Zulie."

"Yes, ma'am."

When Lucy stepped out of the shop, the lane was no longer empty. More than a dozen people stood about in small groups, all of them looking toward the shop. Some of them she knew quite well. Saul's son, Wayland, was there with his wife, Isa, and her father, Gabriel, the gardener. Cheney was with Old Walter. Hayden, a one-time driver, was there, standing alone in the shadows. Several of the younger men, Cawley, Hannibal, and Solon, were there together. And there were others—all of them unnaturally quiet, all of them swiftly looking away from the blacksmith shop and avoiding her eyes.

She started along the lane, started back toward the office. In the past there had been nods, smiles, casual greetings. Now there was nothing. It was as if she were invisible, as if they wished her vanished and out of their lives. She felt the heavy thud of her heart, felt it pounding in her ears, and she realized she was frightened. This was one of the few times in her life that she had been afraid while among her people.

"Good evening, Cheney," she said as she passed the chief driver. Her voice was steadier than she could have hoped.

"Evening, ma'am." Cheney mumbled the words without looking at her. It was as if he were ashamed of having to say them.

"Cheney, please come with me."

He followed silently. She wondered what would have happened if he had refused. The people did that sometimes, as she well knew. *Don't you order me! Won't be no slave to nobody!* And then came the whips. But she was a white woman alone on this vast plantation, and she had never ordered a whipping in her life. She was not certain she was capable of it, and how could she enforce such an order against this damning silence?

If all of her people were to turn against her . . .

Aware of movement behind her, movement that made her heart pound harder, she led the way along the lane. She dared not look back. The office, when they reached it, gave the illusion of sanctuary, and she turned up the lamp.

"Cheney, what is going on?"

Cheney stared at the floor. "Going on, ma'am?"

"Yes, Cheney, what is happening?"

"Ain't nothing happening, ma'am—"

"Tell her." It was Jebediah Hayes, stepping in through the doorway. "You might as well tell her, man, or I will."

Cheney looked at Jebediah defiantly, and Lucy thought he was going to refuse to speak. But after a moment he shrugged. "Ain't nothing for you to worry about, Miss

Lucy. Just people feeling bad 'cause what happen to little Ettalee."

"There's more to it than that, isn't there, Cheney? More than just feeling bad?"

"Lots of bad things happen, Miss Lucy. Time comes when somebody got to be made to pay."

There it was, gently stated: the threat. Or the promise, or the bill overdue. Lucy heard indefinable sounds outside the office. The shuffling of feet, perhaps, and some whispers and sighs.

"But not Miss Lucy," Jebediah said flatly. "Any of the people got any ideas about Miss Lucy paying?"

"Aw, no," Cheney said quickly, apologetically. "Everybody know Miss Lucy a nice lady, always been good to her people. Everybody know she got Ettalee back, even took a shot at that Mr. Skeet. But . . . excuse me, Miss Lucy, you ain't one of *us*."

No, not one of them. And Lucy remembered that when slave insurrections were planned, the slaves often turned against benefactors as well as enemies. And at this very moment they were gathering outside the office; she heard them, she *felt* them; their silence was like a sea she could drown in.

She hurried to the door. The evening was darkening fast, but she could see that there were at least forty or fifty, and the crowd was still growing. But what did they want? Did they themselves know? What did they expect?

She stared at them. Despite Cheney's words, she felt their threat, a threat which perhaps they themselves only partially realized. Her throat was dry, her palms were wet. What should she say to them? That Ettalee's condition was improving? That Vachel Skeet would be punished? They knew better. Should she promise them good times ahead? Bribe them with promises of Christmas gifts and holiday festivities? She did not think she could insult them so.

Then what? Fifty pairs of eyes were gazing into hers, no longer avoiding the sight of her. Fifty pairs of eyes were staring, unblinking, expectantly.

"I need your help," she heard herself say. "You all

know how sick Saul's Ettalee is. You must help make her well. I want you all to go back to your houses now, and I want each of you to say a prayer for Ettalee. And tomorrow I want each of you to go to Ettalee and tell her what you have done. I think it will help her if she knows. Now, please. Please go to your houses and do as I have asked."

For a moment no one moved, and Lucy had the feeling that not a word had been heard. At any instant now they would do something terrible to her, they would drown her in their silence. Then the silence broke, though nothing was said. A few eyes lowered from hers, a few people turned away, and there was movement in the crowd. The incident was over.

Lucy left the doorway. She sank into a chair. She heard Jebediah tell Cheney to see that the people really did go back to their houses. Not until her long shuddering sigh did she realize that she had been holding her breath. She wanted to weep.

"I was frightened, Jebediah," she said.

"Yes, ma'am. You and I know that, but they don't."

"I didn't know what to do."

"You spoke to them very well."

"But the next time . . ." Lucy put her elbows on a desk top and rested her forehead on her hands. "Sometimes I do get so tired. On any other plantation of this size, there would be a master and a mistress and at least one chief overseer and probably two or more assistant overseers. Here there are only you and I. How do we do it, Jebediah?"

"Well, you'll meet some some nice man one of these days, Miss Lucy, and you'll get married, and he'll hire a white overseer, maybe an older, experienced one with a couple of sturdy sons for assistants, and—"

"We need somebody, Jebediah! We really need somebody badly!"

"Yes, ma'am, I think we really do."

"But it's so hard to find the right person."

Somewhere nearby a dog barked, and a second soon joined it. Lucy lifted her forehead from her hands. There was movement in the gathering darkness outside the office doorway. The vague form resolved itself into a tall man in buckskins, a broad-brimmed hat almost concealing his face. He carried a rifle in his right hand, a blanket roll on his left shoulder. As he came into the doorframe, he dropped the roll to the ground and removed his hat. His face was weary and unshaved and aged beyond its years, and for an instant she could not believe it was really he.

"Cousin Lucy?" Justin Sabre said.

Yes, it was most certainly he.

Oh, no, she thought. *Oh, no, no, no, no. . . .*

Three

. . . oh, no, no, no . . .

She heard the chair fall over behind her, and her hand went to her scarred right cheek, the cheek itself averted from him, and she had never done that before.

"I'm sorry," he said, "I didn't mean to startle . . ."

. . . no, no, no, no . . .

Justin: an older face, yes, a face marred by life's uses, but unmistakably his. Her first true love, her only lover. The father of the child she had never had. The spoiler of dreams. The lover she had had to fight not to love, even after he had deserted her. It all came back to her now, everything she had wanted to forget, all that they had had together, and all the nights she had awakened wanting him no matter what he had done to her. All those nights she had awakened weeping, thinking, *It's all a mistake, it's all a misunderstanding, it's all a bad dream, and he'll come back,* knowing he never would.

And now, like a damaged bride, she shrunk from him, hiding her scar.

. . . no, no, no . . .

He had stepped into the room, and now he was saying something, but it might as well have been babble, for all she understood it. She had to brace herself. She had to try. He was saying something about having stopped by the house but nobody had answered, and he had thought to come back here to the office. Jebediah looked puzzled and wary, not understanding what was happening.

Yes, Justin was here, after all this time, and what was she going to *do* about it? Dear God, what?

How dared he!

Anger welled up at last. How dared he come back here! After what he had done, after the pain he had inflicted, not only on herself, but on her father, on Lucinda and Aunt Zule—how dared he!

Did he actually think he would receive a welcome here? A knave and a rogue he was, by the record, but was he such a fool and so insensitive that he thought he could simply stroll back onto Sabrehill after all these years and make himself at home? Did he think that time pardoned all, that they could now sit back together and laugh merrily at his youthful pranks?

How dared he make her turn her scarred face away from him, as if *he,* of all people, made her feel ashamed of it!

The pepperbox pistol she had aimed at Vachel Skeet just two weeks before lay at hand. Jebediah had reloaded it. Her hand moved toward it, and for one long hot moment she wanted to pick it up. She wanted to point it at Justin Sabre and draw back the cock, and if he didn't start running and start damned fast, she would damn well give him a home at Sabrehill—permanently.

But no.

No, she was not going to shoot him, of course not. She leaned against the desk, closed her eyes, and took a deep breath. She was not a hysterical woman. She was not silly, she was not unintelligent. She had too much dignity to go throwing pistol balls at ex-lovers who reappeared, or to scream or weep like a ninny, or for that matter, to smile like a fool. Whatever Justin had taken from her, he had been unable to take her dignity, and she would not allow him to take it now. And she would *not ever* turn her face from him again.

"Cousin Lucy . . . are you all right?"

"Of course, Justin. As you say, you startled me."

"I'm sorry," Justin said again. "I'm sorry to intrude like this."

She straightened up from the desk and turned to face him. She looked at his grave, concerned face and reminded herself that a dozen years had passed. She looked him in the eyes.

"You are not intruding," she said. "You are a Sabre, a member of the family, and as such, always welcome here. Welcome to Sabrehill, Cousin Justin."

Yes, somehow she would take his visit in stride, live through it, and leave it in the past, one more thing to be put out of mind and forgotten. Meanwhile, there were things to be done, orders to be given, and that made matters easier than they might otherwise have been. She dismissed Jebediah, telling him to find Leila and have her report in the passage of the big house. She took a kind of bitter comfort in noting that Justin appeared, if anything, more diffident, more disconcerted by their meeting, than she.

"I wouldn't have bothered you," he said as he followed her toward the big house, "but you see, I was traveling down the river, and . . ."

"And you look weary. You were wise to stop here for a rest. You will stay as long as we can keep you."

"I could use a few days' rest." Justin managed a smile. "I must say, I'm a little surprised to see you here."

"But why?"

"Why . . . I thought most likely you'd married and gone off."

"I'm a widow, Cousin Justin."

"I'm sorry."

"You needn't be. It's an ancient episode." *As is ours.*

"And your father and your uncle?"

"Dead."

"I keep saying I'm sorry. But I am. And your sisters?"

"Gone, Cousin Justin, gone," Lucy said, oddly irritated by his questions, "but we can talk about all that later, if you wish. I am sure you would like to clean up from your journey first and have some supper." And she would ask him no questions about his life, none at all.

The housekeeper met them in the passage. "Leila," Lucy said, "you remember Mr. Justin, don't you?"

Leila looked blankly at Justin. "Yes, ma'am, I sorta do."

"Leila was only about ten, as I recall," Justin said. "She has grown up to be a very pretty young woman."

Leila did not acknowledge the pleasantry. She continued to gaze at Justin in the dull, witless way that she often used as a defense against unfriendly white folks.

"Mr. Justin will be our guest for a nice long stay, Leila. He will be in his old room, the one across from mine. Please have hot water and a tub brought to him as quickly as possible. Tell Lucinda that I want her to prepare a hot meal for him—"

"Please, Cousin Lucy," Justin interrupted, "that's too much trouble."

"Our hospitality is no trouble at all. Can you be ready for your supper in . . . an hour?"

"An hour would be fine, if I can get that hot water right away."

"Leila, when Mr. Justin comes downstairs for his supper, please have your girls make up his room." Lucy was aware that she was sounding too crisply efficient, too demonstratively capable, but she could not help herself. "Ask Irish to assign a boy to Mr. Justin and to have a fire built in his room."

"Yes, Miss Lucy."

Leila headed for the kitchen house. Lucy conducted Justin up the stairs, led him to his room, and saw to it that he had light.

"I hope you will be comfortable."

"I am sure I shall be, Cousin Lucy."

Lucy took a last look around the room and realized that suddenly it was real for her again. Most of her life it had been simply "the room across from mine," a room she rarely entered. For a time, while Justin was at Sabre-hill, it had become the most important room in the house, but afterward she had abandoned it, avoided it, cast all thoughts of it out of her mind. Except for quick inspections of the maids' work, keeping herself blind to everything but dust, she had not really *been in* this room in years . . .

. . . this room where so much had happened between Justin and herself . . . this room where she had given him such love. . . .

"Lucy . . . ?"

"I was . . . I was just wondering . . ." Her voice was dismayingly uncertain. "I was wondering if I had forgotten anything."

"No, I don't think so. I'll be fine, Cousin Lucy."

"Then I shall look forward to seeing you downstairs."

Lucy hurried from the room, quietly closing the door behind her.

Their first two full hours together were less difficult than she had expected. Justin appeared in the dining room in fresh but rumpled clothes, apologetic about his appearance. Traveling, he carried no more with him than was necessary. His clothes could be pressed tomorrow, Lucy said, and perhaps some of her father's clothes would fit him. She immediately regretted the impulsive suggestion and wondered why she had made it.

One of the kitchen girls brought Justin's plate of food to him. Another brought a pot of coffee. Lucy sat at the head of the table. She had thought to put the length of the table between them but had changed her mind. Justin sat on her right, in the circle of soft lamplight, where they could more easily share the coffee. Now that he had refreshed himself, he looked younger, less weary, more at ease.

He soon finished his meal and poured coffee for both of them, and Lucy poured brandy. And they chatted, about the quick and the dead of Sabrehill, about her father and her uncle, her sisters and her cousins, and Lucinda and Aunt Zule and the many others. He sensed that she wished to say nothing of her late husband, and held his peace, and she was grateful. And so she was now all alone here at Sabrehill? Yes, she was, aside from her people. But she had a good overseer? Yes; the young black man he had seen her with earlier. But didn't her neighbors object to that? Occasionally, when they had nothing better to fuss their feathers over.

She gave up her determination to ask him no questions

about his own life. After all, why shouldn't she?—she was growing curious in spite of herself. How was his family, how was his older brother, Zachary? Why, Zachary was fine, still running the plantation in Virginia and fuming about those fools in Washington. And what had Justin been doing all these years? Not planting, as he had expected. He had had some money and had invested well. And he had traveled a great deal. Certain doctors had recommended Switzerland for his ailing wife's health, and certain others had recommended Italy, Greece, the south of France. And how was his wife?

"Rosellen is dead, Lucy."

So he too had left his dead behind. He was a widower, as she was a widow. She might have guessed. "Very ill," he had said of his bride in that awkward letter long ago, "extremely ill, and the doctors can only hope. . . ." He had suffered his own losses over the years. It had never occurred to her that he might, but there was no reason why it should have. He had existed in her life only to be forgotten.

"Do you have any children?"

"Two boys and a girl. They're with Zachary and his family right now."

Two boys and a girl . . . Lucy thought of her own lost child and felt an unexpected pang of jealousy. She could not stop the thought: *They might have been our children . . . yours and mine. . . .*

But she did not wish to have such thoughts. She wished to keep Justin firmly in his place: the distant relative, the guest in the house. She turned resolutely to another subject.

"You haven't told me why you are traveling," she said.

"Time I settled down. My children speak three languages and smatterings of God only knows how many others. Time they saw more of their own country. Anyway, you know how it is with our kind of people—we belong to the land. We're born for it and trained for it, and I've missed that. Zachary got our family plantation, and with one thing and another, I've never gotten one of

my own. So I thought I'd start looking. Thought I'd travel
down through the piedmont, go slowly, ask questions, get
acquainted with the country all over again. Well, I got
this far and thought I'd seen enough in these parts. I
plan now to go to Charleston, take a packet to Savannah,
look around there, and then head for Alabama and Mississippi. Maybe go clear to Texas. Texas sounds mighty
interesting these days."

"But you want your children to see 'our country.'
Texas isn't our 'country.' "

"It will be, one of these days. And maybe, just maybe,
in Texas a man can find a way to raise some kind of
money crop without using slaves."

"You've turned abolitionist, Cousin Justin?"

Justin poured more coffee. He added sugar to his and
stirred it. He stared away from Lucy, into a dark corner
of the room, as if looking at something that she could
not see.

"Lucy," he said, "I came down the river to Sabrehill
on a cotton box. It had some other passengers, ragtag
and bobtail name of Rogan. They were father and grown
son, two of the saddest, meanest, ugliest devils you ever
saw. And with them they had a couple of blacks, blacks
in chains. Now, you wouldn't expect ragtag like that to
own slaves, and I suspect that these were a pair of captured marooners from a camp that was raided about ten
days ago. I don't know. They looked pretty mean themselves, and apparently one of them was wounded. God
knows they were in a pathetic state—underclothed, under-
fed, bleeding. And all the damn drunken Rogans knew to
do with them was to keep on whipping them, keep on
beating them, keep on abusing them. The Rogans said
they planned to sell the blacks, but, Lucy, those boys were
not going to live to be sold. The way they were being
treated, they'd be lucky to last more than a few more
days.

"Now, Lucy, don't tell me that wasn't typical treatment
of a slave—I know that. But that's not the point. The
point is that simply because those two were black, because they were slaves, because of an accident of birth,

there was not a damn thing they could do. Except escape, if they could, or kill the Rogans, if they could, and get hung for it. Because they were black."

Justin sighed and shook his head. "Anyway, Lucy, I've come to realize that I can't live with that. I simply cannot live with slavery, and I cannot understand those who do. Even though I've been one of them. I've been away from the South too long. I've lived out in the world too long, and the world is changing, thank God, and so have I."

Lucy was struck by the quiet passion in Justin's voice, profound and bitter. It almost stilled her. But there was one thing he had said that she could not allow to pass unanswered.

"You say you cannot understand those who do live with slavery, Cousin Justin. You must indeed have been away from the country a great deal. You must indeed have been away from the country a great deal. You seem to have forgotten that some of us consider it a moral obligation to live with slavery."

"A *what?*" Justin looked incredulous.

"I have listened to you, Justin; now hear me out. I can remember my father saying only a few years ago that he had never met a truly intelligent man who believed that slavery was right. Of course, he was living somewhat in the past—"

"He certainly was. Even intelligent Southerners are going mad trying to rationalize slavery."

"I agree, but please listen. Some of us still believe, as most of our forefathers did, that an economy based on slavery is wicked. Like our forefathers, we hope and believe that it will gradually die out."

"But it is not dying out, Lucy, not in the South. It is solidifying."

"I hope you are wrong. But in any case, meanwhile, I have a great many people who depend on me. Somehow I have to keep them adequately sheltered and fed and clothed. Somehow I have to try to give them some semblance of a decent life, even an enjoyable life. It's a moral obligation, Justin. Or am I simply to let my people go free?"

"You could."

"Yes, if the law allowed that, or even against the law. But free for what? Free to starve, Justin. And starving, to get into desperate trouble. And getting into trouble, to die. Because most of them are not ready for freedom; they are illiterate and unskilled and have been sheltered from responsibility. It's as simple as that. I can never leave Sabrehill, not for any great length of time. I could never sell Sabrehill and its people, even if I wanted to, unless I was absolutely certain that the new owners would take at least as good care of the people as I do. I'm trapped here by my obligation, Justin, in much the same way that my people are trapped."

"Trapped at Sabrehill," Justin said ironically. "Trapped in this great empty house with its fifteen or twenty rooms, not to speak of the attic and cellar rooms—"

Lucy's face warmed. "Exactly."

"—while your people are trapped in their comfortable little cabins with their decent enjoyable lives. And what are you doing to prepare your people for freedom, Lucy?"

Lucy refused to be goaded into an angry answer. "Cousin Justin, I have been managing Sabrehill Plantation for only two years. Frankly, I had little idea of what I was doing when I started, and I have had my hands full. But I certainly intend to do everything I can for my people. And I have no illusions that it will be easy. I remember what happened when my father allowed black children into our schoolhouse. Twice our neighbors— somebody—burned it down. But each time it was rebuilt, and we still have it, and one day it will be used again."

"And one day it will be burned down again." Some of his earlier weariness returned to Justin's face. "I'm sorry, Lucy, I've been braying like a pompous Yankee jackass. Of course you'll do your best for your people. And I suppose that sooner or later I'll be like you—I'll wind up buying a Mississippi sugar plantation, and I'll work it with slaves, and I'll tell myself that my people are lucky that I'm such a kindly master and don't work them to death."

"You think I'm a hypocrite?"

"No!" Justin looked stricken. "Lucy, I didn't mean it that way at all!"

"Then what did you mean?"

"I mean that you *will* do your best for your people, and you'll never deceive yourself that slavery is anything but evil. But I'm not as good a person as you. I am more apt to slip into hypocrisy and self-deceit. And that's why I can no longer live with slavery, Lucy. That's why I don't even dare try."

Lucy gazed at Justin's profile. Was this really the same cousin she had known a dozen years before? Yes, it was, in spite of the mature bone that had been added to the high forehead and the long jaw line. But that earlier Justin, it struck her, had been little more than a boy. And this was a man.

They talked on for a time, careful not to let the past intrude too much. Better now to be new acquaintances than old lovers. Lucy caught Justin trying to hide a yawn.

"You stopped at Sabrehill to rest," she said. "I imagine your room is ready by now, and there's no need for you to entertain me. Why don't you go to bed, Justin?"

Justin nodded. "Surprising how tired a man can get, just sitting on a bale of cotton." Lucy remained at the table as he got up and went to the door to the passage. He turned to look at Lucy. "Again," he said, "I am sorry to intrude."

"Again, Justin, you are welcome here."

He nodded again. "Good night, Luz," he said, and he disappeared into the passage.

Luz . . .

Lucy sat paralyzed. The name had come as a stunning blow. She did not think there had been any calculation in Justin's saying it; it had simply slipped out, and he himself was probably unaware of what he had said.

She had forgotten the name. She had forgotten that he had called her that. It was one of those many things she had deliberately put out of mind and not thought of in the past dozen years. And yet it seemed to carry the meaning of everything good they had once had between them.

Luz . . .

"You feeling all right, Lucy-child?"

It was Momma Lucinda, with one of her girls, clearing the table.

"Yes, I'm all right, Lucinda."

"Don't like that man being here. You say so, I run him off myself."

"No need. He won't be here long."

"Glad to hear it. Now, you go get yourself some sleep, you hear me?"

"Yes, Lucinda. Good night."

Lucinda and the girl left. Lucy stayed at the table for a time, lingering over her brandy. When she had finished, she went out into the passage and started up the stairs toward her room.

Twelve years, she thought.

It had been such a long time.

"Ah, Luz . . . Luz . . . Luz . . ."

"Good morning, Lucinda."

"Morning, sir."

Lucinda entered the dining room carrying a tray. A twelve-year-old boy followed her. She was carefully blank faced, as stolid as Leila had been the night before, and her eyes never quite met Justin's as she put his breakfast on the table.

Odd, but he had not been able to recall her face, and yet he recognized her at once, just as he had recognized Lucy. And he now remembered with utmost clarity how she had laughed softly on that Sunday afternoon in the kitchen house long ago and had said, "Whyn't you two get out of here. Go take a walk somewhere." And he and Lucy had taken that walk, and for the first time they had . . . So much was pouring out of the back recesses of his mind, memories that he had long forbidden himself.

"It's nice to see you again," he said.

"Yes, sir."

That was all: a meaningless *yes, sir,* without meeting his eyes. She picked up the tray and started out of the room.

"Thank you, Lucinda."

"Rayburn here your boy. You want something, you tell him."

She left quickly.

So that was how it was to be. Those closest to Lucy

would treat him as a kind of nonpresence while he was here, as a kind of harmless ghost. But he must be a rather substantial ghost, for when he had awakened that morning, after sleeping very late, someone had put a fire on the grate for him, polished his boots, and pressed and rehung his clothes. And for a ghost, he was extraordinarily hungry.

The Ghost of Sabrehill, he thought, wryly amused. Well, he was damned if he was going to spend his few hours or days here brooding on the metaphysics of the situation or on what an intrusive fool he was. Last night Lucy had shown every sign of being able to cope with his presence quite nicely, thank you, and if she could do that, he was not going to stand around with a bowed head, blushing like an idiot. A man could not go around every minute behaving like some kind of two-legged, walking apology. He would simply try not to overburden Lucy with his presence.

He hurried through his breakfast, feeling better every minute and more determined to get this jackassery done with. Actually the prospects seemed brighter than they had the day before—probably because he felt it would be easier to deal with Lucy, a woman, than with Aaron and Joel. If Adaba and Buck managed to reach Sabrehill and find shelter here, they would eventually make contact with Justin. They could rest a few days while Justin bought horses and some kind of carriage. They could meet along the road and then travel together, a Virginia gentleman and his servants. Of course, the "servants" might very well cut his throat, especially that Buck, but somehow Justin trusted Adaba. They would manage to get north together.

Mr. Abolitionist, Adaba had called him.

My God, he thought, *me! a Sabre! a conductor on the Underground Railroad!* He laughed aloud, and the boy, standing nearby, looked startled.

"Rayburn," Justin said, "can you tell me where Miss Lucy is?"

"She be in the office, last I seen."

"Thank you, Rayburn. Somebody gave my boots a nice polish. Did you do that?"

The boy looked pleased. "Yes, sir, master."

"Well, I thank you again. I'll tell you what, I'm going to talk to Miss Lucy. Why don't you go play now, but keep an eye open for me. When I'm through talking to Miss Lucy, I want you to take me around and show me things and say hello to the people for me. Do you think you can do that?"

"Oh, yes, master. I know 'most everybody."

"Good. You go on, then."

The boy sped off. He would be useful, Justin thought, in penetrating the Negro community.

As Rayburn had suggested, he found Lucy in the office, and she was as lovely by daylight at thirty-odd, he decided, as she had been at nineteen by candlelight. In spite of that damned scar. He wondered how she had got it. For some reason he wanted to reach out and touch it.

She looked up brightly and smiled and closed an account book. "And how are you this morning, Cousin Justin?"

"Well rested, thank you, Cousin Lucy."

"I hope Lucinda served you a good breakfast?"

"Nonpareil. The Sabre table continues to be the best in the state." He wondered what was really going on behind that smile and those so-blue eyes.

"Always gallant," she said without irony. "Justin, I've been thinking, we really must arrange some kind of reception or dinner party for you."

"Lucy, no!" Justin was genuinely dismayed. "I'm here for a few days' rest, not to burden your social life. Please, as much as possible, just ignore my presence."

"Now, Justin," Lucy said with gentle firmness, "you must know I cannot do that. My neighbors will soon know that you are here, they will come calling, and you will undoubtedly receive a number of invitations. Now, if you prefer to avoid that, I shall let everyone know that you are here for a badly needed rest but that you look forward to seeing them all, just one time, here at Sabrehill. One party, and no callers until you've had a long rest. It really is the easiest way out for you. And besides," she gave him a quick smile, "I would so like to do it."

"Well . . ." She was right, of course. Justin had long

ago ceased to be a sociable man, and he had not foreseen all of the implications of his return to Sabrehill. Now he began to see what it would cost Lucy in terms of gossip and the everlasting search for scandal. Even though no match had been announced during his last stay, his desertion must have been quite obvious to many people, and now here he was, back after all this time, for a "brief visit." Was she to hide him from the prying eyes and wagging tongues of her neighbors? What could she do, what would she *want* to do, but display him boldly?

"Cousin Lucy," he said, "I shall be honored."

"Bless you. I think perhaps Saturday evening would be best." She turned back to her desk. "Now, if you don't mind, Justin, I do have so much work."

"Not at all. Let me know if I can be helpful. Otherwise, I wonder if you'd mind if I just wandered about Sabrehill a bit, became reacquainted?"

"You do that. Go wherever you please. If you want a horse or a carriage, just ask Zagreus at the stable."

"Thank you."

"And dinner will be at two, Justin, late enough for you to work up an appetite."

"I shall be there, appetite intact."

He stepped out of the office and looked around for Rayburn. Where should he go first? Well, the idea was to let his presence be known here at Sabrehill, known among the slave population as widely as possible, so that the news would reach Adaba and Buck. That should not be too difficult. Justin decided to stroll with Rayburn along the east lane, since that was the closest, stopping at the various outbuildings to chat. He would also do the west lane before dinner if there was time, and later he would—

"Oh, Justin," Lucy called from the doorway of the office.

"Yes, Lucy."

"What are your children's names? You didn't tell me."

"Mark and Catherine Anne and Beau. Born in that order."

"Mark and Catherine Anne and Beau," she repeated, something wistful in her voice. "What lovely names. They must be beautiful children."

Justin waved a dismissive hand. "Savages, all of them. We usually call the girl Katie Anne."

"Katie Anne. I like that." Lucy went back into the office. He though he heard her repeating again, to herself: "Mark and Catherine Anne and Beau."

Skeet was on his way back to Redbird from Riverboro on Wednesday evening when he heard the terrified cry from somewhere in the darkness ahead. He immediately reined up his horse and reached for his pistol. A moment later a shadowy figure broke out of the woods and onto the road. By its carriage and motion, Skeet recognized his overseer.

"Dinkin!"

"Mr. Skeet! Mr. Skeet! That you?"

Skeet urged his horse forward. "It's me, Dinkin. What's the matter?"

"I seen something, Mr. Skeet," Dinkin bawled, "I don't know what! It was in the woods, near the old slave grave-yard. It was moving, Mr. Skeet, kinda swaying, real strange. It was big and dark and giant—it musta been eight feet tall, and it didn't look like nothing I ever seen—"

"Hold on." Skeet got down from his horse. "Now, you tell me what you seen and how you come to see it."

"Well . . ." Dinkin tried to control his panting. "Well, it was 'cause of that goddam Jared. He didn't come out of the fields, and I figured he'd run off again. Or maybe he went over to the Jeppson quarters to see that bitch of his, so I thought I'd go look. And after I started out, I seen these lights, real peculiar, way off in the distance. You know how you can see a light for a mile or more on a clear night. So I figured, hell, I better go look. Might just be the patrol, though what they doing with lights I don't know—"

"Get on with it, Mr. Dinkin."

"So I went walking toward them lights."

"Brave as you please," Skeet said contemptuously.

"Hell, yes. And they was sort of swarming around and blinking and coming and going in the distance, and I got closer and closer until I was almost to the graveyard, and them lights was weaving about, and Mr. Skeet, I thought I heard sounds in there."

"What kind of sounds?"

"Oh, I don't know. A-moaning and a-groaning. Sounds like you never heard on this earth, Mr. Skeet. They was just plumb unnatural! Man'd be a damn fool to get too close to them sounds."

"So you never did find out what was causing them."

"Mr. Skeet, don't you think I was scared. I kept right on going in spite of everything, right straight at them lights till I was 'most to the graveyard. Then all of a sudden, over on the other side of the graveyard, this big dark *thing* came up out of the night—my God, Mr. Skeet, it musta been ten, twelve feet tall, and *big?* I tell you it was big, and it made the goddamnedest noise you ever heard—"

"Was that you I heard yelling when I came down the road, or was it your monster?"

"Well, I . . ." Dinkin hesitated, perhaps preparing a lie. "Well, I don't rightly know, Mr. Skeet. I did yell out, trying to scare that big feller off, but I don't rightly know which you heard, him or me."

Skeet laughed. "And did you scare him off?"

"Don't rightly know that either. He sorta disappeared, and I figured I couldn't find him in the dark all by myself, so I went to get some help, and that's when I saw you coming back to Redbird."

"All right, Mr. Dinkin, let's go look at your mysterious lights and your monster."

"Now?"

"Now, Mr. Dinkin."

He soon saw the lights. They were small, little more than pinpoints. They did not move about, though they did seem to flicker slightly as Skeet got closer. In the near-absolute darkness of the woods at night, it was difficult to judge their distance.

A light had a natural source, Skeet told himself firmly —a candle or a lamp or some other fire.

They came to the edge of the graveyard. On the roots of a tree near the center, several candles stood burning.

Skeet looked about. Starlight penetrated here, and he

could see some of the graves. Many were decorated with broken pottery and colored glass. The rotted remains of an old quilt lay across one grave. There were a number of wooden images, some of them man-size or larger, and most of them snakelike, strangely twisted, and phallic. They were the old idols, the old gods, and it was no use tearing them up and casting them away. That only made the niggers restless, and in time the images would appear again.

"Well, Mr. Dinkin, where's your monster?"

"Guess I scared him off."

Skeet laughed. "Let's take a look at the witching tree." He could have sworn he heard Dinkin swallow.

The half-dozen candles appeared to have been only recently lit. There were patches of wax showing where others had preceded them.

"Don't look like no lights swarming in the night to me, Dinkin. Look like plain ordinary candles."

"I don't like it, Mr. Skeet. Remember what I told you? About them conjure-people over at Sabrehill making spells on us on account of the wench? And not only at Sabrehill, from what I hear. And looks like now they're making spells on us right here at Redbird, right on your own plantation."

"Yeah."

And in the morning there would be dirt freshly strewn on his piazza. If it were not there already. Somehow Skeet knew it.

And he didn't like it. He might laugh and shake his head at the superstitious niggers, but he didn't like it at all. Goddam niggers, Sabrehill niggers, Kimbrough, Buckridge, Devereau niggers, thinking they could spell him, maybe even *his own* niggers, damn their black hides. Didn't make any difference that their spells were a lot of shit—if he caught 'em at it, he would—

"Dinkin," he said, "our niggers talk to the others no matter how you try to keep 'em apart."

"Oh, Mr. Skeet, I don't allow that—"

"Shut up. You tell our niggers, and you tell 'em they can spread the word, I catch any nigger doing voodoo, I'm gonna kill him. Man or woman, I'm gonna nail him up on a wall and cut his parts off'n him a little at a time. He gonna die slow. He gonna pray for the time when I set him on fire so he die. That's *my* kinda voodoo. You tell 'em that, Mr. Dinkin, you tell 'em I'm looking for a nigger to kill."

"Yes, *sir*, Mr. Skeet!" Dinkin was exhilarated by the prospect. "Yes, sir, I surely will tell 'em that!"

Skeet kicked over the candles and stamped them out. He shouldn't leave valuable candles out in a graveyard, he supposed, but he didn't give a damn. The idea of having voodoo candles in his house was disturbing.

Leaving Dinkin behind, he rode swiftly back to the big house. He wanted to find out if dirt had been strewn over the piazza.

It had been.

He stood in the dark, toeing the dirt, feeling it grate under his boot. He felt a force building within himself, the kind of force he had felt that day when he had broken Tag Basset's jaw with a single blow; the kind of force he had felt when he had put the wire loop around Buckley's cock; the kind of force he had felt when the Sabrehill nigger gal had crumbled with fear. Conjure him, would they? Nothing could conjure him. He would break them, shatter them, destroy—

"Mr. Skeet, sir."

He looked around, ready to lash out, though it was Shadrach's voice. Shadrach, who was even more important and useful to him than Dinkin.

"Yeah, Shad?"

"I hear something I think you want to know, sir." There was a kind of satisfaction in the black man's voice, and a touch of contemptuous familiarity. Shadrach took too many liberties.

"Then tell me, goddam it."

"Niggers talking 'bout how Sabrehill got itself a visitor. Old friend of yours."

"What you talking about?"

"Mr. Justin, sir. The minute I hear that name—"

"*Who?*"

"Mr. Justin Sabre. Come on a cotton box a day or two back. They say he—"

"You know what you talking about, boy?"

"Just telling you what the niggers say, Mr. Vachel. Mr. Justin Sabre—"

"Find out if it's the same one. There's lots of Sabres. You find out."

"Yes, sir, I do that."

And if it was . . .

Skeet grinned. He could feel the force growing again, throbbing through him as he stood in the night-dark of the piazza. Break, shatter, destroy. Right was on his side, and nothing could stop him.

There were patterns of debt. Miss Lucy owed him, and he owed Justin. He had never forgotten a debt, and he never would. Payment was due.

Something, somehow, could be arranged.

"Yeah. You do that. . . ."

It was ending, and Buck knew it. His years on the run were almost over. Adaba was all but dead, and Buck was too tired now, too weak and worn for survival.

He had Adaba over his shoulders, and the Rogans' blanket rolls and supply pouches slung at his sides. If he had been willing to abandon Adaba, it would have been a different matter. He would have been able to keep his strength up and take care of himself; he would have found help among the slaves of the countryside. But no one he had met had been able to give Adaba the help he needed, and Buck had forced himself to keep going, as he clung to the feeble hope that Aunt Zule of Sabrehill could save his friend.

He was sure the end was in sight when he blundered into the slave graveyard on Redbird Plantation. At least he thought that was where they were, though he could not be certain after so many years. If he had not been so weary, he would never have made such a mistake; he would have seen the light of the candles, he would have heard the white man. But instead, he had gone groaning, staggering right into the graveyard, Adaba on his shoulders, and the white man had come into full view. Startled, the man had given a yell and run off, but he would certainly be back. These woods would be combed tonight, and before morning . . .

But what could Buck do now but keep on going? And the night's run had hardly begun.

But it was not a run, not any longer. Every step of the way was a pounding, jolting thing, the shoulders sagging under Adaba's weight, the knees threatening to buckle. He stumbled blindly into trees. Limbs tried to sweep Adaba away. Thorned brush clung to Buck's clothes and tore at his flesh, trying to hold him back. And yet he went on . . . and on. . . .

Dawn touched the horizon. Miraculously, there had been no sign of pursuit from the graveyard, and now Buck had to find a place where they could rest again, a place with water and a chance to find food, a place where they could hide through the day.

But there was no such place. In his deep fatigue, he had forgotten how to find one, forgotten how to devise one. Wherever he looked, he saw blacks coming out into the fields, he saw a white man on horseback, and he had to keep going.

No hiding place. No rest, except for stray minutes, before staggering the next few yards.

For all he knew, they had passed Sabrehill.

The sun reached its zenith and moved on.

And Buck knew he could go no farther.

He was at the edge of a patch of woods. The nearby field was lying fallow, and on the far side of a shallow creek was an ancient cabin, apparently abandoned. The roof sagged and the doorway was open. Weeds grew around it, untrampled.

Buck's throat felt like dry stone.

He stepped out of the woods and waded across the stream, heedless of his boots. He carried Adaba into the cabin and lowered him to the floor, trying to be gentle, but Adaba hit and sprawled with a thump. Buck spread one of the blankets over him, then took the other blanket to the stream. After drinking deeply, he soaked one corner of the blanket. Back at the cabin, he squeezed the water into Adaba's mouth and bathed his face.

He stretched out, pulling the damp blanket over himself. The last thing he remembered seeing was a large hole in the sagging roof, and beyond that hole, it seemed, a vast emptiness.

And then he knew they were not alone.

Some sound told him, and he was instantly awake, but he did not move. Every muscle was tense, charged with an energy he had not known he had, ready to defend, to attack, to kill.

He opened his eyes very slowly.

They stood, shadows against the evening, in the open doorway; two boys, aged about fifteen and thirteen. They were staring, fearful, excited, pleased with their discovery, ready to run away at the first alarm. The older of the two nearly ran when he saw Buck's eyes open.

"Please," Buck said softly, "please." He spoke with the thickest field accent he could manage, trying to sound helpless and harmless. "Wheah we at? Don' go 'way. You tell please. Wheah we be?"

"Sabrehill," the younger of the boys said. "This here is Sabrehill."

Four

Sabrehill . . .

It was no dream. By some miracle they had passed through the days and nights of hell to arrive here. Buck felt as if he were awakening from one of his nightmares, but this time with a hope that usually eluded him. Everything would be all right now. If only Adaba were not dead yet, if only he could be helped . . .

"Please," Buck said in the same soft, helpless tone, "you don' tell you massa us heah? You don' tell?"

The boys remained cautiously outside the doorway. "We ain't going tell nobody," the younger one said. "You running away?"

"Yes, sir, we running. Yessirree. That old massa, he whip us so, we run. And he shoot my friend, and we run more. Run all the way down from the hills, a long, long way. And my friend, he so sick."

"Who you?" the older boy asked. He seemed to be the more worried of the two. "Who you, coming 'round Sabrehill?"

Caution was automatic, a survivor's reflex. It was not the time to give the names by which they were best known. Not yet, and perhaps never. Buck wondered who at Sabrehill might recognize him after all these years.

"I'se Samuel," he said. "And my friend, he Jack. Sam and Jack. And who you?"

"Nemo," said the younger of the two. "I'se Nemo and he Tad."

"Nemo and Tad," Buck repeated, sounding as if the names pleased him. "Nemo and Tad, I reckon you know somebody call Aunt Zule at Sabrehill?"

"Aunt Zule?" Tad sounded surprised.

"Nigger way up river, he say at Sabrehill is Aunt Zule. He say Aunt Zule, she help us. Aunt Zule, she make my friend well again."

Tad shook his head. "Aunt Zule dead long time ago."

Out of sheer hope, Buck had discounted that possibility. "Oh, my," he said. "Oh my, oh my."

"But Zulie can help your friend," Nemo said brightly. "Some people say she the best healer at Sabrehill, good as her momma or even better. Some say—"

"Zulie?"

"Aunt Zule's Zulie. She a conjure-woman, make spells just like her—"

"Just like her momma," Buck said. There was hope after all. He had a dim memory of young Zulie, though he had seldom seen her. "She don' tell white massa 'bout me and my friend?"

"Oh, no," Nemo said scornfully, "she don't like white folks at all. She ain't going tell no white masters 'bout you."

"Anyway," Tad said, "ain't no white masters at Sabrehill no more. Is only a white mistress, Miss Lucy. Even the overseer, Mr. Jeb, he nigger like us."

"No Mr. Aaron nor Mr. Joel?" Buck asked wonderingly.

Not that there was any harm, but the words were out before he could stop them. Even with the few hours' rest, even with the defensive surge of energy, Buck's mind felt half-burned out, his cautions inadequate. The boys stared at him.

"What you know about Mr. Aaron and Mr. Joel?" Tad asked. "They long dead too."

"Why, I hear 'bout them from same man tell me 'bout Aunt Zule. Guess he live 'round here long time ago."

The boys accepted that. He could feel their acceptance.

So there was only Miss Lucy here. Buck wondered how in the world that had come about. But it hardly mattered. What mattered was that after their long flight, things were beginning to look considerably better. It seemed that there was indeed help at Sabrehill. And Buck could not believe that a single white person, and a woman at that, posed much of a threat to them on a plantation this big. Not with a conjure-woman who, like Aunt Zule before her, had no love for whites and was willing to help blacks.

"Tad, Nemo," he said, "you don' tell nobody 'bout us? Nobody but Zulie?"

"No," Nemo assured him, "we ain't going tell."

"You, Tad?"

"No," Tad said uncertainly, "I reckon not."

"Aw, he ain't going tell," Nemo said. "We tell Zulie, and she know what to do. You wait here."

Buck nodded. "We wait."

But he did not wait there in the cabin. As soon as the boys had disappeared, he rolled up one of the blankets and slung it from his shoulder. He made sure that Adaba was well covered with the other blanket. He then left the cabin, waded back across the stream, and returned to the woods.

There was nothing more he could do for Adaba. He knew that. But if they were betrayed, he would have one more chance at escape, however slim.

At the edge of the woods he waited.

As he had expected, the boys came back soon after it was fully dark. He was worried at first to see a third figure with them, but then he realized it was a black man.

If they had betrayed Buck and Adaba, almost certainly they would have arrived with a number of whites. Almost certainly, but not quite.

He waited for a minute or two while they looked in the cabin and came back out. He heard their puzzled murmurings. Nemo quietly called out the name Buck had given him: "Sam . . . Sam . . ."

The chance had to be taken. Buck stepped out of the woods. "I'se here," he said.

The cabin was at the corner of the field quarters farthest from the big house. A thin flickering light fell out of the open doorway, and Buck made out three dim figures under the extended front roof. One woman said to another, "Now, don't you worry, them boys ain't going say nothing," and a man said grimly, "They say nothing to nobody. You boys come on!" Tad and Nemo dropped the blankets they were carrying and reluctantly followed their parents away.

On any long march the hardest steps come at the end, after the burden has been laid down. Zagreus, with Adaba across his shoulders, stepped through the doorway as easily as if he were carrying a child, but Buck, following him into the cabin, felt the effort of lifting each foot. He watched as Zag deftly, gently swung Adaba off of his shoulders and onto the bed. The door closed behind him, and he turned to face the woman.

He was perplexed, even faintly shocked. The only light came from a couple of candles and a low fire in the fireplace, but he saw her clearly, and it was like stepping back in time. They must have lied to him: this was Aunt Zule, but an Aunt Zule even younger than he remembered. He thought he even remembered the yellow bandanna that was tied around her small neat head.

For a moment, he thought she must have recognized him. She looked directly and intently into his eyes, as if searching for what might be hidden behind them and taking his measure, but the spark of recognition never came. Without a word, she went past him to the bed where Adaba lay.

She pulled open his shirt, and Buck heard her gasp

when she saw the wounded side. With Zag's help, she
swiftly finished undressing Adaba. She carefully pulled
the crude bandage from his thigh and stared at the wound.
When she turned to look at Buck, her eyes were almost
accusing.

"How long ago he shot?"

How long? A year, a thousand years. "I don't know.
Must be about two weeks now. Seems like forever." He
was too tired to keep up the accent he had been using with
the boys. He never even thought to continue with it.

The woman sat down on the edge of the bed. She put
her ear to Adaba's chest. "Jesus God," she said after a
moment, sitting up again. "Fever, sick in the chest, sick
in the leg and the side—why ain't he dead?"

"You help him?"

"If I can."

"You can help him. I know you can."

The woman's smile was sardonic, pitying, angry. It
was a familiar smile, Aunt Zule's smile. "I guess them
boys, they tell you about me," she said.

Buck nodded. "You're Zulie, the conjure-woman.
Best healer there is in these parts."

"Best anywhere, but that don't mean I can save him."

"You save him, Zulie. You save him, and I do anything
you want for you. Steal, kill, anything."

"I do what I can." Zulie stood up from the bed. "Zag,
you build up the fire and get me some hot water. Light
me more candles." She looked at Buck. "You hungry?"

Buck clutched at a painfully empty stomach and said,
"Oh, Lord, mercy."

"Get some soup or something, Zag. If'n you get it from
Momma Lucinda, don't let her know who for. She'll give
it to you, but she don't want to know."

Perhaps Buck slept. He was dimly aware of Zulie
working over Adaba, as Zag left the cabin and returned
again; Zulie spooning a medicine into Adaba's mouth,
Zulie feeding Adaba the soup that Zag had brought, Zulie
and Zag washing Adaba's body and cleansing his
wounds. He roused up enough to eat some of the soup
himself. Twice Adaba screamed, and Buck was jolted
from his chair to see Zulie with a blood-slick knife in her

hand. When she looked around at him, her face shone with sweat, though the room was anything but hot. "Got to get that poison out," she said. "Got to get it out or it kill him!" With relief, he saw that she was putting fresh dressings on his wounds and drawing blankets up over his body.

She sighed and sat down on the foot of the bed as if exhausted.

"When will he be well?" Buck asked.

"Don't know. He dead already, only he don't know it. If nobody don't tell him, maybe he be all right."

"We got to talk about other things," Zag said. "Sam, them boys—Tad and Nemo—they say your master shot Jack."

"When we try to run away."

"He going to come here looking for you?" Zulie asked.

Buck considered. He was so weary, it was hard to think, and Zulie grew impatient.

"You don't tell us, man, we can't help you. More'n one poor black boy come running here this last year, and now Zag fixed up some good hiding places. But we got to know. We got to know what to expect. Who going come looking for you?"

There was really no choice. "Maybe master—that's Mr. Rogan," he said. "But more likely Mr. Justin, Mr. Justin Sabre."

Zulie's eyes widened. She seemed to be on the verge of exclaiming something, but she remained mute.

"Master caught us running away," Buck explained, altering the truth only as much as necessary. "He says, these niggers no good, going sell them. Takes us down the river on a cotton box, whipping us all the time, like he want to kill us. And Mr. Sabre, he sees, and he act like he don't like it. Helps us get away at night. Go to Sabrehill, he says, and hide. Maybe Aunt Zule will take care of you. And when I get there, I help you. And since then, we been following the river."

"He tell you about my momma?"

"Yes."

"You think he really help you?"

Buck shook his head. "I don't trust him."

"Damn right, you don't trust him." Zulie's eyes flashed. "That man, the way they say he done Miss Lucy . . ."

Buck remembered the house servants' gossip of long ago. "I don't care what he done," he said. "All I know is, I lived long enough not to trust no white man except maybe a Quaker, and even him not too far. For all I know or care, Mr. Justin is just another nigger-stealer."

"Well, you don't need no Mr. Justin. He already here, Sam, been here three days now, and we got to keep him from finding out about you."

"Them boys," Zag said, "they talk a lot."

Zulie shook her head. "They ain't going talk. They scared I spell them." She went to Buck and put a hand on his shoulder. 'Sam, you go with Zag now. He got a nice soft bed for you, hid in a harness room over the coach house. I'm going keep Jack here where I can watch over him. You go get your rest now."

She gave him a pat on the cheek. It made him feel safe, protected, and he was grateful. Adaba was going to recover from his wounds, and everything was going to be all right. He followed Zag out of the cabin.

Zulie watched as they disappeared in the darkness on their way to the coach house, then closed and barred the door. She looked across the room to where Jack lay perfectly motionless, hardly breathing, in her bed.

She would save him.

She refused to doubt it. He was hers now, hers to save, and no fatal miasma, no evil *loa* would take him from her, not from Erzulie, daughter of Erzulie, named for the goddess. As she had been taught, she would refuse to give him up. That was one of her great secrets. Simply that.

There was, of course, more to the story than Sam had told. Zulie had sensed that, had known it, but she had known too that it would be useless to question Sam more closely. Sam was a very cautious man. He was also something other than the simple, uneducated field hand he pretended to be. Something in his speech betrayed him, something he was too weary to hide.

These were dangerous men. Bad niggers.

Zulie drew a chair close to the bedside. She let the fire

on the grate burn down. Candles were precious—she blew out all but one. She wrapped a blanket around her shoulders, and sat down to watch Jack. She would watch him until that hour—it would probably come about dawn—when she would know that he was going to be all right.

She liked Jack's face—the strong bones, the heavy muzzle of black beard.

She smiled. Yes, Sam might try to hide it, but somehow she knew. These were two re-eal bad niggers.

The best kind.

His forge, his hammer, his anvil—these were his drugs. He worked constantly, doing far more than was necessary, laboring at any task he could find. He made nails, he made harness buckles, he made axes and froes and drawknives. It hardly mattered what he made, what he repaired, as long as it occupied his attention and tired his body beyond the ability to think. His ears were alert for any call that Ettalee might give—though she never did cry out—but he tried not to think of her, curled up so still on a corner of the bed. If he thought of anything at all besides his work, it was of Skeet: he saw Skeet's face before him, and then his anvil rang out.

On that day, he left Sabrehill during the afternoon and worked at the Devereau smithy, making repairs and training an apprentice, until almost dark. A good blacksmith —and Saul was the best—was badly needed in the area around Sabrehill, and when his work was finished at home, Miss Lucy allowed him to hire out his time. The practice had long been illegal, but the statute was almost universally ignored. Saul was grateful for that, because when the workday ended, despair began.

Nothing was ever going to change. Zulie's magic had failed to affect Mr. Skeet. Her healing had not helped Ettalee, and the child grew smaller, thinner, more withdrawn each day. She was dying, Saul felt certain, and when she went, he might well go with her.

When his apprentice had deserted him and the Devereau overseer dismissed him, Saul at last closed down the forge and headed back toward Sabrehill. It was a long walk, and he hoped Ettalee would be asleep when he arrived there.

There was at least a kind of peace in sleep—unless she dreamed. If she were still awake when he arrived, he would have to try to coax a smile from her, a smile that never came, and that broke his heart all over again.

It was well after dark when he arrived back at Sabrehill, and as he walked along the east lane, he saw Zag's woman, Binnie, sitting on the bench in front of his shop. As light-skinned as many a white woman, Binnie was pale and ghostlike in the night, and something in her manner as she arose from the bench made Saul wary.

Trouble.

If a man lived long enough, he learned to feel it, to smell it, to taste it in the air. If something more had happened to Ettalee . . .

"My baby," he said, "where she?"

Binnie shushed him. "She's asleep. She's all right, Saul. But something's happened."

Of course. But what?

"Two runaways come here," Binnie said. "Two of the boys, Tad and Nemo, found them out in the fields. And one of them is hurt real bad. Zulie taking care of him right now. We got to help them, Saul."

"Yes," Saul said, " 'course. 'Course we got to help them."

One more act of resistance. One more act of defiance.

Binnie looked past Saul's shoulder, down the lane. "Here come Zag back," she said. "Here he come with one of them now."

She sat quietly, her narrowed eyes never leaving the wounded man's face, and each breath carried a silent prayer: *He going live . . . going live . . . going live. . . .* After a time, she saw the rise and fall of his chest, and they breathed together: *going live . . . going live . . . going live. . . .*

She dreamed then, though she never slept. The images floated freely through her mind, and she saw this man and the other, well again and free, making their way north. She saw them ranging over the countryside, raiding and plundering, and she saw others joining with them, hundreds, even thousands, black people rising up and taking what was rightfully theirs. It would be a black land then, a free land—

Someone was tapping at her door.

She did not want to leave her dreams.

"Zulie!"

The whisper startled her. Jeb's voice? She thought not, but she could not be sure, and there was no time to hide the wounded man. The blanket still around her shoulders, she hurried to the door.

"Who that? What you want?"

"Zulie, this here Saul."

It was all right. Saul had no doubt talked to Zag. She opened the door, and he hurried into her room.

"Zag got Sam hid away all right?" she asked.

Saul looked at the man lying unconscious in the bed and then at Zulie. He was breathing hard, as if he had come running, and his eyes were bright with excitement. "Zag hide him away all right," he said, "but that ain't no Sam, I tell you that."

"What you mean?"

"I mean that ain't no Sam! I know him, Zulie, I know him the minute I set eyes on him."

Zulie was bewildered. "Saul, what you talking about?"

"Now, who I tell you bring back here? Who you be asking Momma Brigitte to set on Mr. Skeet? What kind spells you been making all this time?"

Saul's meaning began to dawn on her. "Saul, you trying tell me—"

"That there is Buckley Skeet come back here. *That there is Black Buck!*"

She stared, hardly able to believe. "You sure?"

"Zulie, I know him! I talk to him just now! 'Buckley Skeet,' I say to him, 'Buckley Skeet, you come back!' And he say, 'Yeah, 'bout time old Black Buck come back here, see his old friends. 'Bout time I come back here.' "

Zulie closed her eyes, as in prayer. It was true. It had to be true. And if it was true . . .

She looked at Saul again. "He say anything about his friend here?"

"He just say, 'Jack, he hurt awful bad.' He say, 'Aunt Zule, her gal taking care of Jack.' "

But if Sam were really Black Buck, might it not be . . .

Some people said he had a mark on his left cheek, the mark that had given him his "basket name" at birth. Of course, that was probably only a story, just as Adaba himself was probably only a story, but just the same . . .

She went to the bed. She leaned down over Jack and searched through the thick black beard that covered half of his left cheek. She found it, down near the jawbone: the odd, birdlike mark.

She didn't think she could breathe. "Saul," she said, "there really is a Black Buck."

" 'Course there is, I tell you that all the time!"

"And there really is a Brown Dove. Ain't no story. Really is, and he come here. Buckley Skeet bring him here to us. Black Buck and Adaba both—they here!"

"Was you bring them, Zulie, you!"

"And you know what that mean, Saul?"

Now she understood her dream. Now she knew why she had seen the two men running free, always beyond capture. Now she knew why she had dreamed of the hundreds and the thousands rising up and taking what was theirs.

"Our time is come, Saul."

He understood. "Our time."

"And there going to be fire and blood at Sabrehill!"

PART FOUR

Avengers

One

Fire and blood, by God, Buck thought, *fire and blood.*
The woman, Zulie, had used the words when she had
looked in on him that morning. "Going be fire and blood,"
she had said, and she was right. He had been more or less
forced back here, but his return was overdue. *Old Vaych,
I'm a-coming for you.*

Zulie now sat on the foot of Buck's bed, looking down
at him as he stretched out fully clothed. Zag and Binnie
stood nearby. Saul sat on the only chair in the room. He
was hunched forward toward Buck, hardly able to check
his excitement.

"You going get him, Buckley?"

"Saul, I'm gonna get him."

They were in a room over the coach house, a dusty,
harness-cluttered room right next to the bright, clean
room occupied by Zag and Binnie. Last night, space had
been cleared, a bed had been put together, and a mattress
and blankets had been thrown on it. Buck had been shown
the nearby hiding place. Thereafter he had slept deeply
and soundly, hardly rousing up, for a night and a day,
and if there had been bad dreams, they were now distant
and forgotten. He had awakened feeling starved, and
Binnie had brought him food. Zag had replaced his filthy,
blood-stained rags with good clothes, old but clean, and
he was washed and even barbered. And in spite of his
long sleep, a full stomach was inducing a comfortable
drowsiness.

But this was not the time for more sleep—not yet. He
looked around the room, weighing what he had learned
of these four people. Saul had no great love for whites
in general, it seemed, but no great hatred of them either.
His hatred was aimed at Vachel Skeet, at Shadrach and
at the overseer, Dinkin. He had told Buck last night what
they had done to his daughter. Zulie certainly had a
hatred of Vachel Skeet, but her hatred was aimed more

toward whites in general. Zag and Binnie seemed to be Buck's weakest allies. They had a positive attachment to the mistress of Sabrehill. And yet, undeniably, they were hiding and sheltering him, and they seemed eager to help him against Vachel. All of them seemed to have a reasonably accurate idea of what had happened at Redbird twelve years ago.

"Buckley," Saul said, "you need you rest, and we going let you get it. But we want to ask you."

"You ask, Saul. Anything you want."

"How you going get him, Buckley? What you going do to him?"

"Well, I ain't rightly made up my mind yet, though I got an idea or two. Trouble is, I don't know how things is around here no more, and you got to tell me. One thing I do know is, old Vaych got to know why he's getting it, and he got to know it's me giving it to him."

"That ain't going make it easy," Zulie said. "It ain't like just stealing a gun and blowing his head off from behind a tree."

"That's right. But I'll figure something out. And now maybe you answer some questions for me."

"Anything you want to know."

"Is it true that Vachel still got a reward out for me?"

Zulie nodded. "Five thousand dollars is what they say. Most anybody ever hear of for a runaway nigger. Mr. Skeet still say one day going get Buckley Skeet."

Saul chuckled. "And ain't he just right!"

"You say Mr. Justin still around here?"

"Still here," Saul said. "Prowl 'round like he looking for you."

"But he ain't gonna find me. Another question. Vachel still got that nigger-jail?"

Saul's eyes darkened. "He got it. Break niggers, same as his daddy. He keep my Ettalee in that jail."

"He got anybody in it right now?"

"Seven," Zag said. "Nemo was snooping around there this morning. Said he counted six men and one woman."

"Any way you can find out where they're from, Zag?" Buck asked. "So we can find out from their friends if they want to run away and go north?"

"I can tell you right now that all but maybe one or two want to run away. Hell, that's why they're in the jail, most of them, Buck—'cause they run away four or five times. Things ain't changed much at Redbird since you went off. Mr. Vachel Skeet just got richer and meaner, is all."

Buck grinned. "Then all I got to do is open up that there jail house, and I got me four or five of the meanest niggers in all South Carolina."

Saul happily slapped a thigh. "Black Buck is surely come. Praise the Lord!"

"Four or five mean niggers like that, and if I can get them out of the jail fast enough, we'll burn goddam Redbird to the ground. With Vachel and Shadrach and that overseer inside it. But I can't lead nobody off after if they ain't got proper things. Guns, axes, good clothes, food."

"Guns hard to get," Saul said, "but steal anything else, all you need."

"We'll have to talk about that some more. Any of you want to run off with me?"

There was a silence. Saul ruefully shook his head. "I got to take care my Ettalee. Can't take her nowhere till she better."

"And Binnie and me," Zag said, "we got us a good place here. But we'll do what we can to help you."

Buck had expected as much. "And you, Zulie?"

Zulie shrugged. "Got to take care of Adaba."

"But that ain't gonna take long, is it?"

"Least a month. Likely a whole lot longer to get his strength back."

Somehow Buck had not expected that, ill though Adaba was. If it was dangerous for either of them to remain too long on any plantation, it was at least twice as dangerous for two of them. Take all the time you need, Adaba had taught him, but never an hour more than you need. Get in and get out.

Perhaps, then, the best course would be to take care of Vachel, lead the Redbird rebels off, and leave Adaba in Zulie's care. It would be the safest course both for Adaba and for himself.

"You know anybody else want to help me? Nigger who want to run away? Live maroon or go up north?"

"Oh, Black Buck," Zulie said, " 'course we know. Ain't hardly a big plantation 'round here ain't got runaways. Only they don't know how, they don't know the way, so most of them, they just get caught. Then maybe get sent to Mr. Skeet so he break them. Buck, Saul and me, we know most all the rebel niggers 'round here."

Rebel niggers . . . rebels on every big plantation. . . . Something stirred in Buck's mind, something of that half-mad vision he had had only a few mornings earlier while sitting in the rain outside the lean-to. Slaves rising up against their masters, black people on the march.

"We got to talk more," he said.

"Lot more."

"But not now. Johnny awake yet?"

"Not yet. Rouse up 'nough for me to feed him, is all."

"Don't tell him nothing about what I aim to do. He knows I aim to get Vachel sooner or later, but don't tell him now, don't tell him how we been planning. You do, he'll worry. He'll want to help, and he ain't ready, not while he's still hurt."

"Won't tell him nothing."

And what about Mr. Justin Sabre? Adaba might not share Buck's and Zulie's distrust.

"If he ask about that Mr. Sabre, tell him . . . just tell him he done come here and left again. Maybe he come back, maybe not. You don't know. And don't let nobody tell him different."

"Ain't nobody going talk to Adaba or even see him 'cept us here."

"Good. That's good."

Soon after that the others left. Buck shrugged out of his clothes, blew out the candle, and curled up in the blankets.

As he lay in the dark, his mind kept reverting to the Skeet jail house. How little he had thought of it in those early days when he had lived happily at Redbird. All that time, black men like himself had been kept in bondage in that house, suffering the chains and whip, while the Old Man tried to make true slaves of them, slaves in their souls. And young Buckley Skeet had found it easiest simply not to think about it. He was not sure he would ever be able to forgive himself for that.

Well, that had been a long time ago. Weep one tear for the dead, brothers and sisters, and move your ass for the living.

I'll get them out, he thought. *I'll get them out of that damn jail house and take them to freedom, take them north, wherever they want to go. Make up a little for the ones I never thought about.* When you got right down to it, that was even more important than evening things with Vachel. A hell of a lot more important.

Buck slept.

On Tuesday morning, immediately after speaking to Justin, Lucy dispatched several riders with invitations to the party. She apologized for the shortness of notice, explaining that her cousin's arrival had been unexpected and that he would be at Sabrehill for only a short time. To her surprise, considering that Christmas was only a few weeks away, most of the invitations were accepted.

A great deal had to be done in a very short time. Those guests who had to travel the farthest for the party would stay the night; rooms had to be aired and beds set up. Every kind of supply had to be checked and arrangements made for musicians. For an affair of this size, house servants had to be trained or retrained, but fortunately Jebediah was available for this. Cheney, the chief driver, could take charge of the fields, and Jebediah could return to his old post as butler. Lucy's bachelor neighbor, Paul Devereau, consented to assist as host, a task that pleased him more than he was willing to admit.

On Saturday afternoon, those guests who had to travel the farthest began to arrive, and Zagreus and his brothers were kept increasingly busy, tending to horses and carriages. By suppertime the entire household was in a kind of happy uproar, and Lucy foresaw that her party was going to be a complete success.

After supper, the nearer neighbors began to arrive: Kimbroughs, Buckridges, Pettigrews, McClintocks, all the most familiar faces. A family at a time, they entered the brightly lit passage, where Jebediah announced them without ever having to ask a name. Justin made a point of being close by at their arrival, and if he had forgotten their names over the years, they never knew it. Lucy watched with hidden amusement as each guest tried to take his measure. This party was somewhat special. While it was common enough to invite neighbors to come meet relatives and friends from distant places—the Sabres had done it often enough in the past—*this* was the cousin who everyone had once thought would marry Lucy, was he not? The one who had run off? *This* was the cousin who had fought the duel over her—it *had* been over her, had it not?—with that rather deplorable Vachel Skeet. And what in the world was he doing back here, after all this time? A breath of old scandal hung over the affair, making it ever so much more fun than it would otherwise have been.

Fiddlers dinned, and the young people danced in the ballroom. Momma Lucinda's Irish served drinks in the larger parlor. The dining room table and a sideboard were loaded with refreshments—candies, cookies, cakes, nutbreads, meats smoked and spiced. Lucy moved about the house swiftly, hardly pausing, going from ballroom to parlor to passage, from passage to dining room to library, keeping her guests happy (she hoped) and seeing that no one monopolized Justin. For one who had long been rather reclusive, she was always surprised at how much she enjoyed these affairs, but then the Sabres had never bowed to anyone in their ability to enjoy their own parties.

From library to ballroom and back again. Paul Devereau and Irish saw to it that glasses were constantly refilled. No male was to be allowed to leave or retire without at least the pretense of being drunk. No lady was to be allowed to go uncharmed. Children, too much underfoot, were to be crammed with goodies until they threatened to become ill and were then to be tucked into bed, where they would be out of the way as the party became livelier. Older daughters sought to evade the parental eye to keep trysts with young blades in the dark chilly gardens. The party would not be a success if a mild scandal or two were not born, and the threat of a duel might be fun, as long as nothing came of it.

From large parlor to passage to small parlor to

ballroom—and Lucy realized that it had been quite some time, more than half an hour, since she had last seen Justin. But of course, he, like the other gentlemen, might have stepped out into the courtyard or onto the piazza for a breath of fresh air and a segar.

She found him with Major Kimbrough, Mr. Buckridge, and Mr. Pettigrew on the piazza, smokes and drinks in hand, caught in a dim light from a parlor window. She was about to step out of the doorway and say, "Gentlemen, you have kept Cousin Justin from the ladies too long," but something stopped her.

". . . glad to see you here," the major was saying. "Fact is that we who know and love Miss Lucy best worry a great deal about her."

"That's right," Mr. Buckridge agreed. "Her all alone here on one of the largest plantations in the region—and not so much as a white overseer to stand by her."

Oh, dear God, Lucy thought, *is* that *starting all over again?* She had heard such sentiments far too often.

"Well, I've only been here a few days, gentlemen," came Justin's murmuring voice, "but I've been under the impression that my cousin has made a resounding success of managing Sabrehill—"

Thank you, Justin!

"—and after all, it's hardly unusual for a widow to have her own plantation and people. In fact, when you get down to it, gentlemen, a great many of our ladies come to that sooner or later."

"Oh, come now, Mr. Sabre," Mr. Pettigrew said irritably, "most widows have small holdings, which means neighbors quite close by. And most widows have sons to assist them. But Miss Lucy doesn't have a single close relative anywhere around here."

"All we are suggesting," the major said, "is that, for Miss Lucy's sake, it would be an act of kindness for some of her family, however distant, to take a close interest in her problems. Perhaps even to settle here and help her run Sabrehill. God knows the poor woman has suffered enough in recent years."

Lucy gritted her teeth. *Poor woman, indeed . . .*

"Well, gentlemen," Justin said mildly, "it's been a long

time since I last visited Sabrehill, and I'm most reluctant
to intrude in my cousin's affairs. I know that you all have
only her best interests at heart, but—" he laughed to take
the edge from his words "—I'm afraid that, like most men,
I have a fair amount of difficulty managing my own life. I
think we might all do best to allow my cousin to manage
hers."

Justin, bless you!

Lucy moved toward the group, but they hardly noticed
her. Certainly Owen Buckridge did not.

"I find it hard to understand your indifference to the
lady's plight, Mr. Sabre."

"Hardly indifference, sir, and I see no plight."

"A woman alone on an exceptionally large plantation,
surrounded by a bunch of ignorant niggers—"

"Ignorant, most of them, I suppose. But I've found her
household to be intelligent, and her overseer is an educated and perceptive man—"

"I am getting goddam sick and tired," Mr. Buckridge
broke in harshly, "of hearing what a bright boy Jebediah
is. My God, man, it was a bright, educated nigger that
led the slaughter up in your own Virginia not long ago.
And nine years before that, it was a bright, educated
nigger that conspired with nine thousand other niggers to
slaughter everybody in this part of South Carolina."

"But wouldn't there have been conspiracies and rebel-
lions in any case? Is the cause of violence education, or is
it slavery per se?"

"That, sir," said Mr. Pettigrew, "is the attitude which
has caused all the laws against educating niggers, clear
back to 1740, to be dead letters. Hell, man, surely you
can't be *for* educating the damn savages!"

Justin shrugged. "Savages are dangerous. How do you
propose to civilize them?"

"I do not, sir. I long ago gave up on that. That's a lot
of abolitionist nonsense. Educate a nigger, and you've got
a book-reading baboon."

"But isn't that true of all of us, Mr. Pettigrew? Our
claims to civilization sometimes seem pretty damned
slight. And how can we blame the Negro for his acts of
violence when he is, after all, a captive? Any captive of

any race can be expected to assert his—his dignity, his independence, his humanity."

"His humanity!" the major laughed. "Assert his humanity by murdering innocent women and children?"

"Now, major, anyone acquainted with the African slave trade knows that the murder of innocent women and children is hardly confined to the colored races. We have all heard of instances where the slaughter was conducted by 'civilized' white men. And yet we persist in blaming the blacks who only want—"

"Are you a nigger-lover, sir?"

Mr. Buckridge's voice shook with passion, and his language stunned the group. "Nigger-lover" was trash talk, po' buckra talk, and it betrayed a crassitude, a stupid hatred of blacks that no gentleman would ever admit to.

"Nigger-lover?" Justin asked softly.

Mr. Buckridge instantly saw his mistake and tried to correct it. "Now—now, you all know what I mean," he went on fumblingly. "Why, I love my people as much as the next man. I *care* for them, and they love and respect me. But I still ask you, sir, are you a—a nigger-lover? By which I mean," his voice began to rise and shake again, "by which I mean, sir, are you one of them goddam William Lloyd Garrison people, spreading their goddam abolitionist poison—"

She could restrain herself no longer. "Mr. Buckridge," Lucy cut in, "I wonder if I might speak to you for a moment?"

The interruption was obviously a relief, even to Owen Buckridge. The entire group at once appeared to relax. Buckridge turned to Lucy, told her, "But of course, my dear," and followed her a few yards along the piazza to the other side of the passage door. The others drifted into the passage, talking and laughing self-consciously.

"Owen," Lucy said, "I did not intend to eavesdrop or to interrupt your conversation."

"Why, of course not, my dear."

"But I could not help but overhear part of it. And I'm afraid I must remind you that Mr. Sabre is a guest in this house, the guest of honor tonight. And I must remind you further that Sabrehill has always been a place where any topic of common interest could be discussed quietly, sanely, without fear of rude contradiction or reprisal. Now, a great many intelligent men in the South have held abolitionist views."

Owen Buckridge's eyes hardened. "No longer, Miss Lucy. The time has passed when we can afford such inflammatory nonsense. People like Garrison should be treated like any other insurrectionists, nigger or otherwise. That man Garrison should be hung on The Lines in Charleston, hung as an example for all the niggers to see."

The man was, Lucy thought, perhaps slightly mad on the subject. But she knew his feeling was scarcely different from that of a great many other people of the time, in the North as well as in the South.

"I have no great love for Mr. Garrison myself, Owen, but that is beside the point. Sabrehill will continue to be, as it was in my father's time, a place for intelligent discussion from any and all points of view, even those abhorrent to us. Any guest in this house may speak his mind freely as long as he does so in a decent and civilized manner."

Mr. Buckridge sighed. "Well . . . I suppose I do sometimes let myself get carried away."

Lucy smiled and patted his arm. Justin had appeared in the doorway, and she was eager to be done with Buckridge. "Owen, dear, we all do. But let's try harder not to. Now, I think Miss Callie is looking for you."

"Yes . . . yes . . ."

It was an excuse for Buckridge to go back into the house. He turned away from Lucy and entered the passage doorway, nodding curtly at Justin as he passed him.

"I'm sorry, Lucy," Justin said, coming toward her in the shadows of the piazza. "I had no intention of making difficulties with your neighbors."

"The difficulties, I'm afraid, existed before your arrival. I thank you for speaking up for me."

"I did what I could. But as for my so-called abolitionist views . . ." He shrugged and made a wry face. "I have no great interest in preaching my views, Lucy, but when the question comes up, I do have a hard time keeping my mouth shut. I'm bad at dissembling, and I hate even to try."

"I understand, Justin. I've always been inclined to speak my mind too quickly myself." She laughed ironically. "And I'm afraid I've even had to learn to lie. I'm not proud of it, but where the survival of my people, and myself, is concerned, I've learned to do it rather well."

"I can hardly blame you."

From within the house came the sound of fiddles, the sound of chatter and laughter.

"Justin, I would like to explain one thing. Whatever those gentlemen may have said, it isn't *my* people who cause trouble around here. In fact, most of the trouble in recent years has been caused by white people. But it seems that whenever there's any disturbance—runaway slaves, a barn-burning—all my neighbors look my way. 'There's that woman at Sabrehill, no white overseers, no other whites at all, black people doing just as they please —how *can* the countryside be safe?'"

"In other words, they make you a scapegoat."

"But I didn't *ask* to be a widow alone at Sabrehill, Justin—my God, I didn't even ask to marry my husband before I *became* a widow—"

She broke off. Why in the world, she wondered, was she telling him this? The events at Sabrehill in recent years had nothing whatever to do with Justin, and why should she try to justify herself to him?

"I'm sorry," she said. "I didn't mean to unburden myself to you."

"Lucy, dear, there is no burden you could place on me that I would not willingly bear."

Lucy smiled. "Always gallant," she said. "Shall we return to the party?"

Saturday night, Buck thought with a nostalgia that surprised him, *oh, for those Saturday nights so long ago!*

Saturday night had always been a time of music and dancing and laughter in the slave quarters. It had been a time of roaming from one quarters to another, of drinking forbidden liquor and chasing girls and making love. And when there was a party in the big house, there was usually an even greater one in the slave quarters.

Well, Buck thought, maybe some things hadn't changed much. Leaving the coach house, he walked west along the lane and stood for a few minutes in the shadows of the overseer's house, looking out at the courtyard. Torches illuminated the yard. The big mansion glowed. Across the way the kitchen house was bright as a jack-o'-lantern, and maids and houseboys ran back and forth along the portico between it and the big house. Lida was nowhere in sight, but to Buck's delight he did see Lucinda, a little heavier but handsome as ever. He would not have minded another encounter with Lucinda after all this time; but since she was a house servant, that was best avoided.

He spent almost an hour with Saul in the shop. The blacksmith assured him that he could make exactly the kind of axe Buck wanted, an axe with a balanced head, and he could supply Buck with a good knife too. In fact, with the help of various friends on nearby plantations, he could get almost any kind of supply Buck wanted. " 'Cause they plenty rich white folk 'round here," he said, "and anything they got, we can take."

But what about getting word to the people in Skeet's jail house? "Best they know the plan," Buck said, "so they know what's happening when the time comes. Is there some way we can get word to them?"

There was, just possibly. The jail house prisoners were largely kept isolated from the other slaves, but perhaps Saul's friend Cato Weston could get word to them. "But if he can't," Saul said, "don't know who can."

"We got to talk to Cato, then. When can we do that?"

"Maybe tomorrow. Tomorrow at the meeting."

"The meeting?"

"There's prayer meeting lots of places on Sunday. Only, the white folk know what some us pray for, they hang us all."

Buck laughed. "Oh, *that* kind of meeting."

When they were finished, they walked out to the field quarters. They kept to the shadows, avoiding the Saturday night festivities, but if anyone saw Buck, he was just a hand from another plantation, some friend of Saul's who had come by to pass the evening.

They found Zulie in her cabin with Adaba. The instant Buck looked at him, all of his good feeling drained away.

"Ain't he any better?"

"He getting better, Buck. Now, don't you fret."

"Don't remember him looking so . . . small."

"You was looking mighty poorly yourself just two nights ago."

Buck wanted to weep. He kept staring at the shrunken figure in the bed and remembering the tall, strong, black-bearded youth who, a dozen years before, had taken him into his camp and taught him how to survive. This was hardly the same man.

He sighed and turned away. Zulie had said it would be weeks before Adaba had recovered his strength, and Buck could believe it now. When he acted, it would have to be on his own.

"You don't tell him nothing, Zulie," he said. "You just get Johnny well again."

"You know I do that."

The three of them—Buck, Zulie, Saul—stepped out into the chilly night. Music and laughter were still in the air, but the sweetness had gone out of the sounds for Buck. On those Saturday nights he had enjoyed so long ago, other men had lain broken and bleeding on the Skeet jail house floor.

Buck looked toward the distant glow of the big house.

That was the enemy, he thought. Even the best of them. The enemy. All of them.

And he would hold Vachel Skeet's beating heart in his hand.

"Zulie," he said, "you told me there's a lot of people around here that want to run away, but they don't know how, and they just get caught. People who will help us."

"That's surely true."

"Well, I do know how to get away from here. And if they want to come with me, I'll take them. All that are strong enough to travel fast and hard and fight like hell if they have to."

"Praise God," Zulie said softly.

"I got to think about it and work out a plan. We'll need a lot of supplies. And everybody has got to do exactly what I say. They do that, and I'll show them the way to get free."

"When?" Saul asked. "When you do that?"

"Soon. Very soon."

Take them to freedom, Buck thought grimly, but first burn Redbird. And take Vachel Skeet's heart.

Fire and blood.

Two

Sometimes he was aware of darkness, sometimes of light, and always in those brief moments there was the Angel of Death, and he felt the beat of wings within his own chest.

Where was he now? In a bed, it seemed. A hand gently lifted his head, and light seared his eyes. The spoon slipped between his teeth, and the warm broth slid down his throat, and he choked; but the next time the broth went down easier. He breathed deeply and felt the beat of wings, and then the gentle wings enclosed him once again in darkness.

Later, cold air swept over his body, and he whimpered as the dressing was pulled away from his side. Something touched him there, something kneaded the flesh, and he knew he was hurt, hurt badly. His leg ached too when the dressing was pulled away, and the Angel seemed to whisper, *Let go . . . let go and come with me. . . .*

But something held him back.

Darkness and light . . . darkness and light . . . the gentle hands on his body . . . the spoon at his lips, the bitter swallow and the warm and soothing . . . and all he wanted was sleep. *Go away, Angel, and let me sleep.*

He slept.

And when he awakened, the Angel of Death was gone.

He lay quietly, his eyes still closed. He was in a bed

with someone, it seemed, and he had no idea who. It hardly mattered. He was weak, oh, so weak, and he was naked as a newborn baby, but he was bandaged and he was breathing and his heart was beating easily and regularly and he was alive.

Alive!

His companion moaned and stirred.

He was not alone!

He had known that from the moment of awakening, and yet he had not known. Now more fully awake, he too stirred, tentatively. Lying on his side, he felt his thighs touch warm bare buttocks. His hand, heavy as lead, moved up a bare back, over a curve of vertebrae.

He wanted to weep, he wanted to laugh. He was definitely not huddled with Buck in some rude lean-to in the woods.

His hand moved from the back to a shoulder—a broad shoulder, but somehow not masculine. He had a sudden suspicion. He remembered a sweet face, candlelit, above his. It could have been a dream. He remembered a hand lifting his head, another hand bringing a spoon to his lips. Somehow he knew that it was not a dream, that this was the woman. His hand moved on.

Yes. He found it. A high, pointed breast, heavy in his hand, astonishingly soft over the hard inner core. He stroked it. He wanted to kiss it. And as he drew at the tautening nipple, his rush of blood gave him further evidence, if he needed it, that he very definitely was not dead.

Oh, Angel of Life!

Suddenly the woman gasped and jumped, pulling away from him. Her hand slapped his away, and she sat up in bed. There was a long moment of silence.

Then she giggled. "Naughty man," she whispered.

He wanted to cackle with glee.

But he did not. He bit his tongue and restrained himself, pretending to be asleep.

She pulled up the blankets and tucked him in, and he watched covertly as she left the bed. Daylight had not yet broken, but as the woman squatted before the fireplace to blow some last ember back to flame, he made out a pleasing curve of back and rump. When she stood up, a lit candle in hand, he saw that she was tall and, as he had thought, broad shouldered, with high, full breasts. Her legs were long, the well-shaped legs of one who could run like a deer, and her waist was narrow.

He wished to God she would come back to bed.

But she did not. She was turning toward him, and unwillingly he shut his eyes. "Hey, you naughty man," she said softly, "you awake? . . . No, guess you ain't."

He heard the creak of floorboards as she turned away, and he looked again through slitted eyes. He watched as, still naked, the woman built up the fire. He watched as she tied a yellow bandanna around her head, her first act of dressing. She pulled on drawers and a shirt and tied something—he could not see what—by a thong around her waist. She pulled a dress on over it all and put on a pair of shoes.

As she came back to the bed, he closed his eyes again. He felt the bed move as she leaned against it, bending down over him.

"Honey-child," she said, "you *sure* you ain't awake?"

He fought back laughter like a happy child—and abruptly fell again into healing sleep.

Justin awakened at dawn, after a very short night's sleep. This was hardly remarkable, since in all his travels he had never become accustomed to sleeping with two other gentlemen in the same bed. Moreover, another two gentlemen slept on cots in the same room, not to mention Rayburn and another boy on pallets on the floor, and the chorus of snores outdid even that of the Rogans, some eleven nights before.

Further sleep, then, was impossible, and Justin got out of bed and quickly and quietly dressed. He washed with cold water, putting off shaving until later. Usually Rayburn had the fire built by the time Justin was awake, but this morning Justin did it himself, taking care to disturb no one. He saw to it that Rayburn and the other boy were still well covered, and left the bedroom.

Minutes later he was in the bright and cheery kitchen

house. Lucinda was just entering, sleep still in her eyes, but the fires had already been built up.

"Mr. Justin," she said disapprovingly, "what you doing up this early, a Sunday morning?"

"Couldn't sleep. Too crowded and too noisy. Thought I might as well get myself up and out of the way. You and Miss Lucy, you're going to be busy this morning with all that crowd."

"Well, you just sit yourself down and I'll get you some breakfast."

"Now, don't you bother, Lucinda—I just thought I could find a biscuit or something. I don't want to make extra work—"

"You ain't gonna mess around my kitchen, boy, you just *sit* like I tell you, and I'll get you some breakfast."

Justin recognized an order when he heard one, and it *was* Lucinda's kitchen; so he sat, and waited, and fifteen minutes later he had a plate of eggs, ham, fried grits, and gravy. And it was delicious.

They had made a truce of sorts. Justin was under no illusion that Lucinda had forgiven him, but he was Miss Lucy's guest, and as such he would be treated decently. Not cordially, but decently and pleasantly. Even Leila volunteered him a brief smile as she passed through the kitchen.

By the time he had finished his breakfast, there was a considerable amount of activity at Sabrehill. Sunday was a day of rest, but not for everybody, and especially not with a house full of visitors. Fires had to be built, water had to be hauled, and servants had to be fed early. The dining room would never accommodate all of the guests, and the ballroom had to be converted into a breakfast hall—and later into a banquet hall for those who stayed for Sunday dinner. Justin figured he had best follow his usual practice since his arrival at Sabrehill: stay out of Lucy's way as much as possible, stay away from the house, and when possible, make himself useful elsewhere on the plantation. But of course, there would be little or nothing to do in the fields today, and he would be expected to help entertain the guests after breakfast. This early morning hour was his best opportunity to take a ramble about the plantation.

He walked along the west lane almost to the mansion quarters, then back again and across the courtyard, and along the east lane. He then walked out to the field quarters, taking a somewhat random stroll along its streets.

No one approached him. Nobody whispered, *"Master Justin . . . you maybe looking . . . for somebody? . . ."*

Where were Adaba and Buck? He had just about given up hope of seeing them again, which probably should have been a relief to him, but somehow was not. He wanted to know they were safe. He had taken a proprietary interest in them. *Yes, proprietary,* he thought ironically, *as if I owned them. As if—*

Aunt Zule.

But of course, it was not Aunt Zule, because she was dead. It could only be that proud conjure-woman's daughter. Not thirty feet away, she was carrying a bucket of water toward the door of a cabin. Startled by the sight of him, she hesitated, then hurried on.

"Zulie!"

Grinning, he hurried toward her, and she stopped again. It was undoubtedly she: he saw the same high-stepping, independent manner, the same bright, world-defying eyes. He remembered how well she had taken care of him and how he had made her laugh in spite of herself.

He stepped between her and the door. "Good morning, Zulie."

Zulie said nothing. She had dropped her gaze, as if conscious only of the bucket she was carrying.

"For a minute I thought you were your mother."

"She dead."

"I know that." For the first time, it occurred to him that Zulie might not recognize him. He laughed, but some part of his happiness died. "You remember me, don't you?"

She raised her eyes, and there was no brightness in them, no intelligence, and certainly no defiance or challenge. He saw only the same dullness that had been in

Leila's eyes when he had arrived, the dullness that said, *I refuse to exist for you.*

His grin faded. "Zulie . . . ?"

"Yeah," she said slowly, dumbly, "reckon I 'member."

"You should. You helped save my life. You and your mother and Miss Lucy."

Zulie said nothing. He might have been speaking a foreign language.

"I've been keeping my eyes open for you, Zulie," he said gently. "Asked around about you, hoping to see you. It's nice to see you again, Zulie."

She lowered her eyes again. "I got to go in now."

She walked around him as if being particularly careful not to touch him. The very care would have been offensive if her eyes had not been so indifferent. She walked to the cabin door, keeping her head down, entered the cabin, and closed the door behind her without a backward glance.

Well, Justin thought, what the hell had he expected? Zulie was one of Lucy's people, wasn't she?

For a time he stood right where he was, feeling a little sick. *Why am I here?* he wondered. *I've given Adaba and Buck almost a week—more than enough time. I'm not wanted here, and for good reason. Lucy's had her party, and there's no further reason to stay.*

Tomorrow, he thought. *Tomorrow will make a full week. Tomorrow all the other guests will be gone, and I'll tell Lucy I've got to be on my way. And she needn't worry about my bothering her ever again.*

He started back toward the big house.

She awakened feeling happy, as happy as she had been in weeks, and she lay abed in a rosy glow, an arm flung across her forehead, her eyes not yet open. She was cramped. She hardly dared move for fear of disturbing her two bed companions. But that hardly mattered. She came up out of dreams to memories of music and the chattering of her guests and the laughter and the toasts drunk and the dancing and . . .

. . . and Justin.

They were friends again.

Of course, they could never be more than friends, not after what had happened those long years ago, but that *had* been long years ago, and they had been so young then, and now . . .

. . . and now she had someone to talk to. Someone besides Jebediah Hayes. Someone who gave her more than household babble or male condescension and who knew there was a real world and civilization outside of South Carolina.

The truth of the matter was that, until last night, Justin had been a considerable failure as a house guest. He had been a boor. He had been at Sabrehill five full days and six nights now, but until last night, it seemed to Lucy, she had hardly seen him. Except for the first morning, when he had slept late, he had always preceded her to the breakfast table and had then disappeared into the outbuildings or the fields. Only twice had he appeared at midday dinner; the other three days he had requested that Lucinda send his dinner out to where he was working. (Working!) Supper times had been better. She always looked forward to civilized conversation, and he had told her about his travels in Europe, and they had discussed the English Reform Bill and the future of railroad transportation and the state of the arts in France. But at the first lull in the conversation—as if one dared not pause for thought—Justin had stifled yawns and announced that he had best retire to his room, as if he were all too eager to be gone from her presence.

But last night had been different. Last night had been a turning point, as if they had rediscovered each other, rediscovered their *real* selves, and everything had changed. At just what point it had happened, she was not quite certain, but she had overheard him defending her, sounding very much like a Sabre, and she had remembered that they both *were* Sabres, and after that . . .

Oh, what did it matter. Her party had been a delight. Justin had been a delight. They had gone back into the house from the piazza and suddenly found themselves dancing together. They had danced quite enough to set tongues wagging again, and she had not cared, not in the slightest. She had felt nineteen years old again, and this morning she still did.

Someone was building a fire in the fireplace: a light thumping of wood, the clink and clatter of metal, a hint of smoke like incense. Lucy did not wish to get up. But it was time: she had to be up and about before her guests, and Leila was gently shaking her. She cast her arm away from her forehead and opened her eyes and saw the full light of day, and oh, my God, it was late, and Leila why did you let me sleep!

Leila went back downstairs. Lucy got out of bed, being careful not to awaken the two girls with her—members of the Kimbrough and Haining clans. She washed hurriedly, dressed, and followed after Leila. She heard guests stirring about downstairs, and others followed after her from upstairs, and oh, it was late! She was relieved to see that the tables were already up in the ballroom and that Jebediah and Irish had the boys and maids busily setting them for breakfast.

Was Justin up yet, she wondered.

She found guests strolling on the piazza. She said good morning to others in the two parlors. Some of the children were already running about the courtyard. But nowhere did she see Justin.

She hurried to the kitchen house and found Momma Lucinda hard at work.

"Good morning, Lucy-child!"

"My God, why didn't someone wake me up! It's so late—"

"Now, you stop that! You just stop that! You think nobody don't know what to do when you ain't around?"

"But Lucinda, I have so much to do—"

"You ain't got to do nothing. We all taking care of it, and will you kindly get out of here? Unless you want something special?"

She did, she wanted something special. Almost diffidently, she asked, "Have you seen Mr. Justin this morning, by any chance?"

"Oh, Lord," Momma Lucinda said with a laugh and a shake of her head, "like always, he was out here long ago.

Out here and had him some breakfast and long gone, I don't know where."

Lucy had a sinking feeling. "On Sunday?"

"Maybe he don't know what day it is. He surely don't ask me."

Out and gone, long gone, like any other morning.

Well, of course.

What in the world had she expected? Had she really thought that in that haze of laughter and dancing and wine there had been some mysterious "turning point," some "rediscovery"? Had she really thought that either of them was other than what he was? He was a road-weary cousin who had paused at Sabrehill to rest. She had given him a party, a party he had not particularly wanted, but he played his part well. *Of course,* he had spoken up for her to her neighbors—would she have expected otherwise? *Of course,* he had fraternized with the men and charmed their ladies. And *of course,* he had been a model of graciousness to his hostess. He was, after all, a Sabre.

But now it was Sunday morning, and the party was over.

"Lucinda," she said, and she was surprised to find that her voice was shaking, "how long will it be until breakfast is ready?"

"Not long. I done fed some of the hungry ones already."

"Good. Breakfast will be quite informal—no one need wait for me. If I'm needed, I'll be in the office."

"But you got to eat first. You ain't eaten—"

Ignoring the admonition, Lucy stepped out of the kitchen. She crossed the courtyard, feeling more irritated by the second. Grazing sheep scattered before her, as if sensing that she was about to kick them out of the way. She flung open the office door, slamming it against the wall, and tossed herself down into a chair.

And was as depressed as earlier she had been happy.

But why? Why should she react so strongly to an incident that really had no significance whatsoever? Why?

Oh, Ga-a-awd, she thought, she knew perfectly well why. Justin Sabre was a big, handsome, attractive man.

And she was thirty-one, almost thirty-two years old and as fully alive as she had ever been in her life. And the body simply did not give a damn about any betrayals the woman had suffered twelve years ago—or for that matter, in the time since. And in all those twelve years, neither the body nor the woman had had any real happiness, any real pleasure, any real fulfillment. Not since Justin had left. And now Justin was back to remind her.

Well, she would get over it. She had before. Justin Sabre was not the first handsome pair of pants to come floating down the river, and he would not be the last.

But just what in the world was Justin here for, anyway? The man comes wandering in out of the night, looking begrimed and exhausted. Supposedly, he stops for a rest—but every morning he is up before dawn and out helping to pull stumps or repairing a sluiceway down on the rice tract or mending a barn roof. Never getting in the way, according to Jebediah, but working as hard as any hand. Getting to know the hands, getting their confidence. And all the while trying to avoid his hostess.

"Good morning."

She looked up, startled. It was Justin, smiling at her through the doorway of the office, as if to give the lie to her thoughts.

"Then you haven't disappeared for the day." She said the words without thinking and more sharply than she would have wished, and the smile faded.

"By no means," Justin said, "and Cousin Lucy, you are looking quite lovely this morning."

But she would not be charmed. If anything, her irritation mounted. "Justin, I would like to speak with you for a moment."

"Of course."

He stepped into the office and at her signal sat down facing her. He waited, the faint shadow of his smile remaining. It struck her as supercilious.

"Cousin Justin, you have been here for five days and six nights."

"Has it been that long?"

"And during that time I have seen very little of you."

"And I all too little of you."

"Spare me." Idle compliments usually annoyed Lucy, and she was not unhappy to see the last of Justin's smile slip away. "I was under the impression, Justin, that you had stopped by here for a rest."

"That was one reason."

"And what other?"

"I think . . ." Justin hesitated. "I think I had some hope of seeing you."

Lucy decided to let that pass for the moment. "You stopped for a rest, and yet each day you have left the house and gone to work—hard work, I understand."

"There are different kinds of rest, Lucy. I've enjoyed what I've been doing. I thank you for the opportunity to do it. And not the least, it gave me a chance to earn my keep while I was here."

"No one asked you to 'earn your keep,' Justin. One does not ask a guest to 'earn his keep.' One asks only for the pleasure of his company. And I have the distinct impression that far from wishing to see me, you have determined to deprive me of your company as much as possible."

To her surprise, Justin's face hardened. Blood darkened it, his mouth drew tight, his hands clenched on the arms of his chair. When he spoke, his voice was thick in his throat.

"Lucy, I've never been much for social conventions—as I think you know. So I'll speak frankly. I was never under the illusion that I would be welcomed back to Sabrehill. I came here unexpected and uninvited, and I am grateful for the reception you've given me. The least I could do was to stay out of your way. And perhaps make myself useful while I was doing it."

He stood up. It seemed to Lucy now that he was restraining great anger, but with himself rather than with her.

"Justin, I have tried to make you understand—"

"I understand that I've put you to a great deal of trouble. I regret that. I was going to tell you tomorrow, after your guests had all left, that I too would be on my way, but—"

"Tomorrow!" Lucy sprang to her feet.

"But since the matter has come up, I may as well say it now. I thank you, Lucy, for a hospitality that I could never have expected. But you need not worry that I'll be back. I'll leave tomorrow—"

"But I don't want you to leave!"

Once again the words were out of her mouth before she could stop them and in a way she would not have wished. She was talking like a fool, embarrassing herself and Justin both. They stared at each other like helpless strangers, speaking different languages.

She tried for a more reasonable tone. "Justin, I didn't mean to imply just now that you aren't welcome here."

"Why should I be?"

"Oh, Justin, don't make this difficult. I'm sorry if—if in any way I've made you feel less than welcome. Your visit did come as a surprise, but . . . I don't see many of the family . . . and I don't meet many people I can talk with as I do with you. I regret that we had a . . . a misunderstanding those years ago—"

"It was not a misunderstanding."

She closed her eyes. She took a deep breath, held it, expelled it slowly. When she opened her eyes, Justin had not moved.

"Very well. If you wish to leave . . . But it seems to me that we've hardly talked. And each day that you've been here, I've looked forward to that all the more. But apparently the inclination was not shared." She sat down again, turning her back to him. "And now if you'll excuse me . . . I think I've made a fool of myself quite enough for one day."

The silence was long, and she wished to God he would leave. She wanted no further explanations or apologies. She wanted only to be left alone.

Would he never leave the office?

Never?

"You really wouldn't mind, then," Justin said, "if I stayed a little longer?"

"Oh, Justin!" She didn't know whether to laugh, cry, or throw something at the man.

"I really will try to be better company."

"Do as you please! Really, I couldn't care less!" Lies, lies, lies.

"If you find me getting in the way, you only have to say so."

"Darling, will you please go shave? We have guests."

He came up behind her. And bent down and kissed her cheek. And left the office.

And she was happy again.

Idiot!

They met on Sunday morning in some woods not far north of the old cabin where Tad and Nemo had found Buck and Adaba. The meeting was a small one: Zulie and Saul had asked only three people. Buck preferred to meet only a few people at a time, gain their confidence, and then build small groups into a larger, more cohesive one.

"I ain't got the whole plan worked out yet," he told Brutus of the Devereau plantation, "but when we open up the Skeet jail and burn Redbird, everything got to happen fast. Fast and sudden and quiet—and in the dark."

Brutus nodded his approval. "Redbird burn—and we all gone."

"Adaba going with us?" Sarah Jane of the McClintock plantation asked. Yes, word that Adaba was nearby had gotten out, and Buck did not like that. Adaba wounded was too vulnerable, too defenseless. "Maybe, maybe not," he said, "but don't you go 'round talking about no Adaba. Somebody gonna hear who ain't supposed to. You hear 'bout plenty John and Buck and Sam and Jack, but only one Adaba—so you whisper that name!"

He turned to Cato Weston, a ginger-haired, freckled man he would hardly have taken for a black. "The people in the Skeet jail house. We break them out, they ain't gonna know what's happening, what to do. Best we tell them first, so they ready. Any way you can do that?"

"Mr. Skeet don't allow us talk with them people," Cato said, "don't allow us near them. But don't you worry, I find a way."

Yes, Cato Weston would find a way. He, like Brutus

and Sarah Jane, had his reasons. "My momma wasn't no darker than my white daddy," he had told Buck, "but she was a slave, and the state wouldn't never let him set her free. So when he die off, they sell us, and that make us black. All right, by God, I *be* black!" He had laughed bitterly. "Couple year ago, before I got sold to Skeet, I run off for a time, maybe four months, got lost wandering 'round the hills. And you be surprised how many buckra bitch I give babies in them four month. And their children and their children children and all their children after—they going talk about how you black and they white, and all the time down deep they is nigger, same as you and me."

The others had laughed with delight. Cato Weston would do fine, just fine.

"You ain't the only one was sold," Brutus of the Devereau plantation had said. "First my baby sold, then my woman sold, then me sold too. Sold like animals, like sow, boar, and shoat. Never see my wife and baby again." Brutus's face had turned as hard as his name sounded. "And know I ain't never going see them. But somewhere I find me a white man, a man with slaves, and he ain't going see his wife and baby no more neither."

And then there was Sarah Jane: "I was at Redbird till the Old Man sold me away, and I still got people there. Got my little sister Serena, that Mr. Skeet and Shadrach treat so bad, and got my man, Tobe, there in that jail house. He there for running them McClintock boys away from me. Someday he kill them, then they hang him up or maybe worse. So we got to get away and take Serena too."

Yes, each of them had good reasons for wishing to flee, to rebel, to take revenge. Each of them had reasons for wishing to destroy their captors. And for each of them there were surely dozens of others on the nearby plantations. Perhaps more than dozens—perhaps hundreds.

And if one considered all of the plantations up and down the sea coast . . . all of the plantations throughout the South . .

"When?" Brutus asked. "When we do it?"

Before Buck could answer that question, he had another of his own. He turned to Sarah Jane. "Maybe Serena can tell you—does Skeet spend much time away from Redbird?"

She shook her head. "I can tell you that. He don't hardly go no place at all, 'cept maybe town on Saturday afternoon. Or ride around, find a nigger like Ettalee to steal. You looking for a time he ain't there, that ain't easy."

"Saturday nights?"

"Oh, maybe he go see Mr. Jeppson or Mr. Tucker, right close by, or maybe they come see him. But mostly he just sit home, maybe drink and wench."

"Then he won't be hard to find?"

"Ain't hardly likely."

Buck smiled. That was exactly what he had hoped to hear.

"Then we'll do it in two weeks," he said. "On Saturday night, just before Christmas. Two weeks, and I pay my respects to Vachel Skeet. And I take you away from this place and march you to freedom. Forever."

And Vachel dies, and Redbird burns.

Three

Two weeks. It was a long time to stay in one place, a long time to live under the noses of the same masters, and thinking about it could bring out a sweat. In two weeks even the best-intentioned of his friends might let a word slip in the wrong place, and suspicions would be aroused, suspicions that could lead to his capture and death. Except when he was in certain maroon camps, Buck tried never to stay in the same place for more than a few days.

But this was different, Buck told himself. This time he wasn't stealing a handful of blacks away from a single plantation, as he had from the Courtney place. No, this time he would be taking them from six or eight planta-tions, perhaps even more, and all at once. He would be doing something he had never done before, something that not even Adaba had done. In a single night he would lead off . . . he hardly dared guess how many.

The word went out from Zulie and Saul. The word went out from Brutus and Sarah Jane and Cato Weston. *Black Buck is here! Black Buck is here, and Adaba too is nearby!* And that same Sunday, in the afternoon, there was still another meeting, this time with people from the Pettigrew, Harmon, Haining, and Kimbrough plantations.

Yes, they would follow him. Yes, they needed only a leader.

They had one now. But they also had followers—people as ready to follow them as they were to follow Black Buck. People who had waited for a Black Buck or an Adaba for most of their lives.

The next morning, Buck started exploring the half-forgotten countryside and planning his escape routes. He had to be cautious, but traveling alone, and with his strength returning, it was not too difficult. But time was precious. In the daytime his potential followers were scattered about the plantations and at work, often under the watchful eyes of their drivers. Only at night could he huddle with the small groups in cabins and enlarge his plans and teach lessons in survival and keep enthusiasm high.

On Wednesday evening Zulie and Cato Weston planned to take Buck to meet some people in the Jeppson quarters. Serena of Redbird might be there too—Buck wondered if she would remember him—and perhaps some people from other nearby plantations. But before he left Sabrehill, Buck stopped by the blacksmith shop to see Ettalee.

"She getting better," Saul said, grinning, but looking as if he wanted to cry; and sure enough, miraculously, it seemed to be true.

On the previous Saturday, when Buck had first seen Ettalee, she had seemed lifeless, a small thing withering away. She lay so still she might have been carved from dark wood, and her eyes had appeared blind. She had been zombielike, one of the living dead, and that, Buck had thought bitterly, was what Claramae might have been like, had she survived the assault made on her.

He had visited Ettalee at least once each day since

Saturday, but he had seen no change. She had continued inert, lifeless, broken. But this evening there was light in the girl's eyes, and she wore a smile that slowly widened as she looked up at Buck from the bed.

"Just sudden this morning," Saul said, "she tell me, 'Daddy, I so hungry! When we going eat?' And I know she be better."

Buck sat down on the edge of the bed. "You feeling better now, Ettalee?"

"Yes, sir," the girl said, "but I sure hungry all day."

Saul laughed happily.

"You know who I am?" Buck asked.

" 'Course I know. You Buckley Skeet, and you come here and talk to my daddy every day. But don't you worry, I ain't going tell nobody."

"Thank you, Ettalee."

Buck got up from the bed and went out into the shop. Saul followed him.

"She's gonna be all right," Buck said. "She's gonna be all right, and we're all gonna be all right." *But Claramae is gone,* he thought, *Claramae is gone,* and the grief was fresh again.

She was content. No, not content, happy. There was no good reason for her happiness, of course—Sabrehill was still a very disturbed place, its atmosphere explosive—but since when had happiness needed a good reason? Justin's presence, that most questionable of reasons, was enough. Lucy liked him. She enjoyed him. He warmed her and made her laugh.

Only once in the next few days was his coming departure mentioned. Justin said he was considering a return to Virginia, before resuming his wanderings, to be with his children at Christmas. That meant he would be at Sabrehill little more than another week. Lucy wanted him to stay longer, much longer—almost a week had already been wasted—but how could she urge the man to stay away from his children? And she could hardly beg him to return to Sabrehill.

She refused to spoil her happiness by brooding on the matter. Or at least she tried.

Starting Monday morning, Justin ate three meals a day with her. He continued to disappear after breakfast, which left her free to do her own work, but he reappeared in the early afternoon for dinner, and they spent the rest of the day together. On Monday afternoon they rode out with Jebediah to inspect the work being done: fences and ditches repaired, cabins under construction, land newly cleared. On Tuesday afternoon they sat in the office, thumbed through old copies of *The Southern Agriculturist*, and lazily debated the merits of various mulches, fertilizers, and rotation schemes. Lucy loved showing off her expertise, since she clearly knew more about cotton and rice culture than Justin did, and he—surprisingly— did not expect her to pretend otherwise. How wise she was, how knowledgeable, how keen! She had to laugh at herself, but when she looked at Justin, she saw admiration in his eyes. Yes, honest-to-God admiration! In a man's eyes! How could she help but be happy?

Late Wednesday afternoon Wayland brought word to the office that his sister had taken a turn for the better. Lucy and Justin at once hurried to the blacksmith shop and found that it was true. Zulie had worked another of her seeming miracles. Ettalee was sitting up in bed, and there was a new, bright light in her eyes.

"You're really feeling better, Ettalee?"

" 'Course I do. But I so hungry!"

"She keep saying that," Saul said happily. "She keep saying that!"

And no wonder—the child looked a fraction of her former weight.

Lucy hurried to the kitchen. Lucinda had to be told. Leila had to be told. All of Sabrehill had to know, was entitled to know. Lucy still remembered all too vividly that evening only nine days ago when the people in their sullen anger had begun to gather outside the office. *"Ain't nothing for you to worry about, Miss Lucy,"* Cheney had said. *"Just people feeling bad 'cause what happen to little Ettalee."* But there had been a great deal to worry about, and there still was.

"Praise Jesus," Lucinda said now, as she heard the news. "Praise Jesus." And Lucy saw that Lucinda was still her friend after all, still the older sister she had always needed. And so was Leila her friend and sister, she thought as they embraced; and after all they had been through together, how could she have thought otherwise? Everything was going to be fine at Sabrehill, just fine.

Perhaps in her heart she knew better. She had been taught from childhood that she was living with an evil, and she never completely forgot it, not even now. So how could everything possibly be "fine at Sabrehill, just fine"?

Wednesday evening, after supper, she and Justin walked out to the field quarters. This was the most popular time, after Saturday night, for socializing, and Lucy often did her visiting on these evenings.

She knew the quarters well. Like most plantation mistresses, she took a special interest in the health, the shelter and clothing, the general welfare of her people. The workday was the province of the master, if there was one, and of the overseer and his drivers. But the domestic realm was that of the mistress, and Lucy had acted as mistress of Sabrehill long before she had taken over its management. She had come to know her people well and had generally been welcomed by them.

On this evening she was not welcome.

She could not have said how she knew. It was rather like that morning some three and a half weeks earlier when she had awakened to find that there was no fire in her room, and two boys were standing out on the parkland, and the house sounds were subtly wrong, and . . . somehow she had known there was trouble. Somehow she had known, even before she had been told that Ettalee was missing.

Now, walking down the quarters street, listening to the laughter and the music, stopping now and then to chat, she felt the same thing. Perhaps the laughter and the music stopped too soon as she and Justin approached. No one frowned at her, everyone smiled, but perhaps they wished to break off conversation and turn away too quickly. Perhaps they had too few requests or complaints. And there was an air, almost palpable, of harbored secrets.

As they came to the south end of the quarters, on their

way back to the mansion, they encountered Jebediah Hayes.

"Jebediah, have you heard that Ettalee is feeling much better today?"

"Yes, ma'am. I've been to see her. I think everybody has heard by now." Jebediah seemed distracted, as if she had interrupted him on some mission.

"How do they feel about it?"

Jebediah fidgeted. "Well, I think . . . relieved . . . and pleased."

"But not as much so as I would have expected. And with Christmas coming soon too. There's usually a better feeling before Christmas, don't you think?"

"I think you just have to give them a little more time, Miss Lucy. After the trouble that Mr. Skeet has caused."

"Perhaps you're right." Lucy shrugged. "Probably it's just my imagination." Certainly Jebediah would know of any special trouble in the quarters, if anyone did. But why did he himself seem so nervous this evening?

"Well . . . if you find out that something is going on . . . anything that I should know about . . ."

"I'll let you know, of course, Miss Lucy."

"Of course. And thank you, Jebediah. Good night."

Jebediah said his good night and hurried past them.

He turned and watched as Miss Lucy and Mr. Justin disappeared into the darkness between the field quarters and the mansion. So Miss Lucy felt that something was wrong in the quarters, did she, something other than Etta-lee's trouble and the long resentments and hatreds that Skeet had stirred up. Well, then, she was probably right, because she was sensitive to such things. And, Jeb felt guiltily, he had let her down. *He* should have known. And in fact, he had known—yes, damn it, something was going on in the quarters, something was amiss—but he had ignored his intuitions, he had put them out of mind, because he had something else on his mind that concerned him far more. His woman.

He headed toward Zulie's cabin.

It had been more than two weeks since he had asked her to marry him, and almost as long since the incident with Skeet when she had come running to his arms. The next ten days or so had been among the happiest in his life. Though she had not given him her answer, she had been warmer and more responsive to him than ever before, and he had been certain that she was about to become his for good. But then, suddenly, inexplicably, she seemed to have lost all interest in him. For about a week now she had been avoiding him, and he knew damned good and well that it was not for the usual woman's reason.

And he wanted her. Wanted her, needed her, badly.

He arrived at the far corner of the quarters just in time to see her step out of her cabin doorway, a faint aureole of candlelight behind her. She hesitated at the sight of him and nearly stepped back into the cabin, but there was no way to avoid him. She pulled the door closed behind her. He hurried up to her in the shadow of her portico.

"Zulie . . ."

"Evening, Jeb." It seemed to him that she wanted to avoid his eyes.

"Well, here you are. I've hardly seen you lately, Zulie."

"No. I been real busy."

"Too busy for me?"

"It do look like it."

"But not too busy now."

She gave him a brief, empty smile. "Got to get my sleep, Jeb."

"But you were just coming out, when I got here."

"Just going for some water. Forgot my bucket, though."

"Want me to get it for you?"

"No. I don't really need it."

He had the feeling that they were not really talking to each other at all. They were merely exchanging words.

"Zulie, honey, do you remember what I asked you?"

She looked at her feet. "Well, I . . . I been thinking about that."

He took her shoulders in his hands and tried to draw her to him, but her lowered head kept them apart. He kissed the top of her head. "You're going to marry me, Zulie. You surely are."

"Well, I got to think more. That's one reason I stay away from you, Jeb. I got to think."

"Now, what could be better than the two of us going up north and being free together?"

Zulie raised her head and laughed softly. "Now, what you talking about, be free together? Ain't no woman, she marry a man, is free."

"It wouldn't have to be like that with us, Zulie."

"You say that now, but a man don't even know when he act like a slavemaster. He been brought up like that." Zulie grinned and showed Jeb a hard fist. "Reckon I ought to marry me a little feller, least no bigger than me. Then when he start treating me like a slave, I just—" Her grin widened, and she shook her fist. "Why, honey, I just plain beat the shit out of that little goober!"

"Yeah, you do that. . . ." With Zulie's head up, Jeb could pull her body to his, and he did. But there was no response; she lay inert against him, and her mouth avoided his, though his own need mounted urgently.

"Zulie, come to my house with me right now." He tried to lead her away. "Come, now—"

"No, Jeb, I so tired—now, Jeb, please—"

"Then we don't have to go to my house." He reached around her and tried to push open her cabin door. "I remember you've got that nice, big bed in there—"

"No!"

The violence of her reaction shocked him. In an instant she was away from him, beating his arm down and standing between him and the door.

"Hey, Zulie!"

"You ain't going in my house without I tell you!"

"I wasn't going—"

"I ain't got much! I can't keep no goddam overseer out, he wants in. But it's my house, and you try to come in without leave, you got to beat me first."

Jeb looked at her with amazement. "I don't want to beat you, Zulie. And I'm not your overseer or your master, and I don't want to be. I'm just somebody who loves you."

Again Zulie avoided his eyes and looked at the ground, and inevitably, anger began to rise in his heart.

"And I'm sorry I even touched your goddam door."

"It's just the way I·feel."

"I can see that."

Anger, yes, but not at the expense of love. For some reason, he was losing Zulie, perhaps had lost her already. But he could not give up so easily.

"I don't want in your house anyway, Zulie," he said. "I want you in my house, I want you there always. Now, it isn't very late yet—why don't you and I—"

She shook her head, quickly, sharply. "No. Not tonight, Jeb. I . . . I just don't want to."

"All right. I'm sorry I bothered you."

He turned and walked away.

The bitch.

He loved her; his heart ached for her. He, more than any other man in the world, even her brothers, recognized her value. And he had enough respect for his own value to believe he was worthy of her. He had taken her into his house, into his bed, into his life. All she had to do was say, "Yes, Jebediah, yes," and they would have each other forever.

But tonight, suddenly, she had barred him from her cabin—as if she were barring him from her life.

What the hell kind of game was she playing?

Was there another man?

He could not believe that. In all honesty he did not think there was another man at Sabrehill who might have usurped her affections. But of course, you could never tell with a woman, and there might be a man on another plantation, a man he did not even know. . . .

Well, to hell with that. She didn't want him, and if it came down to it, he didn't need her. He could have all the women he wanted. Maybe he would get about six of them together and take them all on—he hadn't done anything like that since he had first come to Sabrehill. Yes, sir, he would just get himself about five or six gals and take them all to his house and fill 'em full of whiskey, and he'd strip 'em all down, and then he would . . .

But of course he would not. He would go back to his house alone and throw himself down on his bed in the dark, and think about Zulie, Zulie, Zulie. . . .

Jeb never looked back, and she was glad. She reentered the cabin and latched the door. She leaned against the door, hand and shoulder, as if to bar it from Jeb by her own strength. He must never enter the cabin while Adaba was here.

And perhaps that meant he would never enter it again.

She felt guilty, and guilt brought a whole range of other feelings—anger, self-hatred, defiance. Jeb had offered her love, and she had accepted it. Yes, she had loved him as much as she had ever loved a man—a black man, at any rate—and now she was turning him away. But Adaba and Buck were more important than any feeling she had ever had for Jeb—Buck for the freedom he promised, and Adaba. . . . She did not quite know what he meant to her yet, except that . . . he was like a dream come true.

"I heard some," he said now from the bed, in a voice still pitifully weak. "He gone?"

"Yes. He gone."

She went to the bed and sat down on the edge. She smiled, as she often did when he looked at her, an almost uncontrollable smile, and she felt a surge of protective feelings. This was Adaba, the Brown Dove, she had here, a broken bird that she was healing, and she wasn't sure she wanted to let it go.

"Don't you worry," she told him. "Ain't nobody come in here, I don't tell them so. But just the same, when I leave, you latch the door and put out the candle. And don't you answer for nobody but me."

"Now, why you got to go out, Zulie, and leave me all alone here?"

She stroked the side of his head. "I got to, Adaba! I got to act just like before you come here. That means I go out and talk to people and see my friends."

"Yeah, well, just this one night whyn't you stay here with me. I'll tell you all about Charleston, tell you about the fine houses and how one day you live in one of them, how you go to the fine shops—"

"No, not tonight." He had already discovered her weaknesses, the tales she loved to hear of other, better lives. "You been talking too much anyway, honey. You got to get your rest."

Suddenly she saw alarm in his eyes. He stared at her. "Adaba, what's wrong!"

"Got a chill coming on, Zulie. I feel it! I feel that death chill coming at me! You want to save me, ain't nothing for you to do but peel off that dress and climb into this here bed with me! You got to keep me alive, Zulie— hurry, honey, take off that dress!"

"Oh, you!"

"I'm a dying man, honey! Oops, here I go!"

She gave him a playful slap. "Yes, there you go, I know where you want to go, you naughty man. Now, you shut your mouth and get your rest, and 'fore long Zulie come back again."

"Sleep with me?"

"I got my own place to sleep."

"Mighty cold for you down on the floor. Mighty cold for me in this bed without you."

She laughed and kissed his forehead. "I got to go now. You do like I told you."

As she started to leave, he called to her, "Zulie," and there was something different, something serious in his voice that made her look around.

"Zulie," he said hesitantly, "you hear anything more . . . about that raid . . . on my camp?"

Of course she had heard. Half of the blacks in South Carolina had heard. But she said, "Now, don't you trouble yourself."

"I got to know, Zulie. I got to know. They say how many was hurt? How many killed?"

"Oh, you know how niggers build up tales, each one make it bigger and bigger—"

"How many, Zulie?"

Reluctantly she told him. "Some say thirteen dead." It was the smallest figure she had heard.

Adaba put a hand over his eyes. "Thirteen," he said softly. "Oh, my God. Oh, my God."

"Don't you think about that. Please don't."

He said nothing more. He simply lay there with his hand over his eyes. "I got to go now," she said again, and still he did not answer.

There was no more time. She looked out the door to see that she was unobserved, then waited in the dark outside the door until she heard the click of the latch.

Don't want to go, she thought.

The thought surprised her. The meeting was important. Why, what Black Buck was doing was about the most important thing to happen in her lifetime, and she was part of it.

Don't want to go.

She wanted to stay with Adaba. She wanted to comfort him. And then, when she had brought a smile back to his face, she wanted to hear his jokes, she wanted to be teased by him. Of course, the teasing didn't really mean anything. Men, when they were recovering from illness, often teased like that—some of them got so damn horny they would swear love and fidelity for a lifetime if you would just jump into bed with them once. She knew better than to take Adaba seriously. But just the same . . .

Got to go to the meeting!

And so she did, and as it turned out, it was a good meeting. Cato and Serena from Redbird were there, and Sarah Jane from the McClintock plantation, and three of the Jeppson people. And Buck, of course. That was enough. It was their first real meeting with the Jeppson people, and all three were solidly with them. And ten nights from now . . .

But all the way back to Sabrehill, Zulie thought not of the great flight to freedom but only of Adaba.

Shadrach was drunk. He should not have been drunk, not this drunk on a Wednesday night, unless he was lifting the bottle with Mr. Vachel, but to hell with that. And to hell with Mr. Vachel and Serena and the woman he had been with earlier tonight and all the rest of the world.

He was lying naked on the floor of the cabin when Serena came in, and the other woman was gone—gone before he was finished with her. He still needed a woman.

He struggled to his feet. Serena stared at him warily and started backing away. She knew what he had been up to, even if she hadn't caught him. She had been with him when he had started drinking, hours ago, and he had run her off. But now she was here, and he still hadn't got what he wanted. And needed.

She resisted, of course. She always did, until he frightened her, and sometimes it seemed that her desperation, her hatred of him, was greater than her fear. But not tonight. He tossed her onto the bed and tore at her clothes. She sobbed and cursed him, but the curses meant nothing. The whiskey was fading, and perhaps this time he would achieve the satisfaction he wanted. Sometimes she even gave up and helped him, if only in order to be rid of him sooner.

Why did they hate each other so, he wondered. Even at a moment like this, as she writhed under him, and he struggled to keep her pinned, struggled to keep driving into her, he could wonder. Why? But he knew why.

Serena had hated Shadrach from the very beginning, he knew, because he had been forced on her—because on that summer afternoon so long ago, when she was fourteen years old, she had been made a plaything for Mr. Vachel and Shadrach. And Shadrach hated Serena for much the same reason—because, if it had not been for Mr. Vachel, he could have loved her. But with Mr. Vachel, two niggers ended up hating not only him but also each other.

And themselves.

She was howling now, whimpering, cursing him again and again. He did not mind that; one heavy blow across her face caused her to subside. He simply continued to hold her pinned down, continued doing what he was doing, continued striving for that moment that in his drunkenness might never come.

And then he realized that through her moaning, through her tears, she had said something different, something she had never said to him before. She had threatened him. But not with a knife or a gun or poison. She was talking about Buck, Black Buck, Buckley Skeet. And he did not know what she had said. But it was important. His life might depend on it, and he had to know. What had she said?

What?

Shadrach had been drinking, Skeet could see that, but just how drunk the nigger was—that was hard to say. He walked straight, and his eyes were steady, and there was nothing drunken about his speech. But anger or fear or even plain necessity could clear the whiskey from a man's head mighty fast.

They were in the passage of Redbird. Skeet had grabbed a pistol and come running down the stairs in his nightshirt when he had heard Shadrach's call. Shadrach had lit a lamp. In spite of the chill of the night, the chief driver was barefoot and wore only an old pair of pants, and the girl in the torn dress was not much more covered. She knelt weeping on the floor of the passage, while Shadrach stood over her, cursing and threatening. But Skeet still had no idea of what it was all about.

"Now, tell him," Shadrach commanded. "You tell master just what you tell me."

"Didn't tell nothing," the girl wept. "Didn't mean nothing."

Shadrach swept the hard back of his hand against the girl's cheek—"You tell, goddam you!"—then lifted her head and struck her across the mouth, a lip-bruising blow. Skeet admired the skill.

"You tell, goddam you," Shadrach repeated, "or you don't see this night through!"

Yes, Skeet admired the skill, but sometimes when Shadrach or Mr. Dinkin was particularly brutal, a more gentle approach was helpful.

"Now, now, Shad, maybe the gal don't even know what you're talking about."

"She know!"

"Something you ought to tell me, Serena?" He reached down and patted her head gently, but she flinched away.

"Ain't nothing, nothing!"

"Now, it must be something, Serena, to get old Shad all riled up. What you been saying to Shad?"

"Yeah, Serena," Shadrach said, "what you been telling me about Black Buck?"

Skeet stiffened. Black Buck again. About time to put an end to all that.

"What about Black Buck, Serena?"

"Ain't nothing. It's just a song they sing in the fields. 'Black Buck, he a-coming, Black Buck, he a-coming—' "

"Shad," Skeet said impatiently, "just what the hell is this all about? You must know what she told you. If it's so important, what the hell is it?"

Yes, Shadrach was certainly drunk. He looked around, confused, almost desperate, as if asking himself what the hell *had* Serena said. Skeet knew the look and, for that matter, the feeling of that black, drunken lapse.

"I said, what the hell—"

"Black Buck coming, she say."

"All right, I heard that. Is that all?"

"She say he coming to get me. To get *you!*"

"You afraid of our old Black Buck?"

"No, sir. But when she tell me . . ." A look of recognition spread across Shadrach's face: he had remembered. "She tell me Black Buck is already here, Mr. Vachel—"

"No!" the girl said, too quickly.

"She say he come down the river on a cotton box, and she seen him and talked to him. He was caught, but he got away—"

"No!" Serena said desperately. "No, I never seen him! Ain't no Black Buck! I only say that 'cause Shadrach hurt me! Ain't so, ain't so!"

Which was undoubtedly true. There had been this talk of Black Buck lately, and the wench had made use of it to threaten Shadrach. And the threat had turned against her. Skeet was sourly amused, but it was late, and he was tired.

"Get her the hell out of here. And tomorrow you stripe her butt a few times for her goddam threats. And, Serena, you ain't ever to mention Black Buck again, you hear me?"

Serena nodded.

"And, Shad, you black bastard, you wake me up again for any such nonsense, and I'll stripe you myself."

"Yes, sir! Yes, sir!"

Shad looked relieved that the incident was finished. He yanked the girl to her feet and dragged her through the passage doorway, closing it behind him. He had gotten himself into a drunk mad, Skeet figured, and started something he hardly knew how to finish.

Skeet tossed his pistol into the top drawer of a chest that stood in the passage. The blacks at Redbird didn't dare steal from him, and it would be as safe there as any place. He took the lamp and went into the parlor, where a bottle of whiskey stood handy on a table. He poured himself a drink.

What was it that caused all the niggers from time to time to start talking about Black Buck? Why him rather than another? All that business with Buckley was so long ago. Like yesterday for Skeet, but still . . . so long ago. *Why'd you have to spoil everything, Buckley?*

Instantly the thought was followed by another, deeper, sadder, more sickening: *Why did I have to spoil everything? It could have been so good. . . .*

But that thought, with all it implied, had to be instantly banished. Nothing Skeet had ever done had deserved Buckley's and Claramae's treachery. They had been nigger stud and white slut, nothing more, and he had done what a master was bound to do.

To Claramae, at least.

And to Buckley yet.

He raised his glass in a toast. *To you, Buckley. I'm still waiting.*

Four

They appeared Friday afternoon a little before sundown: a red-bearded man, weathered and gnarled, who could have been ten years older or younger than Jeppson, and a gap-toothed youth with desperation and hunger in his eyes. The sun was red behind them. They carried rifles, and little more, and when the old man hesitantly said that they were George and Lester Carney, Jeppson knew he was lying.

"Food," the old man said. "Some supper and a place to

sleep and some breakfast. That's all we want. And we'll work for it."

Drifters, Jeppson thought contemptuously. Hill people, likely, thieves and scoundrels, and he ought to run them off. But they pretended to be honest, and you didn't run off honest travelers; and he didn't like the way they clutched their rifles, as if they had already been run off one time too many.

"Where you headed for?" he asked.

"Charleston," the youth said too quickly. "We headed downriver, and we going to Charleston. Got people in Charleston. We get to Charleston, we do just fine. Surely looking forward to Charleston."

Spoke too quickly and said too much. And the old bastard knew it and looked at the youth nervously. But he said, "Yeah, me and my honey-boy, we going to Charleston."

Jeppson shrugged. It could just be. Anyway, it didn't really matter as long as the two made no trouble.

"I got wood to split," he said, "a hell of a lot of it. But I got niggers can do the job."

The old man's face darkened. His eyes narrowed, and his mouth pulled, and the youth's face showed the same frustration. "Niggers," old George muttered, "goddam niggers." Because niggers, slaves belonging to people like Jeppson, did the work and took the bread from a white man's mouth. Why should any man hire the likes of him and his honey-boy when he had niggers to do the work? Jeppson saw and approved and laughed to himself.

"Tell you what," he said. "I ain't one to let a white man go hungry. You eat some of my food, and then you chop some of my wood, just to be friendly, and I got a shed you can sleep in, and you can have some breakfast before you're on your way. Give you a poke of something to take with you too."

The frustration faded from the old man's face. "Well, now," he said. "Well, fine. You being right friendly."

"Ain't one to let a white man go hungry."

So he fed them, nothing fancy, just plain hog-and-hominy nigger food, but better than they were used to getting, from the way they wolfed it down. He fed them on the porch, just outside the kitchen, which was part of the house.

"Going to Charleston, eh?"

"Yes, sir," the old man said. "Long time since I been to Charleston. How long you reckon it take us?"

"Damn hard two days' ride. Going afoot, taking time to earn a meal now and then, I don't know. You figure it."

"You figure we're halfway there?" young Lester asked, like an idiot.

"Halfway from where?"

The old man gave Lester a hard look, then turned back to Jeppson. "From where we come from, I reckon that big old Sabrehill plantation is 'bout halfway. Or maybe Redbird. Reckon we passed Redbird by now."

It was hardly inconceivable that George Carney, or whatever the hell his name was, had heard of Sabrehill or even Redbird, but there was a kind of dumb cunning in the man's eyes that Jeppson didn't like.

"No, you ain't passed Redbird," he said. "Redbird is the next place just east of here. And Sabrehill is east beyond that some ways. It's just past the Kimbrough plantation, if you heard of that."

"Sabrehill," George said, "I heard that Sabrehill big house is something to see."

"Pretty fancy, if that's to your liking."

"What it look like?"

"Brick, two and a half stories, big cupola."

"That sound just like a lot of other places."

"Eight pillars on the piazza, straight across. Only place around here with eight pillars, straight across. Oh, it's pretty fancy."

"Might be we take a look at it," George said to Lester, "might be." He turned again to Jeppson. "And Redbird and that Kimbrough place, they worth looking at?"

"Well, Kimbrough Hall, that's pretty fancy too."

Jeppson didn't believe in the apparent innocence of the old man's curiosity, didn't believe in it at all. These two had some special interest in Sabrehill and perhaps in Redbird as well. And perhaps in Kimbrough Hall or in Jeppson's own plantation for that matter. They could be a couple of thieves, getting past the dogs and the niggers and begging a free meal before they used their guns and took what they wanted. If so, they were not about to pull the wool over Balbo Jeppson's eyes. His own gun was handy, and he knew how to use it; and they would do nothing until he turned his back on them. He would simply keep an eye on them while they chopped the wood, then lock them up for the night in the shed, where they could do no harm. Then maybe he would take a ride over to Redbird and tell Vachel to keep his eyes open for this pair. It wouldn't hurt to have Vachel Skeet owe him one more favor.

He was a whisper, a shadow, a ghost . . . a hint, a hope, a rumor. He came and went, seen by only a few, though his presence was felt by others. *"A runaway . . . somewhere in the quarters . . . some say Black Buck, some say Adaba himself . . . don't you say nothing to them kitchen wenches, them house maids . . . don't say nothing to them that might talk. . . ."* Somehow people knew. But whoever was out there, hiding in the quarters, he was one of their own and therefore, to most of them, to be protected.

Early Thursday morning, before daybreak, Buck crossed the lane to see how Ettalee was. To his surprise, she was awake and out of bed. "Can't keep her resting," Saul said, deeply pleased. " 'Fore, can't get her out of that bed hardly. Now, can't hardly keep her there!"

Ettalee giggled. "My knees don't work so good no more."

Buck returned that evening, and the next morning, and yet again on Friday evening. Ettalee delighted him. Her loss of weight had sculpted her down until she was like a thin ebony statuette, a small black angel who might have been a child or an ageless woman. Suffering, Buck knew from experience, seldom beautifies, seldom ennobles. But in Ettalee's case, it did. She was as lively as the squirrels she fed dried crusts to, as quick as the rabbits and the foxes she had once chased through the fields, and every time Buck saw her she seemed more substantial and more radiant.

She was almost exactly half Buck's age, young enough

to be his much younger sister, but almost as old as Claramae had been; and watching her that Friday evening, he
kept thinking of Claramae. To his eyes, they were so
much the same: both so young, so filled with life to live,
so vulnerable. And both so abused. But at least Ettalee
had survived.

The Friday evening meal was finished. Zag and Binnie,
who had joined them, picked up their plates and went
back across the lane to the coach house. Saul went with
them to talk to Zag. And Buck stretched and yawned and
accidentally burped and set Ettalee off on long peals of
laughter. He felt stuffed and lazy and content to stay by
the fire for the rest of the evening or even the night, but
he said what had to be said: "Well, I got to go."

"Now, why you go?"

Buck tried to stir himself from his chair. "Got things
to do, Ettalee."

"That's what you say last night and night before."

"Every night, Ettalee, got to go, got to stir my bones."

"You stay a little longer."

He saw that she meant it: she really did want him to
stay. Stay and make her laugh and tell her tales of his
life on the run.

Buck shook his head, and the girl looked disappointed.
"But I'll come see you tomorrow," he promised. "I'll
come see you every day I can till I leave here."

The girl's eyes were sad. "And then we ain't going see
you no more?"

"Oh, I don't know. Reckon I might just come back for
a visit. That is, if I'm welcome."

"You know you is."

"Well, now, that's fine."

Reluctantly Buck hauled himself up out of his chair.
He crossed the room to where Ettalee sat by the fire and
leaned down over her. Just as he had a time or two
before, he tilted her chin up and started to kiss her cheek.
But this time her head turned, her hand went to the
back of his neck, and her lips met his.

Shock. Fingers lightly on his neck, and warm lips
softly on his, and a shiver of alarm went through him.
Breath stopped, and he could not move.

The kiss lasted only a second or two, then hand and lips dropped away. Ettalee stared into the fire. Her kiss had been without thought or calculation, and she didn't seem to know what it meant to him.

She might have been Claramae, and he thought of everything that might have been.

"Don't you let nothing bad happen to you," she said after a moment.

"No, Ettalee. I won't let nothing bad happen to me." *Nor*, he added silently, *to you neither*.

"Don't want nothing bad to happen to you."

Yes, she might have been Claramae, long ago, saying that, and Buck thought, *Oh, Lord Jesus, I can't let nothing happen to her*. It wasn't that there was anything between them or ever could be. She was so young, as Claramae had been, and after what she had been through, she needed the shelter of Sabrehill, and he had the long hard years of the outlier's life ahead of him. But he could not fail her as he had failed Claramae. She had to live and find her happiness and maybe even someday be free.

He kissed her again, this time on the forehead, and left quickly.

Adaba was awake when Buck arrived at Zulie's cabin. He was stretched out on the bed, bare chested, with the blankets down to his hips as Zulie put a fresh dressing on his wounded side. His voice was weak, and there was still a deep weariness in his eyes, but he grinned up at Buck.

"Well, son," he said, "glad to see you still kicking."

"Glad to see you still the same yourself. Same lazy sonabitch, laying flat on your back."

Adaba laughed. "Yeah, I'm leading the easy life these days. Don't do nothing but laze around, drink juleps, read books stole from the mistress's library."

"He do read wonderful," Zulie said admiringly. "Read good as Mr. Jeb, I reckon."

"Going have to meet this Mr. Jeb one of these days."

"Oh, no, you best not!"

"From what you tell me about him, he ought to be a

real bad nigger. What the hell's he doing busting his ass for a white woman?"

"Maybe that's your answer," Buck said. "Ass."

"Some has said so," Zulie said, "but I sure don't believe it."

"You Jeb's woman?" Adaba asked. The question was deceptively casual.

Zulie looked startled. "Ain't nobody's woman but my own! Where you get that idea?"

"It's somehow in the way you talk about him." Adaba looked at her appraisingly. "Maybe you just *been* his woman."

"Told you, ain't nobody's woman—"

"You?" Adaba was incredulous. "You, Erzulie, name for the love goddess, you ain't got no love-nature in you? You telling me Erzulie is all dry up like a dry well?"

"No, I ain't saying that! I just say—"

"Why, I hope not. Zulie, honey, your Johnny Dove need you! Now, ain't you going give your poor Johnny what he need?" Adaba, hardly covered, started to lift and push down the blankets. "Come on, come see how I need you!"

"Oh, Johnny!"

Zulie tried to push the blankets back up. Adaba grabbed her, and she fell laughing onto the bed on top of him. For a man who sounded weak, Adaba showed surprising strength as they rolled and wrestled on the bed. Or maybe, Buck thought, Zulie did not really wish to escape his arms.

"Ain't gonna stand around here watching you two pleasuring," he said. "Gonna find Saul, talk a little, and go get my rest." He caught Zulie's eye, though she was still laughing and wrestling with Adaba. Yes, he and Saul would talk a little—would talk with their rebels. She would understand. And she understood that Adaba was still not to know.

He said good night and went out into the dark.

The pair on the bed lay still for a moment, watching Buck leave. Zulie was highly conscious of the half-covered body beneath her—the deep chest, the long slope down from the ribs, the hollow of groin between the bandage and the blankets. The chest was cool to her touch but grew warm as her hand lay still on it. She expected, almost anticipated, Adaba to resume the wrestling, but he merely moved a thumb back and forth across her cheek.

"Old Buck," he said thoughtfully, "he sure don't seem in no hurry to leave here."

Zulie let her head fall to Adaba's shoulder. It had the good, clean smell of the harsh lye soap she had used on him. "Ain't no reason he hurry," she said.

"Week is a long time for him and me to stay in a place like this. Time we was on our way."

The suggestion startled Zulie, and she raised her head. "But you can't! You ain't well yet! You can't leave here yet!"

"Maybe I can't, but Buck can. And should. Got to talk to him about that. No sense in him waiting for that Mr. Sabre to come back."

Zulie felt a twinge of guilt. She had followed Buck's instructions in telling Adaba that Mr. Justin Sabre had come and gone and might or might not be back, but if Adaba knew . . .

"That Mr. Justin ain't no good anyway," she said, to make herself feel better.

"Maybe not." Adaba resumed stroking Zulie's cheek, but his thoughts seemed distant. "Honey, you know if old Buck is up to something?"

"Now, why you say that?"

"I don't know. It just ain't *like* him to stay here so long."

"He ain't going to leave here without you!"

"Why not?" He rubbed her nipple through her dress, and she felt it swell. "He know I got my Zulie here to momma me."

She pushed his hand away. "He was wore most to nothing when he come here, Adaba. Not like you, but bad just the same."

He smiled at her and touched a finger to her lips.

"Best not call me that name, Adaba, honey. Adaba is somebody that nobody don't ever see."

She shook her head. "Adaba is what I prayed for and longed for and conjured for. And my Adaba is what I got."

She kissed him then. She had not intended to. It simply happened: her lips moved over his rough beard and found his. And suddenly the well was far from dry; it was flooded, it was hot, it was boiling, and she was groping under the blankets for him, and—

She had to get away from him. Only a few times in her entire life had she felt such an abrupt and powerful surge of passion, and she did not know why, *she had to get away.*

He did not try to stop her. He merely lay there, passive, as she slipped out of his arms and away from the bed. He looked at her, and she turned away and stood trembling.

"I'm sorry," he said after a moment. "I shouldn't teased you the way I been doing. I didn't mean no harm."

She could not answer. She could only shake her head. Of course he had meant no harm.

"One trouble with staying in one place too long," Adaba went on, "is that you begin to feel like you belong there. Even in a few days, people can start meaning something to you, people you can't take with you when you leave. . . . People you can't take with you when you leave," he repeated slowly. "And I don't ever let that happen to me. You understand, Zulie?"

She nodded. Yes, she understood. And she understood now that she had torn herself from Adaba's arms, not because she could not love him, but because she might love him too much, and she had already known what he was telling her: he would allow her no lasting place in his life.

"I leave here," he said, "and it ain't going to be for no Charleston, that you dream about. It ain't going to be for no Boston nor Canada nor any other place up north. At least, not for long. I take them there, but I don't stay."

"I know. That's why you is Adaba."

"I'll be out there in the woods till they kill me, Zulie."

"I know."

"But I'll think about you when I'm out there."

She wanted to weep. *Whyn't I let him do it to me?* she thought miserably. *Wouldn't be no harm. He want me, and I guess I want him, and whyn't I let him do it? Whyn't I take my dress off right now and . . .*

But she knew she would not.

She pulled the blankets up over Adaba's shoulders and tucked them in. "Honey, I got to go out for a while. Nobody going to bother you. You get your rest."

Adaba smiled and closed his eyes.

The quarters were quiet. Last chores were being done before bedtime. Zulie stopped and talked to a few people; she was conscious that her chatter was too bright and that her voice threatened to crack at any moment. *Being silly,* she thought. *Near crawled in bed with that man, like a dang fool. And he ain't nothing to me, ain't nothing at all. Got me a man if I want him, a good man, a better man. . . .*

She walked toward the overseer's house at the head of the lane. Through a window, she saw that Jeb was sitting in the dark in his small parlor, looking at the dying fire. He had a blanket around his shoulders for warmth. When he answered her tap at the door, she slipped quietly into the room.

"You still angry at me 'cause of the other night?" she asked.

"No, I'm not angry, Zulie," he said, still looking at the flickering coals.

She could not see his face in the dark "Can I stay here for a while?"

"You know you can stay as long as you want."

"Just for a while. You really ain't angry?"

Jeb laughed.

"Well, then . . ."

She slipped onto his lap, curled up in his arms. The arms tightened around her, and she put her head on his shoulder. Jeb was one of the few men she knew who was big enough to make her feel small and safe and protected.

"You a good man, Jeb."

"Yeah," he said, not too seriously, "I reckon I am."

"Too good for the likes of me."

He kissed her forehead. "Now, don't talk like that."

"True, though. And if you really want to marry me . . . still . . ."

The big arms tightened around her. "I do, Zulie. You know I do."

She also knew she should not keep him waiting for her answer. She should tell him yes or no, and if she did not intend to say yes, she should never have brought the matter up.

She wanted to tell him yes.

She said, "I'm thinking on it. I really am. And I got such a good feeling for you."

The arms around her grew tighter still.

She stayed there with him a long time without moving. When she returned to her cabin, Adaba was asleep.

The journey had been long and hard. It seemed that the farther they were from home, the less they were trusted. Few people like Jeppson had been willing to let them earn a meal or a place to rest. Again and again they had been delayed by the need to catch a fish, trap a rabbit, steal a turkey. They had damn near got themselves killed, taking some niggers' noon dinner from them at rifle point. They had been shot at and run off for poaching. But somehow they had gotten this far.

Before dawn on Saturday morning, they heard someone rattling the lock on the shed door. That goddam Jeppson hadn't trusted them enough even to turn his back on them—which made his back deserving of a bullet as far as Silas was concerned. Goddam Jeppson with his sly grin and his doubting eyes—he trusted his niggers more than he did a white man. Silas hated the damn son of a bitch who had let them earn their supper and a place to sleep for the night and who was about to feed them again and give them a bit of food to take on their way. He hated Jeppson almost as much as he did Sabre and Tradwell.

They ate their breakfast on the porch outside the kitchen, sullenly accepted a poke of food, and were on their way by the time dawn edged the sky.

Redbird was right next door.

Silas had explained carefully to Lute: "We use your ma's folks' name, call ourselves Carney, so if that Mr. Sabre tells folks to be on the lookout for Rogans, they don't know it's us. Likely he been spreading all kind of lies about us, so's give us trouble if we follow him. And first we go to Redbird and see if Black Buck already been turned in there for the money."

"Likely he been turned in by this time," Lute had said gloomily.

Silas had agreed. "Likely he been. And if he been, then we by God go after that Mr. Sabre, 'cause he stole them niggers from us, and that's just like stealing our money. That there is *our* money, Lute!"

"Yes, sir, it is. And that Adaba, he's our nigger too. We got to get him back."

"Likely they're taking him to Charleston. All right, we follow them. We follow them all the way, and we get the money for Adaba too."

It had all seemed quite reasonable, quite logical, and it still did as Silas and Lute walked through the woods toward Redbird. "We just mosey over," Silas said, "and have us a look-see. Niggers is all going to work at this hour. We just go over and look around real quiet, and maybe we see Black Buck over there, never can tell." He spoke softly, as if they might be overheard.

"But, pa," Lute said, "can't we just walk up to the door and ask? Why can't we—"

"Lute, ain't something struck you as peculiar?"

Lute looked puzzled. "What's that, pa?"

"A murdering, thieving nigger like Black Buck, he was turned in for the reward—don't you reckon we'd heard about it? Don't you reckon that Mr. Jeppson would be telling us about it? Don't you reckon he'd be falling all over hisself to talk about it for the next ten years?"

"Reckon he would."

" 'Course he would. Now, maybe he just misplaced it in his mind. But supposing Mr. Sabre got them niggers over at Sabrehill, and he's dickering to get the price up."

Lute saw the shrewdness of this speculation, saw the possibilities of even greater wealth. "Why, I bet he's doing just that! And if he can do it, we can do it. Why, we get our hands on Black Buck again, he fetch maybe six, seven, eight thousand dollars!"

"Now, now, I ain't saying it's likely Mr. Sabre still got them niggers. I just say it could be. So we got to go look on the quiet first. 'Cause if Black Buck ain't there, we don't want no one to know he could be 'round close by. We got to find him and take him to Redbird ourselves."

But if Black Buck *was* at Redbird?

Silas did not like to think about that. It would mean that Sabre and Tradwell had already collected the reward, and Silas and Lute would have to go after them to get the money. And though he would not admit it to Lute, Silas had a deep, sick doubt that they would be able to do it. But they would have to try. They would have to try, if it was the last, best effort of their lives.

And whether they succeeded or not, they would have to make those snotty nigger-stealing sons of bitches pay. *Pay!*

"There it is, pa."

"Yeah . . ."

Dawn was ahead of them. The main Redbird buildings lay to the southeast. Silas and Lute moved slowly closer, keeping to a line of trees. They expected dogs to start barking at any instant, but the morning remained silent.

"It sure ain't much," Lute said, "for a place that'll put up $5000 for a runaway nigger."

No, not much, compared to some of the other places they had seen as they traveled down the river. Even in the poor light of dawn, it was apparent that both the big house and the outbuildings were shabby and run-down, and there were no vast lawns, no formal gardens. Silas thought he could see the brick nigger-jail—even where the Rogans came from, the Skeets, father and son, had long been known for their ability to break niggers.

"I sure don't see no Black Buck," Lute said, "nor no Adaba either."

"Let's move closer."

Surprisingly, for this hour, few slaves seemed to be up and about. Anyway, Silas figured, if Black Buck were here, he would not be walking about free. Most likely he would be in the nigger-jail.

"Lute," he said, "we got to get a look in that there jail house."

There did not seem to be any difficulty in that. They were within a hundred feet of the building now, a number of trees gave them concealment, and dawn had only begun to spread. All they had to do was keep walking. . . .

They were almost there before Silas realized. They were not alone. Lute gasped and plucked at Silas's arm as he too saw the blacks closing in.

There were half a dozen of them stepping out of the shadows. With them came a white man, a pistol in one hand and a whip in the other. He wore a little grin under his mustache. Two of the blacks held rifles as if they were unaccustomed to them but would use them if so ordered.

Silas and Lute had been expected.

And Silas Rogan knew he had failed. There would be no reward, no recapture of Black Buck or Adaba, no riches after the long years of poverty. The niggers and the rich and the goddam gentry—they would, as always, take it all. And Silas Rogan would die with nothing— nothing but an empty belly, a broken dream, and a curse on his withered lips.

Dinkin and three of the blacks delivered the Carneys, or whatever their name was, to the passage of the big house. It took Skeet a while to get the truth out of them— or at least enough of the truth to be useful.

He knew at once, of course, that Jeppson was right: these two were up to no good. It had been a simple matter to have Dinkin, Shadrach, and a few others keep an eye open for them, and their stealthy approach had soon been observed. But what the hell did they want? The most obvious possibility was that they were thieves, perhaps nigger-stealers. But naturally they denied any such thing.

Skeet sat at ease in a chair in the passage; he held a pistol, taken from a chest drawer, just so these two would get no ideas about getting by him. They had been disarmed, and two of the blacks held their guns. They both looked scared—and humiliated by the fact of being guarded by blacks.

"You come skulking around my place," Skeet said. "You come sneaking up on my jail house, and you tell me you ain't here to steal nothing?"

"We ain't!" old Carney said desperately. "We just passing by on our way to Charleston—"

"What would a dirty old coot like you be doing in Charleston? What business you got in Charleston, tell me that."

"Got kin there. Got kin we ain't seen in a long time. Mister, we don't mean no harm—"

"Lock them up," Skeet told Dinkin. "Lock them up in the jail house till you got time to put shackles on them. Then put them to work with the niggers, and don't spare the whip."

"What you mean?" the old man asked incredulously. "You can't lock us up! You can't shackle us like we was niggers! You can't—"

Skeet pretended to ignore him. "When you going into Riverboro, Mr. Dinkin? Next week sometime?"

"Reckon so," Dinkin said, obviously enjoying the scene. "By the end of next week sometime."

"When you go in, see if you can find the constable. If you do, tell him we got a couple of nigger-stealers and to get his ass out here and pick them up. When he has time, that is. Ain't no hurry, I reckon, long as they earn their keep."

"I don't know, Mr. Skeet," Dinkin said dubiously. "I'd rather have a couple of good niggers, even just one good nigger, than a pair like this anytime."

"But they ain't niggers, Mr. Dinkin, they just a pair of worthless sandhillers, and we ain't got no choice. Hell, yes, you'd rather have just one good nigger, but who's gonna trade for them? Now, get them the hell out of here."

"But you can't—" the old man started, as Dinkin pushed him toward the doorway, and "Pa, don't let them do this!" the younger man yelled; and the old man shouted, "Mister, you got to listen to us!"

"I been listening," Skeet said, "and you ain't told me a goddam thing I don't know already."

"Mister, it ain't like you think!"

Skeet figured the old man might die of apoplexy. "Then what is it?" he asked. "I'm listening."

Old Carney hesitated, and Skeet figured he was groping for a lie. He said, "I'm giving you just one more minute of my time."

"Something . . . something was stole from us."

"Old man, you never in your life had nothing worth stealing but maybe your rifle. Mr. Dinkin—"

"No! No, please! It's true. We was coming down the river on a cotton box with some niggers, and they got stole from us."

Illumination may come at the most unexpected moment. It may come on the slimmest evidence, the slightest testimony, and Skeet made the connection instantly. What had Shadrach said only a few nights before?

"She tell me Black Buck is already here, Mr. Vachel! She say he come down the river on a cotton box, and she seen him and talked to him. He was caught, but he got away!"

The Carneys—with Buckley Skeet?

It was quite impossible, of course. Whatever Serena had said to Shadrach and whatever this old man said now— they had nothing to do with each other. All that had occurred was the coincidence of a few words: *cotton box . . . niggers . . . stole from us . . . Black Buck . . . caught but got away. . . .* When you waited a dozen years for something you craved with all your guts, it never happened. In fact, after a dozen years you could hardly bear to have it happen, for nothing could ever equal the fervor, the power, the sheer lust of that long yearning.

No. Buckley was not back. And he was never coming back. Skeet would never be that lucky.

Nevertheless . . .

"Old man, you better tell me what you talking about."

Even then it was difficult to get the story, and Skeet was not at all certain that he was getting it all.

Old Carney and the boy, it seemed, had captured the

blacks they had brought down the river on the cotton box.

"Why? Why did you bring them down the river?"

The old man reddened, still reluctant to speak. "To get the reward."

"What reward?"

"The reward for Black Buck," young Carney burst out. "That reward for Black Buck is *ours!* Ain't right you give it to nobody else! *We* was the ones caught Black Buck!"

Impossible. Quite impossible.

"You caught Black Buck," Skeet said slowly, "or thought you did, and you was bringing him down the river."

"To you, Mr. Skeet," the old man said, "to you. To claim that reward you had out all these years. You still got that reward out, ain't you?"

"Yes, but—"

"But he got stole from us!"

"How did you know you had Black Buck?"

" 'Cause he look like what they say. And he was with another nigger, a bearded nigger with a dove mark on his chin—Adaba. We had them both, and they both got stole from us."

Black Buck and the Brown Dove. *Both* captured by, and stolen from, the Carneys? The idea that these two mangy, bedraggled, good-for-nothing savages might have captured both Black Buck and the Brown Dove was almost beyond comprehension.

"And who stole them from you?"

"Man name of Tradwell"—yes, Skeet knew the name—"and another name of Sabre."

Skeet did not move. He felt paralyzed.

"Niggers talking 'bout how Sabrehill got itself a visitor. Old friend of yours."

"What you talking about?"

"Mr. Justin, sir. The minute I hear that name—"

"Who?"

"Mr. Justin Sabre. Come on a cotton box a day or two back. . . ."

Suddenly he could believe. Almost.

"Let me get this straight. You caught a couple of run-away niggers. You were bringing them down the river. . . ."

The old man reluctantly, still unsure of his best move, told the story again, and Skeet could see it all. The capture of the blacks had apparently been a matter of sheer luck: that certainly rang true. And to hear old Carney tell it, there was simply no way the two blacks could have escaped from the boat unaided. Skeet did not know Tradwell, but he could see the man warning old Carney to go easier with the whip—the whip that Carney swore was necessary to keep the two killer-niggers cowed. And he could see the look of mutual recognition when Justin's and Buckley's eyes met.

Yes, Skeet could see Justin: pouring whiskey down the Carneys' throats until they passed out. ("Made like he was so friendly, he did, even buying a jug of whiskey and bringing it back to us on the box.") And then, with or without Tradwell's help, stealing Buck and the other nigger away.

Skeet could see it. Skeet could believe it.

Justin and Tradwell would get rid of the Carneys and go on their way. Justin would take Buck to Sabrehill and hide him among the dozens of black families there. Then he would take Buck north with him, both of them laughing at Vachel Skeet, who had come so close to having the black bastard in his hands again after all these years. After all these years, one more laugh on Vachel Skeet.

It had to be that way.

Skeet had one last question. "Why'd you come sneaking up on my place? And don't tell me you didn't."

"Figured on finding out if you had Black Buck yet. If you didn't, we was going to get him back from Mr. Sabre before you found out about him. We was going to bring him here for the reward."

"Or maybe you was going to steal a nigger or two and see what you could get for them." Skeet made a gesture of disgust. "Mr. Dinkin, lock these two fools up."

"Mister, it ain't right!"

"Listen," Skeet said. "I've known the Sabres all my life. Drank with them, ate with them, fought with them. Fought with Justin Sabre and left my mark on him. Ask anybody around here, I don't waste my good words on any Sabre. But one thing they ain't, it's nigger-stealers. Justin Sabre didn't steal your niggers, and I don't reckon Tradwell stole them either. If you lost them, they just plain got away from you. And I haven't a doubt in the world that neither of them was Buck or the Dove."

"They was," the boy insisted. "They was Black Buck and the Brown Dove."

"They was just two no-good runaway niggers, neither of them belong to me, and I never seen either of them in my life. And I don't know what the hell you thought to gain by coming here."

"The reward money—"

"If I'd paid it out, I'd tell you. I don't give a damn who brings Black Buck to me, as long as I get him. But I ain't got him, and neither have you. And Justin Sabre ain't got him either. Now, do you want me to lock you up?"

"No!"

"Then I'm giving you a chance to get out of here. I see you ain't got much. Well, I ain't a hard man, even if you are taking up my time with your goddam nonsense, so I'll have my cook provision you for a few days, and you get the hell back to where you come from. You understand me?"

"Yes, sir," old Carney said.

"And you forget this nonsense about Black Buck. You say one word to anybody, and I'll come after your hide."

"Yes, sir."

"Mr. Dinkin, you heard me. Take care of them. Then come back here."

Dinkin led the two away. Skeet put the pistol back into the chest drawer.

So Buckley was really back.

If Skeet had been incredulous at first, now he had to believe. The need was so great that even the slimmest evidence would have convinced him. He wondered if he should question Serena again, perhaps with a whip, but he doubted that it would do any good. There were times when Serena would rather die than yield to you.

Dinkin returned.

"Mr. Dinkin, you heard all that."

"Yes, sir, I did."

"You and your boys did good work, catching them sand-hillers."

"Why, thank you, sir."

"Now I want you to catch a nigger for me. But not just any nigger. I want Black Buck."

Dinkin looked surprised. "You mean that old man and his boy—"

"I mean that if Buck is around here—and I got reason to believe he is—he's gonna be up to bad mischief. He's gonna be up to trouble. In fact, I got reason to believe he's already stirring it up. Only he don't know yet that we been warned."

Dinkin grinned. "He surely don't!"

"I want guards out patrolling, night and day. Use some of them bad niggers that'll break another nigger's head for a drink of whiskey. Tell our people they catch the right nigger for me, they get rewarded. Extra food, clothes, fancy ribbons for the women. And tell the men . . ." Skeet thought about it. "Tell the guards that the one that gets me Black Buck, he'll get whiskey and extra food and no work for a week and just about any wench he wants. Hell, yes, any wench he wants, and he ain't gonna do nothing but lie around and eat and drink and pleasure that wench for a solid week."

Dinkin's grin broadened. "We got three, four young wenches coming up that the bucks already got it on hard for. Sort of looking forward to them myself."

"Well, you tell them guards they can have all three or four for all I care. A solid week of doing nothing but stud them four wenches. You tell them that, Mr. Dinkin."

"I surely will, Mr. Skeet. They'll catch that nigger for you."

Maybe, or maybe not, but at least Redbird would be guarded against trouble. Meanwhile, there were other steps to be taken. This afternoon he would go into River-boro and talk to some people. Arrange things. This time Buckley Skeet was not going to get away.

Silas and Lute followed the overseer to the kitchen house and stood by silently while Dinkin told the cook what she was to provide for them. They stared at their feet while Dinkin told them to get to the road and to get there damned fast and not to stop until they were back home again. "And if Mr. Skeet or me ever sees your faces, it's gonna be a lot worse for you than just shackles and whips. If you ain't buried at Redbird, you gonna leave here wishing you had been."

They were given back their rifles. They accepted the food without a word of thanks. As they left, they were followed at a discreet distance by three blacks.

They headed west along the narrow rutted road.

When the blacks dropped back out of sight, Silas stopped. He stepped off the road and sat down on the trunk of a fallen tree, leaning his rifle against it. Lute, gnawing a lip and blinking his eyes as if he might burst into tears at any instant, sat down beside him. Neither of them had said a word since leaving the Redbird big house, and they had avoided each other's eyes.

Three weeks, Silas thought. Three weeks to the day, almost to the hour, since they had caught Black Buck and Adaba. Three weeks since the long years of hardship had come to an end and their fortune had been made. Thousands of dollars for Black Buck and maybe for Adaba too.

And it had all slipped through their fingers.

Three weeks of hard travel, of begging and stealing and living off the land, and they had nothing, absolutely nothing to show for it.

No, not three weeks, Silas thought. Years. Years and years and years. All his life, and all of Mrs. Rogan's life, and likely all his honey-boy's life too.

Nothing.

Because the bastards always took it away from you.

Lute gulped audibly. "How long you reckon it'll take us to get home, pa?" he asked.

Silas ignored the question. He still felt shriveled by the humiliation of being dragged before Skeet and having the whole story frightened out of him. He still felt shriveled by the planter's scorn. He sat in silence, thinking.

Buck. Adaba. Skeet. Sabre.

A fortune lost.

And that goddam Mr. Skeet, arrogant as a Sabre or a Tradwell, expected them to just up and walk away.

"No," he said.

"No what, pa?"

"No, we ain't going home. No, they ain't gonna take it away from us. Not this time."

"But that Mr. Skeet said—"

"Don't give a damn what Mr. Skeet said. He ain't got Buck. Maybe nobody got Buck. Don't hardly matter no more. Somebody owes us. *Somebody owes us!*"

"Then what we gonna do, pa?"

Silas stood up from the tree trunk. He picked up his rifle. "Now, what you think we gonna do, honey-boy?" he asked. "We going to Sabrehill."

Five

There is a kind of mad joy born of desperation, a do-or-die and damn-your-eyes joy, and it made Silas laugh. It brought a sudden, broken cackle from his throat, a rasping sound that caused Lute to jump and look startled.

So they thought they would fool Silas Rogan, did they? So they thought they would lie to him and cheat him and send him yelping for home like a cur dog with his tail between his legs. Well, they were wrong. No more would they do that. Never again.

Skeet, he thought. Goddam liar. No matter what Skeet had said, it was likely that he had tried to drive Silas and Lute away so that he could go after Black Buck himself. Go after Black Buck himself, and maybe after Adaba too, and keep the $5000 reward. But he couldn't fool Silas Rogan. Silas might not have book-learning, but he was cunning, he was shrewd. You had to get up pretty early in the morning to fool Silas Rogan.

And Sabre, Silas thought. What about Mr. Justin Sabre? Why hadn't he turned Black Buck in to Skeet? Keeping the nigger for himself, maybe, waiting for the reward money to get even higher? Or maybe Black Buck had just plain escaped from him!

It didn't matter if Black Buck had escaped. He had still been stolen from Silas, and this time Silas would not be cheated.

They left the road, heading into the concealment of woods, and then turned back the way they had come: toward Redbird. They would have to get past Redbird without being seen. Sabrehill was somewhere beyond that, beyond the place called Kimbrough Hall. *"Brick, two and a half storeys, big cupola,"* Jeppson had said. It might take them a half a day or a day or even longer, but they would find Sabrehill without any great difficulty.

And Silas and Lute would not be made fools this time. They would not be caught. No, they would approach Sabrehill with great caution, observing everything, taking no chances. And when at last they closed in . . .

This time it would not be the Rogans who were prisoners.

This time it would be the Sabres.

Saturday morning. A long, leisurely breakfast. Soft domestic clatter in the pantry. Sheep moving across the courtyard in the early sunlight. She kept Justin at the table as long as possible, pouring cup after cup of coffee, talking, laughing, delaying the start of the workday.

"Lucy, you're going to make me fat and lazy."

"Nonsense. You're a braw boy, Mr. Sabre, and I can't imagine you fat."

"You're not going to have to imagine, if you keep on feeding me this way. It's lucky that I'm leaving in a few days, before disillusionment sets in."

"You're not to talk of leaving. Justin, I wish I'd thought of this sooner, but is it too late to send for your children? Couldn't they spend Christmas with you here?"

Justin looked surprised. "My children?"

"Yes. Mark and Katie Anne and Beau. I would so like to meet them."

Justin stared at her for a moment, and she wondered if she were doing something foolish. Finally he lowered his eyes. "I'm afraid it is a little late for that," he said

"Aside from the rush, my brother's family has already planned Christmas for them. And I think they'll want to be with their cousins."

Of course . . .

Justin looked at her again, with a certain curiosity, "You really would like to meet my children?"

"Certainly. Why wouldn't I?"

"Well . . . maybe sometime . . ."

It was a good day, as were all days lately. If there was still some kind of trouble in the quarters, it seemed to have been ameliorated. Perhaps Ettalee's recovery was at last having a good effect on the people, or perhaps it was simply that Christmas was coming. Next Saturday the celebrating would begin, reaching its peak at Christmas and continuing until New Year's Day. Then everything would return to normal.

And Justin Sabre would be long gone. Probably for good.

But she did not want to think about that.

When Lucy could prolong breakfast no longer, they went about their chores. Justin had things to do with Jebediah and Cheney and Zagreus. Lucy had meals to plan with Momma Lucinda. She had work to inspect in the wash house and in the spinning house. There was plenty to keep her busy, and she liked it. Working this way, with Justin taking on the man's role at Sabrehill— it was a sentimental thought, not worth dwelling on— but this was rather the way she had, long ago, envisioned their life together.

The morning passed. The chores were done, and hunger struck. The table was set for the long, early-afternoon dinner, and when Lucy passed through the kitchen, the spicy odor of a stew, the smell of fresh biscuits, made her feel almost faint with anticipation. "Just tell me when," Lucinda said, "and I'll put it on."

Justin would know when it was the dinner hour; there was no need to ring a bell. Lucy followed the portico back to the house, entering by way of the pantry. The pantry led into the dining room.

She was all the way into the dining room before the old man appeared in the doorway.

She stood there, perfectly still, more stunned than frightened. The old man was weather-beaten and red-bearded. He held a rifle pointed directly at Lucy's chest. He was followed into the room by a much younger man, also with a leveled rifle. The younger man wore a gap-toothed grin that was almost idiotic. Both men were bright-eyed and breathing hard with excitement.

It's happened, she thought, hardly knowing what she meant. *It's finally happened.*

The younger man moved carefully around the older man. Their darting eyes covered all doors, all windows, and she knew they would see Justin before he saw them.

"Just tell me what you want," she said quietly. Her heart pounded, but her voice was calm and smooth. "If you need food, I'll be glad to give it to you." She looked at their rags. "Or clothing. Just tell me what you want."

Neither man said a word. Still grinning, the younger man turned his too-wide eyes on her again. He leaned his rifle against the wall, well out of her reach. As he stepped toward her, he reached under his jacket and drew out a knife. She saw that he had an erection.

Then, at last, Lucy knew fear. She knew what some men, men like these, might enjoy doing with a knife, and she already carried one long ugly scar down the side of her face—and worse scars that did not show. She started to move away, but too late: the man's left arm shot out, and he seized the front of her dress at the neck.

As he pulled her to him, she nearly screamed. The blade moved closer, his elbow raised, and she thought he was going to stab her in the breast. Instead, he pulled her garments away from her throat, inserted the knife point-down, and with one swift downward sweep of the blade, ripped open her clothing almost to the waist. By some miracle, she was not cut, but she felt as if she had been eviscerated.

The young man laughed. With both hands he tore the fabric open, exposing her breasts. He seized her right breast with his left hand, twisting it painfully, while his knife-hand went to her back and pulled her hard against him. He ground against her. In an ugly five-word phrase, hoarsely whispered, he told her exactly what he wanted.

The old man chuckled. "That's right," he said. "First him and then maybe me and then him again. Unless you do exactly what we say. Maybe we do it to you anyway, but your only chance is you don't cause us no trouble."

She had not thought that she could be this frightened again. She had thought that all that—fear of the male as an aggressor, larger and stronger than she, with his humiliating phallic weapon—she had thought that all that was behind her. Now she knew it was not. The young man backed off easily enough as she thrust him away, but he still grinned at her and thumbed his upheld blade, and his bone looked larger than ever.

But I must not let them know, she thought, *I must not let them know.*

Covering her breasts, she tried to cling to some shred of dignity. "I asked you," she said as quietly as before, "to tell me what you want. What you really want. Must I ask you again?"

"I reckon you already know what we want," the old man said. "We want what was stole from us. We want that or the money for it. And we aim to get it."

"But I have stolen nothing from you."

"No. Maybe you ain't. But your Mr. Sabre sure as hell did."

"Just turn around real slow."

Justin recognized the voice the instant he heard it, and he knew its meaning, and he felt like a gambler with whom the odds have caught up. Sickened. He thought of his children up in Virginia.

"Turn around, I said."

He was in the blacksmith shop with Saul and Ettalee. Ettalee had the same frightened look in her eyes that had been there when Justin had first seen her. Saul, hammer in hand as he stood by his anvil, was absolutely still. He knew what he was looking at, and he stood like a statue of implacable hatred.

Justin turned around.

The dirty red beard, the greedy eyes, now bright with triumph. Silas stood just outside the doorway in the cold bright light of the December afternoon. The grin and the rifle were held steady.

"We been holding dinner for you," Silas said, "but I figured I better come get you. I told the cook and the houseboy and them all not to let you know about this here surprise, or my honey-boy was gonna do some naughty things to your missus. But I don't never trust a nigger—no more'n I trust you. So I come and got you. . . . You got nothing to say?"

"Not to you, Rogan."

"We'll see about that. Now you and me gonna march back to the big house, or I'm gonna gut-shoot you. Move."

The worst thing one could do with a Rogan, Justin knew, was to show fear. He came out of the shop as if he might walk all over the old man, and Silas backed off. Justin turned contemptuously away from him and walked toward the mansion, taking long, fast strides. Let Silas puff to keep up.

"Through the dining room and into the room with all them books," Silas said. "We got more room to talk in there. And don't you try nothing."

They entered the library. Lute was aiming a rifle at Lucy, who was trying to hold her torn dress closed over her breasts. Her face was white, making her scar more vivid and ugly. Justin stared at her, thinking, *I made this happen.*

"Lute, see he don't have no weapon on him."

His eyes locked with Lucy's, Justin hardly felt Lute's searching hands.

"He ain't got nothing, pa."

"Wrong, Lute. He got our niggers. And we want them, mister."

Justin said nothing.

"I said, we want the niggers you stole from us, mister. We want the niggers, or we want the reward money for them."

"I didn't steal any niggers from you, Rogan, and I know nothing about any reward money."

"We know better. It was you and maybe that Mr. Tradwell. But you was the one that got us drunk—"

"You were drunk from the moment I first laid eyes on you, old man. I didn't have to get you drunk."

"Don't you talk like that!" Lute burst out. "Don't you talk like that to pa! You stole what was ours, and we mean to get it back. 'Cause you know what we aim to do if we don't get it back?"

Justin smiled thinly. "Go for the constable, I suppose, and get me hung for a thief."

"No, we ain't gonna get no constable! What good's a constable for the likes of us!"

"Well, you can always kill me and get yourselves hung."

"But not before we get done fucking your missus! You hear that? Me and pa both. I got a hard-on for her already, and she already felt it, and you're welcome to see it. Now, you get us our niggers, goddam you, or—"

"Justin," Lucy said, "what is this all about? I don't understand. Please, somebody tell me. . . ."

Good. A distraction. More talk. The longer the Rogans could be kept talking, the better chance Lucy and he had.

"Tell her, Rogan. She knows nothing about it."

Silas looked at Justin but spoke to Lucy. "Like Lute says," he said bitterly, "a goddam nigger-stealer is what your mister is. Found out that me and Lute had captured Adaba—"

"Adaba!" Lucy said in surprise. "You actually captured Adaba?" She sounded almost admiring.

"Not only him, but Black Buck too. And everybody knows that Mr. Skeet had a reward out for Black Buck for years."

"Not me," Justin said. "I'd never heard of either of them until you mentioned Adaba's name on the cotton box."

"Now you're lying again. Ain't nobody around here that ain't heard of Adaba and Black Buck."

"Mr. Sabre has been out of the country for many years," Lucy explained. She might have been speaking to a friendly neighbor. "He has only recently returned."

Silas was silent. He glared at Justin. The confrontation had taken a turn and a tone he did not like.

"Rogan," Justin said, "if you missed out on a reward, I don't blame you for being disappointed. If I were in your shoes, I suppose I'd do exactly what you've done. I'd go looking for satisfaction, by God. No, I don't blame you at all. Now, hell, it's dinner time, man, and I'll bet you and Lute are every bit as hungry as I am, and—"

"No," Silas said.

"Now, Rogan—"

"No. You're liars, the both of you. Lute, you go first. Fuck her."

Justin threw himself away from Silas and toward Lute, but he was not fast enough. The back of his head exploded, and he found himself on his knees. Then there was only darkness.

Lucy screamed. The rifle stock, as it slammed into the back of Justin's head, seemed to pick him up and drop him to his knees. As he slumped forward, Lucy tried to reach him, but Lute's fiery backhand blow sent her reeling.

For a few seconds Justin lay still. Then arms and legs began to move, as he tried to struggle to his feet. The Rogans watched him carefully. He got no further than his hands and knees. When he raised his head, Lucy saw that his eyes were opened but glazed, and she knew that his skull might have been crushed.

"I've got to help him!"

"You don't do nothing," Lute said. "He tries anything, pa, hit him again."

The old man pointed his rifle at Justin's head. "He ain't gonna try nothing. Go on, fuck her, Lute. Do it right in front of him, and let him watch. You gonna see something, Mr. Sabre."

Lute turned grinning toward her again. He tossed off his jacket, pulled his shirt over his head and threw it away. Lucy backed away as he came toward her. *My God*, she thought, *he's going to do it, he's really going to do it, and Justin will die, and they'll kill me too. . . .*

Unless . . .

"You can fight it all you want to, lady," Lute said, " 'cause I like that. But you try to run away, and your mister gonna get hurt real bad."

"Please," she sobbed, "don't."

But begging was never going to stop him. As she stumbled backward, he caught her and tried to pull her dress open again; when she resisted, he gave her another burning, head-ringing slap. Grabbing the front of her dress, he ripped it still further. She went for his eyes, but all that got her was more slaps, and he held her too close for her to knee him, as Lucinda had taught her to do. In a matter of seconds he had her dress off of her shoulders and down to her belly, and with one arm he held her half-naked and writhing against his bare chest.

No, this was not a nightmare; it was nothing like a nightmare, it was absolutely real. This was no dark and nameless horror from which she could scream herself awake; this was hard flesh, unwashed and stinking, forcing itself against her. This was what Ettalee had suffered. This was rape.

"Please, please, please, oh, please don't, oh, please, please, please. . . ."

Lute merely laughed and with his free hand unfastened his pants and began pushing them down.

"You know now we mean it," the old man said. "You know now you better give us what we want."

"But I have nothing, nothing!"

"You got what I want," Lute said, plunging his hand down into torn underclothing. His fingers closed on her shockingly, painfully. "You got what I want right here."

"Oh, no, please!"

"And I got what you want."

"Fuck her, Lute."

"I aim to." Lute's pants dropped to his boot tops. "You can see how I aim to."

Yes, he aimed to. And she knew enough about this kind of man to realize that before long he would be unable to stop himself even if it was in his best interest to delay the rape until later. Already he was muttering a single fierce, gutteral verb over and over again, like some frenzied animal imitating human speech. But she had to convince the Rogans that she was utterly broken and that their will was her own.

"Oh, please, no!"

And so she continued to struggle, truly struggle, though

Lute hit her again and again, pummeled her breasts, slapped her face. As he forced her clothing down to her thighs, she thought she heard Justin cry out something, but the old man said, "You just stay still, mister, or I kill you, and you can't do your missus no good then!" Old Rogan, like his son, was almost too excited to know where his best interest lay.

She was weakening. The Rogans had to believe that, but it was no pose. Her strength was almost gone as Lute bent her to the floor and started forcing her thighs apart.

"Please! I'll give you anything you want! But don't do this, don't do this, please! Anything, anything!"

"We want our niggers," the old man said. "We want what was stole from us."

"I don't have your niggers," Lucy sobbed, "but I'll give you all the niggers you want. I'll give you anything!"

"If you ain't got the niggers, we want the reward money."

"Yes! I'll give it to you! I'll give you money—how much money do you want?"

"We want $5000 for Black Buck and . . ." The old man hesitated. "And $5000 for Adaba."

Lucy's eyes widened, but she could scarcely see through her tears. "All that! I—I don't think I—"

"Fuck her, Lute."

"But I'll give you all I have! I might have that much! Please! I'm sure there's 5000! And maybe even more! Much more!"

The younger man, Lute, no longer seemed to hear anything that was being said. Red-faced, panting, he rolled against Lucy, thrust against her, trying to effect entry.

"Stop him, please! I'll give you the money! I swear I will! But stop him!"

"Get off her, Lute."

The younger man whimpered. As Lucy struggled to evade him, he continued to thrust.

"Get off her, I said."

But Lute might have been deaf.

The old man walked over to them. He calmly hit Lute across the temple with his rifle stock.

They let her go to Justin, but there was little she could do for the moment but blot up some blood from the back of his head with a piece of torn linen. His eyes were narrow slits, his jaw slack. Lute, still panting, pulled his clothes back into place, and Lucy tried to hide herself in the tatters of her dress.

"Where is it?" the old man asked. "Where you keep it?"

"I'll have to get it for you."

Lute looked at Justin and picked up his rifle. "Let me club his brains again, pa. That'll make her talk."

"No!" Lucy said quickly. "You don't understand. I'll have to *find* the money for you. I know it's there, because my father always kept it around there somewhere, but I have to find it."

"If you got to find it," the old man said, "reckon we can find it too. You just tell us where to look."

"All right," Lucy said hysterically, "you just go look, for God's sake! Go look in the office, and let me take care of Justin. But if you don't find it, and you won't, don't blame me. My father said it was in a safe place, if ever I needed it, so you just go look!"

The old man looked uneasy. It was not hard for him to believe that there was money cached around Sabrehill some place. Wasn't it said of many a rich planter that he had buried cash, because a man would be a fool to trust all of his money to a bank? But Lucy was right: a man was not about to hide money where anyone who walked in might easily find it.

"You dang right we gonna look," the old man said. "We tear that office down if we got to. But we ain't gonna leave you here to do mischief. You coming along to help us, and the sooner we find it, the better for you. Or maybe I set my honey-boy here loose on you again. You come on, now."

And Lucy knew she had won.

She had to know, had to believe. Any failure of confidence now could be fatal.

She helped Justin to his feet. He seemed dizzy and unsteady, and when she spoke to him, he did not answer.

With him leaning on her, she led the way through the dining room and the passage out into the courtyard.

The sun was as bright as it had been on that afternoon when she had gone to look for Ettalee at Redbird. Lucinda, obviously frightened, watched from the kitchen house door. Irish and Leila were nowhere to be seen. Lucy headed toward the office. Her heart was pounding as hard as ever, and yet she felt perfectly calm, perfectly lucid of mind, almost serene.

She felt like lightning about to strike on a cloudless day.

She and Justin arrived at the office door, the Rogans close behind them. The door was unlocked, and she pushed it open. She helped Justin through the doorway, and left him standing there, leaning against the wall. She continued into the office, the old man behind her, and behind him young Lute.

She walked to a desk. She calmly picked up the six-barreled pepperbox pistol, turned, and fired it at the old man.

Nothing happened.

Nothing but a loud *Click!*

She turned the barrels, pulling back on the cock, and fired again.

Click!

The old man's face was terrible—a face of horror and wrath and madness. His rifle, once loose in his hands, was now swinging up, was swinging toward her, and he was pulling back the cock. This could not be happening to her. But it was. She was about to die, and she had perhaps one more chance with the pepperbox—

Click!

—and the chance was gone, and now the old man was squeezing the trigger, was firing at her—

A gun roared.

But not the old man's. The ball took him in the side of the chest, went crashing through ribs and lungs, knocking him sideways, and the old man's rifle discharged somewhere, and he looked at Lucy with utter astonishment. He turned to look at Lute, now frozen in his own horror, and at Justin with Lute's rifle in his hands.

He looked at Lucy again. Tried to say something.

He went slowly to his knees. Tried again to speak.

His face darkened, and blood appeared on his lips. He continued to the floor, going slowly, as if he were being taken apart, one piece at a time. He fell to one side and rolled onto his back, and more blood came to his lips. His eyes held the sure knowledge that the trail ended here. Every hope, every dream, every hour of struggle in all his life, led only to this. His eyes asked some unanswerable question.

Lucy found that she had her hands at her mouth, holding back a scream. The old man was taking too long to die. Nobody should have to take this long.

But death did come at last. The old man's eyes went blank as a newborn baby's, and he was gone.

Only then did anyone else in the room move. Lute scrambled across the room and threw himself down by the old man, calling to him, *"Pa! Pa! Pa!"* and shaking him as if to recall him to life. His voice became a squeal, and fat tears rolled down his cheeks. Suddenly he was a child again, and lost. *"Pa! Pa!"*

Finally he looked up. Looked at Lucy. Looked at Justin. The tears continued to pour.

"All we wanted was what was ours," he said, "and you know that, mister, you know that. We caught them niggers, and the reward money was ours, and you know that."

Justin said nothing. Lute looked at his father again.

"Ma and Pa, they never had nothing in their whole life, and all they ever asked for was something to make the living a little mite easier. And was that so much to ask? Something to make the living a little easier? A little share of the good things like some other folks got? And when we caught Black Buck and Adaba, it looked like Ma's prayers was answered at last. But now . . . now," Lute sobbed, "now we ain't even got pa. . . ."

Justin stood at the window of the north parlor, looking out at the peaceful, sunlit courtyard. He touched the tender spot on the back of his head. He thought he must have a hard skull, for the ache was already fading. Sheep grazed peacefully in the courtyard.

How could such a thing have happened on a day like this?

My fault, he thought. *All of it. Nearly got Lucy killed, and myself too. Because they would have killed us before they were done. Would have had to.*

But should he have let the Rogans beat the two blacks to death? And what if he had not come to Sabrehill? The Rogans would have appeared here anyway, and Lucy would have had to face them alone. *Not that I was much help . . . until the last possible minute. . . .* That had been the worst of it: having to pretend to be more stunned than he was; not daring to move while Lute Rogan stripped and tried to rape Lucy, because if he did move, he would be dead, and dead he could do nothing, nothing. . . .

He had not known that he could kill with such jubilant savagery, with such a lust for vengeance. Not until he had Lute's rifle in hand and was firing at the old man . . .

Well, it was over now. The old man was lying in a wagon, waiting to be taken into town. Lute was locked up. Lucy had gone to her room. Momma Lucinda had washed the blood from Justin's hair. Maids had gone running up and down the stairs, carrying pails of hot water; there had been whisperings and wide-eyed spyings among the servants, and cries of *Oh, my Lawd!* And Justin thought he heard Lucy's footsteps on the staircase.

Her eyes, as she entered the parlor, were still wide with shock, and her face was ashen. She swayed, but when he reached out to steady her, she snapped her arm away from him as if she could not bear to be touched. Without a word, she crossed the room and settled herself into a chair. She stared up at him and wove her fingers into a white knot.

"I owe you thanks, Justin, for saving my life." Her voice was as tight as her fingers. *No, not shock,* Justin thought. *Anger.*

"You kept your head," he said. "That was what saved us."

"I owe you thanks," she repeated, "but now I think you had better tell me all about it. Tell me what brought those people here."

"I've already told you how I met them, how they were abusing those two blacks on the cotton—"

"The rest of it, Justin. Tell me."

He told her. How he had encouraged the Rogans in their drunkenness. How he had freed the two blacks. How he had told them he would meet them at Sabrehill. Her eyes, hard on him, never blinked, and her lips took on a wry, bitter twist.

"And so," she said, "you came to Sabrehill, not, as you first said, to rest from your journey. Not, as you later claimed, in hope of seeing me. But in order to help your two fugitive friends."

"No, Lucy. It was a damn fool thing, telling those blacks to meet me at Sabrehill. But you were my real reason for coming here. I think you were on my mind before I ever left Virginia."

The wry twist of Lucy's lips did not disappear, and her fingers remained knotted. "How flattering. And now, what do you think we should do about that young man?"

Justin was surprised. "See the son of a bitch hanged," he said, stating the obvious. "Don't they hang for attempted rape in South Carolina?"

"And what good would that do?"

"Lucy, that boy tried to—"

"I know what he tried to do. And I confess that a part of me would dearly like to see him dead. But I ask again, what good would it do?"

"Stop him from ever trying such a thing again."

"True enough. You would stop him from ever again attempting rape. And he, in his turn, will scream his story to high heaven—how you stole two Negroes from him, how you helped two infamous black bandits to escape. And someone is likely to believe him."

"That's a chance I'll have to take."

Lucy's jaw tightened. She seemed near the end of her patience. "Justin, because you are a Sabre and a gentleman, the law in this state will tend to be lenient with you—in most instances. But freeing or stealing Negroes is an extremely serious offense in South Carolina. Now, are you willing to go up in front of a judge and—quite frankly—lie like hell?"

Justin felt a tightening in his chest. In a court he would be under oath. He was capable of an occasional kindly white lie, but to lie under oath, to perjure himself, would be like breaking his word. His respect for himself would never again be the same.

"I have no apologies for doing what I did, Lucy—for freeing those blacks. I'm only sorry that it brought the Rogans here to make trouble for you."

"Then you would not lie."

"I'll have to take my chances."

Lucy closed her eyes. She was silent for a moment, while her hands tried to ruin each other.

"Then this matter must never come to trial," she said.

Justin thought he knew what she was driving at. "You're suggesting that we make a deal with Lute Rogan?"

Lucy nodded. "A life for a life. He goes free, and so do you."

"But after what he did to you—"

"What he did to me was most unpleasant—but ultimately unsuccessful. And you may believe me, Justin, I have experienced far worse in this life. I am prepared to forget about it. I intend to persuade young Mr. Rogan that he unwillingly followed his father to this plantation, where his father attempted a robbery. I shall tell the constable that young Mr. Rogan attempted to dissuade his father. I shall tell him that in the course of the robbery, I tried to kill the elder Mr. Rogan but failed, and that you rescued me. Now, isn't that close to the truth?"

"As close as a lie can get."

Lucy sounded quite calm. "Of course, there must be some reason that the Rogans happened by Sabrehill. There had best be no mention of Black Buck or Adaba. Perhaps the elder Rogan was simply looking for easy plunder, and Sabrehill, known to have a widow as its only white occupant, looked like the best possibility. Yes, I think that story will do quite well."

"Lucy—"

"Now, is there anything I haven't thought of?"

Justin felt sick. "Lucy, I can't let you lie for me."

Lucy's eyes were too bright, and her voice shook. "But why not?"

"It isn't right—"

"It isn't right? But how can you say that, Justin? I'm only a woman, am I not? A member of the weaker sex, the gentler sex?" Her voice rose, and the words came faster. "Don't we women have a very inadequate sense of reality and practically no sense of logic whatsoever? Aren't we supposed to fib a little all the time without hardly knowing it? as we simper and smile at our great big men or stamp our little feet with indignation?" Color returned to Lucy's face, the crimson of anger, as she arose from her chair. "Why, good Lord, Justin, how would you big, strong men ever survive with your magnificent honor, your elephantine rectitude, your aristocrat's code, if you didn't have your women to do your lying for you? Isn't that what the 'little woman' is for—to do the necessary lying, so that the big, strong man can uphold the family honor?"

"Lucy—"

"So for God's sake, Justin, just keep your mouth shut and let me do the lying! And, Justin—*oh! oh!*"

Something broke in her then. He saw it give way as she began to shake. He saw all that she had been trying to hold back—the horror, the dismay, the deep animal fear—he saw it wash over her, saw it flood through her, and suddenly she was in his arms, weeping.

He held her tightly, stroked her, soothed her.

Honor, he thought. Was it something more precious than this? Honor.

For a while he could not remember what the word meant.

It went very easily, far more easily than Justin expected.

Lucy sent for Paul Devereau, her lawyer, who arrived within the hour. He approved of Lucy's plan for handling the situation. "He is just dishonest enough," Lucy had told Justin earlier, "that he may be helpful to us."

Lute Rogan was locked up in an empty room at the

far end of the coach house. Lucy led the way along the east lane, and Justin saw that she was now quite dry-eyed, and her jaw was firmly set. Paul Devereau and Irish stood on each side of the coach house door as Jebediah Hayes opened it. Lute was crouched in a shadowed corner of the empty room. Justin stood by with a pistol in hand, and Lucy reached out and took it from him. Before he could stop or caution her, she walked into the room, straight toward Lute Rogan. She cocked the pistol and, using both hands, aimed it steadily at his head.

"Now, tell me," she said, almost indifferently, "why I shouldn't kill you."

"You killed my pa," the youth whimpered. "Ain't that enough?"

"No. No, that ain't enough. I want to be rid of you, young Mr. Rogan. Reckon your ma is always going to wonder what happened to her man and her boy." Lucy grinned suddenly. Laughed. "Reckon she's going to sit up there somewhere in the hills, wondering and waiting, starving her way through the winter, and maybe if she lives long enough, one day the story will get back to her, how her man and her boy got themselves killed at Sabrehill. Got themselves killed and left her to end her days. . . ."

Lucy laughed again, and Lute Rogan crumbled. He covered his face and bawled.

"When I squeeze this trigger, there won't be anyone but her left, will there, young Mr. Rogan? No one left but your ma, to go on living if she can and to starve if she must. Too old, likely, to find a new man—unless she's got something left to whore with. Because her man and her boy went and got themselves killed on her."

"Lucy," Justin said softly, "for God's sake!" In anger or desperation, he could have killed Lute easily, but he doubted that he could have been this coldly, calculatedly cruel. This was a Lucy he had never met before, strong and savage, fierce protectress of her own.

"Ain't that right, boy?" Lucy asked. The pistol in her hands was as steady as ever. "Ain't that right? You're leaving your ma to starve—"

"All we wanted was our niggers," Lute wept. "All we wanted was the reward money. All we wanted was what was ours."

"Now, you listen to me," Lucy said angrily, "and you hear me right. I know nothing about your niggers. I never set eyes on them in my life. If I had them, I'd show them to you, and I'd keep them, and damn you to hell for what you did to me. I just wish to God I did have them, do you understand me?"

Lute nodded.

"Say it. We're not holding your niggers, and we don't know a thing about them."

"You ain't got them, and you don't know nothing."

Lucy seemed to relax. She sighed. She held the pistol in only one hand, and its muzzle drifted away from Lute's head.

"Lute," she said, almost pityingly, "why did you let your pa talk you into coming here?"

Step by step, then, she led him. Justin and Paul never said a word, merely stood by and listened. Before long, Lute seemed actually to believe that his pa had brought him to Sabrehill against his will. He had meant no harm, but they had been unable to find any steady work; and old Silas, having met Justin on the cotton box, had been convinced that there were easy pickings at Sabrehill. Lute had been unable to stop him.

"And Mr. Justin had no choice but to shoot him, did he?"

"No . . . no choice." That was true enough.

"We're sorry, Lute. We're sorry about what happened to your father. But it was his own fault, wasn't it?"

"Yes . . . his own fault." The boy wept.

"And not yours . . . nobody else's . . . and you've got to go home . . . to your ma. . . ."

Zagreus drove the wagon carrying the old man's blanket-covered body. Lute rode with him, sitting by the body. A hunched, broken figure, he seemed utterly docile, completely submissive. Justin, Lucy, and Paul followed in a buggy. It was late afternoon by the time they arrived in Riverboro and found Constable Wiley Morgan in the sheriff's office.

A man was dead, deliberately, if necessarily, shot; and it seemed to Justin that it took an almost indecently short time to settle the matter. Lucy had hardly started her story and given an idea of its direction when the constable interrupted to say that they had better bury the old bastard in a pauper's grave and do it here and now this afternoon, if Luther Rogan would give his consent— which Luther did, with a mumble and a nod. A coffin was immediately ordered, and the constable sat down again. He was a heavy-set dewlapped man with an amiable hound-dog face.

"Now, you was saying."

Lucy continued her story. In effect, she told exactly what had happened, omitting only the attempted rape and the demands for the two escaped blacks, and asserting that Lute had opposed the robbery.

"You got anything to add?" the constable asked Lute.

Lute shook his head.

"Then we'll just say that your statement agrees in every detail with Miss Lucy's. Save a lot of folderol. And you, Mr. Sabre?"

"I would never contradict a lady," Justin said dryly.

The constable laughed. " 'Course all this got to go to the circuit solicitor, but I doubt that he'll even write up a bill for the grand jury. . . ."

Silas Rogan was buried on a shabby edge of a graveyard, as quickly as he could be shoved underground. Justin was there, on the opposite side of the grave from Lute, while Lucy and Paul remained in the buggy. But he owed that to the man he had killed, Justin figured. Even your enemies, you don't leave to the buzzards.

When the burial was over, Justin walked Lute to the road. He handed Lute the two Rogan rifles, neither of them loaded. He also handed him a poke of grub.

"There's enough in there to last you a week or more."

Lute accepted the poke without a word.

"Lute," Justin said quietly, "you wouldn't be stupid enough to come back here, would you? Miss Lucy is letting you live, and I'm not sure that I approve. You

wouldn't be stupid enough to come back here with a
loaded rifle. . . ."

To his surprise, a broad grin cracked Lute's still tear-
stained face. "You think I'm a damn fool, don't you, Mr.
Sabre? Figure I'm too big a fool to know I'm getting off
easy. Well, I ain't. Pa was a fool, but it weren't his
fault. Ma ain't no fool, but she got no education. Nor do
I. But I got more brains than pa ever let me use.

"But I'm gonna use them from now on, mister. No, I
ain't coming back here with a loaded rifle, but you better
watch out all the same. 'Cause I ain't gonna be satisfied
with no patch of sand for me and mine—not from now
on. I ain't gonna end up like pa, cheated out of everything
he ever wanted by the likes of you and your kind. No,
me and mine, from now on we're gonna take our share,
and there ain't gonna be a damn thing you can do about
it. We're taking it."

As he started to turn away, Lute laughed. "Only one
thing I regret. I regret I didn't fuck your missus."

Justin's hand moved toward his gun.

"Don't bother with that, mister. I ain't no chivalry you
can duel with, and these here rifles ain't loaded, remember? So you ain't gonna shoot me. And I say it again, I
regret I didn't fuck your missus, but one day I'm gonna
do it. Fuck your missus and your daughters and all your
women folk. And what's more, they gonna learn to love
it. 'Cause my day is coming, mister, my day is coming.
And don't you never forget it."

Lute Rogan turned his back and walked away.

Maybe he was right, Justin thought.

The wave of the future.

The news came swiftly to Riverboro, brought by a
couple of blacks from the Kimbrough plantation: two
white men, father and son, had tried to rob Sabrehill, and
one of them had been killed. The news came and spread,
and Skeet knew with a sick heart that Buckley was going
to escape him once again.

From the front steps of the Carstairs tavern, he saw
the mule-drawn wagon coming down the street through
the thinning sunlight of afternoon. The nigger called Za-

greus was at the reins, and young Carney was sitting hunched by a blanket-covered figure on the bed of the wagon. The old man, Skeet thought. The Carneys had disobeyed Skeet's orders and had gone to Sabrehill in search of Black Buck, and the old man had got himself killed. And now Buckley would know that Sabrehill was no longer a safe hiding place.

The wagon was followed at some distance by a buggy carrying Miss Lucy, Justin, and Paul Devereau. It was the first time Skeet had actually seen Justin in the dozen or so days the man had been back, and faintly sick, he stared as the buggy passed over the very spot where Justin had beaten him into the dirt and accepted his challenge. *Not this time,* he thought. *This time it's gonna be a lot different*. He watched as the wagon and buggy passed on down the street and stopped near the courthouse.

Less than an hour later, Skeet found Constable Morgan alone.

"Father and son, name of Rogan," the constable said. "The old bastard tried to rob Sabrehill. Even his own son admits it. Young Rogan tried to stop the old boy, but couldn't. Miss Lucy, Mr. Justin, the son—everybody agrees what happened. It's cut and dried."

Lies. To hide the real reason for the Rogans', or Carneys', visit to Sabrehill: to catch a runaway nigger. Lies, and even the son was in on them, paid off likely as not.

"Miss Lucy," Skeet said, trying to hide his anger, "she was just lucky she had a white man there to look out for her."

"Yeah, and even he ain't gonna be there long. Planning to go back up to Virginia in a day or two. I tell you, it's a crying shame how that woman lives alone out there. . . ."

Skeet felt sweat break out on the palms of his hands. The constable's words seemed to verify his every hope and every fear. Yes, Justin had Buckley at Sabrehill; but warned now, they knew they had to get away. And they would get away, without a doubt.

No. Skeet could not believe that. And there was just a chance . . .

Jeppson, sitting alone at a table, was waiting for him in the Carstairs tavern when he returned.

"You hear what happened at Sabrehill?" Jeppson asked.

"I heard."

"Didn't I say them Carneys was up to no good?"

"I don't give a damn about no Carneys or Rogans or whoever they was."

Skeet sat down. He had for years defied the Carstairs to keep him out of the tavern.

"Jeppson," he said, "I got reason to believe that old Buckley is hiding somewhere on the Sabrehill plantation."

Jeppson stared at him, and Skeet knew what he was thinking: Vachel Skeet has had Buckley on his mind for years. Gone crazy thinking about Buckley. Ain't nobody gonna collect that $5000 reward.

But all he said was: "What reasons?"

"I got 'em."

Jeppson continued to stare, trying to put the pieces together. Maybe Skeet wasn't crazy.

"So you figure on finally getting your Buckley back again."

"I surely do."

"After all these years."

"After all these years. And you're gonna help me."

"Five-thousand-dollars' worth?"

"No, but you'll get your share. Everybody will get his share if he helps and we get Buckley Skeet. I want a posse, Jeppson, one big enough to take that goddam Sabrehill apart like it never been taken apart before. Take it apart brick by brick and board by board if need be. How long you figure it'll take to raise one?"

"The bigger it is, the more have to split the money."

"Well, that's just too goddam bad. Listen, I'll pay fifty dollars a man *if* we find Buckley. And a bonus to them that lays hands on him—say, five hundred dollars. And guarantee you an extra fifty for helping get the posse organized. Reckon we can get fifty men?"

"Don't need no fifty men. Ten or fifteen of us—"

"I said fifty. Now, how long you think it'll take?"

"Two or three days—"

Skeet slammed his fist down on the table. He had a

vision of Buckley running, of Buckley escaping, one last time and forever. "We ain't got two or three days. I want to get out there tomorrow morning at the latest. Before dawn. And I don't want them to know we're coming."

"Now, how you gonna do that? Thirty men, maybe—"

"Then thirty men. More if we can find them. Get the constable to help. Then we'll have a legal posse comitatus, and ain't nobody gonna question our official right."

Jeppson got the point. "All right, with the constable helping, the three of us ought to be able to round up ten or fifteen men each. Round them up tonight, and have them at your place way before first light."

"Fifty dollars a man," Skeet reminded him, *"if* they get Buckley."

"And a hundred each for me and the constable, fifty each guaranteed." Jeppson grinned. "You know, most men, they lucky if they ever see fifty dollars at once in their whole life. They don't find Buckley, they gonna be mighty damn mad."

Skeet massaged his left hand. It ached slightly. It had given him trouble ever since the time he had hit Tag Bassett so hard he had damned near killed him. Now he always wore tight leather gloves whenever he thought he might want to use his fists.

"Yeah, they gonna be mad," he said, rubbing his hand. "And so am I. So am I."

Six

She slept all the way back to Sabrehill. While Paul Devereau drove, she lay back in the curve of Justin's arm, rested her head on his shoulder, and let herself escape into sleep, deep and dark and dreamless.

She woke up slightly when they reached the courtyard. She was dimly aware of being lifted from the carriage, of being moved in Justin's arms, of his carrying her into the house and up the stairs. When he laid her on her bed, she did not want to let him go, but he gently withdrew from her embrace. Then he was gone, but Leila was there, trying to undress her. She resisted, and Leila threw a couple of blankets over her.

Darkness.

Sleep.

And she awakened, not knowing if she had been asleep for an hour or a full day. For a moment she was disoriented. A lamp, turned well down, burned dimly on the mantel, and the windows were dark. What time was it? Was she the only one awake? No, she heard the sudden bray of Irish's laughter somewhere in the house, and a maid shrieked with indignation. Why, it was early yet, she thought with sudden, unreasoning delight—and it was Saturday night!

She threw down the blankets and hopped out of bed. She turned up the lamp. She threw water on her face and brushed her hair, then buttoned her dress and stepped into her shoes. Suddenly she was ravenously hungry, and she hurried downstairs to the dining room.

Justin was there. He had eaten without her and was drinking coffee, and he smiled and rose to his feet as she entered. "I must look a mess," she said, and he said, "You are beautiful," and kissed her smooth left cheek.

Lucinda brought food, and she gulped it down in a most unladylike manner, hardly noticing what she was eating, yet enjoying every mouthful. She thought briefly of the Rogans, but everything that had happened earlier that day now seemed so distant, so long ago, so far away. She had died and been resurrected, and the past was no longer important. She was as happy as she had been in years, and she ate and chattered and laughed.

"What is it, Justin?" she asked, when she realized that he was no longer talking and laughing with her.

And then he had to go and spoil it all.

"Lucy," he said, "I've never really told you why I didn't come back to you. And I think I should."

Oh, no, she thought with dismay. *Not now. Not when we've become friends again. No rationalizations, no excuses, no explanations. Not now.*

"But you did tell me," she said. "You wrote me a letter. I don't think there's anything more to be said."

"There is, though. I never thought I'd tell you more than I did in my letter, but now . . ."

"You need not. I would rather you did not."

"But I feel I owe it to you."

"You owe me nothing. Justin, you saved my life this afternoon. How could you possibly owe me anything?"

But if he owed nothing, perhaps she did. He had never meant to bring the Rogans to Sabrehill, and he had, as she had just said, saved her life.

"I'm not asking for absolution, Lucy, and I have no long heartrending story for you. But there are things you have a right to know."

She shrugged with feigned indifference, trying to hide her distress. "All right, then, once and for all."

"Once and for all," he agreed. "I wrote you, you'll recall, that I had known Rosellen all my life. . . ."

That damned letter. Lucy wondered where it was. She had wanted never to see it again, but at the same time, she had been unable to destroy it. She had put it away in some drawer, purposefully forgotten, God alone knew where.

As Lucy half-listened to Justin, not wanting to hear, almost trying not to, she realized that much of his story had been written between the lines of that awkward letter—much, but by no means all, and she had been too much in pain to read what was there. Yes, Justin had known Rosellen all his life, and had been in love with her, or had thought he was. He had been her most ardent suitor, and her family had approved of him, or at least not disapproved. (Ho-hum. Lucy tried not to yawn.) Rosellen, Justin had thought, had returned his affection but had been reluctant to settle down. A dozen times he had asked for permission to speak to her father, and a dozen times she had refused it. She had teased him with a long line of other suitors, always keeping Justin carefully on her string (what a dull girl, Lucy thought), always promising or hinting that when the right hour came . . . until just before the trip to Charleston, when they had quarreled violently. Justin had lost her, it seemed. He had considered himself a free man.

And then, in Charleston that winter, he had met Lucy.

All right, all right, Lucy knew all this. Yes, they had had a delightful time in Charleston. Yes, Rosellen the fickle, the tease, the butterfly, had been completely swept from Justin's mind. That spring, that summer at Sabrehill had been the most wonderful time of his life, in spite of that damned Vachel Skeet—yes, she believed him. And yes, yes, yes, he had been deeply in love with her and only her. If he said so. But would he please get on with it.

"I had to go back up to Virginia, you'll remember. And when I got home, the very first thing I learned was that Rosellen was dying."

Lucy, recalled to attention, was not sure she had heard correctly. She remembered that Justin, in his letter, had said that his bride was seriously ill, but . . .

"Dying, Justin?"

"Yes. God, I wasn't off my horse, when there was her father, clutching at my arm and trying to tell me that his daughter—the girl most people expected me to marry, the girl who had put me off for so long—was dying of consumption. In the advanced stages, the doctors said, and rapidly growing worse. Somehow she had hidden her illness from everyone else for a long time—she had even hidden it from herself, not wanting to know what was happening to her. But now she knew, and she was in a panic of fear and grief, and so was her family. Do you know what it's like to look your own coming death in the face, Lucy? I think I had some idea, after that damn fool duel. But in a duel you have a chance. I don't think I had the clear sight of death that Rosellen had—fighting not to cough her life up in blood. . . ."

Lucy had a sudden vision, brief but vivid, of Silas Rogan, the blood coming from his lips, the terror in his eyes.

"I thought you promised me no heartrending stories."

"I'm sorry, I didn't mean—"

"No. I shouldn't have said that. Go on."

"She needed someone to give her hope. That was the first thing her father told me, even before I had seen Rosellen. And the doctors agreed. She needed someone

who loved her, whom she could cling to if she was to survive more than a few months. Perhaps I could even give
her a year or two. She needed someone to give her at
least a little happiness in whatever time was left. She had
been waiting for me, wanting me, afraid to write and tell
me what had happened to her. Nobody had wanted to
tell me after I'd got myself shot up—I was close enough
to losing my own life. But the minute I got home . . ."

"And so you married her," Lucy said, wondering how
much of this she could believe.

"Maybe I was wrong. A lot of people would say that
under the circumstances I was a fool to marry Rosellen.
But you had a lifetime ahead of you, a lifetime in which to
forget me. Rosellen had only me—and a few months. I
only know that if I hadn't married her, I would have felt
like her executioner."

"But happily for Rosellen, she survived for a good
many years thereafter and became quite well enough to
bear three children for you." *While you and I had but
one, and it died before it even had a name, and I shall
never tell you.* "You were most fortunate, Justin."

He nodded. If he heard the irony in her voice, he
ignored it. "Three children," he said, "yes. I took her
abroad, Switzerland, Italy. I did my damnedest to keep
her alive. And she did her damnedest to give me a full
and happy life. Eventually, we thought she was completely cured, or at least I tried to believe that. But her
lungs were weakened, and when she finally went . . .
She wasn't afraid the second time she faced death, Lucy.
At least, not in the same way. She was a hell of a lot
braver than I was."

How much to believe? It was all grounded in fact, of
course, but there is always more than one way to tell a
story.

"Your story," she said, "is considerably more detailed
than your letter."

"Lucy, when I wrote that letter, I was still in love
with you. But if I planned to marry another woman, I
would never write a word to anyone that implied that I
did not love her. I wouldn't dishonor my future wife by
doing such a thing."

Lucy sighed. "Well, I've always said that you are gallant," she said dryly, "and to marry a woman that you don't love, and for such noble motives . . ."

She had gone too far. Justin's face darkened. He stood up from his chair, and for a moment she thought he might strike her.

"Lucy," he said harshly, "I never told you that I didn't love my wife. I loved her, or thought I did, before I ever met you. And when I married her, I loved her truly. I put you out of my mind and out of my heart. I devoted myself to Rosellen, and I *did* love her. And she was worth it, every bit of it. When the end came, she was the gallant one, not I. And I—I—" He was shaking uncontrollably; his hand struck a wine glass and knocked it to the floor. "I loved her—I loved her—"

Then he was gone from the table and out of the room. Lucy didn't move.

Now she could believe him.

Yes, it all fitted. It would be exactly like the Justin she had known all those years ago to have acted just as he had done. Call him a fool, but he would have thought it his duty to marry Rosellen. And marrying her, he would give her his full fidelity. A man like Justin had to love something, and he would have loved his wife with all his heart. By a sheer act of will if need be. Why not? Women did it all the time.

And he had loved Lucy too, all those years back. He had truly loved her after all.

The fool, the fool, she thought, *oh, the fool,* feeling somehow proud of him. *Two of us, Justin, two damned fools.*

Well, it had all been a long time ago.

She got up from the table. She thought she had heard Justin leave the house. She found a shawl in the passage, wrapped it around her shoulders, and went out into the courtyard. Justin was standing alone in the dark. Her shoes crunched in the gravel, but he did not look around as she approached him.

They were silent. They could hear the fiddling, filled with Christmas cheer, all the way from the field quarters.

He felt embarrassed as he slid his legs over the side of the bed and sat there naked and shivering. He felt that way in spite of the fact that Zulie had bathed him and bandaged him and carried off his slops for over a week—or maybe because of it. With another woman, he might not have given a damn, but he hated appearing weak in Zulie's sight.

She grinned at him, not embarrassed at all, eager to have his approval of the clothes she had procured for him.

He pulled on first the pants and then the shirt. They were of good woolen material, and they fit him well. Zulie had even found him a heavy leather belt with a highly polished brass buckle—a belt on which to hang the new axe and knife that Saul had given him.

"Where you get clothes like this?" he asked, pleased.

"Just told the old women who do the spinning and sewing to make something Mr. Jeb's size. Maybe they 'spect it ain't for Jeb, but don't worry, they ain't saying nothing."

"And these boots . . ." Adaba pulled on the heavy, well-oiled, hardly used boots; they were as good as any he had ever had. "They for your Mr. Jeb too?"

"Belong to a hand died a while back. Would have end up with Jeb maybe, big boots like that, only now he going find they ain't there no more."

Adaba stood up. His head swam, and his knees shook like reeds. He still felt weak as a baby, weaker than he had expected, but he forced himself to stay on his feet.

"Zulie, I do thank you."

When she tried to steady him, he pulled her into his arms, and she came willingly. He laughed, and she smiled and closed her eyes. He held her, enjoying her softness, her tantalizing nearness, and he wished he could think of her as just another woman, a woman there for the taking if he tried hard enough.

He was tempted. *Got no right to this,* he thought, and yet he didn't let her go . . .

. . . until the knock at the door came. The pattern of knocks, in twos and threes, told them it was Buck.

Reluctantly he released her. She opened her eyes and

smiled uncertainly at him. The knock at the door was repeated.

"Better let him in, honey."

And ain't never gonna have the right. That was the way it was, that was the way it had to be, and he had damn well better keep it firmly in mind from now on.

Buck came in grinning, pleased to see that Adaba was out of bed and on his feet. Like Adaba, he had on new clothes, new to him at any rate, and a knife and an axe, supplied by Saul, hung sheathed from his belt under his heavy jacket.

Adaba nodded his approval. "Look like you're all ready to travel, old son."

Buck smacked a palm with his fist. "Ready for anything!"

"That's good. 'Cause we got to get away from here, fast."

They stared at him, as he had known they would, but to Adaba, the fact was obvious. "Buck, Zulie told me all about what happened with the Rogans here today. Now, you know them coming here ain't just luck—they come after us."

Buck shook his head. "That old man is dead, and the young one is gone away. They ain't no trouble to us no more."

"They're all the trouble we need. We got to go, Buck."

"But you can't travel. Zulie says you can't travel for a long time yet."

"Maybe not on my own, but we got help here, remember? Now that Mr. Justin Sabre is here again." Watching Buck carefully, he voiced his suspicion. "Or maybe Mr. Sabre been here all along."

Buck looked back defiantly. "Wasn't no reason to trust that man long as you was laying here half-dead."

"Adaba," Zulie said, "you can't trust that Mr. Sabre at all. You can't, he ain't no good!"

"Now, how you know that?"

"I know! Ain't never been a white man at Sabrehill you can trust, 'cept maybe old Mr. Aaron, and he long dead. You can't trust him, Adaba!"

"Looks to me like we ain't got much choice. Unless

you want to put me on your back and carry me again, Buck."

Buck sank down into a chair and stared at the floor.

"All right," Adaba said, "we're going. Zulie heard that Mr. Sabre plans to leave in a day or two, head back up for Virginia. Reckon he can use a good body servant or two, couple nice, faithful Sambo boys like you and me. If he's willing—"

"No," Buck said quietly.

"No what?" But Adaba already knew the answer.

"I ain't leaving here yet. I ain't ready yet."

No, Adaba thought, *you ain't ready yet, because you been scheming something. And I reckon I know what it is.*

"Buck, we don't know what all been happening around here. No telling who all them Rogans talked to in these parts, no telling what they said. After the shooting, that Lute Rogan maybe told all about us and most likely did. And whatever they said, it's gonna get spread around, and your old friend Mr. Skeet is gonna hear. And from what you tell me, that Skeet wants you dead just as much as you want the same for him. And this here place ain't gonna be safe."

"But we can hide you," Zulie said, "hide you so they won't never find you!"

"Maybe, but we can't take no chances. We got maybe another day, two days safe here, and that's all. And if Mr. Justin Sabre is willing to help us get away, we're sure as hell going with him."

"No," Buck said. "No."

Adaba ignored him. "Zulie, can you get word to Mr. Justin there's a couple niggers out here in the quarters surely like to talk to him?"

He saw that Zulie was torn, but she nodded.

"Soon, Zulie. First thing in the morning, early."

Buck stood up. "Tell him just one nigger, Zulie, not a couple. When he comes looking, I ain't gonna be here." He looked at Adaba. "You can tell him we split up, took different trails."

Buck meant it. Adaba recognized the stubborn look.

"Why, Buck, why?"

"You know damn well why. It's Vaych's time, Johnny."

"Time to pay." The word was bitter in Adaba's mouth.

"Yes, to pay. And he got a lot to pay for." Buck started for the door.

"Wait, old son. . . ."

Adaba carefully, wearily laid himself down on the bed. His small supply of strength was rapidly draining away.

"You heard what he said, Zulie?" he asked. "Buck wants to make Mr. Skeet pay."

"What I hear tell, he got good reason."

"Yeah, he got good reason. Don't blame him a bit. Feel like that myself many a time. But what good is pay for yesterday—if you throw away tomorrow?"

Zulie was silent, but he felt her resistance. She was with Buck.

"I ain't against justice," Adaba went on. "I ain't against getting what we got coming to us. And people like that Mr. Skeet ought to be shot, hung, and burned. But what's the sense of getting yourself killed trying to kill him?"

"Ain't gonna get myself killed," Buck said.

"But if you wait till a better time—"

"I waited twelve years. I can't wait no longer. You go on with your Mr. Sabre, Johnny, but I'm gonna do what I got to do."

Adaba saw that there would be no persuading Buck. Buck was in the grip of his strongest obsession, and reason counted for nothing now. But Adaba had to save the man from himself if he possibly could.

"Keep yourself alive, Buck. Come with me and keep yourself alive, and you and me'll steal away a thousand niggers from the Skeets. We'll sneak 'em away in the night, we'll head 'em up north, we'll—"

"I got to go." Again Buck turned to the door. "I reckon I'll see you again before you leave. If I don't . . ."

Adaba closed his eyes for a moment. Buck was not going to be saved, and Adaba lacked the strength to argue further. He said, "If you don't . . . you'll see me sometime . . . somewhere."

"Yeah, sometime. Somewhere out in the woods." Buck

grinned, tried to laugh. "Next time you see me out in the woods, Johnny Dove, all my bad dreams gonna be over."

With automatic caution, Buck slipped quietly out of the cabin, closing the door behind him.

No, not everything had changed in the field quarters. There was perhaps a degree more wariness than there had been in happier days. But still she was welcome in the quarters again, at least by some of the people: she felt it. She and Justin walked along the dark, mud streets, looking into a candlelit house now and then, and the greetings came a little easier, and the chatter and the laughter lasted a little longer.

Of course, they all knew. Saul had spread the story, and Irish had told it, and perhaps even the normally closed-mouthed Jebediah had said a word or two, and they all knew how two po' buckra rovers in filthy rags had tried to hold up Miss Lucy, how one of them had put Mr. Justin under the gun and got shot for his trouble, and the other one had been sent packing. And of course, some of the people, the disaffected, would just as soon it had turned out differently and Miss Lucy and Mr. Justin had got their asses shot off. But most of the people . . . what the hell, them Rogans was only nigger-hating sand-hillers, and for all their faults, these here is *our* Miss Lucy and *our* Sabrehill and, yes, *our* Mr. Justin. So them dirty sandhillers—fuck 'em. Lucy noticed some of her people looking at Justin with a certain awe and even admiration.

Yes, she was welcome again, and so was Justin. She had the feeling that working with them daily, he had come to know some of the men far better than she had in her lifetime. They shared jokes that she didn't under-stand and laughter that made her feel left out. Justin might hate slavery, she thought, but he would make an excellent master.

The quarters were bright tonight: the people were be-ing profligate with their candles. They should be warned not to squander them all before Christmas and the dark winter nights that still lay ahead. But that was Jebediah's job and not hers, and besides, she had the feeling that tonight some of those candles burned in her honor. Hers and Justin's.

But where was Jebediah?

Lucy kept her eyes open for him, but he was nowhere to be seen. She made two or three inquiries, but nobody knew where he might be. She saw a light behind Zulie's curtained window, but at Lucy's knock, Zulie said curtly that, no, she had no idea of where Jebediah might be, and the narrow slit of open door quickly closed.

Snippy little witch at times, that Zulie. Lucy shrugged it off.

They headed slowly back toward the big house.

They found Jebediah at home. He asked them to sit down, but remained standing until Lucy told him to sit. He was like that: often independent to the point of arrogance when they were alone together, but always a model of propriety when Justin or any other white person was present. Not out of fear of the others, she knew, but out of affection and respect for her.

She had assured Justin that Jebediah could be trusted, and Justin told him the whole story, briefly but completely.

"I told them that if they came here, I'd try to help them. Maybe that was a damn-fool way to handle it, but I was just freeing them, not stealing them."

"There's not much difference in most white folks' eyes," Jebediah said quietly. He had hardly blinked and never smiled while Justin had been talking.

Justin waved the point away. "Anyway, they may never have come here. Or maybe they came here and left before I ever arrived. Or maybe something happened to them, maybe they were caught somewhere upriver, and we never heard about it."

"If they were Black Buck and Adaba," Jebediah said, "we'd have heard about it."

"Adaba was supposedly wounded, though I didn't notice anything that made it look bad. But I could have been wrong—maybe the man died. Or maybe they decided not to trust me any further. But I'd like to think that they got here all right, and that when they found

that I wasn't here, they moved on. I'd like to think that
they got safely away."

Jebediah sat quietly for a moment, as if he were weighing the situation. Then, to Lucy's surprise, he began to
laugh. It was a low laugh that bubbled up in spite of
him, and he rocked in his chair and shook his head. "Oh,
shit," he muttered between laughs, "oh, shit!" and Justin
raised his eyebrows until he noticed that Lucy was grinning.

"Mr. Justin," Jebediah said, still laughing, tears in his
eyes, "you merely released two of the orneriest niggers
between the Canadian border and the Gulf of Mexico,
and you'd like to think they got *safely away?*"

"I know nothing about their orneriness. I only know—"

"If those two ever show up here, you're going to know
all right. That Adaba will steal every damn thing he can
lay his hands on, and what Adaba leaves, Black Buck
will burn so that *you* can't have it either. Oh, you picked
a fine pair to free, Mr. Justin—speaking frankly, my two
favorite niggers." Jebediah covered his face, trying to
smother laughter.

"All right," Justin said stiffly, "I picked a fine pair. I
think I'd have freed the devil himself from those damned
Rogans."

"And then you killed the old man and scared the boy
off. Excuse me, Mr. Justin, but you must have done some
mighty powerful lying to the constable."

"I did most of the lying for him," Lucy said, not without a touch of complacency, and Jebediah burst into
laughter all over again.

When he had himself under control, he turned to Lucy.
"Well, I'll find out what I can. I'm your overseer, and
the people don't altogether trust me, but most of them
like me, and they're not very good at keeping secrets. At
least, not from me. I don't think Black Buck and Adaba
ever came here, but if they did, I'll find out. It may take
a day or two, maybe even a week, but I'll let you know."

"I'll only be here another couple of days."

"I'll do my best."

"Thank you, Jebediah," Lucy said, and she and Justin
left.

From his window, Jeb watched them walking arm in arm toward the big house. He wondered how much of the tales he had heard about Lucy and Mr. Justin in the old days was true. Not that it mattered, he thought—obviously they were happy now. And he envied them.

He thought of Zulie. Last night she had spent more than an hour curled quietly in his arms. Tonight she had again refused him entrance to her cabin. *"And I ain't coming to your house, Jeb, so you just stop pestering me!"*

I lost her, he thought. *Somehow I lost her, or maybe I never really had her, and I don't understand. . . .*

Well, to hell with her. He loved her still, but he was damned if he was going to act like a moon-struck pup-dog any longer. He had work to do.

Perhaps he knew from the moment he turned his back on Adaba and walked out of Zulie's cabin. Perhaps he knew because his intentions ran so counter to what Adaba wanted and Adaba was almost invariably right. Or perhaps it was something else entirely, a growing realization. In any case, the knowledge already itched at the back of his mind, but he refused to heed it.

Buck saw at once that there was little point in holding a meeting at Sabrehill that evening. Saul agreed. "They all excited 'bout what happen today. That all they want to talk 'bout, how Mr. Justin shoot that man. Saturday night, they want to celebrate for Miss Lucy and Mr. Justin." Well, a meeting of his Sabrehill rebels wasn't important anyway. There were only a few—Hayden and Luther and some others—and he could see them at any time.

He decided to go some distance from Sabrehill—to go to the Buckridge place and work his way east, visiting several plantations. Saul borrowed a couple of Miss Lucy's horses and went with him.

But at the Buckridge place, Buck found that the situation was much what it was at Sabrehill. The news had traveled all over the countryside, and most of the talk was of Miss Lucy and Mr. Justin. Buck had trouble finding his followers. Knowledge was there, and she assured him that the stockpile of stolen supplies was rapidly growing, but Cudjoe, who so much liked to talk of a grand march of blacks to the north, was nowhere to be seen. Off visiting a wench on some other plantation, Knowledge said. After all, it was Saturday night.

Discouraged, Buck decided not to go any farther east. Instead he turned back toward Sabrehill and stopped at the Devereau plantation. Now he thought he knew what to expect, and he was right. Brutus and Faith, the leaders there, assured him that all was going well, that they had recruited new followers, that by next Saturday night everyone would be ready. But what they really wanted to talk about was the pair of robbers who had come to Sabrehill that day. Saul, Buck noticed, was himself more eager to talk about the Rogans than about rebels and runaways.

When they left the Devereau plantation, Saul was ready to return home, but at Buck's urging they both went on past Sabrehill to the Kimbrough plantation. And once again, Buck was disappointed. Most of the conspirators were too busy on a Saturday night to spend much time at a meeting. They met in the cabin of Hector and his woman, Dee, and most of the talk, most of the questions, had to do with the Rogans and with Miss Lucy and Mr. Justin.

" 'Member when Mr. Skeet call out Mr. Justin on the street in Riverboro," one of the men asked, "how he slap Mr. Justin 'round, and Mr. Justin plain beat the shit out of him?"

" 'Member!" another said. "Why, I was there! I see it myself!"

"Yeah, well, I see them fight the duel. Drive the major to the dueling ground, only he was the captain then. Seen them shoot each other up!"

Buck sat quietly as the chatter went on. No one even referred to the plans they had met to discuss, and he felt his spirits sagging still further. He said nothing, as the talk turned to the Christmas season, until Dee mentioned excitedly that *next* Saturday night the *big* parties would start.

"But you won't be here," he said.

It was cruel, though he had not meant it to be. He saw the stricken look on her face; she had forgotten. They had all put it out of mind. Next Saturday night was the night that they would start north, leaving so much of what they loved, as well as what they hated, forever. The room was suddenly quiet.

Hector put his arm around his wife's shoulders. "Never you mind, honey," he said gently. "Next Saturday night you be free."

But Buck wondered if Dee would be with them next Saturday night. Or Hector. Or any of the others.

It was taking too long. Adaba was right: you had to whip up enthusiasm for the flight and act while that feeling was at its peak. More than a few days was too long, for though the dream remained, faith in it quickly withered. Hope had been murdered too often. And furthermore, the incident at Sabrehill that day had given them a new interest, a distraction from their own problems. Skeet's treatment of Ettalee, now that she was getting better, was a thing of the past, and the craving for revenge was dying.

And it was the Christmas season. There was that simple, human fact. There were parties, there were gifts and gaiety, there were family and friends. And who wanted to leave all that behind?

The knowledge that haunted the back of Buck's mind could no longer be denied. His plans were failing.

Oh, there would be runaways next Saturday night, of course. And he would open up Vachel's jail and kill Vachel. The jail people would follow Buck, and so would some of the unhappier blacks from the nearby plantations. But that was all there would be—perhaps a dozen or so runaways. There would be no true rebellion.

And that was what he had been planning, even more than he himself had realized. That was what he had yearned for—not runaways but rebels. Not a few hands from a few plantations sneaking off into the night, but an uprising, a march. It was the vision he had had that morning as he had sat in the rain outside the lean-to thinking that Adaba might well be dying. An army that would grow as it marched north, an army of vengeance that would make every black free. And he would lead it! He tried to be as coldly calculating as Adaba, but in reality he was a man with a skull full of flames, hardly able to keep them banked, and he wanted to let them burn, burn. . . .

But it was not going to happen.

He sat quietly, saying nothing more, hardly listening to the others. He felt very tired, very discouraged. He no longer wished to talk about the plans any more than the others did. He wanted only to return to Sabrehill and perhaps talk to Claramae for a while—

He shook his head. He was confused. He didn't mean Claramae, he meant Ettalee. He would talk to Ettalee, if she were still awake at this hour, and know she was all right, and then he would go to his bed in the room over the coach house.

He suggested to Saul that they leave.

They were out the door, Hector right behind them, when Serena came out of the shadows, and Buck saw at once that something was wrong.

"Hoping maybe you here," Serena said, "hoping I find you."

"Why? What is it—"

"Cato. Mr. Skeet, he done lock Cato up in the jail house!"

"Oh, shit," Hector muttered in a tone of defeat. "That where we all going end up."

That was what *he* now thought of the plans.

Everything was going wrong.

No, there would be no rebellion.

Lucy said her prayers that night kneeling at the side of her bed. It was something she had not done in many years. She was not a particularly religious woman; in fact, she did not think of herself as being religious at all. But her mother had taught her to pray, and the habit had never quite vanished, returning as it did from time to time in periods of stress or happiness. She would find herself lying in bed, the lamp out, murmuring to herself, "Dear heavenly Father . . ."

Tonight the lamp was not out; it still burned quite brightly. And Lucy, her hands clasped and her eyes closed, sank to her knees at the side of the bed without even thinking what she was doing. "Dear heavenly Father . . ."

She finished. She rose to her feet. But she did not put the lamp out, nor did she slide under the covers. The bed was turned down, but she merely sat on it, pulling her feet up and curling her legs under her, and leaned back against the heap of pillows. She was not in the least sleepy. She and Justin both liked to read for a little while at bedtime, and she had a book, but she did not touch it. She reached for the glass of brandy on her bedside table and took a small sip.

How could it be, she wondered, that one of the truly terrible days of her life, a day of fear and near-rape and violent death, could leave her feeling so happy? Why were those terrible events of the afternoon, only a few hours away, so distant?

She thought she knew. Once again she had survived. Once again the perfume, the sweat, the musk of life was fresh in her nostrils, as fresh as spring rain and animals in healthy rut and great banks of green grass and honeysuckle. She lived.

But there was more to it than that. She knew from experience that the mind tried to protect itself by putting painful events at a distance. Only recently she had thought she might be wise to delve into those old memories that she had denied herself for so long, and she had found it difficult, almost impossible. Oh, she could face them as long as she saw them on some distant mental horizon, events that had happened to some other Lucy, some Justin she did not care to know. But to bring back the bone-deep knowledge of happiness destroyed, the hope, the dreams, the exquisite pain of loss—oh, dear God, no!

And now the whole business with the Rogans was at a distance. It was far away on her mental horizon, promising to disappear at any time, taking the last of the panic, the anguish, the terror with it.

While on the other hand . . .

Those old memories which she had denied herself, those old memories that she had been able to face only at a distance because they gave her such pain—she realized that they were now hers again, without pain or shame or useless regret. They were of long ago, but they returned to her with bittersweet pleasure.

She nearly laughed aloud. *Oh, Justin, how young we were!*

She could have sung, remembering that spring: the young cravings, the dreams, the sweet frustrations. On Sundays it had seemed to take forever to escape her father and her sisters and the house to be alone with Justin, alone in the fields or the woods or any distant hidden place where they could hold each other, touch each other, and think of what they must not do. And, oh, the temptation!

There was that Sunday, kept beyond the horizon of memory for so long, when her father had wanted to talk to Justin, and she had gone to her room and stood naked before the open window, the sweat running down her body, and thought, *Justin . . . Justin . . .*

. . . The Sunday when, *Hallelujah!* they had abandoned all clothes for the first time, had rolled naked together in the sweet grass, had crushed the wild flowers, and he had broken into her, plundered her, served her so well.

Yes, they had been foolish. But at least the dreadful shame was gone now, the sickening knowledge that she had been tricked, seduced, used, discarded. No, *that* shameful thing had never happened to her. On that hot dusty afternoon so long ago, she had been loved. . . .

And what a miracle it had seemed to her that first time. For what did she know of the male? Had she ever seen such beautiful shoulders, such an expanse of hard-muscled chest, such a narrow waist and hips? Had she ever seen the full pattern of hair down the length of the torso, and the male aroused above the long graceful thighs? There was her father's library, of course, no books forbidden; but was Justin *really* a figure beyond any Michelangelo, a figure more finely drawn, more fascinating than any stone David? She had stared at the picture of David for hours, had stared at that stone manhood, but David had never responded to her like this, had never been this beautiful. What did she know? . . .

That summer . . . in the woods by the stream . . . in distant fields . . . in her room each night. And after the duel, when he had begun to recover, in his room . . . the two of them in each other's arms, he in her body . . . making such love, such pleasure, such delight. . . .

Oh, Ga-a-awd, you foolish old bawd, she groaned, tucking her gown between her thighs, *yes, it's been a long time, but think of something else.*

And there were other things to think of, good things. Private jokes and shared laughter. Long rides together, into Riverboro and about the countryside, sometimes scandalously unchaperoned. Long, lazy hours, after love, of daydreaming and making plans.

She could remember it all now. She no longer had to disclaim, disown, flee from it. She smiled and sipped her brandy and remembered . . . and somehow, in spite of her, memory kept going back to those summer afternoons, those summer nights. . . .

She stretched out a leg on the bed. The room was growing chilly, but she pulled her sleeping gown to the top of her thigh and looked at the leg. Not bad, she supposed, especially for a woman of her age. Hard work kept her healthy and strong. She looked at her breasts. She put a hand under one and lifted it. Not terribly impressive, but she still looked very good in any dinner or ball gown, better than most younger women. A handsome widow-lady, growing older, being wasted . . . The thought saddened her. She finished her brandy. She had not had much that evening, but she wondered if she were drunk.

The day had been so long, but she was restless, and sleep was still distant. And there was still so much to be said. She wondered if Justin were still awake too. It would be foolish to disturb him, but . . .

She slid her legs over the edge of the bed. She stood up. She found a robe and pulled it over her shoulders. She felt like being foolish, and very well, she would be foolish. Before she had time to think better of it.

Quietly she stepped out into the dark hall. There was a light, barely perceptible, under the edge of Justin's door. Good. He was probably awake.

On silent feet, she crossed the hall. She tapped lightly on the door.

The answering "Yes?" was almost as quiet as her tap.

She opened the door an inch at a time and looked in. Justin was sitting up in bed. He had a book in his hand, though the lamp was turned down low. He put the book on the table beside the lamp. Holding her robe closed, Lucy slipped through the doorway.

"I couldn't sleep," she said in little more than a whisper. "I wondered if you were still awake." She closed the door behind her.

He smiled. "Yes, I'm still awake. Come here, Luz."

She padded, shivering, across the room. For some reason her heart was pounding as hard as it had when the Rogans had appeared that afternoon.

He sat up. She sat on the edge of the bed, facing him. As his arm encircled her shoulders, she let her robe fall to the floor. She had not really thought that this would happen, had not consciously contemplated it at all. But that hardly mattered.

She leaned toward him, and their mouths met, met after all the years. And all the old need flamed up, stronger than ever.

"Luz, Luz, Luz," he said when she drew her mouth away, "Luz, I have no right—"

"Be quiet," she commanded. "Just don't say a thing."

Their mouths met again, met and worked, and she thought with strange amusement that they would have to learn this art all over again, that there was so much to be relearned. And she wanted him to hold her closer, she wanted him to touch her, to stroke her, to bring every part of her alive. She wanted him . . . she wanted . . .

"Come to bed, Luz," he said.

Seven

At first they were like greedy children. They clung too tightly, they kissed too fiercely, as if to gorge themselves on love as quickly as possible. They wanted everything at once. She sat on the side of the bed, swaying in his arms, drunk on something more than brandy, and he tried to touch her everywhere and thus touched her nowhere. She bruised her lips, bruised his, and somehow between their mouths the kiss was lost. He tried to draw her into bed, "Come, Luz, come," but it was all too fast, and she held him off.

He shook his head. His eyes were baffled. "Luz . . . I'm sorry . . . you don't want . . ."

"I do," she said. "I do."

As his arm came around her again, she laid her forehead on his shoulder. How seldom since he had left her had she felt this same sweet heaviness, this honeyed readiness, this desire. How long had she been self-protected against it, knowing that it could never quite be laid to rest, that it always threatened her spinsterish peace. If she were not a fool, wouldn't she slip from his arms and leave this room without another word? That was all she had to do: rise quietly and turn away. . . .

She reached into the open neck of his nightshirt and moved her fingertips lightly down over his chest.

He moved away from her. He pulled up his nightshirt, drew it over his head, and tossed it away. He lifted her chin and kissed her gently, and once again he said, "Come to bed, Luz."

And now it was different. She rolled into the bed with him, and this time when he stroked her, his hand lingered without the painful grasping. When his mouth came down on hers, it was hungry and forceful but without the greed that baffled desire. The old knowledge was returning. They kissed, and kissed again, and his hand moved over her, inviting an ever-stronger need. There was no haste now, but no delay. One took what was given, however quickly or slowly it happened. She moved under his chest, moved against him, reached down to grip and give pleasure to his wanting flesh, and drew up her gown to bare hers.

"Luz . . ."

A flood of jumbled memories came then, as they caressed each other . . . the smell of crushed flowers and the hot summer dust . . . the musk of his body and of her own . . . the stolen moments of hasty love, fully clothed . . . the long naked nights in this same bed . . . the last night, the one last aching time . . . and more . . . and more. . . .

But none of it was as vivid as what was happening

now; the memories were swept away by the intensity of the present—the hand stroking the small of her back . . . the mouth below her breasts as she drew her gown up over them . . . the ache beneath his hand, the taut nipple between his lips, and the need still mounting, demanding always more, like an anger, like a rage, until now, now, now—

—now they could wait no longer. And there was no need to wait. Her gown was gone; she was as naked as he. As he moved over her and she lifted her knees, the remaining covers fell away, all but a bit of sheet. The lamp, dimmed, now seemed blinding as its light flooded between their bodies. She reached for him, lifted herself to him, took him; moved onto him as surely and hungrily as he thrust into her . . .

. . . and they were together again. As if by some miracle, he was with her and within, contained, encompassed, embraced. As if the lost years had no meaning. As if there were only this moment, the moment of complete conquest and surrender.

And now, rest. She wanted to go on, she wanted haste, she was greedy again, but *Not too soon,* she remembered, *not too soon!*

Their breathing, the tension, eased.

Again she looked between their coupled bodies. Yes, this was still the same male body she had known and loved so well. Like her own body, it was a little heavier perhaps, a little coarser, but to her it was still more beautiful than any stone David. She put her hands on the familiar shoulders, moved them to the chest and back she knew so well. She touched the double-diamond of dark hair, raking her fingers through it down from his chest to where it matted against her own blond thatch. Desire blurred her sight. *This is my Justin,* she thought, feeling for him, *my own Justin, home at last.*

He gasped at her touch. She felt his heavy presence within her, felt it move. And she could wait no longer. The tide of need rose again, and she wanted what was still to come, craved it, had to have it. She tightened on that deep presence, gripped and drew on it, bringing a gasp from Justin.

"Oh, God, Luz, I do love—"

"*Shush!*" Stilled, almost frightened by his words, she put a hand to his mouth. "You needn't say that."

"But I—"

"No. I don't want you to say it, not now. You're going away. I know you can't live here, and I can never leave. And we're older now, darling, and we've both changed. But for now, I want to forget all that, oh, please, I want to forget!"

His lips brushed her face, his hand stroked her breast. "Then, forget, Luz, forget," he whispered as they began again. "But I'll still say . . . I love you. . . ."

And afterward, peace, a drowsy delight, a depth of satisfaction such as she had not known in years. A sense of having returned home after a long, hard journey, a feeling of being in her own safe and comfortable place. The two of them clinging together still, with hardly the strength to cling. Justin half asleep. The thought came to her, inevitably, that such happiness must have its price. She might already be with his child. Maybe *this* time she would get to see England or France or Italy; maybe *this* time she would get to visit all those lovely old European ruins. But what did she care tonight?

A resurgence of energy then, and small tasks to be done. Justin tugged at her as she slipped out of bed, but she broke away from him. Her face averted from him, she pursed her lips to hold back a smile. It had really been quite good, she thought with a kind of smug delight. Not perfect, perhaps, not everything one might have wished for, but really quite good. For a first time. After all the long and lonely years. Yes, really quite good.

Small tasks. Still naked, shivering, she went to the fireplace and built up the fire. He protested: he should do that. She insisted: he should not. "Justin, damn you, get back into that bed." She would do all, including an after-love toilette for him, but the water was cold, and her touch set him to laughing, and his little twig shriveled up smaller than ever.

Small tasks. She crossed through the darkness to her

own room. (Maybe Lucinda's instructions would work this time; maybe, with a hope and a prayer, she would *not* see all those lovely old ruins. But on the other hand, what if she simply took her chances?) She found a hair brush. Humming, hardly caring if she disturbed Leila or not, she returned to Justin's room.

"Come here, Luz."

"In a moment, darling."

While she warmed herself by the fire, she unsnarled her hair. She tied it behind with a red ribbon, a loose ribbon taken from her gown, then slipped under the covers and lay over Justin, her breasts against his chest. She purred and nibbled at him and reached down to hold the twig, and he laughed and stretched out his long battle-scarred body and put his arms up behind his head.

"Woman, you're a wanton still."

"Wicked," she whispered. "Shameless. I remember how I shocked you when you first came here."

"You did, a little. You had collected quite an interesting secret vocabulary—"

"Much of which I still don't understand, because you refused to explain. You must teach me, Justin—"

"And I never thought I'd meet a lady quite so . . . well . . . privately uninhibited, I suppose."

"You weren't raised by my father, dear, and taught by Lucinda and Aunt Zule. And I wasn't raised by an Adamina Kimbrough or a Callie Buckridge, thank God. I can remember overhearing Mr. Buckridge saying, 'Whah, a common woman is only a wench, suh, but a true-bred lady don't *have* no dark urges.'" Justin laughed at her imitation. "Dark urges! My God, Justin! Do you mind my dark urges, dear?"

"I love your dark urges."

Lucy sat up, tossing the blankets down to Justin's knees. "And I remember my father shaking his head and saying of one of our neighbors, 'Why, if women had balls, that man would castrate his own daughters.'" She chucked Justin between the legs. "Well, be shocked if you must. But whatever a woman has for balls, my dear, no one has yet cut off mine."

She expected Justin to laugh, but he did not. He merely smiled and said, "No, Luz, no one has yet cut off yours. And I don't think anyone ever will."

It took her a moment to understand: a male expression, a tribute that really had nothing to do with sex. In gratitude she leaned down over him and gave him a quick kiss. But suddenly, as she sat up again, she was saddened.

What if . . . what if . . . ?

They had only this night and perhaps two or three more, and she might never see him again. It was more a fear than a premonition, but it was strong. But what if the years had never been lost? What if Justin had immediately told his family of their marriage plans? What if Vachel and Justin had never fought the duel, and Justin had stayed on and on at Sabrehill, and . . .

"Justin, why did he have to do it?"

"What, Luz? What are you talking about?"

"Vachel Skeet. The duel. His mad idea, somehow, that he had to defend my honor because of you."

"Why, he was in love with you, darling. You know that."

She stared at Justin. What in the world was he talking about?

"Luz, darling, you know . . ."

And of course she did. Perhaps all the world knew. But it was a fact she had not wished to face, over all the years.

"Miss Lucy."

Vachel Skeet, standing there in the passage as she came down the stairs . . . Vachel Skeet, staring at her in her thin dress as if he saw her naked . . .

"Yes, Mr. Skeet?"

Vachel Skeet, his eyes pleading, as if asking her to understand. But she did not want to understand.

"Oh, dear God . . ."

"What is it, Luz?"

No, it was a fact she had not wished to face. Not at any time had she admitted to herself that Vachel had loved her, had come calling on her, and not on her father, on those long-ago Sunday afternoons. Because if she did, she also had to face the fact that she might, just might, have had some small share of the responsibility for what had happened to Justin. And to herself.

"You needn't always feel grateful for love, child," her father had told her long ago, *"but you must always respect it."*

No, she had neither faced the fact nor respected the love.

"Oh, dear God," she said again, and for the first time she admitted to herself that Vachel Skeet had probably suffered as much that summer as she. Poor, wretched, deplorable, unforgivable Vachel Skeet.

Another unwanted thought came to her. "Do you think . . . he suspected about us . . . I mean, that we . . ."

"Luz, I think the whole damned countryside suspected about us, the way we were carrying on. You know how servants talk, how the word gets passed around."

Yes. And that would be quite enough to inflame the imagination of Vachel Skeet, a man sick with love. Lucy covered her face with a hand.

"Luz," Justin said gently. "Lucy, honey, all that is a long time over."

Yes, of course it was. And what had happened had happened, and there was no way of changing it. And she was fortunate. She was alive again, alive with this handsome stranger in her house, and she in his bed, and it was time for gratitude, not for remorse. She was alive again, if only for a little while, and tonight was part of her resurrection. She allowed Justin to draw her hand down from her face. She looked at him and smiled.

"I regret nothing," she said. "Tonight I love you. You keep using those words, though I told you not to, so I'll use them too. Tonight I love you."

"And I love you, Luz."

And it all began again.

She had been wrong, on that Sunday afternoon all those years ago. She had thought that it had to be right that one first time, it had to be perfect, for if it were perfect, it could never be, and need not be, surpassed. But it was surpassed now. For if the hungers of youth had begun to fade, the savoring of the feast had only increased. No hurry now for the final satisfaction. There was time now, after he was deep within her, for sweet whisperings and long caresses and a new kind of quiet laughter. There was time to consider each other's wants and needs, time to feel each slight tremor of pleasure. Time even to part once for the sheer delight of rejoining. Time to build, build, build to that blinding moment, that crescendo, when nothing existed but the ultimate pleasure. Then to find that he was still with her, still deep and hard within, still thrusting and building her toward the next blinding moment.

Had they mastered this art before? Possibly. Some of it. She could not really remember. If the long-ago past had at first enriched the present, the present now wiped the past away. What did it matter now? What was memory, compared to this, the presence of her man over her, the strain of her spread thighs, the lifting to the long penile thrust? What did all that matter? She had been living in a desert for so long, in a scorched, parched land, but now she was back in Eden with her man, and once again their rhythms urged her toward the next explosive ecstasy.

As she reached it, she took him with her. A sharp command, *"Do it! Do it!"* and a clutching, twisting movement of her body, and she felt him come to a sharp halt, trembling on the brink. *"Do it!"* And he could hold back no longer. A soft, wounded cry, and he gave up everything. "Oh, baby, baby, baby," she crooned as he gave it up, "oh, sweet baby love, let it all go, let it all, all . . ."

An ending. A slowing of the rhythms; kisses and tears and soft laughter for their triumph. A softening and a halt. Peace again and the drowsy delight. Another kiss, careful not to put his weight on her, and he slipped out of her and fell to her side. Until the next time, dear, until the next time. She stretched luxuriously. She reached to turn the lamp lower, then pulled the covers up over them and curled into his arms. He murmured love sounds to her and moved his mouth over her face, but he was already half-asleep. She smiled.

What had they done, the two of them? Not much.

Made love. It happened all the time. People did it. This very night, perhaps ten or twenty or thirty couples in the quarters had made love; perhaps some of them were doing it at this very moment. A man turns to his woman, a woman turns to her man, "Honey-love, I needs my pleasure," and it happens. One of the most common acts in the world and one of the sweetest.

She thought of Mr. Buckridge and his "dark urges." Dark urges, indeed!

Still aglow with her love, she snuggled closer to Justin and waited. For the next time.

Later she blew out the lamp. They lay naked together in the bed, unwilling to give up each other's touch; but when she was asleep, she rolled away from him and curled up into a ball, her hands tucked together under her cheek. Suddenly he was alone, and the glow of love was gone, and once again there was a future to be faced.

Christ, he thought, troubled, *where do I go now? What's left of my life after this?*

Perhaps he slept. He thought he only dozed, which was odd because after so much love he should have slept like the dead. But he became aware that hours had slipped by, and he was staring at the dark ceiling, wide awake and still troubled.

He got out of bed. The room was cold. He looked out the window and saw no sign of dawn, but he thought it must be near. The people would be stirring soon, and Rayburn, the boy assigned to him, would be in to build up the fire. Well, that, at least, was easily taken care of: he locked the door and built up the fire himself. He got back into bed and waited for the room to warm.

The question would not go away: *Where do I go?*

He had traveled such a long way already. He had found his woman in that Charleston winter and that Sabrehill spring so long ago. He had loved her and had given her up, perhaps because he was a fool, and had loved another. He had seen the world; he had raised, or half-raised, a family; he had lost a wife. And he had been drawn back here. Had been drawn down the river on a cotton box, drawn back to find his Lucy ill-used and scarred yet still beautiful and strong and ready to love again.

And everything in him said, *Then love her again! Love her!* But did he dare? Had he the right? She would never give up Sabrehill, she would never leave here, and he—

"Are you a nigger-lover, sir? . . . Are you one of them goddam William Lloyd Garrison people, spreading their goddam abolitionist poison?"

—he was increasingly certain that he could not live in the South. At least not in the Southeast, not in South Carolina. Not the way it was going today, charging hysterically into a past that had never really existed, defying the moral and physical might of the rest of the world, defending the indefensible—an institution that, to say the least, was anachronistic.

And vile.

My God, he thought, no wonder that even proslavery Virginians were awed by these South Carolina hotheads. The Turner Revolt had led the Virginia legislature seriously to consider abolition—and for this the Carolinians called the Virginians "fanatics"! Fanatics, for even questioning slavery.

No, he could not live here. And Lucy understood that; she did not expect him to stay. But what was he to do with his life, then? Where was he to go?

To Texas, maybe, as he had suggested to Lucy. Mexico had abolished slavery. Of course, Texas still had it, but from what he had heard, the plantation-slavery system was not yet so deeply entrenched and perhaps never would be. Maybe a man like Justin Sabre could make a future for himself in Texas.

But what would his life be without Lucy? He was hardly an old man, but he was no longer a boy. The seasons were passing for him, and he was not sure there could ever be another woman he could love.

He wanted to see her again. The room had warmed, and he slipped out of bed. He found a splinter by the fireplace, lit it, and used it to light the lamp. Lucy did not move as the light came up.

He climbed back onto the bed and sat there looking at

her. After a moment he slowly pulled the covers down to her knees. She lay on her back now, bent slightly sideways at the waist, legs apart. The red ribbon from her gown still held her long blond hair. In sleep she looked smaller and younger than she was.

Poor abused body, he thought. There was still a welt on her left cheek where Lute Rogan had hit her. There were bruises on her thighs, on her ribs, on one breast, and once again he felt that savage desire for vengeance, that burning need to kill. That anyone should treat her like that . . .

He looked at the long scar down the right side of her face. She had never told him how she had acquired it, and the servants never spoke of it. They respected her silence, and he knew they would not respect him if he asked or even referred to it. But he had gathered that it had something to do with her late husband, a man she could think back on only with pain and bitterness. But how could he have not loved her, how could he have not treated her well? *He must have been as big a fool as I am.*

Justin bent over her. He kissed the scar. It was part of her now, never to be lost, and there was no part of her he did not wish to love.

When he kissed her eyelids, he thought she smiled.

He did not wish to disturb her. His lips barely brushed hers. They barely touched the welt on her left cheek, barely touched her throat, before moving on to her breasts. He kissed each dark bruise. When he touched her nipples and they ripened like fruit between his lips, his own desire stirred, but he tamed it. Let her sleep.

He sat up. He would remember her like this, sleeping peacefully, the faint smile on her slightly open mouth, unmindful of the pain of the day, perhaps dreaming. He would think of her like this, and she would never know.

He bent then and kissed her again. Slid down by her and kissed her bruised thighs, holding one in each hand. Moved closer and kissed her between her legs. Kissed her where she was tenderest and most vulnerable. Kissed her and could not prevent the stirring of his desire . . .

. . . nor the leap of it as she returned his kiss. He cried out and pulled away from her and heard her laughter; he rolled away to escape, but she was after him at once.

"Minx! Siren!"

"Stallion! Bull!"

He laughed with her. They laughed, wrestled, played, sported, and he laid her back and took her once again. He did not believe anyone else in the world could know this woman as he did, no one else ever had or ever would. Whatever others might say of her, whatever they might think, they knew only the cold-eyed lady, the proper and respected mistress of Sabrehill. Only he knew the secret Luz, this sweet and wanton and gentle and eager lover, this treasure trove of affection and desire. How could he ever leave her?

No, he would not think about that. Could not, not now. Not while they were joined in this fine embrace, in this world-well-lost loving. Not now . . .

Later, when they again lay quietly in each other's arms, they heard the horsemen coming.

Eight

He was going to have Buckley Skeet back in his hands again. The need, the craving, had grown all through the night, and now he had to believe that it was going to be satisfied. The need was in his bones, on his tongue, in every breath he took. It was like longing for years for a particular woman and then being told that she would be waiting for you in your bed. When you walked through the doorway, she had to be there.

Buckley, you're mine again.

A misty dawn was breaking as they reined up at the Sabrehill gate at the foot of the long oak-lined avenue that led south to the mansion. The gate was, as always, open, but Skeet made the posse wait there for a few minutes while the sky lightened. He did not want Buckley escaping under cover of darkness.

He looked around him. He had been fortunate. Working through the night, he and Jeppson and the constable had recruited very nearly the fifty men he had wanted. And not just any men—these were men who would have no scruples about tearing hell out of Sabrehill, about burning the damn place down if need be, to collect the money they had been promised. The kind of men who knew how to handle a bad nigger.

"What the hell's holding us up, goddam it?" one of them yelled. "I come here to catch some nigger meat, not to sit here getting saddle sores."

There was approving laughter, much of it drunken, and Skeet joined in with it. He held up his hand to get attention.

"All you men know what to do?"

"We know!"

"Now, we got to do this fast and orderlylike. We don't, them niggers is sure as hell gonna get away from us. Watch out they don't try to make a run for it or maybe sneak away to hide in some place you already searched. Anybody got any questions?"

The constable nervously cleared his throat. "Vachel, like I said before, I really do think we ought to speak to Miss Lucy first."

"Hell, no, we ain't gonna speak to Miss Lucy first! Goddam, I am trying to tell you we got to do this fast! Or there ain't gonna be no Black Buck! Anyway, that bitch is gonna find out what we're doing soon enough. Any more questions?"

Somebody in the crowd laughed and said, "Me, I'm looking forward to getting me some of that prime Sabrehill poontang."

"Now, there ain't gonna be none of that!" the constable said angrily.

"You heard that, men," Vachel said. "There ain't gonna be none of that—while the constable is watching. And not till we got the search all done. We don't want old Black Buck hightailing it while you are wasting time on black pussy, you hear me? But you get Black Buck for me, and I don't give a damn what you do to celebrate."

There was more laughter.

"All right, we're ready to go now. Tag, P. V., get your men moving. The rest of you, *let's go!*"

Skeet led the way across the fields toward the field quarters. Tag Bassett and P. V. Tucker led their men pounding up the road toward the big house and the service lanes. And in the big house, Miss Lucy heard them coming.

Jeb Hayes, in the overseer's house, heard them.

He had awakened and dressed well before dawn. It was an unbreakable habit from the years when he had awakened each morning to the crack of the whip and had been driven into the fields like an animal. Those years were long over now; they were like a fading nightmare. But if the nightmare had faded, it always threatened to return: by a turn of fortune, he could always find himself in the fields again, and he knew it.

He stepped out onto his little veranda. Stood in the half-open doorway. In the still, chill air of dawn, sounds carried far. A horse, a voice. Yes, they were out there.

Christ, he thought irritably, trying to make it seem unimportant, *the goddam patrol!* They were for the most part a lazy, irresponsible bunch, a mere annoynace, unless they chose to beat some poor nigger who wasn't properly "respectful." But why the hell did they have to show up here at this hour and on a Sunday morning?

He knew in some part of himself that this was not an ordinary patrol. He knew somehow that it was going to be bad, and he stepped back inside.

And then they came.

About ten of them came racing between the long lines of live oaks toward the courtyard. Half of them turned onto the west lane and reined up before the butler's cottage. The other half turned toward the east lane and reined up before Jeb's house.

He recognized the first man to leap down from the saddle: Taggart Bassett. Bassett had been to Sabrehill often enough before. A dark compact wiry man, he reached Jeb's porch in four long strides, and with his fifth stride kicked the door in, slamming it against the inner wall, and charged into the house. The other men tied the horses to a porch post and quickly followed.

"Jesus, you sure ain't changed none, have you," Bassett said. "Still got them goddam books on shelves." The books, borrowed from Miss Lucy and neatly shelved, had always seemed particularly offensive to Bassett. With one long sweep of his arm, he sent them flying, scattering them about the floor. The other men laughed, and walked over the books to look into the other two rooms.

"Well, nigger?"

Jeb looked down at Bassett's dark angry face. He smelled the whiskey. He said, "Yes, sir, master?"

More than once, Jeb had stood up to a white man. More than once, he had mocked Bassett, had happy-cooned the man half to death, *Yassah, massa, yassah.* But not this morning. This morning, just a touch of ignorant, dull-witted field accent and nothing more. What the man wanted to hear. Or somebody was going to get killed. Jeb sensed it.

"Yes-sir-master, that's right, nigger. You know why we're here?"

"No, sir, master."

"Don't you lie to me, nigger, we *know* you hiding a runaway nigger here, we *know* you got Black Buck here, we *know* it, nigger."

Justin Sabre's story rushed through Jeb's mind. "Black Buck, sir?"

"Don't you play all innocent with me, you got Black Buck here and most likely Adaba too. We *know* you got Black Buck and Adaba—"

"Black Buck and—oh, no, sir, I don't know no Black Buck nor Adaba—"

"You lying, and you know what you get for lying? You get whipped, by God, and them scars on your face ain't nothing to what you gonna get!"

"Master, sir, I don't know, I swear to you, sir—"

"Gimme that there paddle," Bassett said to one of the other men. "Gimme that there paddle and turn this here nigger 'round."

Yes, the nightmare could always return, but he had not expected this. As in a fever dream, he saw the rawhide paddle, three feet of rough hard leather bored with a dozen holes, being pressed into Bassett's hand. He felt his arms being seized by two of the men. Suddenly his feet were kicked out from under him, and he crashed to his hands and knees. Weight came down on his shoulders, his arms were still held, and he could not rise. This could not truly be happening to him.

"No!"

"What you say, nigger? You say no to me? Get his pants down, goddam it."

He struggled then, but ineffectually, as an arm came around his neck, half-strangling him. He felt his pants going down. This could not be happening, this was Sabrehill and he was the overseer and—

The rawhide paddle seemed to explode in fire across his buttocks, and he screamed, all dignity gone. Once— two years, three years earlier—he might not have screamed at that single blow, but now—

The paddle struck like fire again, and again he screamed, screamed so hard he could barely hear the white men's laughter.

"Now what you got to say, nigger? You gonna tell me where Black Buck is? It's Black Buck we want—"

"I don't know!"

"Leggo his arm," Bassett directed. "Better hang onto your cock, nigger, less'n you want me to bust your balls."

Jeb found his right arm released, and he grabbed at his genitals, drawing them forward.

And the paddle came blazing across him a third time—

"I don't know, I don't know!" he screamed.

And a fourth, a fifth, a sixth, he didn't count the blows, he could only scream through the agony, "I don't know, I don't know, I don't know!" until he realized that the blows had stopped, and Bassett had stepped back, gasping and chuckling.

"Tag," one of the men said, laughing with Bassett, "I think he really don't know!"

"Hell, I know that. Old Buck's most likely out in the field quarters, and they ain't gonna tell no ass-licking white man's nigger where they keeping him. But I been meaning to teach this snotty book-reading jig a lesson for a long time now. Come on, get him on his feet. Let's get out of here.".

Jeb fought back his sobs. His eyes were too blurred to see. He felt himself being lifted to his feet, and someone pulled his pants up for him. His buttocks and the backs of his legs felt wet, and he thought that he must be bleeding. He was afraid that bladder and bowels might release. One of the men laughed and said, "Now, that wasn't so bad, was it?"

Wasn't so bad?

Jeb had spent his life thus far on four plantations. For years he had struggled to maintain some kind of pride, some semblance of manhood, in spite of all that his masters had done to him. And after the first bad months here at Sabrehill, he had thought he had found a kind of haven, a sanctuary. Yes, he had known that his fortunes might be reversed, but it had no longer seemed so important to guard pride and manhood every hour, every minute of his life. And perhaps he had forgotten something, something absolutely vital for a black man in this world. For in less than one full minute, they had taken that pride, that manhood away from him.

It was not shameful to scream—only to scream without a curse.

"Come on," Bassett said. "Like Vachel told us, we got to do this fast. And you come too, nigger. Maybe you don't know about Black Buck, or maybe you do. But I don't trust you."

Staggering with pain, Jeb followed the men out of the house. The horses were still in front of the butler's cottage, on the other side of the courtyard. Something moved within the cottage, and a girl cried out, a cry of helplessness and pain. Jeb hesitated.

"I said, you come with us, nigger!"

It was damn-fool thing to do. There wasn't a thing in the world Jeb could do to help the girl, and he knew it. But he started across the courtyard.

"God damn you, nigger-r-r-r!"

This time he went down not with a scream but a curse.

At first the cries came to Zag in dreams, and that was strange, because his dreams were sweet. He lay deep in his bed with his Binnie in his arms and wondered where those despairing wails could come from. But they were distant, they came from the other side of sunlit fields, they had nothing to do with him and his Binnie as they lay here in their—

The cries were closer. Someone was screaming in the carpenter shop, no more than a few paces away.

And suddenly he was awake, all dreams gone, and boots were pounding on the coach house floor, just below them, pounding on the steps that led up to their room.

"Binnie! Binnie, we got to get him hid!"

Her eyes opened instantly, not dazed with sleep but wide with alarm. Someone shoved at the trapdoor, rattling the bar that held it closed.

"Boy? Boy? I know you up there, nigger. You open this goddam door!"

Binnie flung the covers back and rolled out of bed, and in the same swift motion grabbed a dress and pulled it over her head. She raced for the storage room, and Zag kicked into his pants.

They were pounding at the door now. "Goddam you, nigger, you open up, you hear me? This is a white man talking to you, boy. Don't you know a white man, you hear one? You hear me up there?"

Buck was already stepping into the compartment in the wall, and Binnie shoved the panel back into place. While she hung the harness over it, Zag tore the covers from the bed and gathered up all of Buck's clothes that he saw. Binnie flipped over the old shuck-filled mattress, and Zag threw the clothes and blankets into a chest in the corner. They returned to their bedroom, and Binnie, still in her dress, slipped back into bed.

The pounding at the door continued. "Goddam you, open this door!"

"Ya-a-as, massa-a-ah, ya-a-as." Zag yawned and made his voice as blurry with sleep as he could. "Ah . . . coming . . . massah."

The moment Zag removed the bar, the door was flung

up and open, and the men came running up. Until now, he had been too keyed up, too much in motion to admit fear, but the moment he recognized Bassett, it hit him. Bassett, he knew, was one of those whites who loved to ride with the patrols, the posses, the lynch parties. When they had met before, Bassett had seemed to conceive a special hatred of Zag, and now he was back—with four other men and with a wicked-looking rawhide paddle in his hand. Never had he looked more dangerous.

"You bar a door on a white man, nigger?"

"I—I'm sorry, master, I—"

"All right, men, let's see what we can find."

But they found nothing. There was no place for anyone to hide in the bedroom, no one under the bed or in the chest or in the battered old wardrobe. And there was no one in the harness-cluttered storeroom next door, nor in the rooms beyond that. On the way back to the bedroom, Bassett paused and looked at the empty bed in the storeroom.

"Who sleep here?"

"Nobody, sir," Zag said, "except when some poor nigger gets sick and my Binnie got to look after him. Or me, when my Binnie gets mad at me."

Bassett felt the turned mattress. It was, of course, cold.

Zag hardly knew what hit him. At one instant he was watching Bassett feel the mattress, and at the next the left side of his face was crushed as the paddle pounded across it, and he went blind. He floated backward and down. He was dully aware of the floor crashing against his back. Then he felt himself being dragged out of the cluttered storageroom and into the more spacious bedroom where they could work on him further, and he heard Binnie cry out.

Sight cleared. He was on his feet, held there by two of the men. Two others held Binnie, who was on her knees on the bed, facing Zag.

Bassett stepped in front of Zag. "Now, nigger, you know what we're here for."

"No, sir, Mr.—Mr. Bassett. I don't know, sir—"

"Well, you damn well better know, because that's the only thing will save your ass, is knowing. We're here for Black Buck."

"Mr. Bassett, I don't know about no Black—"

The knee came up squarely between Zag's legs, and the pain bloomed up through his guts, forcing a long, hoarse cry from his throat. He would have fallen, but the men at his sides held him braced up.

"Last couple nigger boys I talked to, I didn't bust their nuts, but I reckon I'll make you an exception." Bassett glanced around. "Look at this here room, boys. Plastered walls, all nice and whitewashed, pictures hung up, curtains at the windows. Lives like he thinks he's a white man. Nigger like that needs busting—gets to thinking he's better than any white man."

The knee came up again, almost gently, and the pain bloomed further. Another groan tore from Zag's throat.

"Not too hard that time. Want to make you last, nigger." Bassett cocked his knee again; Zag, limp legged, had not a chance of evading it. "Now, you tell me where Black Buck is—"

"He don't know," Binnie sobbed. "I swear he don't know, and I don't neither. Please, please, master, please!"

She was straining first one way and then the other between the two men who held her arms. Bassett looked at her. He looked at the paddle, still in his hand, and he looked at Zag. And Zag saw the idea coming into his head.

"Lay that wench belly-down on the bed," he said. "Hang onto her arms and best grab her legs too."

The two men immediately got the idea. The forced Binnie down on the bed, facing Zag. One hooked her left leg with his right to hold it, and pulled her dress up to her shoulder blades; the other grabbed her right ankle. The first one laughed and said, "Goddam, Tilden, she got an ass white as any white woman," and Tilden said, "It ain't gonna be white for very long."

Bassett moved around the bed. Zag cried a hoarse *"No!"* Bassett brought the paddle down.

What happened then seemed to take a very long time. Binnie's eyes slowly opened wider. They grew larger and larger, as large as Zag had ever seen them. They seemed on the verge of leaving their sockets. At the same time, her mouth opened wide, wide, and after an eternity a long animal howl came out of it. And Bassett raised the paddle and brought it down again. And again. And again.

He raised his eyes to Zag. "Now, you tell us, goddam you, where you got Black Buck."

"We ain't got him, we ain't," Binnie sobbed. "Oh, please believe me, master, we ain't got no Black Buck! Oh, please!"

Bassett's face screwed up as he raised the paddle. Harder now, and more rapidly, as in anger, it came down again and again and again, and Zag thought he would die as he saw the blood flow.

"No, no, no, no!" Binnie screamed. "Oh, please!"

Breathing hard, Bassett backed away. He wiped his forehead with the back of his hand.

"That don't make 'em talk," Tilden said, "ain't nothing gonna do it. Ain't no nigger can stand up to the paddle. If he don't know, he either say he don't or he start lying to make you think he do."

"Oh, shit," Bassett said.

He brought the paddle down twice more on Binnie's buttocks, and Zag saw her pass out. Holding the paddle like a club, shaking it, Bassett walked back around the bed to face Zag.

"Something you want to tell us now, boy, before we finish what we gonna do to you?"

Zag's throat was raw. The left side of his face was so swollen it felt as if the skin might split, and he could not see out of his left eye. From his crotch, a swelling pain extended upward through the interior of his body. Bassett slapped the paddle against his own left palm.

"Well, boy?"

Zag began to retch. The two men holding him let him bend forward and lower his head. A thin bitter stream of vomit poured to the floor.

"Hell, he don't know nothing," one of the men said, and Zag felt the fingers on his arms easing. When they let go of him, he could not stand. He fell into the pool of vomit.

"Maybe he don't know nothing," Bassett said, "but we don't find Black Buck, we coming back here." The toe of his boot jabbed at Zag's face. "You hear me, nigger? You hear me?"

Boots tromped out.

How long he lay there, Zag did not know. Like Binnie, he may have passed out. But when he heard her sobbing, he struggled to his knees and crawled to the bed. Still on his knees, he reached for her. They clung together for a long time.

"I didn't tell them nothing, did I?" was the first thing she said.

"No, Binnie, you didn't tell them nothing. But we got to get out of here. That Mr. Bassett is a crazy man, and he might come back here, just like he said. He might come back."

"But Black Buck—"

"Buck is safe now, honey. Buck is safe—unless they burn this here place down!"

Bassett was angry. He knew that Black Buck and Adaba, if they were at Sabrehill, were most likely in the field quarters. But over his protests, Vachel Skeet had sent him to search, first of all, this lane. Of course, Bassett knew he would get his $50, whoever caught Black Buck. But *he* wanted to be the one to lay his hands on that nigger: he figured on getting that $500 bonus money for doing it.

They found no one in the big brick barn nor, heading back along the lane, in the stables, and Bassett's frustration and anger grew. Someone else might be catching Black Buck at this very moment. He had to find that nigger *fast*.

They arrived in front of the blacksmith shop. The shop itself was in the right end of the building, the living quarters in the left. A candle gave light through a window of the living quarters. Bassett shoved open the door and led the way into the living quarters.

The blacksmith seemed quite unsurprised, as if he had been waiting for them. He stood near the bed, fully dressed, quite still, his eyes hard, defiant, unblinking. What was his name? Saul? Bassett stared at him.

"Well, ain't seen you a long time, daddy," he said. "Been here to Sabrehill on patrol, but ain't seen you."

Saul ignored the two men who were going into his shop. He ignored the two who prowled about the room, looking into boxes and cabinets, places where a man could not possibly have hid. He looked only at Bassett.

"No, sir, daddy, ain't seen you. Where you got them two runaway niggers hid, daddy?"

One of the other men raised the paddle. "He ain't talking, we got a way to make him talk."

"Naw," Bassett said, grinning, "that ain't gonna be necessary, is it, daddy? Now, you come on, you tell us where you got them niggers hid."

"I don't know nothing 'bout no hid niggers," Saul said.

"Don't lie to me, nigger." Bassett looked up at the sleeping loft. "You got 'em up there, maybe?"

Saul's hard, direct gaze for the first time wavered. "They . . . they ain't up there."

"No? Well, I reckon something's up there."

Bassett went to the wall ladder that led to the loft and climbed it, taking his time. At the top he peered into the gloom of the loft. He could just make her out.

"Well, my, my, my, what have we here? Ettamae, ain't it? No, Ettalee. Best you come down out of there, Ettalee."

The girl did not move.

"Come on down, now, Ettalee."

The girl remained crouched, unmoving, silent.

Bassett grinned down at Saul. "Daddy, you better tell your wench baby to get down this ladder damn fast, or I'm gonna throw her fucking ass out of that loft."

Saul's mouth moved as if he were getting ready to spit, but after a few seconds he said, "Come on down, Ettalee."

The girl moved. Bassett said, "That's better."

He went back down the ladder and stood at its foot. Ettalee appeared at the edge of the loft, stepped onto the ladder, and followed him down. As she took the last step, he reached for her shoulders and turned her to face him.

"My, my, Ettalee," he said, "you don't look much older than last time I saw you, and that must be way over a year ago. Look skinnier than I remember you too, but just as pretty. Remember what I said then, Ettalee? Said you was black as sin but had a set a man couldn't hardly keep his hands off." He looked around at Saul. "Hey, remember that, daddy? . . . I said, remember that?"

"I 'member."

Bassett drew Ettalee closer. He chucked her chin. "Still can't hardly keep my hands off you, Ettalee." Again he looked at Saul. "Daddy, you *sure* you ain't got no idea where we can find that Black Buck?"

Saul's voice shook. "I ain't got no idea. I don't know nothing."

"That's a shame."

Bassett drew Ettalee still closer, sliding an arm around her shoulders. Her body stiffened as it touched his. He drifted a hand down over her breast.

"Yes, sir, that's a shame. Trying to remember the last time I saw Ettalee. We was looking all over for a murdering white woman. Stopped here, same as everyplace else. Told Ettalee what we was gonna give that white woman when we found her, and said that if we didn't find her, we'd come back here and give it to Ettalee instead. But somehow we got busy and never did come back. Do I remember correctly, Ettalee?"

The girl seemed incapable of speaking, paralyzed in Bassett's arms.

"Sure, I do. . . ."

Bassett found the opening of the girl's dress and reached into it. "Well, here we are, and I reckon the time has come, Ettalee."

Saul roared. *"You take your hands off—"*

He was almost across the room before the others grabbed him, and even then he threw them all off with one gigantic shrug. Bassett had just time to thrust Ettalee away, whirl around, and whip out his pistol.

"Now, don't you make me kill you, nigger!"

The voice fell to a whisper, but it was no less threatening: "Don't you never touch my baby!"

Bassett found himself breathing hard and suddenly more frightened than angry. He had come here to catch a nigger, not to kill one, and certainly not to get killed himself. And now he had the feeling that this big black gray-bearded bastard, half-crouched not three feet away, just might take him. Even if he pulled the trigger. Saul looked at Bassett like a maddened lion, not even noticing the yawning muzzle of the pistol. Yes, he just might. But Bassett could not allow himself to lose face before the other four white men.

Anger returned. Saving anger.

"You don't want your pickaninny touched, you better listen to me, daddy—"

"I don't know where your Black Buck is, white man, or if I do, I don't tell you. Don't give a goddam you believe me or not, one way or the other. I don't tell you nothing, ever, but you touch my baby, white man—"

"I'll blow your goddam heart out and fuck her on your grave, nigger daddy."

It was the wrong thing to say. Saul did not reply, but his hot gaze never wavered, only grew hotter, and Bassett felt himself shriveling. Christ, didn't this crazy nigger know enough to be afraid?

Bassett had to do something. The others were watching. He straightened. Shrugged. Put his pistol away but kept his hand on it. He sighed a sigh he did not feel.

"Well, you can't tell me nothing dead, you damn fool. But I tell you this, daddy. If we don't find Black Buck here at Sabrehill, *this* time me and these here men *is gonna come back*. We gonna come back, and Ettalee gonna get herself all the hard white cock she want for a long time to come. Oh, your Ettalee gonna have herself a joyful time, all right."

A couple of the men guffawed, and Bassett felt better. He slipped past Saul, taking care not to get too close. At the door, he pointed to Tilden. "You, Tilden, you stay right here and make sure that Ettalee and her daddy don't go no place."

Tilden looked disappointed. "But I want to catch Black Buck too. The bonus—"

"You want a share of Ettalee, don't you? Then you'll damn well follow orders and stay."

Bassett and three others went out the door. Tilden sighed. He leaned against the jamb and looked at Ettalee and Saul.

Ettalee slipped into her father's arms, and Saul moved to block her from Tilden's view.

"They going do it to me," she whimpered.

"No, baby, no. They ain't going—"

"They do like Mr. Skeet and them others do." She began to weep. "Daddy, I die, they do that to me again. Daddy, I die, I die, I die. . . ."

"No, Ettalee, they ain't." Saul's tears flowed down over Ettalee's face. "I swear, baby, I don't let them. I swear. . . ."

"I die, I die, I die. . . ."

Sounds.

Lucy had heard them, vaguely, for some time now. But why should there not be sounds, she thought, troubled in spite of herself. It was dawn, or very nearly, and even on a Sunday some of the people would be stirring. Servants would be up the stairs to build the fires, and she knew she should return to her own room. But not yet. She pressed herself to Justin, entangled herself with him, not wanting to leave. She would lose him so soon, lose him forever. . . .

Sounds.

Did someone cry out? Surely not. Ignore . . . She almost sank back into sleep.

More sounds, then; definite, however distant. The wrong sounds. The whinnying of a horse, almost below the windows. A man's shout. A cry, a scream. More horses.

"Justin!" she called in alarm.

Another cry, and she was out of bed, knowing without a doubt that something was very wrong, that there was trouble. She hurried to a window, raised it, and looked out. It was barely first light, barely morngloam, and there was a mist over river and land, but she saw a rider in the east gardens. He shouted, "Ain't nobody out here, Tag," and headed toward the east lane.

When she looked around, Justin was out of bed and dressing: he knew without asking that there was trouble, and he didn't waste time with talk. Lucy, without pausing to put on gown or robe, raced across the passage hall, yelling, "Leila! Leila!" At that moment she could hardly have cared less if her housekeeper had seen her emerging naked from Justin's room. In her own room, she dressed hastily, grabbing the first clothes that came to hand. When she returned to the hall, Leila, clutching a robe about herself, was starting down the stairs.

"Leila, what is it? Did you see what's going on?"

Leila looked frightened. "I don't know. All I know is, Jebediah is hurt. I seen it from my window."

Lucy followed Leila down the stairs, Justin's boots thumping behind them. The moment they stepped out into the courtyard, Lucy saw Jebediah, lying face down on the ground not far from his house. No one else was in sight, and the horses she had heard were gone, disappeared into the mist. She ran to Jebediah, Justin and Leila with her, and knelt by his body. He had an ugly gash on the right side of his head, and his pants were spotted with blood. For a moment Lucy thought he was dead, but then she saw that he was still breathing.

"Who did this, Leila? Did you see?"

"I don't know who all! It was that Mr. Bassett and maybe four or five others." The little housekeeper sounded close to hysteria. "Something woke me up, Miss Lucy, and I just lay there for a time, feeling sick and scared and thinking it was a bad dream. Then I think I hear something, and I go look out the window, and there's Jebediah, laying there like he's dead. And just when he starts to get up, that Mr. Bassett and them others, they come and kick him and hit him with a stick, and he falls down flat again and just lays there, and they keep right on kicking him. Then they get on their horses and ride off like they was heading out to the field quarters. I should called you right away—I'm sorry—I'm sorry—"

"Never mind that now. Get Momma Lucinda. Get Zulie. Get someone who—"

She broke off as she heard sobbing. Looking across the courtyard, she saw Irish and a housemaid, Rolanda, approaching. Irish was supporting the girl, who was weeping into her hands.

"Well, what is it?" Lucy snapped.

"It's . . . it's Rolanda, Miss Lucy," Irish said fumblingly.

"I can see that. What's the matter? Can't you see that Mr. Jeb is hurt?"

"So's Rolanda, Miss Lucy, ma'am." Irish too seemed close to tears—humiliated and angry—and Lucy now saw that there were bruises on his face. "It was them men. You see, Rolanda was—was with me—I mean, just for a little while she stopped by my cottage this morning—"

Lucy was in no mood for niceties. "You mean, they caught you in bed together?"

Irish nodded. "And they . . . they . . ."

"They done it to me, Miss Lucy," Rolanda wept. "Like to Ettalee. That one they call P. V., he make me stand up and the others hold me so that—"

"Oh, dear God!" Lucy was sickened.

"—and they hit Irish and knock him down, and right in front of all of them, he do it to me."

"What are they *doing* here, Irish?" Lucy asked. "What do they want?"

"They say they looking for Black Buck and Adaba, Miss Lucy. They say them niggers is hid here somewhere." Lucy and Justin looked at each other.

"And so they have to hurt Mr. Jeb and beat you, Irish, and abuse Rolanda," Lucy said after a moment. "Are they insane—or simply filth?"

"Where are they now, Irish?" Justin asked.

"After they finish with Rolanda and me, they take their horses and go out the west lane."

"There they go now," Justin said.

Lucy looked where Justin was pointing, to the northwest. Five riders could be seen, dim figures in the mist, coming across the kitchen garden, heading east. They crossed the avenue of oaks and kept on going.

"They're headed for the field quarters too," Lucy said. "I'd better get out there. Leila, I told you to get help for Mr. Jeb, and Rolanda needs it too. Now, *git!*"

"Maybe you had better stay here, Lucy," Justin said, as they started for the field quarters. "Let me handle this."

"No, Justin," Lucy said firmly. "*I* am the mistress of Sabrehill, and I'll be here when you're long gone. I can't afford to let it be said that I needed a man to fight my battles for me. And damn it, I do not. Now, promise me you won't say a thing—give me your word."

Justin gave his word.

Though it was a long quarter-mile to the field quarters, Lucy had walked the distance hundreds of times, and now she ran it, Justin close behind her on the narrow path. As they entered the southwest corner of the square, she saw that there were far more than the ten or a dozen white men she had expected. There were perhaps four times that many, going from cabin to cabin, and they were rapidly making the little village a shambles. Families huddled together out in the open space of the square. Children cried from fear or bewilderment. Windows had been broken. Lucy saw that a couple of cabin doors had literally been torn from their hinges.

She hurried farther into the square, looking about, trying to determine who, if anyone, was leading these white men. She recognized a few of them. Balbo Jeppson, on the west side of the square, was shouting out orders. The man called Bassett stepped out of a cabin. Lucy thought she saw Vachel Skeet passing between rows of cabins on the east side of the square. She was about to turn to Jeppson, as the most likely leader, when Cheney, the chief driver, came hurrying up to her.

"Miss Lucy," he said, "can't you do nothing to stop them? They tearing everything up, they pestering the women folk, they ruin the cabins, the clothes—why, they set about three, four cabins on fire already, and we got to put them out. Miss Lucy—"

"Why, Cheney, why? Why are they doing this?"

"Why, they drunk, half of them, Miss Lucy. And if they ain't drunk, they mean, and they don't need no why nor because. They just come in and tear up and tear down—"

"Constable!" Lucy saw Wiley Morgan hurrying toward her. "Constable, what is happening here? Why are these men treating my people like this? How dare you allow them to come in here—"

"Now, Miss Lucy, Miss Lucy." The constable looked nervous; he held up placatory hands. "It's gonna be all right, Miss Lucy. These here men got a job to do. They don't mean no harm."

"No harm! They have invaded my plantation. They are invading the homes of my people. They are destroying—"

She was interrupted by the sound of shattering glass as a cabin window burst. Two children, a woman, and a man fled from the cabin, and seconds later clothing, bedding, pots and pans flew out the open doorway and fell into the dirt. They were followed by a white man, staggering, who headed for the next cabin.

"No harm, constable?" Justin asked drily, and Lucy shot him a warning glance.

The constable did not look at Justin. "Miss Lucy, I'm sorry some of the men get a little out of hand, but this here is an official search—"

"Search for what? You didn't even ask my permission."

"Only 'cause we couldn't take time to do that. We couldn't take no chances on them niggers getting away.",

"What niggers? What are you talking about?"

The constable looked at Justin for the first time. He drew himself up, as if he felt more sure of his ground. "Seems like that Rogan lad didn't tell us everything yesterday. And the old man couldn't very well tell us after Mr. Justin here shot him dead."

"Constable Morgan, I ask you again, what are you trying to say?"

The constable continued to look at Justin, though he spoke to Lucy. "Seems like the two runaways them Rogans lost wasn't just any two runaways. One they thought to be Adaba—yes, Adaba hisself! And the other was Black Buck, that they was bringing downriver to Mr. Vachel Skeet. Now, Mr. Sabre, sir—"

Lucy was intent on brazening the whole situation out, and she was reasonably confident that she could do it. But she could not tell what Justin, with his ideas of honor, might say if he were questioned now. She cut in quickly: "And you think those two came here? Why in the world would they do that? Whatever gave you such an idea?"

"Well, now, Mr. Skeet and Mr. Jeppson both say the Rogans came by their places inquiring nice and polite about them niggers—"

"That's right, they did." Jeppson, wearing an oily smile, stepped toward them, and Lucy saw Bassett, a vicious-looking paddle in hand, also approaching. She had the feeling of being surrounded.

"And when the Rogans heard about Mr. Justin being nearby," the constable went on, "they thought they'd just ask him too."

"The Rogans," Jeppson said, "figured that Mr. Justin Sabre here might have a fair shrewd idea of how them niggers got away and where they gone to. And considering what we hear about Mr. Sabre's northern abolitionist talk, they just mighta been right!"

"But Mr. Sabre never mentioned the Rogans' asking about them niggers when you brought in the old man's body," the constable said. "No, he just ups and kills the old man—"

"Because that old man tried to rob and kill me. Didn't young Luther Rogan tell you that?"

The constable hesitated. "Well, yes, he did. But that don't mean—"

"It don't mean a goddam thing," Bassett said harshly. "We still got to find them niggers, and I notice that this here goddam Justin Sabre ain't saying nothing."

Lucy glanced at Justin. His lips were tightly compressed, as if he were having trouble restraining himself. She would have to do something to bring this matter to an end, and do it quickly. But she knew these men—Jeppson, Bassett—and she knew that buckling under to them would never be the answer.

"Constable Morgan," she said, "you are paid to uphold the law. You are paid, when necessary, to lead posses. But this obviously is no posse, this is nothing but an irresponsible, riotous pack of rabble intent on destroying the peace and safety of this plantation, and I demand that you take these people and leave here at once."

"Now, now," the constable said, flustered, "you can't oppose a legal posse, Miss Lucy."

"I can and do oppose this mob, and if you wish to put the matter before solicitor and jury—"

"Miss Lucy," Jeppson said, working to keep his voice down, "this here *mob* ain't going nowhere till we find them niggers. So you can just go back to your office house and wait there while we get on with the job." His voice rose and hardened. "When we *want* you, Miss Lucy, we gonna *send* for you!"

Now Lucy was less afraid that Justin would lose his control than that she herself would. "Get that man off of my plantation, constable," she heard herself saying. "Get all of these despicable people off of my plantation, and do it at once. I demand it."

"Oh, you demand it." Bassett's voice shook with anger. "Boys, this little lady here, she don't like us being here, we ain't good enough to be here. She *demands* we get off her plantation. Well, like Mr. Jeppson says, Miss Lucy, we ain't gonna leave till we get done. And you gonna do just like you're told and go back to your office and wait there till you're called. You gonna go right now, you hear me? Or somebody gonna get hurt."

"Mr. Bassett, if that is your name—"

Bassett struck. Cheney had been standing nearby, listening, doing nothing, looking worried. He was totally unprepared when Bassett turned on him and brought the paddle in a wide, hard swing against his buttocks. The sound was like a whipcrack. Cheney cried out and twisted away from Bassett, staring at the man with undisguised hatred.

If Lucy had had a pistol, she surely would have used it. "Mr. Bassett, you dare—"

"You go on now, I said, or somebody gonna get hurt!" And when Lucy hesitated: *"Now,* I said!" And Bassett made his point by raising the paddle. He ran at Cheney, who tried to duck away, and the paddle cracked across the black man's shoulder. He raised the paddle again.

But that was as far as he got. Justin caught him by the arm, whirled him, brought a fist up to Bassett's jaw. Bassett staggered. Justin took the paddle from his hand.

He whirled Bassett back the other way, drew back the paddle, and swung it in a wide, fast arc against Bassett's buttocks. Screaming, Bassett pitched forward onto his hands and knees. Justin raised the paddle again and, using both hands, brought it down, and again Bassett screamed. "Now, crawl, God damn you," Justin said, and he raised the paddle once more.

But this time the paddle did not fall. When Jeppson drew his pistol, Lucy thought Justin was a dead man, and she cried out a warning. Justin turned, the paddle still raised, as Jeppson ran toward him, but he was not fast enough. Jeppson jammed the muzzle of his pistol up under the side of Justin's jaw.

"Gonna kill you," he said furiously. "You drop that paddle, or I'm gonna kill you, and I don't give a goddam what happens. I'm gonna kill you."

Justin did not move.

"Drop it!"

Justin slowly lowered the paddle and tossed it aside. Jeppson, panting, backed off.

"Mister," Justin said quietly, "you had better either use that gun or start running."

Jeppson grinned and shook his head. "Huh-uh. I told you we come here to find them niggers, and we gonna do it if we got to burn down every damn cabin, shack, and outhouse on the whole place. And you ain't gonna try to stop us. You want to know why?"

When there was no answer, Jeppson went on. "I'll tell you why. You seen what Mr. Bassett done to the nigger, and I seen what you done to Mr. Bassett. But that ain't nothing to what some niggers is gonna get if you try to stop us. That's right, every time you make a move to stop us, you gonna get another goddam nigger flayed alive. And maybe you don't care about getting your own goddam brains blown out, but you do bleed for your niggers, don't you. And they gonna do a lot of bleeding for you if you get in our way."

Lucy could not speak. She had never seen Justin look so pale. Jeppson meant every word he said, and they both knew it, and at that moment not even the constable dared say a word.

They were defeated.

Whimpering, Bassett struggled to get up from the ground. Jeppson watched him for a few seconds, then picked up the paddle. He looked at Cheney. He raised the paddle. He said, "Run, nigger, or you gonna bleed." Cheney backed away from Jeppson. After a few steps, he turned and broke into a run.

"And now you," Jeppson said, turning back toward Lucy and Justin. He pointed the paddle at them. "The both of you. You get your asses back to the office house. You wait for us there till we're ready for you, and I mean *there*."

Justin stared at Jeppson. He did not move, though Lucy plucked at his arm. Didn't he realized the extent of their defeat? Didn't he know that some of her people might do more than bleed unless they left right now? They might die.

"Come," she whispered. "Come."

Justin turned and went with her.

Behind them, after a moment, they heard Jeppson snicker. "Nothing changes. Goddam Whore of Sabrehill . . ."

Skeet broke the boy's arm. Snapped it like a twig.

It was the younger boy, the one they called Nemo. Skeet had a chair leg in his hand, and he hardly knew what he was doing. He held the boy's right wrist in his left hand and struck him across the face a couple of times, then brought the chair leg down on the boy's right forearm. Snap. The boy uttered one short, sharp howl, and that was all, though his face was like gray ashes. His mother cried the loudest. "He don't know nothing, master, he don't know. We don't know 'bout no Black Buck." Then the older boy, Tad, was on Skeet's back, and his father, terrified at this attack on a white man, was pulling Tad off, and Skeet wheeled and struck Tad solidly across the temple with the chair leg. The boy dropped like a bundle of rags.

Hell, maybe they didn't know anything. Most black wenches, Skeet was certain, would tell or say or do anything to protect their families. Black daddies too, as often

as not. Skeet had come slamming into their cabin, he had
yanked the boys down from the sleeping loft—a wonder
he had not killed one or both of them—he had questioned,
threatened, beaten all four members of the family. And
still:

"Nemo don't know, master! Tad don't know!"

"Somebody better know, or I'm gonna bust some more
arms."

"No, master, please! None us don't know!"

No, they probably didn't know anything about Buck.

Skeet stomped out of the cabin as abruptly as he had
entered it. It was plenty light now, and the haze was burning off. Goddam, where *was* Buckley hiding?

The field quarters had now been almost completely
searched. Some of the cabins had been searched two and
three times to be sure that Buckley—or Adaba—was not
artfully moving from one to another to elude the posse.
A close watch was being kept to be sure that no one tried
to slip away from the quarters area. And Skeet knew that
the longer it took to find Buckley, the less likely it was
that they would succeed.

And a doubt was growing in his mind. Was it possible
that his whole logic was built upon a wish? Was it possible that Serena had never really spoken to Buckley?
Granting that Justin Sabre had freed the two blacks,
wasn't it likely that they had never come anywhere near
Sabrehill? that Buckley would avoid the vicinity of Redbird, just as he had for years?

No. Skeet could not believe that. He refused to believe
that, and he felt a sweat at the very idea. After all this
time, after all this waiting, he had to have Buckley.

Then Buckley had to be here!

Skeet found himself at the far northeast corner of the
quarters. Looking about, he was certain hat there was
not a cabin anywhere in his sight that had not been
searched at least once.

Except one.

There was no reason that it had not been searched before, except that it was at this far corner and a little separate from the others in the row. It was slightly unusual
in that it had an extended front roof, making a kind of

portico or piazza. As in other cabins at Sabrehill, there were some small glass windows, in this case covered with curtains, and Skeet wondered why the hell the Sabres had wasted good glass and yard goods on nigger cabins.

He hurried to the door, started to fling it open. It was barred. Barred from within. Hope and anger welled up again. How dare a goddam nigger bar his door—bars were for locking niggers in, not white men out. And why should it be barred if Buckley Skeet were not somewhere within?

He pounded on the door, pounded with his fists and slammed the edge of a boot against it. Yelled for whoever was within to open the goddam thing up. As the door began to open, he gave it a shove with all his weight and sent the woman on the other side reeling across the room.

"All right, where you got him? Where is he?"

But the woman seemed to be alone. The bed was empty, though covered with more rumpled blankets than Skeet had ever figured a nigger needed. Two plates with congealed ham fat, the remains of last night's supper, no doubt, lay on a table, and Skeet asked—shouted— "Where's your man?"

"Out. Out somewhere, master."

Christ, nothing. No hiding place. The fireplace was solid. No one was under the bed. There was a sleeping loft, but Skeet knew as he went up the ladder that he would find no one in it, and he was right. Not so much as a scrap of blanket. It probably had not been used in years.

The sense of frustration was like a band around Skeet's chest: he could hardly breathe. He had to do something. *Something.*

"Where is he?" he asked again, as he came down the ladder.

The woman glanced at the plates. "My man, he—"

"Not your man, goddam it," Skeet roared, "Buckley Skeet! Black Buck! Adaba! You know who I mean, you fucking bitch—"

He knew her. He looked directly at her face for the first time since entering the cabin, and he knew—

—screamed as the bitch bit into his hand, and threw

*her a dozen feet into the dust; but she was on her feet
again at once, eight inches of steel in her hand, and coming at him, her eyes mad and her teeth bared, coming at
him like a rabid bitch dog; and he ran, ran and leaped
onto his horse and rode like hell for Redbird while she
pursued him like a nightmare he would have for the rest
of his life—*

—and she recognized him. He saw the remembrance
in those wide eyes. She even glanced down at his left
hand, the hand she had bit.

His own memory had not played false: she was still
about as handsome a piece of black wench as he had
ever seen: tall and broad shouldered, breasts pointed and
carried high, legs long and shapely. She wore no bandanna
around her closely cut hair this morning; her only gar-
ment was an old shift, shrunken to her body, and so often
laundered that he could almost see through it. Skeet
looked, stared openly, at dark nipples, dip of navel,
lift of mound, and all the want he had had for her that
day three weeks ago came rushing back, stronger than
ever, a hot, engorging flood.

She knew. She saw. And she shrank away from him.
But that only made his want the greater.

He went after her. Grabbed her forearms and
laughed softly as she moaned and twisted in his grip. She
tried ineffectually to knee him, never stopped struggling
to escape, and he laughed harder. Christ, she was strong,
stronger than he would have thought, but he was stronger
still. And he had to have her. Had to have something for
this morning, had to!

So he hit her.

His open right hand, swinging up and across, caught
her squarely on the left side of her jaw and raised her,
body arching toward him, up onto her bare toes. The slap
of his left hand sent her twisting and reeling back against
a wall. A third blow twisted her face into a mask of agony.
He caught her as she bounced off the wall and dragged
her toward the bed. He threw her down on it, held her
down, his hands gripping the top of her flimsy shift.

"You got a name, bitch?" He was panting. His voice
was a low growl that he hardly recognized.

"Zulie," the woman whimpered. Blood trickled from a corner of her mouth.

"You know me, Zulie?"

"Know you, master."

"Pulled a knife on me, you did. Pulled a knife on a white man. Ought to kill you for that."

"Please, master."

"Where's Black Buck? Where's Adaba?"

"Don't know. Don't know no Black Buck, no Adaba."

The hands that held the top of the shift wrenched apart. The cloth tore, exposing the high, pointed breasts, pointed even now as she lay on her back, and darkly aureoled. Skeet said something. *Christ!* His tongue thickened, and his throat almost closed. The woman grabbed his wrists as his hands fell on the breasts, palms to nipples, and his fingers worked.

"You gonna tell me, Zulie."

The woman shook her head. "Don't know."

"You gonna tell me."

"No . . . no."

He ripped the shift the rest of the way and pulled it open. The woman lay completely exposed on the bed, her legs dangling. Cupping a hand between her thighs, she rolled over onto her belly and slid off the bed to the floor.

Skeet laughed. "Stop making such a fuss, honey-child. You know you gonna love it. Now, just you don't try to run away. . . ."

He looked around the room. The woman might love it, as he had said, but he knew she was not going to make it easy for him, and he wanted something that would. He decided that the ham fat on the plates would do just fine, and unfastening his pants, he made use of it.

"And now, you fucking bitch . . ."

He was right: she did not make it easy for him. First he had to lift her, thrashing, to the bed again. Then she continued to struggle as he tried to get over her, and his slaps did nothing to stop her. Her teeth were bared, the lips far back, and he knew that no threat of death would keep her from biting him if she could—hands, eyes, anywhere: given half a chance, whe would go for his throat.

There was only one thing to do. He rose up from her, drew back his right fist. Just one blow, not too hard, beside the tip of her chin. He eyes rolled up in her head, and her head fell back.

And he took her.

Afterward, he hit her just one more time. He groaned as he achieved release, lay panting on her for half a minute, and rose up, slipping away from her. He looked down at his limp penis. Then he smiled at her and slapped her with all his strength. He fastened his clothes and said, "Remember me, bitch," and left without another word. The door stood wide open.

Zulie rolled facedown on the bed and wept. There had been times in her life when she had thought that she had no tears left, but she found them now.

She had been unconscious for only a few seconds, but she had come to with the realization that the battle was lost. There was no way she could reach her knife; she could only lie still, choking on her tears and blood, and wait for him to be done. She could only hope that Adaba had not been able to hear all that had been said, could not guess what was happening, could not know of her humiliation. At the same time, she had a fantasy that he might at any instant come crashing out of the compartment under the floor, that he would throw himself on Mr. Skeet, tearing the white man apart. . . ."

But that was impossible. At the first sound, the first outcry, Zulie had hidden him in that coffinlike space that Zagreus had constructed under the floor, and the weight of the bed and their two bodies pressed down on it. Even if the two of them had not been on the bed, Adaba would have had a difficult time getting out without help. He was safe.

"You know you love it, you bitch," Mr. Skeet had said. "All of you, you're like animals, you love it, oh, you love it love it love it love it, *o-o-o-o-oh!*" And he had finished. And had arisen from her and slapped her and left.

When her tears were mostly under control and the bleeding had slowed, she left the bed and closed the cabin door. She could not let Adaba out yet; searchers still might return to the cabin. The tattered shift still hung from her shoulders, and she let it drop to the floor. She poured water from a pitcher into a bowl.

As she washed herself, she remembered things. She remembered the deep tenderness she had felt toward Jeb Hayes. She remembered the almost irresistible love she had felt for Adaba. All of that was gone now. She was a hollow woman. If was as if all sex, all love, had been removed from her, cut out of her with one twist of a bloody knife. What good was sex when a man could use it to make you feel so degraded and defiled? What good was love when its means could be used as a weapon of revenge? She wanted never to be touched by a man again.

She remembered how the meetings of the runaways had diminished in importance for her as she had cared for Adaba, nursing him back to health. *Don't want to go,* she had thought with surprise. She had wanted only to be with Adaba, to care for him, perhaps to yield to her growing love for him. The last few days she had even stopped wearing her knife, as if somehow it hung between Adaba and her.

But that was over now. Mr. Skeet had taken all that away from her. She would never be Adaba's woman. She would never be Jeb's woman. She would start wearing her knife again, and she would be Black Buck's faithful follower, wherever he led. Only that.

She would be a rebel.

No Black Buck, no bonus money, Bassett thought bitterly. Nothing but pain and humiliation from Justin Sabre. But by God, he would have something, something to prove he was still a man. And he knew where to get it.

The instant he stepped through the doorway they understood what he was there for. He had made a promise, a threat, and he had returned to fulfill it. Ettalee, sitting at the head of the bed, drew herself into a tighter ball, and he saw the terror growing in her eyes. Saul slowly stood up, and his eyes held impotent hatred. Tilden, standing by the door, gave Bassett an uneasy grin.

"They found them niggers yet?"

"No, they ain't found them. Not Black Buck, not Adaba."

The grin faded. "Reckon they got away?"

"Maybe, maybe not. I just got tired of looking."

"Then you come back here . . ."

" . . . to get something I figured I got coming to me." To get even.

If there was one thing Tag Bassett could be counted on to do, it was to get even. Walking painfully, unable to hide the pain and hardly able to stop the tears, he had started getting even at once. He had returned to cabins already searched and searched them again. He had bullied the niggers, knocked them about, cursed them . . . but shit, it wasn't enough. It seemed to him that every nigger he looked at must have seen him beaten, must have heard him howl at the two blows Justin Sabre had given him. With those two blows, Justin had reduced him, before the eyes of whites and blacks alike, to just another piece of luckless trash. Bassett felt the niggers' scorn, and the humiliation was as great as the pain.

But now he was going to do something about that.

"No," Saul said softly.

Bassett tossed his hat aside. "You know what I'm here for, Ettalee."

The frightened girl said nothing.

"Don't you worry none, honey. You gonna like it."

Bassett took off his jacket and threw it onto a chair. He unbuckled his belt and slipped his holstered pistol off of it. He handed the holstered pistol to Tilden. He did not bother to rebuckle his belt.

When he stepped toward Ettalee, she strained away from him on the bed. Saul took a step toward him, and Bassett threw him an angry warning look. "Point one of them pistols at daddy," he said to Tilden. "Let him go off into the shop if he want to, just so this wench ain't getting out."

Tilden drew Bassett's pistol from its holster, pulled back the cock, and pointed the gun at Saul. "Go on, old man," he said, his grin returning. "You get your ass out of here."

Saul extended open hands, pleading hands.

"Go on," Bassett snarled. *"Out!"*

Ettalee wailed "Daddy!" as if to stop him, but Saul backed toward the shop door, the pistol following him every step of the way. As he left the room, Ettalee made a sound of despair.

"You might as well get out of that goddam dress, Ettalee," Bassett said, as he started to unfasten his pants. "Come on, let's get this over with."

But Ettalee did not even seem to hear him. Weeping, she moved to the farthest corner of the bed, and Bassett wondered what the hell was the matter with her. She was no goddam virgin, was she? Wasn't she the same wench he had heard that Vachel Skeet had picked up on the road only a few weeks ago? Goddam Vachel had beaten him to her. But she was carrying on like she was some frozen-ass white lady.

He watched her for a moment, and he almost thought to hell with it. She wasn't exciting him at all, this skinny weeping wench. He felt as limp and shriveled as if Justin Sabre had deprived him of his manhood. But he *was* a man, by God, and he was going to prove it. He had sworn to have this wench, and he would have her.

He reached across the bed, grabbed Ettalee, and dragged her to her feet. Holding her close while she struggled against him, he tried to tear off her dress.

He heard Saul's bellow and the pounding of his feet. It was as if some wild animal, a rampaging bull, had burst into the room. He heard a pistol go off, but when he released Ettalee and turned, Saul was still coming, and this time Bassett had no weapon to stop him. And Saul's huge fist was clamped on the handle of a big forty-ounce hammer, holding it high above his head, and he was bringing it down, down, down—

Somehow Bassett deflected the blow, though Saul's forearm nearly crushed his shoulder. Somehow, in spite of the force of the charge, he managed to shove the big blacksmith back. Saul had a stunned look on his face, and he dropped the hammer to the floor. A red spot was spreading rapidly on the right side of his shirt, and Bassett realized that Tilden's shot must have hit him. Saul was looking past Bassett.

"Ettalee," he whispered.

Bassett looked around.

Ettalee was lying face down on the floor. The one open eye he could see was glazed, and blood was welling up from what seemed to be a deep indentation in her head. Arms and legs scratched vainly against the rough floor, like the limbs of a wounded animal.

"My God," Tilden said, "is she—"

"Old daddy here hit her with his hammer," Bassett said, panting. "Ain't nothing wrong with her but that, but she sure as hell ain't gonna be much fun to us now."

"I'm getting out of here," Tilden said, and he dropped Bassett's pistol and holster on the bed and hurried from the room.

Bassett put the holster back on his belt and shoved the pistol into it. He had a sick empty feeling in his gut that he could not account for. "Daddy," he said, "you are just plain lucky that Tilden didn't kill you. And Ettalee, you are just plain *un*lucky that you ain't getting what I promised. But don't you worry, honey-child. I'll be back."

He walked out into the lane thinking that, Christ, nothing was going right. No Black Buck, no bonus money, no Ettalee. And not even the beginning of revenge on Justin Sabre.

He looked across the lane. The carpenter shop. And to the east, right beside it, the coach house.

The wench they called Binnie.

Ass as white as any white woman, one of the men had said.

Well, by God, he would have his ass today all right— he would have that goddam Binnie.

But when he arrived in the upstairs room of the coach house, neither Binnie nor Zagreus was there.

It was too much. God damn all fucking niggers. God damn all Sabrehill niggers. God damn all Sabres and Justin Sabre most of all.

It took Bassett only a few wild, savage minutes to smash the furniture, to break the stove, to rip the mattress, to strew walls, floors, and bed with ashes. Damn them, damn them, damn them all.

Skeet heard the shot but thought nothing about it. His head ached. His eyes stung. He was ready to lash out at any nigger that got in his way, or at any white man. At that moment he could have killed with his bare hands without a thought. He had been defeated again, cheated of his prize, outwitted, outdone, outplayed. And the taste of defeat was bitter.

No Buckley Skeet. Anywhere. Neither Buckley nor Adaba.

But Skeet could not accept that. He was still going to have Buckley. He still believed that, had to believe it, against all odds or evidence. Buckley was here, or somewhere near here, somewhere close by. Serena had seen him. The Rogans had come looking for him. And Justin Sabre, who had been on the cotton box with the Rogans and the two outliers, had shot Silas Rogan, and . . .

Yes, by God, he was going to have Buckley Skeet. If he had to, he would double the reward money in order to keep the posse together. He would search every plantation and farm and scrap of land, including his own, for miles around. But before he did that . . .

"Jeppson, P. V., Rolly Joe! Come with me!"

. . . before he did that, he had someone to talk to.

They rode the narrow path that led southwest from the field quarters toward the courtyard. Jeppson had told Justin and Miss Lucy to wait at the office, and they had damned well better be waiting. Skeet drew a pair of thick tight leather gloves from his jacket pocket and pulled them on. He looked at the leather paddle that Jeppson now carried. Something drummed in his aching head, and his jaw hurt from being clinched for so long.

Justin was not at the office. Glancing down the east lane, Skeet saw him standing outside the blacksmith shop, looking in through the doorway. Skeet turned down the lane, and the others followed. Tag Bassett's horse stood nearby, and Tag was just coming out of the coach house. Good. Skeet had hoped to have Tag here.

The four riders dismounted. Justin continued looking through the doorway. Inside, Skeet saw someone moving around—Miss Lucy.

"Mr. Sabre," Skeet said.

Justin slowly looked around.

"Mr. Sabre, you and me got business."

"I think not, Mr. Skeet."

"Nigger business, Mr. Sabre——"

Before Skeet could say more, Miss Lucy stepped out of the living quarters of the shop. Tears were streaming down her face as she interrupted: "Mr. Skeet, do you know what you have done?"

"Miss Lucy, I ain't gonna stand on formalities——"

"Do you know what you have——"

"Shut up!"

Miss Lucy stopped as if she had been struck. Justin, oddly, did not move. Some men, at such a moment, would have drawn a gun, but Justin just stood as if frozen, white faced and unblinking.

"Mr. Justin Sabre," Skeet said. "I ain't here to waste no time. I'm here to get——"

Justin did not seem to be listening or interested. "You brought these men here, didn't you, Skeet," he said. "Not the constable, but you. You're responsible."

Skeet stared at him. This was the same Justin Sabre of yesteryear. He had not changed at all. This was the same Justin Sabre who had taken Miss Lucy from him, who had humiliated him on the main street of Riverboro, who had somehow contrived to defeat him in a duel by throwing away a shot. The same Justin who looked down on him as if he were some kind of swamp rat, some kind of animal not fit to sniff at Sabre boots, and who let him know it.

Skeet licked his lips. His mouth was dry, and his head drummed harder than ever. "Mister, I said I'm here to get——"

"My God, you've gone downhill in twelve years, Skeet," Justin went on. "Heard you had some good in you once. A little crazy maybe, a little misguided——"

Skeet could not let this go on. "Boys," he said loudly, "this here is a thief!"

The others grinned. They had ranged themselves carefully: Jeppson and P. V. to one side, Rolly Joe and Bassett to the other. They knew what to do.

"If you're done," Justin said, turning away, "you may go."

"You see? He don't even deny it. You stole my Buckley, didn't you, Justin? Stole him and hid him away."

Justin turned slowly back toward Skeet again. "Skeet, I didn't steal your Buckley. And I haven't the slightest idea of where he might be."

"Then you stole him and let him go. I want him, Justin."

Justin smiled faintly. It was a sad smile, more pitying than derisive. It was a Sabre smile.

"Then go find him," he said.

It was like that day in Riverboro, and Skeet remembered it so clearly. Then as now, he had been pushed too far. Then as now, his head had drummed, and suddenly he had gone off, had exploded like a bomb, and his own explosive force had hurled him out into that sunlit street.

And then as now, he had stepped forward and slapped Justin backhand across the face with all his strength—a ripping blow of hard leather, this time, that drew blood.

This time, however, it was going to turn out differently. This time P. V. and Rolly Joe immediately had Justin by the arms. This time Miss Lucy was watching, but when she cried out and leapt forward, Tag Bassett grabbed her and dragged her back.

"Justin, I ain't here to challenge you to a goddam duel," Skeet said, "not this time. I'm here to get my goddam nigger."

"I told you, I don't have your nigger. I told you—"

Even after the slap, even braced by P. V. and Rolly Joe, Justin sounded calm and aloof, but Skeet only grinned. As before: a forehand slap that threatened to break Justin's neck. And then another backhand, that closed Justin's eyes with pain and brought blood from his lips. And this time, when Skeet struck a fourth blow, Justin could do nothing to stop it.

Each blow brought Skeet more sheer pleasure, more sensual gratification, more pure relief than he would have imagined possible. This was even better than forcing himself on the wench Zulie—what was she to him, after all? This was the next best thing to having Buckley himself. He doubled up his fist and drew it back for a fifth blow.

Miss Lucy was crying something: "Don't! Please! He doesn't know!" Crying the same things the niggers cried.

And suddenly Skeet didn't give a damn anymore. Just purely didn't give a damn what Justin might tell him about Buckley. That could wait. The only thing that mattered now was that Justin Sabre was back, Justin Sabre was in his power, Justin Sabre was his to do with as he pleased.

He threw the fifth blow like a battering ram into Justin's belly and had the pleasure of seeing Justin fold forward and retch with pain, and after that he hardly knew what he was doing. He was like a man in a sexual frenzy, striking, thrusting, giving release to all that was within him. He lifted Justin's head again with blows that threatened to break his own knuckles. He ripped at that face with the cruel leather of his gloves. He pounded his fists against ribs, drove them again and again into the belly. His left hand ached. His arms grew heavy. And yet he kept on hitting, kept on and on, hardly seeing his target, hardly aware of Miss Lucy's cries or Tag Bassett's cheering.

P. V. and Rolly Joe were having a hard time holding Justin up. *Dead weight,* Skeet thought. *Dead weight.* And he wondered if Justin were dead.

"Drop him."

Justin dropped to the hard cobblestones.

Skeet gasped for breath. He watched Justin for a moment. Justin moved and tried to raise his battered head.

"You hear me, Justin?"

Justin seemed to be trying to get up. Skeet squatted by him.

"You hear me all right. Justin, I know you stole my Buckley. Stole him, let him go, hid him somewhere. And I want him, and I'm gonna get him. But if I don't find him, Justin, you damn well better get him back for me. 'Cause I'm coming back here for him. And remember, if Buckley ain't here, and if you ain't here—Miss Lucy will be. You hear me, Justin? *Miss Lucy will be here.*"

Justin, his head raised from the stones, seemed to be staring at Skeet through slitted eyes. His head sank back to the ground. Skeet grinned at him. He stood up and grinned at Miss Lucy.

"Reckon he heard me all right. But in case he didn't, you give him the message. All right, Tag, let Miss Lucy go."

Bassett threw Lucy to one side. With a snarl, he rushed at Justin and kicked him in the belly. He snatched the paddle from Jeppson's hands and clubbed Justin three times, across shoulders, back, and buttocks. He then kicked him twice between the legs, and twice more in the belly, rolling him onto his back.

"Hey!" Suddenly frightened, Skeet grabbed Bassett and pulled him away. "Don't kill him, goddam it, he's had enough!"

Yes, Justin had had enough, and Skeet did not like the way he was lying perfectly still, eyes blankly open to a blank sky. To reassure himself, he said, "Don't forget, Miss Lucy. Give him my message."

With that, the five men mounted their horses and rode away.

The lane seemed to darken, and Lucy fell back against the wall of the shop. She thought she was going to faint, but she could not let that happen, not now. She bent far forward, taking deep breaths, trying to pull herself back to full consciousness.

When her mind had cleared, she lifted her head. Justin still lay just as they had left him, unmoving, eyes as lifeless as stone.

He's dead, she thought numbly. *They've killed him. He's dead.* She felt as drained of emotion, as drained of hope and grief and pain as if they had killed her too. And what was there to live for?

She moved toward him. She knelt and lifted his head into her lap. The eyes remained fixed. She saw no sign of breath or heartbeat.

He's dead.

He had come back to her after all this time, they had become lovers again, and now . . .

"Luz," he whispered.

And all the pain returned to her, all the pain and all the grief, racking her, wrenching her, tearing at her, lacerating her soul as if it were her flesh. She screamed his name. She lifted her face to the empty heavens and howled.

And with the grief and the pain came a sense of triumph, a joy that was almost evil in its ruthlessness.

She had won. Justin was hurt, broken, shattered—yes. But he would not be leaving Sabrehill now. He would not be able to leave. He would have to stay here, and she would care for him once again, as she had all those long years past. And this time she would never, never let him go.

Nine

How many hours had he hid in the wall? Buck had no idea. In that small space, in that darkness, time could expand and contract. Muscles grew cramped. The air became summer hot and swamp fetid, until sweat ran down the body and breathing became almost impossible. Only the slow appearance of splinters of light between the boards and through the overhanging harness assured him that time was passing at all.

Outside this coffin that he occupied, people were being hurt. His people. And there was not a thing he could do about it.

As when Adaba's camp had been raided, he was out of bed, some dream of terror still upon him, before he had even known what had awakened him. He had pulled on pants and thrown himself into the hollow in the wall, drawing the panel closed after him. Before he had even latched it, Binnie was hanging harness over it. Everything had been carefully rehearsed, had been practiced a dozen times or more: each had known exactly what to do.

Then had come the worst of it. *"You bar a door on a white man, nigger?"* The search. The questions. The torture. Zag's cries, Binnie's screams. Buck knew the sound of the paddle when he heard it, and he knew well what that instrument could do. These people were suffering because of him. For him.

Afterward, silence; and that was almost as bad. Like time itself, it seemed to expand and contract. It had dimensions like space, and somewhere within it terrible, murderous things were happening, and he could do nothing but wait, wait, wait.

Minutes passed. Hours. The muscle cramps grew worse, and the sweat flowed down his body, and he could hardly breathe, and surely it would not hurt to open the panel, just a little bit, just for one minute, just long enough to let cool air in—

A pistol shot. Not distant, not out in the field quarters, but nearby.

Buck held his breath. It seemed to him that he did not breathe more than three or four full times before he heard that white man's voice again. "Hey, you niggers, where you gone? Goddam you, niggers, I want you, wench!" And then the cursing and the animal growls and the sounds of destruction: the shattering of glass, the smashing of pottery, the clang and clatter of metal. And finally, boots pounding back down the stairs.

More sounds then, no farther away than the lane. A number of horses, hooves clattering on the cobblestones. An angry voice, muffled by the walls. Shouts, a woman crying out. The departure of the horses. And the long desolate wail of the woman.

And still he waited.

She came for him at last. He could not have said how he knew it was Binnie out there, but he did. And as she took down the harness and threw it aside, he unfastened the latches and opened his hiding place. He did not look at her as he came stumbling out. Gasping for air like a man arisen from a grave, he threw himself onto his bed. Binnie's hands fell on his bare shoulders. "You all right?" she asked in a broken voice. "You all right?" Asked him, when he should have been asking her.

"They all gone?"

Binnie nodded. "I think so. All gone now." Her face was smudged with dirt and tears.

"Where's Zag?"

"Outside. With the others."

She helped him get to his feet. He followed her as she went back to her room, helping her when he saw that she could hardly walk. There was dried blood on her skirt and on her bare ankles.

As they went through the doorway, she stopped dead. She looked around, and it was as if she were seeing the room for the first time. Seeing what had happened to it. Before, she had been in too much of a hurry to get him out of the wall. But now she saw.

The windows broken. Curtains ripped to shreds. Pictures torn from the walls and smashed. Bed torn apart and fouled with ashes. Shards of pitcher and bowl and plate strewn about the floor. Handfuls of wet ashes smeared over the white walls.

Her room, hers and Zag's, destroyed. The one place a nigger might have that was his, his own small space on this earth, the one place where a nigger slave, if he had the guts and the will and the need, might make a little bit of beauty of one kind or another—ruined.

Buck saw the anguish in her eyes. He watched her hands go to her mouth. He watched her face crumple. He watched the tears come, blinding her. He listened as the sobs, almost silent, racked her. This, he knew—the desecration, the defilement of this room—was even worse than the beating she had suffered. And there was nothing he could do for her except draw her into his arms for a little while and hold her and stroke her and swear silently that this was one more debt that would never be forgiven.

Something was happening outside. Buck heard a stirring in the lane. Zag was "outside, with the others," Binnie had said. Letting go of her, he crossed the room and edged up to a broken window. Down below, facing the blacksmith shop, there must have been at least a couple dozen of the people, and more were arriving. He saw no white faces.

"What is it?" he asked. "What's happening down there?"

"Ettalee," Binnie sobbed. "Ettalee . . ."

Buck looked at her sharply. "What about Ettalee?"

She could only shake her head.

He had to know, had to know fast. Dozens of people gathering outside the blacksmith shop, and Ettalee—

He knew where his clothes would be hidden. He rushed to the chest, threw the lid up, pulled them out. Dressed as hurriedly as possible. His axe and his knife were kept hidden in the wall compartment, and he went back for them.

He abandoned virtually all caution. He hurried down the stairs and out into the lane and began breaking his way through the crowd. People turned and stared. Many of them had heard the tale of his presence at Sabrehill or somewhere nearby, but this was the first time most of them had laid eyes on him. Yet they knew him, knew who he was.

He went directly to the door of the living quarters of the blacksmith shop. Stepping through the open doorway, he saw that Ettalee was lying on the bed, apparently unconscious or asleep. Saul was sitting in a chair, bent forward, his eyes hidden by one hand. Lying across another chair was a bloody shirt, and there was a bloodstain on the floor.

"Saul," Buck said, "what happened?"

Saul raised his head slowly. He turned and looked at Buck.

"She dead, Buck," he said after a moment. "My Ettalee dead. That Mr. Bassett, he come here and . . ."

He could say no more. And did not have to. *Ettalee,* Buck thought. *Ettalee and Claramae and how many others?* (For he never thought of Claramae as one of *them.*) *How many others you gonna let them take, O Lord, how many?*

None. None, by God, without they die too.

The vision returned: it burned in his head as never before. An insurrection, bloody and murderous. Not merely a few runaways. Not merely a handful of killers from Vachel Skeet's jailhouse to burn down Redbird. No, a growing army to burn everything, everything. He was a man with a skull full of flames, and no longer would he keep them banked. From now on, he would let them rage.

And now the people would follow him. He felt that in his hot bones, in the beat of his heart. Ettalee's death would not go unavenged, those blacks gathering in the lane would not allow it to go unavenged. Now he had what he wanted. His army was beginning to gather, right outside this building.

He took his axe from its sheath. He went to the door, stepped down a step, and looked out at the crowd. There was not a single white face out there, but he would hardly have cared if there had been. He raised his axe and shook it as if he were threatening the very heavens.

"We gonna kill 'em," he yelled at the top of his voice. "You hear me, you niggers? *We gonna kill 'em all!*"

It was back: the same hatred, sickness, and despair that she had felt growing among her people from the time she had brought Ettalee back from Redbird. She had thought that with the news of Ettalee's improvement a few days ago, it had begun to dissipate, but now it was worse than ever.

She saw it, felt it, that afternoon when she went out to the field quarters to inspect the damage. In the evening, after supper, she went out again, went to talk to the people, to reassure them, to promise them repairs, replacements, reparations, whatever they needed to restore their lives. Now she felt no fright, as she had that night two weeks ago, when the people had gathered so silently outside the office. She felt neither welcome nor unwelcome. The people seemed almost indifferent to her, hardly listened to her promises. Their minds were on the bitter realities of the day. Ettalee was dead—had died in those brief moments while Lucy and Justin had stood in the office, listening for another shot, Justin trying to hold her back from danger. Several women had been raped—Rolanda, Lida, others. Children had been hurt. Personal property, if a slave could be said to have such a thing, had been destroyed—things too precious to their owners ever to be replaced. The sickness, the despair, the bitterness was a fog, an evil miasma, a thing that hung almost palpable in the air.

Finally Lucy returned to the big house. Justin had been placed in the downstairs bedchamber, just as he had after the duel. A young woman, Reba, was watching over him. "You may go for a while if you wish, Reba. I'll stay with him. . . ."

Zulie had refused to look after Justin. "I got my own people to care for," she had said, and Lucy had nearly struck her. *Miserable little bitch, I'll have you whipped!* But there would have been no point in ordering a whipping even if Lucy had been capable of it, and besides she knew that Zulie was right: she was more useful elsewhere.

Lucinda had looked after Justin until, several hours later, Dr. Paulson had been found and brought to Sabrehill.

"How bad is it, doctor?"

The doctor had shrugged. "He's banged up pretty bad, Lucy-girl. Don't think anything's broken up inside, but sometimes it's hard to tell. He's lucky he doesn't have any of those stove-in ribs shoved through a lung. He's going to be in this here bed for a mighty long time."

"But he'll be all right?"

The doctor had shrugged again. "I think so. All we can do now, though, is keep a sharp eye on him and wait. A day or two will tell the tale."

Wait. God, she thought, how much of her life had been spent waiting.

For the second time since Justin's return to Sabrehill, she slipped to her knees beside a bed. *O Lord, please don't let him die. . . .*

And then: *I* won't *lose you this time, Justin,* she swore silently, almost angrily. *I won't, I won't, I won't!*

Part of Monday morning was devoted to burying Ettalee, and most of the Sabrehill people were at the graveyard—sullen and angry, every last one of them, in a way that Lucy had rarely seen. Feeling like an outsider, she attended the burial but remained outside the fringes of the crowd.

Later in the morning, Major Kimbrough paid a call, meeting with Lucy in the office. "I just wanted to know if that damned posse has caused as much trouble here at Sabrehill as it has at Kimbrough Plantation—which, I can tell you, was considerable."

Lucy gave him a brief account of the posse's visit. To her surprise, he expressed no particular indignation over the beating Justin had been given.

"And they're still riding around," the major said, "riding around like a bunch of drunks, abusing our people, tearing their homes apart—apparently just because that fool Vachel Skeet has some idiotic idea that his long-lost Buckley and that damned Adaba are around here somewhere. My God, they think they can get away with anything in the name of searching for Adaba and Black Buck. And maybe they can." Abruptly he added, "Lucy, I don't like the way the niggers are acting. Do you think you're safe here? Especially now that Justin can't help you?"

"Why, of course," Lucy said, surprised. "My people feel very badly about what's happened, but I think they're loyal to me—most of them."

"Most of them," the major said ironically. "*I* don't like the way this posse is stirring them up. These searches are putting them in a damned ugly mood. And remember, my dear, there are far more blacks than whites in our fair state, and the blacks know it."

Lucy was glad to see the major leave.

She spent most of the rest of the day continuing her inventory of the damage done by the posse and checking on the wounded—among them, young Nemo, with his broken arm, and Jebediah, so battered he could hardly move. But no one else had been hurt as badly as Justin, who seemed to be asleep or unconscious most of the time. He lay perfectly still, eyes closed, and rarely so much as whispered a syllable. Lucy spent what little time she could spare at his bedside.

Thus it was Monday evening before she could consult with Paul Devereau, and well after dark when she arrived at the Devereau mansion.

"My God, Lucy," he said as a maid ushered her into the library, "what are you doing out at this hour?"

She looked at him with mild astonishment. "Why, Paul, I'm sorry. I thought you were rather a night owl."

"But don't you know what's going on?"

"If you're referring to that bunch of ruffians that calls itself a posse—"

Paul settled her into a deep, comfortable chair. "I'm referring to the trouble the posse is making with the blacks. That posse has been riding all over these parts for two full days now, and God only knows how many slaves have been abused. And don't think they're incapable of retaliating. Push them too far, and they will, no matter what the consequences."

Lucy remembered Major Kimbrough's words: *"I don't like the way the niggers are acting. Do you think you're safe here?"* She thought of the bleak and bitter mood she had felt among the people of Sabrehill, and somewhere within her an alarm sounded.

"You really think there's danger?"

"Lucy, there have already been a couple of barn-burnings on the McClintock and the Haining plantations. And last night at least two white men were attacked by blacks and nearly beaten to death. Yes, there is a great deal of danger."

"But isn't there anything we can do to stop this posse?"

Paul's laugh was humorless. "Oh, yes, of course. Complain to the sheriff." The posse was supposedly led by Constable Morgan, and in theory he was under the sheriff's direction. "Or politely ask Skeet to send his friends home. Just try any of that and see how far you get."

"But after what they did to Justin—"

"I heard what they did to Justin. From Major Kimbrough. But what do you expect to do about it? There were five of them, the major told me, quite enough to alibi each other. There were only two of you, since Negro witnesses don't count—the word of two against five. And furthermore, Justin is by no means a popular man around here. He expressed some most unacceptable views at that party you gave for him, views on the dignity and educability of the Negro, for instance."

"But he hardly said a thing!"

"Apparently he said quite enough. Lucy, you must realize that to challenge the common view of the nigger in these parts—to question the status quo of slavery—why, it's enough to get a man tarred and feathered. You can be sure that Vachel Skeet and his friends aren't the only ones delighted to see Justin beaten damned near dead. South

Carolina is no place for a man like Justin—unless he can learn to keep his mouth shut."

"I don't think Justin can ever learn that. At least, not well enough."

"Then get him back on his feet and send him home."

Never, Lucy swore silently, *never.* But what if she kept him here, only to get him hurt again? perhaps killed the next time? Had she the right?

When she arrived back at Sabrehill, Justin was conscious, and he smiled wanly at her as she entered the bed-chamber. That seemed a good omen. Careful not to disturb the bed, she leaned down and gently kissed him on the mouth. And Paul Devereau's warning was completely forgotten. And once again she thought, *Oh, yes, I'll keep him here. I'll keep him here and never, never let him go. . . .*

Rebellion, insurrection, escape to freedom—it did not matter what you called it. It was going to happen. From the moment he looked down at Ettalee's body, so still on the bed; and as he raised his axe over his head and yelled, *"We gonna kill 'em all!";* and as he walked recklessly through the crowd, heading toward Zulie's cabin; he knew it was going to happen after all.

He felt it in the crowd. He had not the slightest doubt. Not that everyone in that crowd would follow him—oh, no. But at that moment there were perhaps a dozen or even more, ready and eager to follow him, ready to commit any violence to avenge Ettalee and their own years of captivity and to find freedom in the North. And if the same fever spread to the other nearby plantations . . .

It did spread, thanks to Vachel Skeet and his posse, as Buck learned by evening. The posse had spent the entire day on other plantations, doing exactly what they had done at Sabrehill—doing Buck's missionary work for him —and the next day they were still at it. Buck, following in their wake, sampled the hatred they left behind. "They whip Knowledge," Cudjoe of the Buckridge plantation told him on Monday morning. He was trembling, almost weeping, as he thought of what had happened. "They take off her dress and whip her naked, I don't know why. But she don't say nothing. She don't tell nothing at all." He wiped tears away. "Buck, we all follow you, seven us here. But ain't only us and them on near plantations. Word pass along, you know, all up and down the river. 'Black Buck lead us, maybe Adaba too. Time come soon, time to shake off the shackles and go follow Black Buck and Adaba. Then run for the woods, and the white masters never catch us.' "

Could such a thing happen? Buck was recruiting his band mainly from ten large plantations on the north side of the river, and he estimated he would have about sixty or seventy followers. But if Cudjoe were right, if the entire countryside were to rise up, if the number to rebel and march to freedom were in the hundreds or even the thousands . . .

It would be Nat Turner's dream come true. It would be Black Buck's fiery vision fulfilled. And how many white men would die. . . .

At the evening meetings, Buck now found no lack of excitement and enthusiasm among his followers. They were eagerly gathering the supplies they would need, and they listened to every word he said. "Still don't see how I can steal me a gun yet," Brutus said, worried, when Buck visited the Devereau plantation on Wednesday night. "Don't you worry about it," Buck told him. "If you get one, that's fine, get lead and molds and powder too. But if you got to choose, what you want is a good short-handled axe. One like this, if you can find it." He drew his new axe from its sheath and showed it to the half-dozen people gathered in the little cabin. "You got an axe like this, you can make a snare for a rabbit. You can build a shelter. You can make a spear. This axe here, he'll keep you alive in the wilderness the way a gun can't never do. You got the right kind of axe, like this one, and learn about it the way I teach you, you can even bring down a deer with it or—" the axe flashed across the room and struck with a solid *thunk* deeply into the wall "—split open a white man's skull!" There was approving laughter, and the excitement built to a new height. These people were ready to rise up. Ready to rebel. Ready to follow Buck anywhere he led.

At these meetings Buck inspected stolen supplies, went over the plan again, answered questions, refined details. The plan was really quite simple. The rallying place would be some woods on Sabrehill, just north of the field quarters. On Saturday afternoon those who lived on the plantations farthest from Sabrehill would start for those woods. On that day, and that evening, there would be a lot of visiting back and forth, with or without passes, between the plantations, providing a degree of cover for the runaways. Some of the visitors would even be on mule-back or in wagons, making it easier for the runaways to transport stolen animals and supplies without being detected.

Those from the farther plantations would arrive at the rallying point after dark, when the evening's parties were starting. Those from the nearer plantations would wait until the Redbird big house was on fire—runners would carry the word to them. They would then set fire to barns, big houses, whatever they could, thus giving the white people a great deal to think about, and in the confusion they would hurry to Sabrehill to join the others. And Buck would lead the whole band north—to freedom.

Wednesday evening passed, Thursday came.

Thursday evening.

Forty-eight hours. Less. A little more scouting of Redbird, a few more meetings.

It was going to happen. Nothing could stop it.

He wanted Zulie.

He wanted her more than anything else he had ever wanted in his life, unless it was freedom and life itself, and wherever Jeb wandered through the field quarters that evening, whoever he spoke to, he was looking for her and thinking of her. He wanted to say, *Let me take the curse of Skeet off of you. Let me make you forget him. Let me heal you, as you are healing me. Let me take away your pain, as you are taking away mine. . . .*

The pain had been terrible. They had beaten him, as

nearly as he could remember, three times: first, when they had invaded his house; then, when he had tried to answer Rolanda's cries; and finally, when he had regained consciousness and tried to climb to his feet.

Of what followed the beatings, he remembered little. He found himself lying face down on his bed, and he realized that Momma Lucinda and Leila were washing the blood away. Later, Zulie came and took care of him. Her fingers moved gently over his back, carefully laying on the ointments, miraculously soothing the pain, and he drifted off into sleep.

She returned the next day, and he awakened to the touch of her fingers on his back. "You just stay still, Jeb," she said softly. "You going be all right."

There was superficial pain, little stabs of fire, as she touched back, buttocks, and legs, but the deeper aches seemed to be drawn away.

When she examined his head wound, he knew she was almost finished, but he did not want her to leave.

"What happened?" he asked. "What happened—was it yesterday?"

"Posse," Zulie said.

"Posse for what?"

"Black Buck. And Adaba."

Mr. Justin, Jeb thought . . . Black Buck and Adaba . . . the Rogans. . . . He tried to get it all straight in his mind, but for the moment, it was too much for him.

"They find anybody?"

"No."

"Make much trouble? Anybody else hurt—"

"Ettalee dead. 'Cause that Bassett man."

"Oh, no. Oh, dear Lord, no." Jeb was sickened enough to forget his own pain.

Zulie finished rebandaging his head. When he could speak again, he asked, "Who . . . who led the posse?"

Pulling the blankets up over him, Zulie got up to leave. "Mr. Skeet," she said.

It was then that Jeb noticed the curiously dead quality of Zulie's voice, as if all the tears had gone out of it, leaving it dusty and dry. It had been that way from the first word she had spoken to him. And a terrible thought came to him.

He remembered that Sunday afternoon three weeks ago when Mr. Skeet had attacked Zulie, almost certainly with the intention of carrying her off as he had carried off Ettalee—and undoubtedly with the intention of treating her in the same way. And he remembered that Zulie had defended herself—had run Mr. Skeet off with a knife. It was an offense that such a man could never forget or forgive.

And if Mr. Skeet had brought the posse here for a search . . .

Jeb had to know.

"Zulie, wait. Mr. Skeet . . . did he find you?"

Zulie, in the doorway, stared at the floor.

"Zulie, did he . . . did he bother you again?"

She shrugged. "Don't matter."

"It does matter. What did he do to you?"

"No worse than some others, I reckon. Jeb, you get your rest."

She left before he could ask her anything more.

No worse than some others. So Mr. Skeet had gotten what he wanted. Had taken it.

From my woman, Jeb thought, hating the man as he had hated no other. *From my woman.*

Those first two days, Sunday and Monday, he hardly moved from his bed. He had other visitors, Leila in particular, but he looked forward only to seeing Zulie, to hearing her voice, to feeling her hands on his back. She came twice a day with her medicines—voodoo medicines, some said—and each time her hands eased a little more of the pain out of his body.

And his body knew want again. By the third day, as she touched him, he knew how well he was recovering.

Had she no idea of how much he loved her? Of how much he desired her? Had she forgotten? He tried to talk to her as he lay there, her hands moving over his battered body. He tried to tell her of his love, of his desire. He tried to make her smile, to make her laugh—at the very least, to bring some life back into her voice. But without success. When he reminded her of his marriage proposal, she was evasive, and when he tried to talk of Skeet, tried to comfort her, she would not speak to him at all.

By the fourth day, Wednesday, he was up and moving about, slowly, cautiously, trying to do some of his duties, but Zulie continued to come to his house twice a day. And twice a day, as he shrugged out of his clothes and she ministered to him, he suffered. How long had it been since they had slept together, how long since they had pleasured? A matter of weeks? of days? It seemed like months. And didn't she see what she was doing to him now? How could she fail to see—she who had always known? Was she doing it purposely for some perverse reason? No, she was not. When he looked up at her over his shoulder, her face was blank, her eyes dull and empty, as if her mind were a world away.

On Thursday morning it came to an end. He tried to distract himself from his needs, tried to talk to Zulie of other things, but she hardly answered. And he could stand it no longer. Lying on his belly, every muscle tense, he was erect, hard, throbbing. And as she finished her work, he found himself rolling over onto his back, and roughly pulling her to him. "Zulie, please—"

She fought silently. Lust turned to anger, and as he put her onto her back and rose over her, he was close to hitting her. But then he saw her face. Saw the sickness in it and the fear in her eyes. And he had to let her go.

"Zulie! I'm sorry! Zulie!"

She fled from his house.

He sat on the edge of the bed, his cock wilting, sickened with himself; hating himself almost as much as he did Skeet. Maybe he was worse than Skeet, because he claimed to love Zulie and yet had allowed his lust to make him forget what she had been through. How did he dare to think of her as his woman? He knew nothing of love, and he could never deserve her.

Yet the love and the need did remain, no matter how much he reviled himself, and when Zulie failed to return that afternoon, he was more wretched than ever. By evening he could no longer wait for her. He headed through the darkness out toward the field quarters.

He tried to keep some pride. He told himself that he had other reasons for going to the quarters besides seeking Zulie, that it was most unlikely that she would be out at this hour and that there was no point in going to her cabin, since her door was closed to him. He told himself that he was looking for signs of trouble in the quarters, signs of Adaba and Black Buck, since he had promised to do so, and the posse's failed search did not change that promise. And yet he kept thinking, *Let me help you forget that man, let me heal your pain,* and he found himself standing before Zulie's door, staring at it.

The door had an inside latch: Zulie did not like uninvited visitors. Perhaps tonight she had forgotten to use the latch. Or perhaps she had just taken it off.

Jeb put his hand on the door. He did it simply because it was Zulie's door. Quite likely he would have knocked next, no matter how futile the gesture. He had no intention of simply walking in, of intruding. But with the weight of his hand on it, the door began to swing in; and without even thinking about it, Jeb pressed harder, and the door swung faster.

In the dim candlelight he saw Zulie's startled face.

But he was looking beyond that face to another. A face with a muzzle of black beard.

He knew instantly. He would have known even if he had not heard that face described. This was no slave from a neighboring plantation, no secret sweetheart of Zulie. Or even if he were, he was something more than that. He was Adaba—the Brown Dove.

Jeb turned and walked rapidly away.

One moment of carelessness, and she had ruined everything. One small act of forgetfulness, a latch left unfastened, and Adaba was discovered and, quite likely, the rebellion ended.

No, she could not let that happen. She stood frozen as Jeb disappeared. And then she was out the door and running.

"Jeb!" she cried fiercely. "Jebediah, God damn you! Jeb!"

Ahead of her in the darkness, Jeb stopped and turned slowly.

"Jeb, please," she said as she reached him, "don't tell!" Jeb stared down at her. She could read nothing in his starlit face. On an off chance, she said, "That there ain't nobody. That there is only—"

But of course, he knew. "Only Adaba," he said. "What I want to know now is, where is Black Buck?"

"I don't know! Adaba, he say Buck take a different trail long ago."

"Maybe so. But they were together, and since you've been hiding Adaba, Black Buck could be here too. And if he is, I'm going to find him."

Jeb again started to leave, and Zulie grabbed his arm. "No! Wait! He ain't here! Don't tell, Jeb!"

"Zulie, your friend can start running if he wants to. But I'm not going to tell anyone but Miss Lucy and Mr. Justin, and Miss Lucy isn't going to let Adaba get hung— you know that's not in her nature. And Mr. Justin only wants to help him get away."

"No! That ain't so! Jeb, you don't know that man like I do. Know him from a long time back. You got any idea what he done to Miss Lucy?"

"Miss Lucy happens to think the world of Mr. Justin. Any fool can see that. Zulie, you just naturally hate and distrust anything with a white skin."

For days Zulie had been living in a kind of gray haze, emotionally dead except for a kind of low-burning hatred, and this was the first time she had felt anything as strong as desperation or anger. Her hand itched for the knife beneath her dress. And she exploded.

"Well, don't you, you damn fool? Any white skin ever do anything good for you, except Miss Lucy? And I guess that's only 'cause she's a dried-up old-maid widow-woman, likes her big-cock nigger buck!"

The shoulder bunched, and the big hand came up, and she thought he was going to hit her. For the first time the whip-cut face showed emotion, the eyes widening, the teeth glittering between the taut lips. But he slowly lowered the hand.

"Zulie, I love you, but don't you ever talk like that about Miss Lucy."

She controlled herself. Somehow she had to find an

argument, a bargaining point. She looked wildly for it, but only one thing occurred to her.

"Jeb, don't tell—and I be your woman again. I promise."

Something showed in his eyes, as if he were caught between hope and pain, but he shook his head.

"We get married, Jeb. Like you want. We go north, and I be your woman and a good wife forever. Ain't that what you want, Jeb?"

The pain, the hope, in Jeb's eyes deepened, and for a moment she thought he was going to accept her offer. But again he shook his head.

"Zulie, I can't take you on those terms—selling yourself—"

"Well, what the hell more you want?" Zulie was on the verge of tears. "What more you want, boy? Tell me!"

"I want you to listen to me. Zulie, that Black Buck is trouble. A lot more than Adaba. From what I've heard, all Adaba does is steal a few niggers and take them north, and for that I say God bless him. But that Black Buck—"

"Oh, for that you say God bless him! But you tell Miss Lucy when he don't want you to. God bless, you say, but you ain't helping him none. Jeb, it's true—it's true what they say about you. Just another goddam white man's nigger!"

When Jeb spoke again, his voice shook. "I started to say, Black Buck is a killer—"

"Yeah, shot him a couple of white skins!"

"And from what I hear, he's a burner. Now, I don't give a damn what you think about white skins, Miss Lucy is my friend. I'm not going to let any goddam Black Buck hurt Miss Lucy or her Mr. Justin. I'm not going to let him put his torch to Sabrehill. And if he tries, he's going to find one mean black man out after his ass. He's going to find—"

The voice came out of the shadows, a purr: "Black Buck isn't going to burn Sabrehill, Mr. Hayes."

Zulie looked around, startled, as Adaba came toward them. *Why ain't you running?* she thought. *Damn fool, run and hide!*

"Black Buck isn't going to hurt your Miss Lucy or your Mr. Justin," Adaba went on, speaking every bit as well as Jeb. "Of course, he might take away some of your people, and so might I. But I take it you have no strenuous objection to that."

Jeb stared. "Adaba," he said.

Adaba smiled. "Yes."

Zulie looked from one man to the other, half-expecting one or the other to attack at any instant. But Adaba merely went on smiling, and Jeb seemed to relax, as if relieved to be talking to him.

"How do you know what Black Buck is going to do or not do?" he asked.

"Buck does as I tell him. At least, most of the time. About this, I can promise for him."

"Then he is around here."

"Around here somewhere. But not for long. Planning to leave. I'm surprised he hasn't left already."

"And you?"

Adaba shrugged. "Unlike Zulie and Buck, I am inclined to trust Mr. Justin Sabre. I was hoping that once my wounds were healed, he'd help me get away from these parts. But Zulie tells me that thanks to Mr. Skeet and his friends, Mr. Justin is now worse off than I am."

"That's true."

Adaba laughed sadly and shook his head. "He seems to have made some nasty enemies around here. Maybe *I'll* have to help *him* get away from these parts. Steal him north."

"He told me how he helped you get away from the Rogans."

Adaba nodded. "And Mr. Hayes, regardless of how Zulie feels about white pelts in general and Mr. Justin in particular, I am making that man an honorary nigger."

In a matter of a few seconds, something had changed. Zulie sensed it. It was as if, having spoken to each other, the two men sensed something in each other that could be trusted. And Zulie remembered what she should never have forgotten: that, "white man's nigger" or not, Jeb had never hesitated to stand up for a black man.

"Please, Jeb," she said, "don't tell Miss Lucy. Maybe

you right, maybe best for Adaba and Buck if you did, but ain't they got a right to a choice?"

"Mr. Justin can't help Buck and me now, Mr. Hayes," Adaba said, "and I don't see any good in worrying your Miss Lucy. And again I promise you: whatever else he may do, Buck is not going to harm your Miss Lucy or Sabrehill."

"Please, Jeb . . ."

Jeb sighed. "All right. I'll keep my mouth shut. For now, at least. But if there's any trouble . . ."

"Oh, thank you!" Impulsively Zulie stepped up to Jeb, pulled his head down, and kissed him. "Thank you. And like I said . . . 'bout going north . . . you got my promise."

Jeb shook his head. "I can't hold you to such a promise, Zulie." He looked at Adaba, looked him up and down. "You've got my boots," he said, and once again he turned and walked away.

The danger was past. Better than that: there was no longer any reason to worry about Jeb finding out about Adaba and Buck. His word, Zulie knew, was good, and he would not inform Miss Lucy. That meant one less threat to Buck's plans.

And the rebellion would come. No matter what Adaba had promised Jeb in respect to Sabrehill, the rebellion grew more certain with every hour, and it would tear the countryside apart. Zulie had made the proper sacrifices, had performed the proper rites, and Momma Brigitte smiled on her.

For perhaps the ten-thousandth time, she thought the words: *Fire and blood. Fire and blood.*

I could kill him now, Buck thought.

He still had no gun, but Theron was sure he could steal a pistol at the last moment from Kimbrough Hall. Failing that, Saul said there was a not very reliable pepperbox in Miss Lucy's office. But of course, Buck did not need a gun to kill Skeet. His knife or his axe would do as well as anything.

He stood in the woods looking toward the night-dark Redbird big house. His problem was simple: to find the best route to the jailhouse. He would not know for a certainty what it was until Saturday night—it would depend on the weather. But meanwhile he had approached the main buildings of Redbird from every angle. He had circled them several times, and he had seen them both by day and by night. And he felt very much at home again.

Too bad this wasn't Saturday night. It was almost ideal. The little starlight that earlier had penetrated the woods was now gone, obscured by clouds. The jail house was between him and the big house, and the wind was blowing toward him, carrying his scent away.

A dog barked, but the sound was muffled. Buck grinned. His luck was running true. Not only did the wind favor him, but the dog was locked up, making it even harder for him to get Buck's scent.

He moved closer, ready to cut and run if he had to, but with growing confidence. The jail house was now little more than a hundred yards away. Since he had come back, he had never before been this close to it.

Yeah, I could kill him right now.

The idea was tempting. Obviously Redbird had been put to bed for the night. The best way, he supposed, would be to circle wide and reapproach on the piazza side of the big house. As likely as not, the door would be unlocked—in any case, he could find a way to get in. Go up the stairs, remembering which steps creaked. Enter the bedroom they had once shared. Light a lamp. Then have a quiet little chat with good old Vaych. Talk for a little while, and then . . . put the lights out.

Tempting, yes. But it did not fit in with Buck's plans. Patience, he told himself. Adaba had always taught him to be patient. Two more nights, that was as long as he had to wait, and on Saturday night—

It struck him then, the enormity of it, and his head seemed to go up in those flames that he could no longer keep banked. He, Black Buck, would be marching north with a small army at his command. An army that would grow daily larger, an army that could not be stopped. An army that would ravage the white man's land. An army of thousands, perhaps tens of thousands, endless black legions, that would pillage and plunder and kill and rape

—yes, that too. The white man's nightmare: that the black man would do to the white woman what the white man had done to the black. Let it happen. Let the land burn. Let the skies fall. Let all be destroyed. And Johnny Dove, Adaba, would join them when he was well and ready; he would see the necessity of it all. Johnny and Claramae and he would lead their army north, relentless, invincible, merciless—

Buck shook his head, trying to clear it. Increasingly, as his visions carried him away, he became confused. Claramae was dead now, and it was Ettalee who—

No. No. Ettalee was dead too. Of course.

Buck sobbed, the first sound he had made in the night.

They were all dying, one by one, or sometimes a great many at once, as at Adaba's camp during the raid. It was said that a lot of niggers had died there. Yes, they were all dying, that was inevitable, Buck knew that now, but first, before they died—

Jesus, he thought, *I got to pull myself together. Only two more nights to wait. And then I'll be all right.*

But would he?

Trouble was, there were times when he just didn't give a damn anymore. Didn't give a damn about anything. You dreamed of vengeance, but Johnny Dove was right: even that, what good did it do?

A lot of good. One dead Skeet could mean a lot of live niggers. Even if Buck wasn't there to lead them away. Even if he went ahead and killed Vachel tonight.

He moved closer to the jail house. Closer to the big house.

No, not tonight. Stay with the plan. The others were counting on him. Time to turn now and head back and—

For an instant he thought he had been shot through the head. His skull seemed to burst into a hundred blazing fragments that burned themselves out, leaving him in darkness. As he felt himself fall, his skull burst again, and the darkness deepened.

Slowly it cleared. Flickering light pressed through his eyelids. His head ached. He realized that he was lying on a rough plank floor. He felt heat on one side of his face and smelled a wood fire.

He opened his eyes, to look up at a man towering above him, a man with the long gray face of Vachel Skeet.

"Good evening, Buckley," the man said, smiling. "We've been waiting for you to come around here. Welcome back to Redbird."

PART FIVE

Rebels

One

"It's been a long time, Buckley."

Yes, it had been.

"Don't just sit there. Talk to me."

No.

"We got a lot to say to each other."

It's all been said, Vaych.

"No, no. Don't close your eyes. Got something to show you. Open 'em up. You know I got ways to open 'em if I want to. Ever see a nigger without eyelids?"

The other white man, Mr. Dinkin, cackled with laughter.

"That's better, Buckley. Don't want you falling asleep on me. Know what I'm gonna show you, Buckley? . . . No, don't turn your head away. Look. Lookee here."

A length of wire with a loop at the end.

"Yes, sir. You may not believe it, but this is the exact same one. Kept it greased so it wouldn't rust away or nothing. Been saving it for you."

Buck had often wished he had carried that wire away with him and saved it for Vachel. Futile wish.

"Now, don't bust out crying, Buckley. Look at him, Mr. Dinkin, I swear he's gonna bust out crying. Did you ever see a nigger so grateful?"

"No, sir, I never did."

"Just for a little gift, a little piece of wire. Don't never say that our Buckley Skeet is an ungrateful nigger."

So this was the way it ended. The circle was closed at last, and he had returned to the heart of the horror. It seemed to Buck that he could almost hear the echoes of Claramae's last screams.

He wanted to cry out, *Get it over with, you bastard, get it over with,* but he could not. He was afraid: the sweat of fear seemed to drip from him. His body crawled with the horror of what might come next. But even greater than the fear was the vast weariness that consumed him. He felt that even if he had been untied, he would have been unable to act. He would have continued to sit right where he was, waiting for whatever came next.

Buck tore his eyes away from the loop of wire. He looked around the room. Nothing had changed. There was the table they had held him against as Vachel had put the loop around Buck's genitals: it stood in exactly the same place. There was Vachel's desk, Buck's knife and axe and hat now lying on it. And he was tied to the same chair from which he had broken free. Vachel's jug was on a shelf, and a small fire crackled in the fireplace.

Circles, Buck thought. Maybe this ending had been inevitable from the start. Didn't most men spend their lives running in circles, large and small?

Skeet was saying something. ". . . them four wenches we talked about, Mr. Dinkin. Might as well rouse 'em out right now and give 'em to Ako and Prince. Put 'em all together in that empty cabin, you know the one, and see they got some whiskey and anything else they need. They got a big week ahead of 'em."

"Nothing to do but eat and drink and sleep and spread them gals, by God," Mr. Dinkin said, grinning.

"Yeah, maybe tomorrow we'll go watch 'em at it. Maybe even help 'em out a little. Now you get out of here till I call you. I got to have a little private talk with my old friend Buckley Skeet."

When the other man had departed, Skeet took down the jug and drank from it. He held it out to Buck, who shook his head, and he set it down on the table. He turned a chair and sat on it backward, his arms resting on its back. The wire loop dangled from his fingers. He looked steadily at Buck, and it was a long time before he smiled and spoke.

"We surely had a lot of good times together, didn't we, Buckley?"

Buck nodded. "We did, Vachel." His voice was weak.

"God, yes. Swimming together when we was kids. Going to town on Saturday afternoons. Wenching together Saturday nights. Planning things together. My God, the plans we had."

Yes, Vachel.

"Remember the time I had a row with Caley Carstairs and damn near killed him before you pulled me off? Remember?"

I remember.

"And the night Claramae was born? You and me and Caley playing out in front of the tavern, and we could hear all that howling and shrieking while your ma and mine was helping old Mrs. Carstairs to pop out Claramae? Remember that?"

I remember, Vachel.

"Liked to scared the hell out of me, all that howling. And remember how we used to go riding over to Sabrehill on Sunday afternoons? I'd go talk to Miss Lucy and her pa, and I guess you spent most of your time sniffing around that damn Lucinda. Remember that? . . . Hey. I said, remember?"

"I remember, Vaych."

"But mostly I think it was the planning that was best. When the Old Man was failing and we was taking over the place. All the things we was gonna do with it. The way we was gonna make it one of the grandest places around here, maybe even as grand as Sabrehill or Kimbrough Hall. Dreaming, Buckley. I reckon that's half the fun, ain't it?"

"I reckon, Vaych."

Vachel Skeet's smile faded. "Why'd you have to go and spoil it all, Buckley?"

"Wasn't me that spoiled it."

"You and Claramae. Now, there just ain't no denying it, Buckley. You know what you and her done."

"It was what you done to her, Vachel. You turned plumb . . ." Buck faltered.

"Go ahead and say it. You can say anything you want tonight, I ain't gonna hurt you. Ain't gonna lay a hand on you, 'cause I'm saving that pleasure for later. And I ain't gonna punish you tomorrow for anything you say tonight, 'cause I want to hear what you got to say. So go right ahead."

Buck looked at Skeet and tried to read his eyes. He did

not trust the white man, but he thought Skeet probably meant what he said. Anyway, there were moments when a man, black or white, had to speak.

"It was what you done to her," he repeated. "You turned plumb mean. She loved you, Vachel, same as I did. And she tried to please you, we both did, but you just wasn't having love no more. And somehow we both found out, Claramae and me, that all we had was each other."

Skeet's mouth had compressed into a short tight line. "Now, that is just plain shit," he said. "I treated you good, Buck. I always treated you good. Oh, maybe I put you down in your place when you got out of line, but hell, how many times did I ever lay a whip on you? And Claramae, that slut, she wasn't worth a diddle. Tricked me into marrying her, couldn't do nothing right to help run the place, couldn't move her lazy ass around the house—just spread it out like on a platter for you. Got hot for nigger cock, and I reckon you wasn't the only one that pronged her. I reckon—"

"That ain't true!"

"I reckon more'n one stud around here dipped his wick in that honey pot—"

"That ain't true, Vaych!"

"Hurts, don't it? To hear the truth. Hurts like hell. Why, Buckley, I do think you're crying!"

Perhaps he was. He hardly knew. His head had fallen to his chest, and now he raised it. Looked at Vachel Skeet.

Skeet grinned. "Now try telling how it really was."

"You want to know? You really want to know?"

"It's your one chance to say what you like. It may never come again."

"Then I'll tell you."

"I'm waiting."

Buck took a deep breath and plunged in. "For a long time I didn't understand it. For a long, long time. But out there in the woods you get a chance to think. And when I did finally understand—oh, maybe five, six years ago—Vachel, I damn near forgave you. Damn near, but not quite. Not after Claramae."

"What the hell are you talking about?"

"Vachel, you're a scared man. You was scared back then, scared when we was kids, and I reckon you're still scared now."

"Nigger, there ain't a thing in the world that scares me."

"You was scared of the Old Man, till you got big enough to lick him. You was scared 'cause you didn't feel smart as other people, didn't go to some big college. You was scared of the gentry that you wanted so much to be part of, scared they'd laugh at you—"

"That's crazy, nigger. I'm a Skeet, I got a good name—"

"And you was scared of women. God, was you scared of them. Scared of Miss Lucy, scared of the wenches— hell, I think you was even scared of Claramae."

Skeet's eyes were hard. "That's a damn lie, and you know it."

Buck ignored him. "Guess I can't blame you for that, though. Guess I was scared too."

"What you said about me being scared of women—"

"Yeah, I guess it's kinda natural when you're first starting out. But I don't think you ever did get over it, Vaych. Remember how we used to go wenching together? There always was a kinda mean streak in you, like you had to scare a gal, maybe slap her butt a little harder than you shoulda, before you could spread her. Show you was master, that kinda excited you, didn't it, Vaych?"

"Ah, shit!"

"And then there was the drinking. Swear, you could drink more'n any nigger I ever met and still get it up and off. It was like, 'stead of stopping you, the drinking *helped* you do it. 'Cause a drunk man ain't scared, see? Ain't scared of nothing, not even a woman. And if you could have you a couple drinks and then slap ass a while, why, then you didn't have no trouble *at all* doing it!"

"You about finished?"

"But what I think helped most was me. At least, up till near the end. Reckon not even you would have felt right, asking me to come right into the bedroom with you and Claramae."

Skeet stiffened. "What the hell do you mean?"

"You always wanted me along when you went wenching. It was always you and me and one or two gals."

"You never had no objections."

"Hell, no. When we first started out, you helped *me* feel brave too."

"I didn't need you, never. We had good times, was all—you and me and a couple of wenches and some whiskey—"

"And me there to watch you. Me there to tell you how good you was. What a stud you was. How nobody could be better than you. Remember how you used to show it to me? 'Go ahead, Buckley,' you'd say, 'touch it. Ain't that hard?' Not them giggling gals, but me. Like we was still a couple of goddam pickaninnies, just finding out."

Vachel Skeet's face was ashen. "You're twisting it all around, Buckley. You're making it sound like—"

"I'm making it sound like it was, like maybe in your heart you was scared of them gals. Well, I ain't blaming you. Reckon I was a lot like you, Vaych. When I was alone with a woman, I reckon it was more like rape than pleasuring. But somehow I got over that. I learned to do my pleasuring with love, Vachel, with love. And you, you poor bastard, you never did." Buck shrugged again and looked away. He sighed. "And to be fair, maybe I helped make it so you never could. You still ain't got no woman all your own, from what I hear, no family to love. No more than me, out there in the woods. So maybe Claramae and me ruined your last chance. If that's so, maybe we owed you something. But not what you made us pay."

"It ain't nothing to what you're gonna pay, nigger!"

Skeet's voice was a harsh, rasping whisper. When Buck looked around at him, his face was more pale than ever. Buck thought of the glowing, sun-brightened, happy face of the boy of long ago. Truly that Vachel was dead, murdered by this one. This one was a man of ice, a creature of arctic winters of the soul.

"No, it ain't nothing to what you're gonna pay." Skeet held up the loop of wire. "Oh, I ain't gonna use this tonight. Maybe not tomorrow or the next day or even next week or next month. But I am gonna use it on you. Maybe use it to take just a little off you at a time.

"Because I'm gonna make you last, Buckley. Twelve years I've been waiting to get my hands on you, and that's something that can't be wiped out in an hour or two. No, sir, I'm gonna have that twelve years back. I'm gonna have payment for it. And you know how I'm gonna get that payment? . . .

"I'm gonna get it by making you last twelve years. That's right, I ain't about to kill you, nigger boy. I'm gonna make you last twelve years at least, and the time is gonna come when you hope for death every hour. But you ain't gonna get it. It's gonna go on . . . and on . . . and on."

A touch of color came back to Skeet's face. He grinned and stood up. He opened the office door and called out into the night: "Mr. Dinkin! Shad! Come a-running, goddam it, I need you!"

He again turned, grinning, to Buck. "Why, I couldn't just up and kill you, Buckley," he said. "I love you too much."

"We get married, Jeb," she had said. *"We go north, and I be your woman and a good wife forever."* Jeb had said he could not hold her to such a promise, but still the promise had been made. And Adaba, listening, had known that she would never be his.

The thought stunned him, though he knew he had no claim on Zulie, and he had never meant to make one. Hadn't he warned her? She could mean nothing to him, nothing of any importance, because he had to leave. And when he did leave, it would be without her. He could ask no woman to share the kind of life he led.

Then why should he now feel such a profound sense of loss?

They watched until Jebediah had disappeared in the darkness, then walked slowly back toward Zulie's cabin. Most of the quarters were asleep by that time, and there was little chance that they would be observed. The night was chilly, even for December, and Adaba impulsively put an arm around Zulie's shoulders, trying to warm her, but she was stiff against his side, as if forever frozen.

She had been like that since the morning of the posse, and he thought he knew why. He knew that the man called Skeet had hurt her. He knew Skeet had beaten her, and he was certain the white man had done worse. Adaha had lain in his dark cramped shelter under the floor, feeling craven, feeling enraged that he could not defend Zulie, and he had heard her cries. Without being able to make out the words, he had heard the harsh muffled whispers. He had heard the rustling of the bed over his head.

Later, when Zulie had released him from his hiding place, he had held the shaking, sickened, frightened girl in his arms for an hour without either of them saying a word. And still later, when he had asked, "Zulie, what that man do?" she had shaken her head and moved away from him, and he had soon come to understand that he was not to ask again. The hurt went too deep for her to speak of it, thus validating his certainty. And now he too had a personal reason for wanting to kill Skeet.

He watched as Zulie laid out her pallet on the floor. When she started building up the fire, he tried to help her, but she brushed him aside. Firewood was precious, but Zulie insisted for his sake on keeping the cabin warm.

He sat on the edge of the bed, pulling off his boots, pulling his shirt over his head, and watched her. When she had finished with the fire, she took off her shoes and, otherwise fully clothed for warmth, slid into her pallet.

"Zulie," he said, "let me sleep there."

"No." She settled in, facing the wall, her back turned to him. He saw only her curled shape and the yellow scarf on her head.

"Please. I'm well enough now. And I'm more used to that kind of bed than—"

"No."

By now he knew better than to argue with her. She could be as strong willed as he. He stared at her back, his sense of loss growing ever stronger, knowing of no way the loss could be avoided.

"Zulie. You going north with your Mr. Jeb?"

"You hear all that?"

"I heard most of what you said."

"Then you hear me promise."

"But he won't hold you to it."

There was no answer, and Adaba wondered why he was talking. And yet he had to keep on, like someone pressing wounded flesh, testing the ache.

"I think you should go with him, Zulie. If what you say is true, that Miss Lucy will let him go north. And let you go with him."

Zulie lay perfectly still. She might have been asleep and unhearing.

"Most what you tell me, you make him sound like a good man. And he sure ain't no uneducated field hand, you're right about that. I knew that 'fore he said six words. I tell you something, Zulie. Nigger goes north, and for plenty it ain't so easy. Free? Maybe. But a nigger can starve up there. And sometimes I think there's more nigger-haters up there than there is down here. No, it ain't easy. But with a man like that Jeb . . . he could maybe be a very important man up there someday. You could be the wife of a very important man."

He sat quietly on the edge of the bed, feeling the ache, feeling the loss, feeling it deepen. Zulie was unnaturally still. He should blow out the candle, he knew, and climb into the bed, but he sat there while the candle burned down another fraction of an inch.

Maybe he should tell her again, he thought. Maybe he should make sure she understood.

He got up from the bed and went to her. He dropped to one knee and put a hand on her blanketed shoulder. Her face was in shadows.

"Zulie, honey, like I said . . . I got no right . . . I can't take no woman off with me to live my kind of life. Oh, I know some do, but it ain't no life for you. . . . Zulie, honey, 'less you got a real need to escape to your freedom, better you stay at Sabrehill than be with me. Sure better than most plantations I seen. . . .

"So you see, that's the only smart choice for you—up north with your Jeb or down here by yourself . . . or with someone else you find. 'Cause I *can't* take you with me—I *won't* take you with me—and if you *was* my woman, you wouldn't hardly see me."

Zulie was utterly unmoving, as if indifferent to every word. He stood up and turned away from her. For Christ's sake, he thought, what kind of fool was he making of himself? But he went on.

"No, you wouldn't hardly see me, and I wouldn't hardly see you. Taking 'em north, weeks and months gonna go by when I can't get back here to you. And always have to take care I don't get caught with you, 'cause that would be bad trouble for you too."

Then, without having planned to, he said what had been inevitable from the moment he had heard Zulie promise herself to Jeb; perhaps even from the moment when she had kissed him and touched his manhood and then torn herself from his arms: "Zulie, I know I ain't got the right . . . but I want you so much . . . care for you so much . . . and if there ain't nobody else for you . . ." Inevitable, yet the hardest question he had ever asked. "If you could see your way clear to being my woman . . . Zulie, darling, if you be my woman . . . I promise you . . ."

He heard her then, a sharp sob like something breaking free within her, a sound like something melting, a sound like none other he had ever heard before. She was on her feet before he could turn back to her. And as she threw herself weeping into his arms, he knew she was his.

Weeping and laughing. The both of them. Weeping and laughing and clinging together. Clinging and moving against each other in the dim and flickering candlelight, beginning the dance of love. Tears slowing and laughter softening, the kisses growing longer and warmer and more languorous, and lightning striking him as her tongue darts swiftly, deeply into his mouth.

Nothing sweeter than this, nothing in his life or in hers. Clothes begin to drop away. She gasps as he strokes her, yields to his touch. He laughs as he finds the knife hanging from her waist and pulls it away. Only one of us needs one of these, he says, and I got it already; and

show me, she says, and he does, and again their laughter
turns to gasps, moans, sobs, as they abandon the last
piece of clothing and kiss, explore, hold, fondle.

Then, naked, they dance to the bed. For a time they
play, prolonging this extraordinary event that has been a
thousand years in arriving, but at last she lets him lay her
back on the bed. Carefully. Gently. And as he approaches
her, rising over her, he sees what a miracle she is—
mounded and hollowed and revealed and hidden. And
she, seeing the miracle of him, must open those nether
lips for him so that he may enter between them with that
lower, scapelike tongue. And enter he does, and tastes
love's mouth. He draws back from her, then tastes again,
deeper. Draws back, and tastes deeper still. And she lifts
her strong thighs high about his chest so that he can drive
in the deepest ever and, with the tip of that tongue, taste
the very source of life.

An ordinary act, more ordinary than murder. More
ordinary than whipping and torture, almost as ordinary
as pain and hatred, even in this dark and violent land.

She lowers her thighs. She plants her heels. Then, after
a moment's rest, they begin again.

No. Wrong. *Not* ordinary. Impossible to conceive that
this could ever be ordinary, that it could have taken place
between any other two people at any time in history.
Once before in her adult life she has had passion, but
without tenderness. And she has had tenderness, but without this passion. But now Erzulie, voodoo goddess of love,
has given her this man, and he and this moment, this
hour, are like no other. He is driving her mindless with
his hard, fast thrusts, burning her mindless, burning away
everything that Skeet has done to her. For five terrible
days she has carried Skeet within her like an evil spirit,
but now, in one great mindless moment, he is driven from
her forever.

Not ordinary at all. Not to lie here, laughing, gasping,
smiling, even talking sweetly, even chattering, while he
takes his pleasure more slowly. Seeing his smile, the smile
she loves more than any other in the world, as he talks to
her and strokes her cheek and kisses her nose, while he
moves slowly, slowly, steadily, steadily, within her. Paus-

ing for a while. Continuing. And he seeing that faraway look come into her eyes as she begins again, ever so slightly, to tighten and strike back at him.

Ordinary, extraordinary. He does not know. He knows only that there was never anything like this in that darkness he came out of, nor will there be in that darkness that he must return to. He, thrusting harder, faster, knows only that he has found his woman, his only woman, his one true mate. He is that kind of man. He must leave her, but he will always return. There will be no other for him. When some creatures die, their mates die too. Perhaps he is one of these.

And so they have each other. She pulls her feet up higher on the bed, so that she can lift herself higher and strike back harder. Her head whips from side to side, and she looks as if she is in pain, as if she is giving birth. His hands cup her shoulders, her fingers claw at his buttocks. And when at the height of her frenzy she stills for an instant and cries out, he is with her. He rises above her at his arms' length. He too is stilled, poised, for a mere instant. And then, in a dozen scalding thrusts, a hundred, a countless number, he throws out his seed, flings it into her, shoots it against the mouth of her womb.

The womb that will one day give, in return, his son. Another Adaba. O little Brown Dove.

Later she lies against him in such a way that they can hold each other intimately, as if claiming possession. Is he asleep?

Guilt gnaws at her. In all the world he is now the person closest to her, and she is the person he should most be able to trust. But she still has not told him about Buck's plans. And she knows she should. He would want to know about them. But if he did know, he would surely insist on helping Buck. And he is not ready yet. His wounds are healing well, but he is still so weak, and it will be a long time before he has his full strength back again. Surely it would be wrong to tell him.

Yet the guilt remains.

Then tell him.

Yes.

But he stirs in her arms. She feels his hand moving over her body, stroking her, and he chuckles softly. No, she must not tell him. Not yet. She must keep him here with her. She must. She must. . . .

Two pairs of large iron hooks were securely fastened to the face of the thick, solid door, and in each pair of hooks lay a beam, holding the door closed. Buck knew there was absolutely no way the door could be opened from the inside.

Shadrach lifted the beams out of the hooks and set them aside. An odor that turned the stomach had already reached Buck's nostrils as they had approached the building, and as Shadrach shoved open the door and quickly stepped back, it became far worse.

Dinkin shoved Buck toward the door. There was little point in resisting, and only the terrible stench made Buck hang back. Dinkin prodded him up one step. Before Buck could take the next, the overseer and Vachel Skeet grabbed his arms and threw him bodily through the doorway. He could do nothing to save himself—his wrists were still tied behind him, and his ankles were connected with a two-foot length of rope—and he fell heavily, painfully to the plank floor.

Then, Skeet's voice again: "And don't think your friend Adaba is gonna get you loose, Buckley. We ain't given up watching for him. I got guards all around this place. Sweet dreams."

The door closed, and Buck heard the beams falling into place.

The stench was overpowering. Buck began to retch.

Somewhere in the darkness a woman laughed. "You, you ain't got no stomach for that, boy?"

Buck raised his head and tried to look around, but he could see nothing in the darkness.

"You get use to it, boy. You get use or you die."

Buck retched again, retched and whimpered, and again the woman laughed, the most mirthless laugh he had ever heard in his life.

"Buck?" another voice whispered. "Buck, that you?"

"Cato . . ."

"Yeah."

A faint scuffing sound, coming closer. Silence. Hands touched Buck's arm and moved lightly along it.

"I'm tied up."

"I get you loose."

"So," the woman said. "Is Buck. Is Black Buck."

Quickly, deftly, Cato's hands found the knot on Buck's wrists and worked it loose.

"Why he put you here, Cato?"

"Well, you tell me get word to these here people what we going do. And Mr. Skeet, he catch me talking to Big Tildy—that's who you hear—so he say, 'You like Big Tildy so much, you go live with her.' So here I is."

"Jesus. I'm sorry, Cato."

"What for? I got word to them, ain't I?"

His wrists free, Buck sat up and worked at the rope on his ankles.

"Buck," Cato said worriedly, "he got you now. We going get out of here, ain't we?"

What could he say? Only one thing. "Hell, yes, we're gonna get out of here."

"When, Buck? Adaba coming after us?"

"Can't say when. Leave that up to Adaba."

But Adaba didn't know he was here. Adaba knew nothing of the rebellion, of the escape to freedom.

Buck shivered and fought his nausea. He put his back against a wall, and Cato laid his blanket over the two of them. The despair he had felt in the office, the great weariness, was almost overwhelming, and he knew he must not communicate it to Cato and the others. He must force himself to believe against all odds that there was still a chance.

"The others here," he said, "they all ready?"

"You open that door, Buck, they follow you anywhere you say. They burn what you say, steal what you say, kill what you say."

"Tell me about them."

"All asleep 'cept Big Tildy. From Haining plantation, meanest nigger you ever know. Tobe, he's Sarah Jane's man, you know about. Josiah and Isaac from Breakline plantation. Hear tell they kill a bad overseer once." Cato laughed. "But you can't hang a couple 'spensive niggers just 'cause they kill a mean-bad overseer. They get whipped bad and sent here to get broken. But that's long ago, and here they is again."

"Any others?"

"Two. Iba and Kimbo, from Harmon. They only talk Gullah, but they understand our talk good."

"That's six. Eight, including us. Eight bad niggers, and that's just fine."

"And Saturday night we be free? . . ."

"Yes. We be free."

They had to be. Buck felt a kind of mad resolve returning to him. No matter how deep his own despair, he could not let these people down. Cato was in this jail house because of him, and he had to do something about it. And he would.

The two men slid down onto the floor and tried to find some position in which they could sleep, but Buck found it impossible to distract himself from the odor that made him want to retch almost every instant. There was something familiar about the smell—bad meat, excrement, decay—but he did not remember the jail ever having been this bad.

"Jesus, Cato," he whispered, "don't old Vachel ever let you clean up in here? How did it ever get this bad? The smell, I mean."

For a moment Cato was silent.

"That there is Joseph," he said.

"What?"

"Joseph, from the Haining plantation. He dead."

"*Dead!*"

"Been dead 'bout four, five day now. Lesson for the niggers."

Somewhere in the darkness Big Tildy laughed.

Somehow he managed to snatch an hour's sleep, but the nausea and the retching began again the moment he awakened. He heard the rattling of chains. The overseer was yelling: "Come on, you black bastards, get your lazy asses up and out of there, come on, come on, come on!" Buck and Cato struggled to their feet and followed the others out the door. On his way out, Buck saw a small dark form lying unmoving on the floor. The last of Joseph.

It was not yet first light, and a couple of torches burned nearby. There was light in the office. Buck filled his lungs with the comparatively fresh air a few yards from the jail house, and his stomach eased. He looked about. From now on, he must be watching every instant for a chance to escape. His seven companions, he noted, stayed in a small group, almost huddled together, as if trained to do so. When he tried to stray away from them, a guard immediately raised a whip and ordered him back. Of the group, he was the only one who was not chain-hobbled. There were only three guards, two with whips and one with a rifle—Buck recognized none of them—but they all kept their distance, and the hobbles made running impossible. There would be no way to evade a rifle shot.

But there had to be a way. . . .

"Buckley," a cheerful voice called. "Buckley Skeet, boy, you get over here!"

It was Vachel, coming out of the office. As Buck went to meet him, walking slowly, watchfully, Dinkin moved in on his right, and Shadrach, a coiled whip in hand, came out of the darkness on his left, the two of them flanking him.

When Vachel stopped, six feet away, Buck stopped too. Vachel stood, hands on hips, and smiled. "Buckley," he said, "just so we get off on the right foot, so to speak . . . just so we know where we stand . . ."

Shadrach grinned. His whip arm went back, and the whip uncoiled. He shot it forward with all his strength. The whip caught Buck across the shoulders, like the rip of a deep-cutting claw. He fell past Vachel and found himself on his hands and knees, a terrible inrush of breath scouring his tightened throat, a harsh groan following. Somewhere, distantly, he heard Dinkin's hyena-laugh.

And so began his first day back at Redbird.

His first task was to go back into the jail house, back past that corpse and into that stench, to get the ropes that had bound him. His second task was to retie his own ankles. "Gonna have new chains made for you special,"

Vachel said, as Buck sat on the ground tying the knots. "Been needing some made up. But meantime this'll do fine." When Buck was done, Vachel squatted down to inspect the job. He looked up at Shadrach and nodded. This time Buck half-expected the blow, but the anticipation only made it worse. He waited, feeling the muscles tense in his still-burning back. And waited, the seconds stretching out. And waited. When the blow came, it sent him rolling to one side, and this time, in spite of all effort to stop it, a cry of pain tore from his throat.

"Now, untie that hobble," Vachel said, "and tie it again, and this time do it right."

When the hobble was tied to Vachel's satisfaction, Shadrach and Dinkin marched him to the kitchen house in the slave quarters where the other seven were having their breakfast. He was given some mush on a shingle, to be eaten with his fingers. The stench of the jail house, the pain of his back, had taken away all appetite, but he forced the food down his throat. No escape was possible if he failed to keep up his strength.

After the breakfast had been hastily downed, Buck was given his next task. Dinkin called him and Big Tildy over. He tossed each one a shovel, and Buck noted with a certain grim satisfaction that he took care not to get too close to either of them: there was a touch of fear in the man's eyes. When he lost that fear, when he became careless . . .

"You two got a grave to dig," he said. "You dig it deep, and you dig it fast, 'cause if you don't, you know what you get."

He had been right that night, more than two weeks before, when he had come stumbling through the graveyard, carrying Adaba on his shoulders: he had been on Redbird Plantation. The half-dozen or so candles, broken now, still lay scattered about the roots of the witching tree. Zulie's work, putting a curse on Vachel Skeet— might it send him to some everlasting voodoo hell.

As dawn broke, a guard marked off a rectangle, and they began to dig, Buck at one end and Big Tildy at the other. The two guards with which they had been honored stood watching them, one on each side of the grave, and kept their distance. The work soon brought a sweat, cool though the day was, and when Buck paused to wipe his forehead, he felt a whip across his shoulders for a third time that day. It was a light blow, hardly comparable to the others, but it hurt, and it brought new fire to the earlier cuts.

Buck looked angrily at the guard. "Why you do that?"

"You hear Mr. Dinkin," the man said nervously. "He say deep and fast. You ain't done fast, we in trouble too. Now, you get digging, nigger. You hear me, dig!"

Buck dug.

Without seeming to, he watched Big Tildy. She was big boned and muscular and one of the tallest—altogether one of the biggest—women Buck had ever seen. Hot hard eyes and a mouthful of rotten teeth that she might have chewed a guard up with—*a real evil nigger woman,* Buck thought, *and maybe a little crazy, just like me.* The grave grew deeper, and Buck wondered: if only he could get Big Tildy out of the grave, if she had the wit to distract one of the guards . . .

"Tildy, you get out of here and rest," he said. "Hell, we're just in each other's way in this hole."

The whip came across his shoulders, harder this time. Buck cursed and grabbed at it, but the guard yanked it away. "You don't talk, goddam you," he said. "You hear me, you don't talk! Mr. Dinkin hear you, he cut your damn tongue out."

"What the hell's the matter with you, man?" Buck shouted back. "You hit a black man without reason, what the hell kind of driver are you, you do that—"

"I don't hit you, some bastard nigger going hit me, you don't know that? There going be a bastard nigger around here, he going be *me!* Now, shut your goddam mouth and *dig!*"

He went back to digging, but continued to stay alert for an opportunity. With or without Tildy's help, it might be possible for him to overcome both guards. Put on a show of greater weariness and pain than he felt. Lure a guard into carelessness, then—one blow of the shovel. Go after the other guard, run him off, fight him off, kill him.

Only one guard with a whip—what the hell. *Old Vaych,* he thought, *you're being mighty careful, putting two guards on me, but you've got the meanest, baddest nigger on your hands you ever dreamed of.*

Still, Vachel Skeet knew what he was doing, and two guards who kept their distance and handled their whips well could cut Buck to ribbons in a minute, and Buck knew it. And when the grave was dug, he still had not found his chance. But he kept on looking for it, looked for it every step of the way back to the jail house.

"Now," Vachel said, "bury that little piece of shit."

Joseph.

Buck was not sure he could force himself back into the jail house. To his shame, he was not sure he could make himself touch the corpse that had once been a black brother. Perhaps Big Tildy saw that. She glanced at Buck and said, "I get him." It was the first thing he had heard her say that morning.

Stolid-faced, the woman entered the jail house. A moment later she reappeared with Joseph in her arms. As she walked toward them, Buck had all he could do not to close his eyes and turn away.

"Where the box?" Big Tildy asked.

Vachel smiled. "What? What box?"

Big Tildy frowned. "Where the box for him?"

"Don't need no box for the likes of that, Tildy."

The woman stared at Vachel as if she could not believe what she had heard. Not even a white man could be this low.

She turned back toward the jail house. "I wrap him in a blanket."

"Oh, no, you ain't gonna waste no blanket like that."

"I give him my blanket," Tildy said without looking around. "Put Joseph's blanket on top of the grave." She started toward the jail house.

"Hell, no, you ain't gonna waste none of my good blankets!" Vachel yelled. "Stop her!"

The whip sizzled through the air and caught Big Tildy across the back. She stopped in her tracks, but otherwise gave no sign that she had felt the blow. Blood slowly seeped through her dress.

"Now, carry him out to the grave," Vachel said. "Let's stop wasting time."

This time Vachel accompanied them to the graveyard, he and the two guards walking behind. Buck, walking beside Big Tildy, tried to keep from retching, and the effort brought tears to his eyes. He hated himself for it. This thing in Big Tildy's arms had been a man, after all, and deserving of more respect than this primitive revulsion. Big Tildy's face showed utterly nothing.

The walk to the graveyard seemed to take forever. Halfway there, Buck forced himself to say it: "You want me to carry him?"

"No."

"He your man?"

"No. My friend."

They reached the gravesite at last. Big Tildy very gently, very respectfully laid Joseph down beside it. She stood up, her face still impassive.

"A moment of silence for the dear departed," Vachel said, and immediately added, "All right, Tildy, dump him in."

Big Tildy made no move.

"I said, dump him in, goddam it."

Big Tildy was a statue carved from dark African wood.

"Kick him in, God damn you! I'm telling you—"

"No." Big Tildy's hands went to her mouth. Great tears appeared in her eyes. "No, it ain't right."

"Jesus Christ, I ain't got all day—"

"No box, no blanket, it ain't right, Mr. Skeet!"

"Look, you big bitch, if you don't—"

The tears poured from Big Tildy's eyes. "No, no, no, no," she sobbed. "Ain't right to treat Joseph that way, Mr. Skeet! It ain't right, it ain't right, it ain't—"

This time, when the whip cut across Big Tildy's back, Buck knew she felt it. He felt it himself. And he could not stand it. He never knew how he had reached the guard, how, hobbled, he had flung himself so far. But he was on the guard's back, had the guard's whip in hand, was twisting it around the guard's throat. Was strangling the man, was dragging him to the ground, was trying to break his neck. A whip cut across Buck's back, but that didn't matter. He was killing, killing, killing—

Until the blow across the side of his head.

He found himself lying on the ground beside Joseph. He heard the guard he had attacked painfully sucking air. He heard Vachel laugh. It seemed to Buck that Vachel did a lot of laughing these days. A very happy man.

"All right, Buck," he said. "You asked for it. Now you gonna get it."

Vachel had made certain improvements at Redbird. In the slave quarters he had planted two tall posts several feet apart, with a pole extended across the top of them. This was the whipping scaffold. Cato had told Buck about it. Sometimes, after a whipping, the victim would hang crucified from it for a full day or longer.

After having Buck stripped by the guards, Vachel personally tied a rope to each of his wrists. The ropes were tossed over the top corners of the scaffold, and Buck was hoisted up, a wrist to each corner. His legs were spread and an ankle tied to each post. He was almost two feet off the ground and thus visible to every slave who had been brought to watch. Every straining at the bonds, every humiliation could be seen.

And they were all there, to the last man, woman, and child on Redbird, for this was an occasion. Buck looked out at all the faces and, except for the younger children, was surprised at the number he still knew. He thought he recognized Jared, who had spoiled his clothes all those years ago *("You just 'nother nigger . . . you dirty nigger slave!")*, but there was no triumph on the man's face now. A few of the faces showed an odd fascination, but most of those present looked humiliated and sick. Serena took one look at Buck and hung her head and wept.

Jeppson and Bassett had stopped by Redbird by some chance, or more likely because Vachel had sent for them. Together with Dinkin, they grinned up at him.

"He sure ain't hung with much, is he?" Bassett said contemptuously. "Not much for a nigger."

"It's fear that does that to 'em," Jeppson said with relish, "fear and pain and cold. Put old Buckley to stud, and I reckon he's good as any of 'em. But right now he knows what's a-coming."

"I still say he ain't got much. Not like Shad here, I bet. Ain't that right, Shad?"

Shadrach grinned and turned to Vachel. "How many you want me give him, Mr. Skeet? Thirty-nine now and another thirty-nine—"

"None yet. I got something to say first." Vachel looked around at the silent black faces. "Now, you all listen to me," he said loudly. "You all know who this is hanging up here, don't you?"

There was no answer.

"Yes, you all know. This here is your old friend Buckley. Buckley Skeet, called hisself. Black Buck, that's who. You all hear of Black Buck—killer, burner, marooner?"

And still no answer.

"Some Sabrehill niggers thought they was gonna sic him on me. Gonna voodoo him back on me. If they did, all they did was help me, 'cause I been looking for Black Buck for twelve years. Slave runs from me, I don't never give up! There just ain't no getting away from Mr. Vachel Skeet, you all hear me? There just ain't no getting away!"

Somewhere in the crowd a child began to cry.

"Now, I treat you all good. Good enough food, good enough clothes, more whiskey than you deserve, and time off for a little pleasuring. I treated Buckley good too, better than any other nigger was ever treated. But he abused me, Buckley did, he abused me and run off. Run off for twelve years." Vachel took a deep breath and shouted his final words. "And for the next twelve years, you niggers, you gonna see what an ungrateful nigger gets! You gonna see, starting now!"

You niggers could kill him, Buck thought, shaking, *you could kill them all four, but you won't. Not without me. Even though they're gonna kill you all, sooner or later.*

Vachel turned to Shad. "You lay it on now, you lay it on so it hurts. I'll tell you when to stop. But I don't want him so crippled up he can't work tomorrow. I want him working even if it's on his knees. Now, get to it. Lay it on."

Later they threw him back into the jail house and tossed his clothes in after him. But he just lay there naked in the cold and the stench, unable to move. He had not been hobbled again: he wasn't going anywhere.

He heard the others coming in that evening. "Black Buck," one of them said softly, with a kind of pitying contempt. *"He* the one going take us all away from here?"

Gonna, Buck said silently. *Gonna . . . gonna . . . gonna . . .* But it was more a prayer than a promise.

A tap-tap-tap-tapping. She wanted to dream it was a woodpecker in a tree over the stream where she and Adaba bathed so happily together on a sunny spring afternoon. She wanted to keep on dreaming in the warmth of Adaba's arms. But . . .

The tapping grew louder. Stopped. Became a pounding. And then she was awake, alarmed, because who could be at her door at this hour?

She slipped out of bed, careful not to disturb Adaba, and wrapped the top blanket around her bare body. Shivering, she hurried to the door.

"Who that?" she whispered.

"Serena."

Now? in the middle of the night? Serena?

"Please. Let me in."

But Zulie could not do that. She glanced over her shoulder to see that Adaba lay still; then, drawing the blanket more tightly about her, she opened the door and stepped outside.

"Serena, how you get here!"

"I run. Run most ever' step of the way. And I got to run back. Shad drunk, but if he wake and find me gone—oh, Zulie!" Serena sounded as if she had been crying, and now she burst into tears again.

"Now, don't you do that. He ain't going find out—"

"Oh, it ain't that! It's Buck, Zulie, Buck!"

The sense of alarm grew. "What about Buck?"

"Mr. Skeet, he—he catch Buck, Zulie."

Impossible. Impossible after all this time, after all their efforts, after all they had gone through.

"Serena, you—are—wrong! You don't know! Why, Mr. Skeet, he can't never catch Buck, he—"

"I tell you true! He got him, he got him now! I seen . . ."

Serena told all she knew . . . how Buck had been caught by two guards at Redbird on Thursday night . . . how on Friday morning he had been put to work . . . how he had attacked one of his guards and been whipped and even now lay in the Skeet jail house.

"And this the first chance I get to come tell you. . . ."

When Zagreus had mentioned that Buck had been gone on Thursday night, Zulie had not been surprised or concerned. Buck had frequently stayed overnight at other plantations. She had been a little surprised when he had not reappeared by Friday evening, but the fact was that all day long Adaba had been on her mind far more than Buck's plans. She had only been waiting for evening, waiting for the time when she could return to her cabin and once more slip into Adaba's arms, and . . .

"There ain't going be no runaway," Serena wept. "Never be free now. And poor Buck, Mr. Skeet kill him, you wait and see."

No runaway, no escape for those who had so long dreamed of freedom—the thought was intolerable. "Now, you listen to me, Serena. It's all going happen. Just like Buck planned."

"But if we got no Buck—"

"Who all you tell this?"

"Nobody, just you."

"Then don't tell nobody, nobody at all."

"Everybody know soon. Mr. Skeet ain't keeping it quiet, how he catch Buck. Tomorrow, next day—"

"You all be gone by then. You all going run off tonight, Saturday night, just like we planned."

"But how—"

"I don't know yet. But anybody asks you, you say nothing is changed. Tell them Buck say, do just like he told you. You taking care of Mr. Skeet's dogs tonight?"

"Yes. Poison them. Beat their head, if'n I got to."

"You do that. From what you say, Buck is a long way from dead yet. And he'll get out of that jail house somehow."

"Ain't *nobody* ever get out of that jail house."

"Serena!" Zulie raised her hand. In her sudden anger she could have slapped the other woman's face off. "Serena, you do like I say, or I take it out of your hide! I ain't going let nothing stop us now!"

"All right. All right, I do like Buck say."

"And best you get back to Redbird now, before Shadrach find you gone."

Serena hurried off into the night.

Couldn't let them be stopped now, couldn't!

But what could she do, what was the best thing?

When she went back into the cabin, Adaba startled her by asking, "Who was that?"

"Just a gal had trouble with her man. Wanted me to give her a love spell." Zulie put the blanket back on the bed and slid in beside Adaba.

"Love spell," he said sleepily, as he stroked her tense body. "You put a love spell on me, Zulie? Sure don't need none."

At any other time she would not have allowed him to drift back to sleep, not yet, but now she was glad when he did. She had to think.

What should she do? What should she do?

Two

"All right, you lazy niggers, come on, let's go, let's get your lazy asses out of there!"

Gonna get away from here . . . gonna get these niggers free . . . gonna . . .

He awakened to the sound of Dinkin's voice, with the idea of escape still pounding in his head. He found himself fully clothed and wrapped in a blanket, though he had no idea of how he had got that way. Then he remembered Big Tildy's gentle hands.

"Come on, you lazy niggers!"

"Tonight, Buck?" Cato whispered as he helped Buck, shivering, to his feet. "We still do it tonight?"

"Yes. Tonight."

Gonna get away from here. He had to believe that. Had to. Even if he were not free to burn Redbird, signaling the nearby plantations, something would happen to set the rebellion off. His people were ready; surely nothing could hold them back. And they would come here, they would storm Redbird, they would open up the jail house . . . something would happen.

Every muscle ached, and he felt as stiff as old dried-up leather, but with Cato's help, he went out into the yard with the other prisoners. Once again they huddled together, watched by the guards in the light of the torches. Once again Vachel stepped out of the office and called to Buck. Buck could only move slowly toward him, but he held his head high and tried to keep his dignity.

Vachel grinned. "Reckon we ain't even gonna have to hobble you today, are we, Buckley? Feeling a mite stiff, are you?"

Buck waited for Vachel to say something worth answering.

"Well, you gonna have an easy day today, don't you worry. Noticed you didn't much like the smell of that dead nigger yesterday. Can't say I blame you. So I'm gonna give you a chance to get that smell out of the jail house. What you gonna do today is scrub it down. Scrub it and scrub it with hot soap and water, and then scrub it some more, and see if you can't get rid of that smell. You think you'd like that job?"

Buck stared at Vachel.

"What's the matter, Buck? You figure on not talking to me no more?"

"Ain't got much to say to you, have I, Vachel?"

Vachel laughed and slapped his thigh. Happy Vachel.

Scrubbing out the jail house was not an easy job. The terrible smell began to bother Buck again, but he learned to fight it by filling his nostrils with the clean odor of the strong soap. He worked steadily all morning, pausing only to relieve himself at an outhouse, and the guard, who stood in the open doorway, never once touched him with his whip. Once Vachel stopped by and said, "Come on, Buckley, put your back into it. Let's see those elbows move," and Buck increased his pace. Vachel told the guard, "Now, just see he keeps going like that," and walked away. After a moment the guard said, "It's all right, he ain't looking now," and Buck laughed. At least this guard wasn't the same poor frightened bastard he had had yesterday.

Noon passed. The dinner hour came. Buck was astonished to be handed a full plate of excellent food: ham, yams, corn bread, and gravy, and plenty of it, served up hot. It was as good as the best he had got at Sabrehill. When he had finished eating, the guard allowed him a full half-hour's dozing in the cool wintry sunlight before putting him back to work.

He scrubbed the jail house repeatedly, scrubbed it and doused it down. He noticed the webs and spider balls in the rafters, knocked them down with a broom, crushed them, and washed some more. By the middle of the afternoon, Buck realized what a favor Vachel had done him in giving him this kind of work. In spite of his fatigue, he was gradually working the pain from his muscles, and as the pain went, his hopes rose sharply. He found himself with a kind of heady optimism, feeling better than at any time since his capture. Of course everything was going to be all right. Evening was coming on, and before long the runaways from the farthest plantations would be starting toward Sabrehill. Possibly some of them had started already. Yes, by God, tonight they would rise up.

In the late afternoon, a boy came, saying that Buck was to finish his work and go see Mr. Skeet in the office. Buck washed away the last of the soap and returned his bucket and brush to the storehouse. He found Vachel lounging back in a chair, one boot up on the table, and his jug at his elbow.

"Sit down, Buckley," he said. "But not too close. You'd likely kill me if you had a chance."

Buck glanced at the guard, who had stayed just outside the door. "Don't worry, Vaych," he said, "I ain't moving so fast these days."

"Well, I am. So don't try nothing, or I'll kick your silly goddam teeth in."

Buck glanced at the jug. Vachel had been drinking, all right.

Vachel noticed the glance. "Want one, Buckley?"

"No, thank you, Vachel."

Vachel nodded his approval. "Polite goddam nigger. You always was a polite nigger, Buckley."

"If you say so, Vachel."

Vachel put a finger through the jug handle, rolled the jug to his shoulder, and took a large sip. He rolled the jug back down and set it back on the table. Swallowed and sighed.

"God," he said. "Remember how Saturday afternoons you and me'd come in here after work . . . sit down and have a couple of drinks . . . and talk about what we'd done and all we was gonna do?"

"Yeah, I remember."

"I'll tell you something. Every once in a while I wish we could be like that again. In spite of everything that happened. It hits me like a pain in the gut, if only . . . we could . . ." Vachel's gaze was distant; after a moment he pulled it back. "You ever feel that way, Buckley?"

He had. Not often, but a time or two. And he had hated himself for it, had felt that he was betraying Claramae.

"What the hell's the difference, Vaych?"

"Yeah, you're right, what the hell's the difference?" Vachel brightened. "Hey! Enjoy your work today?"

"I've done worse, and harder, right here at Redbird."

"And dinner was good, wasn't it?"

"Excellent, Vachel, excellent."

"Excellent!" Vachel laughed. The man could not stop laughing these days. He was happy as a lover. "You know, Buckley, I been thinking about you, thinking about you hard."

"I bet you have, Vaych."

"Want to know what I been thinking?"

"No, but I can't stop you telling me."

"That's right." Vachel thumped his boot down from the table. He hunched forward in his chair, elbows on knees, and looked at Buck with shining eyes. "Black Buck," he said. "Outlier. Burner. Slave-stealer. A real wild, savage nigger. That's supposed to be you. And if it is, I bet you got all kinds of crazy ideas about how you gonna bust outa the jail house, how you gonna set Redbird on fire, ain't that right? Ideas about Adaba is gonna come rescue you, ideas about stealing my niggers away, all kinds of crazy ideas, ain't that right, now? Ain't it?"

Oh, you bastard.

Vachel grinned and pointed a forefinger at Buck's face, as if he saw something there. "Ah? Ah-ha? Ha? That's right, ain't it! I guessed right, didn't I?"

There was a leaden, sinking sensation in Buck's guts. He felt as if Vachel had been listening in on his thoughts and laughing at them. As if Vachel were determined to rob him of every last hope.

But he only said, "Why, whatever made you think that, Massa Vachel, suh?"

Vachel dismissed the matter with a wave of his hand and sat back in his chair. "Whatever you been thinking, forget it. I got niggers all over this place just looking for that Adaba. Wish to God he *would* come here after you. But that ain't all I been thinking. I been thinking I was wrong, Buckley."

"Wrong, Vaych?"

"Yeah. Wrong about punishing you all the next twelve years or longer. Oh, I got to punish you all right, and you never gonna know when I'm gonna put that wire on you and maybe pull it all the way next time. But, hell, I don't want you, like I said, *hoping* to die, maybe pining yourself away or cutting your own throat. Hell, no, I want you begging to *live!* Now, don't that make more sense?"

"I don't understand you, Vachel." But Buck feared that he did.

"I want you begging to live, Buckley, and that means you got to have something to live *for*. You don't want to die *now*, do you?"

"No."

" 'Course not. You live on hope. And another thing you live on is small pleasures. So you just think about that nice dinner you had today and sitting in the sun for a while after. You're gonna have lots of nice dinners like that Buckley, you really are. You believe me?"

"Yes, Vachel. I believe you."

"Sure, you do. You're my slave, Buckley, and I got to punish you for what you done. And I'm gonna punish you, my Christ, how I'm gonna punish you. But that ain't all of it. Hell, we're gonna have some *good* times together, Buckley, lots of good times, just like in the old days. Reckon you still like a woman from time to time? Well, you're gonna have a woman, yes, sir, you are. You don't want to live in that damn jail house all the time. Well, by God, you ain't gonna have to live there all the time. We'll build you a nice little brick cabin all your own, lock you up in it nights, let you stay there with your woman. My God, you're gonna live *good,* Buckley, better than most niggers ever dream of!

"But anytime . . . when I figure it's time . . . when you make one little mistake, or maybe just when I damn well feel like it . . . it's all gonna change. You're gonna find yourself back in the jail house. You're gonna find yourself up on that whipping rack again or maybe tied to this table with the wire 'round your cock. And every time a week or a month or six months goes by, and you figure, oh, hell, old Vaych has got tired of it and given up . . . it's gonna happen again, worse than ever.

"The way I see it, that can happen a hundred times or five hundred or a thousand before you die, Buck. All you ever gonna know is, it can go on like that for years . . . or *this* time, while the wire's tightening around your cock, *this* time may be the last.

"You think you ain't gonna learn to beg?"

Buck saw it: the rest of his life, being reduced to Vachel's plaything. Slowly having all resistance, all dignity eroded away by small hopes, random pleasures, and the fear of pain as much as the pain itself. A life of watching Vachel's every movement, every look, every reaction. A life of cringing and fawning and groveling, in spite of himself. A life rewarded by a bit of good food, warm enough clothing, an occasional casual fuck.

And then, once again, the pain, the horror.

A slave's life. A nigger's life.

Vachel laughed. "Know what you're thinking. Thinking I'm giving you up to twelve years to get loose again and somehow kill me, ain't that right?"

Yes! Buck thought, trying to believe it. *Yes!*

"It ain't gonna happen, of course, but I want you to think that. That's what they call hope. You gonna hang onto it till I'm ready to take it away from you. And then . . . Sure you wouldn't like a little drink, Buckley?"

But Vachel Skeet was killing hope better than he knew. As Buck walked slowly back to the jail house, he had never felt more defeated. And ready to die.

Carefully, so as not to be seen, Adaba looked out the north window of Zulie's cabin. The shortest days of the year had come, and the sun was already lowering in the west, but he could hazily see into some woods to the north, between the field quarters and the road. There was some movement in those woods: several people and a mule. Perhaps a couple of mules.

What were they doing there?

He knew that six days a week some of the hands passed through those woods on their way to and from the fields. But this was Saturday, and the hands had long ago come back to the quarters. By now they would have completed most of their home chores and would be looking forward to supper. And after that there would be the Saturday night celebration. Why would anyone want to loiter in the woods at this hour—and with mules?

He knew why *he* might want to. Or Buck.

He didn't like it.

Well, he would find out.

He wandered restlessly away from the window, prowling the cabin like a caged animal, stretching and straining his muscles until he shook. He felt housebound, and the books Zulie had "borrowed" from the big house library no longer distracted him. *Time to get away from here,* he. thought. Past time. He was still far from fully recovered, still quite weak, but he thought he could travel and survive now, at least with Buck's help.

But where was Buck? Adaba had hardly seen him since the posse had come to Sabrehill. Come to think of it, not since . . . Wednesday. Three days now. And he hadn't taken care of Skeet and lit out, or Adaba would have heard. Buck should have been right here at Sabrehill, lying low. Then what the hell was he up to?

That was another thing Adaba would have to find out.

There was a tapping at the door, Zag's tap. Adaba checked carefully at the window before letting him in. To his surprise, Zag handed him a plate of food. Surprise, because it was quite early for supper. One more little thing that was not quite right.

"So soon, Zag?"

"Zulie ask me to fetch it to you. Guess Miss Lucy's been keeping her real busy at the big house."

"Well, thank you, Zag."

"Oh, you're real welcome, Ada—I mean Johnny." Zag turned to leave. "Well, I better—"

"Wait a minute, old son."

There was something out of the ordinary in Zag's manner, something hurried, nervous, excited. Maybe all he wanted to do was get back to that pretty little Binnie gal of his. But with everything else . . .

He smiled at Zag. "Want to tell me about it?"

Zag's face went blank. "About what?"

Adaba winked and nodded his head toward the north window—toward the woods. "Oh, you know," he said. Sometimes it worked, sometimes it did not.

"No . . . no . . ." Zag looked confused, almost too puzzled. He wiped his palms on his pants. "No, I don't know what you mean, Johnny."

"Those people out in the woods, out north of here."

Zag went to the window and looked out. "Ain't nobody out there now."

Adaba looked, and indeed, the figures in the woods had disappeared. But he said, "Oh, they're out there, all right. They just moved farther back. Like they was hiding. If you don't know what they're doing there, maybe you ought to tell Mr. Jeb. Ask him to come out here and talk to me. Maybe together, him and me—"

"Oh, there ain't nobody out there, Johnny," Zag said too quickly, too positively. "You think you saw somebody out there, I go look myself. I find somebody out there, I find out what they doing and come back and tell you. Why don't I do that, just go out there myself? And I'll come back and tell you."

So Zag knew something. Something he did not want Adaba to know. Adaba, still smiling, kept a steady gaze on him, but he did not wish to alienate the man by pressing too hard.

"It's all right, Zag. You don't have to go out there. But please get word to Zulie that I want to see her just as soon as possible."

Zag gave assurance that he would do exactly that and left hurriedly.

Answers, Adaba thought. One way or another, he intended to have them.

Standing in the dark of the portico, holding the supper tray, Lucy shivered and listened.

Silence.

It seemed to her that as the evening grew darker, Sabrehill grew quieter. And on this night, the Saturday night before Christmas, that was wrong, all wrong. This was traditionally a night of merrymaking. Momma Lucinda and Maybelle and Olympia should have been chattering happily in the kitchen house. Irish should have been teasing the maids. There should have been happy shouts in the darkness and bits of music floating over the fields.

Instead—silence.

Once again she remembered that nightmare evening less than three weeks ago when her people had damned her with silence and had moved in on the office, all those pairs of eyes staring, unblinking, waiting, sowing terror in her heart. It had been one of the few times she had been afraid, truly afraid, of her own people.

But she refused to think of that now. Refused. She had Justin to think of.

Followed by Zulie and Reba, she carried the tray into

the house to the downstairs bedchamber. Zulie and Reba ever so carefully lifted Justin, helping him sit up just enough to put pillows behind him. It was a slow and painful process. Lucy put the tray on the bedside table. She laid a napkin across Justin's chest and sat down on the edge of the bed, preparing to feed him. She picked up a bowl of broth and a spoon.

"Please, Lucy," he said, his first words since she had entered the room. His face was pale and drawn, and he had given her nothing but the bleakest and wannest of smiles since regaining consciousness.

She knew what he meant. "But you need help, Justin."

"No, really. I can manage."

"But I want to help you."

He frowned slightly and barely shook his head, and she knew her insistence would only upset him.

She tried to understand. A man who had suffered a brutal beating and been left with a half-dozen or more broken ribs, wanted nothing more than to be left alone, to be left to sleep and to mend. But there were things that had to be done for him, some of them not very pleasant things, and she wanted to do them. She was his woman, not merely his "lady." But he seemed humiliated that she wished to help him. He did not even wish her to see him being helped by others, though she knew he had little objection to Reba feeding him when she was out of the room. She felt that out of some strange, twisted pride he was rejecting her, and it hurt.

But she had pride of her own, and she pretended to shrug the matter off. She put the bowl and spoon back on the tray and stood up from the bed. Zulie had already left the room, so she turned to Reba. "Stay with him," she said. "Give him his food as he wants it, and whatever help he needs." But Reba knew by now what to do. Lucy promised to look in on Justin later, knowing he would probably be asleep. They had said so little in the last six days, and he had seemed so distant, that she sometimes had the feeling that he had departed from Sabrehill on that terrible Sunday morning.

She returned to the kitchen house. Again, as she walked

along the portico, she felt, as much as she heard, the silence.

Momma Lucinda was still there, along with Leila. Neither said anything as Lucy entered the room.

"Well," she said with forced gaiety, "I must say, this is a lively Saturday night!"

"Yeah," Leila said quietly, "everybody celebrating. Celebrating how for three days that damn posse rode all over everywhere, starting right here. Celebrating who got raped and who got whipped and who got his arm broke like our Nemo. Celebrating houses broke in and belongings busted. Celebrating Ettalee dead."

Lucy's face burned. She wondered how she could have been so insensitive. She wanted to say, *I'm sorry,* to ask for pardon, but she was not at all certain she had the right even to do that.

She said, instead, after a moment: "Yes, of course. I think I'll go out to the field quarters and see if there's anything I can—"

"Now, don't you do that!" Momma Lucinda cut in sharply. "Just you stay away from out there!"

"Yeah, Lucy-child," Leila said more slowly, "maybe you better just stay away from there for a while, specially at night."

And yet again she saw those staring eyes in the dark. "Do you mean to say I wouldn't be safe—"

"Miss Lucy," Lucinda said, "them people been all stirred up, and they're sorrowing. And maybe some of them loves you, but some of them hates you, and even them that loves you—"

She broke off, as if she were saying too much. And Lucy remembered a warning Jebediah had given her long before: even those of her people who loved her, even a Momma Lucinda, would be capable of harming her when they grieved for the crippled, wasted lives of their own enslaved children.

And of course, he was right. The danger was there, never more than tonight.

Then what was she to do?

She had to talk to Jebediah. He would know.

A light glowed in his house on the other side of the courtyard, and she thought she saw his shadowy figure on the porch. After giving her promise not to visit the field quarters, she hurried across the courtyard. Jebediah stood up to greet her.

She went right to the point. "Jebediah, we've got trouble on our hands, haven't we?"

He did not soothe her fears by pretending not to know what she was talking about. "We may, Miss Lucy. Bad feeling has been building up for a long time, and especially since Mr. Skeet carried off Ettalee a month ago. And now, these last few days . . . I get the idea it's spread all up and down the river, thanks to Mr. Skeet and that posse."

"But is anything going to happen *here*? I mean, might our people . . ." She left the worst unsaid.

"I don't think so, but I truly don't know. Miss Lucy, if it'll make you feel better, I can put some armed men around the big house. Do it discreetly . . ."

Far from making her feel better, the thought frightened her.

"Do you think it's necessary?"

"It's just a suggestion."

"Who would you trust with arms?"

"Zagreus. Maybe Orion. Cheney. Myself."

"Well . . . I don't like the idea, but do as you think best."

"Don't worry about it. Leave it to me."

"Thank God for you, Jebediah."

Lucy walked slowly back to the big house, feeling oddly exposed and vulnerable. *Nothing is going to happen,* she thought, *nothing bad, nothing at all*. Tomorrow would bring Christmas one day closer, and the danger would pass, would be forgotten. Yes, the people grieved, they were wretched, they were in pain, but Christmas was, somehow, the anodyne, and if only they could reach it . . . Lucy clung to the hope.

"I think he knows."

"Zag, how can he? He ain't hardly been out of my house, and who going tell him—"

"He knows, Zulie. That man look right through you and smile and smile and ask questions, just teasing at you, and all the time he *knows!* He seen them people out in the woods, they come from the Haining place and get here *way* too early, and right away he starts figuring. And you know Adaba ain't no fool."

Zulie considered. "Well, I reckon he was bound to find out sooner or later. Or have to be told. But he still ain't all well, and Buck didn't want him all worried and fretting."

"He say for you to come see him."

"I will, first chance I get."

But the chance did not come until well after dark. The day had been an agony. From the moment she had spoken with Serena, Zulie had thought of nothing but Buck and how he could be saved. Everything depended upon that, everything they had hoped for, everything they had planned. She had consulted no one but Saul and Zag.

"Tell Adaba?"

"No," Saul had said. "Ain't no use in that. I get Buck away from Mr. Skeet, don't you worry."

But now she looked forward to sharing the entire matter with Adaba and being rid of the guilt feelings that haunted her for not having confided in him before.

When she entered the cabin, he gave her a bearlike hug that lifted her from her feet, and he kissed her long and hard. His strength was coming back just fine, she thought—as if she had not known that from the last two nights! And tonight, after Buck and his people were on their way . . .

Adaba set her back on the floor. "You kept me waiting a long time, woman!"

"I'm sorry. Been running around like a chicken with its head cut off."

"Well, now you're back, honey, and I got some questions to ask."

" 'Bout . . . 'bout Buck, I reckon."

"About Buck . . . and maybe some other things. Things that been going on around here, Zulie. But since you thinking about Buck, first you tell me about him."

"Well, the thing is . . ." Zulie hesitated. How to tell

him? "First of all, Adaba, maybe this ain't bad as it sounds. But Buck . . . I just hear about it this morning." Nothing to do but blurt it out. "Couple nights back, Mr. Skeet—he done catch Buck."

Adaba's face was suddenly that of a stranger looking at a stranger. It was a moment before he could speak. "Skeet caught Buck?"

"But like I say, maybe it ain't so bad—"

"Oh, Lord." All of Adaba's newly gained strength seemed to drain from him as he sank into a chair. "Oh, Lord. I warned him. I tried to tell him. After all this time, he has to go and get hisself caught. How did it happen?"

"It was night 'fore last. Guess Buck was snooping 'round Redbird, and Mr. Skeet had guards out watching him. And Serena—that's a gal from Redbird—she say two them guards catch him. But, Adaba, we think he's all right! Yesterday Mr. Skeet work him and—and whip him, but he ain't dead! He's just there waiting, waiting for us to come get him out!"

Adaba did not seem to hear her. "Buck caught," he said softly. "Oh, Lord, Lord. What that Skeet will do to him . . ."

"But we going get him out, Adaba!"

Adaba looked around slowly, as if remembering her presence. "How?" he asked dully. "Oh, Lord, how?"

"We find a way! We got to! Saul gone on his way to Redbird right now to see what he can do."

"And if he gets hisself caught by them guards too?"

Zulie dared not think of that possibility. "No, he ain't going to! Likely there won't be no guards, now that Mr. Skeet got Buck. Never was before. Just dogs, and Serena, she going take care the dogs, poison them and kill them, and—"

"And Saul will just break into the jail house and carry Buck off?

Adaba's obvious skepticism worried Zulie, and she hastened to reassure both him and herself. "He can do it, Adaba!"

"He's wounded, Zulie, shot by that man—"

"He can do it! And after that—oh, Adaba, after that!"

"After that, what, honey?"

This was the most exciting part. Surely he would understand. She went to him, knelt so that she could look up into his face. "Buck is going take them niggers out of the jail—there's 'bout seven 'sides Buck—and he's going burn Redbird and kill Mr. Skeet!"

Adaba nodded. "He'll do that, all right, given half a chance."

"But that ain't all! That there is just the signal for the beginning."

"The beginning of what, Zulie?"

"The uprising!"

"The . . . uprising?" It might have been a foreign word.

"Them people you seen out in the woods, them that you told Zag about. They come from the Haining place, down the river. And there's others coming, lots of others, people from plantations all 'round here, people from the little farms, so many people—"

"Woman," Adaba said, and his face looked drawn now, "please tell me what the hell you are talking about." And yet she had a feeling that he already suspected.

"They going run off, Adaba. Rise up and run off! While the white people 'round here fight the fires, the black people going to follow Buck north—north to freedom!"

"Are you trying to tell me—"

"Tonight, Adaba, tonight! And that's why we got to get Buck out of that jail house. More people coming here all the time, and others just waiting to start the fires. There going be an army, Adaba! An army on the march!"

"Oh, my God, my God . . ."

The words came out a moan, and she did not understand him. She kept trying to spark his enthusiasm, to communicate her excitement, but somehow he did not respond. Far from being enthused, he looked appalled.

"Zulie, why didn't you tell me this before?"

"You been sick. You still ain't well. And you can't help, being like that, but Buck say you going want to, so best not to say nothing to you 'bout it—"

"And he went ahead and . . . and . . ." Brushing her aside, Adaba got up from his chair. He paced the room. His hands went to his head as if to keep his skull from bursting. He turned back to Zulie again.

"Honey, who all is involved in this? I mean, how many people does Buck expect to lead off from here?"

"From all the plantations, all come who say they will, there be about eighty. Some get scared, maybe only sixty. But Buck say when others see them going, could be they join in too. There could be *more* than eighty. Others along the way see them, they join too, and there could be hundreds! Buck say—"

"And Buck is right. There could be hundreds. Oh, my Lord God."

Zulie was utterly baffled by Adaba's reaction. She had expected him to be angry, perhaps, at not being included in the plans. She had expected him to be disappointed that he was still not strong enough to participate in them. She had expected almost anything but this: that he should act as if this uprising were the worst thing that could possibly happen.

"It's going be all right," she said. "We get Black Buck out of that jail house, he'll lead the people north—"

"Zulie," Adaba said gently, "I have some things to tell you, and I want you to listen to me very carefully." He took her hands, led her to the bed, and sat down with her on the edge. "Zulie, for a long time now, I been taking black people north. You know about that."

"Everybody heard about Adaba."

"I don't do it alone. Others been doing the same thing. We work together, we teach each other, and we learn all the best ways. It was me taught Buck. And little by little we been making what some people call the Underground Railroad. You heard about the Underground Railroad, Zulie?"

She had. Of course she had.

"Mostly we take people a few at a time. One or two people here. Maybe a family there. Always quiet, always careful. It's a long way north to freedom, Zulie, a long, long way. It takes weeks, sometimes months. You understand?"

She resisted. She wanted *him* to understand. "Yes, but Buck, he say—"

"Honey, there just ain't no way Buck can lead eighty people away from here, all at one time, and keep them safe. There ain't no way he can lead half that many or even a quarter. Maybe eight or ten people if he's careful and lucky—no more. How he gonna hide eighty people? The country around here is too built up, too crowded. Eighty people travel slow. How he keep them moving fast enough so the militia don't catch up with them? How get all them people far enough into the swamps or the wilds to hide them? How, Zulie? *There just ain't no way!*"

Zulie looked for answers, but these were questions that had never even occurred to her. That way why they had needed Buck: to raise and answer the important questions. And she had needed desperately to believe in him.

"And if Buck starts burning," Adaba went on, "if others join up with him, if it turns into a march—that's what they call an insurrection. And a lot of people are gonna get killed—most of them black."

"But if there's enough of our people—"

"No, Zulie. There ain't never been an insurrection in South Carolina that ain't turned out bad for us. I don't think there been one in the whole country. They just shoot us down like animals, then hang anybody left."

Zulie felt dazed. Adaba spoke with such conviction that he made what he said seem obvious. She had a vision of hundreds of black people surrounded by whites with rifles, the whites closing in and firing, firing, while black people fell. And Adaba was saying that that was what was going to happen tonight.

He went on talking, trying to persuade Zulie to his view, but she hardly listened. She didn't have to listen any longer.

Some dreams die hard. Zulie had long dreamed of freedom, and not only for herself. She had dreamed of it for all those who had come together for the Sunday meetings, risking their lives to share the dream. For the sake of the dream she had conjured, she had spelled, and it had all come to this: that they could not let the uprising take place tonight. Zulie saw that clearly and quickly, but only with pain.

"Then why Buck do this?" she asked. "Why?"

Adaba shook his head. "Honey, I don't know. There ain't a man in the world cares more for our people than Buck. There ain't a man in the world who's a better friend. But some mighty bad things happened to him in his time—"

"We hear tales 'bout him and Mr. Skeet's woman."

"That's part of it, but I don't think it's all. Some men hurt more than others, Zulie, and maybe Buck's one of them. He's seen too much, had too much happen to him. And the last two, three years . . . more and more he made mistakes. He's careless, he's reckless, like he don't hardly give a damn no more, and that makes him dangerous to other people, even his friends. Like at the Courtney plantation—so crazy to burn it, he got one of his own people killed. Then he led the posse right into my camp and got a lot more people killed. He ain't good for our people no more, Zulie, he ain't good. I been telling him to go up north and stay there. Black Buck has had his day, and if he don't stop, he's gonna get us all killed.

"And I reckon in his heart he knows that. That's the real reason he didn't want you to tell me what he was up to. He knew I'd try to stop him."

Adaba had had his say. He sat quietly, watching Zulie, still holding her hands. She wanted to cry.

"We got to stop him, Adaba."

"Yes."

"But we can't just leave him in Mr. Skeet's jail."

"We ain't going to." Adaba stood up. "Saul been gone long?"

"A little while. I don't know 'zactly when he left."

"On foot?"

"No, he took a mule."

"Then I got to get there fast. Think Zag can give me a horse?"

"I think so. Miss Lucy ain't going nowhere tonight. Take the cabriolet and go by road is fastest, and tonight ain't likely be no patrol."

"Then we'll do that. Because if Saul beats me to Redbird and opens up that jail house—if Buck sets Redbird on fire . . ."

He didn't finish. There was no need to.

My fault, Zulie thought, remembering all the spells she had cast. *My fault, more than Buck's, they all going die . . .*

Defeated and ready to die . . .

Vachel was right. There would be no uprising, no burning, no revenge. There would be no final blow, however futile, struck for black dignity. That, at the very least, he had hoped for. But it was not to be. The years might stretch out ahead of Buck, but they led to nothing. Except death, and perhaps a slim chance of killing Vachel Skeet first. Even if he succeeded in that, he had no hope of escape. His luck had run out, and he would be hung or shot or something worse.

But if only he *could* get Vachel . . .

To hell with it, he thought.

He was weary now, weary beyond belief, and in the jail house he rolled up in a blanket, knees drawn up, chin down, arms crossed over his chest, and escaped into sleep. He was almost too weary to dream, and the catalogue of horrors he had collected over the years flickered only dimly through his mind, inspiring less terror than sorrow—a vain regret that nothing could have been changed, that the world could not have been different.

The feeling stayed with him even as Vachel Skeet's booted toe prodded him awake.

"Supper time, Buckley," Vachel said, his voice gentle.

Buck climbed stiffly to his feet. There was just enough light so that he could see that Vachel was smiling. The smile was as gentle, as friendly as his voice.

" 'Fraid there ain't no fine meal this time, Buckley. Just cold mush. But I reckon you'll get used to it."

Buck gave no sign that he had heard. *There ain't a damn thing you can do to me anymore,* he thought, *even if you don't know it.* For the present, at least, he felt no fear whatever of whips or knives or even loops of wire. He felt as if he had moved beyond hope or despair. Indeed, his only possible weakness, the one thing that might make him vulnerable, would be the rebirth of hope.

The prisoners of the jail house usually worked much later than the other slaves, even on Saturdays, and it was quite dark as Vachel and a guard took Buck to join the others for supper. Cato looked up and smiled at him, but the other six seemed to avoid looking at him. No one said a thing. Though he was not hungry, Buck made himself eat his mush, swallowing it without tasting it. He was aware that Vachel was watching closely, his smile fading at Buck's obvious indifference, but Buck hardly cared. He had no interest in small victories over Vachel Skeet.

With the others, he walked back to the jail house, walking slowly, as if he too were hobbled.

"Good night, Buckley. Sleep well. This ain't been much of a day for you, but I think you'll find tomorrow more interesting. I got plans for you. . . ."

As the door was drawn closed, they found their habitual places on the floor and curled up in their blankets. A thump and thud told them that the timbers were falling into place in the iron hooks. They were secured for the night.

Buck felt Cato's touch in the dark.

"You all right, Buck?"

"I'm all right."

"Yeah, we all going be fine."

The two Sea Island blacks murmured a few words in Gullah and fell silent. Nothing more was said. No one spoke of the promised escape, the escape that was not happening, the escape that was never to be. They all understood by now. Black Buck had failed, and the last hope, if there had ever been one, was gone.

Claramae, Buck thought, as he closed his eyes, *Claramae, I'm just sorry I didn't get him for you, honey.* He tried to picture her. It saddened him that at times he could hardly remember what she had looked like, but then some fresh recollection would come to him, and she would live for him again, as vividly as when he had first loved her. *Claramae, I'm sorry . . .*

"That you, Buck?"

"It's me, all right, honey."

" 'Bout time you came back here to me, Buck."

"Now, couldn't nothing keep me away from you for long, Claramae."

"*Sure seems like a long time to me. Any time away from you seems like a long time to me.*"

"*Well, maybe soon now we can be together for good, honey.*"

"*Won't never leave me again?*"

"*Won't never . . .*"

The dream never had a chance to go bad. Buck became aware of a faint scratching noise that brought him up resentfully from sleep. It sounded as if someone was quietly and carefully removing the bars from the door. Was it morning already? And if not, what the hell was Vachel up to now?

The door opened a few inches.

Buck found himself holding his breath.

"Buck?" a voice whispered from the outside. "Buck, you in there?"

He could not believe it. He knew this was no dream. He was wide awake and lying on the floor of Vachel Skeet's jail house. But he could not believe that he was truly hearing Saul's voice.

"Buck? . . . Buck?"

Buck sat up. "*Saul!*"

The door opened a few more inches, and a shadowy figure slipped into the room.

"We all ready to go, Buck."

Cato crowed triumphantly. He could hardly keep his voice down. "You see, you niggers? What I tell you? Black Buck going open up this here jail, going bust us out! And here is Black Buck and old Saul from Sabrehill, and Saturday night is come at last, and . . ."

Buck sat where he was, unmoving, but around him there was a rustling sound like a great wind coming up. Blankets were tossed aside. Chains clanked. There was low excited laughter, and Big Tildy said, "I guess you really *is* Black Buck!"

Yes, he was Black Buck. And now, with this miracle, new strength flooded his body—new strength and all the old wrath. The aches, the whip-stripes, the burdens of the day were nothing. He leapt to his feet. It seemed to him that even if the door had been barred at that moment, he could have burst through the walls. *I've come back for you, Vachel! By God, I've come back to get you!*

"And now we going strike a blow, ain't we, Buck!" Cato said excitedly. "Going strike a blow for niggers!"

"That's right!" Buck said, and his voice had never sounded more savage. "That's right! Strike a blow for niggers!"

Even if it had to be the last one.

Three

Buck looked out through the barely opened door of the jail house. He saw no one. The night was silent. The office and the kitchen house were dark. The only light he could see anywhere came from the downstairs of the big house. And that, Buck thought with satisfaction, almost certainly meant that Vachel was at home. It spared Buck the trouble of looking for him.

He turned back to Saul. "How you get here? Vachel told me there was guards."

"Was. Seen two. They talking 'bout how they going catch Adaba. If they ain't sleeping, they dead now, and I don't give a damn. That kind nigger—"

Buck laughed. "You did better than me. You got everything?"

There was a faint clatter as Saul held up the cloth bag he carried. "Got knives, got hammer, chisel, all I need to strike the chains. Got the gooseneck for you, and got this here too. Stole it just 'fore I come." Buck felt something begin pressed into his hand. "It don't always work so good, but it got six barrels, all loaded. One don't work, use another."

Six barrels. A six-barreled pepperbox. Suddenly his luck was running strong again.

"Lord bless you, Saul. Cato, your people here all with us?"

"All with you, Buck, every one."

There were sounds of agreement in the darkness, and Big Tildy growled, "You just tell us what we do."

"Soon as Saul gets those chains off you, you go after Mr. Dinkin and Shadrach. Don't make noise—go quiet like shadows. And kill them."

"*Ban!*" said one of the Sea Islanders. *It is done!*

"I'll take care of Mr. Skeet myself. With those three out of the way, we ain't gonna have trouble from nobody else at Redbird."

The pistol in his belt and the gooseneck in his right hand, he moved through the night shadows to the office. The gooseneck, or socket-lock chisel, was a long metal mortise tool that made an excellent pry bar. Buck slipped the sharp edge between the door and its jamb. Every sound he made seemed like thunder in his ears, and he kept glancing toward the big house, but in a matter of seconds he had the office door open.

He stepped inside, closing the door behind him. He put the gooseneck on the table where it would be easily found. In the old days the Old Man and Vachel had kept weapons locked in a cabinet in this room, and Buck figured they would still be there. Now that he had the pepperbox, however, he did not have to pause to get them. He could leave that to the others.

He laughed to himself. So little had changed in this room, he was feeling right at home. Even in the dark he could still find his way without missing a step.

His hat, knife, and axe were on Vachel's desk, right where they had been left two nights before. He put on the hat and hung the axe and knife from his belt. He was about to leave the office when he thought of something.

"*Want one, Buckley?*"

Hell, yes, Vaych. I'll drink with you now.

He lifted the jug down from the shelf. He pulled the cork. He rolled the jug up onto his shoulder and sipped from it, and the whiskey flowed over his tongue, warm and smooth and tangy. He took another, larger swallow and felt the fire bloom like a rose in his stomach.

Good stuff, Vachel. We always did make good stuff here at Redbird. Wish I had time to sit down and drink some more with you, but . . .

He did drink some more, drank slowly, curiously reluctant to leave the office. *"Do you remember, Buckley? . ." I remember, Vachel. . . .* He did remember, too much, things he had forgotten and had no business remembering ever again. He remembered a hot summer afternoon when their mothers had taken them for a picnic in the woods and afterward had carried them out into the cooling stream . . . the spring morning when Vachel had scotched the copperhead that almost got Buckley, and then, frightened, had bawled so hard that Buckley had had to carry him home. . . . He remembered . . . remembered. . . .

He shook his head hard to clear it. What was he doing here in the dark office, drinking and dreaming back? The time, goddam it, was *now*. And Vachel was in the big house, waiting to be killed.

He took one long last drink. By now Saul would have freed enough of the prisoners to go after Dinkin and Shadrach, would have given the prisoners knives to cut throats. Buck carefully corked the jug and set it back on the shelf. Maybe he would take it with him later. No point in wasting good liquor.

Again he looked carefully about the courtyard before leaving the building. He saw no one, not even the freed prisoners. He drew the pepperbox and cocked it. It was probably a little bastard of a gun, he thought, highly inaccurate as well as unreliable, but at short range it would blow a big enough hole in a man.

He left the office and walked toward the big house. His breathing was labored, and time seemed to be passing much too quickly. He wanted to hold it back. He caught a glimpse of Vachel through a parlor window, and he had a mad wish that Vachel would see him coming. See him and start running. *Run, goddam it, Vaych, or I'm gonna get you!*

He was at the door of the big house. (*Too soon! Too*

soon!) He tried the handle very slowly, very carefully, and had a sick feeling as he found it unlocked. Nothing was going to stop him now. He slipped into the passage.

He stood there for long minutes, looking about. There was not much light in the passage. What little there was came from a parlor. But there was enough light for Buck to see that the woodwork was out of repair and there was dust and clutter on the furniture. And on a chest sat three scattered books—yes, Buck was certain of it—the same three books that Vachel had borrowed from Sabrehill and never returned. Unexpectedly he felt pain, and he thought, *Damn, Vaych, you ain't kept this place up right—you need me. . . .*

But this was no time for such thoughts.

He was here. Back. At Redbird. Not in the fields, not in the jail house, but in the big house, the house he had called home for so many years.

And Vachel was in the next room.

Gun leveled, Buck walked in without making more than a whisper of sound. Vachel was sitting at an escritoire, looking over an account book he had evidently brought in from the office. Buck waited for him to hear the shuffle of a footstep, the heavy breath.

Vachel slowly looked up and around. For a moment he stared at Buck with dull-eyed incomprehension. When understanding dawned, he got up so quickly that his chair was flung over backward, and he stood in the crouched, hands-raised position of shock.

Buck gave him time to take it all in.

"I don't think *you'll* find tomorrow more interesting, Vachel," he said. "In fact, I don't think you'll be around tomorrow. So you can forget them plans you got for me."

"How . . . how did you. . . ?"

"How'd I get out? What's the difference? I'm out."

Vachel looked frantically around for some possible way to escape—a window, a door.

"You can't make it, Vachel. You might try calling for your overseer or Shadrach if you want. I kinda guess they're dead by now."

Vachel's gaze returned to Buck. "Ain't you even gonna give me a chance?" His shaking voice had a paper-thin sound.

"A chance, Vachel? Like you gave Claramae? Like you gave the nigger you buried yesterday? Like you was gonna give me?"

"I told you—it wouldn't be so bad—"

"I know what you told me. While you dangled a loop of wire in front of my face. I know what you did to me with that loop"

"But I didn't *kill* you, for Christ's sake! I couldn't have killed you—"

"Not for twelve years. I was to be a long time dying, wasn't I Vachel?"

Vachel's voice rose. "For God's sake, Buckley, a *chance!* You woulda had a chance! Twelve years was a big chance! I got a right to a chance—"

"Forget it, Vaych. We ain't a couple of fine gentlemen fighting a duel. We're just a nigger killing off a white man."

The flat statement seemed to do something to Vachel. The panic began to leave his eyes and intelligence to return. He slowly straightened from his shock-crouched position and lowered his hands. It was as if he knew the verdict was in and that begging would get him nothing.

"Yeah," he said, and his voice was stronger and steadier. There was even a hint of mockery in it. "Yeah, the nigger who was my friend."

"Your black brother, Vaych." Buck tried to say it lightly, with his own mockery, but there was pain in his breast. "The one who slept in your bed with you."

"Yeah. But you and me . . . I guess we didn't treat each other like brothers, did we?"

"Oh, we did, Vaych, we did. For most of our lives, all but the last twelve years and a little more. We did, Vaych—"

"Yet all that time . . . before Claramae . . . it don't mean nothing?"

"Nothing. No more to me than to you."

But it does! It does!

Vachel smiled. "You're lying, Buckley. We was brothers, just like you said. And no matter what we done to each other later. And brothers is brothers always, come love or come hate. That's why it hurts so much. Ain't that so?"

The pain in Buck's breast grew. "Why don't you just say a prayer, Vachel?"

"You know damn well it's so. You ain't forgot about us growing up together . . . growing into men . . . taking over running Redbird. That was the happiest time of my whole life. I tell you, Buckley, I worked hard since, and I done all right, but I ain't had a truly happy day in twelve years. Can you say that you have?"

"Yeah, I can say that. When I took a nigger north. When I burned a place like this. When I shot a hole through a white man's guts."

"Then I reckon you been better off than me, ain't you?"

"I reckon. But you ain't gonna have to worry about that no more."

Vachel sighed. Nodded. For the first time Buck noticed the dark circles under his eyes, the weary slant of his head. Once more, Vachel looked around the room as if for some way of escape. He shrugged, accepting the fact that there was none.

"Then do it," he said.

"When I'm ready."

"Oh, you're ready, Buckley. Do it."

Buck raised the pistol higher, holding it with both hands. Twelve years of waiting for this. Twelve years of hating the man. Twelve years of circling, going farther and farther from the horror of that last night at Redbird, and then coming closer and closer to it again. And then to face Vachel and see the growing sheen of sweat on his forehead—and somehow, after the first fright, more dignity than Buck would ever have expected.

"Go ahead, Buckley. Or are you gonna make me wait and sweat for twelve years too?"

Twelve years of waiting . . .

"Do it." Vachel's voice had sunk to a whisper.

Buck's hands tightened on the pistol. His right forefinger pressed against the trigger. He tried to pull. Tried and tried again. It was as if his hand were paralyzed.

Slowly he lowered the pistol. His vision was blurred.

"You know, Vaych . . . it's funny . . . but after waiting all this time . . . after all the hoping and praying and planning . . . I ain't sure I can."

Something like disbelief, or hope, came into Vachel's eyes—almost an astonishment that this was not the end.

Buck closed his eyes. He raised the pistol again. As he squeezed the trigger, he opened his eyes, and in the midst of the roar he saw Vachel slammed back against the wall. His arms were crossed before him as if, too late, for protection. His eyes were unfocused and wide with shock. His mouth was agape.

The eyes came to focus on Buck. They denied that this could happen, that this was right. The mouth was still open. It moved, and Buck waited for words to come, but it said nothing.

He pulled back the cock and turned the barrels and fired again.

The ball hit Vachel's chest, crushing him to the wall. Blood spread over his chest from the first wound. He took a step toward Buck and fell sprawling to the floor, face down.

He tried to crawl. Buck went to the next barrel and fired one more time, aiming at Vachel's head. But his hand shook so badly that the ball hit his back.

Vachel lay still.

"Vachel," Buck called softly after a moment. "Vachel?"

There was no answer.

"Vaych . . ."

Then he broke. His sobs doubled him over, almost brought him to his knees. Twelve years he had waited for this, and at no time in those twelve years had he felt such pain. Twelve years, and now there was no more Vachel Skeet to hate, no more Vachel Skeet to love. Nothing more, really, to live for.

He could hardly accept it. It should not have ended this quickly, this easily, this definitely. Vachel had been right: it should have taken years. But now it was over.

And he was left with all his old anger, all his mad rage—and a sense of having been cheated. It was finished forever and all, but he still wanted to kill Vachel, to kill him and kill him again. Vachel had cheated him by dying so easily.

"Oh, you bastard," he sobbed, "you bastard, you bastard, you bastard. . . ."

He wept until he remembered that this was no time for tears. They must come later, if at all. Others depended upon him, and they were waiting. He had to pull himself together and move fast now. Loot, burn, and run—that was what he must do next.

He forced calm. He wiped his eyes and took another look at the parlor floor. Vachel lay perfectly still. There was something in the parlor Buck had wanted—*the pistols,* he remembered. The case that held the matched set of dueling pistols, together with their accessories, had always been kept in a cabinet in this room, and Buck quickly found it.

He then picked up the lamp and ran up the stairs. He opened wardrobes and drawers and grabbed out all clothing that might be useful, hardly bothering with any kind of selection. He kicked out the windows and threw the clothing out through them. Blankets from the beds followed. He looked for weapons but found none.

When he was finished upstairs, he took one last look at the rooms he and Vachel had occupied, knowing that he would never see them again. No one in the world would ever see them again, because he was about to burn them. But he hesitated, stopped by the thought that this had been *his* house, *his* home. He had loved it, and in a way he still did. He remembered the boy, Henry, on the Courtney plantation: *"Don't need no fire! . . . Ain't no need for no fire!"*

But there was a need, and Buck forced himself to act on it. With the lamp, he set fire to drapes, furniture, anything that would burn.

He raced back down the stairs. There was little of value in the house—a little silver, which he took, and on impulse he picked up the three books that had come from Sabrehill. Again he set fire to everything that would burn easily. The whole process took only a few minutes.

In the passage, he paused to look into the parlor at Vachel again. Vachel still lay there, and Buck tried to capture a sense of his presence. He could not do it. Vachel was dead; Vachel was gone. All that was left of him were a few fading scratch marks on a slate that had been wiped clean.

Buck said, "Good-bye, Vaych," and ran for the passage door.

In the parlor, Vachel Skeet slowly raised his head. Buckley was nowhere in sight. An inch at a time, painfully, Skeet began crawling toward the passage.

It was as if the natural order of things had been disrupted: for some, as if dawn had come to the east many hours early; for others, as if the sun had reversed its direction and was rising in the west. And like any such disruption, it brought fear and awe and a kind of mad joy: *Look! It's happening!*

Sarah Jane, of the McClintock plantation, saw it first. She and her people, seven in all, were on Redbird land, headed west toward Sabrehill. After her sister, Serena, had told her of Buck's capture—making her swear to tell no one else—Sarah Jane had almost abandoned hope. But Zulie, according to Serena, had said to follow Buck's instructions faithfully, and for Tobe's sake she had done so. Now she had to reach Tobe, and no longer fearing Mr. Skeet's guards, she led her people toward the Redbird big house.

A slave named Ruff saw it, the very slightest lightening of the sky to the east, over Redbird. He wished he dared move closer in order to be certain. Then the flames grew higher and redder, and he very nearly cheered aloud. It was really going to happen, this grand defiance, this rebellion, this escape to the north! He watched the glowing sky a few minutes longer, then started back home as fast as he could run. Within the hour, the Jeppson big house would be burning too—burning, Ruff hoped, with Mr. Jeppson in it.

On the other side of Redbird, Theron and Lize also watched the fire, and they did laugh aloud. Let Mr. Skeet's guards hear them—what did it matter now? The chances were that Mr. Skeet was dead. And Ettalee was avenged.

People were already moving through the night toward Sabrehill. The runaways from the Haining place had arrived there long ago. Those from the Pettigrew plantation, well on their way, looked back over their shoulders to see the fire at Redbird. People from the Harmon plantation were on their way, and others, from the Buckridge and Devereau plantations, joined them as they passed by.

An uprising, a rebellion, a march.

Buck's dream.

Look! It's happening!

"You're free!" Buck yelled at the top of his voice. "You hear me, you niggers, you're free! Say it out loud, you hear me? You're free!"

"You free!" Saul yelled, and there was laughter around the flame-illumined courtyard. Sarah Jane and her people had arrived, and she was embracing her Tobe. The people of Redbird stood around the edges of the courtyard, observing and marveling, as the flames rose higher.

As quickly as it had come, the pain had vanished. Suddenly Buck wanted to sing, he wanted to shout. By God, he had done it. All he had dreamed of, all he had planned, was happening, and Vachel Skeet was dead at last. *Got him for you, Claramae. And for you too, Ettalee. And the bastard's burning—burning in his own house.*

"You're free, and you're going north! Anybody, everybody, all that wants to go! You're going north, and ain't nobody gonna stop you! Mr. Vachel Skeet is dead, and he ain't never gonna whip another slave! 'Cause he ain't got no slaves no more! You're free, we all are free! Free forever!"

Buck laughed and sobbed. Not since his time with Claramae had he felt so released, so buoyant, so triumphant, and yet tears kept coming to his eyes. What the hell difference did it matter if they killed him now, he thought, what the hell difference did anything make? Vachel was dead. And as Cato had said, they were striking a blow for niggers. And that was enough.

He put the dueling pistols into Cato's keeping, and he gave Saul instructions as to what to do with the three books. He jammed the pepperbox under his belt, and standing before the office, the three of them drank from Vachel's jug.

"Dinkin and Shadrach," Buck said. "You get them yet?"

Cato shook his head. "They gone, Buck. Don't find them nowhere."

"Jesus, and I wanted them. I want them for Ettalee." Buck saw Saul tighten up. "Well, I'll get them yet. You got any idea where they might be hiding?"

"Most likely just ran off. Saw what was going on and got scared. They ain't going stay here, they think Mr. Skeet is dead."

"But they don't know he dead," Saul said. "Maybe they go for help."

"That's right," Buck agreed. "Let's get the weapons from the office and get our people moving out of here fast."

But they found no weapons in the office. At some time past, they had been removed. It was a disappointment, but not the worst in the world. Buck felt as he had when Saul had appeared at the jail house door: nothing could stop him now. Nothing but death. That was bound to come, but he planned to be mighty hard to kill.

"All right," he said as he stepped back out of the office, "burn the place, and I'll—"

"Just don't move," Dinkin said.

Buck could see him clearly in the light of the flames. He was a good fifty feet away, coming across the courtyard, Shadrach at his side. Both men carried rifles, and Dinkin had a couple of pistols in his belt as well. As he approached, he kept his rifle pointed at Buck's chest.

"Well, by God," Buck said with delight, "we don't have to go looking for them. They coming right to us."

He pulled his jacket over the butt of the pepperbox.

"Don't you move," Dinkin said, " 'cause I'd as soon kill you as not."

You ain't gonna kill nobody. Just wait till you get close enough. . . .

Buck looked about the courtyard, taking in the situation. Most of the Redbird people, on the edges of the courtyard, were rapidly fading back into the shadows. Others, caught in the firelight, stood as if frozen. Among them, he saw some of the jail house prisoners—Iba, Kimbo, Tobe, Josiah. Shadrach was about six feet to Dinkin's left, and fanning out behind them to cover the courtyard area were three more blacks with rifles and several with whips.

Dinkin and Shadrach came to a halt ten feet away, close enough for a pepperbox shot, but Dinkin kept his rifle pointed steadily at Buck's chest.

"Why, good evening, Mr. Dinkin, sir," Buck said, grinning and taking off his hat. He held the hat in front of his waist.

"You shut up," Dinkin said. "Now, I'll tell you what we're gonna do. All you Redbird people, you get back to your houses. Do it now, fast. And you jail house niggers, you don't move till I tell you, and then we're gonna herd you back into that jail house. And if any of you gives us trouble—"

"Mr. Dinkin, sir," Buck said in his softest, friendliest manner, "don't you realize, sir—"

"I said, shut up. You shut up, or I'll pull this trigger."

"And my men will cut you down," Buck bluffed. "They got you covered, sir, covered from inside the office."

Dinkin's rifle wavered, but not enough. When he spoke again, his voice shook.

"Now, you listen to me. I'm gonna give you one last chance—"

"You still got the idea that you, a white man, can walk up to any bunch of niggers and give an order, and they gonna do just like you say. Just 'cause you got a whip or a gun and a white skin."

"Goddam you—"

"You forgetting two things, Mr. Dinkin, sir. One is, we all here are bad niggers. So bad we just purely don't give a shit no more."

"One last—"

"And the other is, you ain't got us no more, Mr. Dinkin. Mr. Dinkin, sir—*we got you!*"

That got what Buck wanted. There was a sudden burst of laughter from the prisoners and, better yet, a triumphant shriek from one of the Sea Island blacks. It was as bloodcurdling a cry as Buck had ever heard, and it caused Shadrach to spin left and fire at it. The shot went wild. Dinkin too started to turn toward the cry, and that was all Buck needed. Flinging away his hat, he dived to his left and dropped to one knee. The pepperbox came out and swung up toward Dinkin as Buck pulled the cock and went to the fourth barrel. Dinkin saw. His face bright with fear, he tried to swing his rifle toward Buck again. Buck fired. Dinkin was knocked backward, and he fell like a puppet whose strings had been cut.

He lay still.

No more Dinkin.

The armed blacks at the edge of the courtyard immediately moved away. Buck had expected that. One of them threw down his rifle and ran. But Shadrach stood only a few feet away from Buck, an easy target.

"For Ettalee, Shad," Buck said. "Remember Ettalee? For Ettalee and Serena and all the others . . ."

Buck saw the fear in the man's eyes. He saw the hatred. One of them was going to die.

Drawing his empty rifle back behind him like a club, Shadrach charged. A single blow of that heavy barrel would be enough to brain a man.

Buck smiled. His pistol was already leveled at Shadrach. He cocked and went to the fifth barrel.

Shadrach lifted the rifle high above his head. Every muscle strained to bring it down with all his force.

Buck pulled the trigger.
Click!

And he knew it was over.

He tried desperately to get the cock back, to get to the last barrel, but he knew it was too late. And he was down on one knee—he could never escape the blow. He was finished.

With a triumphant howl, Shadrach brought the rifle smashing down.

An inch at a time. Painfully.

If there were any way at all, if it took a miracle, Skeet was going to get Buckley. He was not going to die this way, unavenged, killed by the nigger who had betrayed him so long ago. Killed by the nigger who had called himself a friend. Killed after twelve long years of waiting.

Somehow he made it to the passage. The heat of the flames beat on him. On hands and knees he crossed the passage. The pistol was in the chest—if Buckley had not taken it. Clinging to the chest, he managed to pull himself up on his knees and get the drawer open. The pistol was still there.

By sheer will he forced himself to his feet. For a moment a black cloud seemed to envelope him, and he thought he was going to pass out—or die. He drove the cloud away. He had to find Buckley, had to. He staggered toward the open door and the courtyard.

He could not make it. He would never make it. He fell full length, and the pistol flew from his hand, skidding over the floor. Sobbing, Skeet crawled toward it. *Buckley, goddam you, I'm gonna take you with me.*

The black cloud overcame him again, but it drifted away, and he found he had the pistol once more in hand. He crawled on toward the doorway.

He saw Buckley. Saw Dinkin and Shadrach. Buckley was much too far away for a shot, he was a hundred miles away, but Skeet saw him.

The black cloud.

Something happened, because even through the cloud Skeet heard two shots. When he could see again, Dinkin was on his back and Buckley was down on one knee.

Skeet pulled back the cock and tried to line up his sights. An impossible shot, but it was his one last chance.

Then he heard Shadrach howl and saw him bringing the rifle barrel down on Buckley.

No, goddam it, he's mine!

The barrel came down sickeningly on Buckley's shoulder. Through Buckley's scream, Skeet thought he heard bones breaking. The barrel rose high and came down again.

No, damn you, don't . . .

Skeet watched in horror. The barrel came down a third time. Buckley lay huddled on the ground, unmoving. Shadrach reversed the rifle, holding it by the barrel, and brought it down again and yet again.

No! No, don't!

The horror grew. He had never meant it to be this way, never in all the years of waiting. He had dreamed of revenge, but not this. He could not let this happen to Buckley, he could not. Not to the friend he had loved and hated for so long. No one could do this to Buckley, no one in the world. *He's Buckley Skeet, God damn you, and you can't . . .*

Shadrach raised the rifle again.

Skeet shifted his sights. He squeezed the trigger.

It was an impossible shot, a shot of a hundred miles. But it was the best shot of Skeet's life, and the ball flew true. It struck Shadrach in the side of the chest, and the rifle went flying. Shadrach jumped and spun. And fell unmoving to the ground.

Ha!

I got him for you, Buckley! I got him!

Nobody touches old Buckley.

Nobody . . .

The black cloud came, and Skeet felt his forehead hit the floor. It was the last thing he ever felt.

Vachel Skeet died a happy man.

Adaba watched from behind the jail for a few minutes, then, followed by Zulie, circled to watch from behind the

Redbird office. By then he was reasonably certain they were safe. He saw no whites anywhere. Every black at Redbird seemed to be in the courtyard, and Zulie said some people from the McClintock plantation were there too. He spotted Saul among them. They were strangely silent, and only a few of them looked at the burning house. Somewhere among them a woman was weeping.

Someone had died. Skeet of course. But not only Skeet. Adaba felt it in the strange paralysis of the crowd. He had known they were too late from the moment they had seen the flames in the sky, but somehow he had never doubted that Buck would leave Redbird alive.

Still followed by Zulie, he walked around to the front of the office, threading his way between people. Saul looked up toward them, new pain in his eyes.

"What happened, Saul?" Adaba asked. "Is Buck. . . ?"

"Johnny Dove!" he heard Buck say, his voice little more than a whisper. "Adaba!"

He saw then, and it was even worse than he had feared. They lay scattered on the ground. Two white men shot dead, and one of them must have been Skeet, and that was all right. One black shot dead, and maybe that was all right too. But—*Oh, my Christ,* he thought—what had they done to Buck?

His face was savagely battered. One shoulder was down almost to his waist, and a leg was oddly twisted. His chest looked caved in, and he was soaked with blood.

Oh, my sweet Jesus . . .

Adaba sank to his knees beside him.

"Guess my luck run out," Buck whispered, his lips barely moving.

"Buck . . ."

"But I got him, Johnny. I got old Vachel at last."

Adaba looked at Buck through a blur of pain. Nothing to do now but accept what had happened. Speak calmly, if that was possible. Not make it any harder for Buck than was necessary.

"Yeah, you got him," he said, when he could speak again. "Always knew you would."

"Got him and the overseer. But Shadrach got me. He

was one mean bastard, that Shadrach. He really got me good."

Adaba looked at the dead black man. "But how did he. . . ?"

Buck made a sound that might have been a laugh. "They tell me Vachel shot him. Son of a bitch, I put three balls in Vachel, and he still lived long enough to shoot Shadrach. All the way from the door of the house. Don't know what the hell he thought he was doing."

Adaba looked toward the burning house. He had heard enough about it over the years, and knew so well what it had meant to Buck, in the good times and the bad, that he almost felt that it was part of his own history.

"Hell of a shot," he said.

"Probably shooting at me."

"Maybe. Maybe not."

"I asked them to drag him out here 'fore the house burned down on him. Didn't reckon Vachel would want to be burned. What I mean is . . . never a man whose guts I hated more or for better reason . . . but I just couldn't let that happen to him, Johnny."

"I understand."

Buck lay still and silent, his eyes closed, and for a moment Adaba thought he had lost consciousness. When he spoke again, his voice was weaker.

"I'm dying, Johnny."

"No, you ain't." Adaba struggled to keep his voice steady and purposeful. "I'm taking you to Sabrehill, Buck, the same as you took me. And Zulie will fix you up—"

"No. I'm all busted up. Sometimes a man knows. Like you said, you can feel the Angel getting closer. And I want to stay here."

Adaba could think of nothing to say, no word of comfort, no word of hope.

"Zulie tell you what I was gonna do?" Buck asked.

"She told me."

"Reckon you think I'm a goddam fool."

"No, Buck. No, I don't."

"True?"

"True, Buck."

"Then . . . I wish I told you."

"That's all right. You let me get well without no worries. That was a nice thing to do."

"We was gonna go north. Maybe sixty, eighty of us. You think we could done it?"

"With you leading? 'Course you could."

"Thought others would join us."

"They would, Buck. They *will!*"

"Could be hundreds. Thousands. Black people on the march. Taking what's rightly theirs. Can't hold them down no longer."

"That's right. That's exactly what's gonna happen."

Hope came into Buck's fading voice. "You lead them now, Johnny?"

"I'll lead them. I promise you. I'll take them north."

"I should known you would."

"Buck, there gonna be a march like not even you ever dreamed of. Oh, Buck . . . there gonna be such a march. . . ."

"They can't catch the Brown Dove. Never."

Adaba looked up at the faces that surrounded them and realized that they would be counting on him from now on: he was their hope.

A sigh from Buck made him look down again. "Buck, is there anything . . . anything I can do?"

"You mean, finish me off? No. I don't feel much now. Not much pain. And I won't be much longer. Johnny, you know, I sort of like the idea of being buried at Redbird. Me and Vachel both." Again, that sound that might have been a laugh. "Me and Vachel both—guess that was what Vachel wanted too."

"That what you want, you get it. Saul will see to it. He knows you belong here."

"Yeah. A man can count on Saul. And, Johnny . . ."

"Yes, Buck?"

". . . better . . . leave . . ."

Buck's voice drifted off, and his face turned away. After a moment Adaba gently took his wrist, afraid of causing pain, but if there was a pulse, he could not find it.

He felt Zulie's touch on his shoulder. "He gone?" she asked.

For a time Adaba could not answer. When he could, he said, "I reckon. Close enough to it, anyway, it don't make no difference."

He thought about the ragged, frightened, half-starved youth who had stumbled into his camp those years ago. He thought about their adventures and their laughter and the trip to Sabrehill. He wondered how long this pain he felt would last. A long, long time, he had no doubt.

Well, you're home now, old son, he thought. *Won't say good-bye. Won't never say good-bye. Just say—you're home.*

But Buck was not dead.

When he opened his eyes, Adaba and the others had left, some for the quarters, others for Sabrehill. He was alone with what remained of Vachel and the two others, overseer and chief driver. And the joy of release, the sense of triumph, was gone.

He had failed.

Oh, there would be a march—Adaba had promised. And that was the most important thing. But he himself had failed, and now, alone, he wept.

Twelve years, and he had at last killed Vachel Skeet. Twelve years, and he had at last avenged Claramae. And what the hell difference did it make?

What difference did it make to Claramae, who was still just as dead as ever?

What difference did it make to Vachel Skeet, who was now beyond suffering or joy?

What difference did it make to Buck, who in his last moments was left with only his bitterness and hatred—that not even Vachel's death could purge?

What difference? Buck lay still and wept at the profound futility of his revenge and asked, *What difference, what difference, what difference?*

Until suddenly, like a touch of grace, a revelation, a star breaking through eastern darkness, he understood. He knew what he had to do. He was not dead yet, and there was one final act, one more thing to be done.

Using his good arm, he struggled to sit up. The effort and the movement brought back much of the pain, and he screamed, though the sound was more like a sob. When he was up, he used the good arm and his one good leg to move himself toward Vachel. This brought still more pain, and he knew he was using the last of his strength. But fortunately Vachel was not far away, and Buck persisted. Before long he managed to get Vachel's head up onto his lap.

"I'm sorry, Vachel," he said, still weeping. "I'm sorry."

Sorry. Not sorry that he had killed Vachel. Not sorry he had taken Vachel's woman. Not sorry for most of what he had done in his lifetime, and certainly not forgiving of Vachel's evil. Simply sorry, sorry for Vachel, sorry for Vachel's sake that Vachel had been what he had been. Sorry that Vachel had suffered and that his suffering had made him an evil man. Helped to do it, at any rate. Sorry for Vachel Skeet.

"I'm sorry, Vachel. I'm sorry it had to be the way it was. I'm sorry it didn't all turn out different. For both of us. I'm sorry."

Vachel showed no sign of hearing. The light of the burning house was reflected in his dead, unseeing eyes. And yet . . .

"God, Buck," he said after a moment, "it really is burning good, ain't it?"

"I *had* to burn it," Buck said, trying to make Vachel understand. "Like everything else I done. I *had* to do it."

"It don't matter. We was always gonna rebuild it anyway, remember? This way we can start from scratch."

A profound sense of relief swept over Buck. He laughed, and even his tears were tears of relief. "Yeah," he said, "yeah, that's right. Now we can start from scratch!"

"Still a hell of a lot of work to do around here."

" 'Course there is! Ain't never no end to it, running a plantation, we both know that. Always something to be done."

"Specially since you left. Hell, I can't take care of a house right, not the way you do. And I ain't found nobody else that can do it."

Buck felt pleased, too deeply pleased to answer. He could only go on weeping.

"I'm glad you come back, Buckley," Vachel said after a time.

"I'm glad to be back, Vaych."

The roar of the burning house grew louder. Buck had done a good job, and it was going fast.

Vachel's face took on a troubled look. He never moved; he kept his dead eyes on the burning house, but Buck saw it.

"Buckley . . ."

"Yes, Vachel?"

"I'm sorry about Claramae."

"Never mind, now."

"No. I want to say I'm sorry. Fact was, she always was more yours than mine. Wasn't like I had any real love for her, not like you did. And I guess I treated her pretty bad. I'm sorry about that."

"It's all past, Vaych, all past."

"Yeah, all past."

Buck felt light-headed, almost as if he were drifting. *Not much longer,* he thought, *not much longer.*

"You know," Vachel mused, "they never did find Claramae's body."

"I know."

"Could be she wasn't dead at all when they got rid of her. Could be she's still out there somewhere hiding."

"I guess it could be, Vaych."

"I wouldn't do nothing to her if she came back now."

"I know you wouldn't, Vaych."

"The three of us . . . we could do an awful lot with the old Redbird."

"We sure could, Vachel, we sure could."

Vachel was silent a moment. A slow grin spread over his face.

"Buck . . ."

"Yeah?"

"Look over there."

"Where?"

"Over there. Ain't that . . . coming this way. . . ?"

Buck strained his eyes toward the darkness beyond the firelight. He saw something moving toward them.

"Yeah," he said after a moment. "I think it is."

And it was.

Smiling.

Balbo Jeppson and P. V. Tucker found them.

Tucker had stopped at Jeppson's place, and the two of them had decided to ride over to see Vachel Skeet. They saw the flames long before they reached Redbird, and when they passed the slave jail, they understood at once what must have happened: somehow the bad niggers had gotten loose and had set the big house and several outbuildings on fire. And moving toward the courtyard, they saw the bodies: Skeet, Dinkin, Shadrach. Skeet's head lay on a nigger's lap.

"Would you look at that boy," Tucker said, "babbling and bawling away like he don't even know Vachel's dead?"

"Like maybe he don't know he's just about dead too," Jeppson said, and he stepped closer to get a better look. "Well, I'll be damned. He ain't got much face left, but do you see who this here is?"

"Hell, yes," Tucker said, "that's Buckley Skeet. He musta had something to do with all this."

"You damn right he did." Calmly Jeppson took out a pistol, pointed it at Buckley Skeet's head, and blew a hole in it. Buckley fell back dead.

"Come on," Jeppson said, "we're gonna be right busy the next day or two. We got more niggers to kill."

Four

Look! It's happening!

First Redbird, and then the Jeppson plantation. Most of the people on the Jeppson plantation stayed behind their doors, not knowing what violence the night might lead to. They knew that something was about to happen, that rebellion had been close for a long time, but they had closed their eyes and ears to it. Let others whisper about Black Buck, let others hint that the time was drawing near. It was the white folks' problem; let Mr. Jeppson worry about it.

They heard the slave Ruff breaking open the door of the cabin that held his brother and his brother's wife. Two bad niggers, those, and Mr. Jeppson had them locked up nightly. They heard the shouts when a driver discovered what was happening and tried to interfere. Later they found the driver lying in the dust with his scalp laid open. They heard the runaways in the slave street, and through their windows, before the alarm sounded, they saw the flames of the big house begin to rise.

It was only a short time after that the fires started at Kimbrough Hall. Mrs. Kimbrough, in her darkened bedroom, happened to glance out a window. At first she could not understand what she was seeing down below, it was so unexpected, so unusual. Two bright lights moved through the darkness, and she thought she recognized the slave Hector, carrying torches. One of the torches swirled about, then sailed skyward, and never fell back to earth. Hector moved the other torch, and a third light was born from it, one torch igniting another. Again, a light sailed skyward, never to fall, while Mrs. Kimbrough watched, dumbfounded. Another torch was lit and sailed high.

Then Mrs. Kimbrough understood. She screamed.

It was sometime later that the Devereau fires were set.

And still later, the Buckridge big house. The Buckridge house, that had been rebuilt after having been burnt to the ground less than two years before. Owen Buckridge, stunned, gazed at the growing inferno, while at his side Callie Buckridge wept. His son, Royal, and his overseer, Mr. Dwyer, ran about, futilely trying to organize the fire fighters. This could not be happening to him again, Owen Buckridge thought, it could not. But it was.

Fire, up and down the river.

And meanwhile, the rebels, the runaways, moved through the night toward Sabrehill.

Look! It's happening!

It was happening; Adaba was too late to stop it, and now, with his best friend dead, he was not sure he wanted to. But he could not allow it to happen in the way Buck had intended. He could not allow eighty or a hundred or a thousand black people to die in a futile, if heroic, gesture. Somehow he had to find a way to keep at least some of these people alive.

Redbird might burn for hours before any whites found out about it, or they might appear at any time. From the moment Buck breathed his last words, it was imperative to act quickly, and the first thing Adaba did, with Zulie's and Saul's help, was to move the runaways to some woods several hundred yards to the east of the burning house.

There he looked them over, and their eyes peered back excitedly, expectantly, in the dark. There were seven people from the jail, another seven from the McClintock plantation, and ten or eleven from Redbird—about two dozen people altogether, and several mules packed with supplies. And this was only the beginning. Zulie had told him that there would be runaways from about eight other plantations and a couple of small farms. *Christ, it's impossible,* he thought despairingly, *impossible!* Some of them would have to turn back, some remain behind. But how was he to persuade them of that?

First of all, he had to take command and keep it.

"Now, you all know who I am, don't you?" he said,

and it was more a statement than a question. There was a murmur of general assent: "We know . . . we know . . . you Adaba. . . ."

"And you know what I do?"

Another murmur, excited: "Like Black Buck . . . take us north . . . steal black folk free. . . ."

"That's right. Steal black folk free. And that's what I'm gonna do for you. I'm gonna do what Black Buck wanted to do, I'm gonna take every last one of you north, every last one that wants to go. You believe that?"

"We believe," several voices said.

"Gonna get you all up there safe—*if* there's any way I can do it. You believe that?"

Excitement seemed to grow with the reassurance. "We believe, we believe!"

Adaba raised his voice. "But you got to believe this too. There's a good chance some of you gonna get killed. Maybe a lot of you. Spite of anything I can do. A damn good chance." He all but shouted: "Maybe we *all* get killed! You believe *that?*"

They did not. There was skeptical laughter. The woman called Sarah Jane said, "Don't you worry 'bout us, Mr. Adaba. Black Buck, he tell us the chance we take—"

"I said *killed!*" Adaba roared. "A month ago a posse found one of my camps. You heard about it. Slaughtered the people there like goddam pigs. They dead now, and dead is dead. You believe *that?*"

Momentarily there was a shocked silence, and Adaba hoped that the reality of what he had said was sinking in. If Buck had warned these runaways of the dangers, he had probably not put them so forcefully. He had given them a vision of an uprising that ultimately would be successful, no matter what the losses meanwhile. And in visions wasn't it always someone else who did the dying?

"But if us all rises up together—" a man began.

"Ain't gonna be no uprising," Adaba said flatly. "Ain't gonna be no insurrection. Just gonna be us, running like hell by night, laying in a dirty ditch by day, starving most of the time, goddam militia hot after us, trying to shoot us down."

"But Buck say—"

Buck: their hero before they had even set eyes on Adaba. Should he tell them that Buck was a noble fool, driven half-mad, grown so careless of life that he would fling theirs away along with his own? No, he could not have done that even if they would have listened to him.

"I know what Buck said," he told them. "But Buck's way ain't my way. I try to take you Buck's way, you all get killed for sure. I ain't saying Buck couldn't do it, but *I can't!*"

"But if we just do like Buck say—"

"Ain't nobody turning back now—"

"Ain't scared of nothing!"

"You ain't scared," Adaba said, "you a damn fool, and I ain't leading no damn fools nowhere. You hear me? I turn my back on you."

Now they began to understand: they needed him, but he was threatening them. There was no more laughter, and as they stared at him, he saw the excitement in their eyes turning to bewilderment and fear. Black Buck had made them promises, and now he, Adaba, was breaking them.

The silence stretched out until the woman called Big Tildy broke it. "Mr. Adaba, sir," she said quietly, "us can't go back. Mr. Skeet and Mr. Dinkin, they dead, and we hang for it. They catch us now, every last one they hang."

Adaba had no doubt that she was right.

He had given hope. He had taken it away. Now it was time to give hope back again.

"All right," he said. "I ain't gonna let them hang you. All you from the nigger jail, I'm taking you away where they won't never find you. And just like I said, I'll take the rest of you too. But you got to understand, I can't take all of you at once. Some of you gonna have to wait."

"But what we going do?" Sarah Jane asked tearfully. "I can't go back to McClintock now. My Tobe can't stay here, and I got to go with him—"

"He's your man, you go with him," Adaba agreed. "But all you others, I'm asking you to stay here for now.

You do that, and I'll come back for you, I promise. I'll take you away from here just like I said."

"When?" someone asked. "When you come back?"

"I don't know," Adaba answered honestly. "It won't be in a month or even two months. It won't be till the white masters get tired of looking for me around here. It may be as long as a year, it may be longer. But I will come back!"

"Adaba don't lie to you," Zulie said. "He come back for you, and I come with him."

Adaba turned and looked at her. She shrugged. "Like you say, he your man, you go with him."

"But my sister," Sarah Jane said, "my sister, Serena. I can't leave her here. Her and Tobe all I got—"

"Never you mind," Serena cut in quietly. "I stay here if it help you and Tobe get away."

"But after all they done to you—"

"Mr. Skeet, Mr. Dinkin, they dead now, they ain't going do nothing to nobody. I stay and wait. And a year from now, I see you again." Serena looked at Adaba. "Ain't that right?"

Thank you, Serena, he thought, *thank you. Show the others the way. . . .*

"That's right," he said. "I promise you. Maybe not even that long. And since you understand so good, Serena —since you're willing to stay here to give these others a better chance—you the first one I'm coming back for. Even if something happens you get sold away, I'll find you and take you north. I promise that too."

"Then we want to go with Serena," a man said quickly. He had his arms around a woman and a boy, his family. "We stay here now, we go with Serena?"

Adaba grinned. "Well, now . . ."

He had made his point. They would do as he told them. But the larger task still remained: he still had to meet with the runaways from the other plantations and farms. He would tell them how they could be of help. They could stall in putting out the fires, they could set new fires, they could do any number of things that would delay and frustrate pursuit. And he would promise them that one day he would return for them.

Sometimes he wondered if Buck's way were not the best way. Rage against the white masters. Make them free you or kill you. But he, Adaba, was too much on the side of life. And it was to life, rather than to death, that he would lead his people.

It was never called the Night of the Runaways or the Night of the Killings or even the Night That Adaba Took Our People Away. It was always afterward referred to as the Night of the Fires.

There were fires on five plantations along that stretch of the river. Oddly enough, Sabrehill, in the midst of the others, was spared.

The first fires that Sabrehill learned of were on the Kimbrough plantation. Miss Lucy at once sent Jebediah and all able hands to be of help, and there Jeb learned of the capture and death of Black Buck. He also learned that both the Redbird and the Jeppson big houses were burning. And when a rider came with the news that the Devereau plantation too had fires and was seeking assistance, he knew he had to get back to Sabrehill as quickly as possible. The fires could be no coincidence, and they had to have something to do with Black Buck and Adaba. Adaba was still at large, and how far could his word be trusted?

Jeb arrived back at Sabrehill in the early morning hours, to learn from Miss Lucy that the Buckridge big house was also burning. It was already almost a total loss, and there was no point in trying to be of help. The Devereau big house had been saved, though a couple of other buildings were burning to the ground.

Jeb set up a guard system he thought he could trust. He had no difficulty in urging the rest of the people to their beds. But he was dissatisfied. With his knack for keeping track of his people, he knew that not everyone who should have, had gone to the Kimbrough plantation. A number had been missing—Zulie, for instance. And he would not feel that Sabrehill was safe until he knew exactly where Adaba was and what his plans were. And so, weary though he was at this hour, he set out exploring the field quarters, speaking to anyone who was still awake, and looking for Zulie.

He soon found her. She was just leaving her cabin, pausing to look about carefully as if afraid of being seen. She failed to see him; he was just around the corner of another cabin, and some instinct kept him silent. Lifting a rather large bundle to her shoulder, Zulie closed her door and swiftly but silently moved toward the woods to the north of the quarters. Jeb followed.

Entering the woods, he heard soft laughter, whispers, a few muttered words of Gullah. A moment later he saw, like indistinct shadows, the runaways and their loaded mules. Moving on to a starlit clearing, he recognized some of them. The chief driver from the Buckridge place. Hector and Dee from Kimbrough. Faith from Devereau.

And Zulie.

She cried out when she saw him, a mixture of fear and defiance on her face. Her hand darted toward the knife that hung from her waist under her dress. As if he were her enemy. As if she needed a knife, when she could cut his heart out with a look.

Adaba appeared from somewhere in the darkness. The outlier smiled as he stepped forward, Zulie at his side. "Well, son," he said, "you arrive just in time to wish us luck." His voice was weak with fatigue.

"You set the fires," Jeb said.

Adaba shook his head. "Buck arranged for all that. Then he went and got himself killed. I didn't know anything about his plans until just tonight. Our good friend here," he glanced at Zulie, "seems to have been keeping secrets from both of us. So now there's no help for it, I've got to take over. I take it you still have no objection to my stealing a few niggers?"

Jeb looked about, trying to penetrate the darkness. "How many are you taking with you?"

"If I've counted correctly, there are thirty-three of us."

"It's impossible!"

"Yeah, it's impossible," Adaba agreed, "and I've told them that."

"But, my God, man, you'll all be killed—"

"No. No, we won't all be killed. Somehow I'll get them through, I'll get them north, impossible or not. These people here, they're the ones that either can't turn back now, Jeb, or I can't make 'em."

"How many did you turn back?"

"Must have been about fifty I sent home again. But I'm coming back for them too, you can count on it."

Yes, he would come back for them—if he lived to do it. Somehow Jeb had no doubt of it.

Adaba raised his face to the breeze that cut through the woods. "Seems to me I can almost smell the dawn coming. But we've still got a few hours of dark left, and we'd better make good use of them."

He smiled and held out his hand. He kept it out until Jeb took it.

"And thank you," he said. "Thank you for your silence."

He turned and disappeared once more into the darkness. The others followed him, and Jeb heard a faint rustling sound as the band of runaways started on its way. But Zulie remained, standing before Jeb and looking up at him.

"You said you won't hold me to my promise, Jeb."

What good were promises if they were not willingly given?

"He need me, Jeb," Zulie said when he did not answer. "You don't need me like he do. He sick, and he ain't hardly back on his feet, and here he is, taking these folks off and trying to keep them alive. He *need* me, Jeb!"

And didn't Jeb need her? Didn't she know she was his life?

She stepped closer to him. "Aw, Jeb, I ain't the right gal for you. I never was, you got to see that. You going north one day soon and stay north and be a big important

man. And I'm going hear about it and be so proud. But
that ain't my way, Jeb, just following you around up
there. Maybe 'cause I'm just plain mean-ass trouble-
making nigger gal. Maybe I just got to stay 'round where
I got a chance to stick my knife in somebody. Sometimes
I think I got more hate in me for *them* than I got love
for my own."

"But you've got love for Adaba," Jeb said, and the
words brought pain to his throat.

"Yes, I do. Like none I ever known. And I got to
grab it, 'cause the voodoo ain't going give me no more
like it." She reached up and touched his cheek, and he
wanted to hold her fingers there forever. "But I got real
love for you too, Jeb, and I ain't going forget it. Ain't
going forget it never."

She leaned forward and kissed his cheek where she
had touched him. She peered intently into his eyes for
a moment, as if to put something into them and to take
something away. And then she too was gone into the
darkness.

He stood there for a time in the starlit clearing. It
was over, his time with Zulie. It was finished, and he had
not known such a sense of loss, such a loneliness, such a
feeling of being adrift in an indifferent universe for many
years. And he knew that nothing, not a thing in the world,
could be done about it.

There were simply some things a man could not have.

He thought of all he had been through, all he had
achieved. House-raised and self-educated, he had been
sold into the fields. He had endured the most sadistic
treatment and survivied every loss. He had arrived at
Sabrehill a rebellious, whip-crazed runaway, had very
nearly died, and yet had risen to be overseer. He was,
whatever the law might say, virtually a free man, be-
holden to none.

But Zulie was gone. And there was nothing left for
him at Sabrehill.

He raised his eyes until he saw the pole star.

Maybe, he thought, it was time to leave Sabrehill.

Maybe it was time to head north. Perhaps that would help him to forget.

Good-bye, Zulie. Good-bye. . . .

He headed back for the big house.

She soon caught up with Adaba. He was assisting himself with a staff she had found for him, but she arrived just in time to save him from stumbling. He paused for a moment, panting with fatigue, and Zulie was frightened for him. She recalled Jeb's words: *"It's impossible!"* And Adaba's reply: *"Yeah, it's impossible. . . ."*

"You all right?"

"I'm fine, I'm fine."

Adaba forced a smile, but his voice shook, and there was sadness as well as weariness in his eyes. He put an arm around her shoulders.

"It's gonna be hard, Zulie."

"I don't mind."

"Never no easy life in Charleston."

"That don't matter."

He looked back the way they had come. "You ought to be back safe at Sabrehill."

"I'm going be with you. Always."

"I kinda liked the idea of you being back at Sabrehill. It was like I had some place to come home to."

"We going have a home of our own, Adaba. Someday." You could dream of it, even if it wasn't true. You had to have some kind of dream.

"Yeah," Adaba said, and his arm tightened around her. "Someday."

They hurried on through the night.

Five

And they made it!

Made it away from Sabrehill. Made it to Adaba's camps. Made it all the way north, all the way to Canada.

Oh, there were desertions and there were deaths, but the survivors, the determined, made it. Because, as Zulie learned, there were still heroes, and not all adventures ended in failure.

The first few days were, of course, the most dangerous. Fortunately the first day was a Sunday, and they traveled well into daylight without being seen—or at least without being seen by anyone who informed on them. And this time Buck's use of fire as a diversion worked beautifully—the plantations were thrown into such confusion that not all of the runaways were discovered until Monday, and it was Tuesday before any kind of pursuit could be organized.

But pursuit in what direction?

Nobody knew. There was no trail to be followed.

Adaba went the first two nights and a day with barely an hour of sleep, driving himself, driving the runaways, organizing them, getting them away from Sabrehill as far and as quickly as possible. By then he looked like a walking corpse, a zombie, and Zulie was sick with worry about him. She had no idea of where he found the strength to keep going. But after a day's sleep, he seemed well revived, and he led his people on through the next night. And the next. And the next . . .

He had one great, happy surprise. He found that in the time he and Buck had been at Sabrehill, Buck had trained his followers exceptionally well. He had instructed them in the necessary skills—keeping to shadows, moving silently, avoiding the crest of hills. He had instilled them with discipline. He had inspired them. Thus their chances of success were greater than Adaba had supposed.

But there were losses. By Tuesday morning, Hayden and Luther of Sabrehill had had enough. If this was freedom, or what led to it, it was no kind of life for them, and to hell with it. They headed back home.

And on Wednesday morning, just before dawn, Big Tildy and a family of five from the Haining plantation were killed. Adaba heard the shots and went back to see what had happened. He found them lying near the edge of the woods with a party of hunters standing over them. Perhaps they had grown careless, perhaps their luck had gone bad. In any case, they must have been discovered and given resistance. And now they were dead.

There was no time for tears. Adaba returned silently to the others, and they all pushed on.

And a couple of days later, a man who had run away from a farm near Sabrehill simply disappeared. He might have wandered off, lost, in the dark; he might have preferred traveling on his own. Perhaps he had friends or family nearby. Perhaps he had died.

But there were twenty-four of them left, and they would be all right. Twenty-four traveling through the wastes and wilds toward the nearest of Adaba's camps. And late one night, after Adaba had exchanged hoots with an owl, he turned to them and laughed aloud. "Hey, you niggers," he said to the others in the loudest voice they had heard in days, *"hey,* you niggers, we're here!"

In the days that followed, they went on to other camps. Breaking up into smaller groups, twenty-two of the twenty-four, all but Adaba and Zulie, made their way to the northern states and to Canada. It was a long hard dangerous journey, a journey for heroes.

And they were heroes, all.

Meanwhile, up and down the river, as Lucy noted with both worry and amusement, all was confusion.

Mr. Jeppson organized a posse and rode about the countryside swearing to "catch me some runaway niggers and kill 'em"—but where were the runaways to be found? The patrol rode from plantation to plantation but found nothing—nothing but slaves preparing for the Christmas celebrations, with rather unusually high spirits. A few hysterical whites cried "Insurrection!" and "Rebellion!" and demanded that the militia be called out, but there seemed to be no insurrection or rebellion for the militia to put down. Indeed, most thoughtful people were extremely reluctant to feed the news of a "rebellion" to the northern agitators. In their view, the worst that could be said was that a "handful of bad niggers had set fire to a few buildings and run off." And the nigger who had killed Skeet and Dinkin (no tears there) was dead.

Mr. Jeppson helped promulgate not only this view, but also the idea that Adaba had been the leader of the runaways and that Justin Sabre had had something to do with the whole affair. Yes, he said, Vachel Skeet had told him a thing or two, and Vachel had told Constable Morgan too, you just ask. Now, of course, Vachel coulda been wrong, but Black Buck—Buckley Skeet, that was—*had* showed up, and he was a known companion of that damn Adaba, and moreover—

The result was that a self-appointed committee came to Sabrehill to question Justin: Major Kimbrough and Messieurs Buckridge, Pettigrew, McClintock, and Haining. Lucy indignantly informed them that they would do no such thing. Justin was in bed, badly injured, and asleep. Furthermore, no guest in her house would ever be subjected to their inquisitions. They could leave now and stay away until they had learned better manners. "Now—now —Miss Lucy—" "Mr. Buckridge, I mean it! Out! *Out!*"

However, Justin was not asleep, and lying in the downstairs bed chamber, he overheard.

There was a substantial increase in the number of whippings in the weeks that followed, and several more outbuildings burned down, as if in retaliation. No doubt, since two white men had been killed, blacks would have been hung (yours, not mine, damn it; niggers cost money) if there had been the slightest excuse. But there was none. And the punishments merely caused more discontent among the slaves, more sabotage, more dreams of freedom, more tales, true or not, of Adaba. Soon it was being told that he was now traveling with a woman—and a conjure-woman, at that. "Zulie from Sabrehill—'member her? Knows all the wicked voodoo spells, like her momma and *her* momma afore her. . . ."

And early one morning a man named Courtney found dirt scattered over his piazza and candles burning around a tree in his slave graveyard. And later he found that

five of his people—Nita and Henry and three others—
had disappeared, never to be seen again. . . .

This time she would keep Justin; she would never again
lose him. It was more than a vow that Lucy renewed each
day, it was a bone-deep need, a savage determination,
something as feral as any primitive mating. Every act of
the day was dedicated to him, and almost every thought.
It was as if she existed only to be with Justin. Once again
he was in her blood, in her soul, surely more so than ever
before, and no, she simply would not let him go.

And as she sensed his mending, desire returned. It was
no romantic wish, no vague dream of fulfillment, but a
fierce animal want. When she thought of making love with
Justin, her head swam. Preparing for bed, she would stand
naked before her mirror, just as she had as a girl, and look
at herself with desire-glazed eyes. She would stand before
an open window and let the chill night air sweep over her
fevered body. And, *Oh, Justin,* she would think, *I love
you so much, and I'm going to keep you. And I want
you, I want you so very much. And soon now, darling,
you and I . . .*

But not yet. First Christmas had to come, and the New
Year, as quiet a holiday season as Lucy remembered.
And then, once again, Zachary Sabre arrived at Sabrehill
to check on Justin, and once again he departed in a flurry
of "goddams." A few days later Dr. Paulson stopped by
and examined Justin and announced that he was coming
along very well, very well indeed, though he was by no
means ready to leave his bed. That became quite evident
when they moved Justin from the downstairs bed chamber
up to his own room. There was no joking this time, no
laughter. Justin's face was white and drawn, and he held
himself as if he sensed his own fragility. Lucy could not
help noticing that he automatically reached out to Lucinda
and Reba for assistance rather than to her.

He accepted almost nothing from her. He would plead
a lack of hunger rather than allow her to feed him. When
she brought his razor and hot water and soap, he said,

no, let Reba shave him later. He slept a great deal of the
time, and often, when she was reading to him, she was
certain that he feigned falling asleep so that she would
leave him.

He was, if anything, even more distant from her than
when he had first returned to Sabrehill. *Pride,* she thought,
it's wounded pride, and he'll get over it. But in her heart
she knew it was not that simple. Under the apparent
apathy, there was a deep, brooding anger, and she could
not tell if it was directed inward toward himself, or outward
toward his attackers, or perhaps toward both. It seemed
to be the very opposite of her own love, which was preoc-
cupied both with Justin and with her own desires, and she
wanted to say to him, *Oh, give it up, Justin, give it up!
We have something else so much better!*

But physically, at least, he was improving. The time
came when he could sit up in bed, could even raise himself without assistance. And then one afternoon, when she
brought his dinner up to him, she caught him out of bed.

"Justin, what in the world. . . ?"

Still in his nightshirt, he stood at the foot of the bed,
one hand on a bedpost to steady himself and the other
protectively over his chest. Lucy rushed to put the tray
down and to get to him.

"You see, Lucy . . ." For the first time in days, he
smiled at her. Carefully, his hand still against his chest,
he walked along the foot of the bed, turned, and walked
back. "You see, I am recovering quite nicely."

"But what are you doing up! You should be in bed!"

"Not necessarily. Didn't Aunt Zule ever tell you that
staying in bed too long is bad? She certainly told me. A
black man regains his strength faster than his master, she
said, simply because his master kicks him out of bed
sooner."

"Well, you get right back again!" she said, laughing.
"You've had your exercise for today!" When had he
last made such a long speech? She tried to lead him to the
side of the bed, but he resisted.

"Lucy . . ."

"Yes, Justin?"

His smile had vanished. "I just want to say, I'm sorry. You've been better to me than I deserve. And for the last few weeks . . . Lucy, I've suddenly realized that I've been even poorer company than when I first arrived here. I've been a terrible guest."

"No, Justin. You've been hurt—"

"That's no excuse. I'll try to do better."

She was standing very close to him, her hands still on his arms as she urged him back to bed, and she wanted terribly for him to kiss her. Perhaps he felt that. The arm that protected his chest dropped and went around her. He touched the small of her back, leaned down, and kissed her. It was hardly a kiss at all, just a brush at the corner of her mouth, but she went weak all over.

"Now, get out of here, woman."

"Can I get anything more for you? Would you like me to have coffee with you?"

"No. I know you have things to do, and I can feed myself now. I'll be perfectly all right."

"Perhaps you'd like company for supper. I could bring up a tray for both of us." She knew she was pressing him, perhaps too hard, but she could not help herself.

Justin smiled again. "I'd like that very much."

She sensed that he did not want her to see him climbing back into bed, as if that were a symbol of his weakness, and she left. But for the first time in weeks, she was happy.

She startled Leila and Lucinda by singing her way through the afternoon. For some time a plan had been shaping in her mind, and she knew exactly what she was going to do.

She told Lucinda that she wanted an especially delicious supper for two to be arranged on a tray, and Lucinda, who was nobody's fool, looked marvelously pleased. Lucy made certain other arrangements. In the late afternoon she she had a hot bath brought to her room, and she enjoyed a leisurely soak in it. Afterward, she dressed in fresh clothes, and when supper was ready, she carried it up to Justin's room herself.

It was pleasant, so pleasant that a time or two she found herself on the verge of tears, and she thought there was a special softness in Justin's eyes too. She told him all that had happened since the Night of the Fires, even things she had told him before, because now for the first time he seemed to be listening to her.

One of the most peculiar things, she said, had happened right at Sabrehill. One morning she discovered that some-one had broken into the office and returned three books—Irving, Milton, and Locke—that had disappeared from the library years before; she thought they had been lent to Vachel Skeet and never returned. And lying near the books had been the old pepperbox pistol, with four barrels fired.

"I would hazard a guess," Justin said slowly, "that someone from Sabrehill had recently visited Redbird."

"So would I. And if that pistol had been found at Red-bird and recognized—and that could have happened—Sabrehill would have been implicated in the affair."

"Then someone has done you a great favor," Justin said, "and I advise you to say nothing about it."

"Oh, believe me, I shall not." Lucy had a delicious sense of complicity with Justin.

When supper was over and they had had their coffee, Lucy stacked the tray. Before leaving the room, she leaned over Justin and kissed him. She kissed him good night every night, but this was the first time he had given her more than a shadow of a response, and again she went weak, thinking of what was yet to come.

"Don't go to sleep, darling. I have a few things to do, and then I'll be back."

She took the tray out to the scullery in the kitchen house. After finishing a few chores, she informed Leila and Lucinda that she did not wish to be disturbed any-more that night and that she would see them in the morn-ing.

The champagne, in its ice bucket, and the glasses were already in her room, waiting. Humming rather unsteadily, she took off all her clothes. She glanced at herself in a mirror and wondered if she were not a fool to feel so gloriously happy. Her nightgown was already laid out. It was one of her very prettiest. More than a week ago she had taken it out, inspected it, and readied it for such a night as this. *Justin, soon* . . .

She pulled her gown on, smoothed it, and looked down at herself. Yes, he would be able to see her, just enough of her. She threw her best silk robe over her shoulders and picked up the tray with the champagne and the glasses. Slippers? Not necessary. Trying to rein back her excitement, she peeked out into the hallway, then crossed unobserved toward the light that shown under Justin's door.

She tapped on the door and, at Justin's answer, entered.

As she had half-expected, he looked stunned. He was sitting up in bed reading, and his book fell to the floor. For a moment she was uncertain of herself, but then, slowly, he smiled. It was a soft smile, almost a sad smile, but she was sure he was pleased, and she smiled back. She elbowed the door closed and carried the tray to the bedside table.

"Lucy," he said, "you're beautiful."

"Thank you, darling. You're feeling so much better that I thought we might celebrate."

"You're the most beautiful thing I have ever seen."

She sat down on the edge of the bed, moving carefully so as to avoid hurting him. She sat facing him, just as she had the last time she had come to him in the night. She moved closer, until her hip pressed against his thigh, and once again her robe fell from her shoulders.

"No one like you in the world, Lucy. . . ."

"And you're the most handsome, gallant. . . ."

She leaned forward and kissed him. She knew how to now: gently but firmly, not greedily but savoring, letting desire mount, but never forcing it. As she pressed his head back on the pillows, his lips moved beneath hers, a gentle, almost too gentle reply, and she wished he would lift his hand and touch her breast.

"Well, I told you I'd be back," she said softly after a moment.

He said nothing. His eyes were closed, and his smile was gone. She leaned forward and kissed him on the mouth, then moved her lips over the familiar slopes and angles of his face. She felt dazed with love, as if in a dream.

"Would you like the wine now," she asked, "or . . . after?"

His eyes slowly opened, and she was surprised at the depths of their sadness.

"Lucy . . ."

A spark of fear was born. "You were expecting me, weren't you?"

"Yes, but . . . not like this."

"Wouldn't you like me to sleep with you tonight?"

"I'd like nothing better under heaven, but Lucy . . ."

What was he trying to tell her? "I think it would be all right now, wouldn't it?"

He shook his head hopelessly.

She laid a hand on him just below the bandages, careful not to hurt him. She dared not be bolder. "We wouldn't have to make love if you don't want to. But if . . . if you'd like to . . ." She found she was embarrassed. "I could . . . I could do everything for us."

"Lucy . . . oh, Lucy . . ."

Giddy with desire, she put her forehead down on his shoulder. But why didn't he touch her? Why, oh, why didn't he put his arms around her? "Wouldn't you like to, darling? I'd like . . . you know . . . just to have you in me."

"Lucy, darling . . . Lucy, you know I'd like to, but . . . right now . . ." He blurted it out. "I don't even think I could."

It took a moment for his meaning to sink in. Then, appalled, she lifted her head and stared at him. "You don't mean—that Bassett creature, when he kicked you —he didn't—"

"No, not that. I don't think it's that."

The fright vanished as quickly as it had come, and she almost laughed with relief. "Then, my God, Justin, what's the matter? Is it something I can help you with? Please let me try!"

Again, he shook his head. "Lucy, we've got to talk. What happened to us . . . that one night . . ."

"Was a miracle."

"Yes. But we both knew then that it was a miracle that couldn't last. You yourself said—"

"Oh, Justin, I don't care what I said then. That was weeks ago!"

"But nothing has changed since then. Except, perhaps, to get worse. You still intend to stay at Sabrehill, don't you?"

"Of course. I have no choice. But—"

"And I still can't live here. And furthermore, my presence here can only make trouble for you."

"Darling, you don't know what you're talking about!"

"I do. You thought I was asleep when those gentlemen came calling on you—the major and Buckridge and Pettigrew and the rest. But I wasn't asleep, and I heard. As long as I'm here, they'll give you trouble."

"Oh, they will anyway. They always have, and you're only their latest excuse. Darling, I love you—"

"And I love you, more than you'll ever know. But I'll be leaving here soon, Lucy—"

Oh, no, you won't! "Justin, listen to me, please—"

"I'll be leaving here, and the sooner, the better. I've never in all these years brought you anything but grief."

"That's not true!"

"It is true. And I'll never forget that morning when I heard that man call you what he did . . . use the word whore . . . and I walked away without ever doing a thing about it. Without ever saying a word. Walked away as if I hadn't even heard—"

"Oh, for God's sake, Justin!" Was *that* what had wounded him so? Not the beating he had taken, but merely a stupid insult he had overheard? "You had to walk away, we both did, for our people's sake. And for the love of heaven, what does it matter?"

"It matters to me. A great deal."

"We'll talk about it tomorrow—"

"No. We don't have to talk about it, ever." He hesitated. He was as drawn and pale as the day Lucinda and Reba had helped him up the stairs. "Don't you see,

Lucy, any way you care to look at it, I have no right to you. And I never will."

"No right to me!" She stared at him, unbelieving. "And what about my rights? Don't I have any rights? I've waited a long time for you, Justin. I want my man. I have a right to him, don't you think?"

Justin refused to meet her eyes. He shook his head. "Lucy, I'm sorry. But I've told you. I don't think . . . I don't think I even could."

And would not. Would not try. Would not allow her into his bed, would never allow himself to be seduced. For some foolish principle, for honor or pride—she hardly knew what—he was still shutting her out of his life, as he had done for weeks. Like a wife, a mate, a lover, she had come half-naked to his bed, and he was sending her away, rejected, and feeling like a complete fool.

And yet she could not help trying to embrace him once more. "Please, Justin . . ."

His eyes closed again. The shake of his head was infinitely sad, but his decision was absolute: "Lucy, no."

She could not stop the tears that welled up. She could not stop the shaking, the trembling. All dignity was gone. "Oh, God damn you, Justin Sabre," she cried, and grabbing her robe, she fled from the room, slamming Justin's door behind her, slamming her own door in turn.

She threw herself across her bed. Sobbing, she tore at her pillow. She had been so determined to keep him that it had been inconceivable that she might fail, but now—

I won't let him leave me, she vowed through her tears. *I won't, I won't, I won't!*

But her neighbors had other ideas about that. Justin was not welcome in their midst, and they were determined to let him know it—even those who considered themselves to be Lucy's friends. At her party, a few weeks earlier, Justin had said a few words that might be considered critical of slavery. Only a few words, but they had been quite enough. And the Night of the Fires had seemed to confirm that Justin's views were highly dangerous.

Certainly it was clear that Major Kimbrough had not forgotten his conversation with Justin at the party. In mid-January, when Justin began to be up and about, the major and Mrs. Kimbrough were the first guests Lucy invited for Sunday dinner. It was a mistake. The major spent virtually the entire afternoon lecturing on a variety of subjects—the justification of slavery, the superiority of the Southern way of life, the place of the South in national politics—in a prodding, abrasive way that clearly challenged Justin to disagree. Justin grew increasingly quiet, and Lucy noted that he was taking on what she thought of as his "storm-cloud look." *Don't, Justin,* she thought, *please don't, don't, don't!*

But Justin did.

After dwelling for some twenty minutes on the subject of nullification—the theory that a state could legally "nullify" federal law—the major smiled with satisfaction and said, "But I haven't asked: what do *you* think of the nullification question?"

"I think, major," Justin said with ill-concealed disgust, "that there is no such thing as a nullification question."

"No such thing?" The major sounded surprised.

"There is no such thing, because, for all the chatter about it, it is no longer a live issue."

The major bridled. "My dear sir—"

"Nullification, sir," Justin said flatly, "is dead."

So much for everything the major had said during the last twenty minutes. But he was not to be put off. "Nevertheless," he said with some asperity, "what do you think of the matter philosophically?"

Lucy looked at Justin and though, *Oh, please, darling, please do be tactful!* But the aggressive glitter in Justin's eyes told her that this was not to be.

He gave a snorting laugh. "It's sheer nonsense, of course."

"Now, really," the major said, "one may question some of Calhoun's points, but his arguments can hardly be called nonsense."

Justin's smile was twisted by contempt. "I find Calhoun's arguments to be tortured, trivial, and pathetic."

The statement was almost blasphemous. John C. Calhoun had been, by many, all but canonized. "Why—why, by God, sir," the major sputtered, "why—I find such a statement to be downright insulting!"

Justin shrugged. "You asked my opinion, and I gave it to you."

Socially, the afternoon was a shambles. Within minutes, a semblance of polite farewells was made, and Lucy and Justin saw the Kimbroughs to their carriage. Final curt nods were exchanged by the gentlemen, and excessively fond words by the ladies, and the carriage rolled away.

"Justin, really," Lucy said, as they watched it go, "you didn't have to agree with the major, but you could have been more . . . gentle."

"That was what the major expected. At some point I would demur quietly, he would preach to me the error of my ways, and he would then tell the world how he had told off that 'Virginia radical, with his fanatic ideas.'" Justin laughed, a surprisingly happy laugh. "But he forgot that if you persist in trying to ride a man down, sooner or later he's apt to shoot you out of the saddle."

The incident was repeated, in variation, a week later. Word of the Kimbroughs' visit to Sabrehill soon reached the Buckridges. Mrs. Buckridge at once invited Lucy and Justin to dinner in town. Lucy declined the invitation— Justin was not all *that* well yet—but out of courtesy returned one of her own. And so, on the next Sunday, the Buckridges came to dinner.

This too was a mistake. At the end of the meal the gentlemen retired to the library for their coffee and brandy, and Lucy and Mrs. Buckridge went to the north parlor. For more than an hour, all was well. Then gradually Lucy became aware that men's voices—or at least Mr. Buckridge's voice—had been raised so that they could be heard from one end of the house to the other. "Oh, my, politics," Mrs. Buckridge sighed, and Lucy suggested, "Perhaps we had better join the gentlemen."

But the subject was not politics.

". . . an unintelligent race!" Mr. Buckridge was ranting as the ladies entered the library. "Why, sir, the very concept of intelligence fails to apply to the Negro except insofar as it can be said to apply to any other inferior animal!"

"Thirty-odd Negroes from around these parts contrive to vanish without leaving a trace," Justin said angrily, "and you can tell me with a straight face that they are an unintelligent race?"

"Animal cunning, sir! It shows nothing at all but animal cunning!"

"If a white man does it," Justin said, exasperated, "it is sheer genius. If a black man does it, it is ipso facto mere animal cunning? Is that your argument, sir?"

"But we already *know* that the black is an inferior race! Why, those niggers could never have gotten away if they hadn't had superior leadership! It *had* to be someone like that damned Adaba that led them off! Otherwise they could never have done it!"

"Well," Justin laughed, "I am happy to know that this inferior race is capable of producing superior leadership."

"I do think," Mrs. Buckridge said, "it is time to end this discussion."

Mr. Buckridge gave no sign of hearing her. "I do not wish to appear rude while a guest in this house," he said, "but apparently I took your measure quite correctly, sir, when you first arrived here. And I can tell you, sir, that your kind of pernicious doctrines of racial equality are not welcome in South Carolina. No, sir! Come, Callie, it is time we left."

No, Justin's "pernicious doctrines" were not welcome, and that meant that Justin was not welcome either.

Of course, as Lucy knew would happen, the stories of these two encounters were quickly spread far and wide. And it became apparent to one and all that, while they had long wished Lucy to take a husband, Justin Sabre simply would not do for that role.

Near the end of January this hostility came completely out into the open. Messieurs Buckridge, Pettigrew, and McClintock paid a visit to Sabrehill, and Mr. McClintock came right to the point. "We all want to know, Mr. Sabre, just how long you plan to stay on here?"

The interview took place in the north parlor, and Lucy was present. "My cousin," she said coldly, "will remain here as long as I can persuade him to do so."

Justin held up a hand to silence her. He said, "With all respect, Mr. McClintock, I don't think my plans are any of your business."

McClintock's eyes hardened, but Pettigrew cut in before he could speak. "Now, let's all go about this in a civilized way. It really is our business, Mr. Sabre. These are troubled times, and you know we've had a lot of problems around here lately. Niggers running off, houses being burned—"

"We're sorry about your difficulties," Lucy said, "but what do they have to do with Justin?"

"What they have to do is," Buckridge said, "we've got to get rid of any agitation around here and settle our niggers down. And with Mr. Sabre spreading his opinions around—"

"I keep my opinions to myself, Mr. Buckridge," Justin said, "unless they're asked for. But when they're asked for—"

"You give 'em," McClintock said, "and that's what makes you dangerous, both to the community and to yourself."

Pettigrew tried to strike a more reasonable tone. "Mr. Sabre, there's not a man here who doesn't like you personally and hold that you're entitled to your own views. After all, you're a gentleman, like us. But it's your kind of talk that gets the damned Jeppsons and Bassetts and all that rabble worked up so they start pestering our people, the way they did back before Christmas. And that, in turn, makes our people so damned mad they start burning and stealing and running off. Now, presumably, you will be leaving here sooner or later. But we've got to go on living here, right along with the Jeppsons and the Bassetts—"

"Are you trying to tell me," Justin interrupted, "that you can't control that kind of trash?"

"Can you?" Buckridge asked angrily. "Can you? Seems

to me you're a hell of a one to talk about controlling anyone! They damn near killed you, Mr. Sabre!"

"And don't tell us there wasn't no connection between that and your abolitionist talk," McClintock said.

"Now, we all realize," Pettigrew went on, turning to Lucy, "that Mr. Sabre has got to have time to recover. But we would like to know—in fact, everybody around here would like to know—just how long he intends to continue his sojourn among us."

It was really too much. The situation called for diplomacy, but Lucy saw Justin's temper flaring, and for once she hardly cared. She felt as angry as he.

"All right, Justin," she said, "tell them. Tell them anything you please." She knew he caught her meaning, and she felt as if she were telling a mean dog, *Sic 'em!*

"I don't mind giving you an answer," Justin said, his voice faintly shaking. "I'll give you my answer just once, plain and clear. I shall leave here, gentlemen—*when I damned well please!*"

The three visitors stared at Justin.

"You have heard, gentlemen," Lucy said, "my cousin will leave here when he damned well pleases. And now if you'll excuse us . . ."

Justin showed the men to the door. When he returned to the north parlor, he looked grim. "Well, that should convince you," he said. "This part of the country is no place for Justin Sabre."

Lucy felt the whole thrust of her anger shifting.

"Oh . . . *God!*"

Justin looked at her in surprise. "What's the matter?"

I have had enough, she thought.

Enough of intrusive neighbors. Enough of being treated like a "mere woman," incapable of managing her own affairs. Enough of—yes, enough of Justin's air of—of what?—of petulant self-defeat.

"Is that the real reason you want to leave here, Justin? Because you can't live with slavery?"

"It's one reason, yes."

"But is it *your* reason, the *true* reason? Do you really

think you're the only man in the South who detests slavery?"

"Of course not. There are a great many—"

"Or the only one who feels he must speak his convictions?"

"Lucy—"

"And do you love me, Justin Sabre, as I love you—"

"You know I do!"

"—because I'm too proud a woman to stand on false pride, Justin Sabre, and I do love you, and you know it. And maybe that frightens you. Are you one of those men who are frightened by love, Justin?"

"You know better than that—"

"Not anymore, I don't. Maybe you simply aren't man enough to stay here and be the master of Sabrehill and its notorious whore."

Justin's face had gone white. "Lucy, don't you talk like that."

But she could no longer stop herself, even if she had wanted to. "Not man enough, Justin? No guts, as my father would say? Maybe they were beaten out of you —that happens to a man sometimes, doesn't it? Is that what happened to you, Justin?"

Justin's lips barely moved. "There's more involved than that, and you know it well."

"What, that I know so well?"

"Lucy, I've told you. I've never brought you anything but grief. I don't think I could ever make you happy here."

She tossed her head. Her laugh was sharp and ironic. "And so you're going to make me happy by leaving here. You're going to leave, knowing I can't be happy without you. Well, I think you're right, Justin. You've convinced me that you should leave. That way at least one of us will be happy, isn't that so? And how fortunate for you that you'll be the one."

"You think I'm being selfish?"

"Well, aren't you? You know Sabrehill needs you. You know I need you. And Mark and Katie Anne and Beau, don't they need a home and a mother?"

"Lucy, you've no right—that's unfair!"

"Is it, now!" For an instant she thought she had gone too far, that he might actually attack her, and she could not have cared less. "Forgive me, Justin, if I suspect your scruples of being less than selfless. Go if you must, my dear. Leave Sabrehill anytime you please. But please, Justin, do not try to tell me you are making this large and noble sacrifice for the sake of the woman you love."

"You are a bitch," Justin said, shaking. "You really can be a bitch."

"I'm surprised you've noticed."

"Lucy, what the hell do you want from me?"

"Not a thing, my dear. I no longer want a thing."

"For God's sake, don't you think I'm tempted to stay here with you? Don't you think I'm tempted to say to hell with it all and marry you—"

"Oh, thank you, my dear! Thank you for your ardent declaration of love. It's exactly what every woman dreams of." The anger began to fade into something else, perhaps disgust, perhaps sorrow. *God,* she thought, *even if they don't drive him away, they're tearing us apart.* "Just go, Justin, whenever you please. You leave Sabrehill with my compliments. . . ."

She hurried from the room before she burst into tears. Justin watched as she hurried up the stairs in the passage.

The bitch! he thought again.

All right, she had been right—in almost every word she had said. He *had* for a time felt unmanned by the craven way—in his view—that he had walked away from the posse and by the beating he had taken. To some extent he still did. And loving Lucy, he certainly should consider the unhappiness his leaving would cause her. And without question, he was obliged to weigh what would be best for his children. She was right.

But did she really think it was as simple as all that? Did she think he was lying when he said he didn't believe he could live with slavery? Had she no idea of how important that was to him? He loved her with all his heart, but could he bear to spend the rest of his life either curbing his tongue or quarreling with his neighbors? How long could he keep her love under such conditions?

And as for his children, did he want to raise them in this land? *Could* he raise them decently in a land of slavery?

He didn't know.

Then maybe, goddam it, he thought, *I'd better get away from here. Once and for all.*

I won't let him leave me, she had sworn, but how was she to stop him? By reasoning with him? What lover was ever held by mere reason. By passion? He would never give her the chance. And in a few more days he would be gone.

Where was he now, Lucy wondered on that Saturday afternoon as she sat alone in the office. At work somewhere, no doubt, though the work week was over. Justin was again rising before dawn and going out with the hands. According to Jebediah, he could maul fence rails, grub stumps, and split firewood with the best of them. If his battered body still gave him trouble, he showed no signs of it, and he gave every indication of having regained his full strength. Lucy was a little surprised that she had managed to keep him at Sabrehill this long.

Her thoughts were interrupted by a sound outside, the crunch of gravel under hooves, and she got up to see if Justin had returned. Instead, she was confronted by a Negro on a mule.

"Looking for Mr. Justin Sabre, please, ma'am," he said as he dismounted.

Lucy stepped out of the office. "Mr. Sabre isn't here right now."

"Got to find him, ma'am." The man took something from his coat pocket. "Got to give him this here."

It was a letter apparently, but who would be sending Justin a letter by messenger? The crumpled, stained envelope did not have the look of a social invitation.

She held out her hand. "You may leave it with me. I'll see that he gets it."

The man looked worried. "Ain't suppose to give it to nobody but him, ma'am."

"Do you know who I am?"

"Yes, ma'am. You just got to be Miss Lucy."

"Then you must know that the letter will be safe with me. Please give it to me."

The man's brow furrowed deeper. The idea of refusing a direct command from a white lady bothered him, but evidently he was under very strong and specific orders.

"What's your name?" she asked. "Who sent you here?"

The man avoided her eyes. "Ain't . . . ain't suppose to say, ma'am. Just suppose to give Mr. Justin Sabre this here letter and light out fast."

"Aren't you supposed to wait for a reply?"

"No, ma'am. Master say, don't wait for nothing, don't answer no questions, just light out like they's a bee under the saddle."

It was an odd kind of instruction, and the man knew it. That was why he had been so nervous from the moment he had appeared.

"Very well," Lucy said, "you may do as you were told. And while we wait here for Mr. Justin, you may show me your pass."

The man started to dip a hand into his pocket again, then realized his predicament. To show his pass would be to reveal the very information he had been told to keep to himself. He looked at Lucy resentfully for a moment.

"You give Mr. Sabre this here letter for sure?" he asked.

"Of course. I'll give it to him today."

Almost fearfully, the messenger stepped forward and thrust the letter out to Lucy. The instant she took it, he rushed back to his mule, mounted, and rode away.

Lucy looked down at the soiled envelope in her hand. The two misspelled words were printed out in crude letters: *Justan Sabar.*

Dear God, she thought as she went back into the office, what now? One more unpleasant incident with the community? One more incident to persuade Justin that

Sabrehill and South Carolina were not for him? Obviously the letter was not from any of her more literate friends, and her thoughts automatically turned to Balbo Jeppson and his kind. What would they want, what would they have to say to Justin? She might have guessed, but she preferred not to follow that train of thought.

She continued to look at the envelope. A small fire was burning in the grate, and she moved closer to it. She was tempted. Get rid of the envelope and whatever was in it. Forget all about it.

Burn it.

But of course, one did not burn other people's mail.

"I've fixed up that broken gin," Justin said as he entered the office behind her. "I wanted to get it done so you wouldn't have to worry about it."

Lucy turned and held up the envelope. Justin glanced at it and saw his name. Frowning slightly, he took it from her hand and looked at it. Obviously he had not been expecting it.

"A messenger brought it just a few minutes ago," she said. "He was a bit strange. He said he was to give it to you personally and leave without waiting for an answer. I persuaded him to give it to me."

Justin tore open the envelope. "Did he say who sent him?"

"No, he said he wasn't supposed to answer any questions. 'Just light out like they's a bee under the saddle.'" Lucy spoke with a lightness she did not feel.

Justin pulled a scrap of paper out of the envelope and unfolded it. He read it.

She knew almost at once that it was bad, even worse then she had anticipated. For a moment Justin's face was stonily blank. She saw his eyes move, perhaps reading the letter a second time. Then the familiar transformation took place: the darkening of the face, the growing tautness about the mouth, the hardening of the eyes.

"Justin, what is it?"

He thrust the letter into a pocket. "I have to go into town," he said quietly.

"Darling, please don't—"

"I have to go into town," he repeated, "right now."

"Is it Jeppson? or Tucker or Bassett or any of those people? They are nothing, Justin, nothing. Don't let them push you into something foolish—"

"Nobody is pushing me, Lucy. Nobody."

"Then stay right here—"

He seemed to explode, his force driving her back across the room. *"Nobody is pushing me, goddam it! By God, they'll learn! Nobody is pushing me, nobody—"*

"Justin!"

Her cry was like a slap that brought him back to his senses. He looked at her uncomprehendingly for a moment, then seemed to calm. But she knew the calm was only on the surface.

"Justin, I don't know what's in that letter, but think what you're doing."

"I'm sorry, Lucy, but I know what I'm doing. What I've got to do. I'll be back as soon as I can. I don't know when that will be, but it shouldn't be too long."

"But what's it about, what—"

"Just a little personal business. Nothing for you to worry about. It's nothing I can't handle."

"But Justin—"

"Please. No questions. Not now. I'm leaving as soon as I can get Thunder saddled. The sooner I get this done, the better."

And so he left. She watched as he rode down the long avenue of oaks away from the Sabrehill mansion and turned toward the town of Riverboro. And she learned once again that dreams and vows of love were not enough. Justin Sabre was his own man, and he would die if need be to remain his own man. And there was not a thing in the world she could do about it.

His anger was under control now. It was still hot, it was murderous, but it was a tool to do what had to be done. It was a cleansing anger, and it felt good. He gave the big Morgan horse its head and let it gallop. Its strength seemed to be his own.

Perhaps this was what he had been waiting for. He

could have left Sabrehill days ago, even weeks ago, if he had really wanted to, but he had stopped resisting Lucy's insistence that he stay on. He had spent the days regaining his strength and waiting—for this.

Lucy simply did not understand, he thought, and he doubted that he could ever explain to her. It was not just a matter of being beaten half to death by a bunch of white trash, though that was bad enough. But to be unable to get up and fight back . . . to be rendered helpless for weeks, to feel impotent and worthless . . . and to think that perhaps your own mistakes, however well meant, had helped bring all the grief about . . . how could a man help but start hating himself? How could he help but feel unworthy? It became necessary, then, for a man to find a sense of his own worth again. He could not afford to be "gentle" with a Kimbrough's challenges or to remain silent in the face of a Buckridge's bigotries. It had been a matter of reaffirming that he was still Justin Sabre.

Well, that was over now. He knew who he was. Justin Sabre was back in the saddle.

At the edge of Riverboro he slowed Thunder to a walk. He had already begun looking. The note had been anonymous, signed *Yore frends,* but he knew very well who his "friends" were. He had sorted them out, talking to Reba and Lucinda, and he would recognize any of them on sight. The two who had held his arms while Skeet did the hard work were called P. V. Tucker and Rolly Joe Macon. Taggart Bassett was the one who had held Lucy and who had kicked him. Balbo Jeppson had neither hit him nor kicked him, as far as he could remember, but he had been part of it all.

He could literally see the word spreading ahead of him: *Justin Sabre is in town.* The road by which he had come led directly through Riverboro, its main street, and he reined up and watched. A man stared at him, a woman, another man. Heads turned. There were whispers. A boy listened to them, ran down the street, and entered a dry goods store. A man and a woman came to the door and looked out at Justin.

He moved on slowly, watching carefully. More people appeared on the street, but nowhere did he see Jeppson, Bassett, Tucker, or Macon. He saw Owen Buckridge and Monroe Pettigrew and exchanged nods with them.

When he reached the courthouse, he still had not seen any of his "friends." He was disappointed. On a Saturday afternoon, he had hoped for better luck. But he had time.

He found Constable Wiley Morgan alone in the sheriff's office. The constable did not appear at all happy to see him. His pouched eyes watered, and his dewlaps quivered. "Mr. Sabre," he whined, "Miss Lucy told me you was hurt pretty bad that day, but since there was only her for a witness against all them—"

"Shut up," Justin cut him off. He took the letter out of his pocket and held it before the constable's eyes. When the constable tried to take it, he said, "Never mind, just read it."

He himself remembered every word, and his anger again threatened to break loose. *Ant you lerned yore lesson? You ben here long enuf. We dont need no nigger stealin abolishunist round here. If you out workin like a nigger you are well enuf to travel. And you better travel or you git wors than last time. This here is yore final worning.*

"Is that a threatening letter or is it not?"

"Why, now—"

"Is it or is it not?"

"Why, I reckon it is."

"And who sent it to me, constable?"

"Now, how would I know that? It just says your friends."

"But we both know who my 'friends' are, don't we, constable?"

The constable was sweating. "Mr. Sabre, I wish there was something I could do—"

"We both know. Have you read the last line of the letter?"

"Yes—yes, sir, I read it."

After the anonymous valediction, a final line had been

added: *And after we git rid of you we goin to take keer of yore whore.* It had been an afterthought, no doubt, greeted with snorts of bawdy laughter and much crotch-scratching. But if nothing else in the letter had been enough to send Justin to Riverboro, those words had done it.

"What do you think of that line, constable?"

"Why . . . why, it's terrible."

"Remember it. And keep out of my way."

As he came out onto the street from the courthouse, afternoon was fading into evening. The light was soft and dusky. A number of people were still out on the street, looking his way, as if they expected something to happen. He hoped they would not be disappointed.

And then he saw one of them.

Justin could hardly have said if it was anger or joy that flooded through him. It was Bassett, striding along the board sidewalk, he was quite sure. Bassett, who had kicked and clubbed him. Bassett, who had caused the little black girl's death. Leaving his horse tied in front of the courthouse, Justin followed the man at a near-run. People stared, but Bassett, unaware of what was happening, did not turn around. He entered the Carstairs tavern.

Justin slowed, saving his energy and his breath. He had plenty of time now.

A moment later he entered the tavern. Without pausing at the door, he saw that there were a half-dozen other people in the room. Directly ahead of him, P. V. Tucker was sitting behind a table. Bassett was standing beside the table on Tucker's right. Tucker, surprised, looked up at Justin. Bassett, equally surprised, followed Tucker's gaze. Then he grinned. "You can't do it, boy," he said contemptuously, turning back toward the table, "so don't even try—"

As Justin reached the table, his open left hand swung up and around hard and fast and caught Bassett on the back on the head. Bassett's hat flew off, he broke forward at the hips, and Justin smashed his face down on the table. His right hand had Bassett's right wrist, and he twisted the arm high behind the back, holding the man pinned. With his left hand, he lifted Bassett's coat. The expected knife was there in a sheath, and he drew it and tossed it onto a counter across the room. Still, holding Bassett pinned, he dipped into the man's sagging right-hand coat pocket and pulled out a small pistol, which he tossed after the knife.

By that time Tucker had recovered from his surprise and was moving around the table to Justin's left. Justin welcomed him. Releasing Bassett and pivoting, he brought his right fist up hard and deep into Tucker's belly. Tucker gagged wildly and painfully, and fell to the floor, straining for air.

"I'll take care of you another time," Justin said. He looked around the room. "Anyone else?"

No one moved—no one but Bassett, who was rolling over on the table and trying to regain his feet. Justin helped him, jerking him to his feet, then stood back, waiting.

Bassett swung a wild right. The blow never came close, and Justin planted a right jab in the man's mouth, staggering him back against another table. But Bassett returned with a flurry of blows that pounded Justin to the wall, and he automatically protected his ribs. It occurred to him that this might take a while. But that was all right. He was in no hurry.

He grabbed Bassett's coat front, tripped him up, and threw him to the floor. As Bassett tried to roll away, Justin seized him by the back of the collar and the belt and lifted him to his feet. Bassett was off balance, and Justin ran him out though the open doorway, heaving him with all his strength out into the street. Again Bassett fell, and went rolling, slithering through the mud.

Justin followed, taking his time. Bassett was not going anywhere. The others followed them out of the tavern, and people came running from up and down the street.

As Bassett began struggling to get up, Justin took off his hat and handed it to someone nearby. He did not even notice who it was. He did notice that Bassett was wearing gloves, and that reminded him: he pulled a pair of heavy well-fitting leather gloves of his own from his pocket. At least he had learned one useful thing from Vachel Skeet.

"All right, Bassett," he said, as he pulled on the gloves, "let us begin."

Justin Sabre did not consider himself to be a violent man, but he was disappointed that Bassett lasted no longer than he did. It seemed to him that the fight was over in a matter of minutes, though later some witnesses assured him that it had lasted considerably longer than that. Afterward, his principal recollections were of his own fury, of pounding Bassett down into the mud time and again, and of warning Bassett that he had better continue defending himself, because he, Justin, had no intention of stopping.

But eventually there was simply no one left to fight. The man who had clubbed and kicked Justin, the man who had caused Ettalee's death, was nothing but a mass of muddy, bloody rags lying in the street, and for a moment Justin thought he was dead.

Then Bassett groaned, twitched, sobbed.

One finished, three to go, Justin thought savagely, the anger still pounding in his veins.

But he was not done with Bassett yet.

Ignoring the dirt and the blood, he leaned down, grabbed the man, and hoisted him up over a shoulder. He carried him like that all the way to the courthouse, the crowd still milling around them. Someone opened the door, and Justin went down a corridor to the sheriff's office. Constable Wiley Morgan was still there, as if in hiding. Justin, without excessive gentleness, dumped Bassett onto the floor.

"If you can't do anything about my 'friends,' constable," he said, "I can."

"Now, Mr. Sabre—"

"Bassett and his crowd have given enough trouble to me and to mine and to everyone around here. You tell them that if they want to give me more, they know where to find me. But if they don't want what Bassett got, they had damned well better stay out of my way."

The constable made futile gestures, which Justin ignored. He turned to the door to find himself looking at Pettigrew and Buckridge. Pettigrew, grinning, handed Justin his hat. There was such a wild light in Buckridge's eyes that at first Justin thought he was angry. He was wrong.

"By damnation, sir," Buckridge said excitedly, "you surely did take care of that Bassett right!"

Justin looked blank-faced at the man, not sure that he was understanding correctly.

"Bassett *bastard*," Pettigrew said, "everlasting bastards, every damn one of them, and if only I was ten years younger, sir—"

"Yes, *sir!*" Buckridge said. "That bunch, riding around the countryside, giving our people hell—no wonder our people want to burn everything and run off. Can you blame 'em? It's about time somebody let the Bassetts and their like know we're not going to take it any longer. By God, sir, we do have our differences, but we're all gentlemen here together, and I would like to buy you a drink!"

No, dreams and vows were not enough, and Justin would soon be leaving. What could she do now but accept that?

She had supper alone that evening: one woman alone at the end of the long dinner table, a maid standing silently by in case she wanted something. The room was dimly lit, because there was no need for more light. The only sound was that of silver on china. How often had she eaten like this before Justin had returned, she wondered. Hundreds of times. Now there was a second place set at the table, but no one in the chair. Justin had not returned from Riverboro.

Halfway through supper she had the frightening thought that perhaps he never would.

Often on Saturday evenings she would go out to the

field quarters to visit with her people. Tonight she did not. She said a quiet good night to Lucinda and Leila and went to bed early, intending to escape into sleep. She took some brandy with her and, as usual, a book. But once in bed, the book did not hold her, and her eyes refused to tire, even in the softened light of the lamp.

Why did it have to be, she wondered. Why did so many hopes and expectations come to nothing? As a small child, she had been struck by the horrible injustice of it all: that God had thrust certain wishes and longings upon her—she had not asked for them; they were simply there, a part of her—and He had made the rest of the world in such a way as to baffle those wishes and longings. Why had she been made to want certain things, if she could not have them? Why? Why?

Why was Justin going away?

There was the answer he had given her: he felt that he could no more live here than she could leave. But there were also two other possibilities, fearful possibilities, which she had refused to contemplate. One was that Justin was truly and completely impotent—that Taggart Bassett had incapacitated him permanently. He had denied that, but since it was something that most men would rather die than admit, it remained a possibility. And the idea was a horror to Lucy. She wanted to believe that she could love under any circumstances, that her love could survive any blow. But the fact was that she wanted physical love and the physical expression of love. She wanted it, she knew now, about as much as she wanted anything in the world.

The other possibility was that, whatever he said, Justin simply did not love her. They had been drawn to each other; she had gone to his bed—not he to hers—and in the heat of the moment he had declared his love. Perhaps he had thought he had to, in spite of her protestations. And afterward he had felt obliged to affirm the declaration, obliged to save her from shame. But love was another thing altogether.

But why should she torture herself with such speculations? She refused to believe either possibility. The important thing, the real thing, was that Justin had come back to her and they had fallen in love again. *And I'm going to keep him,* she swore in a sudden surge of feeling, even knowing the uselessness of such vows, *I won't let him leave me, I won't, I won't!*

The feeling was so strong that it brought her to her knees on the bed. Her eyes were tightly closed, her fists were clenched, and she had to fight not to cry out. She wanted Justin, she wanted him now. He had awakened her again, as no other man could, and she needed him as she needed air to breathe. Better to die than to face the long empty years ahead without him.

A door opened and closed.

Justin, she thought.

It had to be he, safely back from Riverboro. Or it might only have been Leila, if she had not yet come up to bed. Sobbing quietly, Lucy sat back again and pulled the covers over her. She listened.

Boots on the stairs. That told her it was Justin. The step was his, though tonight it was quicker and lighter than usual.

Why must I feel this way? she asked some anonymous god. *It's so useless! Why can't I let him go!*

Justin seemed to be humming or singing a song. She could not remember having heard him sing before in all the past weeks. The sound broke off for a moment outside her door, and for some reason she held her breath. Then it resumed, and Justin's door opened and closed.

Lucy put her hand to her eyes and wept. *So useless, so useless . . .*

When she heard the soft tapping at her door a few minutes later, her tears were gone. What good were tears?

"Come in, Justin," she said, knowing it was he.

Justin came into the room and closed the door behind him. His boots were off, and he was in shirtsleeves. He stood at the door for a minute, his hand still on the knob, smiling at her. It was a soft smile, hardly a smile at all, just the kind of look a man gives someone of whom he is very fond.

"I saw the light under your door," he said. "I hope you don't mind. . . ."

"Of course not. Are you all right?"

"I'm quite all right. I'm sorry if you were worried."

"Well, I was. The way you ran off . . ."

"As I told you . . . it was just a little personal business."

He came to the side of her bed. Still smiling, he looked down at her for a long moment.

"Am I too late?" he asked.

"I don't understand."

He shrugged. He pulled a chair closer to the bed and threw himself down in it.

"I thought you might be interested in knowing why I'm so late getting back."

"Really, Justin, whatever you do is your own—"

"After I had concluded my personal business, I ran into Buckridge and Pettigrew, and you know how it is. Buckridge wanted to buy me a drink, so of course I had to buy a round, and then Pettigrew bought one too."

"Justin, what in the world are you talking about?" She wondered why he was teasing her. *"You* and Mr. Buckridge and Mr. Pettigrew?"

"Why not? We have a lot in common, those gentlemen and I."

"And you spent the evening drinking with them?"

"Oh, no. I spent most of it, as a matter of fact, at Kimbrough Hall. I thought I might as well stop off there, since I had the time, and I ended up staying for supper."

"Because you and the major have so much in common."

Justin laughed. "Of course. We're both admirers of Johnny Calhoun, aren't we?"

"Not the last I heard."

"Actually we are. Hell, the major got me irritated that day, and I had to hit back. I don't agree with everything Calhoun says, but he still represents a certain Southern point of view better than anyone else I know."

Fence-mending, Lucy thought. *That's what he's been doing, he's been out fence-mending, but . . .*

"Why?" she asked. "Why are you doing it, Justin?"

"Doing what?"

"You know perfectly well what."

"They're your friends, Lucy. You may sometimes find that hard to believe. They may give you a lot of problems from time to time. But I've noticed something else. They may cuss you up and down, but they respect and admire you, and some of them even have a kind of love for you. As old friends should."

"But what's that to you? Why should you care?"

Justin's smile faded. "I care because you may be needing your friends, Lucy, and I don't want to come between you and them. I've got reason to believe that the trouble around here is far from over. We were talking about it this evening. It's always hard to maintain proper discipline in the patrol, and a posse like the last one is even worse. It can cause more trouble for both blacks and whites than all the Adabas and Black Bucks put together. Now, Skeet's out of it, of course, but from what I've been told, Balbo Jeppson has always been the real ringleader of the troublemakers, and he's still here. And somehow those people have got to be brought back into line."

"Well, I do thank you, Mr. Sabre, sir, for thinking of my well-being."

Justin laughed. He got up from the chair and sat with her on the bed. He touched her cheek, and a tremor went through her entire body.

"Why, Luz, honey, you've been crying."

"I do, sometimes."

"Don't," he said. "Please don't cry."

He leaned toward her to kiss her about the eyes. His hand drifted from her cheek to her breast, and her breath caught. *Oh, don't, if you don't mean it,* she thought at first, but then: *Oh, don't stop,* and she raised her face to his, her mouth open. Her hand went to the back of his head and drew him closer, as his hand slipped beneath her gown to stroke the swelling flesh.

"Then I haven't lost the right?" he asked a moment later.

She shook her head. Let him do as he pleased, let him

stay with her, or let him run to Texas. She still wanted him to make love to her.

"Because I do love you, Luz," he said.

"I've told you, Justin, you don't have to say that."

"But I love you so much, and I want you to believe me."

"Then I do believe you." *Just make love to me, make love to me.*

His mouth went to hers again, his fingers drew at her breast, and she was carried away.

No one else in the world knew her as he did. No one else ever would. With no one else could she ever be this free, this open, this loving. As she lowered herself in the bed, she reached for him and heard herself moan commands of love.

He obeyed. And for the moment she could forget that she was losing him. She could forget all the disappointments and the worry and the bitterness of the past weeks, as they gave to each other gently, hungrily, fiercely. He tossed his shirt off, and she slipped her gown down, slipped it away as he followed it with caresses and kisses. She reached for his belt, wanting him to be as naked as she, wanting to return every pleasure, but he brushed her hand away as if determined that all the first and best should be hers.

But then, in spite of everything, she remembered.

"Oh, God, Justin," she sobbed, "don't leave me!"

"I won't."

"Because I won't let you go, I won't ever, somehow I'll find a way to keep you."

"You already have. You've helped me to become a man again."

"You don't even have to marry me. Just stay. I'll be your mistress, your whore."

"You'll be everything to me. Wife, mistress—"

"I can't live without you. How can you live without me?"

"I don't think I can. And you need me, Luz, as much as I need you. . . ."

Only then did she realize what he had been telling her.

She stilled his hands and looked at him with dazed eyes.
The tension of her passion eased, and she lay perfectly
still, trying to be absolutely certain that she did not mis-
understand.

"You need me," he repeated, "and I'll be damned if
I'm going to let them drive me away from you—not the
Bassetts or the Buckridges or anyone else. They're not
going to do it, and I think they know that now."

She did not want to believe too quickly. She wanted the
luxury of understanding and believing a little at a time.

"Are you saying . . ."

"I love you, Luz."

"But you've told me so often, you can't live here."

"It's still my little part of the world. And if there's a
lot I hate about it—maybe it needs me too."

"Then you've decided . . ."

"Will you marry me, Luz?"

It was a question that took a great deal of listening to,
and she was still listening to it when she found herself
saying, *"Oh, Justin, yes, yes, yes!"* and they were both
laughing, and in the next moments any lingering worries
she might have had about his lost manhood vanished
forever.

And suddenly it was summer. The sun beat down
through the leaves, warming their bare bodies, and the
gentle breezes caressed them, and the scent of wildflowers
and crushed grass was love's perfume. And this was no
stone David she was rolling about with in shared ecstasy;
he was too alive, too loving, a naked godlike creature
with the powers of a ram, ready for her as no David
could ever be. And she was his match, no genteel widow-
lady living in frozen loneliness, but a pagan woodland
creature, insatiable, inexhaustible, and every bit as ready
as he.

And when at last he took her, she cried out *"Hallelujah!"*

Dirt on a piazza, candles in a graveyard. A planter
cursed with bad luck, a few more slaves vanished in the
night. For years they blamed it on Adaba and his woman,

Zulie. Some, of course, said there was no such person as Adaba, the Brown Dove, that he was only a rumor, a myth, a dream. But whatever else he might have been, he was a hope of freedom. And by the hundreds and the thousands, the slaves continued to vanish.

As for Black Buck, it was said, in the manner of legends, that he too was somewhere out in the night, fighting for his people, stealing them north, demanding that all debts be paid. It was said that he had never been killed at Redbird, that he had somehow escaped, that Black Buck would live forever. Just as with Adaba and Zulie, there would always be a Black Buck when his people needed him.

So it was said.

And perhaps it was true.

Also by Raymond Giles in the Sabrehill series

SABREHILL

X3506 $1.75

Jeb was just one slave among many. But he was a man no one could ignore. Women noticed him. Men envied him. With his lean, muscular body and a flash of arrogance in his face, Jeb made heads turn when he strode by. Jeb knew what he had going for him. But he wanted more. He wanted his freedom. And he would have it—or die trying to get it.

SLAVES OF SABREHILL

X3304 $1.75

This big, turbulent novel of plantation life unfolds a richly detailed story of the antebellum South and the men and women whose passions shaped its destiny . . .

Here is a vivid and lusty portrait of the Old South. It is a story of lovers and haters, of killers and heroes, of black and white in a world that will never be forgotten.

Also by Raymond Giles

DARK MASTER   1-3622-1 $1.75

This novel tells the story of black passions and forbidden love involving the black master of a great Southern plantation and a white woman. Hannibal was master of Duquesne. He was also master of Libby Drummond. Would this be his death sentence?

ROGUE BLACK   Q3534 $1.50

This passionate and dramatic tale of a handsome young slave and his white mistress brings into shocking focus all the savagery and terror of the Old South.